CW01188361

THE *NEGRO MOTORIST* GREEN BOOK
COMPENDIUM

A compilation of four volumes of the classic Jim Crow-era travel guide for African Americans covering all four decades during which the series was published, from the 1930s to the 1960s

Victor H. Green

Compiled and notes by Nat Gertler

About Comics   *Camarillo, California*

The Negro Motorist Green Book Compendium

Copyright 2019 About Comics
Includes material published 1938, 1947, 1954, and 1963 by Victor H. Green & Co.

Hardcover ISBN-13: 978-1-949996-10-4, continuous printing starting March, 2019
Paperback ISBN-13: 978-1-949996-06-7, continuous printing starting January, 2019

Customized editions available

Direct all queries to *questions@aboutcomics.com*

CONTENTS

About the Green Book..page 5

The Negro Motorist Green Book 1938...........................page 7

The Negro Motorist Green Book 1947.........................page 39

The Negro Travelers' Green Book 1954.....................page 123

Travelers' Green Book 1963–64.................................page 207

Green Book advertising rate card..................................page 310

Carry Your Green Book with you
. . . you may need it . . .

About the *Green Book*

The Green Book was created in 1936 in an America where it was sadly necessary. The rising African-American middle class had the finances and vehicles for travel but faced a nation where social and legal restrictions barred them from many accommodations. At the time, there were thousands of "sundown towns," places that legally barred Black people from spending the night there at all. Traveling through unknown territory, you could not count on finding a place to stay the night or even to get a meal.

This problem was addressed by Victor Hugo Green, an African-American postman who delivered the mail in Hackensack, New Jersey, but lived in Harlem. He began compiling what was launched as *The Negro Motorist Green Book*, which was at first a guide that covered only the New York area, filled with ads for Black-friendly (and often Black-owned) New York City businesses. By the 1938 volume reprinted within, the guide would cover hotels, restaurants, and other vital Black-accessible businesses for all states east of the Mississippi. The next year its coverage would reach out to the west coast (and the guide dropped its visually annoying green interior printing for more traditional black ink.) Information for locations beyond New York were generally provided by the book's customers, and often by other African-American mailmen across the nation. The demand was as clear as the need. Green retired from postal work in 1952 to focus on his company, both publishing the guide and expanding into providing travel services.

Victor H. Green
1892 – 1960

The guide grew, both with more listings and various articles – travelogues, travel advice, automotive reviews, and other things that might be of interest to the those journeying beyond their hometown. In 1952, the title changed to *The Negro Traveler's Green Book*, with the explanation that the change was "due to the fact, the name was confusing and a good many people thought that it was intended for the motorist only, but is used for any mode of travel." In 1956, the frequency briefly switched to two volumes per year, in the spring and fall. It was sold largely through mail order and through service stations – specifically, through Esso stations, as Esso not only served African-American customers, they were willing to franchise their stations to African Americans, unlike most petroleum companies of the day. The guide was also offered by AAA and distributed elsewhere with advice from the United States Travel Bureau, a government agency.

Victor Green died in 1960, having already been out of the masthead of the guide for several years. Others, including his widow Alma, would continue his efforts. *The Green Book* lost its apparent vitality when the civil rights laws of the 1960s brought about the end of legal segregation, and it disappeared a couple years later.

PRICE — 25 Cents

THE
NEGRO MOTORIST
GREEN BOOK

HOTELS
ROAD HOUSES
TAVERNS
NIGHT CLUBS
TOURIST HOMES
TRAILER PARKS & CAMPS
RESTAURANTS
GARAGES
SERVICE STATIONS
SUMMER RESORTS

1 9 3 8
EDITION

Listing all of the
States east of the
Mississippi River

BARBER SHOPS
BEAUTY PARLORS
DANCE HALLS
THEATERS

Keep This Guide In Your Car For Ready Reference

For Information Concerning this Guide
Communicate with
Victor H. Green, Publisher
938 Nicholas Ave.   New York City

COPYRIGHTED

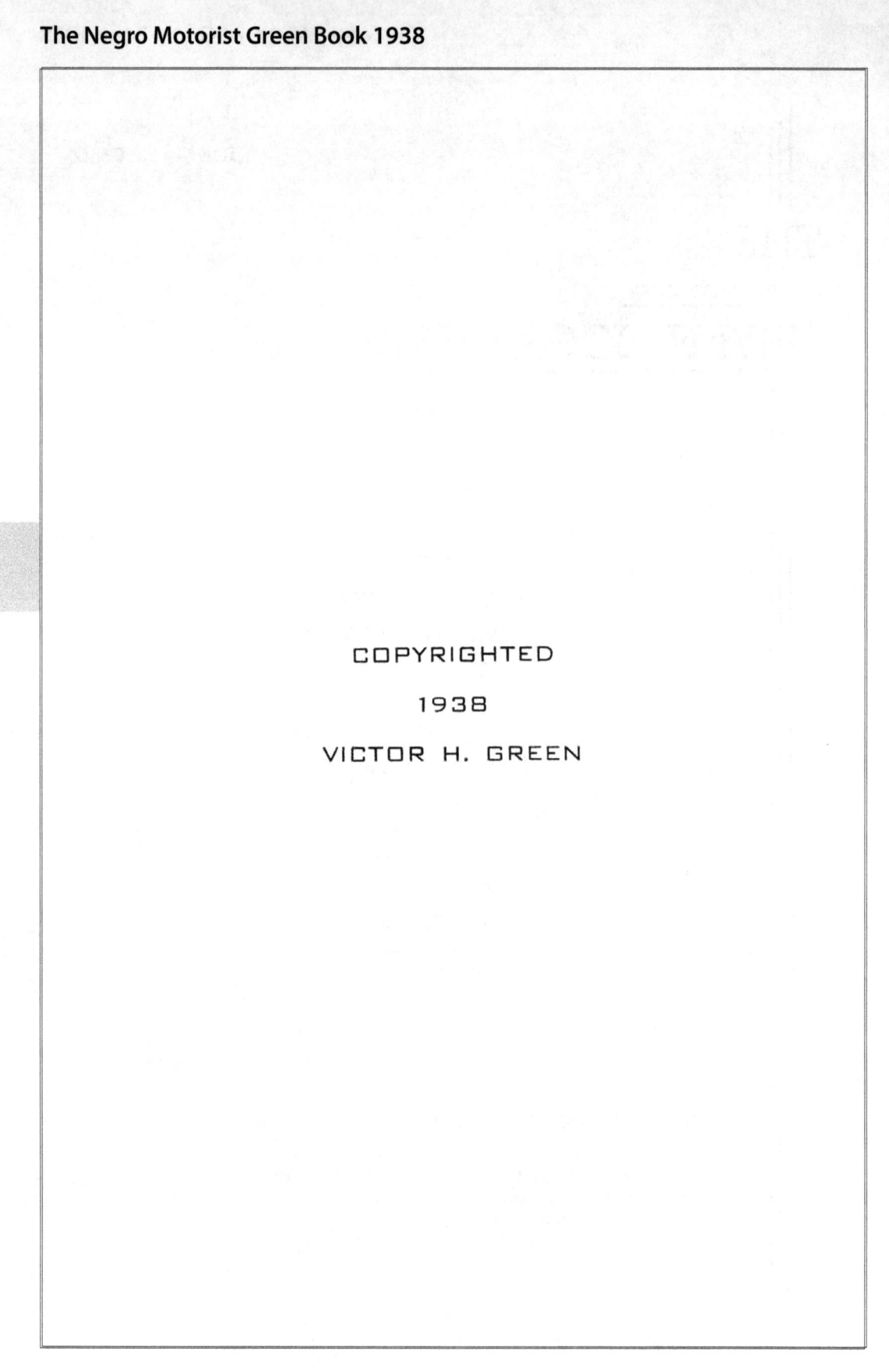

1938

VICTOR H. GREEN

THE
NEGRO MOTORIST
GREEN BOOK

INTRODUCTION

The idea of "The Green Book" is to give the Motorist and Tourist a Guide not only of the Hotels in all of the large cities East of the Mississippi River, but other Classifications that will be found useful whereever he may be. Also facts and imformation that the Negro Motorist can use and depend upon.

There are thousands of places that the public doesn't know about and aren't listed. Perhaps you might know of some? If so send in their names and addresses and the kind of business, so that we might pass it along to the rest of your fellow Motorists.

You will find it handy on your travels and up to date. Each year we are compiling new lists; as some of these places move, or go out of business and new business is started.

All of our Advertisers have been selected with care and are the best represenative and responsible in their field. One will always find them willing and ready to serve the best that there is.

When you are traveling mention "The Green Book" so as to let these people know just how you found out about their place of business. If they haven't heard about This Guide, tell them to get in touch with us.

If this Guide is useful, let us know, if not tell us also, as we appreciate your criticisms.

If any errors are found, kindly notify the publishers so that they can be corrected in the next issue.

Published yearly in the month of April by Victor H. Green. Executive & Advertising office at 938 St. Nicholas Ave., New York, N. Y. Advertising office at 938 St. Nicholas Ave, Tel. ED. 4-3425. Copyrighted — 1938 by Victor H. Green. Manuscripts submitted for publication should be sent to 938 St. Nicholas Ave. New York, N. Y., and must be accompanied by return postage. No liability can be assumed for the loss or damage to manuscripts although every possible precaution will be taken.

Subscription: Twenty-five cents per copy.

Advertising: For rates, Write to the publisher.

Last forms close on March 15th. We reserve the right to reject any advertising which in our opinion that does not conform to our standards.

PUBLISHED BY

VICTOR H. GREEN

938 ST. NICHOLAS AVE.

NEW YORK, N. Y.

Correspondence to the Editor

327 Railroad Ave.,
Hackensack, N. J.

Victor H. Green
Publisher
938 St. Nicholas Ave.
New York, N. Y.

Dear Sir;

    It is a great pleasure for me to give credit where credit is due. Many of my friends have joined me in admitting that "The Negro Motorist Green Book" is a credit to the Negro Race. It is a book badly needed among our Race since the advance of the motor age. Realizing the only way we knew where and how to reach our pleasure resorts was in a way of speaking, by word of mouth, until the publication of "The Negro Motorist Green book". With our wishes of your success, and your ernest efforts. We earnestly believe "The Negro Motorist Green Book" will mean as much if not more to us as the A. A. A. means to the white race.

Respectfully Yours,

Wm. Smith.

SAFE DRIVING RULES

1. Watch out for the drvier who crosses the White Line.

2. When the other car passes you, watch out that he doesn't cut in on you.

3. Watch out for the driver who doesn't know any better than to pass on a hill.

4. Even when the light is Green, look out for the reckless driver comming from left or right, who is ignorant that the Red light is against him.

5. Watch the driver ahead — you can't be sure whether or not he'll signal when he turns.

6. Even on highways, look out for parked cars.

7. Watch the car comming down the steep hilltowards you. Maybe the driver doesn't know enough to go into second.

8. Don't assume that the other fellow has good breakes.

9. At night look out for pedestrains walking on your side of the highway.

10. On Icy Roads look out! Some drivers don't know any better than to brake suddenly on ice.

11. Going over a hill, be ready for drivers who may be fools hardly as to make a turn across the road.

12. When you are passing, look out for the car that may be suddenly pulling out to pass just ahead of you.

13. Maybe the cop won't catch the car that passes you at 80, but "sudden death" is liable to.

14. On a three lane highway, watch out for the driver who thinks the middle lane is his exclusively.

15. Remember that Junior thinks that the ignition key is something to play with.

INDEX

ALABAMA	1
CONNECTICUT	1
DISTRUCT OF COLUMBIA (Washington)	1
FLORIDA	2
GEORGIA	2
ILLIONIS	3
KENTUCKY	3
LOUISIANIA	3
MAINE	,3
MARYLAND	4
MASSACHUSETTS	4
MICHIGAN	4
NEW JERSEY	4
NEW YORK	8
NORTH CAROLINA	14
OHIO	14
PENNSYLVANIA	15
RHODE ISLAND	16
SOUTH CAROLINA	17
TENNESSEE	17
VIRGINIA	17
WEST VIRGINA	19
SUMMER RESORTS	20

EXPLANATION

We are making this Guide as near complete as possible, until such time as we can get the information from the different sections of the country. The 1939 issue will contain the western section of the United States and will be complete.

The business classifications listed have been arranged under the different cities and towns, so that one won't have any trouble finding what they want.

ALABAMA

ANDALUSIA
TOURIST HOMES
   Mrs. Ed. Andrews—
      69 N. Cotton St.

BIRMINGHAM
HOTELS
   Dunbar Hotel—316 N. 17th St.
   Fraternal Hotel—1619 N. 4th St.
   Palm Leaf Hotel—318 N. 18th St.
   Rush Hotel—316 N. 18th St.

DECATUR
TOURIST
   Mrs. F. Hayes—207 W. Church St.

GADSDEN
HOTELS
   Smith Hotel—902 Garden Ave.
TOURIST
   Mrs. S. Neal—1317 4th Aev.
   J. C. Oliver—1335 4th Ave.
   Mrs. A. Sheperd—1324 4th Ave.
   Mrs. J. Simons—233 N. 6th St.

GENEVA
TOURIST
   Joe Dondal
   Susie M. Sharp
   Sallie Edwards

MOBILE
TOURIST
   Mrs. E. Reed—950 Lyons St.
   Mrs. E. Jordan—256 N. Dearborn
   Mrs. G. B. Sylvester—355 Cuba St.

SHEFFIELD
McClain Hotel—19th St.
TOURIST
   Mrs. I. Hawkins—S. Atlantic Ave.

TROY
TOURIST
   Mrs. S. A. Benton—
      113 E. FairView St.
   Mrs. J. Thomas—E. Academy St.

TUSCALOOSO
TOURIST
   Mrs. G. W. Baugh—2526 12th St.
   Mrs. M. A. Barnes—419 30th Ave.
   Mrs. G. W. Clopton—1516 25th Ave.
   Mrs. G. Robinson—11th St.

CONNECTICUT

BRIDGEPORT
   Hotel Broad—468 Broad St.

BRIDGEPORT
TOURIST
   Mrs. M. Barrett—83 Summer St.
   Mrs. E. Lawrence—68 Fulton St.
   Mrs. R. Williams—101 Church St.

HARTFORD
HOTELS
   Log Cabin Cottage—2016 Main St.
   Mme. S. A. Reed—12 Canton St.

NEW HAVEN
   Majestic—359 Beach St.
   Hotel Portsmouth—91 Webster St.
   Phyllis Wheatley Home—
      108 Canal St.

CONNECTICUT

A new express Highway, The Merritt Parkway, about 40 miles in length connecting with the Hutchinson River Parkway in New York State will carry one clear on the other side of Norwalk and connect with Route No. 1 the old Boston Post Road. By using this road one will eliminate the necessity of going through so many small towns in Connecticut and being held up by lights. This highway has been completed thus far and in time will take one into Boston Mass.

Motorists traveling from the South or West going to the New England States on reaching New York by way of the Holland Tunnel or the Geo. Washington Bridge can use the West Side express Highway Connecting with the New Hendrick Hudson Parkway, north on Saw Mill River Parkway and at the Hawthorne Circle connect with the Hutchinson River Parkway and then the Merritt Parkway. By using these routes one finds very few lights and doesn't have to enter any of the towns, hence much time will be saved.

NEW HAVEN
TOURIST
   Dr. M. F. Allen—65 Dixwell Ave.
   Mrs. S. Robinson—54 Dixwell Ave.
   Mrs. C. Raine—68 Dixwell Ave.
   Mrs. S. Jackson—55 Dwxiell Ave.

NEW LONDON
TOURIST HOMES
   Home of the Bachelor—
      20 Brewer St.
   Mrs. Wm. Gambles—45 Shapley St.
   Hempstead Cottage—
      73 Hempstead St.

WASHINGTON, D. C.   KEEP THIS GUIDE WITH YOU   FLORIDA — GA.

    The Gertrude—88 Bank St.
    Mrs. E. Whittle—785 Bank St.
STAMFORD
    Bladstone—Gay St.
    The Byron—33 Beekley Ave.
WATERBURY
    Mrs. J. Carter—57 Bishop St.
    Mrs. A. Dunham—208 Bridge St.
TOURIST
    Rob't Graham—37 Hanrahan Ave.
    Community House—81 Pearl St.
    Mrs. M. Kefford—99 Pearl St.
    Mrs. Ed. Jones—51 Pearl St.
Mrs. E. McKinney—25 Pearl St.
    Mrs. B. Smith—56 Pearl St.

DELAWARE

DOVER
    Cannon's Hotel—Kirkwood St.
    Cannon's—Division St.
    Caleb Brown—Lincoln St.
    Dean's—Forrest St.
    Moseley's—Division St.
    Weston's....Division St.
    The Bells—Lincoln St.
WILMINGTON
TOURIST
    Mrs. E. W. America—
      1106 Tatnall St.
    Mrs. G. Cooper—110 W. 12th St.
    Mrs. E. Till—1008 French St.
    Mrs. M. Wilson—1317 Tatnall St.

DISTRICT OF COLUMBIA

WASHINGTON
    Glover Hotel—N. J. Ave &
      D St. N. W.
    Henry Hotel—1825 13th St. N. W.
    Johnson Hotel—1502 13th St. N. W.
    Mid City—7th & N St. N. W.
    Whitelaw—13th & T St. N. W.
    Y. M. C. A.—1816 12th St. N. W.
    Y. W. C. A.—
      901 Rhode Island Ave. N. W.

North 9065
Satisfaction Plus Quality
Equals Service

FEATHERSTONE'S

SERVICE ANGLE GAS and OIL
Battery and Ignition Service—oil
Changed and Cars Greased New Tires
1305 New Jersey Ave. N. W.
Washington, D. C.

WASHINGTON
TOURIST
    Mrs. L. O. Diggs—
      215 Florida Ave. N. W.
    Mrs. M. J. Hines—
      1929 13th St. N. W.
    Mrs. R. Lee—1212 Girad St. N. W.

    Mrs. E. H. Watson—
      1435 "Q" St. N. W.
TAVERNS
    Liberty—910 5th St. N. W.
RESTAURANTS
    Green Parrot—1218 'U' St. N. W.
    Key's—7th & 'T' St. N. W.
BEAUTY PARLORS
    Apex—1417 'U' St. N. W.
THEATERS
    Bookert T.—'U' St. Bet 13 & 15 St.
    Lincoln—'U' St. Bet. 13 & 15th St.
    Republic—'U' St. Bet. 13 & 15 St.
SERVICE STATIONS

FLORIDA

JACKSONVILLE
HOTELS
    Blue Chip Hotel—514 Broad St.
    Hotel Eggmont—635 W. Ashley St.
    Hotel Sanders—636 W. Ashley St.
    Richmond Hotel—422 Broad St.
TOURIST
    Mrs. E. H. Flipper—
      739 W. Church St.
    Mrs. L. D. Jefferson—
      2140 Moncrief St.
    Mrs. B. Robinson—
      128 Orange St.
LAKELAND
    Cowell's Hotel—827 Florida Ave.
MIAMI
    Dorsey Hotel—941 N. W. 2nd Ave.
    Mary Elizabeth 700 N. W. 2nd Ave.
PENSACOLA
    Hotel Belmont—
      311 N. Tarragonia St.
ST. AUGUSTINE
TOURIST
    Mrs. P. C. Farrior—
      129 Central Ave.
    F. H. Kelley—83 Bridge St.
    H. G. Tye Apts.—132 Central Ave.
(ST. PETERSBURG)
(TOURIST HOMES)
    Mrs. J. A. Barrett 28th St. &
      6th Ave. S.
    Mrs. C. A. Sanders 1505 5th Ave.
    J. A. Bailey—942 3rd Ave. S.
TAMPA
    Beatrice Hotel—1515 Central Ave.
    Central Hotel—1028 Central Ave.
    Dallas Hotel—829 Zack St.
    Delux Hotel—822 Contant St.

(GEORGIA)

(ALBANY)
TOURIST
    Mrs. A. Bentley 525 Mercer St.
    Mrs. L. Davis 313 South St.
    Mrs. A. J. Ross 514 Mercer St.
    Mrs. C. Washington 214 S.
      Jackson St.

GEORGIA — ILL. USE IT AS YOUR IDENTIFICATION KEN. — LA. — MD.

ATLANTA
    Hotel Shaw—245 Auburn Ave.
    James Hotel—211 Auburn Ave. N.E
    McKay Hotel—Auburn Ave.

**Butler Y. M. C. A. 22 Butler St.

GEORGIA
(ATLANTA)
TOURIST
    Mrs. E. B. Jackson 49 Davis St. N. W.
Night Clubs
    The Top Hat—Auburn Ave. N. E.
Restaurant
    Mrs. Suttons 312 Auburn Ave. N. E.
Barber Shops
    Artistic 55 Decatur St.
Beaty Parlors
    Poro Auburn & Belle St. N. E.
Theaters
    Royal Auburn Ave. N. E.
Ashly Hunter St. N. E.
Dance Halls
Sunset Casino
Service Stations
Halls Auburn Ave. N. E.
COLUMBUS
    Lowes Hotel
(DUBLIN)
TOURIST
    Mrs. H. T. Banyon 316 S. Jefferson
    Mrs. M. Burden, 508 McCall St.
    Mrs. R. Hunter 504 S. Jefferson
    Mrs. M. Kea 105 S. Jefferson St.
(EASTMAN)
TOURIST
    J. P. Cooper 211 College St.
    Mrs. M. Mariano 408 1st Ave.
(GREENSBORO)
TOURIST
    Mrs. C. Brown Caanen Section
    Mrs. E. Jeter Railroad Sec.
    Mrs. B. Walker Springfield Sec.
MACON
    Douglas Hotel—361-3 Broadway
    Richmond Hotel—319 Broadway
(MACON)
TOURIST
    Mrs. M. Clemons 104 Spring St.
    Mrs. E. C. Moore 122 Spring St.
    Mrs. F. W. Henndon 139 1st Aev.
    Mrs. C. A. Monroe 108 Spring St.
SAVANNAH
(TRAILERS PARK)
    Jerry Cox
(WAY CROSS)
TOURIST
    Mrs. E. Duggar 964 Renolds St.
    Mrs. K. G. Scarlett 843 Reynolds

(ILLINOIS)
CHICAGO
HOTELS
    Brookmont—3953 S. Michigan Ave.
    Claridge—51st & Mhichigan Ave.
    Grand—5018 S. Parkway
    Huntington—619 E. 37th. St.
    Monogram—3449 S. State St.
    Ritz—409 E. Oakwood Blvd.
    Southway—6014 S. Park Aae.
    Trenier—409 Oakwood Blvd.
    Tyson—4259 S. Parkway
    Vincennes—601 E. 36th St.
    Y. M. C. A.—3763 S. Wabash Ave.
    Y. W. C. A.—4559 S. Parkway
    Franklin—3942 Indiana Ave.
CENTRALIA

Mrs. E. B. Clayborne
303 N. Pine St.

Barber Shops
    P. Coleman 503 N. Poplar St.
Beauty Shops
    M. Coleman 503 N. Poplar St.
Service Stations
    Langenfield 120 N. Poplar St.
DANVILLE
TOURIST
    Stewart—E. North St.
SPRINGFIELD
HOTELS
    Dudley—130 S. 11th St.

KENTUCKY
LOUISVILLE
HOTELS
    Allen—2516 W. Madison
    Walnut—615 Walnut St.
    Y. W. C. A.—528 S. Walnut St.
MOMMOUTH CAVE
HOTELS
    Brantsford
MT. STERLING
HOTELS
    Dew Drop Inn—E. Locust St.
PADUCAH
    Jefferson—514 S. 8th St.
    Metropolitan—724 Jackson St.
    Washington—805 Washington St.

LOUISIANA
NEW ORLEANS
HOTELS
    Astoria—225 S. Rampart St.
    Chicago—Bienville
    Patterson—761 S. Rampart St.
    Page—1038 Dryades
SHREVEPORT
    Lloyd—Milom St.

MAINE
PORTLAND
    The Thomas House—28 "A" St.

MARYLAND
HOTELS
ANNAPOLIS
    Wright's—26 Calvert St.

MD. — MASS. — MICH.   KEEP THIS GUIDE WITH YOU   NEW JERSEY

BALTIMORE
    Clark—Dolphin & Marison Ave.
    Hawkins—902 Madison Ave.
    Dru Moore Inn—
      839 N. Fremont Ave.
    Majestic—1602 McColloh St.
    Penn—1631 Pennsylvania Ave.
    Reed—1002 McCulloh St.
    Banks—1217 Madison Ave.
    Stokes—1624 Madison Ave.
    Y. M. C. A.—1600 Druid Hill Ave.
    Y. W. C. A.—1200 Druid Hill Ave.
        (MARYLAND)

Watch out for a new type signal light installed on the highways of Maryland. They are designed for high speed traffic and the main beam can be seen for 2000 ft. even on a bright day, while the secondary beam can be seen at short range. Each lens has a presmatic band which is used to intenify the beams. The presmatic bands in the Red Lens is horizontal, The Amber Lens is diagonal while the Green Lens is vertical. By having these bands at different angles one can tell at a distance which light is being read.

(FREDERICK)
TOURIST
    Mrs. E. W. Grinage 22 W. All Saints
    Mrs. J. Makel 119 E. 5th St.
    Mrs. W. W. Roberts 316 W. South
        (SALISBURY)
TOURIST HOMES
    Mrs. M. L. Parker 110 Delaware Ave.

HAGERSTOWN
TOURIST
    Frank Long—Jonathan St.
    Harmon—226 N. Jonathan St.

MARLBORO
HOTELS
    Wilson

        MASSACHUSETTS
BOSTON
HOTELS
    Harriett Tubman—25 Holyoke St.
    Melbourne—815 Tremont St.

        MICHIGAN
HOTELS
DETROIT
    Biltmore—1926 St. Antoine St.
    Dunbar—550 E. Adams St.
    Tansey—2474 Antoine St.
    Eizabeth—413 E. Elizabeth St.
    Fox—715 Madison St.
    Le Grande—1365 Lafayette St.
    Norwood—550E. Adams St.
    Northcross—
      St. Antoine & Columbia
    Russell—615 E. Adams St.
Night Clubs
    Plantation—550 E. Adams St.
SERVICE STATION
    Cobb's Maple & Chene Sts.

        New Jersey
ARENEL
RESTAURANT
    Tyler's Chicken Farm
ASBURY PARK
HOTELS
    Adore—104 Myrtle Ave.
    Metropolitan—
      1200 Springwood Ave.
    Whitelead—25 Atkins Ave.
TOURIST
    Mrs. A. Arch—23 Atkins Ave.
    Mrs. E. C. Burgess—
      1200 Springwood Ave.
    Mrs. Brown—135 Ridge Ave.
    Mrs. W. Greenlow—
      1317 Summerfield Ave.
    Mrs. C. Jones—141 Sylvan Ave.
    Mrs. V. Maupin—25 Atkins Ave.
    Mrs. Minyard—1106 Adams Ave.
    Mrs. M. Wigfall—1112 Adams Ave.
    Mrs. S. Wilks—1112 Mattison Ave.
    Mrs. E. C. Yesger—1406 Mattison Ave.
RESTAURANTS
    Danny's—Springwood Ave.
    George's—159 Springwood Ave.
    Pop's—1511Springwood Ave.
    West Side—1136 Springwood Ave.
TAVERNS
    Aztex Room—1147 Springwood Ave.
    Capitol—1212 Springwood Ave.
    Hollywood—1318 Springwood Ave.
    2 Door—1512 Springwood Ave.
BARBER SHOPS
    Consolidated—
      1216 Springwood Ave.
BEAUTY PARLORS
    Imperial—1107 Springwood Ave.
    Little Hollywood—
      1138 Springwood Ave.
    LaRoberts—1402 Springwood Ave.
    Opal—1146 Springwood Ave.
    Willie's—37 Sylvan Ave.
GARAGES
    West Side—1206 Springwood Ave.
ATLANTIC CITY
HOTELS
    Attucks—134 N. No. Carolina Ave.
    Bay State—334 N. Tennessee Ave.
    Liberty Apt.—
      Baltic & Kentucky Ave.
    Randell— 1601 Arctic Ave.
    Russell—23 N. Kentucky Ave.
    Ridley—1806 Arctic Ave.
    Scott—15 Illinois Ave.
    Swan—1326 Virginia Ave. N.
    Wright—1702 Arctic Ave.
ATLANTIC HIGHLANDS
RESTAURANTS
    Tennis Club Tea Room—
      Prospect Ave.
BAYONNE
TAVERNS
    Doc's—67 W. 23rd St.

4

NEW JERSEY   KEEP THIS GUIDE WITH YOU   NEW JERSEY

BRIDGESTON
TAVERNS
   The Ram's Inn—
      Bridgeston & Millville Pike
CAMDEN
TAVERNS
   Green Gold—3rd & Cherry
CAPE MAY
HOTELS
   De Griff—830 Corgie St.
   Richardson—Jackson St.
CAPE MAY
TOURIST HOMES
   Mrs. S. Giles—806 Corgie St.
   Mrs. M. Green—728 Lafayette St.
CEDAR KNOLL
COUNTRY CLUBS
   The Shady Oak Lodge
EATONTOWN
NIGHT CLUBS
   The Greenbrier—Pine Bush
EAST ORANGE
BEAUTY PARLORS
   Matties—186 Amherst St.
   Ritz—276 Main St.
ELIZABETH
TOURIST HOMES
   Mrs. L. G. Brown—173 Madison St.
   Mrs. T. T. Davis—27 Dayton St.
   Mrs. G. Pierson—1093 Williams St.
   Mrs. J. Pryde—1125 Fanny St.
RESTAURANTS
   Paradise—1129 E. Grand St.
ENGLEWOOD
LIQUOR STORES
   Giles—107 Williams St.

ENGLEWOOD-CLIFFS
NIGHT CLUBS
   Harlem on The Hudson
HACKENSACK
BARBER SHOPS
   Central Service—174 Central Ave.
   Dotson—234 1st St.
BEAUTY PARLORS
   Mary—206 Central Ave.

Central Bootblack Parlor

240 1st St.   Hackensack, N. J.

FIRST CLASS SHOE SHINE

ALL COLORED PAPERS

TOBACCO   CIGARETTES

Maurice Boswell
  Prop.

DRUGGIST
   Taper—259 1st St.

Hackensack 2-9233

Phone Englewood 3-2128

TAXI'S

AND

CARS FOR HIRE

DWIGHT MANOR GARAGE

STORAGE and REPAIRING

Washing -- Polishing — Simonizng

Cars Called For and Delivered

25 So. Van Brunt St. Englewood N. J.

CENTRAL TAXI SERVICE

Under the New Management of

CAREY E. McCALL

COURTEOUS — SAFE CONVENIENT

240 First Street .... Hackensack, N. J.

5

NEW JERSEY — USE IT AS YOUR IDENTIFICATION — NEW JERSEY

GENERAL REPAIRING

GAS   OIL   ACCESSORIES

Ignition & Carburetor

Work a Specialty

Tel. Hack. 2-6888 — Res. 3-0485

BROOKS BROS. SERVICE STATION

Hackensack, N. J.

WINE — DINE — DANCE

The Best Whiskies Wines & Beer

RIDEOUT'S BAR AND GRILL

204 CENTRAL AVE.

HACKENSACK, N. J.

Rideouts Swing Band
                    Two Floor Shows

HASKELL
RECREATION PARKS
   Thomas Lake
KINGSTON
ROAD HOUSES
   Merrill's
LAWNSIDE
TAVERNS
   Acorn Inn—Whitehorse Pike
   Dreamland
ROAD HOUSES
   Hi-Hat
   Lawnside Inn
LINDEN
NIGHT CLUBS
   4th Ward Club—
     1035 Baltimore Ave.
LONG BRANCH
RESTAURANTS
   The Main Stem—163 Belmont Ave.
   Woodson's—198 Belmont Ave.
TAVERNS
   Club "45"—Liberty St.
   Cosmopolitan—192 Belhont Ave.
   Sam Hall—18 Academy St.
   Tally-Ho—185 Belmont Ave.
MAGNOLIA
TAVERNS
   Green's
MONTCLAIR
RESTAURANTS
   Jack O'Lantern—
     193 Bloomfield Ave.
   J. & M.—213 Bloomfield Ave.
TAVERNS
   Spring Gardens—35 Spring St.
NIGHT CLUBS
   Rrecreation—Glenridge Cor. Bay St.
SCHOOL OF BEAUTY CULTURE
   Hair Dressing—207 Bloomfield Ave.
BARBER SHOPS
   Paramount—211 Bloomfield Ave.
BEAUTY PARLORS
   Quality—235 Bloomfield Ave.
NEWARK
HOTELS
   Grand—78 W. Market St.
TOURIST HOMES
   Mrs. M. Johnson—
     151 Pennsylvania Ave.
   Mrs. E. Morris—39 Chester Ave.
   Mrs. Spence—506 Washington St.
RESTAURANTS
   Dixie Chicken Club—
     178 Orange St.
   Eva's—126 West St.
TAVERNS
   Alcaza—72 Waverly Pl.
   Bert's—174 W. Kinny St.
   Charles—125 Broome St.
   Club Cuban—115 Broome St.
   Colony—Broome & W. Kinny Sts.
   Dan's—245 Academy St.
   Dodgers—8 Bedford Pl.
   Little Jonny's—47 Montgomery St.
   Lestbaders—175 Spruce St.

NEW JERSEY　　　　KEEP THIS GUIDE WITH YOU　　　　N. J.

 Reiff's—94 So. Orange Ave.
 Rim Tim Inn—179 Orange St.
 Saul's—60 Waverly Ave.
 The Hi Spot—173 W. Kinny St.
 Vito's—648 N. 6th St.
 Warren & Norfolk—256 Warren St.
 Woods—258 Prinnce St.
 Zan's—88 Waverly St.
BARBER SHOPS
 El Idelio—28 Wright St.
 Teals—137 Somerset St.
BEAUTY PARLORS
 Gomes—230 W. Kinny St.
 La Vogue—227 W. Kinny St.
 Harrison & Douglas—
  125 Somerset St.
NIGHT CLUBS
 Boston Plaza—4 Boston St.
 Golden Inn—150 Charleston St.
 Nest Club—Warren & Newark St.
 New Kinny Club—36 Arlington St.
 Villa Maurice—375 Washington St.
CHINESE RESTAURANTS
 Spruce Chinnese—191 Spruce St.
DRUGGIST
 Mendelsohn's—132 Spruce St.

NEW BRUNSWICK
ROAD HOUSES
 Green's Barn—RT 27
  Bet. Princeton & New Brunswick

ORANGE
TAVERNS
 Frank's—120 Hickory St.
NIGHT CLUBS
 Dave & Manney's Paradise—
  Parrow & Chestnut Pl.
CHINESE RESTAURANTS
 Orange Gardens—132 Parrow St.

OCEAN CITY
HOTELS
 Comfort—201 Bay Ave.
 Neal—4th St.

PATERSON
RESTAURANTS
 Governor—130 Governor St.
TAVERNS
 Blue Chip—10 Bridge St.

POINT PLEASANT
TAVERNS
 Joe's—337 Railroad Ave.

UP - TO - DATE
PEOPLE
USE
THE GREEN BOOK'
ON THEIR TRIPS

The Choicest Spot Of New Jersey
Special Entertainment On Thursday —
Saturday & Sunday

CHARLIE'S PARADISE
80 1st St.　　　　Passaic, N. J.

BAR & GRILL

Best Wines and Liquors

Good Old Fashion

Southern Fried Chicken

OPEN AT ALL HOURS

Catering to clubs　Charles Jones Prop.

PLAINFIELD
TAVERNS
 Liberty—4th St.

RAHWAY
NIGHT CLUBS
 Rainbow Inn—257 Union Pl.

RED BANK
RESTAURANTS
 Vincents Dining Room—
  263 Shewsbury Ave.
TAVERNS
 West Bergen—103 W. Bergen Pl.
BARBER SHOPS
 A. Dillard—250 Shewsbury Ave.
BEAUTY PARLORS
 R. Alleyne—124 W. Bergen Pl.
 Surles—214 Shewsbury Ave.
SERVICE STATION
 Galatres—Shewsbury & Catherine
TAILORS
 Dudley's—79 Sunset Ave.

REVEYTOWN
ROAD HOUSES
 Bob Jones

SCOTCH PLAINS
RESTAURANTS
 Hill Top—60 Jerusalem Road
ROAD HOUSES
 Villa Casanova—Jerusalem Road

7

NEW JERSEY — USE IT AS YOUR IDENTIFICATION — N. Y.

COUNTRY CLUBS
Shady Rest Jerusalem Road

SEA BRIGHT
RESTAURANTS
Essie Kings—11 New St.

VAUX HALL
BEAUTY PARLORS
Celeste—211 Springwood Ave.

NEW YORK

HOTELS
BUFFALO
Francis—Exchange St.
Little Harlem—44 Michigan Ave.
Montgomery—486 Michigan Ave.
Vendome—177 Clinton St.

NEW YORK CITY
HOTELS
Adrienne—2053 7th Ave.
Braddock—126th St. & 8th Ave.
Dewey Square—201 W. 117th St.

**Fane-Dumas—205 W. 135th St.

**Garrett House—314 W. 127th St.

Grampion—182 St. Nicholas Ave.

**Martha—6 W. 135th St.

Mariette—017 7th Ave.
Olga—695 Lenox Ave.

**Press—23 W. 135th St.

The Harreit—271 W. 127th St.
50 W. 112th St.
Woodside—2424 7th Ave.

RESTAURANTS
Ansonia, 2230 8th Ave.
Aunt Dinah's Kitchen, 172 W. 135th
Bolivia Rotisserie, 2143 7th Ave.
Bozans Cor. 116th & 8th Ave.

Cafe California, 730 St. Nicholas A.

Central, 569 Lenox Ave.
Cherry Blossom, 338 Lenox Ave.
Clara's Open Kitchen,
  275 St. Nicholas Ave.
Cotton, 630 Lenox Ave.
Cozy Shoppe, 2154 7th Ave.
Dixie Cafeteria, 2657 8th Ave.
Drake, 2170 7th Ave.
Edgecombe Rotisserie,
  431 Edgecombe Ave.
El Mundilal, 222 W. 116th St.
Harlem Sea Food, 2126 7th Ave.
Holly Mount, 2210 8th Ave.
Ideal, 247 W. 145th St.
Jimmie's Shicken Shack
  763 St. Nicholas Ave.
Craig's 55 St. Nicholas Pl.
Little Gray Shop No. 2,
  2465 7th Ave.
Little Gray Shop No. 3,
  266 W. 145th St.

Liberty, 2230 8th Ave.
Lou's Kitchen, 2297 7th Ave.
Luxor, 2394 7th Ave.
Max's, St. Nicholas Ave. & 145th St
Monterey, 2339 7th Ave.
Millicent's, 826 St. Nicholas Ave.
New York Lunch, 2723 8th Ave.
Oyster Bay, 2288 7th Ave.
Pete's, 2534 8th Ave.
Regal Cafeteria, 303 W. 125th St.
Ritz Luncheonette, 2310 7th Ave.
Sheffield, 2343 8th Ave.
Solar Cafeteria, 104 W. 116th St.
Southern, 2201 7th Ave.
Thomfords, 351 W. 125th St.
Tillie's, 227 Lenox Ave.
Willow, 207 W. 125th St.

TAVERNS
Alhambra, Cor. 126th St. & 7th Ave
Arthur's, 2481 8th Ave.
Big Apple, 2300 7th Ave.
Bird Cage, 2308 7th Ave.
Blackbirds Inn, 2130 7th Ave.
Blue Heaven, 378 Lenox Ave.
Brittwood, 594 Lenox Ave.
Calvacade, 2104 7th Ave.
Chicks, Cor 148th St. & 7th Ave.
Colonial, 2321 8th Ave.
Colonial Krazy House,
  116 Bradhurst Ave.
Doonan's, 2307 8th Ave.
Eddie's, 714 St. Nicholas Ave.
Elbow Inn, 658 Lenox Ave.
Elk Scene, 469 Lenox Ave.
Florentine, 2175 7th Ave.
Golden, 356 W. 145th St.
Gotham, 2440 7th Ave.
Gus', 565 Lenox Ave.
Harlem, 2418 7th Ave.
Harlem Grill, 2140 7th Ave.
Harlem Hollywood, 105 W. 116th St
Harlem Moon, 2320 7th Ave.
Heat Wave, 1991 7th Ave.
Hot-Cha, 2280 7th Ave.
Horse Shoe, 2474 7th Ave.
Jay's, 400 W. 148th St.
Knickerbocker, Cor. 126th &
  St. Nicholas Ave.
La Mar Cheri, 739 St. Nicholas Ave
Lenox Empire, 281 Lenox Ave.
Lincoln, 518 Lenox Ave.
Lincoln Grill, 2046 7th Ave.
Lildale, 2469 7th Ave.
Logas, 2496 7th Ave.
Long's Golden Grill, 356 W. 145th
Metropolitan, 2056 Lenox Ave.
Moon Glow, 220 W. 145th St.
Monte Carlo, 2247 7th Av. e

The Green Book is always ready
To Serve You
Use it on each trip
Patronize these Listed Places

| NEW YORK CITY | KEEP THIS GUIDE WITH YOU | NEW YORK CITY |

NEW YORK, N. Y.

The Geo. Washington Bridge Tunnel, crosstown to Amsterdam Ave. will carry traffic under Manhattan streets so to avoid other street traffic to the Bronx an the Tri-Borough Bridge and to the Worlds Fair, located on the Flushing meadows. This improvement will be finished in time for the Worlds Fair.

Moulin Rouge, 2454 7th Ave.
Murrain, 635 Lenox Ave.
New Harlem, 515 Lenox Ave.
New Manhattan, 503 Lenox Ave.
New Thrill, 2 Bradhurst Ave.
Orange Blossom, 570 Lenox Ave.
Palace, 535 Lenox Ave.
Paradise Inn, 2342 8th Ave.
Pedro Montanez, 22 Lenox Ave.
Roma Gardens, 257 W. 116th St.
Red Arrow, 2259 7th Ave.
Reliance, 207 W. 116th St.
Renaissance, 2359 7th Ave.
Roma Gardens, 257 W. 116th St.
Rythm Club, 2245 7th Ave.
Saratoga, 575 Lenox Ave.
Shanty Inn, 2191 8th Ave.
Silver Cup, 2430 8th Ave.
Speedway, 92 St. Nicholas Ave.
Sports Innn, 2308 8th Ave.
Swanee, 218 St. Nicholas Ave.
The Partridge Inn,
 106 St. Nicholas Ave.
Tom's Cabin, 760 St. Nicholas Ave.
Victoria, 2418 7th Ave.
Welcome Inn, 2895 8th Ave.
Wonder Bar, 2193 7th Ave.
Wonder Bar, 302 W. 145th Ave.
Yeah Man 2350 7th Ave.
721 St. Nicholas Ave. Grill

NIGHT CLUBS

Capitol, 115 Lenox Ave.
Elks Rendezvous, 133rd St.
 & Lenox Ave.
Harlem Hollywood, 105 W. 116th St
Plantation, 142nd St & Lenox Ave.
Small's Paradise, 7th Ave. &
 135th St.
101 Ranch, 101 W. 139th St.

BARBER SHOPS

A. McCargo, 242 W. 145th St.
B. Carey, 2521 8th Ave.
B. Garrett, 2311 7th Ave.
Eldorado, 203 W. 116th St.
Esquire, 2265 7th Ave.
Hi-Hat, 2276 7th Ave.
Hoghie Rayford, 2013 7th Ave.
H. Parks, 200 W. 146th St.
Latin America, 2395 8th Ave.
Leon & Teddy's, 353 W. 145th St.
Lud, 166 W. 116th St.
Park Lane, 2206 7th Ave.
Manhattan, 2456 8th Ave.
Majestic, 130 W. 116th St.
Modernistic, 2132 7th Ave.

Renaissance, 2349 7th Ave.

Roxy, 2322 7th Ave.
Royal, 749 St. Nicholas Ave.
Edean, 237 W. 145th St.
Spanish America, 2637 8th Ave.
Spooner's, 2435 8th Ave.
World, 2621 8th Ave.

BEAUTY PARLORS

B. Pierce, 2370 7th Ave.
Beard's, 322 St. Nicholas Ave.
Beulah,s 350 Manhattan Ave,
Chassie 2148 7th Ave,
Constance, 2192 7th Ave.
De Lux 2422 8th Ave.
Dutchess, 2392 7th Ave.
Evelyn's, 713 St. Nicholas Ave.
Frances, 2446 7th Ave.
G. Warren, 348 W. 145th St.
Glady's, 472 Convent Ave.
Harris, 2194 7th Ave.
Helen's, 217 W. 145th St.
Ideal, 245 W. 116th St.
Irene's, 152nd St. & Convent Ave.
Josephine's, 212 St. Nicholas Ave.
La Bolita, 19 St. Nichalos Ave.

Tillinghast 5-9791 Call for Appointment
LA RITZ BEAUTY SALON
Bernice Bruton—Billy Bouknight
2205 7th Ave.   New York City
Near 130th Street

Lotties, 2468 7th Ave.
Lu Audra, 2352 7th Ave.
Mae's, 720 St. Nicholas Ave.
Mamies, 345 W. 116th St.
Murians, 402 St. Nicholas Ave.
New Way, 143 W. 116th St.
Park Lane, 2166 7th Ave.
Personality, 2124 7th Ave.
Powder Puff, 2487 7th Ave.
Sybils, 2124 7th Ave.
Silver Leaf, 461 W. 150th St.

SCHOOL OF BEAUTY CULTURE

Apex, 200 W. 135th St.
Mme. C. J. Walker, 239 W. 125th St

NEW YORK CITY   USE IT AS YOUR IDENTIFICATION   NEW YORK CITY

AUTOMOTIVE

   Andy Radiator, 416 W. 127th St.
   A. Eastmond Auto Blacksmith, 31 W. 144th St.
   C. Jones, Technician, 25 E. 136th St.
   Daly Bros., 484 St. Nicholas Ave.
   Green's Auto, 110 W. 145th St.
   H. Facey Painting, 705 Lenox Ave.
   J. Jones Repairs, 120 W. 145th St.
   L. Martinez, 612 Lenox Ave.
   Meisel Tire, 2079 7th Ave.
   Nathan Auto Parts, 34 W. 145th St.
   R. & S Auto Elec., 626 Lenox Ave.
   Richards Auto Repairing, 112 W 145th St.
   Stanley Brake, 1020 St. Nicholas A.
   Simons Supply, 133 W. 145th St.
   Ullman & Hauser, 27 St. Claire Pl.
   Viaduct Garage, 101 Edgecombe A.
   W. J. McAvoy, Ignition, 703 Lenox

THE WORLD'S FAIR 1939

Contract Now For

Your Add Space

LET THE MOTORIST KNOW WHERE YOU ARE

AUTO LOANS
   Community, 2368 7th Ave.

GARAGES
   Colonial Park, 310 W. 144th St.

DANCE HALLS
   Club Danceland, 322 W. 125th St.
   Lido, 7th Ave. & 146th St.
   Follies Ball Room, 2356 8th Ave.
   Renaissane, 7th Ave. & 138th St.
   Savoy, Lenox Ave. & 140th St.

Phone: AU. 3-0671

THE TALK OF THE TOWN WHEN IN NEW YORK

Little Alpha Service
THE COMPLETE CLEANERS

ONE OF NEW YORK'S PIONEER CLEANERS, WHERE SERVICE IS JUST A SMILE.

6-8 HOUR SERVICE—R. E. EUBANKS, MGR.

200 WEST 136th St. Cor. 7th Ave.

84 West 120th St. Cor Lenox Ave.

ALWAYS ON DUTY

YOUR ADD!

Is Seen

NOT FOR A DAY

BUT FOR A YEAR

THEATERS
   Apollo, 253 W. 125th St.
   Lafaytte, 7th Ave. & 131st St.

PEP 'EM UP
AUTO ELECTRIC SERVICE
GORDON SEALE
Armatures and Ignition
W. 145th St.   New York City

10

USE IT AS YOUR IDENTIFICATION

"THE AUTOMOBILE AND WHAT IT HAS DONE FOR THE NEGRO"
by BENJ. J. THOMAS
FORMER STATE EXAMINER
and
PROPRITOR OF THE BROADWAY AUTO SCHOOL

In 1890 the Automobile first made its appearance in the United States, and since that time up until to-day, the automobile has been steadily increasing with leaps and bounds, and till today the automobile industry is the second largest industry in the world, giving employment to more people than any industry in the world.

In 1937 there were about thirty million automobiles being operated in the United States alone. This amount being made up of pleasure cars. Added to this there ar millions of trucks in the commercial fields, Vans in the local and long distance moving fields, and millions of buses in the transportation fields.

The automobile has been a special blessing to the Negro, for the Negro is getting better wages and doing more business in the automobile industry than any other industry in the world. Take for instance 25 years ago, the average young colored man was either doing porter work, bell hopping, running an elevator or waiting on table, and the average wage at that time was $5.00 per week. That same young man as soon as he learned to operate an automobile, instead of paying him

$5.00 per week, he would begin at not less than $15.00 per week, and as he progressed and became a mechanic his wages would be railed to $25.00 per week until today, men that are good mechanics and can master the trade, both as a chauffeur and mechanic, are being paid anyway from $25.00 to $50.00 per week, therefore, taking men out of the servant class and placing them in the mechanical class.

In New York City alone, one third of the Mechanical work is being done by Colored men, and the same that applied to New York, applies to all other cities and towns through the country. There is one automobile manufacturing company alone that employes 5000 Colored men, saying nothing about the thousand of Colored men that are employed by other automobile companies.

The Negro owns and controls a large percentage of the taxicab business throughout the country, and the garage and repair shop business is held in the same proportion.

NEW YORK CITY   USE IT AS YOUR IDENTIFICATION   WESTCHESTER

Katherine Fontaine   Elliott Fontaine

We call and Deliver Anywhere

La FONTAINE SERVICE

Valet — Tailoring — Dyeing — Cleaning

Phones: EDgecombe 4-1365
AU. 3-7976

470 Convent Avenue   764 St. Nicholas Avenue
New York City

Call Audubon 3-8340 Prompt Delivery

Open 8 A. M. to 12 P. M.

GOLDMAN'S
WINES AND LIQUORS

New York State Retail Wine and Liquor Store Lincense L-761

483 W. 155th St.   New York City
Cor. Amsterdam Avenue

The Most Dependable Place on Washington Heights

Phone: WAdsworth 3-9417

LOU PRICE AUTO SALES, Inc.

"Used Cars Of The Better Kind"

As Low As $5.00   20 Mo. To Pay

ALL CARS GUARANTEED

No Red Tape — Trades Accepted

4330 B'way.   New York, N. Y.

Formally Located At 124th St. & 8th A.

Tel. MO. 2-1056
UN. 4-8351

GENERAL AUTO REPAIRING
SA-MED BRAKE & AUTO SERVICE CORP.

Brake & Ignition Specialists

ALL WORK GUARANTEED
MODERATE PRICES

517-519 WEST 125th ST.
NEW YORK, N. Y.

WESTCHESTER   KEEP THIS GUIDE WITH YOU   N. Y.

ELMSFORD
TAVERNS
   Clarke, 91 Saw Mill River Road
NEW ROCHELLE
RESTAURANTS
   Betsy Ann, 442 North Ave.
   City Park, 521 5th Ave.
   Harris, 29 Morris St.
   Rogers, 50 Winyah
   Week's, 68 Winyah
TAVERNS
   Bal-Mo-Ral, 56 Brook St.
NIGHT CLUBS
   Sky Vue, Wingah & Brook St.
BEAUTY PARLORS
   A. Berry, 50 DeWitts Pl.
   B. Miller, 8 Brook Ave.
   H. Johnson, 97 Winthrop Ave.
   Maion's, 108 Winthrop Ave.
   Ocie, 41 Rochelle Pl.
   Orchid, 57 Winyah Ave.
BARBER SHOPS
   The Royal Salon, 4 Brook Ave.

Phone N. R. 9694   A. B. Fields, Prop.

FIELDS BARBER SHOP

10 YEARS IN ONE PLACE

Latest Modernistic Shop in W'chester

66 Winyah Ave.   New Rochelle, N. Y.

Telephones: N. R. 10409 or 10017
Dolly Madison Ice Cream
Cigars, Cigarettes
**QUALITY CHEMICALS
PROMPT SERVICE**

DANIEL'S PHARMACY
C. H. Daniels, Ph. G.
57 WINYAH AVE.
New Rochelle, N. Y.
Our Motto: Purity, Promptness,
Accuracy

USEFUL INFORMATION

Key to Street Numbers in N. Y. C.L To find what street is nearest, take the street numer, cancel last figure, divide by 2, add or subtract key number by 2, add or subtract key number found below. The result will be the nearest street.

Ave. A ....Add 3
Ave. B ....Add 3
Ave. C ....Add 3
Ave. D ....Add 3
1st Ave ....Add 3
2nd Ave. ....Add 3
3rd Ave. ....Add 9 or 10
4th Ave. ....Add 8
5th Ave.

  Up to 200 ....Add 13
  Up to 400 ....Add 16
  Up to 600 ....Add 18
  Up to 775 ....Add 20
  Above 2000 ....Add 24

6th Ave. ....Subt. 12 or 13
7th Ave. ....Add 12
8th Ave. ....Add 9 or 10
9th Ave. ....Add 13
10th Ave. ....Add 14
11th Ave. ....Add 15
Amsterdam ....Add 59 or 60
Audubon ....Add 165
Columbus ....Add 59 or 60
Convent ....Add 127
Edgecombe ....Add 134
Ft. Washington ....Add 158
Lenox ....Add 110
Lexington ....Add 22
Madison ....Add 26
Manhattan ....Add 100
Park ....Add 34 or 35
Pleasant ....Add 101
St. Nicholas ....Add 110
Wadsworth ....Add 173
West End ....Add 59 or 60
B'way ab. 23, Subt. 30 or 31

Central Pak West—Divide house number by 10 and add 60.

Riverside Drive—Divide house number by 10 and add 72.

Streets—To find nearest avenue, count 100 numbers to the block, east or west

WESTCHESTER   KEEP THIS GUIDE WITH YOU   BKLYN.

LARCHMONT
TAVERNS
   Park, 1 5th Ave.

HILLCREST 5080

THE FAVORITE GRILL
JOHN B. STEWARD, Prop.

WINES — LIQUORS — BEER

Dining and Dancing Every Night
Music with the Harlem Touch

154 So. 7th Ave.   Mt. Vernon, N. Y.

MT. VERNON
ROAD HOUSES
   Pitts, 24 W. 3rd St.
   Mohawk Inn, 142 S. 7th Ave.
SCHOOL OF BEAUTY CULTURE
   Okeh, 224 S. 7th Ave.
   Orchid, 48 W. 3rd St.
OSSINING
ROAD HOUSES
   Goodie Shop, 51 Hunter St.
PLEASANTVILLE
ROAD HOUSES
   White Towers
PORTCHESTER
NIGHT CLUBS
   Famous Royal Gardens,
     14 New Broad St.
TUCKAHOE
RESTAURANTS
   Major's, 48 Washington St.
   Butterfly Inn, 47 Washington St.
BARBER SHOPS
   Al's, 144 Main St.
BEAUTY PARLORS
   Shahana, 144 Main St.
WHITE PLAINS
RESTAURANTS
   Goody Shop, Brookfield St.

Tel. White Plains 10386

Dine and Dance

At   L

LLOYD'S
OF WHITE PLAINS

Entertainers BAR & GRILL Orchestra
Fine Wines and Best Food
At Moderate Prices
LOOK FOR LLOYD'S SIGN
88 MARTINE AVENUE
W. Bernard, Prop. White Plains, N. Y.

Phone W. P. 10250

"A Delight in Every Bite'

SOUTHERN
RESTAURANT

Wines and Liquors
Dancing
Open Day and Night

118 Martine Ave.
White Plains, N. Y.

TAVERNS
   Kingfish, 129 Martine Ave.
   Oasis, 115 Tarrytown Road
BEAUTY PARLORS
   Marie's, 94 Brookfield St.
NORTH TARRYTOWN
BARBER SHOPS
   Lemon's, Valley St.
   J. Brown, Valley St.
BEAUTY PARLOR
   J. Prioleau, 88 Valley St.

BROOKLYN
RESTAURANTS

Bagley's Restaurant & Summer Garden—2561 E. 16th St.

Sheepshead Bay, Brooklyn, N. Y.

   Dew Drop—363 Halsey St.
   Lucille's—923 Fulton St.
   M. & M.—1455 Fulton St.
   Richardson—1686 Fulton St.
   Rosebud—1081 Fulton St.
TAVERNS
   Moonlight—589 Franklin St.
   Royal—1073 Fulton St.
   Utopia—1093 Fulton St.
NIGHT CLUBS
   Hanlew—334 Lewis St.
   Lion's—307 Ralph Ave.
   Sadelle's—
     Atlantic & Saratoga Aves.
DANCE HALLS
   Bedford—1153 Atlantic Ave.
   Palm Gardens—Summer Ave.
   Palm Gardens—Bainbridge St.
THEATERS
   Apollo—Fulton & Throop Ave.
   New Casino—Broadway & DeKalb
   New United—Myrtle & Hudson Ave
   Regent—Fulton St. & Bedford Ave.
   Tompkins—Tompkins & Gates Ave

Brooklyn   USE IT AS YOUR IDENTIFICATION   N. C. — OHIO

BEAUTY PARLORS
    Bartley's—514 Classon Ave.
    Cloverleaf—425 Gates Ave.
    C. Bogan—1720 Fulton St.
    Diddy's—1518 Fulton St.
    Emma's—1391 Fulton St.
    La Mae—525 Classon Ave.
    Victoria—486 Halsey St.
SCHOOLS OF BEAUTY CULTURE
    Almanello—1345 Fulton St.
    J. K.—417 Tompkins Ave.
    Ritz—1358 Fulton St.
    Theresa—304 Livonia Ave.
JAMAICA L. I.
TAVERNS
    Monarch—171st St. & Liberty Ave.
NIGHT CLUBS
    High Hat—108th St. & Merrick Rd.

NEW YORK
NIAGARA FALLS
    The Parker House—627 Erie Ave.
Beauty Parlors
    La Belle—Erie Ave.
    The Parker House—627 Erie Ave.
Barber Shops
    Ashford—Erie Ave.
    Garland—Erie Ave.
ROCHESTER
    Gibson—461 Clarissa St.
    Johnson—86 Industrial St.
Night Clubs
    Cotton—Joseph St.
SARATOGA SPRINGS
    Geneva—27 Walworth St.
    Green Tree—52 Washington St.
SYRACUSE
    The Savoy—210 Almond St.
ELMIRA
    Wilson—307 E. Clinton St

NORTH CAROLINA
CHARLOTTE
HOTELS
    Charlomac—1st & Brevard Sts.
    Sanders—2nd St.
DURHAM
HOTELS
    Biltmore—E. Pettigrew St.
    Jones—502 Ramsey St.

ENLARGE YOUR SALES AREA

PEOPLE ARE TRAVELING ....

THE YEAR ROUND

A D V E R T I S E

IN

THE GREEN BOOK

NORTH CAROLINA
TOURIST HOMES
    Mrs. Mary Sims, 909 Fayettesville
    Mrs. S. A. Morris, 902 Fayettesville
    Mrs. N. O'Daniel,
      1005 Fayetteville St.
FAYETTEVILLE
HOTELS
    Bedford Inn—203 Moore St.
GASTONIA
HOTELS
    Union Sq.
GREENSBORO
HOTELS
    Travelers Inn—612 E. Market St.
    Legion Club—829 E. Market St.
TOURIST HOMES
    T. Daniel, 912 E. Market
    Mrs. E. Evans, 906 E. Market
NEW BERN
HOTELS
    Rhone—42 Queen St.
TOURIST
    H. C. Sparrow, 68 West St.
RALEIGH
HOTELS
    Arcade
SANFORD
HOTELS
    Philipps—Pearl St.
WILSON
HOTELS
    Biltmore—E. Washington St.
    The Wilson Biltmore—539 E. Nash
WINSTON-SALEM
HOTELS
    Ideal—11th & Woodland Ave.
    Lincoln—9 E. 3rd St.
TOURIST HOMES
    Mrs. J. Penn, 115 N. Ridge Ave.
    Mrs. H. L. Christian, 302 E. 9th St.
    Mrs. N. Jones, 859 N Liberty St.
    Mrs. R. B. Williams,
      1225 N. Ridge Ave.
BEAUTY PARLORS
    Orchid
WELDON
HOTELS
    Pope
    Terminal Inn—Washington Ave.

AKRON   OHIO
HOTELS
    Garden City—Howard &
      Furnace Sts.
    Mathews—77 N. Howard St.
    The Mecca—76 Furnace St.
    The Upperman—197 Bluff St.
CLEVELAND
HOTELS
    Geraldine—2212 E. 40th St.

    Majestic—2291 E. 55th

    Ward—4113 Cedar Ave.
    Y. M. C. A.—E. 76th St. & Cedar
BARBER SHOPS
    Majestic, 2290 E. 55th St.

PENNSYLVANIA   KEEP THIS GUIDE WITH YOU   PENN.

CLEVELAND
NIGHT CLUBS
   Heat Wave, 2291 E. 55th St.
BEAUTY PARLORS
   Lu Zell, 2211 E. 55th St.
THEATERS
   Globe, E. 55th & Woodland
RESTAURANTS
   The Chicken Coop, 9615 Cedar Ave.
GARAGES
   Rollin, E. 40th & Central
SERVICE STATIONS
   Wrights, E. 92nd & Cedar

COLUMBUS
HOTELS
   Fulton, 403 E. Fulton St.
   Litchferd, N. 4th St.
   Macon, 368 N. 20th St.
   Plaza, Long St. & Hamilton Ave.

SPRINGFIELD
HOTELS
   Posey, 209 S. Fountain Ave.

TOLEDO
HOTELS
   Kea, 720 Washington St.
   Pleasant, 15 N. Erie St.

ZANESVILLE
HOTELS
   Park, 1561 W. Main St.
   Stevens, 657 W. Main St.

PENNSYLVANIA

ALLENTOWN
TOURIST HOMES
   Mrs. D. Taliaferro, 378 Union St.
   Mrs. W. Washington, 207 Leigh St.

BEDFORD
HOTELS
   Harris

BRISTOL
TOURIST
   Mrs. L. Willhite, 414 Cedar St.

COATESVILLE
HOTELS
   Subway

CHAMBERSBURG
HOTELS
   Liberty Inn, Liberty & Water St.
TOURIST HOMES
   Mrs. H. Pinns, 68 W. Liberty St.
   Mrs. C. Stevenson, 619 S. Main St.

CHESTER
TOURIST HOMES
   R. L. Bennett Home For Women
   830 W. 2nd St.

WEST CHESTER
HOTELS
   Magnolia, 300 E. Miner St.

ERIE
HOTELS
   Pope, 1318 French St.

HARRISBURG
HOTELS
   Jackson, 1004 N. 6th St.

TOURIST HOMES
   Mrs. H. Carter, 606 Foster St.
   Mrs. H. Hall, Herr & Montgomery

LANCASTER
TOURIST HOMES
   Mrs. E. Clark, 462 Rockland St.
   J. Carter, 143 S. Duke St.
   A. L. Polite, 540 North St.

OIL CITY
TOURIST HOMES
   Mrs. Jackson, 258 Bissel Ave.
   Mrs. M. Moore, 8 Bishop St.

PHILADELPHIA
HOTELS
   Attucks, 801 S. 15th St.
   Baltimore, 1438 Lombard St.
   Citizens, 420 S. 15th St.
   Douglas, Broad & Lombard Sts.
   Elrae, 805 N. 13th St,
   Elizaeth Fry, 756 S. 16th St.
   La Salle, 2026 Ridge Ave.
   Maceo Cafe, Van Pelt & Norris St.
   New Roadside, 514 S. 15th St.
   Paradise, 1627 Fitzwater St.
   Blue Bowl, 22nd & Montgomery A.
   The Alston, 2333 Catherine St.
   Y. M. C. A., 1724 Christian St.
   Y. W. C. A., 1605 Catherine St.
   Y. W. C. A., 6128 Germantown Ave.

TAVERNS
   Dixon's Wonder Bar,
     19th & Montgomery Sts.
   Harlem, 13th & Lombard Sts.
   Lenox, Popular — Jessup Sts.
   Roseland, 5404 Arch St.
   Parrish, 10th & Parrish Sts.
   Sam's, 1612 South St.
   Wander Inn, 18th & Federal Sts.

NIGHT CLUBS
   Butler's Paradise, Ridge &
     Jefferson
   The Progressive Club,
     1415 S. 20th St.

RESTAURANTS
   Marion's, 20th & Bainridge Sts.
   Wilson's, 21st & Burke Sts.

BARBER SHOPS
   S. Jones, 2064 Ridge St.

BEAUTY PARLORS
   Agnes, 705 South 18th St.
   At's, 661 N. 13th St.
   Effie's, 5502 Girad Ave.
   Elizabeth's, 5003 Brown St.
   A. Henson, 1318 Fairmont Ave.
   Jennie's, 1618 French St.
   La Salle, 2036 Ridge St.
   Lady Ross, 718 S. 18th St.
   A. Reynolds, 2133 Christian St.
   Redmond's, 710 N. 48th St.
   Rose's, 16th & South Sts.

GARAGES
   Burrel, 1210 N. 19th Sts.

SERVICE STATIONS
   Dorsey Bros., 2009 Oxford St.

15

PENNSYLVANIA USE IT AS YOUR IDENTIFICATION R. I.

PHILADELPHIA
THEATERS
- Lincoln, Broad & Lombard Sts.
- Nixon's Grand, Broad & Montgomery Sts.
- Pearl, Ridge & Jefferson Sts.
- Royal, 16th & South Sts.

GERMANTOWN-PHIL.
TOURIST HOMES
- M. Foote, 221 N. Penn St.

BARBER SHOPS
- G. Taylor, 60 W. Duval St.

BEAUTY PARLORS
- M. Harris, 42 W. Rittenhouse St.

TAVERNS
- The Terrace Grill, 75 E. Sharpnack St.

PITTSBURGH
HOTELS
- Ave—1538 Wylie Ave.
- Bailey's Stagg, 1308 Wylie Ave.
- Bailey's, 1533 Center Ave.
- Colonial, Wylie Ave. & Fulton St.
- Park, 2215 Wylie Ave.
- Potter, 1304 Wylie Ave.
- Station, Station St. E. End

TOURIST HOMES
- Mrs. R. Lewis, 2600 Wylie Ave.
- Mrse. J. Williams, 5518 Claybourne St.

Mr. ADVERTISER!
Your Name is Before the Public
NOT FOR A DAY OR WEEK BUT A YEAR

READING
TOURIST HOMES
- Mrs. W. Isaacs, 131 Green St.
- Mrs. C. Dawson, 441 Buttonwood St.

SCRANTON
TOURIST HOMES
- Mrs. E. King, 1312 Linden St.
- Mrs. C. Jenkins, 424 Moir Ct.
- Mrs. J. Taylor, 14151 Penn Ave.

WILLIAMSPORT
TOURIST HOMES
- M. Nash, 612 Walnut St.
- Mrs. W. Gordon, 646 Walnut St.
- Mrs. R. Lightfoot, 603 Walnut St.
- Mrs. E. Johnson, 621 Spruce St.

WILKES BARRE
HOTELS
- Shaw, 15 S. State St.

WASHINTON
HOTELS
- Jimmie Fishers, 120 E. Chestnut St

WASHINGTON
TOURIST HOMES

Booker T. Washington
36 N. College St.

- A. Banks, 143 E. Chestnut St.

RESTAURANTS
- W. Allen, N. Lincoln St.
- J. Fisher, 120 E. Chestnut St.
- M. Thomas, N. Lincoln St.

NIGHT CLUBS
- Dreamland Inn, E. Hallan Ave.

BARBER SHOPS
- Yancey's, E. Spruce St.
- T. Wheeler, E. Chestnut St.
- J. Baker, E. Chestnut St.

DANCE HALLS
- Odd Fellows, E. Chestnut St.

IF YOU WANT MORE BUSINESS YOU CAN GET-IT! BY USING SPACE AND MAKE YOUR BUSINESS KNOWN TO THE TOURIST

YORK
HOTELS
- Howard, Beaver & Princess Sts.
- Y. W. C. A., N. Lincoln St.

TOURIST HOMES
- Mrs. E. Armstrong, 116 E. King St.
- Mrs. I. Grayson, 32 W. Princess
- John Miller, 307 E. King St.
- S. Green, 103 S. Duke St.

RHODE ISLAND

NEWPORT
HOTELS
- Glover, Brindley & Center Sts.

PROVIDENCE
HOTELS
- Hill Top Inn, 72 Meeting St.
- The Bertha, 54 Meeting St.

KEEP THIS GUIDE WITH YOU

BAD DRIVING WASTES FUEL

With the high tax on gasoline in the different states, it behoves all motorists to get the most out of his car. This is particularly true of the newest cars because of their great capacity for performance. Many driving customs should be revised when driving for milage with the modern car. With the automatic choke, if the car is backed out of the driveway, it shouldn't be left running; but switched off. If this precaution is not observed the engine will load up and cause the wasting of a lot of gas.

More and more drivers shoot their machines up to 20 miles per hour in low and more than 30 in second. Also this spurt in low gears serves no good purpose at all. As soon as the car is rolling along easily in low it should be shifted to second. This same rule should be appleed when shifting from second to high.

The good care that you give your car regularly also plays an important part. New spark plugs, keeping the ignition timing up to its highest point of efficiency will cause improvement. The proper lubrication is important and the right oil in the crank case. The oil filter is important so that the engine doesn't suffer from increased wear. Tires should be well inflated and seeing that the brakes don't drag.

Clutch slippages also wastes fuel. The braking of a car causes the lost of fuel as the brakes shouldn't be applied suddenly when approaching a traffic light or halting for an emergency. One should always be on the watch for same as it requires added fuel to build up momentum.

SOUTH CAROLINA

AIKEN
TOURIST HOMES
  Mrs. S. Bryant, 915 Fairfield St.
  Mrs. M. H. Harrison, Richland Avenue
ROAD HOUSES
  Chauffeurs Inn, 1102 Sumter Street

CHARLESTON
TOURIST HOMES
  Mrs. Alston, 43 South St.
  Mrs. Gladsden, 15 Nassau St.
  Mrs. H. L. Harleston, 250 Ashley Avenue
  Mrs. Mayes, 47 Sotuh Street.

COLUMBIA
HOTELS
  TAYLOR, 1016 Washington St.
TOURIST HOMES
  Mrs. H. Cornwell, 1713 Wayne
  Mrs. W. D. Chappelle, 1301 Pine St.
  Mrs. T. H. Pinckney, 1406 Park St.
  Mrs. B. Vincent, 1712 Wayne
  Mrs. J. P. Wakefield, 1323 Heidt St.

FLORENCE
TOURIST HOMES
  Mrs. C. C. Godblood, 227 E. Marion
  Mrs. B. Wright, 1004 E. Cheeve St.

GEORGETOWN
TOURIST HOMES
  Mrs. R. Anderson, 424 Broad
  Mrs. D. Atkinson, 811 Duke
  Jas. Becote, 118 Oronge
  T. W. Brown, Merriman & Emanuel
  Mrs. A. A. Smith, 317 Emanuel

SPARTANBURG
TOURIST HOMES
  Mrs. H. Cloeman, N. Dean St.
  Mrs. S. McElroy, Silver Hill St.
  Mrs. M. Young, S. Liberty St.
  Mrs. M. H. Wright, 400 S. Liberty St.

MILES?

&

MISSES?

DEPEND ON

THE GREEN BOOK

Don't Go Miles Out of the Way

And Miss the Place

TENNESSEE

CHATTANOOGA
HOTELS
  Lincoln, 1101 Carter St.
  Martin, 204 E. 9th St.
  Peoples, 1104 Carter St.
TOURIST HOMES
  Mrs. J. Baker, 843 E. 8th St.
  Mrs. E. Brown, 1133 E. 8th St.
  Mrs. D. Lowe, 803 Fairview Ave.
  Mrs. A. Jackson, 1416 College St.
  Y. W. C. A., 839 E. 8th St.

CLARKSVILLE
HOTELS
  Central, 535 Franklin St.
TOURIST HOMES
  Mrs. E. F. Thompkins, 411 Poston St.
  Mrs. H. Northington, 717 Main St.

BRISTOL
TOURIST HOMES
  A. D. Henderson, 301 McDowell St.

LEXINGTON
TOURIST HOMES
  C. Timberlake, Holly St.
  W. Kiser, Holly St.

MEMPHIS
HOTELS
  Clarke, 144 Beale Ave.
  Travelers, 347 Vauce

MURFREESBORO
TOURIST HOMES
  Mrs. R. Moore, Cor. University & State Sts.

NASHVILLE
HOTELS
  Bryant, 500 8th Ave. S.
  Fred Douglas, 501 4th Ave. N.
  Washington, 422 Cedar St.

VIRGINIA

ABINGDON
TOURIST HOMES
  Mrs. H. Anderson, Near Fairgrounds, E. End.
  Mrs. N. Brown, High St.
  Mrs. A. Monroe, 300 "A" St.
  B. Nicholas, Park St.

ALEXANDRIA
TOURIST HOMES
  J. T. Holms, 803 Gibbon St.
  J. A. Barrett, 724 Gibbon St.

BRISTOL
HOTELS
  Palace, 210 Front St.

CHRISTIANBURG
HOTELS
  Eureka

FREDERICKSBURG
HOTELS
  McGuire, 521 Princess Ann St.
  Rappshsnock, 520 Princess Ann St.
TOURIST HOMES
  Mrs. B. Scott, 207 5th St.

17

VIRGINIA — USE IT AS YOUR IDENTIFICATION — VA.

DANVILLE
TOURIST HOMES
  Mrs. M. K. Page, 434 Holbrook St.
  Mrs. S. A. Overbey, Holbrook St.
LYNCHBURG
HOTELS
  Manhattan, 1001 5th St.
  Petersburg
TOURIST HOMES
  Mrs. C. Harper, 1109 8th St.
  Mrs. M. Thomas, 919 Polk
  Mrs. Smith, 504 Jackson
ROAD HOUSES
  Goldendale Inn, 1001 5th St.
BEAUTY PARLORS
  Selma's, 1002 5th St.
NORFOLK
HOTELS
  Douglas, 716 Smith St.
  MT. VERNON, Brambleton Ave.
  Prince George, 1751 Church St.
  Wheaton, 633 E. Brambleton Ave.
TOURIST HOMES
  Mrs. S. Noble, 7 23Chaple St.
TAVERNS
  Peoples, Church & Calvert Sts.
  Tatem's, Charlotte & Brewer Sts.
NEWPORT NEWS
TOURIST HOMES
  Mrs. W. E. Barron, 758 25th St.
  Mrs. W. R. Cooks, 2211 Marshall A.
  Mrs. W. Herndon, 753 26th St.
  Mrs. C. Stephens, 1909 Marshall A.
  Mrs. J. H. Taliaferro,
    2206 Marshall Ave.
SERVICE STATIONS
  Ridley's, Orcutt Ave. & 30th St.
BEAUTY PARLORS
  Black & White, 300 Chestnut Ave.
  Rattrie's, 300 Chestnut Ave.
PETERSBURG
HOTELS
  The Walker House, 116 South
TOURIST
  Mrs. E. Johnson, 116 South Ave.
PHOEBUS
RESTAURANTS
  Ye Shingle Inn, 17 E. County St.

RICHMOND
HOTELS
  Miller's, 2nd & Leigh Ets.
  Slaughters, 514 N. 2nd St.
TOURIST HOMES
  Mrs. E. Brice, 14 W. Clay St.
  Y. W. C. A., 515 N. 7th St.
RESTAURANTS
  Cora's Waffle Shop, Leigh & 5th St
BEAUTY PARLORS
  Jimmies, 735 N 2nd St.
  Rest-A-Bit, 619 N. 3rd St.
DANCE HALLS
  ROSELAND, E. Leigh St.
  Casino, N. 2nd St.
DRUGGIST
  Williams Prof., 414 N. 3rd St.
ROANOKE
HOTELS
  Dumas, 106 Hnry St. N. W.
TAVERNS
  Tom's Place
STAUNTON
HOTELS
  Pannell's Inn, 613 N. Augusta St.
WINCHESTER
  New Evans Hotel, Sharp St.
TOURIST HOMES
  Mrs. Jos. Willis, N. Main St.
  Dunbar Tea Room, 21 W. Hart St.

HOW TO KEEP FROM GROWING OLD

Always race with locomotive to Crossings. Engineers like it; it; it breaks the monotony of their jobs.

Always pass the car ahead on curves or turns. Don't use horn, it may unnerve the fellow and cause him to turn outout too far.

Demand half the road—the middle half. Insist on your rights.

Always speed; it shows them you are a man of pep even tho an amateur driver.
Never Stop, look or listen at railroad crossings. It consumes time.

Always lock your brakes when skidding. It makes the job more artistic.

In Sloppy weather drive close to pedestrians. Dry cleaners appreciate this.

Never look around when you back up; there is never anything behind you.

Drive confidently, just as tho there were not eighteen million other cars in service.

HELPFUL?

Use It on Your Next Trip

Use It When You are Out for a ride

18

VT. — W. VA.　　　USE IT AS YOUR IDENTIFICATION　　　WEST VIRGINIA

VERMONT

BURLINGTON
HOTELS
 Pate's, 86 Archibald St.

WEST VIRGINIA

CHARLESTON
HOTELS
 Ferguson
TOURIST HOMES
 A. Brown, 1001 Washington St.

HUNTINGTON
HOTELS
 Fair
 Massey's, 837 7th Ave.
 Southern, 21 8th Ave.
 The Ross, 911 8th Ave.

TOURIST HOMES
 E. Washington, 1657 8th Ave.
RESTAURANTS
 J. Gross, 839 7th Ave.
TAVERNS
 Monroe's, 1616 8th Ave.
NIGHT CLUBS
 Appomattox Club, 1659 8th Ave.
BARBER SHOPS
 J. Harriston, 1615 8th Ave.
BEAUTY PARLORS
 Mrs. Pack, 1612 Artisen Ave.
SERVICE STATION
 Sterling, Cor 12th St. & 3rd Ave.
GARAGE
 South Side, 716 8th Ave.
THEATERS
 Fox, 1640 8th Ave.
DANCE HALLS
 Alpha, 1636 8th Av.

(Continued)

 There is a great many branches to the automobile industry, mainly, the manufacturing, the painting, repairing, driving, cars for hire, express business, tires and repairing of tires, gasoline fiilling and oiling stations, radiator repairing, upholstering, body and fender repairing besde the long distance hauling of all goods and the transportation of coal from the mines along with local moving and jobing.

 You will find the Negro doing his part in each and every branch of the industry in certain sections of the country, where the so-called jim-crow laws are being enforced. Negroes are operating bus lines to transport passengers as they prefer to ride in a bus rather than be jim-crowed, and that, of coure, give employment to a great many persons, both chauffeurs and mechanics in this same section, Persons that can afford an automobiel use their cars exclusively for transportation for the same reason. And taking it as a whole, the Negro has made, and is making more money in the automobile industry than any other industry in the world. And the future looks bright, as the automobile business has just begun.

KEEP THIS GUIDE WITH YOU

SUMMER RESORTS

Advertise your place in this section. Let the Public know where you are and What you have to offer.

CONNECTICUT
South Glastenbury,

**Camp Bennett,
Independent Social Center
2076 Main St.
Hartford**

West Haven ....Hotel Majestic

MAINE
Smithfield ....Camp Beulah

MARYLAND
Annapolis ....Sparrow's Beach
Shadyside ....Mrs. M. Carter
Benedict ....Violet Belles Hotel

MASSACHUSETTS
Plymouth ....Camp Twin Oaks
East Brookfield ....Camp Atwwater
Sheffield ....Elm Court Inn
N. Egrmont ....Elm Court Inn
Cape Cod ....Gladstone Manor
Oak Bluffs ....Nungessers's Chateau
Great Barrington ....Sunset Inn

NEW JERSEY
Atlantic Highlands ....Maplewood Villa
Atlantic City ....Apex Rest
                               Wright's
Belmar ....Brighton Inn
                               Morris
               Sea Breeze Rest
Cape May ....Bryan's Villa
Asbury Park ....Overton Cottage
                          Hotel Adore
                     Hotel Metropolitan
                     The Federal Hotel
                      Wright Cottage
East Riverton ....Idle Hour

Telephone 151

REST

An Ideal Place   Good Food & Water
Near the Shore — Still in the Country

WESTVIEW COTTAGE
Mrs. Della Weaver
R. F. D., Box 180   Eatontown, N. J.

EATONTOWN
                             Greenbrier Inn
Fair Haven ....Lula Mae Villa
                              Fair Haven
                              Cedar Grove
Long Branch ....Arlington House
                   No. Baptist Conference
                          Mrs. R. Patton

**Metropolitan Seashore House
8 Cottage Ave., West End.**

Oceanport ....Goose Neck Inn
Ocean City ....Hotel Comfort
Red Bank

**Foreman's Camp
I. A. Foreman, P. O. Box 325**

Spring Lake ....Laster Cottage
Garwood ....Mrs. M. DeCassers
Zion ....Rainbow's End

NEW YORK
Allaben ....Camp Bryton Rock
Avern ....Alberhta Inn
Catskill ....English House
Coxsakie ....Hudson View
Didell ....Hill Top Farm
Elmont, L. I. ....Blue Bird Inn
Glen Cove ....Continental Cottage
Greenwood Lake ....Forest Farm House
                     The Justice House
                        Mrs. L. Taylor

**KEEP YOUR NAME
BEFORE THE PUBLIC
IT PAYS**

USE IT AS YOUR IDENTIFICATION

THE ROYAL SERVICE HOUSE

GORDON HEIGHTS   **MEDFORD, L. I., N. Y.**

BESSIE RICH, PROP.

HIKEING

FISHING

SWIMMING

COMFORTABLE

AIRY

ROOMS

FOR A QUIET REST AMONG THE OAK TREES AND CEDARS
Special Attention To Convalescents — Calory and Vitamin Diets
Vegeterian Service — Special Milk
ADULTS $14.00 — CHILDREN UNDER SEVEN, $7.00
Reservation, 141 West 118th St., New York City   Phone: UN. 4-2886

NEW YORK

Hunter ....Notch Mountain House
Montrose ....Montrose Country Club
                                 Villa Orlando
Mt. Beacon ....Vincent Rest
Niagara Falls ....Johnson Cottage
New York City ....Loafing Holt
                             Fern Rock Camp
                           Rising Sun Golf Club
                                  Mrs. G. Hill
Otisville ....Mountainside Farms
Patterson ....Magnolia Farms
Pawling ....The Hill Cottage
Poughkeepsie ....Mrs. L. Sullivan
Prattsville ....Red-Falls-on-the-Catskill
Quogue, L. I. ....William's Cottage
                             Shinnecock Arms
Rockaway ....Eddie's Boarding House
                              The Club House
                                      Regina
Roosa Gap ....Anderson's Farm
Roxbury ....Mountain View House
                                   Hill House
                                 Miner Cottage
                           Jessie Manna Farms
Saranac Lake ....Mrs. V. Ramsey
Sag Harbor

   (Ivy Cottage)
   Mrs. A. Johnson
   P. O. Box 156

Saratoga ....Greentree Inn
                             Branchcomb Cottage
   Washington Cottage
   128 Washington St.
   M. Ryder, Prop.

Schroon Lake
   Claver Villa
   P. O. Box 404

Spring Valley ....Gail's Cottage
Stormville
   Mountain View Farms
   R. F. D. No. 16

Sheepshead Bay ......Virginia Chateau
Salt Point ....Wappinger Creek Farm
White Plains ....Mrs. B. Anderson
Wingdale ....Camp Unity
PENNSYLVANIA
Cannonsbough ....Willow Beach
Monroeton
   Dorsey Wood Park Farms
   Mrs. J. D. Holden

Montrose ....Naylor's Lake View Rest
Pipersville ....Camp Green Acres
Mt. Pocono ....Rose Tree Inn
Swiftwater ....The Swiftwater
SOUTH CAROLINA
Ocean Drive ....Atlantic Beach
WEST VIRGINIA
Harpers Ferry ....River View Cottage
CANADA
Montreal ....Mrs. G. Potter
NEW HAMPSHIRE
Portsmouth ....
                 Blank's Riverview Cottage
West Rummey ....
                 Sivertip Poultry **Farms**

"The Negro Motorist Green Book" a Motorist and Tourist Guide for 1938 is ready for circulation and is yours for the asking.

You will find it handy on your travels, whether at home or in some other state, and is up to date. Each year we are compiling new lists as some of these places move, or go out of business and new business places are started giving added employament to members of our race.

Where shall we go over the week end or spend our vacation are two of the many questions that people are asking. In order for one to know where to go and to stop without worrying a long time ahead; we have mdae the Green Book larger and as your medium so as to give you this information.

Perhaps you might know of others who would be interested in receiving a free copy. If so you might list a few of your friends; send it along with your name and address and we will be glad to send them copies.

Name ....

    Address ....

Name ....

    Address ....

Name ....

    Address ....

Name ....

    Address ....

Name ....

    Address ....

Your Name ....

City .... State ....

We thank you and believe your friends also will thank you, for making it "The Negro Motorist Green Book" known to them.

                              Your Truly,
                              Victor H. Green,
                                  Publisher

MEMO

MEMO

THE NEGRO MOTORIST

GREEN-BOOK
1947
ESTABLISHED 1936

A Classified
MOTORIST'S & TOURIST'S GUIDE
Covering the United States

Carry Your Green Book with you
... you may need it ...

PRICE
75¢

ESTABLISHED 1936

THE Negro Motorist GREEN BOOK

INTRODUCTION

The idea of "The Green Book" is to give the Motorist and tourist a Guide not only of the Hotels and Tourist Homes in all of the large cities, but other classifications that will be found useful wherever he may be. Also facts and information that the Negro Motorist can use and depend upon.

There are thousands of places that the public doesn't know about and aren't listed. Perhaps you might know of some? If so, send in their names and addresses and the kind of business, so that we might pass it along to the rest of your fellow Motorists.

You will find it handy on your travels, whether at home or in some other state, and is up to date. Each year we are compiling new lists as some of these places move, or go out of business and new business places are started giving added employment to members of our race.

When you are traveling mention "The Green Book" so as to let these people know just how you found out about their place of business. If they haven't heard about This Guide, tell them to get in touch with us.

If this Guide is useful, let us know, if not tell us also, as we appreciate your criticisms.

If any errors are found, kindly notify the publishers so that they can be corrected in the next issue.

Publication Office—Leonia, N. J.—Victor H. Green, Editor.
 Published yearly by Victor H. Green & Co.
Advertising Office—200 West 135th St., Room 215-A, New York City, N. Y.
Copyrighted—1947 by Victor H. Green. Manuscripts submitted for publication should be sent to 200 West 135th St., Room 215-A, New York 30, N. Y., and must be accompanied by return postage. No liability can be assumed for the loss or damage to manuscripts although every possible precaution will be taken.
District Advertising Representative:—
Western Representative—Elmer Jackson-2605 Euclid Ave., Kansas City, Mo.
 Subscription: Seventy Five cents per copy.
 Advertising: For rates, Write to the publisher.
Last forms close on Nov. 1st. We reserve the right to reject any advertising which in our opinion does not conform to our standards.

PHOTO CREDIT—(Cover,) Maine Development Comm. "Orr's Island" to the Mainland

INDEX

Negro Schools & Colleges 3	MISSISSIPPI 46
NEGRO NEWSPAPERS 7	MISSOURI 47
GREEN BOOK TRAVELING 10	MONTANA 49
GENERAL MOTOR CARS 13	NEBRASKA 49
FACTS ON FUTURE AUTOMOTIVE DESIGN 17	NEW JERSEY 49
	NEW YORK STATE 54
FORD CARS 19	NEW YORK CITY 56
ALABAMA 26	New York City (Brooklyn) 61
ARKANSAS 26	New York City (Bronx) 62
ARIZONA 28	LONG ISLAND 62
CALIFORNIA 28	WESTCHESTER 63
COLORADO 30	NEW MEXICO 63
CONNECTICUT 31	NORTH CAROLINA 63
DELAWARE 32	OHIO 66
DISTRICT OF COLUMBIA 32	OKLAHOMA 68
FLORIDA 33	OREGON 69
GEORGIA 34	PENNSYLVANIA 70
ILLINOIS 35	RHODE ISLAND 72
INDIANA 36	SOUTH CAROLINA 72
IDAHO 36	SOUTH DAKOTA 73
IOWA 37	TENNESSEE 74
KANSAS 38	TEXAS 75
KENTUCKY 39	UTAH 77
LOUISIANA 40	VERMONT 77
MAINE 42	VIRGINIA 77
MARYLAND 42	WASHINGTON STATE 80
MASSACHUSETTS 43	WEST VIRGINIA 80
MICHIGAN 44	WISCONSIN ...... (Cover) 81
MINNESOTA 45	WYOMING ...... (Cover) 81

EXPLANATION

No travel guide is complete with the multitude of business places that are unheard of. The principal value is its completeness for which reason we are endeavoring to make this guide actually the most complete possible.

We have given you a selection of listings that you might choose from, under no circumstances do these listings imply that the place is recommended.

The business classifications listed have been arranged under the different cities and towns, so that one won't have any trouble finding what they want.

MONEY FOR NEGRO COLLEGES

This year more than ever we must see to it that our colleges are prepared to carry a maximum load of work, and ready to do it well. One group of colleges deserves special attention in this respect: the institutions that devote themselves to education of the Negro. Under the leadership of the United Negro College Fund thirty-three of these private colleges are beginning a campaign for $1,300,000. John D. Rockefeller Jr. is chairman of the advisory committee for this third annual fund drive, and a number of other prominent men and women have interested themselves in the cause.

The need for full subscription is more pressing this year because of the unusual burden thrown on all educational facilities by the returning veteran. The Negro played an important and often heroic, part in the war. He shared the mud, the danger, the sweat and the tears. Now he has the right to continue his interrupted education if he wants to do so. Many college doors will be closed to him, and to others regardless of race, color or creed, simply because there are too many returning veterans to be cared for at once in the colleges of their choice. But we cannot allow these thirty-three Negro private colleges to turn away any applicant because they lack funds, or to curtail their programs because of it.

The educated Negro was once a rarity. His numbers are increasing year by year, and his contributions to the arts, science and education steadily gain a wider and juster recognition for his abilities. From these we all gain, regardless of color. And, as we mutually put a proper, unprejudiced estimate on the contributions of all races to the common good, we move surely closer to the goal of living together in harmony.

REPRINTED WITH PERMISSION OF THE N. Y. TIMES

Negro Schools and Colleges in the United States

Just a few pages ahead you will find a list of Negro schools and colleges in the United States.

As you visit the various states you will have a splendid opportunity of visiting the great educational centers, where students receive a sound, enlightened humanistic education and where they are prepared for life with a fine linguistic equipment, a trained ability to examine facts critically, a sharpened and heightened sensibility to values, a developed capacity for historical and philosophical reflection, and as a culminative result of all these disciplines, an enhanced capacity for reflective decision and action.

Take time out to read or to see these great homes of learning where the young folks of today and tomorrow are having their characters moulded. Plan for the future of your children so that in time to come they will face life with a fine equipment. Let us not forget that with this question of schools the whole of education is bound up, for the greatest thought of mankind is in books and the greatest living teachers are in our schools and colleges in the United States.

ERNESTINE L. HOPPS, Director

IN PATRONIZING THESE PLACES

"Negro Schools and Colleges in the United States"

ALABAMA
Birmingham
   Miles Memorial College
Huntsville
   Oakwood College
Selma
   Selma University
Montgomery
   State Teachers College
Tuscaloosa
   Stillman Institute
Talladega
   Talladega College
Tuskegee
   Tuskegee Normal and Industrial Institute

ARKANSAS
Pine Bluff
   Agricultural Mechanical, and Normal College
Little Rock
   Arkansas Baptist College
   Dunbar Junior College
   Philander Smith College
North Little Rock
   Shorter College

DELAWARE
Dover
   State College for Colored Students

DISTRICT OF COLUMBIA
Washington
   Howard University
   Miner Teachers College

FLORIDA
Daytona Beach
   Bethune-Cookman College
Jacksonville
   Edward Waters College
St. Augustine
   Florida Normal and Industrial Institute
Tallahassee
   Florida Agricultural and Mechanical College

GEORGIA
Atlanta
   Atlanta School of Social Work
   Atlanta University
   Morehouse College
   Spelman College
   Clark University
   Gammon Theological Seminary
   Morris Brown University
Albany
   Georgia Normal and Agricultural College
Augusta
   Paine College
Fort Valley
   Fort Valley Normal and Industrial School
Industrial College
   Georgia State College

KENTUCKY
Frankfort
   Kentucky State Industrial College
Louisville
   Louisville Municipal College for Negroes

LOUISIANA
New Orleans
   Dillard University
   Xavier University
Baker
   Leland College
Grambling
   Louisiana Normal and Industrial Institute
Scotlandville
   Southern University and Agricultural and Mechanical College

4

PLEASE MENTION "THE GREEN BOOK"

MARYLAND
Baltimore
  Morgan College
  Coppin Normal School
Bowie
  Maryland State Teachers College
Princess Anne
  Princess Anne College

MISSISSIPPI
Alcorn
  Alcorn Agricultural and Mechanical College
Jackson
  Campbell College
  Jackson College
Holly Springs
  Rust College
Edwards
  Southern Christian Institute
Tougaloo
  Tougaloo College

MISSOURI
Jefferson City
  Lincoln University
St. Louis
  Stowe Teachers College

NORTH CAROLINA
Greensboro
  Bennett College
Fayetteville
  Fayetteville State Normal School
Charlotte
  Johnson C. Smith University
Salisbury
  Livingstone College
Greensboro
  Agricultural and Technical College
Durham
  North Carolina State College

Raleigh
  Shaw University
Elizabeth City
  State Teachers College
Winston-Salem
  Winston-Salem Teachers College

OHIO
Wilberforce
  Wilberforce University

OKLAHOMA
Langston
  Agricultural and Normal University

PENNSYLVANIA
Cheyney
  Cheynly Training School for Teachers
Lincoln University
  Lincoln University

SOUTH CAROLINA
Columbia
  Allen University
Charleston
  Avery Institute
Columbia
  Benedict College
Trenton
  Bettis Academy
Chester
  Brainerd Junior College
Orangeburg
  Clafflin College
Rock Hill
  Clinton Normal and Industrial Institute
Cheraw
  Coulter Memorial Academy
Rock Hill
  Friendship College
Sumter
  Morris College

IN PATRONIZING THESE PLACES

Seneca
  Seneca Junior College
Orangeburg
  State Normal, Industrial, Agricultural and Mechanical College
Denmark
  Voorhees Normal and Industrial School

TENNESSEE

Nashville
  Fisk University
Knoxville
  Knoxville College
Jackson
  Lane College
Memphis
  Le Moyne College
Nashville
  Meharry Medical College
Morristown
  Morristown Normal and Industrial College
Rogersville
  Swift Memorial Junior College
Nashville
  Tennessee Agricultural and Industrial State Teachers College

TEXAS

Marshall
  Bishop College
Tyler
  Butler College
Seguin
  Guadalupe College
Houston
  Houton College for Negroes
Hawkins
  Jarvis Christian College
Crockett
  Mary Allen Junior College
Waco
  Paul Quinn College
Prairie View
  Prairie View State College
San Antonio
  St. Philip's Junior College and Vocational Institute
Austin
  Samuel Houton College
Tyler
  Texas College
Austin
  Tillotson
Marshall
  Wiley College

VIRGINIA

Petersburg
  Bishop Payne Divinity School
Hampton
  Hampton Institute
Suffolk
  Nansemond Collegiate Institute
Lawrenceville
  St. Paul Normal and Industrial School
Ettrick
  Virginia State College
Lynchburg
  Virginia Theological Seminary and College
Richmond
  Virginia Union University

WEST VIRGINIA

Bluefield
  Bluefield State Teachers College
Harpers Ferry
  Storer College
Institute
  West Virginia State College

PLEASE MENTION "THE GREEN BOOK"

Leading Negro Publications of the United States

Listed below are the countries leading newspapers. When you reach your destination, from the list below, purchase a copy of their paper and enjoy the latest news from all over the world.

ALABAMA
Birmingham
   Newspic Magazine
   Weekly Review
Gadsden
   Call Post
Mobile
   Gulf Informer
Montgomery
   Alabama Tribune
Tuscaloosa
   Alabama Black Citizen

ARKANSAS
Hot Springs
   Crusader Journal
Little Rock
   Arkansas Survey Journal
   State Press
   Arkansas World
Pine Bluff
   Negro Spokesman

CALIFORNIA
Los Angeles
   California Eagle
   Sentinel
   Tribune
Oakland
   California Voice

COLORADO
Denver
   Colorado Statesman
   Star
   Pueblo Western Ideal

DISTRICT OF COLUMBIA
Washington
   Afro-American
   Tribune

FLORIDA
Jacksonville
   Florida Tattler
Miami
   Florida Times
   Whip
Pensacola
   Courier
   Junior Press
Tampa
   Bulletin

GEORGIA
Albany
   Enterprise
Atlanta
   World Syndicate
   World
Augusta
   Echo
Columbus
   World
Rome
   Enterprise
Savannah
   Tribune

ILLINOIS
Champaign
   Illinois Times
Chicago
   Bee
   Defender
Springfield
   Illinois Conservator

INDIANA
Gary
   American
Indianapolis
   Recorder

IN PATRONIZING THESE PLACES

IOWA
Des Moines
   Iowa Bystander
   Iowa Observer

KANSAS
Kansas City
   Plaindealer
Wichita
   Negro Star

KENTUCKY
Louisville
   Defender
   Leader

LOUISIANA
New Orleans
   Informer-Sentinel
   Louisiana Weekly
   Sepia Socialite
Shreveport
   Sun

MARYLAND
Baltimore
   Afro-American

MASSACHUSETTS
Boston
   Chronicle
   Times

MICHIGAN
Detroit
   Michigan Chronicle
   Tribune

MINNESOTA
Minneapolis
   Spokesman
St. Paul
   Recorder

MISSISSIPPI
Greenville
   Delta Leader

Jackson
   Advocate
Meridan
   Weekly Echo

MISSOURI
Jefferson City
   Lincoln Clarion
Kansas City
   Call
St. Louis
   American
   Argus

NEBRASKA
Omaha
   Guide
   Star

NEW JERSEY
Newark
   New Jersey Afro-American
   New Jersey Herald-News
   Record

NEW YORK
Buffalo
   The Star
New York
   Age
   Amsterdam News
   Crisis
   Music Dial (Magazine)
   Peoples' Voice
Syracuse
   Progressive (Herald)

NORTH CAROLINA
Durham
   Carolina Times
Raleigh
   Carolinian
Wilmington
   Cape Fear Journal

PLEASE MENTION "THE GREEN BOOK"

OHIO

Cincinnati
   Independent

Cleveland
   Call & Post

Columbus
   Ohio State News

Dayton
   Bulletin
   Dayton-Cincinnati Forum

Youngstown
   Buckeye Review

OKLAHOMA

Muskogee
   Oklahoma Independent

Oklahoma City
   Black Dispatch

Tulsa
   Oklahoma Eagle

PENNSYLVANIA

Philadelphia
   Afro-American
   Christian Review
   Independent
   Tribune

Pittsburg
   Courier

RHODE ISLAND

Providence
   Chronicle

SOUTH CAROLINA

Columbia
   Lighthouse and Informer
   Palmetto Leader

TENNESSEE

Chattanooga
   Observer

Knoxville
   Flashlight Herald

Memphis
   World

Nashville
   Globe & Independent
   National Baptist Union Review

TEXAS

Dallas
   Express

Fort Worth
   Mind

Galveston
   Voice

Houston
   Defender
   Informer
   Negro Labor News

San Antonio
   Informer
   Register

Waco
   Messenger

VIRGINIA

Norfolk
   Journal and Guide

Richmond
   Afro-American

Roanoke
   Tribune

WASHINGTON

Seattle
   Northwest Enterprise

WEST VIRGINIA

Charleston
   West Virginia Digest
   Color Magazine

IN PATRONIZING THESE PLACES

Not only Happy Motoring
But Happy Travelling by any method, is obtainable
through Green Book Routing
Say the ESSO Special Representatives

Editors Note:-The following article is as nearly as is possible, a reproduction of a discussion between Wendall P. Alston and James A. Jackson, both Special Representatives of the Esso Marketers.

JAMES A. JACKSON, the senior has attempted to reproduce his reactions to the book and its field of usefulness, by reminiscing a bit about his early travels. In the pursuit of a livlihood since the dawn of the century, Mr. Jackson has covered a lot of territory. He has actually visited 1997 towns and cities in the United States and on several trips abroad has been in Nineteen foreign countries. He has been in so many communities in America as to be quite at home in most of them, because of his frequent visits, as time went on.

His present position, held for the past twelve years, after seven years in the U. S. Dept. of Commerce and six with the Billboard, a theatrical magazine is with the Public Relations Department of the Standard Oil Co. and its affiliated companies. Mr. W. P. Alston has for the past two years been his traveling companion, and his potential successor. Together they go about to the extent of around 20,000 miles per year.

But let them tell their own story:-

When this article reaches print in the 1947 issue of the Green Book, the authors of this little brochure will be wandering down in Louisiana, and Arkansas; and in fact one of us will have been across the border and into Texas. For about six weeks beginning right after Xmas, we will be on a trip of more than three thousand miles, involving fourteen stops in each state.

Both of us are experienced travellers and one is especially fortified with contacts in many towns and cities which he has been visiting at intervals for, in some instances, more than forty years. The gray headed member of the team, whose experiences indicate his age, but whose energy and will to get about this and other countries, seems to be undiminished.

Of course, like all old codgers, he is inclined to reminisce at almost any opportunity. Talk of the Green Book and mention of comparisons since its first publication a scant half dozen years ago, has just set him off.

"Gee" said he, "If there had been any such publication as this when I started travelling 'way back in the Nineties, I would have missed a lot of anxieties, worries and saved a lot of mental energy which, had it been conserved and used solely to the advancement of the business interests for which I traveled, my years "on the road' might have been concluded long ago, with enough savings to permit my living a life of peace and quiet, now that I am becoming an old codger."

10

PLEASE MENTION "THE GREEN BOOK"

JAMES A. JACKSON (SEATED) AND WENDEL P. ALSTON, SPECIAL REPRESENTATIVES OF THE ESSO MARKETERS IN THEIR NEW YORK OFFICE.

Of course, he could not be stopped traveling any more than one could stop him from talking about "Back when;" but make no mistake about his yarns, they are factual experiences and one, by one, as we go about, somewhere we encounter people familiar with the incident, or incidents, about which he has talked at sometime or another.

"When I first started jumping from place to place, just like white commercial travellers have been doing for time immemorial" he continued; the folk in many, many places looked with fear and doubt upon the traveling man from beyond the borders of their own county. In like manner, I, said he "wondered if my bags were safe, and if the bed I acquired for the night would be mine alone; or if I would have the night companions such as those for which D. D. T. has been created."

IN PATRONIZING THESE PLACES

Hotels, such as they were had been designed solely as a place for the too inebriated man to occupy rather than to go home to an angry spouse in his unfortunate condition, according to the elder of this team. At other places, the doors were innocent of locks; and much of the equipment for bathrooms, such as are common place today, were unknown where Negro travellers might stop. It seems that the major bit of bathroom equipment could be found anywhere from fifty to a hundred feet down the yard and on the way, a grape arbor afforded the only shelter from storm.

Slowly the more modern hotels conducted for our patronage came into being during the past four or five decades, and as slowly, or even more slowly, have the minds of the owners and managers of these improved institutions of comfort and service, realized that to obtain patronage, the Negroes of the country must be informed of heir existence.

How much nicer it is today, when one in contemplating a trip by train, motor or plane, is able to have determined in advance the places he may stop at while in the different communities; and how much more is the peace of mind of the traveller; and of his family and associates left at home, knowing that in emergency, just where one may be found.

I believe the Green Book was created in response to growing auto tourist business that would support it. However, what difference does it make to the traveller, or to the hotel and tourist home keeper, about what means of travel may be involved. The traveller needs a "home away from home" to the profit of those who make such homes available.

Just in case some of the Green Book readers may identify us form either the pictures or recognize the owner of the gray head from his talk as quoted here, Jack reminds the editor that "I am broad minded enough to want the traveler by train and plane to enjoy their stops anywhere just the same as if they had traveled by car. I am broad minded that way: and besides, Planes use petroleum products for motive power, so do a lot of railway engines, and all of them have to have lubrication, so my employer is not being cheated too badly, not enough to warrant them having an objection to all travelling colored people being able to obtain some degree of peace and comfort when they go away from home regardless of how they travel.

They're nice that way, therefore those who may be motoring may express their gratitude to Mr. Green for making possible the serenity of the trip; and insure themselves of Happy motoring by using Esso products while on tour, thereby adding to the writers a degree of Job insurance and enhance the social security of our families as they enjoy Happy motoring with ESSO.

12

PLEASE MENTION "THE GREEN BOOK"

GENERAL MOTORS CARS

At the time our guide went to press the 1947 Models of General Motors Cars had not been announced.

CHEVROLET

The new Chevrolet uses the valve-in-head Thrift-Master engine famous for its rare combination of economy and performance. This engine extracts more power from a given quantity of fuel than do other types of engines of the same displacement. Durability and ease of servicing also are important advantages of the valve-in-head construction.

Chevrolet alone, among the lowest-priced cars, has the famous Body by Fisher and all that it provides in styling, safety comfort, luxury, and durability. A distinctive feature of this body is its steel construction. The thoroughly reinforced cowl, side, rear, and floor panels and Turret Top are welded to form an all-steel unit of tremendous strength.

Still another Chevrolet feature is a vacuum cylinder which does nearly all of the gear shifting work. All the driver has to do is move the lever and the lever works so easy that you can move it with your forefinger without taking your hand off the steering wheel. You shift the gears but not your grip.

PONTIAC

Your first impression of the big, new Pontiac is that here is a car of outstanding beauty. Its clean, sweeping lines accentuate its length and size. Every detail of design adds to its stunning beauty. But its extra value is even more evident when you open the wide doors and get a glimpse of the luxurious interior. Here again, every detail of appointment adds up to comfort and luxury unmatched in its price class, and gives you the beauty of custom-type appointments at low cost.

Pontiac interiors are roomy, comfortable and in trim good taste. Soft, pleasing colors and smart hardware combine with plenty of elbow and headroom to add to passenger comfort. Upholstery is rich and luxurious. Ash trays and built-in arm rests are another "plus value" feature of all Pontiac models.

Pontiac's reputation for trouble-free performance is the result of advanced engineering and good craftsmanship. From drawing board to assembly line, Pontiac is designed and built to give mile after mile of trouble-free, economical performance, as the experience of owners has proved over and over again.

Many Pontiacs have been driven 100,000 miles and more with unbelievably little care and expense. New mechanical improvements combined with scores of time-proved features prove that in operating economy and dependability the 1946 Pontiac brings new perfection to its price class.

13

IN PATRONIZING THESE PLACES

Oldsmobile "98" 4 Door Sedan

OLDSMOBILE

Ever since the days of the "Curved Dash Runabout," Oldsmobile has been famous for combining new ideas with proved features . . .in the right proportion to create a fine automobile. This tradition is carried out in the new Oldsmobiles.

Yet it takes the experience of actually driving the Oldsmobile to gain a real appreciation of how it combines many new improvements—in engine and body and chassis—with proved quality features and basic soundness of design. Add to these advantages the New Hydra-Matic Drive—the famous General Motors feature that gives you fully automatic gear-shifting and eliminates the clutch pedal entirely.

Built for the owner who wants quality construction plus outstanding economy, the Oldsmobile Special is a roomy, roadworthy automobile, offering many unusual extra-value features. The 1946 Oldsmobile Special "66" is 204 inches long overall—a full 17 feet from bumper to bumper. Its wheelbase is 119 inches. Its precision-balanced Fire-Power Engine delivers 100 horsepower. And this fine economy car is a true Oldsmobile through and through —in styling, in engineering, and in every detail of construction.

The Custom 8 Cruiser is truly the finest Oldsmobile ever built, a car for the owner who demands the finest in styling, in comfort, and in performance. It is a big impressive-looking car, 18 feet long from bumper to bumper, with a wheelbase of 127 inches It is a modern car, with floors so low that running boards are not needed, and with bodies that are

PLEASE MENTION "THE GREEN BOOK"

wider than they are high. It is a luxurious car, with custom-quality appointments and DeLuxe equipment throughout. And this fine big Oldsmobile is so perfectly balanced that it is one of the easiest-handling cars on the road. Beneath its broad hood is a 110-horsepower "Straight 8" Engine, with outstanding new features that contribute to new standards of smoothness and performance.

BUICK

Buick's line includes the Special, Series 40; the Super, Series 50; and the Roadmaster, Series 70. Here we picture the interior of Model 51, the sleek, clean-lined four-door SUPER sedan.

In many instances in this 1946 Buick Fireball valve-in-head engine, parts are held to closer tolerances than in precision power plants of the air.

There's a closer fit between the pistons and the cylinder walls than in an aircraft engine. There's quieter action because of closer fits in the valve mechanism.

Connecting rods ride on crankshaft bearings more closely fitted to journals. Oil pump gears mesh more precisely. Camshaft bearings meet closer standards of fit.

This all means extra fine, smooth performance and longer engine life. And this meticulous matching is only part of the whole Buick engine story.

There is the valve-in-head principle with the Dynaflash combustion chamber which rolls the fuel into a power-packed charge, squeezes it into a flattened ball so that it lets go with a super-stout wallop.

Yes, this Buick Fireball straight-eight for 1946 is a great engine. More brilliantly agile, more frugal with fuel and oil, and definitely proof that "When Better Automobiles Are Built Buick Will Build Them."

CADILLAC

First among automobile companies, Cadillac was singled out by the government for war production. During those war years when no civilian cars were produced, Cadillac's precision workmanship continued uninterrupted . . . the Cadillac engine and transmission assembly lines never stopped. Cadillac's contribution to Victory remained, to a large extent, in the familiar realm of automotive-type production.

Naturally, automotive progress went far ahead at Cadillac. Over 50,000 of the famous Cadillac V-type engines and Hydra-Matic transmissions went into tanks and other motorized weapons . . . met the grueling tests of the battlefields . . . to emerge toughened and hardened to new standards of efficiency and dependability. Their development was far greater than would have been possible during four peacetime years.

This new mechanical perfection of engine and Hydra-Matic transmission is but one reflection of how Cadillac is able to resume fine car production with the most advanced new cars in

IN PATRONIZING THESE PLACES

This is Cadillac's 62 Model

PLEASE MENTION "THE GREEN BOOK"

its distinguished history . . . why the new, Cadillac is the greatest of all time, improved even beyond expectations.

In this basic mechanical improvement alone is the assurance that Cadillac—whose leadership long ago established its cars as "Standard of the World"—again today is creating fine cars which advance comfort, luxury and automotive performance to a new, far higher standard.

Facts on Future Automotive Design

APPEARANCE

Henry Ford II has said that new cars, meaning the 1947 models, will be "evolutionary" and not "revolutionary." There won't be any radical changes although the '47 models will certainly feature more changes than any previous models in company history. In general, however, the trend is toward smoother, aerodynamically clean lines.

RIDE

Cars of the future will provide progressively better rides. Possibilities for suspension include: torsion bars, rubber, air, oil, conventional and coil spring arrangements. Whatever is used, the motorist can count on getting an increasingly smoother ride from his motor car.

TIRES

According to Mr. James, natural rubber tires should not be counted out. There is much to recommend them. At the present time, they are not only cheaper, but easier on gasoline. Experiments show that they enable the motorist to get at least an extra mile to the gallon.

There is no evidence that synthetic tires, at present, last longer than the natural product.

Big synthetic winner is the butyl rubber inner tube. Due to less porosity they have much better air retention properties.

ENGINES

Mr. James feels that the conventional, reciprocating engine is still the best power source available for the present automobile. He sees lighter, more compact engines creating far greater horsepower for a given displacement. He is not so sure compressions will go much higher. Higher compressions, he says, impose greater strains on bearings, create higher temperatures, result in a "high strung" or tempermental engine in frequent need of attention.

He says there is a possibility the same end—greater horsepower for a given displacement and weight—may be achieved by the use of superchargers.

According to Mr. James, gas turbines as power plants for "tomorrow's" automobiles leave much to be desired—at least in their present stage

17

IN PATRONIZING THESE PLACES

of development. He says they have a bright future in the heavy power plant field, i. e. airplanes, sea-going vessels, trains and special power plants requiring 1,000 or more horsepower.

Advantages of the gas turbine are: compactness, fewer-moving parts, low initial cost and weight, ability to use low volatile fuels. Chief disadvantages are: Higher fuel consumption and their inability, in the present state of development, to be produced satisfactorily as small power units.

TRANSMISSIONS

Mr. James says that "easier to shift" transmissions are on their way. Clutch pedals are likely to disappear on all models in the near future. He is not sure that the gear shift lever will disappear entirely, although smaller, easier-to-manage levers are definitely in the picture. The matter of selectivity is something motorists must decide. Do they want a transmission that is fully automatic or do they want to exercise some choice in the matter? Semi-automatic and fully automatic transmissions are already a reality.

FUELS

The cars of the future will determine the kind of fuel we get according to Mr. James. He points out that a car lasts seven years; a fuel only seven weeks from refinery to engine.

LIGHT METAL AND PLASTICS

There is little likelihood of an aluminum, magnesium or all plastic automobile in the future, says Mr. James. Chief trouble with aluminum is that it is too expensive. It now costs from 15 to 16 cents a pound. The industry will get interested when it gets down to 4 or 5 cents. This seems unlikely since it takes two cents of electricity to make a pound of the meatl.

On the other hand the present cost of steel is around 2 cents a pound.

Fabricating problems of aluminum could be licked, Mr. James believes. It's a matter of basic cost that is the stumbling block.

The plastics picture is the same as aluminum or magnesium. Basic costs are high, and in addition there is a higher cost of fabrication to consider.

REAR ENGINE DRIVE AND FRONT ENGINE DRIVE

Prme advantages of either of these arrangements, Mr. James says, is that both permit lower floors. This is an important design consideration. He forsees considerable experimentation with both in the near future.

A secondary advantage of the rear engine design, one not possessed by the front drive, is improved visibility.

Problems of rear engine desgns are: weight distribution difficulties and cooling.

AIR CONDITIONING

There is a good chance that motor cars in the near future may feature controlled year-around temperature, obviating the necessity for opening the windows at any time. Humidity, too, will be controlled, eliminating interior fogging.

PLEASE MENTION "THE GREEN BOOK"

THE FORD CAR

At the time our guide went to press the 1947 Ford Motors Cars had not been announced.

Ford's New Sportsman's Convertible

Seven reasons why the Ford Motor Company's new Sportsman's Convertible combines custom craftsmanship with production cost are shown here.

Outstanding feature of the Sportsman's convertible is the use of wood panels on a steel frame, combining strength with station wagon appeal.

Examining the new model at Dearborn are seven of the nation's outstanding custom automobile designers, all of whom have recently joined Ford's expanded styling department. They are, left to right:

John F. Dobben, formerly with J. B. Judkins Company, Merrimac, Mass., builders of custom bodies for Lincoln, Pierce-Arrow, Packard, Deusenberg, and other luxury cars. He designed special bodies for Tom Mix, W. C. Fields and other screen notables.

Tom Hibbard, formerly of Hibbard and Darrin, Paris France. Hibbard's firm built custom bodies for Rolls Royce, Packard, Lincoln, Mercedes, Renault, Hispano Suiza, Pierce-Arrow, Isotta-Frachinni and othr famed continental makes. He designed a special Deusenberg for ex-King Alphonso of Spain.

Martin Regitko, formerly with the Willoughby Company of Utica, N. Y., custom body builders for Lincoln, Rolls Royce, Deusenberg and others. He helped design special cars for presidents including Coolidge and Hoover. All were built on Lincoln chassis.

George Tasman, designer for Locke & Company, and J. S. Inkskip, both of New York. The latter was agent for Rolls Royce and Bentley. He has designed scores of custom bodies.

IN PATRONIZING THESE PLACES

Herman Brunn, son and partner of Herman A. Brunn, of Brunn & Company, Buffalo. He was stylist and designer for his father and later for Kellner and Company, Paris France. He once designed an all-white ceremonial car with solid gold trim for the Shah of Iran.

Victor Lang, formerly with Brunn and Company, custom body builders for Lincoln, Pierce-Arrow, Rolls Royce and other. He designed a special Lincoln body on a 150-inch ambulance chassis for the late President Roosevelt. The car now is being used by President Truman.

Paul Weichbrodt, formerly with Willoughby and Brunn of Utica, N. Y., custom body designers for many notables, including numerous film stars.

The 1946 Ford is not a "stop-gap" model hurriedly produced but is the result of four years of research and production know-how, Ford Motor Company officials said today.

The 1946 Ford is designed and built without compromise of traditional Ford quality in workmanship and material. It contains more mechanical improvements than were included in any previous year to year model.

Outstanding features of the car are: a more powerful engine, better performance, longer life, improved economy and a better ride.

The new V-8 engine develops 100 horsepower, making it the most powerful Ford in the history of the company. Pre-war Fords were equipped with V-8 engines developing 90 horsepower.

The chief exterior change is a newly designed radiator grille. The louvres are fewer in number and larger. They

1946 Super De Luxe Fordor

20

PLEASE MENTION "THE GREEN BOOK"

extend horizontally from fender to fender, enhancing a lower, broader appearance.

Other exterior changes include a new hood ornament and a more elaborate rear deck ornamentation. In addition a complete line of colors will be available in the long-wearing, durable Ford synthetic enamel paints.

Luxury and eye-appeal are accentuated in the interiors. Instrumentation is generally the same, but the styling and color schemes of the instrument panel are new.

Upholstery will be available in mohair-broadcloth of several shades. Imitation wood grain panels have given way to subdued panels that blend into the general interior color scheme.

Durable, eye-appealing art-leather decorates the door panels and interior trim.

An improved ride and better roadability, especially at high speeds in cross winds or on curves is assured by the use of improved-type springs and shock absorbers and the addition of a rear-end sway bar.

The thickness of the spring leaves has been reduced and their number increased.

Shock absorbers have improved oil seals to prevent loss of fluid.

The brakes also have received considerable attention. They are new and require less pedal pressure. They are easier to adjust and feature a floating type shoe that seats itself.

A Lincoln-type hand brake lever has been adopted as standard equipment on all Ford Models.

Radiator brackets have been redesigned to prevent radiator corners from breaking and causing leakage. In addition, the hood latch has been changed to a stamping to eliminate possibility of breakage.

Other improvements are: the use of self-locking nuts wherever possible to eliminate the necessity for using cotter pins; a tool bag that is made from artificial leather in place of burlap, and a car jack of ratchet type design. The latter replaces the friction type formerly used.

Improved cooling has been achieved by the adoption of a new radiator pressure cap that maintains a constant pressure of five pounds inside the radiator. Evaporation is reduced and winter anti-freeze preserved. Ford is first in the low-priced field to incorporate this feature in regular production.

Aluminum pistons equipped with four rings will be standard on all models. This, coupled with an improved rear main bearing seal, will effect further economies in oil consumption and prevent loss.

A new standard in fuel economy has been achieved despite an increase in horsepower. Higher engine compression, a change in the engine-axle ratio and the adoption of a new carburetor has made this possible.

Longer life for the camshaft timing gear has been obtained by changing over to aluminum.

21

IN PATRONIZING THESE PLACES

A newly designed distributor virtually eliminates possibility of motor interference or stoppage resulting from condensation or water seepage. The use of oil repellant and long lasting Neoprene covering for ignition wires has eliminated another troublesome feature of pre-war motoring.

All Ford models will feature oil bath air and oil cleaners as standard equipment, wartime use of these accessories having demonstrated their value in prolonging engine life.

Valves on the new engines have been moved outward form the cylinders permitting improved water jacketing and better cooling. Intake and exhaust valves have been equipped with hardened, heat-resisting alloy steel inserts to save the cost of adjustments and regrinding. Using inserts for both intake and exhaust valves is an exclusive Ford feature.

Cylinder block heads for new V-8 engines have been made interchangeable, requiring a change in gasket design.

Possibility of over heating under adverse conditions has been dealt another blow by the development of a new oil pump that circulates a greater volume of oil through the engine lubrication system at a higher pressure.

Valve springs are shot-peened and rust proofed for longer life. The main leaf on each spring is also shot-peened for added strength.

As in the past, sturdy, high-torque Ford 6-cylinder engines well be available for those who prefer the in-line type.

A number of changes have been made in this rugged engine, thousands of which power various military vehicles.

Like the V-8, the new 6-cylinder engine features aluminum pistons and 4 rings for greater oil economy, the new improved distributor, oil filter and oil filtered air cleaner. It also has shot-peened and rust-proofed valve springs and a number of other features incorporated on the larger engine.

In addition new front motor supports have been added. These are made from Neoprene, a synthetic product that is unaffected by oil.

The exhaust manifold has been redesigned so that it is removed far enough from the fuel pump to eliminate possibility of vapor lock.

General engine performance of the Ford 6 has been stepped up by the use of a new, higher lift cam. It develops 90 horsepower at 3300 rpm.

THE 1946 MERCURY

DETROIT, Mich.,—The 1946 Mercury, according to Frank J. Denney, general sales manager for the Lincoln-Mercury Division of the Ford Motor Company, has a heavier, lower and wider appearance, resulting from a wider hood and re-designed front grille.

The new grille consists of die-cast, vertical louvres extending across the

22

PLEASE MENTION "THE GREEN BOOK"

1946 Mercury Two Door Sedan

front. The lines of the hood ornament also have been changed to connote fleetness and beauty.

Separate "Mercury" and "Eight" nameplates have been added, and mouldings have been widened all around the car to accentuate the length and low center of gravity.

The new Mercury is available in eight exterior colors, with harmonizing instrument panels, upholstery and trim.

Two distinctive interior treatments are used. One features gray-green broadcloth upholstery and a modernistic gray-green lacquered instrument panel with contrasting plastic trim. Doors are paneled with gray-green art leather.

The other interior features rust brown cord upholstery with a golden brown lacquered instrument panel and brown art leather paneling on the doors.

Engineering knowledge gained during research and production of wartime goods is reflected in the mechanical changes incorporated in the 1946 Mercury engine.

These include such outstanding features as tri-alloy bearings, crank-case ventilation, improved oil pump, four-ring aluminum pistons, and interchangeable cylinder heads.

Riding comfort in the new Mercury has been increased through redesigning of the springs. The spring leaves are thinner and their number has been increased.

A track bar has been added in the rear, to prevent "wander" on the road in high winds, and a floating-shoe brake has been developed. Brake pedal

IN PATRONIZING THESE PLACES

1946 Lincoln (Four Door Sedan)

PLEASE MENTION "THE GREEN BOOK"

pressure is softer, increasing driving comfort.

The wheelbase is 118 inches.

Mr. Denney has announced that plans are progressing for establishment of an exclusive Mercury dealer organization, as well as separation of production facilities. Prior to the war, Mercury cars were merchandised largely through the Ford dealer organization.

Assembly locations for the post-war Mercury will include the three plants of the Lincoln Division—the Detroit Lincoln plant at Warren and Livernois, and the two new Lincoln-Mercury plants now under construction on the East and West coasts.

THE 1946 LINCOLN

Detroit, Mich.-The 1946 Lincoln was the first of the post-war luxury automobiles to be shown to the public in dealer showrooms throughout the nation.

According to Frank J. Denney, general sales manager, the new model retains the graceful lines first introduced to the quality field by Lincoln, but a number of improvements give the cars a larger and more luxurious appearance.

Exterior improvements include wider bumpers, to provide more protection for fenders, and completely new bumper guards, heavier at the top to prevent override and possible damage to fenders and grille.

The new grille, a massive die-casting with a quadrated pattern, gives the front a lower, broader appearance, and provision for built-in fog lights is a new safety feature that adds an attractive note as well.

Electrically operated hydraulic mechanism for raising and lowering windows is a standard feature on all 1946 Lincoln cars. This is more convenient and safer than the conventional mechanism, since the driver can, with the pressure of one finger, raise or lower either of the car's front windows at any time.

Mr. Denney said that, with new grilles, new bumpers, new color combinations, new rich upholstery, new hardware throughout, new panel instruments, new steering wheel and automatic window lifts, the new Lincoln is by all odds the most beautiful and finest automobile yet offered the American public.

Two models of the 1946 Lincoln are now in production, the four-door sedan and the club coupe, with other models to be added soon. The new Lincolns will be available in eight different exterior colors.

Prices for the 1946 Lincolns, as announced by OPA are:

F. O. B. Detroit—Club Coupe, $1,986.40; Club Coupe with custom interior, $2,112.28; Four-Door Sedan, $2,002.65 and Sedan with custom interior, $2,128.55. These prices include state and federal taxes, gasoline and oil.

IN PATRONIZING THESE PLACES

ALABAMA

ANNISTON
HOTELS
St. Thomas—127 W. 10th St.

ANDALUSIA
TOURIST HOMES
Mrs. Ed. Andrews—69 Cotton St.

BIRMINGHAM
HOTELS
Dunbar—323 N. 17th St.
Palm Leaf—328½ N. 18th St.
Rush—316 N. 18th St.
New Home—1718½—4th Ave.

GADSDEN
TOURISTS HOMES
Mrs. A. Sheperd—1324 4th Ave.
Mrs. J. Simons—233 N. 6th St.

GENEVA
TOURISTS HOMES
Joe Dondal
Susie M. Sharp

MOBILE
TOURISTS HOMES
E. Reed—950 Lyons St.
E. Jordan—256 N. Dearborn St.
F. Wildins 254 N. Dearborn St.
BEAUTY PARLORS
Ritz—607 Congress St.

MONTGOMERY
HOTELS
Douglass—121 Monroe Ave.
Royal Palm—109 Monore Ave.
RESTAURANTS
Bonnie's—390 W. Jeff Davis Ave.
TAVERNS
Douglas—121 Monroe St.

SHEFFIELD
HOTELS
McClain—19th St.

TUSCALOOSO
TOURISTS HOMES
M. A. Barnes—419 30th Ave.
G. W. Clopton—1516 25th Ave.

ARKANSAS

ARKADELPHIA
HOTELS
Hill's—1601 W. Piine St.
TOURIST HOMES
Mrs. B. Dedman—W. Caddo St.
Mrs. L. Cooper—W. Pine St.

RESTAURANTS
Richie Square Deal—Caddo St.
Hill's—River St.
BARBER SHOPS
Scott's—6th & Clay St.
Richie's Upright—16th St.

BRINKLEY
TOURIST HOMES
Davis—709 S. Main St.

EL DORADO
HOTELS
Brewster—E. & B. Sts.
Green's—303 Hill St.
TOURIST HOMES
C. W. Moore—5th & Lincoln Ave.
Dr. Dunning—7th & Columbia Ave.
BARBER SHOPS
Leaders—301 1/2 Hill St.
GARAGES
Williams—1305 E. 1st St.

FAYETTEVILLE
HOTELS
Mebbs—9 N. Willow St.
TOURIST HOMES
Mrs. S. Manuel—313 Olive St.
N. Smith—259 E. Center St.

FORT SMITH
HOTELS
M. Stratford—803 No. 9th St.
Ullery Inn—719 N. 9th St.
TOURIST HOMES
E. O. Trent—1301 N. 9th St.

HOPE
HOTELS
Lewis-Wilson

HOT SPRINGS
HOTELS
Crittenden—314 Cottage St.
The Reed House—115 Cottage St.
Crussader—501 Malvern Ave.
Poro Flat—410 Cottage Ave.
TOURIST HOMES
Barabin Villa—717 Pleasant St.
J. W. Rife—347 1/2 Malvern Ave.
Mrs. N. Fletcher—416 Pleasant Ave.
Mrs. C. C. Wilson—232 Garden St.
Mrs. H. Stilson—735 Pleasant St.
E. E. Lawson—706 Pleasant St.
Edmondson's—243 Ash Street
SANITARIUMS
Pyschean Baths—415 1/2 Malvern Ave.

26

PLEASE MENTION "THE GREEN BOOK"

LITTLE ROCK

HOTELS
The Marquette—522 W. 9th St.
Graysonia—809 Gaines St.
New Vincent—522½ West 9th St.
Tuckers—700½ W. 9th St.
C & C—522½ W. 9th St.

TOURIST HOMES
Mrs. T. Thomas—1901 High St.
Lafayette—904 State Street

RESTAURANTS
Lafayette—904 State St.
College—16th & Bishop
Johnson's—610 W. 9th St.
DeLuxe—203 E. Washington
DeLuxe—724 W. 9th St.
Dean's—904 State Street
Brown Bomber—W. 9th Street

BEAUTY PARLORS
Myrtles—1822 High St.
Woods—16th & High St.
Sue's—919 W. 9th St.
Lafayette—914 State Street

BEAUTY CULTURE SCHOOLS
Velvatex—1004 State Street
Velvia—814 Chester Ave.

TAVERNS
Ferguson's—14th & High Street

NIGHT CLUBS
Shangri-La—904 State Street
Lafayette—9th & State Street

BARBER SHOPS
Whitney—524 W. 9th St.
East End—1005½ Apperson
Century—609 W. 9th St.
Elite—622 W. 9th St.
Fontaine's—710 W. 9th St.
Century—610 West 9th Street
Woods—1523—High Street

LIQUOR STORES
Ritz—1511 Wright Ave.
Jones—528 W. 9th St.

SERVICE STATIONS
Lee's—1401 High St.
Spoon's—14th & High St.
Anderson—8th & State St.

GARAGES
Fosters—1400 W. 10th St.
Lee's—9th & Chester Street

In Our Next Edition
Make it a Point to Have Your Name Inserted Under the Proper Classification

---

DRUG STORES
Floyd—602 W. 9th St.
Children's—9th & Gaines

TAILORS
Miller—916 Gaines St.
Crenshaw—709 W. 9th St.
Dunn—2719 E. 2nd St.
Metropolitan—618 W. 10th St.
B & F—1005 Apperson St.

North LITTLE ROCK

HOTELS
Oasis—1311 E. 3rd St.

TOURIST HOMES
De Lux Court—2720 E. Broadway

RESTAURANTS
Jim's—908 Cedar St. N. L. R.
Nore Vean's—1101 E. 6th St.
Ceats—Henry—No. 67

ROAD HOUSE
Oasis—1311 East 3rd Street

BARBER SHOPS
College—1523 High St.

CAMDEN

TOURIST HOMES
Mrs. Benj. Williams—N. Main Street
Mrs. Hugh Hill—S. Main Street

RESTAURANT
Jim Summers—717 S. Main Street

BEAUTY SHOPS
Glady's—219 E. Washington St.

BARBER SHOPS
Lincoln—215 E. Washington St.

TAVERNS
Patton's—212 Short St.
Daniel's—North Adams St.
Jones—309 Monroe St.

LIQUOR STORES
Package—715½ Main St.
Summers—715½ S. Main Street

GARAGE
Mollette—N. Main Street

SOUTH CAMDEN

ROAD HOUSE
Henry Hanson—Cross Street

PINE BLUFF

HOTELS
P. K.—3rd & Alabama Sts.
Marietta—3rd & Louisiana Sts.
Smith's—East Third St.
Pee Kay—300 E. 3rd Street

TOURIST HOMES
Mrs. K. L. Bell—1111 W. 2nd Ave.
M. J. Hollis—1108 W. 2nd Ave.

RESTAURANTS
Shelton's—200 E. 3rd Street
Duck Inn—405 N. Cedar Street

BARBER SHOP
Nappy Chin—217 State Street

IN PATRONIZING THESE PLACES

BEAUTY PARLOR
  Pruitt's—1317 W. Baraque Street
BEAUTY SCHOOLS
  DeLuxe—221 E. 3rd St.
  Jefferson—1818 W. 6th Ave.
SERVICE STATION
  Anderson—100 S. Mulberry St.
GARAGE
  Alley's—1101 N. Cedar Street

FORDYSE
RESTAURANTS
  Harlem—211 1st St.

HELENA
SERVICE STATIONS
  Stark's—Rightor & Walnut Sts.

RUSSELLVILLE
TOURIST HOMES
  Mrs. M. Jackson—Herman St.
  E. Latimore—318 S. Huston Ave.

TEXARKANA
HOTELS
  Brown's—312 W. Elm St.
TOURIST HOMES
  G. C. Mackey—102 E. 9th St.
RESTAURANTS
  Grant's Cafe—830 Laurel St.
BEAUTY PARLORS
  M. B. Randall—1105 Laurel St.
BARBER SHOPS
  G. Powell—106 E. 9th St.
  Williams—121 E. 9th St.
SERVICE STATIONS
  Smith & Rand—723 W. 7th St.

ARIZONA

DOUGLAS
TOURIST HOMES
  Faustina Wilson—1002-16th St.
RESTAURANTS
  Blue Bird Inn—361-9th St.

NOGALES
RESTAURANTS
  Bell's Cafe—325 Morley Ave.

PHOENIX
HOTELS
  Winston Inn—1342 E. Jefferson St.
  Rice's—535 E. Jefferson St.
TOURIST HOMES
  Mrs. L. Stewart—1134 E. Jefferson
  Gardener's—1229 E. Washington St.
RESTAURANTS
  Alhambia—1246-48 E. Wash. St.
  Town Talk—1202 E. Jefferson Street
  H & H—537 E. Jefferson Street
  Walker's—1303 E. Jefferson Street
BEAUTY PARLORS
  Thelma's—533 E. Jefferson St.
  Copelands—1316 E. Jefferson St.
  M. Parker—547 E. Jefferson St.
  C. Jackson—1238 E. Madison St.

BARBER SHOPS
  Hagler's—111 So. 2nd Street
  Bryant's—620 S. 7th Ave.
TAVERNS
  Vaughn's—1248 E. Washington Ave.
  May's—1645 E. Madison Street
NIGHT CLUBS
  Elks—7th Avenue & Tonto
SERVICE STATION
  Super—13th & Washington Street
GARAGES
  Tourist—126 S. 1st St.
  Burly Ridue—126 So. 1st Street
DRUG STORES
  R. D. Davis—1127 W. Buckeye Rd.
  Johnson's—1140 E. Washington Street

TUSCON
TOURIST HOMES
  Criterion Rooms—138 W. Ochoa St.
RESTAURANTS
  Hill's Cafe—354 S. Meyer St.

YUMA
HOTELS
  Brown's—196 N. Main St.

CALIFORNIA

BERKLEY
BEAUTY PARLORS
  Little Gem—1511 Russell St.
BARBER SHOPS
  Success—2946 Sacramento St.
TAVERNS
  Schaeffer's—2940 Sacramento St.

EL CENTRO
HOTELS
  The Roland—201 E. Main St.
TOURIST HOMES
  Mrs. L. Augustas—420 Commercial Ave.
RESTAURANTS
  Pearl McKinney Lunch—301 Main St.

FRESNO
HOTELS
  Claren—145 N. Front Street
TOURIST HOMES
  La Silve—841 F St.
RESTAURANTS
  Taylor's—1402 C St.
  Collins—847 'G' St.
  DeLuxe—1228 'F' St.
  Stella's—1861 'G' St.
  Stella's—1861-G. Street
  New Jerico—101 Church Street
BEAUTY PARLORS
  Rosebud—835 G. Street
  Clara's—855 'G' St.
  Ruth's—1816 F. Street
  Clara's—855 G. Street
  Golden West—1032 - F. Street

PLEASE MENTION "THE GREEN BOOK"

BARBER SHOPS
  DeLuxe—725 'G' St.
  Golden West—1032—'F' St.
  Magnolia—602 F. Street
  Sportman's—855 G. Street
  Esquire—1011 G. Street
TAVERNS
  20th Century—1401 - F. Street
GARAGE
  Buddy Lang's—1335 - F. Street
  Frank's—1326 Fresno Street
TRAILER PARKS & CAMPS
  Barnes Drive In—1412 "F" St.
TAILORS
  Jackson's—1205 Sacramento Street

LOS ANGELES

HOTELS
  Clark—1824 Central Ave.
  Arcade—542 Ceres Avenue
  Lincoln—549 Ceres Ave.
  Sheridan—1824 Central Avenue
  McAlpin—648 Stanford Ave.
  Elite—1217 Central Avenue
  Olympic—843 S. Central Avenue
  Regal—815 E. 6th St.
  Sojourner's—1119 E. Adams Blvd.
  Kentucky—1123 Central Ave.
  Avon—405 S. Hewitt
  Dunbar—4225 S. Central Ave.
  Morris—809 E. 5th Street
  Glacier—523 Stanford Street
TOURIST HOMES
  Mrs. B. Hoffman—760 W. 17th St.
RESTAURANTS
  Marble Inn—1820 Imperial H'way
  Robertson's—4815 S. Central Avenue
  Chief—4400 S. Avalon Blvd.
  Ivie's—1105½ E. Vernon Avenue
  Pig N' Pat—4200 S. Central Avenue
  Henry Bros.—10359 Wilmington (WATTS)
  Banks—4019 S. Avalon Blvd.
  Nita's—125 W. Vernon Avenue
  John's—3519 S. Western
  Woodson's—Jefferson & Raymond Sts.
  Eddie's—4201 S. Central Avenue
  Blue Room—9900 S. Central Avenue
  Casa Blanca—2801 S. San Pedro St.
  Gingham—111 N. San Pedro Avenue
  Zombie—5432 S. Central Avenue
  Bobbie's—4001 Avalon Avenue
  The Fawn—Western & 29th St.
  Arc—4067 S. Central Avenue
  Shadowland—4505 Avalon Avenue
  Hi Jenks—4428 Avalon Avenue
  Waffle Shop—1063 E. 43 Street
  Clifton's—618 S. Olive Street
  Digby—1st & Alameda Street
BEAUTY PARLORS
  Creole—2221 Central Ave.
  Mary Esther—1709 E. 103rd St.
  Tex—2830 S. San Pedro St.
  Sherwoods—5113 S. Central Avenue
  Studio—2515 S. Central
  Continental—5203 Hopper Avenue
  Anna Mae's—4436 Avalon Avenue

  Gorum—5440 S. Central Avenue
  Louise—816 E. 5th St.
  Triangle—43 San Pedro & Walls Sts.
  Colonial—1813½ S. Central Avenue
  Dunbar—4225 S. Central Avenue
  M. Wilson—2818 S. Central Avenue
  Beauty Salon—1195 East 35th Street
BARBER SHOPS
  Hotel—1808 S. Central Ave.
  Elite—4204 S. Central Avenue
  Connie's—2204 S. Central Avenue
  Bertha's—1434 W. Jefferson Boulevard
  Personality—4222 S. Central Ave.
  Williams—3615 S. Western
  Echo—43rd & Central Ave.
TAVERNS
  Marble Inn—1820 Imperial Highway
  Margot—5259 S. Central Avenue
  Emeral Room—901 E. 6th St.
  Emerald Room—901 E. 6th St.
  Golden Gate—1719 E. 103rd St.
  Paradise—5505 S. Central Avenue
  Samba—5th & Towns Avenue
  Onyx—1808 S. Central Avenue
  Crisbar—2829 S. Western Avenue
  Reney's—2023 S. Central Avenue
  Johnson's—4201 S. Main Street
  Casa Blanca—2801 S. San Pedro.
NIGHT CLUBS
  Club Alabam—4215 S. Central Avenue
  Down Beat—4201 S. Central Avenue
  Plantation—108th & Central
  Cafe Society—2711 S. San Pedro Avenue
  Basket Room—3219 S. Central Avenue
  Harlem—118th & Parmalee Sts.
  Rumboogie—1751½ E. 103rd St. (WATTS)
  Harlem—11812 Parmalee
  Tommy Brookins—1808 S. Central Ave.
  Billy Bergs—1354 N. Vine Street
ROAD HOUSE
  Casa Blanca—2801 S. San Pedro St.
LIQUOR STORES
  House of Morgan—2729 S. Central
  Mike's—10959 Wilmington (WATTS)
  Dunbar—4223 S. Central Avenue
  Jackson's—5501 S. Central Avenue
SERVICE STATIONS
  Valentine's Service—2657 S. Western Ave.
  Newton's—3903 S. Central Avenue
  Hopkins Signal Ser.—3426 Central Ave.
  Long's—2732 S. Central Ave.
  Carner's—4500 S. Avalon Avenue
  Simpkins & Cower—2227 S. Central Ave.
  Si Johnson's—3500 S. Western Ave.
  Tom's—1424 W. Jefferson Blvd.
  Hughes—2901 W. Jefferson Blvd.
  Brock—1246 W. Jefferson Blvd.
  R. A. & S.—Jefferson & Griffith
  Garcia—52nd Pl. and Central
GARAGES
  Parkers—2100 E. 103rd St.
  La Clare—Jefferson at Hill
  McAdam's—1448 W. Jefferson Blvd.
  Bill's—4106 Avalon Blvd.
  Alexander's—Jefferson & Griffith

29

IN PATRONIZING THESE PLACES

AUTOMOTIVE
Lee's—4820 S .Central Avenue
Auto Parts—864 N. Virgil Avenue

DRUG STORES
Allums—4375 S. Central Avenue
Doctor's—4012 S. Central Avenue
Medical—3112 S. Western Avenue
Martinas—4406 Avalon Avenue
Slopers—2100—W. Jefferson Blvd.

TAILORS
Bader's—1840 E. 103rd St.
Delta—8512 Compton Avenue
Duver Bros.—811 E. 5th St.
Progressive—4302 S. Central Avenue
Beason—2901 S. Western Ave.

ELSINORE
MOTEL
Geo. Moore—407 Scrivener Street

HOLLYWOOD
TOURIST HOME
Jam. W. Brown—2881 Seattle Dr.

OAKLAND
HOTELS
Warren—1252 7th St.

TOURIST HOMES
Mrs. A. C. Clark—805 Linden St.
Mrs. H. Williams—3521 Grove St.

RESTAURANTS
The Villa—1724 7th St.

BEAUTY PARLORS
Personality—3613 San Dablo Avenue

TAVERNS
Overland Cafe—1719 7th St.
Rythm Buffet—1704 7th St.

SERVICE STATIONS
Summers—1251-7th St.
McCabe—5901 Adeline St.
Signal—800 Center St.

GARAGES
Bufford's—5901 Aldine St.

PASADENA
RESTAURANTS
Hub—Orange Grove at Fair Oaks

TAVERNS
Kentucky—1067 N. Fair Oaks

SERVICE STATIONS
Penn. Mobile—1096 Lincoln Ave.
Stacy's—920 N. Fair Oaks Avenue

SAN BERNADINO
TOURIST HOMES
S. M. Carlton—939 W. 6th St.

SAN DIEGO
HOTELS
Douglass—206 Market St.
Simmons—542 6th Avenue
Y. W. C. A.—2905 Clay St.
Y. M. C. A.—2905 Clay St.

TOURIST HOMES
Johnson's—18 N. 30th St.

RESTAURANTS
Sun—421 Market Street
Brown Hostess—2816 Imperial Ave.

SERVICE STATION
Weber's—2nd & Market Street
Woodson's—30th & K Streets

TAVERNS
Night Hawk—2971 Market Street

TAILORS
Clever—2606 Imperial Avenue
Imperial—2751 Imperial Avenue

DRUG STORES
Imperial—30th & Imperial Avenue

SAN FRANCISCO
HOTELS
Buford—1969 Sutter St.
The Scaggs—1715 Webster St.
Powell—Powell & Market Sts.

TOURIST HOMES
Mrs. F. Johnson—1788 Sutter St.
Helen's Guest House—1951 Sutter St.

RESTAURANTS
Calif. Theatre—1605 Post Street

BEAUTY PARLORS
Arineica's—1928 Fillmore St.

TAVERNS
Jack's—1931 Sutter St.

NIGHT CLUBS
Town Club—1963 Sutter St.

DRUG STORES
Riggan's—2600 Sutter St.

SANTA MONICA
TAVERNS
La Nobita—1807 Belmont Place

TULARE
TOURIST HOMES
South "K" St.—330 South "K" St.

TAVERNS
King's—322-24 South K. St.

VALLEJO
TAVERNS
Cotton Club—Virginia & Branciforte

VICTORVILLE
TOURIST HOMES
Murray's Dude Ranch

COLORADO

COLORADO SPRINGS
TOURIST HOMES
G. Roberts—418 E. Cucharras St.
L. C. Alford—509 N. Boyer St.

PLEASE MENTION "THE GREEN BOOK"

DENVER

HOTEL
Hildreth—2152 Arapahoe Street

TOURIST HOMES
Mrs. G. Anderson—2119 Marion St.
Mrs. W. Graham—2544 Emerson St.
R. B. Anderson—2421 Ogden St.
Mrs. A. S. Fisher—2355 High St.

RESTAURANTS
King's—2359 Marion St.
Red Booster—2622 Welton St.
Sugar Bowl—2832 Welton St.
Mac's—2635 Welton St.
Royal—2536 Washington St.
Mary's—714 E. 26th Avenue
A & A—2359 Marion St.
Warners—1857 Champa St.
St. Louis—2856 Welton St.
Green Lantern—2859 Fremont
Da-Nite—1430 22nd Avenue
B & E—2847 Gilpin St.
Dew Drop Inn—2715 Welton St.
Nu Way—1025 21st St.
Sugar Bowl—2832 Welton Street
Two Friends—1857 Champa Street
Down Beat—609 - 27 Street

BEAUTY PARLORS
Landers 2460 Marion St.
Unique—2547 Welton St.

Modern Costemologists

UP TO DATE BEAUTY SHOP

For High Class Work

For Appointment - Tel. TA-9444

•

Mrs. MYRTLE FOSTER, Prop.
Miss RUTH ALLEN, Operator

Ford—2527 Humboldt St.
Myrtle's—2404 Clarkson St.

BARBER SHOPS
Dunbar—2741 Welton St.
Roxy—2559 Welton St.
20th Century—2727 Welton St.
W. A. Stephens—2650 Welton St.

TAVERNS
Rossonian Lounge—2650 Welton Street
Andersons—715 E. 26th Avenue
Arcade—739 E. 26th Avenue
Archie's—2449 Larimer St.

LIQUOR STORES
Lincoln—2636 Welton St.
18th Ave.—1108 E. 18th Avenue
Aristocrat—3101 William St.

SERVICE STATIONS
Mac's—2637 Welton St.
Da-Nite—728 E. 26th Avenue
White—2655 Downing St.
Plazer—E. 22nd & Humboldt Sts.

GARAGES
Mattherson's—2637 Welton St.
Mac's—2637 Welton Street

TAXI CABS
Ritz—2721 Welton St.

DRUG STORES
Rocy Mt.—23rd and Champa Sts.
T. K.—27th and Larimer Sts.
Ideal—28th & Downing
V. H. Meyers—22nd & Downing Sts.
Atlas—2701 Welton St.

TAILORS
Arcade—739 E. 26th St.
White House—2863 Welton St.
B & B—1710 E. 25th Avenue
Ace—2220 Downing St.

GREENLEY

TOURIST HOMES
Mrs. E. Alexander—106 E. 12th St.

LA JUNTA

TOURIST HOMES
Mrs. R. Mitchell—322 W. 1st St.
Mrs. Moore—301 Lewis Avenue
Mrs. H. Tittsworth—325 Maple Avenue

PUEBLO

HOTELS
Perry—231 S. Victoria St.

TOURIST HOMES
Mrs. T. Protho—918 E. Evans Avenue
C. Forehand—1003 Spruce St.

TRINIDAD

TOURIST HOMES
Mrs. C. Brooks—114 W. 3rd St.

CONNECTICUT

BRIDGEPORT

HOTELS
Y. W. C. A.—237 John St.

TOURIST HOMES
Mrs. M. Barrett—83 Summer St.
Mrs. E. Lawrence—68 Fulton St.

GARAGES
W & T—179 William St.

IN PATRONIZING THESE PLACES

HARTFORD

HOTELS
  Parrish Rooming House—26 Walnut St.
TOURIST HOMES
  Mrs. Johnson—2016 Main St.
BEAUTY SHOPS
  Quaility—1762 Main St.
BARBER SHOPS
  Williams—1978 Main Street
TAVERNS
  Turf Club—2243 Main St.

NEW HAVEN

HOTELS
  Phyllis Wheatley—108 Canal St.
  Hotel Portsmouth—91 Webster Avenue
TOURIST HOMES
  Dr. M. F. Allen—65 Dixwell Avenue
  Mrs. S. Robinson—54 Dixwell Avenue
  Mrs. C. Raone—68 Dixwell Avenue
RESTAURANTS
  Mrs. Griggs—146 Dixwell Avenue
  Ruth's—222 Dixwell Avenue
  Montrey—265 Dixwell Avenue
BEAUTY PARLORS
  Mme. Ruby—175 Goffe St.
  Harris—138 Goffe St.
  Glady's—624 Orchard Street
  Ethel's—152 Dixwell Avenue
SCHOOL OF BEAUTY CULTURE
  Modern—170 Goffe St.

NEW LONDON

TOURIST HOMES
  Home of the Bachelor—20 Brewer St.
  Hempstead Cottage— 73 Hempstead St.
  Mrs. E. Whittle—785 Bank St.
BEAUTY PARLOR
  Boone's—96 Main Street

STAMFORD

HOTELS
  GLADSTONE—Gay St.
TOURIST HOMES
  Robert Graham—37 Hanrahan Ave.
NIGHT CLUBS
  Sizone—136 W. Main St.

WATERBURY

HOTELS
  Jones—64 Bishop St.
TOURIST HOMES
  Mrs. A. Dunham—208 Bridge St.
  Community House—34 Hopkins St.

WEST HAVEN

TAVERNS
  Hoot Owl—374 Beach St.

DELAWARE

DOVER

HOTELS
  Cannon's—Kirkwood St.
  Cannon's—Division St.
  Caleb Brown—Lincoln St.
  Dean's—Forrest St.
  Mosely's—Division St.
  Moseley's—Division St.
  Weston's—Division St.

TOWNSEND

HOTELS
  Rodney—Dupont Highway-Rt. 13

WILMINGTON

HOTELS
  Royal—703 French St.
  Anderson—716 French St.
  Y. M. C. A.—10th Ave. and Walnut St.
  Y. W. C. A.—10th Ave. and Walnut St.
TOURIST HOMES
  Miss W. A. Brown—1306 Tatnall St.
  Mrs. E. Till—1008 French St.
RESTAURANTS
  Christian Assn. Bldg.—10th & Walnut St.
BEAUTY PARLORS
  Mrs. M. Anderson—916 French St.
BARBER SHOPS
  Burton's—8th and Walnut St.
NIGHT CLUB
  Spot—7th and 8th on French St.
SERVICE STATIONS
  Esso—8th and 9th on King

DISTRICT OF COLUMBIA
WASHINGTON

HOTELS

JOHNSON'S HOTEL
1502 - 13TH ST., N. W.
ALL OUTSIDE ROOMS
HOT & COLD WATER IN EVERY ROOM
Joseph M. Johnson, Prop. Phone No. 6510

Henry—1825 13th St. N. W.
Mid-City—7th & 'N' Sts. N. W.

JOHNSON'S Jr. HOTEL
1509 VERMONT AVE., N. W.
HOT & COLD WATER IN EVERY ROOM
ALL OUTSIDE ROOMS
JOSEPH R. JOHNSON, PROP.

PLEASE MENTION "THE GREEN BOOK"

HOTELS
  Whitelaw—13th & 'T' Sts. N. W.
  J. Y's—16th & 'G' Sts. N. W.
  Dunbar—U St. & 15th St., N. W.
  Y. M. C. A.—1816 12th St. N. W.
  Y. W. C. A.—901 Rhode Is. Ave. N. W.

TOURIST HOMES
  Mrs. L. Fowler—1449 'Q' St. N. W.
  Mrs. R. Lee—1212 Girad St. N. W.
  Towles—1342 Vermont Ave., N. W.
  Bailey's—2533 - 13th St., N. W.
  Modern—3006 - 13th St., N. W.

TAVERNS
  Holleywood—1940 9th St. N. W.
  Liberty—910 5th St. N. W.
  Harrison's Cafe—455 Florida Ave. N. W.
  Service Grill—12th & 'V' Sts. N. W.
  Off Beat—1849 - 7th St., N. W.
  Kenyon—Ga. Avenue & Kenyon St., N. W.
  Brentwood—4526 Rhode Island Ave., N. E.
  Capitol—1224 U St., N. W.
  Chuck's 1334 V St., N. W.
  Club Liberty—910 - 5th St., N. W.

RESTAURANTS
  Keys—7th & 'T' St. N. W.
  Clore—7th & 'T' Sts. N. W.
  Chicken Paradise—1210 U. St., N. W.
  Earl's—1218 U St., N. W.
  Sugar Bowl—2830 Georgia Ave., N. W.
  Pig N Pit—1214 - 14th St., N. W.
  Shrimp Hut—807 Florida Aveneue, N. W.
  Casbah—1211 U St., N. W.
  Uptown—807 Florida, N. W.
  Johnson's—1909 - 14th St., N. W.
  Mother Froman's—1108 9th St., N. W.
  The Hour—1937 - 11th St., N. W.
  Jackson's—1831 Weltberger St., N. W.

LIQUOR STORES
  Peoples—719 - 11th St., N. W.
  S & W—1428 - 9th St., N. W.
  Ney's—1013 Penna. Ave., N. W.
  Shuster's—101 H St., N. W.
  Masters—714 K St., N. W.

BARBER SHOPS
  Florida—1803 Florida Ave., N. W.

BEAUTY PARLORS
  Apex—1417 'U' St. N. W.
  The Royal—1800 'T' St. N. W.
  Elite—1806 Florida Ave., N. W.
  Vanity Box—1515 - 9th St., N. W.
  Lil's—1327 - 11th St., N. W.
  Green's - 1825 - 18th St., N. W.
  A. Marie—3114 - 11th St., N. W.
  Bandbox—2036 - 18th St., N. W.

NIGHT CLUBS
  Bali—1901 14th St. N. W.
  Caverns—11th & 'U' St. N. W.
  Republic Gardens—1355 'U' St. N. W.
  Grand Terrace—3925 Benning Rd., N. E.
  Club Bali—1901 - 14th St., N. W.
  Club Caverns—11th & U St., N. W.

SERVICE STATIONS
  Brown's—Georgia Ave. & 'V' St.
  B. Barker—Florida Ave. & 8th St.
  Engelberg—1783 Florida Ave., N. W.

GARAGES
  University—Rear 1019 Columbia Rd. N. W.

TAILORS
  W. R. Reynolds—1808 Florida Ave., N. W.

FLORIDA

DAYTONA BEACH

TOURIST HOMES
  M. Littleton—522 S. Campbell St.

RESTAURANTS
  Rotisserie—2nd & walnut St.
  Casa Blanca 899 Cypress St.
  C & B 566 Capbell St.

TAVERNS
  Palms—walnut & 2nd Sts.

LIQUOR STORE
  Hank's—610 S. Campbell St.

SERVICE STATIONS
  Kirkland—Campbell & Orange Ave.

DELRAY BEACH

TAVERNS
  Manfield—N. W. 1st St.

FORT LANDERDALE

HOTELS
  Hill—430 N. W. 7th Ave.

TAVERNS
  Windsor

JACKSONVILLE

HOTELS
  Blue Chip—514 Broad St.
  Richmond—422 Broad St.

TOURIST HOMES
  Craddock—45th & Moncrief
  Alpine Cottage—714 W. Ashley St.
  E. H. Flipper—739 W. Church St.
  L. D. Jefferson—1834 Moncrief Rd.
  B. Robinson—128 Orange St.
  G. L. Martin—702 W. Beaver St.
  C. H. Simmons—434 W. Ashley St.

NIGHT CLUBS
  Two Spot—45th & Moncrief Rd.

LAKE CITY

TOURIST HOMES
  Ben-Flo—720 E. Leon St.

LAKELAND

TOURIST HOMES
  Mrs. A. Davis—518 W. 1st St.
  Mrs. J. Davis—842½ N. Florida Ave.
  Mrs. J. Boyd—Missouri Ave.

LIBERIA

LIQUOR STORES
  Blue Chip—2200 Simon Street

MIAMI

HOTELS
  Mary Elizabeth—642 N. W. 2nd Ave.
  Dorsey—941 N. W. 2nd Avenue

IN PATRONIZING THESE PLACES

BEAUTY PARLORS
  Progressive—1324 N. W. 1st Court
  Williams—1214 N. W. 3rd Avenue
  Elizabeth—175 N. W. 11th Terrace
  Charlows—1730 N. W. 1st Court
  Minnie's—1469½ N. W. 5th Avenue
BEAUTY SCHOOLS
  Sunlight—1011 N. W. 2nd Avenue
BARBER SHOPS
  Smith's—262 N. W. 17th St.
TAVERNS
  Star—3rd Ave. & 15th St. N. W.
NIGHT CLUBS
  Fiesta—627 N. W. 2nd Avenue
LIQUOR STORES
  Cuban—1701 N. W. 4th Avenue
  Ideal—175 N. W. 11th St.
  Plantation—N. W. 14th St. & 3rd Ave.
  Henry's—379 N. W. 14th St.
TAILORS
  Valet—506 N. W. 14th St.
TAXI
  Brown's—N. W. 8th St. & 2nd Ave.

ORLANDO
HOTELS
  Wells Bilt—509 W. South St.

PENSACOLA
RESTAURANTS
  Rhumboogie—509 E. Salamanca Street
TAILORS
  Reese—307 E. Wright Street

SEBRING
RESTAURANTS
  Brown's—406 Lemon St.

ST. AUGUSTINE
TOURIST HOMES
  F. H. Kelley—83 Bridge St.
  H. G. Tye Apts.—132 Central Avenue

TAMPA
HOTELS
  Central—1028 Central Avenue
  Dallas—829 Zack St.
  DeLux—822 Constant St.
RESTAURANTS
  Bruce's—813 Scott St.
TAVERNS
  Little Savory—Central & Scott

WEST PALM BEACH
RESTAURANTS
  Silver Bar Grill—615 8th St.

GEORGIA

ALBANY
TOURIST HOMES
  Mrs. A. J. Ross—514 Mercer St.
  Mrs. L. Davis—313 South St.
  Mrs. C. Washington—228 S. Jackson St.

ATLANTA
HOTELS
  Hotel Royal—214 Auburn Ave., N. E.
  Mack—548 Bedford Place, N. E.
  Savoy—239 Auburn A. (formerly Roosevelt)
  Shaw—245 Auburn Ave.
  James—241 Auburn Ave. N. E.
  McKay—Auburn Ave.
  Y. M. C. A.—22 Butler St.
TOURIST HOMES
  Mrs. Connally-125 Walnut St. N. W.
RESTAURANTS
  Suttons—312 Auburn Ave. N. E.
  Dew Drop Inn—11 Ashby St. N. E.
  Smitty's—Auburn Ave. N. E.
  Hawk's 306 Auburn
TAVERNS
  Yeah Man—256 Auburn Ave. N. E.
  Sportmans Smoke Shop—242 Auburn N. E.
  Butler's—1868 Simpson Road
BEAUTY PARLORS
  Poro—250½ Auburn Avenue
BARBER SHOPS
  Artistic—55 Decatur
  Gate City—240 Auburn Ave., N. W.
NIGHT CLUBS
  The Top Hat—Auburn Ave. N. E.
  Posnciana—143 Auburn Avenue
SERVICE STATIONS
  Harden's—848 Hunter Ave. Cor. Belle
  Hall's 215 Auburn Ave., N. E.
GARAGES
  South Side—539 Fraser St., N. E.

AUGUSTA
HOTELS
  Crimm's—725 9th St.
  Harlem—1145 9th St.
TOURIST HOMES
  Mrs. M. Beaseley—1412 Twigg St.
WINE & LIQUOR STORES
  Bollinger's—1114 Gwennett St.

BRUNSWICK
TOURIST HOMES
  The Palms—1309 Glouster St.

COLUMBUS
HOTELS
  Lowes—724 5th Ave.
  Y. M. C. A.—521 9th St.
RESTAURANTS
  Economy Cafe—519 8th St.
BEAUTY PARLORS
  Ann's—832 4th Ave.
BARBER SHOPS
  Sherrell's—First Avenue
NIGHT CLUB
  Golden Rest—1026 7th Ave.
GARAGES
  Seventh Avenue—816 7th Ave.

PLEASE MENTION "THE GREEN BOOK"

DUBLIN
TOURIST HOMES
Mrs. M. Burden—508 McCall St.
Mrs. R. Hunter—504 S. Jefferson
Mrs. M. Kea—405 S. Jefferson

EASTMAN
TOURIST HOMES
J. P. Cooper—211 College St.
Mrs. M. Mariano—408 1st Ave.

GREENSBORO
TOURIST HOMES
Mrs. C. Brown—Caanen Section
Mrs. E. Jeter—Railroad Section
Mrs. B. Walker—Springfield Section

MACON
HOTELS
Douglas—361 Broadway
Richmond—319 Broadway
TOURIST HOMES
Mrs. E. C. Moore—122 Spring St.
Brs. F. W. Henndon—139 1st Ave.
RESTAURANTS
Mables—Main Street
Red Front—417 Wall St.
Jean's—429 Cotton Avenue
West Side—222 Dempsey Avenue
BEAUTY PARLORS
Marquiata—554 New Street
La Bonita—455 Cotton Avenue
Carrie's—133 Forest Avenue
Lula Life—425 E. 2nd Street
TAILORS
Huschel—264 Broadway
Community—550 - 3rd Avenue
SERVICE STATION
Anderson's—Pursley at Pond Street

SAVANNAH
RESTAURANTS
Dreamland—43rd & Hopkins St.
BEAUTY PARLORS
Rudies'—1827 Ogeechee Road
Rose—348 Price St.
SCHOOL OF BEAUTY CULTURE
456 Montgomery St.
SERVICE STATIONS
Gibson's—442 West Broad Street
DRUG STORES
Moores'—37th & Florence
TAILORS
Halls—1014 W. Broad St.
TRAILERS PARK
Cocoanut Grove—Mrs. J. Cox

WAY CROSS
TOURIST HOMES
Mrs. K. G. Scarlett—843 Reynoids

ILLINOIS
CHICAGO
HOTELS
Ritz—409 E. Oakwood Blvd.
Alpha—2945 S. Michigan Blvd.
Como—5204 S. Parkway
Green Gables—3920 S. Lake Park Ave.
Du Sable—764 E. Oakwood Blvd.
Strode—820 E. Oakwood Blvd.
Almo—3800 Lake Park Ave.
Evans—733 E. 61st St.
Oakwood—820 E. Oakwood Blvd.
Perishing—6400 Cottage Grove Ave.
Praire—2836 Praire Ave.
S & S—4142 S. Park Ave.
Southway—6014 S. Parkway
Spencer—300 E. Garfield
Western—6357 Champlain Ave.
Grand—5044 S. Parkway
Tyson—4259 S. Parkway
Vincennes—601 E. 36th St.
Y. M. C. A.—3763 S. Wabash Ave.
Y. W. C. A.—4559 S. Parkway
Franklin—3942 Indianna Ave.
Lincoln—2901 State St.
Pompeii—20 E. 31st St.
New Hazie—3910 Indianna Ave.
Clarilge—51st & Michigan Ave.

TOURIST HOMES
Mabel Bank—712 E. 44th St.
Poro College—4415 S. Parkway

RESTAURANTS
Morris'—410 E. 47th St.
Wrights—3753 S. Wabash Ave.
A & J—105 E. 51st St.
Hurricane—345 E. Garfield Blvd.
Pitts—812 E. 39th St.
Palm Gardens—720 E. Oakwood Blvd.
400 Club—715 E. 63rd St.
Pioneer—533 E. 43rd St.
Pershing—755 East 64th Street

BEAUTY PARLORS
Matties'—4212 Cottage Grove Ave.

BARBER SHOPS
Bank's—209 E. 39th St.

TAVERNS
The palm—466 E. 47th St.
El Casino—823 E. 39th St.
Key Hole—3965 S. Parkway

NIGHT CLUBS
Boulevard Lounge—104 E. 51st St.
El Grotto—6400 Cottage Grove Ave.
Rhum-Boogie—353 E. Garfield Blvd.
820 Club—820 E. 39th St.
Show Boat—6109 S. Parkway

SERVICE STATIONS
Parkway—5036 S. Parkway
Waterford's—6000 S. Wabash Ave.
Standard—Garfield & S. Parkway
American Giants—5900 S. Wabash Ave.
Roosevelt—4600 S. Wabash Ave.

35

IN PATRONIZING THESE PLACES

GARAGES
Grove—4751 S. Cottage Grove Ave.
Zephyr—4535 S. Cottage Grove Ave.
DRUG STORES
Partee—4308 S. Parkway
Thompson—545 E. 47th St.

CENTRALIA
TOURIST HOMES
Mrs. Claybourne—303 N. Pine St.
BEAUTY SHOPS
M. Coleman—503 N. Poplar St.
BARBER SHOPS
P. Coleman—503 N. Poplar St.
SERVICE STATIONS
Langenfield—120 N. Poular St.

DANVILLE
HOTELS
Just A Mere Hotel—218 E. North St.
TOURIST HOMES
Stewart—214 E. Main St.

EAST ST. LOUIS
TOURIST HOMES
P. B. Reeves—1803 Bond Ave.
W. E. Officer—2200 Missouri Ave.
NIGHT CLUBS
Cotton Club—1236 Mississippi Ave.

PEORIA
TOURIST HOMES
Clara Gibbons—923 Monson St.
RESTAURANTS
Twenty Grand—523 Smith St.
BEAUTY PARLORS
S. Thompson—809 Sanford Street
BARBER SHOP
Stone's—323 N. Adams St.
NIGHT CLUB
Bris Collins—405 N. Washington St.

SPRINGFIELD
HOTELS
Dudley—130 S. 11th St.
TOURIST HOMES
Mrs. M. Rollins—844 S. College St.
Mrs. B. Mosby—1614 E. Jackson St.
Mrs. H. Robbins—1616 E. Jackson St.
Mrs. G. Bell—625 N. 2nd St.
Mrs. E. Brooks—705 N. 2nd St.
Dr. Ware—1520 E. Washington St.

OTTAWA
TOURIST HOMES
Mrs. G. Danile—605 S. 3rd Ave.

ROCKFORD
HOTELS
Briggs—429 S. Court St.
TOURIST HOMES
Mrs. C. Gorum—301 Steward Ave.
Mrs. G. Wright—422 S. Court St.
S. Westbrook—515 N. Winnebago

WAUKEGAN
TOURIST HOMES
Mrs. R. Norwood—819 Mott Ave.

IDAHO
BOISE
TOURIST HOMES
Mrs. S. Love—1164 River St.

POCATEELLO
TOURIST HOMES
A. M. E. Parsnage—625 E. Fremont St.
Tourist Park—E. Fremont St.

INDIANA
ANDERSON
TAVERNS
Terrance Cafe—1411 Madison Ave.
RECREATION PARKS
Fox Lake Summer Resort 1½ miles S. W. of Angola

ELKHART
TOURIST HOMES
Miss E. Botts—336 St. Joe St.

EVANSVILLE
TOURIST HOMES
Mrs. B. Bell—672 Lincoln Ave.
Mrs. Lauderdale—309 Locust St.
Miss F. Snow—719 Oak St.
Community Ass'n—620 Cherry St.

FORT WAYNE
RESTAURANT
Leo Manuals'—1329 Lafayette St.

GARY
HOTELS
States'—1700 Washington St.

FRENCH LICK
HOTELS
Thurman—222 Indianna Ave.

INDIANAPOLIS
HOTELS
Y. M. C. A.—450 N. Senate Ave.
Y. W. C. A.—653 N. West St.
Anderson—Indianna Ave.
Ferguson—1102 N. Capitol Ave.
Marquis—1523 N. Capitol Avenue
HOTELS
Hawaii—406 Indiana Ave.
Zanzibar—420 N. Sinate Ave.
TOURIST HOMES
Morris Fur. Rms.—518 N. West St.

36

PLEASE MENTION "THE GREEN BOOK"

RESTAURANTS
 Lasley's—510 Indiana Ave.
 A. B.'s—413 Indiana Ave.
 Broaden's—1645 N. Western Ave.
 Parkview—321 N. California Ave.
 Green's—709 Indiana Ave.
 Stormy Weather—319 Indiana Ave.
 Log Cabin—524 Indiana Ave.
CHINESE RESTAURANT
 Yee Sen—545 Indiana
BEAUTY PARLORS
 Petite—420 W. Michigan St.
 Stephens & Childs—527 Indiana Ave.
 Beauty Box—2704 Clifton St.
 Dancy's—436 N. California Ave.
 Smith's—446 Douglas St.
TAVERNS
 Mayes Cafe—503 Indiana
 Hambric Cafe—510 Indiana
 Ritz—Sinate & Indiana
 Sunset—875 Indiana
 M. C.—544 W. Maryland St.
 Blue Eagle—648 Indiana
 Midway—736 Indiana
 Panama—304 Indiana
SERVICE STATIONS
 Harris—458 West 16th St.
GARAGES
 25th St. Garage—553 W. 25th St.
DRUG STORES
 Ethical—642 Indiana
TAILORS
 Neighborhood—1642 Northwestern Ave.
 Lee's—401 W. 29th St.

JEFFERSONVILLE
TOURIST HOMES
 Charles Thomas—607 Missouri Ave.
 Leonard Redd—711 Missouri Ave.

MARION
RESTAURANTS
 Marshall's—414 E. 4th St.

KOKOMO
TOURIST HOMES
 Mrs. C. W. Winburn—1015 Kennedy St.
 Mrs. Charles Hardinson—812 Kennedy St.
 Mrs. A. Woods—1107 N. Purdun St.
 Mrs. S. D. Hughes—1045 N. Kennedy St.

LAFAYETTE
TAVERNS
 Pekin Cafe—1702 Hartford St.

MICHIGAN CITY
TOURIST HOMES
 Allen's—210 E. 2nd St.

MUNCIE
HOTELS
 Y. M. C. A.—905½ Willard St.

SOUTH BEND
RESTAURANTS
 Smokes—432 S. Chapin St.

NEW ALBANY
TOURIST HOMES
 J. D. Clay—513 Pearl St.

TERRE HAUTE
HOTELS
 Booker—306 Cherry St.
TAVERNS
 Dreamland Cafe—306 Cherry St.

WEST BADEN SPRINGS
HOTELS
 Waddy

EVANSVILLE
TOURIST HOMES
 Z. Knight—410 S. E. 9th St.

IOWA
CEDAR RAPIDS
TOURIST HOMES
 Mrs. W. H. Lavelle—812 9th Ave. E.
 Brown's—818 9th Ave. S. E.

DES MOINES
HOTELS
 Y. W. C. A.—1407 Center St.
 Parker-Roach—762½ 9th St.
 La Marguerita—1425 Center Street
RESTAURANTS
 Sampson—1246 E. 17th St.
 Cunningham's—1602 E. University
 Ida Bell's—783 11th St.
 Watkins—833 Keo Way
 Corinne's—1450 Walker Street
 Bryson's—1115 Center Street
 Gertrudes'—1308 Keo Way
 Peck's—1180 - 13th Street
 Community—1202 Center Street
 Ida Bell's—783 Eleventh
 Wilber & Mac's—1792 Walker Street
 Buzz Inn—1000 Center Street
 Herb's—1002 Center Street
 Erma & Carrie's—1008 Center Street
 William's—1200 East 16th St.
 Welcome Inn—1545 Walker St.
BEAUTY PARLORS
 Vo-Pon—1656 Walker St.
 Berline—1206 Center St.
 Polly's—1544 Walker St.
 Evalon—762 W. 9th St.
 Bernice's—911 W. 16th St.
 Murlians—933 16th St.
 Miniature—1143 Enis
 Louie's—1204 Center Street
 Ruth's—1049 4th Street

IN PATRONIZING THESE PLACES

TAVERNS
  Herb's—1002 Center St.
SERVICE STATIONS
  Eagle—1955 Hubble Blvd.
  Mumford's—4th & Euclid Avenue
  Holgates—6th & Oak Park
  E & G Keo Way & Crocker
GARAGES
  4th Street—417 4th St.
  Hiland—205 - 6th Avenue
AUTOMOTIVES
  Andy's—E. University & Hubble
TAILORS
  National—808 - 12th Street
  Clean Craft—1300 - 6th Avenue
DRUG STORE
  Adams—E. 5th & Locust St.

DUBUQUE
TOURIST HOMES
  Mrs. P. Martin—712 University Ave.
  Mrs. Edwin Weaver—795 Roberts Ave.

OTTUMWA
TOURIST HOMES
  Mrs. J. Rose—802 N. Fellows
  William Bailey—526 Center Ave.
  J. H. Hewitt—512 Grant
  Harry Owens—814 W. Pershing

WATERLOO
TOURIST HOMES
  Mrs. B. F. Tredwell—928 Beach St.
  Mrs. Spencer—220 Summer St.
  Mrs. E. Lee—745 Vinton St.

KANSAS

ATCHISON
TOURIST HOMES
  Mrs. Geneva Miles—924 N. 9th St.
NIGHT CLUB
  Mrs. M. McDonald—10th & Spruce
DRUG STORES
  Henderson—7th & Division St.

BOGUE
TOURIST HOMES
  Tourist Court—Juntion Rt. U. S. 24

COFFEYVILLE
TOURIST HOMES
  Tourist Home—618 E. 5th St.

CONCORDIA
TOURIST HOMES
  Mrs. B. Johnson—102 E. 2nd St.
  Mrs. Glen McVey—328 East St.

EMPORIA
TOURIST HOMES
  Elliott's—816 Congress St.

EDWARDSVILLE
TOURIST HOMES
  Road House—Anderson's Highway 32 & Bitts Creek

FORT SCOTT
HOTELS
  Hall's—223½ E. Wall St.
TOURIST HOMES
  Peter Thomasun—114 S. Ransom St.

HIAWATHA
TOURIST HOMES
  Mrs. Mary Sanders—1014 Shawnee

HUTCHINSON
TOURIST HOMES
  Mrs. C. Lewis—400 W. Sherman

INDEPENDENCE
TOURIST HOMES
  Major McBee—418 S. 3rd St.

JUNCTION CITY
HOTELS
  Bridgeforth—311 E. 11th St.
TOURIST HOMES
  Mrs. B. Jones—229 E. 14th St.

LARNED
TOURIST HOMES
  Mrs. C. M. Madison—828 W. 12th St.
  Mrs. Mose Madison—518 W. 10th St.
  Mrs. John Caro—E. 16th St. & Johnson Av.

LAURENCE
HOTELS
  Snowden's—1933 Tennessee St.

LEAVENWORTH
TOURIST HOMES
  Mrs. J. Hamilton—720 N. 3rd St.
  Mrs. W. Shelton—216 Poplar St.

KANSAS CITY
RESTAURANT
  Keystone Club—4th & Freemen
  Duck Inn—5th & State Street
  Famous—12th & Forest
  Chat-Chew—1908 N. 5th Street
  Virgil's Place—1622 Gray Road
  M & T—2013 E. 12th Street
ROAD HOUSE
  De Moss—37th & Ben Balance Road
NIGHT CLUBS
  Flamingo—1916 N. 5th St.
  Congo—1932 - 5th St.
SERVICE STATION
  Dunn & McGee—7th & Garfield

PLEASE MENTION "THE GREEN BOOK"

GARAGE
Economy—1935 N. 5th St.
DRUG STORES
Whitney's—5th & Virginia
Cundiff—5th & Quindarf

MANHATTAN

TOURIST HOMES
Mrs. E. Dawson—1010 Yuma St.
Mrs. H. Jackson—830 Yuma St.

OTTAWA

TOURIST HOMES
Mrs. Folson—112 N. Poplar
Mrs. R. W. White—821 Cypress

PARSONS

TOURIST HOMES
Mrs. F. Williams—2216 Grand Ave.
Womack—2109 Morgan

TOPEKA

HOTELS
Dunbar—400 Vuincy St.
TOURIST HOMES
Mrs. E. Slaughter—1407 Monroe
TAVERNS
Macks'—400 Quincy St.
Power's Cafe—116 E. 4th St.

WICHITA

TOURIST HOMES
Oklahoma House—517½ N. Main St.
RESTAURANTS
Oklahoma Cafe—517 N. Main St.

KENTUCKY

ELIZABETHTOWN

TOURIST HOMES
A. Johnson—Valley Creek Road
Mrs. B. Tyler—Mile Stt.
M. E. Wintersmith—S. Dixie Ave.

HAZARD

TOURIST HOMES
Mrs. J. Razor—436 E. Main St.
Mrs. Jessie Richardson—

PADUCAH

TOURIST HOMES
Amy Cox—813 Washington St.

HOPKINSVILLE

TOURIST HOMES
Mrs. M. McGregor—200 E. First St.
L. McNary—113 Liberty St.
J. C. Hopkins—128 Liberty St.

LANCASTER

TOURIST HOMES
Burn's—Buford St.
Hord's—Buford St.
RESTAURANTS
Plum's—Buford St.
BARBER SHOPS
Hyatt's—Buford St.
BEAUTY PARLORS
Hilltop—Buford St.
GARAGES
Warren & Francis—N. Campbell St.

LINCOLN RIDGE

TOURIST HOMES
Lincoln Institute

LOUISVILLE

HOTELS
Allen—2516 W. Madison St.
Pythian Temple—10th & Chestnut
Walnut—615 Walnut St.
Y. W. C. A.—528 S. 6th St.
May's—623 S. 10th St.
TOURIST HOMES
Lee L. Brown—1014 W. Chestnut
Hattie Daniels—1512 W. Chestnut
RESTAURANTS
Eatmore—964 S. 12th St.
White Swann—1208 W. Walnut
Honey Dripper—1208 Breckinridge St.
jones—525 S. 13th St.
Du Rez—Madison & 26th St.
Honey Dripper—1212 W. Breckenridge St.
Thompson's—419 So. 19th St.
Harry's—28th & Chestnut Sts.
W. & H.—432 S. 18th St.
California—1604 Gallagher St.
Club Hollywood—813 S. 6th St.
Jone's—525 S. 13th St.
West End—1929 W. Walnut St.
BEAUTY PARLORS
Scotty's—442 So. 21st St.
Bellonia—1625 Callagher St.
Mae Ella's—1110 W. Walnut St.
McKissick's—505 S. 8th St.
Scotty—422 S. 21st St.
Elizabeth's—962 S. 12th St.
Jones—409 S. 18th St.
Beauty Box—922 W. Walnut St.
Rose's—1813 W. Walnut St.
Willie's—639 S. 10th St.
BARBER SHOPS
Hunter's—1501 W. Chestnut St.
TAVERNS
Herman—1601 W. Walnut St.
Dave's—13th & Magazine
NIGHT CLUBS
Del Rey—Madison & 26th St.
LIQUOR STORES
Palace—12th & Walnut St.
Lyons—16th & Walnut St.
GARAGES
Eade's—2420 Cedar St.

39

PLEASE MENTION "THE GREEN BOOK"

TAXI CABS
Lincoln—705 W. Walnut
Dependable—1835 W. Walnut St.
Ave.—620 W. Walnut St.

LOUISIANA

BATON ROUGE
HOTELS
Ever-Ready 1325 Government St.
TOURIST HOMES
T. Harrison—1236 Louisiana Ave.
RESTAURANTS
Ideal Cafeteria—1501 E. Blvd.
TAVERNS
Waldo's—864 S. 13th St.
BEAUTY PARLORS
Carrie's—561 S. 13th St.
BARBER SHOPS
Malacher's—1310 Government St.
NIGHT CLUBS
Paradise—220 Boatnes St.
SERVICE STATIONS
Horatio's No. 1—1150 South St.
Horatio's No. 3—1607 Gov't. St.
ROAD HOUSES
Apex—Louise St.

BOGALUSA
TOURIST HOMES
Mrs. E. L. Raine—508 North Ave.

LAFAYETTE
TOURIST HOMES
Bourges—416 Washington St.
Mrs. A. Miles—302 Johns St.
J. Bondreaux—315 Stewart St.

LAKE CHARLES
TOURIST HOMES
Combre's Place—601 Boulevard

MANSFIELD
TOURIST HOMES
S. A. Wilson—N. Jefferson St.
W. Simpkins—Jenkins St.
BEAUTY SCHOOL
Annie Lou—615 Jenkins St.

MONROE
HOTELS
Turner's—1015 Desiard St.
TOURIST HOMES
R. H. Burns—700 Adams
L. B. Hortons—Congo St.

MORGAN CITY
TOURIST HOMES
Mrs. L. Williams— 719 Federal Ave.
Mrs. V. Williams—208 Union St.

NEW ORLEANS
HOTELS
Patterson—802½ S. Rampert St.
Vogue—2231 Thalia St.
North Side—1518 La Harpe St.
Gladstone—3435 Dryades St.
Astoria—225 S. Rampart St.
The Chicago—1310 Iberville St.
Paige—1038 Dryades Ave.
Riley—759 S. Rampart St.
Palace—1834 Annette St.
New Roxy—759 S. Rampart St.
Golden Leaf—1209 Saratoga St.
TOURIST HOMES
Mrs. F. Livaudais—1954 Jackson
N. J. Bailey—2426 Jackson Ave.
Mrs. King—2826 Louisiana Ave.
RESTAURANTS
Honey Dew Inn—115 Front St.
Club Crystal—1601 Dumaine
Place-of-Joy—2700 Melpomene St.
Pelican—S. Rampart at Gravier
Dooky—Cor. Orleans & Miro
Foster's Chicken Den—Cor. LaSalle &7th St.
92nd Club—2119 Orleans St.
The Gem—2601 Orleans St.
Hayes Chicken Shack—La. & Saratoga St.
Hide-away Inn—28 Desire St. & Rampart
Beck's—1520 N. Claiborne Ave.
Playhouse—2441 London Ave.
Portia's—2426 Louisiana Ave.
BARBER SHOPS
Lopez's—447 S. Rampart St.
BEAUTY PARLORS
Bessie's—1841 St. Ann St.
Thompson's—3429 Dryades St.
Ola's—1320 St. Bernard Ave.
SCHOOL OF BEAUTY CULTURE
Josephine's—1206 Pine
Poro—2217 Dryades St.
TAVERNS
Astoria—235 S. Rampart St.
Monte's—Jackson & S. Claiborne Ave.
Club Crystal—1601 Dumaine
Le Rendez-vous-7 Mille Post Gentilly H'way
Di Leo's—Ursuline & N. Robertson
NIGHT CLUBS
Dew Drop Inn—2836 La Salle St.
Shadowland—1921 Washington Ave.
Graystone—1900 Eagle St.
SERVICE STATIONS
Bill Board—2900 Claiborne Ave.
Ross—2620 S. Claiborne
Ross—1330 S. Broad St.
TAXICABS
Ed's—St. Bernard & N. Claiborne
Haney Dripper—Phone B—y3071
V-8 Cab Line—Felicity & Howard Sts.
Logan—2730 Felicity St.
DRUG STORES
Aprill—LaSalle & Washington
TAILORS
Martin's—1341 St. Anthony St.
Autocrat—1609 LaHarpe St.

Phone Jackson 9617 On U. S. No. 90

E. L. Marsalis J. L. Wicker

2900 S. Claiborne Ave. New Orleans, La.

Repairs, Washing, Greasing, Tire—Battery Service & Complete line of Standard Products. Tourist Information

E. L. Marsalis Sr. Prop. Phone: CEDAR 4009

RIVERSIDE TOURIST COURT
3501 Riverside Drive - Jefferson Parish - New Orleans 20, La.
In Connection With - Bill Board Esso Service

IN PATRONIZING THESE PLACES

TRAILER COURTS
Greenwood—Rt. 90—7½ miles P. T.

NEW IBERIA
TOURIST HOMES
M. Robertson—116 Hopkins St.
N. E. Cooper—913 Providence St.

OPELCUSAS
TOURIST HOMES
V. Arceneaux—723 E. Landry
H. Johnson—N. Market St.
B. Giron—S. Lombard St.

SCOTLAND
SERVICE STATIONS
Horatio's No. 2—Highway No. 61

SHREVEPORT
HOTELS
Hardy's—1726 Ford St.
Lloyd's—1229 Reynolds St.
RESTAURANTS
Wilson's—840 Williamson St.
Lighthouse Inn—2321 Milam St.
Saphronia's—815 Lawerence St.
Grand Terrace—Pierre & Looney St.
TOURIST HOMES
Grant Flats—1239 Reynolds
Mrs. J. Jones—1950 Hotchkiss
Mrs. A. Webb—1245 Reynolds
Mrs. W. Elder—1920 Hotchkiss
TAVERNS
A-Jack's—1836 Perrin St.
New Tuxedo—611 East 70th St.
Goldie's—238 Baker St.
SERVICE STATIONS
Ross'—901 Pierre St.
Pat's—Milan & Lawerence Sts.
William's-Milan & Ross-Milan & Pierre Ave.
TAILORS
3-Way—2415 Milan St.
Jones—1837 Looney St.
3 Way—2415 Milam St.

MAINE
AUGUSTA
TOURIST HOMES
Mrs. J. E. McLean—16 Drew St.

BANGOR
TOURIST HOMES
Mr. E. Dymond—339 Hancock Street

GARDNIER
TOURIST HOMES
Pond View—Pleasant Pond Road

OLD ORCHARD
TOURIST HOME
Mrs. Rose Cumming's—110 Portland Ave.

PORTLAND
HOTELS
The Thomas House—28 'A' St.

MARYLAND
ANNAPOLIS
HOTELS
Wright's—26 Calvert St.
NIGHT CLUBS
Washington—61 Washington St.

BALTIMORE
HOTELS
York—1200 Madison Ave.
New Albert—1224 Penna. Ave.
Smith's—Druid Hill Ave. & Paca St.
Majestic—1602 McCulloh St.
Y. W. C. A.—1916 Madison Ave.
Stokes—1500 Argylle Ave.
Y. M. C. A.—1600 Druid Hill Ave.
TOURIST HOMES
Mrs. E. Watsons—340 Blum St.
RESTAURANTS
Gorden's—1533 Druid Hill Ave.
Murry's—1423 Penn. Avenue
Spot Bar-B-Q—1530 Penna. Ave.
Club Barbeque—1519 Penna. Ave.
BEAUTY PARLORS
M. King—1510 Penna. Ave.
Scott's—1526 Penna. Ave.
Young's—613 W. Lafayette Ave.
La Blanche—1531 Penna. Ave.
BARBER SHOPS
Nottingham—1619 Penna Ave.
TAVERNS
Sugar Hill—2361 Druid Hill Ave.
Velma—Cor. Penn & Baker St.
Wagon Wheel—1638 Penna. Ave.
The Alhambra—1520 Penna. Ave.
Dreamland—1007 Penna. Ave.
Gamby's—1504 Penna. Ave.
Frolic—1401 Penna. Ave.
NIGHT CLUBS
Little Comedy—1418 Penna
Ubangi—2213 Penna Ave.
Wonderland—2043-Penna
Casino—1517 Penna Ave.
20th Century—21 W. Oliver
LIQUOR STORES
D & D—890, Linden Ave.
Berman's—1439 Penna Ave.
Fine's—1817 Penna Ave.
Hackerman's—1733 Penna
TRAILER CAMP
Scott's—Eastern Ave. Rd., Box 593
SERVICE STATION
Esso-Presstman & Fremont
GARAGES
Jacks'—514 Wilson St.
Service—1415 Etting St.

42

PLEASE MENTION "THE GREEN BOOK"

BUENA VISTA
RESTAURANT
 Eddie Bells—Defense Highway

COLTON
HOTELS
 Shirley K
 Conway's
 Golden's

FREDERICK
TOURIST HOMES
 Mrs. J. Makel—119 E. 5th St.
 Mrs. W. W. Roberts—316 W. South
 E. W. Grinage—22 W. All Saints
RESTAURANTS
 Crescent—16 W. All Saint St.

HAGERSTOWN
TOURIST HOMES
 Harmon—226 N. Jonat an St.

SALISBURY
TOURIST HOMES
 M. L. Parker—110 Delaware Ave.

TURNERS CORNER
NIGHT CLUBS
 Adam's

UPPER MARLBORO
TOURIST HOMES
 Wm. Eaton—Leland Rd. & Cainds H'way

MASSACHUSETTS

ATTLEBORO
TOURIST HOMES
 J. R. Brooks Jr.—54 James St.

BOSTON
HOTELS
 Harriett Tubman—25 Holyoke St.
 Mothers Lunch—510 Columbus Av.
 Lucille—52 Rutland Sq.
TOURIST HOMES
 Mrs. Williams—555 Columbus Ave.
 Julia Walters-912 Tremont
 Holeman—212 W. Springfield St.
 M. Johnson—616 Columbus Ave.
 Mrs. E. A. Taylor—192 W. Springfield St.
 Guest House—193 Humbolt St.
RESTAURANTS
 Western—431 Mass. Ave
 Lonie Lee's—536 Columbus Ave.
 Village—422 Mass. Ave.
 Slades—958 Tremont St.
 Estelle's—889 Tremont St.
 Southern—505 Mass. Ave.
 Oklahoma—975 Tremont Ave.
 LaBid—708A Tremont St.
 Charlie's—429 Columbus Ave.
 Green Candle—395 Mass. Ave.

BEAUTY PARLORS
 Clark-Merrill—505 Shawnut Ave.
 Amy's—796 Tremont St.
 Geneva's—808 Tremont St.
 Estelle's—15 Greenwich Ave.
 Mme. F. S. Blake—363 Mass. Ave.
 E. L. Crosby—11 Greenwich Park
 Mme. Enslow's—977 Tremont St.
 W. Williams—62 Hammond St.
 Victory—46 W. Canton St.
 E. West—609 Columbus Ave.
 Ruth Evans—563 Columbus Ave.
 Doris—795 Tremont St.
 Rubinetta—961 Tremont St.
 Beauty Box—781C Tremont St.
 Lucile's—226 W. Springfield St.
 Constance—414 Mass. Ave.
 Atlas—716 Shawnut Ave.
 Ester's—169A Springfield St.
 Arizona—563 Columbus Ave.
 Washington—985 Tremont
 Lititia's—140 Linox St.
 Jovennette's—109 Humbolt Ave.
 Betty's—609 Columbus Ave.
BARBER SHOPS
 Amity—1028 Tremont St.
 Abbott's—974 Tremont St.
NIGHT CLUBS
 Little Dixie—417 Mass. Ave.
 Savoy—410 Mass. Ave.
SERVICE STATIONS
 Maryland—690 Columbus Ave.
GARAGES
 DePrest—255 Northampton
TAILORS
 Garfield's—657 Shawnut Ave.
 Savannah—612 Shawnut St.
 Baltimore—1013 Tremont St.
 Corry's—431 A Mass. Ave.
 Chester's—189 W. Newton St.
 Grady & Oliver—525 Shawnut St.

CAMBRIDGE
TOURIST HOMES
 Mrs. S. P. Bennett—26 Mead St.

GREAT BARRINGTON
TOURIST HOMES
 Mrs. I. Anderson—28 Rossiter St.

HYAMIS
TOURIST HOMES
 Zilphas Cottages—134 Oakneck Rd.

NORTH ADAMS
TOURIST HOMES
 F. Adams—32 Washington Ave.

NEEDHAM
TOURIST HOMES
 B. Chapman—799 Central Ave.

IN PATRONIZING THESE PLACES

PITTSFIELD
TOURIST HOMES
M. E. Grant—53 King St.
Mrs. T. Dillard—109 Linden St.
Mrs. B. Jasper—66 Dewey Ave.
J. Marshall—124 Danforth Ave.

PLYMOUTH
TOURIST HOMES
Mrs. Taylor—11 Oak St.
W. A. Gray—47 Davis St.

RANDOLPH
RESTAURANTS
Mary Lee Chicken Shack—482 Main St.

ROXBURY
TOURIST HOMES
Mrs. S. Gale—168 Townsend St.
BEAUTY PARLORS
Ruth's—64 Humboldt St.
Charm Grove—90 Humboldt St.
Mme. Lovett—68 Humboldt St.
SERVICE STATIONS
Mac's—8 Coventry St.
Thompson's—1105 Tremont St.
TAILORS
Garfield's—657 Shawnut St.
Morgan's—355 Warren St.
Roxbury—52 Laurel St.
DRUG STORE
Douglas Square—1002 Tremont St.
Jaspan's—134 Harold St.

SOUTH HANSON
TOURIST HOMES
Modern—26 Reed St.
TRAILOR PARKS
Mrs. Mary B. Pina—26 Reed St.

STOCKBRIDGE
HOTELS
Park View House—Park St.

SPRINGFIELD
HOTELS
Springfield
BARBER SHOPS
Joiner's—97 Hancock Street
BEAUTY PARLORS
Law's—18 Hawley St.
TAILORS
American Cleaners—433 Eastern Ave.

SWAMPSCOTT
TOURIST HOMES
Mrs. M. Home—3 Boynton St.

WORCESTER
HOTELS
Worcester—Washington Square

RESTAURANTS
Dixie—143 Summer St.
Moffett's—47 Summer St.
BARBER SHOP
Buddy's—118 Summer St.
BEAUTY PARLORS
Bea's—8 Carwell St.
SERVICE STATION
Kozarian's—53 Summer St.
GARAGE
Bancroft—24 Portland St.
DRUG STORE
Bergwall—238 Main St.

WOBURN
TOURIST HOMES
Watts—10 High St.

MICHIGAN
ANN ARBOR
HOTELS
American—123 Washinggton St.
Allenel—126 El Huron St.
TOURIST HOMES
Mrs. E. M. Dickson—144 Hill St.

BATTLE CREEK
TOURIST HOMES
Mrs. F. Brown—76 Walters Ave.
Mrs. P. Grayson—22 Willow
Mrs. C. S. Walker—709 W. Van Buren

BALDWIN
SERVICE STATIONS
Bayak's—. Morgan, Prop.
Nolph's Super Service

BENTON HARBOR
NIGHT CLUBS
Research Pleasure Club—362 8th St.

BITELY
HOTELS
Kelsonia Inn—R. R. No. 1
Royal Breeze—On State Rt. 37

DETROIT
HOTELS
Touraine—4614 John R. St.
Gotham—111 Orchestra Place
Mark Twain—E. Garfield & Woodward
Biltmore—1926 St. Antoine St.
Tansey—2474 Antoine St.
Elizabeth—413 E. Elizabeth St.
Fox—715 Madison St.
Le Grande 1365 Lafayette St.
Norwood—550 E. Adams St.
Russell—615 E. Adams St.
Preyer—2476 St. Antoine St.
Crosstown—4652 Hastings St.

44

PLEASE MENTION "THE GREEN BOOK"

Touraine—4614 John R. St.
Terraine—John R. & Garfield
Northcross—2205 St. Antoine
Dewey—505 E. Adams St.
Davidson—556 E. Forest Ave.
Edenburgh—758 Westchester Ave.
Hotel - McGraw—5605 Junction
Old Rivers—2036 Hastings
Sportman's—3761 W. Warren Ave.

TOURIST HOME
Labland—39 Orchestra Place

RESTAURANTS
Blue Goose—4121 Hastings St.
Lunchonette—1949 Hastings St.
Pelican—4613 John R. St.
De Luxe—5423 Hastings
Jean's—6066 Brush
Vera's—John R & Palmer

BEAUTY PARLORS
Cleo's—4848 Hastings St.
Touraine—4626 John R. St.
Oakland—9313 Oakland Ave.
Powder Box—3737 Hastings St.
Elizabeth's—4848 Hastings St.
West Warren—4815 W. Warren Ave.

BARBER SHOPS
Swanson's—3415 Hastings St.
Bob's—4564 W. Warren Ave.

TAVERNS
Champion—Oakland & Holbrook
Horseshoe—606 Club
Bizerto—9006 Oakland Ave.
Owl—1540 Chene St.
Broad's—8825 Oakland

NIGHT CLUBS
666—666 E. Adams St.
Sportree's—2014 Hastings St.

ROAD HOUSES
Brown Bomber—421 E. Vernon H'way

SERVICE STATIONS
Murray's—1104 Holbrook St.
Johnson's—McGraw & 25th St.
Cobb's—Maple & Chene Sts.
Homer's—589 Madison Ave.

AUTOMOBILES
Davis Motor Co.—421 E. Vernon H'way

TAILORS
Kenilworth—131 Kenilworth
Blair—277 Gratist
Thomas—1024 Caniff Ave.
Hill's—8954 Oakland Ave.
Raglin—3636 W. Warren Ave.

DRUG STORES
Clay—Clay & Cameron Ave.
M. Dorsey—2201 St. Antoine St.
Kay—4766 McGraw Ave.
Barthwell's—Hastings & Benton

FLINT
TOURIST HOMES
T. Kelley—407 Wellington Ave.
T. L. Wheeler—1512 Liberty St.
Mrs. F. Taylor—1615 Clifford St.

GRAND JUNCTION
TOURIST HOME
Hamilton Farms—RFD No. 1

HARTFORD
TOURIST HOMES
Mrs. R. E. J. Wilson—210 E. 4th St.
Crosby's Farm

IDLEWILD
HOTELS
Eagles Nest
TOURIST HOMES
Edinburgh Cottage—Miss Herrone
B. Riddles
Meadow Lark Haven—Pine St.
RESTAURANTS
Lottie Roxborough—Box 837
Lorine Lunch—Baldwin Road

JACKSON
TOURIST HOMES
Mrs. W. Harrison—1215 Greenwood Ave.
Mrs. S. Collins—835 Adrian Ave.

LANSING
TOURIST HOMES
Mrs. M. Gray—1216 St. Joseph St.
M. Busher—1212 W. St. Joseph St.
Mrs. Lewis—816 S. Butler St.
Mrs. Cook—1220 W. St. Joseph St.
Mrs. Gaines—1406 Albert St.

MUSKEGON
TOURIST HOMES
R. C. Merrick—65 E. Muskegon Ave.
Rev. Fowler—937 McIllwraigh St.
R. A. Swift—472 W. Monroe

OSCODA
TOURIST HOMES
Jesse Colbath—Van Eten Lake

SHELBY TOWNSHIP
ROAD HOUSES
Joe Louis Farm—9700 Hamlin Road

SAGINAW
TOURIST HOMES
Mrs. E. Gant—312 S. Baum St.
Mrs. J. Curtley—439 N. Third St.
Mrs. P. Burnette—406 Emerson St.

SOUTH HAVEN
TOURIST HOME
Mrs. M. Johnson—Shady Nook Farm

WOODLAND
TOURIST HOME
Mrs. C. P. Tucker—Shangri - La

MINNESOTA

DULUTH
TOURIST HOMES
Jefferson—1119 W. Michigan Ave.

IN PATRONIZING THESE PLACES

MINNEAPOLIS
HOTELS
Y. W. C. A.—809 N. Aldrich Ave.
Serville—246½ 4th Ave.
TOURIST HOMES
Phyllis Wheatley House—809 N. Aldrich Av.
RESTAURANTS
Bells Cafe—207 South 3rd St.

ST. PAUL
TOURIST HOMES
Villa Wilson—697 St. Anthony Ave.
RESTAURANTS
G. & G. Bar-B-Q—291 No. St. Albans

MISSISSIPPI

BILOXI
TOURIST HOMES
Mrs. L. Scott—421 Washington St.
Mrs. G. Bess—630 Main St.
A. Alcina—437 Washington St.

CLEVELAND
SERVICE STATIONS
7-11—Highway 61 at 8

COLUMBUS
HOTELS
Queen City—15th St. & 7th Ave.
TOURIST HOMES
M. J. Harrison—915 N. 14th St.
H. Sommerville—906 N. 14th St.
Mrs. L. Alexander—N. 12th St.
Mrs. I. Roberts—12th & 5th Ave. N.
Mrs. Chevis—1425 11th Ave. N.

GREENVILLE
TOURIST HOMES
Mrs. B. B. Clark—508 Ohea St.
SERVICE STATION
Peoples—Nelson & Eddie St.

GRENADA
TOURIST HOMES
Mrs. K. D. Fisher—72 Adams St.
F. Williams—H'way 51 & Fairground Rd.
Henry's Lodge—H'way 51 & Fairground Rd.

HATTIESBURG
TOURIST HOMES
W. A. Godbolt—409 E. 7th St.
Mrs. A. Crosby—413 E. 6th St.
Mrs. S. Vann—636 Mobile St.

JACKSON
HOTELS
Wilson House—154 W. Oakley St.
TOURIST HOMES
Mrs. B. Marino—937 Grayson St.

RESTAURANTS
Shepherd's—604 North Farish St.
Home Dining Room—400 N. Farrish St.
BEAUTY PARLORS
Davis Salon—703 N. Farish
BARBER SHOPS
City—127 N. Farish
SERVICE STATIONS
Johnson's—536 N. Farish
GARAGES
Farish St.—748½ N. Farish

LAUREL
HOTELS
Bass—S. Pine St.
TOURIST HOMES
Mrs. S. Lawrence—902 Meridian
Mrs. E. L. Brown—522 E. Kingston
Mrs. F. Garner—909 Joe Wheeler's Ave.
Mrs. S. G. Wilson—802 S. 7th

MACOMB
HOTELS
Townsend—534 Summit St.
TOURIST HOMES
D. Mason—218 Denwidde St.

MERIDIAN
HOTELS
Beales—2411 Fifth St.
TOURIST HOMES
C. W. Williams—1208-31st St.
Mrs. H. Waters—1201 26th Ave.
Mrs. M. Simmons—5th St. betw. 16 & 17 A.
Charley Leigh—5th St. & 16th Ave.

MOUND BAYOU
TOURIST HOMES
Mrs. Sallie Price
Smith's
Mrs. Charlotte Strong
GARAGES
Liddle's

NEW ALBANY
HOTELS
Foot's—Railroad Ave.
TOURIST HOMES
S. Drewery—Church St.
Patt Knox—Cleveland St.
C. Morganfield—Cleveland St.

YAZOO CITY
HOTELS
Caldwell—Water & Broadway Sts.
TOURIST HOMES
Mrs. A. J. Walker—321 S. Monroe
Mrs. C. A. Wright—234 S. Yazoo

PLEASE MENTION "THE GREEN BOOK"

MISSOURI

CAPE GIRADEAU
TOURIST HOMES
G. Williams—408 S. Frederick St.
W. Martin—38 N. Hanover St.
J. Randol—422 North St.

CARTHAGE
TOURIST HOMES
Mrs. M. Webb—S. Fulton St.

COLUMBIA
HOTELS
Austin House—108 E. Walnut St.
TOURIST HOMES
Mrs. W. Harvey—417 N. 3rd St.

CHARLESTON
TAVERNS
Creole Cafe—311 Elm St.

EXCELSIOR SPRINGS
HOTELS
The Albany—408 South St.
Moore's—302 Maine St.

HANNIBAL
TOURIST HOMES
Mrs. E. Julius—1218 Gerard St.

JEFFERSON CITY
HOTELS
Lincoln—600 Lafayette St.
Booker T.
TOURIST HOMES
Miss C. Woodridge—418 Adams St.
R. Graves—314 E. Dunklin St.
RESTAURANTS
University—Lafayette & Dunklin Sts.
De Luxe—601 Lafayette St.
Blue Tiger—Chestnut & E Atchenson St.
College—905 E. Atchenson St.
BARBER SHOP
University—Lafayette & Dunklin St.
Tayes—Elm & Lafayette Sts.
BEAUTY PARLORS
Poro—818 Lafayette St.
SERVICE STATION
C. Little—Chestnut & Dunklin
TAVERNS
Tops—626 Lafayette St.
NIGHT CLUBS
Subway—600 Lafayette St.
Lone Star—930 E. Miller St.
TAXICABS
Veteran—515 Lafayette St.
TAILOR
Rightway—903 E. Atchenson St.

JOPLIN
HOTELS
Williams—308 Penna. St.
J. Lindsay—1702 Penna. St.
Mrs. F. Echols—901 Missouri Ave.
TOURIST HOMES
Mrs. Lindsay—1702 Penn. St.

KANSAS CITY
HOTELS
Booker T. Hotel—1823 Vine St.
Cadillac Hotel—1429 Forest
921 Hotel   921 East 17th Street
Watson—1211 S. Highland St.
Street's—1510 E. 18th St.
Lincoln Hotel—13th & Woodland Sts.
TOURIST HOMES
Mrs. Vallie Lamb—1914 E. 24th St.
Thomas Wilson—2600 Euclid Ave.
RESTAURANTS
Lill's Buffet—2458 Charlotte Ave.
Top Hat—1008 Garfield
Nashe's—1200 E. 18th St.
Oven—17th & Vine St.
Elnora's Cafe—1518 E. 18th St.
Dorothy's—2614 Prospect St.
Tasty Sandwich—1323½ E. 18th St.
Square Deal—1312 E. 15th St.
Porter's—1813 Vine
New Hollywood   907 E. 18th St.
TAVERNS
Vine St.—1519 E. 12th St.
NIGHT CLUBS
Chez Paree—1822 Vine St.
Scott's—2432 Vine St.
BEAUTY PARLORS
Hazel Graham—1836 Vine St.
Arlene—2409 Vine St.
Euthola—1602 E. 19th St.
Alexander—2429 Vine St.
Modern—1811½ Vine St.
LIQUOR STORES
Cardinal—1515 E. 18th St.
Monarch—2300 Prospect Ave.
Dundee—1701 Troost
Virginia—1601 Virginia
Chester's—18th & Charlotte St.
Golden Crown—2218 Vine
Ace—2404 Vine
Donnell—18th & Troost Sts.
SERVICE STATIONS
Stone's—2001 E. 31st St.
Mobile Station—1502 E. 19th St.
GARAGES
19th St.—1510 E. 19th St.
DRUG STORES
Community—2432 Vine St.
TAILORS
Spotless—2303 Prospect Ave.
COUNTRY CLUBS
Hillcrest—H'way 132 - 12 miles West of Kansas City

47

IN PATRONIZING THESE PLACES

Penrod—H'way 40—13 milee W. of Kansas City

LEBANON
TOURIST HOMES
Mrs. J. Osborne—Rt. 5
Mrs. Ann Wilson—Rt. 3
Mrs. Eliza Turner—Rt. 3

MOBERLY
TOURIST HOMES
Mrs. F. Davis—212 N. Ault St.
Ralph Bass—517 Winchester St.
W. Johnson—N. 5th St. 400 blk.

POPLAR BLUFF
TOURIST HOMES
Mrs. W. Brooks—1800 N. Alice St.

SEDALIA
TOURIST HOMES
Mrs. T. L. Moore—505 W. Cooper
Mrs. C. Walker—217 E. Morgan
W. Williams—317 E. Johnson

SPRINGFIELD
TOURIST HOMES
U. G. Hardrick—238 Dollison Ave.

ST. JOSEPH
TOURIST HOMES
Mrs. T. J. Coleman—1713 Angelique St.

ST. LOUIS
HOTELS
Midtown—2935 Lawton Boulevard
Booker Washington—Jefferson at Pine
Poro—Pendleton & St. Ferdinand
West End—3900 W. Beele St.
Grand Central—Jefferson & Pine
Calumet—611 N. Jefferson Ave.
Corona—2840 Olive St.
Harlem—3438 Franklin
Antler—3502 Franklin Ave.

RESTAURANTS
Bob's—2816 Easton Avenue
Oak Leaf—4269 W. Easton Ave.
Society—900 N. Taylor Ave.-8
DeLuxe—10 N. Jefferson Ave.
Seashore—2829 Easton Ave.
Northside—2422 N. Pendleton Ave.
Lindsey's—3805 Page Blvd.
Snack Shop—1105 N. Taylor
Highway—1239 N. 20th St.
Wike's—1804 N. Taylor Ave.

BEAUTY PARLORS
Allen's—2343 Market St.
Shaw's—4356 Easton-13
Juvill—4141 Easton-13
Rosa's—1222 Armstrong
Artistic—1014 N. Whittier
Young's—2005 Pine St.
Artistic—909 N. Taylor-8

Azalie's—4621 Easton Ave.-13
Amanda's—1021 N. Cardinal Ave.-6
Ollie's—3803 Page Blvd.
Boulevard—1023 N. Grand Ave.-6
Parkway—4284 W. St. & Ferdinand-13
Argus—1008 N. Sarah St.
Hall's—3038 Franklin Ave.
Beauty Nook—3303 Lucas Ave.
Montgomery—3406 Franklin Ave.
Lottie's—3026 Lawton
Harris—919 Ohio Avenue
McCain—4702 A Newberry Terrace
Superior—219 A N. Jefferson
De Luxe—3604 Finnery Ave.
Clay's—613 N. 18th St.
2 Sisters—4126 Kennerly Ave.
Marcella's—2306 Cole St.
Estrella's—4629 W. Aldine Ave.
Tillie's—2600 Cole St.

BARBER SHOPS
Bullock's—3320 Franklin Ave.

TAVERNS
Silver Slipper—2817 Easton Ave.
Glass Bar—2933 Lawton St.
Rio—18 South Jefferson
Carioca—1112 N. Sarah St.
Zanzibar—215 Cardinal-3
20th Century—718 N. Vanderventer-8
West End—939 N. Vanderventer Ave.
Hawaiian—3839 Finney Ave.
Play House—4071 Page Blvd.
Casablanca—4111 Finney Ave.
Manhattan—1115 N. Sarah
Zanzibar—215 N. Cardinal

NIGHT CLUBS
Paradise—930 N. Sarah St.
Riviera—4460 Delmar Blvd.
Sunset—6th & Peggot St.
West End—911 N. Vanderventer
Key—211 N. Cardinal Ave.-3
El Grotto—6412 Cottage Grove Ave.

SERVICE STATIONS
Midville—1913 Pendleton Ave.
Mac's—4102 Delmar
Anderson's—930 N. Compton
Merritt's—1701 Bond

GARAGES
Davis—3811 Finney Ave.
Fred Cooper's—Pine at Ewing Ave.

TAILORS
Jackson's—4501 W. Easton Ave.

LIQUOR STORES
Siegel's—1300 Franklin Ave.
K & F—3901 Olive St.
Harlem—4161 Easton Ave.
West End—937 N. Vanderventer Ave.

TAXICABS
Blue Jay—2811 Easton Ave.
DeLuxe—16 N. Jefferson Ave.

DRUG STORES
Taylor-Page—1301 N. Taylor
Douglas—3339 Laclede
Williams—2801 Cole St.
Harper's—3145 Franklin
Kinlock—Hugh St. & Carson Road
Ream's—1112 N. Sarah St.

48

PLEASE MENTION "THE GREEN BOOK"

EAST ST. LOUIS
HOTELS
  Thigpin—1425 E. Broadway
RESTAURANTS
  Uutra-Modern—114 S. 15th St.
  J. F. Sugg's—4305 Trendley Ave.
  Del-Rio—1504 Broadway
  Whiteway—4246 Market Ave.
  Magnet—306 Broadway
BEAUTY PARLORS
  Whitehead—8 N. 17th St.
SERVICE STATIONS
  King's—1741 Bond Ave.
TAVERNS
  Thigpin—1425 E. Broadway
  South End—1527 Russell Ave.
  Victory Club—4833 Tudor Ave.
  Jolly Corner—1433 E. Broadway
TAILORS
  Attucks—2217 Missouri Ave.
DRUG STORES
  South End—1652 Central Ave.

MONTANA
HELENA
TOURIST HOMES
  Mrs. M. Stitt—204 S. Park

NEBRASKA
FREMONT
C. M. Brannon—1550 N. 'C' St.
Gus Henderson—1725 N. Irving St.

GRAND ISLAND
TOURIST HOMES
  Mrs. M. Hunter—217 E. 5th St.

OMAHA
HOTELS
  Broadview—2060 N. 19th St.
  Patton—1014-18 S. 11th St.
  Walker—2504 Charles St.
  Willis—22nd & Willis
TOURIST HOMES
  L. Strawther—2220 Willis Ave.
  Mrs. M. Smith—2211 Ohio St.
  Miss W. M. Anderson—2207 N. 25th St.
  G. H. Ashby—2228 Willis Ave.
  Dave Brown—2619 Caldwell St.
RESTAURANTS
  Sharp Inn—2318 N. 24th St.
  Neal's—N. 24th & Lake
  Cozy—2615 No 24th St.
TAVERNS
  Red Brick—2723 'Q' St.
  Myrtis—2229 Lake St.
  Len's—25th & Q St.
  Apex—1818 N. 24th St.

NIGHT CLUBS
  Railroad Men's—2701 N. 24th St.
LIQUOR STORES
  Thrifty—24th & Lake St.
  Crown—1512 N. 24th St.
  Liquor—24th & Cumming
SERVICE STATIONS
  Villone's—24th & Ohio
  Gabby's—24th & Ohio
  Kaplan—24th & Grant
  Deep Rock—24th & Charles
DRUG STORES
  Hermansky's—2725 Q St.
  Duffy—24th & Lake St.
  Johnson—2306 N. 24th St.
  Reid's—24th & Seward Sts.
TAILORS
  Tip Top—1804 N. 24th St.

LINCOLN
TOURIST HOMES
  Mrs. E. Edwards—2420 'P' St.
RESTAURANTS
  Roosevelt—610 N. 20th St.
BARBER SHOP
  Service—237 N. 13th St.
DRUG STORE
  Smith's—2146 Vine St.
TAILORS
  Zimmerman—2355 O St.

NEW JERSEY
ASBURY PARK
TOURIST HOMES
  Mrs. A. Arch—23 Atkins Ave.
  Mrs. E. C. Burgess—1200 Springwood
  Mrs. W. Greenlow—1317 Summerfield Ave.
  Mrs. Brown—135 Ridge Ave.
  Mrs. C. Jones—141 Sylvan Ave.
  Mrs. V. Maupin—25 Atkins Ave.
  E. C. Yeager—1406 Mattison Ave.
  Anna Eaton—23 Atkins Ave.
HOTELS
  Metropolitan—1200 Springwood
  Reevy's—135 DeWitt Ave.
  Whitehead—25 Atkins Ave.
RESTAURANTS
  West Side—1136 Springwood Ave.
  Nellie Fritts—Springwood Ave.
  Tip Top Lunch—1143 Springwood Ave.
  Nellie Tutt's—1207 Springwood Ave.
BEAUTY PARLORS
  Imperial—1107 Springwood Ave.
  Opal—1146 Springwood Ave.
  Marions—1119 Springwood Ave.
BARBER SHOPS
  Consolidated—1216 Springwood
  John Milby—1216 Springwood Ave.

IN PATRONIZING THESE PLACES

TAVERNS
  Aztex Room—1147 Springwood Ave.
  Capitol—1212 Springwood Ave.
  Hollywood—1318 Springwood Ave.
  2-Door—1512 Springwood Ave.
NIGHT CLUBS
  Cuba's—Springwood Ave.
SERVICE STATIONS
  Johnson—Springwood & DeWitt Place
GARAGES
  Arrington—153 Ridge Ave.
  West Side—1206 Springwood Ave.

ATLANTIC CITY

HOTELS
  Liberty—1519 Baltic Avenue
  Bay State—N. Tenn. Ave.
  Randell—1601 Arctic Ave.
  Ridley—1806 Arctic Ave.
  Swan—136 N. Virginia Ave.
  Wright—1702 Arctic Ave.
  Capitol—37 N. Ky. Ave.
  Lincoln—911 N. Indiana Ave.
  Luzon—601 N. Ohio Ave.
  Attucks—1120 Drexel Ave.
  Apex Rest—Indiana & Ontario
TOURIST HOMES
  A. R. S. Goss—324 N. Indiana Ave.
  Mrs. V. Jones—1720 Arctic Ave.
  M. Conte—111 N. Indiana Ave.
  E. Satchell—27 N. Michigan Ave.
  Bailey's Cottage—1812 Arctic Ave.
  D. Austin—813 Battle Ave.
  R. Brown—113 N. Penn. Ave.
RESTAURANTS
  Golden's—41 N. Kentucky Ave.
  Little Diner—104 N. Kentucky Ave.
  Smack Shack—40 N. Kentucky Ave.
  Eddie's—1702 Arctic Ave.
  Perry's—Kentucky Ave.
  Young's—18 N. Ohio Ave.
  Anderson's—1702 Arctic Ave.
  Bedford's—Artic & S. Carolina Ave.
  Kelly's—1311 Arctic Ave.
BARBER SHOPS
  42 N. Illinois Ave.
  Hollywood—811 Arctic Ave.
  Hunter's—1814 Arctic Ave.
BEAUTY PARLORS
  Mme. Newson's—225 N. Indiana Ave.
  Grace's—43 Kentucky Ave.
TAVERNS
  Wonder Bar—1601 Arctic Ave.
  Little Belmont—37 N. Kentucky Ave.
  Hattie's—1913 Arctic Ave.
  Daddy Lew's—Bay & Baltic Ave.
  Mack's—1590 Baltic Ave.
  Popular—1923 Artic Ave.
  Elite—Baltic & Chalfonte Ave.
  Herman's—Maryland & Artic
  Prince's—37 N. Michigan Ave.
  Austins—Maryland & Baltic
  Golden's—41 N. Ky. Ave.
  Elks Bar &Grill—1613 Artic
  Lighthouse—1613 Baltic Ave.
  New Jersey—N. J. & Mediterranean
  Circus—37 N. Michigan Ave.
  My Own—701 Baltic Ave.
  Tim Buck Two—1600 Artic Ave.
NIGHT CLUBS
  Harlem—32 N. Kentucky Ave.
  Paradise—N. Illinois Ave.
LIQUOR STORES
  Mark's—1923 Arctic Ave.
  Timbucktu—1608 Arctic Ave.
  Tumble Inn—Delaware & Baltic
  Goodman's—1317 Arctic Ave.
SERVICE STATIONS
  Mundy's—1814 Arctic Ave.
GARAGES
  Johnson's—11-15 Ohio Ave.
DRUG STORES
  London's—Cor. Ky. & Arctic Ave.

ATLANTIC HIGHLANDS

RESTAURANTS
  Tennis Club Tea Room—Prospect Ave.
TAVERNS
  New Way Inn—71 Ave. 'A'

BAYONNE

TAVERNS
  Doc's—67 W. 23rd St.
  John's—463 Ave 'C'
  Golden Arrow—545 Hudson Blvd.

BELL MEADE

HOTELS
  Bell Meade—Rt. 31

BRIDGESTON

TAVERNS
  The Ram's Inn—Bridgeston & Millville Pike

CAMDEN

RESTAURANTS
  Bar-B-Q—818 S. 9th St.
CHINESE RESTAURANTS
  Lon's—806 Kaign Ave.
TAVERNS
  Nick's—7th & Central Ave.
TAILORS
  Merchant—741 Kaign Ave.

CAPE MAY

HOTELS
  Richardson—Broad & Jackson Sts.
  De Griff—839 Corgie St.
TOURIST HOMES
  Mrs. M. Green—728 Lafayette St.

CEDAR KNOLL

COUNTRY CLUBS
  The Shady Oak Lodge

50

PLEASE MENTION "THE GREEN BOOK"

EAST ORANGE
BEAUTY PARLORS
　The Ritz—214 Main St.
　Milan's—232 Halstead St.
TAILORS
　Vernon's—182 Amherst St.
　Charles—63 N Park St.

EATONTOWN
NIGHT CLUBS
　The Greenbriar—Pine Bush

EGG HARBOR
HOTELS
　Allen House—625 Cincinnati Ave.
TAVERNS
　Red, White & Blue Inn—701 Phila. Ave.

ELIZABETH
TOURIST HOMES
　Mrs. L. G. Brown—178 Madison St.
　Mrs. T. T. Dtvis—27 Dayton St.
TAVERNS
　Hunter's—1155 Dickerson St.
　One & Only—1112 Dickerson St.

ENGLEWOOD
TAVERNS
　The Lincoln—1-3 Englewood Ave.
LIQUOR STORES
　W. E. Beverage Co.-107 William St.
　Giles—107 Williams St.

HACKENSACK
BEAUTY PARLORS
　Mary—206 Central Ave.

HACK. 2-9733

5 POINT SERVICE STATION

SERVICE SUPREME

BUY AT THE **ESSO** SIGN

Walter Levin, Prop.

First and　　　　Hackensack
Susquehanna St.　　　N. J.

BARBER SHOPS
　Tip Top—174 Central Ave.
　Crosson—Railroad Place
TAVERNS
　Rideout's—204 Central Ave.

NIGHT CLUB
　Majestic Lodge—351 - 1st St.

HASKELL
RECREATION PARKS
　Thomas Lake

HIGHTSTOWN
TAVERNS
　Paul's Inn—Rt. 33 East Windsor TWP
　Old Barn—104 Daws St.

JERSEY CITY
BEAUTY PARLORS
　Beauty—74A Atlantic Ave.
TAILORS
　Bell's—630 Cummunipaw Ave.
　E. & E.—11A Oak St.

KINGSTON
ROAD HOUSES
　Merrill's

KEYPORT
TAVERNS
　Green Grove Inn—Atlantic & Halsey Street
　Major's—215 Atlantic Ave.

KENNELWORTH
TAVERNS
　Driver's—17th & Monroe Ave.

LAWNSIDE
TOURIST HOMES
　Hi-Hat—White Horse Pike
TAVERNS
　Acorn Inn—Whitehorse Pike
　Dreamland
　La Belle Inn—Gloucester Ave.
BEAUTY PARLORS
　Thelma Thomas—Warwick Blvd.
BARBER SHOPS
　Henry Smith—Mouldy Road
RECREATION PARKS
　Lawnside Park

LINDEN
NIGHT CLUBS
　4th Ward Club—1035 Baltimore
TAVERNS
　Victory—1307 Baltimore Avenue
TAILORS
　Quality—1140 E. St. George Ave.

LONG BRANCH
TAVERNS
　Club '45'—Liberty St.
　Sam Hall—18 Academy St.
　Tally-Ho—185 Belmont Ave.

51

IN PATRONIZING THESE PLACES

LAKEWOOD
BEAUTY SALON
 Hollywood—17-4th St.

MADISON
TAXICABS
 Madison—18 Lincoln Place
 Yellow—14 Lincoln Place

MAHWAH
TAVERNS
 Paul's Lunch—Brook St.

MOMOUTH JUNCTION
TOURIST HOMES
 Macon's Inn—H'way Rt. No. 1-26

MONTCLAIR
SCHOOL OF BEAUTY CULTURE
 Hair Dressing—207 Bloomfield Ave.
 Scientfiic—146 Bloomfield Ave.
BARBER SHOPS
 Paramount—211 Bloomfield Ave.
NIGHT CLUBS
 Recreation—Glenridge Cor. Bay
GARAGES
 Maple Ave.—80 Maple Ave.

MORRISTOWN
NIGHT CLUBS
 Eureka—118 Spring St.

NEPTUNE
RESTAURANTS
 Hampton Inn—1718 Sringwood Ave.
BEAUTY PARLORS
 Priscilla's—261 Myrtle Ave.

NEWARK
HOTELS
 Grand—78 W. Market St.
 Y. M. C. A.—153 Court St.
 Y. W. C. A.—20 Jones St.
 Harwin Terrace—27 Sterling St.
TOURIST HOMES
 Mrs. E. Morris—39 Chester Ave.
 Mrs. Spence—506 Washington Ave.
RESTAURANTS
 Cabin Grill—54 Waverly Ave.
 Royal Palm—123 Waverly Ave.
 Alpine—197 W. Kinney St.
 Bar-B-Q—9 Monmouth St.
 Easter—154 Prince St.
BEAUTY PARLORS
 La Vogue—227 W. Kinney St.
 Irene's 125 Somerset St.
 Farrar—35 Prince St.
 Billy's—206 Belmont Ave.
 Chapman's—96 Belmont Ave.

BEAUTY PARLORS
 Virginia Salon—132 West St.
 Paris Salon—368 Washington St.
 Dutcher's—156 Spruce St.
 Mae's—271 Sringfield Ave.
 Algene's—120 Spruce St.
 Rene's—97 West St.
 Queen—155 Barclay St.
BARBER SHOPS
 Cochran's—323 Mulberry St.
 El Idellio—30 Wright St.
TAVERNS
 Bert's—211 Renner Ave.
 Dodger's—8 Bedford Street
 Dan's—245 Academy St.
 Little Johnny's—47 Montgomery
 Lestbaders—175 Spruce St.
 Kesselman's—13th & Rutgers St.
 Alcazar—72 Waverly Place
 Rosen's—164 Spruce St.
 Dave's—202 Court St.
 Wtrren & Norfolk—256 Warren Stt.
 Woods—258 Prince St.
 Kleinbergs—88 Waverly St.
 Afro—19 Quitman St.
 Welcome Inn—87 West St.
 Del Mar—133 Howard St.
 '570'—570 Market St.
 Boyd's—70 Boyd St.
 Corprew's—297 Sprinfield Ave.
 Dug-Out—188 Belmont Ave.
 Harry's—60 Waverly Ave.
 Ernie's—104 Wallace St.
 Trippe's—121 Halstead St.
 Mulberry—302 Mulberry St.
 Frederick—2 Boston St.
NIGHT CLUBS
 New Kinney Club—36 Arlington St.
 Boston Plaza—4 Boston St.
 Golden Inn—150 Charleston St.
 Nest Club—Warren & Norfolk St.
 Villa Maurice—375 Washington St.
 Alcazar—72 Waverly Ave.
 Picadilly—1 Peshine Tve.
 Dodgers—8 Bedford St.
CHINESE RESTAURANTS
 Chinese-American—603 W. Market
SERVICE STATIONS
 Estes—39 Belmont Ave.
 Livingston—300 W. Kinney St.
GARAGES
 Branch—45 Rankin St.
TAILORS
 I. Jordan—178 W. Kinney St.

OCEAN CITY
HOTELS
 Washington—6th & Sampson Ave.

ORANGE
HOTELS
 Y. M. C. A.—84 Oakwood Ave.
 Y. W. C. A.—66 Oakwood Ave.
 Oakwood Dep't—84 Oakland Ave.

52

PLEASE MENTION "THE GREEN BOOK"

RESTAURANTS
  Triangle—152 Barrow St.
  Jeter's—77 Barrow St.
  Joe's—120 Barrow St.
  Bar-B-Q—153 South St.
CHINESE RESTAURANTS
  Orange Garden—157 Barrow St.
BEAUTY PARLORS
  Park View—473 Central Ave.
  Clarise—81 South St.
  Elizabeth—159 South St.
  Baugh—76 S. Center St.
  Frank's—120 Hickory St.
NIGHT CLUBS
  Paradise—Barrow & Chestnut St.
DRUG STORES
  Bynum & Catlette—Barrow & Hickory St.
TAILORS
  Fitchitt—99 Oakwood Ave.
  Triangle—101 Hickory St.

PAULSBORO
RESTAURANTS
  Elsie's—246 W. Adams St.

PATERSON
HOTELS
  Joymakers—38 Bridge St.
TAVERNS
  Idle Hour Bar—53 Bridge St.
  Joymakers—38 Bridge St.
GARAGES
  Brown's—57 Godwin St.

PERTH AMBOY
HOTELS
  Lenora—550 Hartford St.
BARBER SHOPS
  Kelly's—128 Fayette St.

POINT PLEASANT
TAVERNS
  Joe's—337 Railroad Ave.

PINE BROOK
TOURIST HOMES
  Wilson's
RESTAURANTS
  Grigg's—58-60 Witherspoon St.
BEAUTY PARLORS
  Vanity Box—188 John St.

PLAINFIELD
TAVERNS
  Liberty—4th St.

PLEASANTVILLE
TAVERNS
  Harlem Inn—1117 Washington Ave.
ROAD HOUSES
  Martin's—304 W. Wright St.

RAHWAY
ROAD HOUSE
  O. Paterson—Edwards Ave. & Potters Crossing

RED BANK
HOTELS
  Robins Rest—615 River Road
RESTAURANTS
  Vincents—263 Shrewsbury Ave.
  Dan Logan's—W. Bergen Place
TAVERNS
  West Bergen—103 W. Bergen Place
  Charlie's—W. Bergen Place
BARBER SHOPS
  A. Dillard—250 Shrewsbury Ave.
BEAUTY PARLORS
  R. Alleyne—124 W. Bergen Place
  Suries—214 Shrewsbury Ave.
SERVICE STATIONS
  Galatres—Shrewsbury & Catherine
TAILORS
  Dudley's—79 Sunset Ave.

ROSELLE
TAVERNS
  Omega—302 E. 9th St.
  St. George—1139 St. George Ave.

SCOTCH PLAINS
RESTAURANTS
  Hill Top—60 Jerusalem Road
ROAD HOUSES
  Villa Casanova—Jerusalem Road
COUNTRY CLUBS
  Shady Rest—Jerusalem Road

SALEM
TAVERNS
  Stith's—111 Market St.

SEA BRIGHT
RESTAURANTS
  Castle Inn—11 New Street

SHREWSBURY
SERVICE STATIONS
  Rodney's—Shrewsbury Ave.

SUMMIT
HOTELS
  Y. M. C. A.—393 Broad St.

TOMS RIVER
TAVERNS
  Casaloma—Manitan Park

TRENTON
HOTELS
  Y. M. C. A.—105 Spring St.

IN PATRONIZING THESE PLACES

TOURIST HOMES
- Mrs. C. Taylor—92 Spring St.
- Mrs. M. Morris—116 Spring St.
- Mrs. Pleash—88 Spring St.
- Mrs. Garland—62 Spring St.

RESTAURANTS
- Spot Sandwich—121 Spring St.

BEAUTY PARLORS
- Bea's—83 Spring St.
- Geraldine's—17 Trent St.

BARBER SHOPS
- Sanitary—199 N. Willow St.
- Bill's—81 Spring St.

NIGHT CLUBS
- Famous—228 N. Willow Street

ROAD HOUSE
- Crossing Inn—Eggertt's Crossing

POOL PARLOR
- Reid's—219 Fall St.

VAUX HALL

BEAUTY PARLORS
- Celeste—211 Springwood Ave.

TAVERNS
- Carnegie—380 Carnegie Place

ROAD HOUSES
- Lloyd Chicken Farm—26 Valley

WILDWOOD

HOTELS
- Glen Oak—100 E. Lincoln St.
- The Marion—Artic & Spicer Ave.
- Artic Ave.—3600 Artic Ave.

TOURIST HOMES
- The Denmond—129 W. Spicer Ave.
- Mrs. A. H. Brown—3811 Artic
- Mrs. E. Crawley—3816 Artic

RESTAURANTS
- Palm Leaf—3812 Artic Ave.

BEAUTY PARLORS
- B. Johnson's—407 Garfield Ave.

BARBER SHOPS
- R. Morton—4010 New Jersey Ave.

NIGHT CLUBS
- High Steppers—437 Lincoln Ave.

WOODSBURY

RESTAURANTS
- Robinson's—225 Park Ave.

WEST PLEASANTVILLE

COUNTRY CLUB
- Pine Acres Country Club—Atlantic City

NEW YORK STATE

ALBANY

HOTELS
- Broadway—603 Broadway

TOURIST HOMES
- Mrs. Aaron J. Oliver—42 Spring St.

RESTAURANTS
- Broadway—603 Broadway

BEAUTY PARLORS
- Buelah Fords—96 2nd St.

BARBER SHOPS
- Martin's—4 Vantromp St.

SERVICE STATIONS
- Ten Eyck—137 Lark St.

NIGHT CLUBS
- Harlem Grill—Hamilton St.
- Rythm Club—Madison Ave.

BUFFALO

HOTELS
- Little Harlem—494 Michigan Ave.
- Y. M. C. A.—585 Michigan Ave.
- Montgomery—486 Michigan Ave.
- Vendome—177 Clinton St.
- Claridge—38 Broadway

TOURIST HOMES
- Miss R. Scott—244 N. Division St.
- Mrs. F. Washington—172 Clinton St.
- Mrs. G. Chase—192 Clinton St.
- William Campbell—22 Milnor

RESTAURANTS
- Horseshoe—198 Pine St.
- Lou's—154 Williams St.
- Rozer's—Williams & Bennett
- Crystal—534 Broadway
- Bar-B-Q—413 Michigan Ave.
- Empire—454 Michigan Ave.
- Silver Star—175 Williams
- Elite—168 Clinton
- Alma's—314 Williams
- Chet & Als—486 William St.
- Standard—66 Ridge St.
- Pepper Pot—377 Jefferson St.
- Apex—311 William St.
- Arnold's—348 William St.

CHINESE RESTAURANTS
- Kam Wing Loo—433 Michigan Ave.

BEAUTY PARLORS
- Orchid—419 Pratt St.
- Melisey's—236 William St.
- Artisian—271 Spring St.
- La Ritz—348 Jefferson Ave.
- Matchless—169 Willam St.
- Edwards—530 William St.
- Lady Esther 243 E. Ferry St.
- Jean's—142 Adams St.
- La Grace—620 Brodway
- Laura's—643 Broadway
- Rena's—494 Jefferson Ave.
- Modern's—170 Clinton St.
- La Mae—437 Jefferson Ave.
- Jessie's—560 Spring St.

BARBER SHOPS
- Elite—171 William St.
- People's—433 Williams St.

TAVERNS
- Pearls—474 Michigan Ave.
- Clover Leaf—443 Michigan Ave.
- Jefferson—381 Jefferson
- Apex—311 Williams St.

54

PLEASE MENTION "THE GREEN BOOK"

TAVERNS
　Hickory—Hickory & Williams
　Horse Shoe—Williams & Pine
　Little Harlem—496 Michigan
　Toussaint—292 Williams St.
　Joe's—416 William St.
　Tuxedo—121 Williams St.
　Glass Horseshoe—214 Williams St.
　Jamboree—339 Williams St.
　Mandy's—278 Williams St.
　Polly's—483 Jefferson St.
NIGHT CLUBS
　Moonglow—Michigan & Williams
　Jamboree—339 Williams
　Cotton Club—349 Broadway
LIQUOR STORES
　Zarin—557 Clinton St.
　Parkside—452 William St.
　Swan—Swan & Hickory St.
　Aqui-Line—141 Broadway
　Ferry—192 E. Ferry St.
　Totton's—344 Jefferson Ave.
　Stenson's—133 William St.
SERVICE STATIONS
　Fraas—Clinton & Jefferson
　Burns—120 Willilams St.
　Spring St.—240 Spring St.
　Oab's—90 Williams St.
　Al's—Clinton & Enslie Sts.
　Klein's—Clinton & Emslie St.
TAILORS
　Twi-Light—458 Williams St.
　Eagle—414 Eagle St.
　Reeve's—119 Clinton St.
　Mickey's—541 Williams St.
　Shirley's 533 Broadway
　Tidwell—561 Eagle St.
TAXICAB
　Veteran—63 William St.

ELMIRA
HOTELS
　Wilson—307 E. Clinton St.
TOURIST HOMES
　J. A. Wilson—307 E. Clinton St.

ITHACA
NIGHT CLUBS
　Forest City Lodge—119 S. Tioga St.

GLEN FALLS
TOURIST HOMES
　Mrs. M. Mayberry—16 Ferry St.

JAMESTOWN
TOURIST HOMES
　Mrs. I. W. Herald—51 W. 10th St.
　Mrs. J. M. Brown—108 W. 11th St.

LACKAWANNA
RESTAURANTS
　Little Swan—25 Wasson Ave.
　Standard—68 Ridge Road

　Chicken Shack—23 Simon Ave.
　Merriweathers—73 Ridge Rd.
TAVERNS
　Little Harlem—26 Gates Ave.

NIAGARA FALLS
TOURIST HOMES
　Mack-Hayes House—437 1st St.
　Mrs. Alice Ford—413 Main St.
　Fairview—413 Main St.
　Mrs. Brown—1202 Haeberie Ave.
　Parker House—627 Erie Avenue
　A. E. Gabriel—635 Erie Ave.
　C. A. Brown—3106 Highland Ave.
BARBER SHOPS
　Garland—Erie Ave.
TAVERNS
　Sunset Cafe—619 Erie Ave.
　Chef. W. Martin—609 Erie Ave.
　Cephas—621 Erie Ave.
　Andrew's—135 Memorial Park
GARAGES
　Smith & Bradberry—150 Memorial P'kway.

PORT JERVIS
TOURIST HOMES
　R. Pendleton—26 Bruce St.

POUGHKEEPSIE
TOURIST HOMES
　Mrs. S. Osterholt—16 Crannell St.
　Mrs. S. Le Fever—217 Union St.
　G. W. Hayes—93 N. Hamilton

ROCHESTER
HOTELS
　Gibson—461 Clariss St.
　Freeman House—112 Industrial St.
TOURIST HOMES
　G. W. Burke—221 Columbia Ave.
　Mrs. Latimer—179 Clarissa St.
NIGHT CLUBS
　Cotton Club—222 Joseph Avenue

SCHENECTADY
HOTELS
　Clefton—516 Broadway
TOURIST HOMES
　R. Rhinehart—125 S. Church St.
　S. Kearney—857 McDonald Ave.
　G. D. Thomas—123 S. Church St.

SYRACUSE
HOTELS
　The Savoy—518 E. Washington St.
　Almond House—210 Almond St.
TOURIST HOMES
　W. R. Farrish—809 E. Faytte. St.
RESTAURANTS
　Little Harlem—449 E. Washington St.
　Aunt Edith's—601½ Harrison St.
　Field's—E. Adams & S. Townsend St.

IN PATRONIZING THESE PLACES

TAVERNS
Penquin—822 S. State St.
BARBER SHOPS
Cameron—401 E. Washington St.
Smith's—600½ E. Washington St.
NIGHT CLUBS
Goldie's—423 Harrison St.
LIQUOR STORE
Mulroy's—301 E. Genesse St.
GARAGES
Ben's—829 S. Townsend St.
DRUG STORES
Allen's—928 S. Townsend St.

UTICA

TOURIST HOMES
Broad St. Inn—415 Broad St.
Mrs. S. Burns—318 Broad St.
Howard Home—413 Broad St.

WATERTOWN

TOURIST HOMES
E. F. Thomas—123 Union St.
V. H. Brown—502 Binase St.
G. E. Deputy—711 Morrison St.

NEW YORK CITY
(HARLEM)

STOP AT

The HARRIET HOTELS
and EXTENSIONS

313 WEST 127TH ST.
N.E. COR. ST. NICHOLAS AVE.
8TH AVE. SUBWAY AT DOOR

◆◆

271-5 WEST 127TH ST.
NEAR 8TH AVENUE
ALL TRANSPORTATION FACILITIES

250 Rooms Available
DAY or NIGHT

OUR DINING ROOM SPECIALTY
SOUTHERN FRIED CHICKEN
AND WAFFLES

PHONE: UN 4-9053 & 4-8248

E. T. RHODES, PROP.

Cambridge—141 W. 10th St.
El-Melrah—21 W. 135th St.
Martha—6 W. 135th St.
Garrett House—314 W. 127th St.
Press—23 W. 135th St.
The Viola—227 W. 135th St.

HOTEL FANE
Formerly Hotel Dumas
205 WEST 135TH STREET

"In The Heart of Harlem"

RATES REASONABLE

Hot & Cold Water in Rooms

For Reservations
PHONE: AU 3-8396

Frank G. Lightener, Mgr.

DEWEY SQUARE HOTEL
OFFICE PHONE UN 4-1593
250 LUXURIOUS ROOMS
WHEN IN NEW YORK VISIT US
FOR COMFORT, LUXURY AND PRESTIGE
201—203 WEST 117TH STREET
FROM 7TH TO ST. NICHOLAS AVES.

HOTELS
CROSSTOWN HOTEL
515 WEST 145th STREET
The Tenrub—328 St. Nicholas
Elks—608 St. Nicholas
Beakford—300 W. 116th St.
Braddock—126th & 8th Ave.
Theresa—125th St. & 7th Ave.
Grampion—182 St. Nicholas
Olgo—695 Lenox Ave.
Woodside—2424 7th Ave.

DOUGLAS

809 St. Nicholas Ave., Nr. 151st St.

Transients Accomodated

Tel. ED 4-7560-7561

Y. M. C. A.—180 W. 135th St.
Y. W. C. A.—175 W. 137th St.
Currie—101 W. 145th St.
Mariette—170 W. 121st St.
Cecil—208 W. 118th St.
Revella—307 W. 116th St.

PLEASE MENTION "THE GREEN BOOK"

HOTELS
Barbera—501 West 142 St.

Brown's—210 W. 135th St.
E & M—2016 7th Ave.
Em & Bee—458 Lenox Ave.
Davis'—2066 7th Ave.

Tel: AU 3-9122

For Comfort & Courtesy

HOTEL ELMENEH

RADIOS IN ROOMS

845 St. Nicholas Avenue

N. W. Corner 152nd Street

HOTEL McCLENDON

23 WEST 123rd STREET

ALL IMPROVEMENTS

LOW RATES

TRANSIENTS $1.50 UP

SPECIAL 7 DAY RATES

Joseph McClendon, *Prop.*

PALS INN

"A Good Place To Eat"
Twenty-Four Hours Service
Always Reasonable Prices

307 WEST 125TH ST.

TEL. UN 4-9893

EDDIE WALCOTT, MGR.

Harris' Corner—132nd & 7th Ave.
Little Shack—2267 7th Ave.
Elsie's—975 St. Nicholas Ave.
Doris'—2066 7th Ave.

"Come Revel in
Gastronomical Luxury"

BELL'S RESTAURANT

3618 BROADWAY at 149th St.

COCKTAIL LOUNGE BAR
FINE WINES & LIQUORS

When Epicures gather, this smart address is known for generous tasty well cooked portions it serves here; Dining and Drinking regains its alluring appeal.
For a perfect Luncheon, Dinner, Supper. No more intimate rendezvous can be found.

Bob Bell and George Bell

RESTAURANTS
Otis Coles—108 West 145th St.
Jimmie's Chicken Shack—763 St. Nicholas A.
Pete's—2534 8th Ave.
Virginia—271 W. 119th St.
Clarkson Bros.—2499 - 7th Ave.
Lulu Belle—229 W. 125th St.
Pete's Creole Restaurant—2230 7th Ave.
Bob's Lounge—2165 8th Ave.
Lulu Belle's—317 W. 126th St.
Four Star—2433 7th Ave.
Jim's Cuban Lunchionette—2346 8th Ave.

RITZ TEAROOM
2310—7th AVENUE

"The Squeeze Inn"—2125-7th Ave.
Helen's Haven—2930 8th Ave.
Pauline's—1627 Amsterdam Ave.
Tabb's—2354 7th Ave.
Watson's—127 Lenox Ave.
El Mundial—2201 7th Ave.
James Bar-B-Q—1815 Amsterdam Ave.
Esquire Lunchonette—2201 7th Ave.
Bee Bee's Blueplate—2373-7th Ave.
Al's—57 Lenox Ave.
Sherman's Bar-B-Q—1835 Amsterdam Ave.

Empire—125th St. & Lenox Ave.
Jimmy's—763 St. Nicholas Ave.

57

IN PATRONIZING THESE PLACES

RESTAURANTS
Gertrude's—267 West 141st St.
Four Star—2433 - 7th Ave.
George's—1921 Amsterdam Ave.
Jennie Lou's—2297 - 7th Ave.
Hamburg Paradise—377 West 125th St.
Bodden & Clark—2150 - 7th Ave.

CHINESE RESTAURANT
Mayling—1723 Amsterdam Ave.

BEAUTY PARLORS
Elite—2544-7th Ave.
Myers & Griffin—65 W. 134th St.
Your Pal—22 W. 133rd St.
National—301 W. 144th St.
Neuway—143 W. 116th St.
A. L. Smith—2411 7th Ave.
Oneda's—231 Edgecombe Ave.
Sibley's—301 W. 126th St.
Beard's—322 St. Nicholas Ave.
Bonnie's—165 W. 127th St.
Dorothy's—247 West 144th St.
Rose Meta's—148th St. & St. Nicholas Ave.
Lillette's—1308 Amsterdam Ave.

BARBER SHOPS
Sportsmen's Barber Shop—2224-7th Ave.
Davis—69 W. 138th St.

DE LUX
90 St. Nicholas Place

The Best On The Hill

James Monroe, Mgr.—Tel. AU 3-9186

Renaissance—2349 7th Ave.
DeLux—2799 8th Ave.
WORLD BARBER SHOP
2621 - 8th AVENUE
Bob Cary's—2521 8th Ave.
Spooner's—2435 8th Ave.
DUNBAR BARBER SHOP
2808—8th AVENUE
B. Garrett—2311 7th Ave.
Eldorado—203 W. 116th St.
Hi-Hat—2276 7th Ave.
Hoghie Rayford—2013 7th Ave.
IDEAL BARBER SHOP
716 ST. NICHOLAS AVENUE
Leon & Eddie's—353 W. 145th St.
Roxy—2322 7th Ave.
Modernistic—2132 7th Ave.
Service—7th Ave. & 135th St.

TAVERNS
Lenox Lounge—290 Lenox Ave.
El Favorito Bar—2055 Eighth Ave.
Old Time Tavern—2160 5th Ave.
International—2150 5th Ave.
GOLDEN BAR & GRILL
366 WEST 145th STREET
Arthur's—2481 8th Ave.

Red Tip—2470-7th Avenue
Bird Cage—2308 7th Ave.
John Allen's—207 W. 116th St.
Brittwood—594 Lenox Ave.
POP'S BAR & LOUNGE
1981 AMSTERDAM AVENUE
Big Apple—2300 7th Ave.
Frank Lezama—3578 Broadway
Frankie's Cafe—2328-7th Ave.
Bank's—2338 - 8th Ave.
Paradise—2033-8th Ave.
JENNINGS BAR & GRILL
Cor. Amsterdam Ave. & 162nd St.
Little Zhack—2267 - 7th Ave.
Ray's—165th St. & Broadway

PHONES: AU3-8445—3-8155

HARRIS' CORNER

132nd Street & 7th Avenue

Featuring—
Chicken In The Rough
SHRIMPS — SCALLOPS

Best of Wines and Liquors

PERCY R. HARRIS, PROP.

Shalimar—3638 Broadway
Palm—209 West 125th St.
Frank's—313 West 125th St.
Covan's—371 West 125th St.
Renny—2359 - 7th Ave.
Parkway—2063 - 8th Ave.
Dolen-Taylor—134 Hamilton Place
S. S. Francois—2104 - 7th Ave.
Chick's—2501 - 7th Ave.
C. L. D. - 1948 - 7th Ave.
Mac's—267 West 125th St.
William's—2011 - 7th Ave.

BROWNIE'S

2571—8th AVE. ——— 2557—8th AVE.

Choice Wines, Liquors & Beer

AU 3-9761   Janice Brown, Prop.

Dawn—1931 Amsterdam Ave.
Pasadena—2350 - 8th Ave.
Barfield—2379 - 7th Ave.
Joe Louis—11 West 125th St.
Jack Carters—1890 - 7th Ave.
Poor John's—2268 - 8th Ave.

PLEASE MENTION "THE GREEN BOOK"

Baby Grand—319 West 125th St.

PHONE: AU 3-8244

MEET YOUR FRIENDS
—AT—
WELL'S MUSICAL BAR
2249—7th AVENUE

Charles Stewart at the Organ

Marlow Morris at the Piano

**Finest of Wines & Liquors
Chicken, Steak & Chops
Our Specialty**

Al's—415 West 125th St.
Horseshoe—2474 - 7th Ave.
Lou's—1985 Amsterdam Ave.
Welcome Inn—2895 - 8th Ave.
Dick Wheaton's—7th Ave. & 137th St.

A MUST ON YOUR LIST
...On The Hill...

L. BOWMAN'S

Famous For Its

**FOOD
WINES
LIQUOR**

VISIT OUR MUSIC ROOM

AT
92 ST. NICHOLAS PLACE
Phone: AUdubon 3-8515

1996 AMSTERDAM AVE.
Cor. 159th St.   Tel. WA 3-9187

Blue Heaven—378 Lenox Ave.
Calvacade—2104 7th Ave.
Colonial—116 Bradhurst Ave.

TAVERNS
Eddie's—714 St. Nicholas Ave.
Elk Scene—469 Lenox Ave.

FIRPO'S

503 LENOX AVE., Nr. 135th St.

Fine Food, Wines & Liquors

A. S. Porco, Prop.   AU3-9255

Hot-Cha—2280 7th Ave.
Jay's—400 W. 148th St.
La Mar Cheri—739 St. Nichollas Ave.
Logas—2496 7th Ave.
Monte Carlo—2247 7th Ave.
Murrain—635 Lenox Ave.
Orange Blossom—570 Lenox Ave.
Speedway—92 St. Nicholas Ave.
Victoria—2418 7th Ave.
721 St. Nicholas Ave. Grill
Fat Man—St. Nicholas Ave. & 155th St.
Mayfair—773 St. Nicholas Ave.
C. L. D. Grill—1958-7th Ave.
Jimmie Daniels—114 W. 116th St.
Chick's—2501 7th Ave.
Moon Glow—2461 7th Ave.
Palm Cafe—209 W. 125th St.

EUGENE E. KEMP
LESTER A. KEMP   PROPS.

CAFE CASBAH
VERY UNIQUE

WINES & LIQUORS
OF THE BETTER KIND

163rd St. & St. Nicholas Avenue

TEL. WA 3-9142

Palace Bar & Grill—247 Lenox
George Farrell's—2711 8th Ave.
Novelty Bar & Grill—1965 Amsterdam Ave.
Johnson's—614 Lenox Ave.
L-Bar—3601 Broadway
Chick's Bar & Grill—2501 7th Ave.
Well's Cocktail Bar—2249 7th Ave.
Sport's Inn—2308 8th Ave.
The Colonial—2321 8th Ave.
Clover Bar & Grill 1735 Amsterdam Ave.
Swanky Bar & Grill—1744 Amsterdam Ave.
Welcome Inn—2895 8th Ave.
Lou's—1985 Amsterdam Ave.
Daniel"s—2461 7th Ave.

IN PATRONIZING THESE PLACES

THE TALK OF THE TOWN

Little Alpha Service
THE COMPLETE CLEANERS

200 WEST 136th STREET
(NEAR 7th AVENUE)

Phone: AU 3-0671

6 - 8 HOUR SERVICE

ONE OF NEW YORK'S PIONEER CLEANERS

R.E EUBANKS, MGR.

TAVERNS
Horseshoe—2474 7th Ave.
Mac's—267 W. 125th St.
Coran's—2359 7th Ave.

Tel: UN 4-8577

HARLEM
BAR and GRILL

Visit Our
  Newly Decorated "U" Bar

Dine In The Avenue's Only
  Fountain Cocktail Lounge

MODERATE PRICES——
  ——SATISFACTORY SERVICE

2140—7th Avenue   Cor. 127th St.

Parkway—2063 8th Ave.
Pelican—45 Lenox Ave.
Bar '61'—61 W. 125th St.
Jock's—2350 7th Ave.
Randolph's Shangri La—1978 Amsterdam Av.
Mandalay—2201 7th Ave.
Broadway Palace—147th & Broadway
Williams'—2011 7th Ave.
Bell's Bar—Broadway & 149th St.
Dawn Cafe—1931 Amsterdam Ave.
Old Pasadena—2350 8th Ave.
Chateau Lounge—379 W. 125th St.
Jerry's Bar—2091-8th Ave.

NIGHT CLUBS
Small's Paradise—229417th Avve.
Elk's Rendezvous—133rd & Lenox Ave.
Celebrity Club—35 E. 125th St.

NIGHT CLUBS
Murrain's—132nd & 7th Ave.
Caribbean Club—2387 7th Ave.
Hollywood Club—116th & Lenox Ave.
Lenox Rendezvous—75 Lenox Ave.
Club Sudan—640 Lenox Ave.
Hollywood—105 West 116th St., N. Y. C.
Club Baron—132nd St. & Lenox Ave.

LIQUOR STORES
Friedland's—605 Lenox Ave.
J & D—271 West 141st St.

Call AU 3-8340

Free Prompt Delivery

WE RECOMMEND

GOLDMAN'S
WINES AND Liquors

New York State Retail Wine
& Liquor Store License L-761

483 W. 155th St. — New York

Corner Amsterdam Avenue

LIQUOR STORES
Square Wine & Liquor—209 W. 127th St.
Leslie T. Turner—26 Macombs Place
Margaret B. Gray—394 Manhattan Ave.
Dave's—472 Lenox Ave.

PLEASE MENTION "THE GREEN BOOK"

GARAGES
  Viaduct—101 Macombs Place
  Colonial Park—310 W. 144th St.
  Polo Grounds—155th St. & St. Nicholas Ave.
  McClary's—163 West 132nd St.

AUTOMOTIVE
  The New Deal—30 W. 140th St.

TAILORS

For De Luxe Service

PHONE: ED 4-2574

Work Called For & Delivered

GLOBE

Ladies' & Gents' Tailor—Furrier
Garments Relined — Repaired
Remodeled — Dry Cleaning

**2894—8TH AVE., E. L. CAUSEY, PROP.
NR. 153RD ST.**

Robert Lewis—1980-7th Ave.
La Fontaine—470 Convent Ave.
Broadway—92 St. Nicholas Ave.

UN 4-9177

It Pays To Look Well

DIG-BY CLEANERS

300 WEST 111th STREET
Cor. 8th Avenue

Dyeing — Cleaning — Tailoring

We Call And Deliver Anywhere

W. D. TUCKER Prop.

DANCE HALLS
  Savoy—Lenox Ave. & 140th St.
  Golden Gate—Lenox Ave. & 142nd St.

BROOKLYN

HOTELS
  Y. M. C. A.—405 Carlton Ave.
  Burma—145 Gates Ave.
  T. C. U.—1124 Fulton St.

RESTAURANTS
  Dew Drop—363 Halsey St.
  El Rose—1093 Fulton St.
  Little Roxy—490A Summer Ave.
  Bernice's Cafeteria—105 Kingston Ave.
  Spick & Span—70 Kingston Ave.

BEAUTY PARLORS
  Bartley's—1125 Fulton St.
  Lamae—545 Classon Ave.
  Katerine's—345 Sumner Ave.
  Ideal—285-A Sumner Ave.

SCHOOLS OF BEAUTY CULTURE
  Theresa—304 Livonia Ave.

TAVERNS
  Palm Gardens—491 Summer Ave.
  Royal—1073 Fulton St.
  Goodwill—1942 Fulton St.
  Parkside—759 Gates Ave.
  Stuyvesant—Hancock & Lewis Ave.
  Capitol Bar—1550 Fulton St.
  Turner's—1698 Fulton St.
  Decatur Bar & Grill—301 Reid Ave.
  Kingston Tavern—1496 Fulton St.
  Arlington Inn—1253 Fulton St.
  McGorem's—1253 Bedford Ave.
  Gallagher's Bar—249 Reid Ave.
  Kingston Lounge—Kingston Cor. Bergen
  Rainbow Inn—1630 Fulton St.
  Durkin Tavern—1289 Fulton St.
  Disler's—759 Gates Ave.
  Elegant Bar & Grill—1420 Fulton St.
  Verona Leafe—1330 Fulton St.
  Frank's—Kingston & Atlantic Ave.
  K & C Tavern—588 Gates Ave.
  George's—328 Tompkins Ave.
  Smitty's—286 Patchen Ave.
  Casablanca—300 Reid Ave.
  Tropic Moon—1304 Fulton St.
  Buckham's—399 Nostrand Ave.
  Ten-Twelve—Sumner & Myrtle Aves.
  Bedford Rest—1253 Bedford Ave.
  Country Cottage—375 Franklin Ave.
  Bombay—377 Christppher St.
  Bedford Lounge—1194 Fulton St.
  Marion's—125 Marion St.
  Capitol—1550 Fulton St.
  Corba—1593 E. New York Ave.

NIGHT CLUBS
  Hanlew—334 Lewis St.
  Lion's—307 Ralph Ave.

WINE & LIQUOR STORES
  Yak—1361 Fulton St.
  Lincoln—401 Tompkins Ave.
  York—1361 Fulton St.
  Stuyvesant—1551 Fulton St.
  Gottlesman's—41 Albany St.
  Allen Rose—106 Kingston Ave.
  Turner's—249 Sumner St
  Gottesman's—41 Albany Ave.
  Sexton's—616 Halsey St.

TAILORS
  G & O—84 Troy Ave.

IN PATRONIZING THESE PLACES

For Comfort and Service
HOTEL CARVER
IN THE BRONX
980 PROSPECT AVENUE
PHONE: DA 9-7233
MONTAGUE J. ELLIS, MGR.

(BRONX)
HOTELS
Carver—980 Prospect Ave.

RESTAURANTS
Fischer's—1086 Boston Road
Betty's Blue Room—1363 Stebbins Ave.
The Blue Way—3269 3rd Ave.
Dick's—699 E. 163rd St.
Denton's—1300 Boston Road
Shrimp's—734 East 165th St.
Daniel's—1107 Prospect Ave.

BEAUTY PARLORS
Grayson—974 Prospect Ave.
Glennada—875 Longwood Ave.

TAVERNS
Freddie's Cafe—1204 Boston Road
Uncle Curley's—3589 Third Ave.
Prospect Cafe—845 Prospect Ave.
The Fair Play—1260 Boston Road
Boston Road Cafe—1078 Boston Road
Sun Brite 921 Prospect Ave.
Harty's Mid-Way—458 E. 165th St.
Louis' Ambosino—737 E. 165th St.
Neighborhood—3344 Third Ave.
Third Ave. Rendezvous—3377 Third Ave.
Prospect Bar & Grill 1431 Prospect Ave.
Louis' Tavern—3510 Third Ave.
Kennie's—853 Freeman St.
Lucille's—3800 Third Ave.
Jimmy's—267 E. 161st St.
Zombie Bar—1745 Boston Road
Rainbow Gardens—977 Prospect Ave.
The Forest Lounge—750 E. 165th St.
Boston Road Tavern—1429 Prospect Ave.
Johnny's—1048 Boston Road
B & P—823 E. 169th St.
Trinity—163rd & Trinity Ave.
Ralph Rida's—1155 Tinton Ave.
Triangle—849 E. 169th St.
Old Harlem Union Cafe—1087 Union Ave.
Rendez-Vous—907 Prospect Ave.

Bronxwood—3950 Bronxwood Ave.
Crystal Lounge—1035 Prospect Ave.
Happy Hour—1183 Boston Road
Four Aces—1306 Boston Road

TAVERNS
Central—271 East 161st Street
Kelly's—430 East 169th St.
Fair Play—1260 Boston Road
Kennie's—853 Freeman St.
Prospect—1431 Prospect Ave.
Step Inn—1308 Washington Ave.
Five Corners—169th St. & Boston Road
Third Ave.—3377 - 3rd Ave.
Freddie's—1204 Boston Road
Uncle Curley's—3589 3rd Ave.
Sporting Life—950 Prospect Ave.
Louis Ambrosino—737 East 165th St.
Central—267 East 161st St.
DeLuxe—270 East 161st St.
Johnny's—1056 Boston Road
Elk's—980 Prospect Ave.
Midway—458 East 165th St.
Forest Lounge—750 East 165th St.
Boston Road—1078 Boston Road
Rendezvous—907 Prospect Ave.
Hilltop—947 Forest Ave.
Trinity—163rd St. & Trinity Ave.
SunBrite—921 Prospect Ave.
Hi-Spot—3824 - 3rd Ave.

WINE & LIQUORS
Franklin Ave.—1214 Franklin Ave.
Prospect—889 Prospect Ave.
Jack's—1309 Prospect Ave.
West Farms—2026 Boston Road
O'Connell's—1311 Boston Road
Prospect—889 Prospect Ave.

NIGHT CLUBS
845—845 Prospect Ave.

BALLROOM
McKinley—1258 Boston Road

PLEASE MENTION "THE GREEN BOOK"

TAILORS
 Hendrix's—1202 Union Ave.
 DeLux—857 Freeman St.

LONG ISLAND

AMITYVILLE
RESTAURANTS
 Watervliet—158 Dixon Ave.
ROAD HOUSE
 Freddy's—Albany & Banbury Court
BARBER SHOP
 Jimmy's—Albany & Brewster
BEAUTY PARLORS
 Boyd's—21 Banbury Court

CORONA
TAVERNS
 Big George—106 Northern Blvd.
 Prosperity—32-19 103rd St.
NIGHT CLUBS
 New Cameo—108 Northern Blvd.

FLUSHING
ROAD HOUSE
 Club Forty—40 Lawrence St.

HEMPSTEAD
TAVERNS
 Eddie Bar & Grill—28 S. Franklin

JAMAICA
TAVERNS
 Tolliver's—112 New York Blvd.
 Hank's—108 New York Blvd.
BEAUTY PARLORS
 Roslyn—106 New York Blvd.
TAILORS
 Klugh's—109 Union Hall St.
 Merit—109 Merrick Blvd.

WESTCHESTER

ELMSFORD
TAVERNS
 Clarke—91 Saw Mill River Road

MT. VERNON
RESTAURANTS
 Hamburger Bar—15 W. 3rd St.
 Southern Tea Room—44 W. 3rd St.
 Friendship—50 W. 3rd St.
SCHOOL OF BEAUTY CULTURE
 Orchid—48 W. 3rd St.
TAVERNS
 Mohawk Inn—142 S. 7th Ave.
 Friendship Center—50 W. 3rd St.
 Golden Lion—50 S. 8th St.

NEW ROCHELLE
RESTAURANTS
 City Park—521 5th Ave.
 Harris—29 Morris St.
 Week's—68 Winyah Ave.

BEAUTY PARLORS
 A. Berry—50 DeWitts Place
 B. Miller—8 Brook Ave.
 Ocie—41 Rochelle Place
BARBER SHOPS
 The Royal Salon—4 Brook Ave.
 Field's—66 Winyah Ave.
 Bal-Mo-Ral—56 Brook St.
LIQUOR STORE
 A. Edwards—112 Union Ave.
DRUGGIST
 Daniels—57 Winyah Ave.

NORTH CASTLE
ROAD HOUSE
 Carolina Lodge

OSSINING
BEAUTY PARLOR
 Leona's—13 Hunter St.

NORTH TARRYTOWN
BARBER SHOPS
 Lemon's—Valley St.
 J. Brown—Valley St.
BEAUTY PARLOR
 J. Prioleau—88 Valley St.

TUCKAHOE
RESTAURANTS
 Major's—48 Washington St.
 Butterfly Inn—47 Washington St.
BEAUTY PARLORS
 Shanhana—144 Main St.
BARBER SHOPS
 Al's—144 Main St.

WHITE PLAINS
RESTAURANTS
 Carver Lunch—168 Whitfield St.

YONKERS
TAVERNS
 The Brown Derby—125 Nepperham Ave.

NEW MEXICO

ALBUQUERQUE
TOURIST HOMES
 Mrs. W. Bailey—1127 N. 2nd St.
RESTAURANTS
 Bon Ton—115 N. First St.

CARLSBAD
TOURIST HOMES
 Mrs. A. Sherrell—502 S. Haloquens
 L. M. Smith—514 South Canyon

DEMING
TOURIST HOMES
 M. Wilson—Iron & 2nd St.

IN PATRONIZING THESE PLACES

LASCRICES
TOURIST HOMES
Mrs. R. B. McCoy—545 N. Church

ROSWELL
TOURIST HOMES
Mrs. Mary Collins—121 E. 10th St.
R. Brown—115 E. Walnut St.
RESTAURANTS
Sunset Cafe—115 E. Walnut St.

TUCMCARI
TOURIST HOMES
Rockett Inn—524 N. Campbell St.

NORTH CAROLINA

ASHEVILLE
HOTELS
Y. W. C. A.—360 College St.
Booker T. Washington—409 Southside Ave.
Savoy—Eagle & Market St.
RESTAURANTS
Palace Grille—19 Eagle St.
BEAUTY PARLORS
Butler's—Eagle & Market St.
BARBER SHOPS
Wilson's—13 Eagle St.
TAVERNS
Wilson's—Eagle & Market Sts.
GARAGES
Wilkin's—Eagle & Market Sts.

BLADENBORO
BEAUTY PARLORS
Lacy's Beauty Shop

CARTHAGE
HOTELS
Carthage Hotel

CHARLOTTE
SERVICE STATIONS
Bishop Dale—First & Brevard Sts.

DURHAM
HOTELS
Biltmore—E. Pettigrew St.
Jones—502 Ramsey St.
RESTAURANTS
Congo Grill—Pettigrew St.
Catlett's—1502 Pettigrew St.
Elivira's—801 Fayetteville St.
BEAUTY PARLORS
De Shazors—809 Fayetteville St.
D'Orsay—120 S. Mangum St.
BARBER SHOPS
Friendly—711 Fayetteville St.
TAVERNS
Blue Tavern—801 Fayetteville St.
Hollywood—118 S. Mangum St.

SERVICE STATIONS
Granite—Main & 9th St.
Midway—Pine & Poplar Sts.
Pine Street—1102 Pine St.
TAILORS
Union—112 Parrish St.
Royal—538 E. Pettegrew St.

ELIZABETH CITY
TAVERNS
Blue Duck Inn—404½ Ehringhaus

ELIZABETHTOWN
RESTAURANT
Royal Cafe
BEAUTY PARLORS
Liola's Beauty Salon
TAVERNS
Gill's Grill
Royal Cafe

FAYETTEVILLE
HOTELS
Bedford Inn—203 Moore St.
Restful Inn—418 Gillespie St.
TOURIST HOMES
Mrs. L. McNeill—418 Gillespie St.
RESTAURANTS
Mayflower Grill—N. Hillsboro St.
BEAUTY PARLORS
Mrs. Brown—Person St.
Ethel's—Gillespie St.
BARBER SHOPS
DeLuxr—Pesno St.
Mack's—117 Gillespie St.
TAVERNS
Bedford Inn—203 Moore St.
Big Buster—Gillespie St.
SERVICE STATIONS
Moore's—613 Ramsey St.
GARAGES
Jeffrie's—Blount St.

GASTONIA
HOTELS
Union Square

GREENSBORO
HOTELS
Travelers Inn—612 E. Market St.
Legion Club—829 E. Market St.
Dixie—423 Lindsay St.
TOURIST HOMES
T. Daniels—912 E. Market St.
Mrs. E. Evans—906 E. Market St.
Mrs. Lewis—829 E. Market St.
I. W. Wooten—423 Lindsay St.
TAVERNS
Paramount—907 E. Market St.
TAILORS
Shoffners—922 E. Market St.
TAXICABS
MakRae—106 S. Macon St.

64

PLEASE MENTION "THE GREEN BOOK"

GREENVILLE
RESTAURANTS
 Paradise—314 Albermale Ave.
 Bell's—310 Albermale Ave.
BEAUTY SHOPS
 Spain—614 Atlantic Ave.
 Midgett's—212 Clark St.
SERVICE STATION
 Eagle's
DRUG Stores
 Harrison's—908 Dickerson St.

HALLSBORO
BEAUTY PARLORS
 Leigh's—Route No. 1

HENDERSON
TAXICABS
 Green & Chavis—720 Eaton St.

HIGH POINT
HOTELS
 Kilby's—627½ E. Washington St.

LITTLETON
HOTELS
 Young's Hotel

MT. OLIVE
RESTAURANTS
 Black Beauty Tea Room

NEW BERN
HOTELS
 Rhone—42 Queen St.
TOURIST HOMES
 H. C. Sparrow—68 West St.
TAVERNS
 Palm Garden—192 Broad St.

LEXINGTON
SERVICE STATIONS
 D. T. Taylor—Esso Service

RALEIGH
HOTELS
 Lewis—220 E. Cabarrus St.
 Arcade—122 E. Hargett St.
RESTAURANTS
 B & H Cafe—411 S. Blount St.
 Chicken Shack—Cross & Lake St.
BEAUTY SHOPS
 Sales—222 S. Tarboro St.
TAVERNS
 Savoy—410 S. Blount St.
 Savoy—410 S. Bount St.
TAXICABS
 Capitol—Phone 9137
 Hooper's—402½ W. South St.
TAILORS
 Peerless—103 W. Jones St.
 Provressive—Smithfield & Bloodworth Sts.
GARAGES
 Richardson & Smith—108 E. Lenoir St.

PINEHURST
TOURIST HOMES
 Foster's
SERVICE STATIONS
 Foster's

SANFORD
BEAUTY PARLORS
 Douglas'—310 Wall St.
GARAGES
 Campbell's—Pearl St.
DRUG STORES
 Bland's—300 S. Steele St.

SALISBURY
TAXICABS
 Safety—122 N. Lee St.

SUMTER
TAVERNS
 Silver Moon—20 W. Liberty St.

WHITEVILLE
TOURIST HOMES
 Mrs. F. Jeffries—Mill St.

WILSON
HOTELS
 Biltmore—E. Washington St.
 The Wilson Biltmore—539 E. Nash
TAXICABS
 M. Jones—1209 E. Queen St.

WINDSOR
TOURIST HOMES
 W. Payton

WINSTON-SALEM
HOTELS
 Y. M. C. A.—410 N. Church St.
 Lincoln—9 E. Third St.
TOURIST HOMES
 Charles H. Jones—1611 E. 14th St.
 Mrs. H. L. Christian—302 E. 9th St
 R. B. Williams—1225 N. Ridge Ave.
NIGHT CLUBS
 Club 709—709 Patterson Ave.

WASHINGTON
DRUG STORES
 Lloyd's—408 Gladden St.

WELDON
HOTELS
 Pope
 Terminal Inn—Washington Ave.

WILMINGTON
HOTELS
 Paynes—417 N. 6th St.
 Murphy—813 Castle St.

IN PATRONIZING THESE PLACES

RESTAURANTS
- Harris—10th & Worcester Sts.
- Johnson's—1007 Chestnut St.
- Hillcrest—1118 Dawson St.
- Manhattan—816 S. 13th St.
- Ollie's—415½ S. 7th St.

BEAUTY PARLORS
- Beth's—416 Anderson St.
- Lizora's—609 Red Cross St.
- Germany's—715 Red Cross St.
- Lou's—830 Red Cross St.
- Newkirk's—1217 Castle St.
- Pierce's—615 Kidder St.
- Apex—613 Red Cross St.
- Dickson—1101 S. 7th St.
- Gertrude's—415 S. 7th St.
- Howard's—121 S. 13th St.
- Vanity Box—115 S. 13th St.
- La Celeste—508 Nixon St.
- La May—703 S. 15th St.
- Dixie—512½ Nixon St.

BARBER SHOPS
- Johnson's—6 Market St.

NIGHT CLUBS
- High Hat—Market St. Rd. (4 miles out)
- Del Morocco—1405 Dawson St.

TAVERNS
- Happy Hour—6tth & Brunswick Sts.
- High Hat—713 Castle St.
- Black Cat—922 N. 7th St.
- William's—8th & Dawson Sts.
- Blinker Cafe—605 Red Cross St.

TAXICABS
- Star—601½ Red Cross St.
- Mack's—520 N. 7th St.
- Dixie—516 S. 7th St.
- Blue Bird—517 N. 8th St.
- Tom's—418 McRae St.
- Crosby's—124 S. 13th St.
- Greyhound—Phone 2-1342

OHIO

AKRON

HOTELS
- Green Turtle—Federal & Howard
- Exchange—32 N. Howard St.
- Garden City—Howard & Furnace
- Mathews—77 N. Howard St.
- The Upperman—197 Bluff St.

TOURIST HOME
- R. Wilson—370 Robert St.

BEAUTY PARLORS
- Beauty Salon—70 N. Howard St.

BARBER SHOP
- Goodwill's—422 Robert St.
- Matthew's—77 N. Howard St.
- Allen's—43 N. Howard St.

TAVERNS
- Brook's—42 N. Howard St.
- Garden City—124 N. Howard St.

NIGHT CLUBS
- Cosmopolitan—33½ N. Howard St.

SERVICE STATIONS
- Dunagan—834 Rhoades Ave.
- Zuber's—47 Cuyhaga St.

ALLIANCE

TOURIST HOMES
- Mrs. W. Jackson—774 N. Webb Ave.

CANTON

HOTELS
- Phillis Wheatly Asso.—612 Market Ave. So.

TOURIST HOMES
- Smallwood—1203 Housel St. S. W.

RESTAURANTS
- Hunters—527 Cherry Ave. S. E.

BEAUTY PARLORS
- Vanitie—528 Cherry Ave. S. E.

BARBER SHOPS
- Barbes—525 Cherry Ave. S. E.

DRUG STORE
- Southside—415 Cherry Ave. S. E.

CINCINNATI

HOTELS
- Y. W. C. A.—702 W. 8th St.
- Terminal—1103 Hopkins St.
- Cotton Club
- Club Tavern—540 W. 7th St.

HOTELS
- Sterling—6th & Mound Sts.
- Cordella—612 N. 6th St.
- Manse—1004 Chapel St.

TOURIST HOMES
- O. Steele—3065 Kerper St.

RESTAURANTS
- **Miniature Grill—1132 Chapel St.**
- Grand—600 W. Court St.
- Kitty Kat—417 W. 5th St.
- Ann—503 W. 5th St.
- Mom's—6th & John Sts.
- Davis—118 Opera Place
- Perkins—430 West 5th St.
- Loc-Fre—1634 Freeman St.
- 8-16—816 W. Court St.
- Williams—1051 Freeman St.
- Hide Away—4th & Smith St.
- 7th & Mound Sts.

CHINESE RESTAURANTS
- Tim Pang—514 W. 6th St.

BEAUTY PARLORS
- **Efficiency—878 Beecher Street**
- The Hosmer—920 Churchill Ave.
- Poro—1524 Linn Street
- Mill's—2639 Park Ave.

BARBER SHOPS
- Collegiate—906 Churchill Ave.
- Clark's—422 Central
- 5th Ave.—528 W. 5th Ave.

TAVERNS
- Edgemont Inn—2950 Gilbert Ave.
- Travelers Inn—1115 Hopkins St.
- Log Cabin—608 John Street
- **Kitty Kat—417 W. 5th St.**
- Log Cabin—602 John St.

66

PLEASE MENTION "THE GREEN BOOK"

DRUG STORES
  Sky Pharmacy—5th & John Sts.
  Hoard's—937 Central Ave.
  Fallon's—6th & Mound Sts.
  West End—709 W. Court St.
NIGHT CLUBS
  Cotton Club—6th & Mound Street
  Cotton Club—6th & Mound St.
ROAD HOUSE
  Shuffle Inn—7th & Carr Streets
TAILORS
  De Luxe—1217 Linn St.
SERVICE STATIONS
  Coursey—Gilbert & Beuna Vista
  S. & W.—9th & Mound Sts.
  Coursey—2985 Gilbert Ave.
GARAGES
  Adams—2915 Gilbert Ave.
  7th St.—328 W. 7th St.
TAXICABS
  Calvin—9th & Mound St.
  Ferguson's—Alms Pl. & Lincoln Ave.

CLEVELAND

HOTELS
  Ward—4113 Cedar Ave.
  Phyllis Wheatly—4300 Cedar Ave.
  Geraldine—2212 E. 40th St.
  Y. M. C. A.—E. 76th & Cedar
  Majestic—2291 E. 55th St.
  Carnegie—6903 Carnegie Ave.
TOURIST HOMES
  Mrs. Edith Wilkins—2121 E. 46th St.
RESTAURANTS
  Williams—Central & E. 49th St.
  Cassie's—2284 E. 55th St.
  Manhattan—9903 Cedar Ave.
  Cassie's—2284 E 55th St.
  State—7817 Cedar
BEAUTY PARLORS
  Cosmetology—Phyllis Wheatly Bldg.
  Alberta's—8203 Cedar Ave.
  Alberta's—81st & Cedar
  Wilkin's—12813 Kinsman Road
  Unique De Luxe—2408 E. 79th St.
  Parisian—53 N. Howard St.
  Poro—48 N. Howard St.
  Smart—249 Euclid Ave.
  Morris—46 N. Howard St.
BARBER SHOPS
  Bryant's—9808 Cedar Ave.
  Driskill—1243 E. 105th St.
TAVERNS
  Brown Derby—40th & Woodland Ave.
  Cedar Gardens—9706 Cedar Ave.
  Gold Bar—Massie & E. 105th St.
  Log Cabin—2294 E. 55th St.
  Cafe Society—966 E. 105th St.
  Gold Bar—105th St. & Massie Ave.
NIGHT CLUBS
  Douglas—7917 Cedar Ave.
BEAUTY SCHOOLS
  Wilkins—2112 East 46th St.

SERVICE STATIONS
  Kyer's—Cedar & 79th St.
  Douglas—E. 93rd & Cedar Ave.
  Wrights Ohio Service—7 Stations
  K & R—Garfield & E. 105th St.
  Amoco—Ashbury & E. 105th St.
GARAGES
  Rollin—E. 40th St. & Central
  Sykes—13618 Emily Avenue
  Ben's—834 E. 105th St.
DRUG STORES
  Benjamin's—E. 55th St. & Central
TAILORS
  Gant's—10026 Cedar Ave.
  Serv-well—1283 E. 105th St.
  Primrose—2928 Woodland Ave.
  Yale—876 E. 105th St.

COLUMBUS

HOTELS
  Madonna Apts.—Tayor & Long St.
  Ford—179 N. 6th St.
  Lexington—180 Lexington Ave.
  Norfolk—430 N. Monroe Ave.
  Plaza—Long St. & Hamilton Ave.
  Macon Hotel—366 N. 20th St.
  Charlton—439 Hamilton Ave.
  Flints—703 E. Long St.
  Hawkins—65 N. Monroe Ave.
  Litchferd—N. 4th St.
  Fulton—403 E. Fulton St.
TOURIST HOMES
  Hawkins—70 N. Monroe Ave.
RESTAURANTS
  Belmont—689 E. Long St.
TAVERNS
  Poinciana—758 E. Lony St.
NIGHT CLUBS
  Club Rogue—772½ E. Long St.
  Turf Club—Champion at Mt. Vernon
SERVICE STATIONS
  King's—E. Long & Monroe
  Peyton Sohio's—E. Long & Monroe
TAILORS
  Prince's—677 E. Long St.

DAYTON

HOTELS
  Y. M. C. A.—907 W. 5th St.
TOURIST HOMES
  B. Lawrence—206 Norwood St.

LIMA

TOURIST HOMES
  Sol Downton—1124 W. Spring St.
  Edward Holt—406 E. High St.
  Amos Turner—1215 W. Spring St.
  George Cook—230 S. Union St.

IN PATRONIZING THESE PLACES

LORAIN
TOURIST HOMES
 Mrs. Alex Cooley—114 W. 26th St.
 Mrs. W. H. Redmond—201 E. 22nd St.
 Worthington—209 W. 16th Stt.
 Porter Wood—1759 Broadway
 H. P. Jackson—2383 Apple Ave.

MANSFIELD
HOTELS
 Lincoln—757 N. Bowman St.

MARIETTA
HOTELS
 St. James—Butler St.
TOURIST HOMES
 Mrs. E. Jackson—213 Church St.

MIDDLETOWN
RESTAURANTS
 Dew Drop Inn—1232 Garfield
BARBER SHOPS
 Acme—808 Lincoln Ave.
TAILORS
 Tramell—1308 Garfield

OBERLIN
HOTELS
 Oberlin Inn—College & Main

SPRINGFIELD
HOTELS
 Posey—209 S. Fountain Ave.
 Y. M. C. A.—Center St.
 Y. W. C. A.—Clarke St.
 Burtons—120 Center St.
TOURIST HOMES
 Mrs. M. E. Wilborn—220 Fair St.
 H. Sydes—902 S. Yellow Spring St.
 Mrs. C. Seward—1090 Mound St.
RESTAURANTS
 Burton's—642 S. Yellow Spring St.
 Mrs. J. Johnson—416 W. Southern
 Posey—211 S. Fountain Ave.
 Stewart's—217 E. Main St.
BEAUTY PARLORS
 Louise—902 Innesfallen Ave.
 Powder Puff—638 S. Wittenberg Ave.
BARBER SHOPS
 Harris—39 W. Clark Street
 Griffith & Martin—127 S. Center St.
TAVERNS
 Posey's—211 S. Fountain Ave.
NIGHT CLUBS
 K. P. Imp. Club—S. Yellow Spring
SERVICE STATIONS
 Underwood-1303 S. Yellow Sp'ng. St.
GARAGES
 Green's—1371 W. Pleasant St.
 Ben's—935 Sherman Ave.

STEUBENVILLE
TOURIST HOMES
 W. Jackson—648 Adam St.
 H. Jackson—650 Adam St.

TOLEDO
HOTELS
 Y. M. C. A.—669 Indiana Ave.
 Pleasant—15 N. Erie Ave.
TOURIST HOMES
 G. Davis—532 Woodland Ave.
 J. F. Watson—399 Pinewood Ave.
 P. Johnson—1102 Collingwood Blvd.
BEAUTY PARLORS
 Personality—913 Collingwood Blvd.
BARBER SHOPS
 Chiles—Indiana & Collingwood
TAVERNS
 Indiana—529 Indiana Ave.
 Midway—764 Tecumsik St.
SERVICE STATIONS
 Darling's—858 Pinewood Ave.
 Hobb's—City Park & Belmont
 South—Dorr & City Park

YOUNGSTOWN
HOTELS
 Y. M. C. A.—962 W. Federal St.
NIGHT CLUBS
 40 Club—399 E. Federal St.

ZANESVILLE
HOTELS
 Park—1561 W. Main St.
RESTAURANTS
 Little Harlem—Lee St.
TOURIST HOMES
 L. E. Coston—1545 N. Main St.
BARBER SHOPS
 Nap Love—Second St.
BEAUTY PARLORS
 Celeste—South St.

OKLAHOMA
BOLEY
HOTELS
 Berry's—South Main St.

CHICKASHA
TOURIST HOMES
 Boyd's—1022 Shepard St.

ENID
TOURIST HOMES
 Allen Crumb—222 E. Park St.
 Mrs. Eliza Baty—520 E. State St.
 Mrs. Johnson—217 E. Market St.
 Edward's—222 E. Park St.
 Vandorf—Broadway & Washington

GUTHRIE
TOURIST HOMES
 James—1002 E. Springer Ave.
 Mrs. M. A. Smith—317 E. Second St.

PLEASE MENTION "THE GREEN BOOK"

MUSKOGEE

HOTELS
Elliot's—111½ S. Second St.
Bozeman
Peoples—316 N. Second St.
RESTAURANTS
Do-Drop Inn-220 S. 2nd St.
BARBER SHOPS
Central—228 N.Second St.
Peoples—312 N. Second St.
Robbins—Second at Court
BEAUTY PARLORS
Pete's—312 N. 2nd St.
TAVERNS
Eagle Bar—Second at Court
Crazy Rock Inn—318 N. Second St.
ROAD HOUSES
Blue Willow Inn—1008 S. 24th St.
SERVICE STATIONS
Smith Tire Co.—2nd at Dennison
GARAGES
Middleton's—420 N. Second St.
Nelson's—940 S. 20th St.
TAILORS
Williams—321 N. 2nd St.
Ezell's—208 S. 2nd St.

OKLAHOMA CITY

HOTELS
Little Page—219 N. Central Ave.
Hall—308½ N. Central
M. & M.—219 N. Central
Magnolia Inn—629 E. 4th
Wilson's—200 N. E. 2nd St.
TOURIST HOMES
COrtland Rms.—629 N. E. 4th
Scrugg's—420 N. Laird St.
Tucker's—315½ N. E. 2nd St.
RESTAURANTS
Eastside Food Shop—904 N. E. 2nd St.
Scales—322 A. N. E. 2nd St.
Ruby—322½ N. E. 2nd St.
King's—905 N. E. 4th St.
BEAUTY PARLORS
Chambers—531 N. Kelly St.
Lyons—316 North Central
N. B. Ellis—331½ N. E. 2nd St.
BARBER SHOPS
Elks—300 Block N. E. 2nd St.
Golden Oak—300 Block N. E. 2nd
Clover Leaf—300 Block N. E. 2nd St.
TAVERNS
Lyons—304 E. 2nd St.
Scales—322A N. E. 2nd St.
Ruby's—322½ N. E. 2nd St.
King's—905 N. E. 4th St.
SERVICE STATIONS
Richardson—400 N. E. 2nd St.
Deep Rock—400 N. E. 2nd St.
Harry"s—547 N. E. 3rd St.
Mathues—1023 N. E. 4th St.

GARAGES
Ed's—220 N. E. 1st St.
DRUG STORES
Randolph—331 N. E. 2nd St.
Cut Rate—301 N. E. 2nd St.

OKMULGEE

RESTAURANTS
Louisiana
Simmons—407 E. 5th St.
BEAUTY PARLORS
Walker—717 N. Porter
SERVICE STATIONS
Phillips—5th & Delaware Sts.
TAXICABS
H. & H.—421 E. 5th St.

SHAWNEE

HOTELS
Olison—501 S. Bell St.
Slugg's—410 So. Bell St.
TOURIST HOMES
M. Gross—602 S. Bell St.

TULSA

HOTELS
Small—615 E. Archer St.
Lincoln—E. Archer St.
Red Wing—206 N. Greenwood
Royal—605 E. Archer St.
McHunt—1121 N. Greenwood Ave.
Warren Hotel
Y. W. C. A.—621 E. Oklahoma Pl.
TOURIST HOMES
W. H. Smith—124½ N. Greenwood
Gentry—537 N. Detroit Ave.
C. LL. Netherland—542 N. Eigin St.
RESTAURANTS
Your Cab—517 E. Beady St.
Barbeque—1111 N. Greenwood Ave.
BEAUTY PARLORS
Cotton Blossom—308 E. Haskell
May's—523 N. Greenwood Ave.
BARBER SHOPS
Swindall's—203 N. Greenwood
SERVICE STATIONS
Mince—2nd & Eigin Sts.
GARAGES
Pine Street—906 E. Pine St.
DRUG STORES
Meharry Drugs—101 Greenwood St.

OREGON

PORTLAND

HOTELS
Medley—2272 N. Interstate Ave.
Y. W. C. A.—N. E. Williams Ave. & Till.

69

IN PATRONIZING THESE PLACES

RESTAURANTS
  Ballot Box—1504 N. Williams Ave.
  Barno's—84 N. E. Broadway St.
  Barno's—84 N. E. Broadway
  Cozy Inn 66 N. W. Broadway
BEAUTY PARLORS
  Bakers—6535 N. E. Grand Ave.
  Redmond—2862 S. E. Ankeny
  Mott Sisters—2107 Vancouver Ave.
BARBER SHOPS
  Holliday's—511 N. W. 6th Ave.
NIGHT CLUBS
  Oregon Frat.—1412 N. Wms.
  Fraternal Ass'n.—1412 N. William Avenue
ROAD HOUSE
  Spicers—1734 N. Williams Ave.
GARAGE
  English—N. E. Williams & Weidler
TAXICABS
  **Broadway DeLuxe
  Phone: BR 1-2-314**

PENNSYLVANIA

ALLENTOWN
RESTAURANTS
  Southern—372 Union Street
  Elsie's—372 Union St.
BEAUTY PARLORS
  Baker's—382½ Union St.

ALTOONA
TOURIST HOMES
  C. Bell—1420 Wash. Ave.
  Mrs. E. Jackson—2138-18th St.
  Mrs. H. Shorter—2620-8th St.
RESTAURANTS
  Mac's—1710 Union Ave.

BEDFORD
HOTELS
  Harris—200 West St.

COATESVILLE
HOTELS
  Subway

CHESTER
HOTELS
  Harlem—1909 W. 3rd St.
  Moonglow 225 Market Street
RESTAURANTS
  Rio—321 Central Ave.
BEAUTY PARLORS
  Rosella—413 Concord Ave.
  Alex. Davis—123 Reaney St.
BARBER SHOPS
  Bouldin—1710 W. 3rd St.

TAVERNS
  Wright's—3rd St. & Central Ave.
TAILORS
  Tailor Shop—601 Tilgaman

DARBY
TAVERNS
  Golden Star—10th & Forrester

ERIE
HOTELS
  Pope—1318 French Street

GETTYBURG
TOURIST HOMES
  Mrs. J. Forsett—210 W. High

GERMANTOWN PHIL
HOTELS
  Y. M. C. A.—132 W. Rittenhouse
TOURIST HOMES
  M. Foote—5560 Blakmore St.
TAVERNS
  Terrace Grill—75 E. Sharpnack St.

GREENSBURG
RESTAURANT
  Breeze Inn—618 W. Otterman St.

HARRISBURG
HOTELS
  Alexander—7th & Boas Sts.
  Jackson—1004 N. 6th St.
  Jack's—1208 N. 6th St.
TOURIST HOMES
  Mrs. H. Carter—606 Foster St.
  Mrs. W. D. Jones—613 Forester St.
BEAUTY PARLORS
  Rowland—1321 N. 6th St.
BARBER SHOP
  Jack's—1002 N. 6th St.
SERVICE STATION
  Broad St.—417 Broad St.

LANCASTER
TOURIST HOMES
  E. Clark—449 S. Duke St.
  J. Carter—143 S. Duke St.
  A. LL. Polite—540 North St.

NEW CASTLE
HOTELS
  Y. W. C. A.—140 Elm St.

OIL CITY
TOURIST HOMES
  Mrs. Jackson—258 Bissel Ave.
  Mrs. M. Moore—8 Bishop St.

70

PLEASE MENTION "THE GREEN BOOK"

PHILADELPHIA

HOTELS
Baltimore—1438 Lombard Street
Attucks—801 S. 15th Street
Elizabeth—756 S. 16th St.
Woodson—17th & Lombard
Gilchriest—319 N. 40 St.
Dixie—606 S. 13th St.
The Grand—420 So. 15th St.
Citizens—420 So. 15th St.
Douglas—Broad & Lombard Sts.
Elrae—805 N. 13th St.
LaSalle—2026 Ridge Ave.
New Roadside—514 S. 15th St.
Paradise—1627 Fitzwater St.
James—2052 Catherine St.
Y. M. C. A.—1724 Christian St.
Y. W. C. A.—1605 Catherine St.
Y. W. C. A.—6128 Germantown Ave.
Horseshoe—12th & Lombard
New Phain—2059 Fitzwater
La Reve—Cor. 9th & Columbia Ave.
Chesterfield—Broad & Oxford St.
Ridge—1610 Ridge Ave.
Bilclore—1432 Catherine St.

RESTAURANTS
Marion's—20th & Bainbridge Sts.
Wilson's—21st & Burke Sts.
Seattle—113 South St.
Trott Inn—5030 Haverford Ave.
Mattie's—4225 Pennsgrove St.
Ruth's—1848 N. 17th St.
Luke & Carl's—3901 N. 17th St.
Cost to Cost—1334 South St.
Brigg's—2510 Ridge Ave.

BEAUTY PARLORS
Effie's—5502 W. Girard Ave.
A. Henson—1318 Fairmont Ave.
Jennie's—1618 French St.
LaSalle—2036 Ridge St.
Lady Ross—718 S. 18th St.
Reynolds—1612 N. 13th St.
Rose's—16th & South St.
F. Franklin—2115 W. York St.
Morton's—17th & Bainbridge
Redmond's—4823 Fairmount Ave.
A. B. Tooks—1913 W. Diamond St.

SCHOOL OF BEAUTY CULTURE
Hill School—3610 Haverford Ave.
Carter's School—1811 W. Columbia Ave.

BARBER SHOPS
S. Jones 2064 Ridge Ave.

TAVERNS
Wander Inn—18th & Federal St.
Musical Bar—9th & Columbia Ave.
Butler's Tavern—17th & Carpenter
Campbell's—18th & South St.
Loyal Grill—16th & South St.
Irene's—2200 Ridge Ave.
Lyons—12th & South St.
Blue Moon—1702 Federal St.
Butler's—2066 Ridge Ave.
Modern—11th & Fitzwater
Cotton Grove—1329 South St.
Wayside Inn—13th & Oxford St.

TAVERNS
Wonder Bar—19th & Montgomery
Lenox—Popular & Jessup Sts.
Fred's—1320 South St.
Preston's—4043 Market St.
Jimmy's—1508 Catherine St.
Casbah—39th & Fairmount St.
Dixon's—19th & Montgomery
Last Word—Haveriford & 51st St.
Cathrine's—1350 South St.
Postal Card—1504 South St.
Emerson's—15th & Bainbridge St.
Irene's—2200 Ridge Ave.
Brass Rail—2302 W. Columbia Ave.
Club 421—5601 Wyalusing Ave.

NIGHT CLUBS
Cotton Club—2106 Ridge Ave.
Cafe Society—1306 W. Columbia Ave.
Paradise—Ridge & Jefferson
Crystal Room—1935 W. Columbia Ave.
Progressive—1415 S. 20th St.
Zanzibar—1833 W. Columbia Ave.
Cotton Bowl—Master St. & 13th St.

GARAGES
Bond Motor Service—561 N. 20th St.
Booker Bros.—1811 Fitzwater St.
Garage—5732 Westminister Ave.
Garage—1823 Baingridge St.

SERVICE STATIONS
Dorsey Bros.—2009 Oxford St.

PITTSBURGH

HOTELS
Ave'—1538 Wylie Ave.
Bailey's—1308 Wylie Ave.
Bailey's—1533 Center Ave.
Colonial—Wylie & Fulton St.
Park—2215 Wylie Ave.
Potter—1304 Wylie Ave.
Palace—1545 Wylie Ave.

TOURIST HOMES
Godfrey House—1604 Cliff St.
B. Williams—1537 Howard St.
Mrs. William—5518 Claybourne St.

RESTAURANTS
Scotty's—2414 Center Ave.
Dearling's—2524 Wylie Ave.

READING

TOURIST HOMES
C. Dawson—441 Buttonwood St.

SCRANTON

TOURIST HOMES
Elvira R. King—1312 Linden St.
Mrs. J. Taylor—1415 Penn. Ave.
Mrs. C. Jenkins—610 N. Washington Avenue

SHARON HILL

TAVERNS
Dixie Cafe—Hook Rd.—Howard St.

71

IN PATRONIZING THESE PLACES

WASHINGTON
TOURIST HOMES
  Richardson—140 E. Chestnut St.
  B. T. Washington—32 N. College
RESTAURANTS
  W. Allen—N. Lincoln St.
  M. Thomas—N. Lincoln St.
BARBER SHOPS
  Yancey's—E. Spruce St.
NIGHT CLUBS
  Thomas Grill—N. Lincoln St.

WAYNE
NIGHT CLUB
  Plantation—Gulf Rd. & Henry Av.

WILLIAMSPORT
TOURIST HOMES
  Mrs. Edward Randall—605 Maple St.

WILKES BARRE
HOTELS
  Shaw—15 So. State St.

YORK
TOURIST HOMES
  Mrs. I. Grayson—32 W. Princess St.

RHODE ISLAND
NEWPORT
TOURIST HOMES
  Mrs. F. Jackson—28 Hall Ave.
  Mrs. L. Jacgson—35 Bath Road

PROVIDENCE
HOTELS
  Biltmore
TOURIST HOMES
  Mrs. M. A. Greene—85 Meeting St.
  W. W. Joyce—12 Benefit St.
  Dinah's—462-4 N. Main St.
  Hines—462-4 N. Main St.
TAVERN
  Dixieland—1049 Westminster St.
BEAUTY PARLORS
  B. Boyd's—43 Camp St.
  Geraldine's—205 Thurbus Ave.
  Marie Wells—18 Benefit St.
AUTOMOBILES
  George's—203 Plainfield St.

SOUTH CAROLINA
AIKEN
TOURIST HOMES
  C. F. Holland—1118 Richland Ave.
  M. H. Harrison—Richland Ave.
DRUGGIST
  Dr. C. C. Johnson—1432 Park Ave.

BEAUFORD
SERVICE STATIONS
  Peoples—D. Brofn, Prop.

CHARLESTON
TOURIST HOMES
  Mrs. Gladsen—15 Nassau St.
  Mrs. Mayes—82½ Spring St.
  L. Harleston—250 Ashley Ave.
  A. Serrant—99 Coming St.
TAVERNS
  Harleston's—250 Ashley Ave.

COLUMBIA
HOTELS
  Y. W. C. A.—1429 Park St.
  Taylor—1016 Washington St.
  Community Center—831 Hampton St.
TOURIST HOMES
  Mrs. S. H. Smith—929 Pine St.
  College Inn—1609 Harden Street
  Mrs. H. Cornwel—1713 Wayne
  Mrs. W. D. Chappelle—1301 Pine St.
  Beachum—2212 Gervais Street
  Mrs. J. P. Wakefield—1323 Heidt
  Mrs. S. H. Smith—929 Pine St.
RESTAURANTS
  Green Leaf—1117 Wash. St.
  Magnolia—2108 Gervais
  Savoy—Old Winnsboro Rd.
  Waverly—2315 Gervais St.
  White Way—2330 Gervais
  Cozy Inn—1509 Harden St.
  Mom's—1005 Washington St.
  Treye's—2103 Gervais St.
  Brown's—1014 Lady St.
BEAUTY PARLORS
  Amy's—1125½ Washington St.
  Obbie's—1119½ Washington St.
BARBER SHOPS
  Holman's—2138 Gervais St.
  Stratfords—1003½ Washington St.
  Macks—1110 Harden St.
TAVERNS
  Taylor's—Broad River Rd.
  Mrs. I. Goodum—922 Harden St.
NIGHT CLUBS
  Chauffer's—2314 Pendleton
ROAD HOUSES
  Macks—1110 Harden St.
SERVICE STATIONS
  A. W. Simkins—1331 Park St.
  Waverly—2200 Taylor St.
  Caldwell's—Oak & Taylor Sts.
GARAGES
  Johnson's—1609 Gregg St.
TAXICABS
  Blue Ribbon—1072 Washington St.
DRUG STORES
  Counts—1105 Washington Street

PLEASE MENTION "THE GREEN BOOK"

CHERAW
TOURIST HOMES
  Mrs. M. B. Robinson—211 Church St.
  Mrs. Maggie Green—Church St.
RESTAURANT
  Gate Grill—2nd Street
  Watson—2nd Street
TAVERN
  College Inn—2nd St.
ROAD HOUSE
  Hill Top—Society Hill Road
NIGHT CLUB
  Rommie's—High Street
BARBER SHOPS
  Imperial—2nd Street
BEAUTY SHOPS
  Bell's—Huger St.
SERVICE STATION
  Motor Inn—2nd Street

FLORENCE
TOURIST HOMES
  Mrs. B. Wright—1004 E. Cheeve St.
  J. McDonald—501 S. Irby St.

GEORGETOWN
TOURIST HOMES
  Mrs. R. Anderson—424 Broad
  Mrs. D. Atkinson—811 Duke
  Jas. Becote—118 Orange
  T. W. Brown—Merriman & Emanuel
  Mrs. A. A. Smith—317 Emanuel

GREENVILLE
HOTELS
  Imperial—8 Nelson St.
  Liberty—18 Spring St.
TOURIST HOMES
  Miss M. J. Grimes—210 Mean St.
  Mrs. W. H. Smith—212 John St.
RESTAURANTS
  Fowlers—16 Spring St.
BEAUTY PARLORS
  Broadway—11 Spring St.
BARBER SHOPS
  Broadway—8 Spring St.
DRUG STORES
  Gibb's—Broad & Fall St.

MULLENS
HOTELS
  283 W. Front St.
  Ace Hi—148 Front St.
TOURIST HOMES
  E. Calhoun's—535 N. Smith St.
RESTAURANTS
  Ace Hi—148 Front St.
BEAUTY PARLORS
  Bessie Pitts'—Smith St.
BARBER SHOPS
  Noham Ham—Front St.

NIGHT CLUBS
  Calhoun Nite Club—535 Smith St.
ROAD HOUSES
  Kate Odom—76 H'way
SERVICE STATIONS
  Ed. Owins'—Front St.
GARAGES
  C. B. Pegues—76 H'way

ORANGEBURG
DRUG STORES
  Danzler—121 W. Russell St.

SPARTANBURG
TOURIST HOMES
  Mrs. O. Jones—255 N. Dean St.
  Mrs. L. Johnson—307 N. Dean
RESTAURANTS
  Beatty—N. View
  Mrs. M. Davis—S. Wofford
  Howard's—415 S. Liberty St.
BEAUTY PARLORS
  Harmon—221 N. Dean St.
  Callaham—226 N. Dean St.
  Clowney's—445 S. Liberty St.
BARBER SHOPS
  R. Browning—122 Short Wofford
TAVERNS
  Moonlight—N. Vito & Chasander
  Victory—Union Highway
NIGHT CLUBS
  Club Paradise—491 S. Liberty
SERVICE STATIONS
  Collins—398 S. Liberty St.
  South Side—S. Liberty St.
  Magnolia—217 Magnolia St.
TAXICABS
  Collin's—389 S. Liberty St.

SUMTER
TOURIST HOMES
  Mrs. Julia E. Byrd—504 N. Main
  Edmonia Shaw—206 Manning Ave.
  C. H. Bracey—210 W. Oakland
TAVERNS
  Steve Bradford—N. Main St.
SERVICE STATIONS
  Esso Gas Station
DRUG STORES
  Peoples—5 W. Liberty St.

SOUTH DAKOTA
ABERDEEN
HOTELS
  Alonzo Ward—S. Main St.
RESTAURANTS
  Virginia—303 S. Main St.
BEAUTY PARLORS
  Marland—321 S. Main St.

73

IN PATRONIZING THESE PLACES

BARBER SHOPS
Olson—103½ S. Main St.
SERVICE STATIONS
Swanson—H'way 12 & Main Sts.
GARAGES
Spaulding—S. Lincoln St.
Wallace—S. Lincoln St.

PIERRE
TOURIST CAMPS
U. S. No. 14 (Inquire)

SIOUX FALLS
TOURIST HOMES
Mrs. J. Moxley—915 N. Main
Chamber of Commerce—131 S. Phillips Ave.
(Inquire)

TENNESSEE
BRISTOL
HOTELS
Palace—210 Front St.
TOURIST HOMES
A. D. Henderson—301 McDowell

CHATTANOOGA
HOTELS
Y. M. C. A.—793 E. 9th St.
Lincoln—1101 Carter St.
Martin—204 E. 9th St.
Peoples—1104 Carter St.
TOURIST HOMES
Mrs. J. Baker—843 E. 8th St.
Mrs. E. Brown—1129 E. 8th St.
Mrs. D. Lowe—803 Fairview Ave.
Y. W. C. A.—839 E. 8th St.
J. Carter—1022 E. 8th St.
RESTAURANTS
Chief—215 W. 9th St.
BEAUTY PARLORS
May's—208 E. 9th Street
SERVICE STATIONS
Mann Bros.—528 E. 9th St.
GARAGES
Volunteer—E. 9th St. & Lindsay
TAXICABS
Simms—915 University Ave.

CLARKSVILLE
HOTELS
Central—535 Franklin St.
RESTAURANTS
Foston's—851 College St.
TOURIST HOMES
Mrs. H. Northington—717 Main St.
Mrs. Kate Stewart—500 Poston St. (Blk)
Black & White—S. Clarksville St.
BARBER SHOPS
Wilson's—900 Franklin St. (Blk).

BEAUTY PARLORS
Johnson's—10th St.

KNOXVILLE
HOTELS
Y. W. C. A.—329 Temperance St.
Brownlow—219 E. Vine St.
Hartford—219 E. Vine St.
TOURIST HOMES
N. Smith—E. Vine St.
Walker's—E. Church St.

LEXINGTON
TOURIST HOMES
C. Timberlake—Holly St.

MEMPHIS
HOTELS
Clarke—144 Beale Ave.
Travelers—347 Vance
Mitchells—160 Hernando St.
Marquette—406 Mulberry St.
RESTAURANTS
The Parkview—516 N. 3rd St.
Bob's—195 S. 3rd St.
Scott's—368 Vance Ave.
Davidson's—345 S. 4th St.
Bessie's—338 Vance Ave.
Moonlight—900 S. Landerdale
BEAUTY PARLORS
Chiles'—341 Beale Ave.
BEAUTY SCHOOLS
Burchitts'—201 Hernando St.
Superior—1550 Florida Ave.
Johnson—316 S. 4th St.
TAILORS
Parks—697 Landerdale
DRUG STORES
So. Memphis—907 Florida Ave.

MURFREESBORO
TOURIST HOMES
Mrs. M. E. Howland—439 E. State
R. Moore—University & State St.

NASHVILLE
HOTELS
Carver—1122 Charlotte Ave.
Y. M. C. A.—4th & Charlotte Aves.
Carver Courts—White's Creek Pike
Y. W. C. A.—436 5th Ave. N.
Bryant—500 8th Ave. S.
Y. M. C. A.—436-5th Ave., N.
Fred Douglas—501 4th Ave. N.
TOURIST HOMES
Mrs. C. James—1902 18th St. N.
BEAUTY PARLORS
Queen of Sheba—1503 14th Ave. N.
Queen of Shebra—1503 14th Ave. N.
Estelle—405 Charlotte Ave.
RESTAURANTS
Dew Drop Inn—2514 Booker St.
Black Hawk—1124 Cedar St.
Martha's—309 Cedar St.

PLEASE MENTION "THE GREEN BOOK"

BARBER SHOPS
'Y'—34 4th Ave. N.
BEAUTY PARLORS
Myrtles—2423 Eden St.

TEXAS
ABILENE
TAVERNS
Hammond Cafe—620 Plum St.

AMARILLO
HOTELS
Mayfair—119 Van Buren St.
RESTAURANTS
Murphy Crain—400 W. 3rd St.
BEAUTY PARLORS
Mal-Ber School—116 Harrison St.
ROAD HOUSES
Working Man's Club—202 Harrison

AUSTIN
TOURIST HOMES
Mrs. J. W. Frazier—810 E. 13th St.
Mrs. J. W. Duncan—1214 E. 7th St.
Mrs. W. M. Tears—1203 E. 12th St.
Porter's—1315 E. 12th St.

BEAUMONT
TOURIST HOMES
Mrs. B. Rivers—730 Forsythe St.
RESTAURANTS
Long Bar-B-Q—539 Forsythe St.

CORPUS CHRISTIE
RESTAURANTS
Avalon—1510 Ramirez
Skylark—1216 N. Staples
Liberty—1406 N. Alemeda
Blue Willow—806 Winnebago
Little Aisle—1530 Ramirez
Square Deal—810 Winnebago
Savoy—1007 N. Taneahua
Royal—1222 N. Staples St.
Fortuna—1307 N. Staples St.
BEAUTY PARLORS
Johnson's—1405 Chipito St.
Edna's—921 San Rankin
Just-a-Mere—901 Parker St.
Mitchell's—1519 Ramirez St.
BARBER SHOPS
Steen's—1303 N. Alameda St.
NIGHT CLUBS
Alabam—1503 Ramirez
Elite—1216 N. Staples St.
LIQUOR STORES
Pier—821 Winnebago St.
Savoy—1220 N. Staples St.
TAILORS
Burley's—1223 N. Alameda St.
McIntyre's—1426 Ramirez

CORSICANA
TOURIST HOMES
Rev. Conner—E. 4th Ave.
Robert Lee—712 E. 4th
RESTAURANTS
Early Birds Cafe—220 E. 5th Ave.
BARBER SHOPS
Mrs. Dellum—117 E. 5th Ave.

DALLAS
HOTELS
Grand Terrace—Boll & Juliett
Lewis—302½ N. Central St.
Powell—3115 State St.
Y. M. C. A.—2700 Flora St.
Y. W. C. A.—3525 State St.
Hall's—1825½ Hall St.
Lone Star—3118 San Jacinto St.
RESTAURANTS
Beaumont Barbeque—1815 Orange
Tommie & Fred's—Washington & Thomas A.
Davis—6806 Lemmon Ave.
Palm Cafe—2213 Halls St.
BEAUTY PARLORS
S. Brown's—1721 Hall St.
BARBER SHOPS
Washington's—3205 Thomas Ave.
TAVERNS
Hall St.—1804 Hall St.
NIGHT CLUBS
Regal—3216 Thomas Ave.
GARAGES
Givens—2201 Leonard Ave.
DRUG STORE
Smith's—2221 Hall St.

EL PASO
HOTELS
Hotel Murray—214-224 S. Mesa Ave.
Phillips Manor—704 S. Vrain St.
Jordan's—104 Kemp St.
Daniel Hotel—413 S. Oregon St.
TOURIST HOMES
A. Winston—3205 Almeda St.
Mrs. S. W. Stull—511 Tornillo
C. Williams—1507 Wyoming St.
L. Walker—2923 E. San Antnio
E. Phillips—704 S. St. Vrain St.
TAVERNS
Daniel's—403 S. Orange St.
DRUG STORES
Donnel—3201 Nanzana St.

FORT WORTH
HOTELS
Del Rey—901 Jones St.
Jim—413-15 E. Fifth St.
TOURIST HOMES
Evan's—1213 E. Terrell St.

75

IN PATRONIZING THESE PLACES

RESTAURANTS
  Y. M. C. A.—1604 Jones St.
  Green Leaf—315 E. 9th St.
BEAUTY PARLORS
  Dickerson's—1015 E. Rosedale
SERVICE STATIONS
  South Side—1151 New York St.

GALVESTON
HOTELS
  Oleander—421½ 25th St.
RESTAURANT
  Mitchell's—417 25th St.
TOURIST HOMES
  G. H. Freeman—1414 29th St.
  Mrs. J. Pope—2824 Ave. M
  Cotton's—2907 Ave. L
TAVERNS
  Gulf View—28th & Blvd. Houston

HOUSTON
HOTELS
  Y. M. C. A.—1217 Bagby St.
  Y. W. C. A.—506 Louisiana St.
  Cooper's—1011 Dart St.
  Dowling—3111 Dowling St.
RESTAURANTS
  Eva's—1617 Dowling St.
BEAUTY PARLORS
  School & Parlor—222 W. Dallas
  Lou Lillie's—2714 Lee St.
BARBER SHOP
  —Harris—508 Louisiana St.
TAVERNS
  Welcome Cafe—2409 Pease Ave.
LIQUOR STORE
  Joe's—2506 Posto......ce
DRUG STORES
  Langford's—3026 Pierce St.
  Lion's—618 Prarie & Louisiana

MARSHALL
TOURIST HOMES
  Rev. Bailey—1103 W. Grand Ave.

MEXIA
HOTELS
  Carleton—1 W. Commerce St.
RESTAURANTS
  Mrs. M. Carroll—109 N. Belknap St.
BEAUTY PARLORS
  Mrs. B. Smith—N. Denton
BARBER SHOPS
  Mr. C. Carter—N. Belknap
TAVERNS
  R. Houston—N. Belknap
NIGHT CLUBS
  Payne's—West Side
ROAD HOUSES
  Jim Ransom—N. Carthage

SERVICE STATIONS
  Joe Brooks—107 N. Belknap
GARAGES
  Rev. T. Sparks—N. Belknap

MIDLAND
HOTELS
  Watson's Hotel
  Nuf Sed—Moody Addition
RESTAURANTS
  King Sandwich—Moody Addition
BEAUTY PARLORS
  Beauty Shop Jeanett
  Manbd-Nuf Sed—Moody Addition
BARBER SHOPS
  James Moore's—Moody Addition
SERVICE STATIONS
  Buster & Bates—Moody Addition
TAXICABS
  Johnnie's—Moody Addition

PARIS
HOTELS
  Brownrigg—88 N. 22nd St.
TOURIST HOMES
  Mrs. I. Scott—405-2nd St., N. E.
  Mrs. I. Scott—115 N. 22nd St.

PITTSBURG
TOURIST HOMES
  Bobbie's Place—Happy Hollow
  S. E. Crawford—Happy Hollow

SAN ANTONIO
HOTELS
  Dunbar
TOURIST HOMES
  Mundy—129 N. Mesquite St.
RESTAURANTS
  Cactus—524 E. Commerce St.
  Houston's—318 Hedges St.
  Rick's—602 S. Olive St.
  Mamie's—1833 E. Houston St.
BEAUTY SHOPS
  Optimistic—107 Anderson St.
  Jones—209 N. Swiss St.
  Band Box—135 N. Mesquite St.
  Mitts—115 N. Swiss St.
  Arritha's—113 Alabama St.
  R & B—126 N. Mesquite St.
  Hick's—1515 E. Houston St.
  Briscoe's—518 S. Pine St.
  Three Point—716 Virginia Blvd.
NIGHT CLUBS
  Wood Lake Country Club—New Sulphur Spring Road
  Zanzibar—108 N. Center St.
  Eldorado—1918 Wyoming St.
LIQUOR STORES
  Good's—106 Pearl St.
SERVICE STATIONS
  Eason's—1605 E. Houston
  Mitchell's—805 S. Hackberry St.

PLEASE MENTION "THE GREEN BOOK"

TYLER
TOURIST HOMES
 Mrs. Thomas—516 N. Border St.
 W. Langston—1010 N. Border

TEXARKANA
RESTAURANTS
 Casino—504 West 3rd Street
TAVERNS
 Dutahess Tea Room—1115 Capp St.
GARAGES
 Carl Hill—925 W. 20th St.

WACO
TOURIST HOMES
 B. Ashford—902 N. 8th St.
RESTAURANTS
 Kirk's—1114 S. First St.
 Harlem—123 Bridge
 Ideal—109 N. 2nd St.
ROAD HOUSE
 Golden Lilly—426 Clifton
TAVERN
 Green Tree—1325 S. 4th St.
BARBER SHOP
 Jockey Club—2nd & Franklin St.
BEAUTY PARLORS
 Cendivilla—107½ N. Second St.
 Cinderella—1133 Earle St.
 Ideal—1029 Taylor St.
 Earle St.—1113 Earle St.
 Mayfair—112 Bridge St.
 Modern—1406 Taylor St.
 Hine's—1125 Earle St.
 Murphy's—115 So. 2nd St.
SERVICE STATION
 Hick's—2nd & Franklin St.
GARAGE
 Malone—Clay & River St.

WAXAHACHIE
TOURIST HOMES
 Mrs. A. Nunn—413 E. Main St.
 Mrs. M. Johnson—427 E. Main St.
 Mrs. N. Lowe—418 E. Main St.
 Mrs. N. Jones—430 E. Main St.

WICHITA FALLS
HOTELS
 Bridges—404 Sullivan St.
TOURIST HOMES
 E. B. Jeffrey—509 Juarez St.
 T. S. Jackson—Park St.

UTAH

SALT LAKE CITY
HOTELS
 New Hotel J. H.—250 West So. Temple

VERMONT

BURLINGTON
HOTELS
 The Pates—86-90 Archibald St.
TOURIST HOMES
 George E. Braxton—191 Champlain St.
 Mrs. William Sharper—242 North St.
SERVICE STATIONS
 McDermotts Esso Station

MANCHESTER
HOTELS
 Clyde Blackwells

RUTLAND
TOURIST HOMES
 J. H. Meade—83 Strongs Ave.

NORTHFIELD
TOURIST HOMES
 Mrs. A. J. Cole—7 Sherman Ave.

VIRGINIA

ABINGTON
TOURIST HOMES
 H. Anderson—Near Fairgrounds E. End
 Mrs. N. Brown—High St.

ALEXANDRIA
TOURIST HOMES
 J. T. Holmes—803 Gibbon St.
 J. A. Barrett—724 Gibbon St.

BUCKROE BEACH
HOTELS
 Bay Shore
NIGHT CLUBS
 Club 400

CARET
TAVERNS
 Sessons Tavern

CHARLOTTESVILLE
TOURIST HOMES
 Virginia Inn—W. Main St.
 Chauffeur's Rest—129 Preston Ave.
 Alerander's—413 Dyce St.
BEAUTY PARLORS
 Apex—211 W. Main St.
BARBER SHOPS
 Jokers—North 4th St.

CHRISTIANBURG
HOTELS
 Eureka

DANVILLE
TOURIST HOMES
 Yancey's—320 Holbrook Street
 Mrs. M. K. Page—434 Holbrook St.
 Mrs. S. A. Overby—Holbrook St.

IN PATRONIZING THESE PLACES

DUNBARTON
TOURIST HOMES
 H. Jackson—Route No. 1, Box 322

FARMVILLE
TOURIST HOMES
 Wiley's—626 S. Main St.
RESTAURANTS
 Reid's—236 Main Street
TAVERNS
 Ried's—200 Block, Main St.
SERVICE STATIONS
 Clark's—Main Street

FREDERICKSBURG
HOTELS
 McGuire—521 Princess Ann St.
 Rappahannock—520 Princess St.

HAMPTON
RESTAURANTS
 Paul's—216 W. King St.
BARBER SHOP
 Paul's—154 Queen St.
BEAUTY PARLORS
 Tillie's—215 N. King St.
SERVICE STATION
 Lyle's—40 Armitsead Ave.
GARAGES
 Walton's—W. Mallory Ave.

HARRISONBURG
RESTAURANTS
 Frank's—145 E. Wolf St.

LEXINGTON
TOURIST HOMES
 The Franklin—9 Tucker St.
RESTAURANTS
 Washington—16 N. Main St.
TAVERNS
 Rose Inn—331 N. Main St.

LURAY
TOURIST HOMES
 Camp Lewis Mountain—Skyline Drive

LYNCHBURG
HOTELS
 Phyllis Wheatley YWCA—613 Monroe Street
 Manhattan—1001 Fifth St.
 Petersburg—66 Ninth St.
TOURIST HOMES
 Mrs. C. Harper—1109 8th St.
 Mrs. M. Thomas—919 Polk St.
 Mrs. Smith—504 Jackson
 Happyland Lake—812 5th Ave.
BEAUTY PARLORS
 Selma's—1002 5th St.

SERVICE STATIONS
 United—1016 Fifth St.

NATURAL BRIDGE
TOURIST HOMES
 Mountain View Cottage

NEWPORT NEWS
TOURIST HOMES
 Mrs. W. E. Barron—2123 Jefferson
 Mrs. W. R. Cooks—221 Marshall Ave.
 Thomas E. Reese—636-25th St.
TOURIST HOMES
 Mrs. W. Herndon—752 26th St.
 Mrs. C. Stephens—1909 Marshall Ave.
 J. H. Tallaferro—2206 Marshall Ave.
RESTAURANTS
 Tavern Rest—2108 Jefferson
BEAUTY PARLORS
 Rattrie's—300 Chestnut St.
SERVICE STATION
 Ridley's—Orcutt Ave. & 30th St.

NORFOLK
HOTELS
 Prince George—1757 Church St.
 Y. M. C. A.—729 Washington Ave.
 Ambrose—616 Brambleton Ave.

Phone 29554

TATUM'S INN
453 Brewer St.   Norfolk, Va.

MAKE THIS
YOUR HOME
AWAY FROM HOME

Open Day & Night

Rooms by Day or Night

Dining Room Service

W. M. Tatum, Prop.

TOURIST HOMES
 Mrs. S. Noble—725 Chaple St.

MRS. GEO. COLLETTE
                                923 Wood St.
ENJOY HOME COMFORTS
GARAGE ACCOMODATIONS
Tel. NOrfolk 27425

BEAUTY PARLORS
 Jordan's—526 Brambleton Ave.
 Vel-Ber St. Ann—1008 Church St.
 Yeargen's—1685 Church St.

PLEASE MENTION "THE GREEN BOOK"

TAVERNS
  Peoples—Church & Calvert Sts.
  Russell's—835 Church St.
SERVICE STATIONS
  Alston's—Cor. 20th & Church St.
  Mac's—1625 Church St.

PETERSBURG
HOTELS
  The Walker House—116 South

PHONE: CHESTER 3953

♦

COLBROOK INN

Rest In Home Surroundings

♦

GOOD FOOD

COMFORTABLE CABINS

♦

U. S. HIGHWAY NO. 1

8 Mi. N. of Petersburg

15 Mi. S. of Richmond

—♦—

W. E. BROOKS, Mgr.

NIGHT CLUBS
  Chatter Boy—143 Harrison St.

PHOEBUS
BARBER SHOPS
  118 S. Mallory St.

RICHMOND
HOTELS
  Slaughters—514 N. 2nd St.
  Harris—200 E. Clay St.
  Eggleston (Miller's)—2nd & Leigh St.
TOURIST HOMES
  Mrs. E. Brice—14 W. Clay St.
  Y. W. C. A.—515 N. 7th St.
  Jack's—on Rt. No. 1-6 m. N. of Richmond
RESTAURANTS
  Cora's—427 E. Leigh St.

BEAUTY PARLORS
  Rest-a-Bit—619 N. 3rd St.
BARBER SHOPS
  Wright's—412 E. Leigh St.
  Scotty's—505 N. 2nd St.
TAVERNS
  Market Inn—Washington Park
NIGHT CLUBS
  Terrace Club—1212 N. 26th St.
SERVICE STATIONS
  Cameron's—Brook Ave. & W. Clay St.
  Harris—400 N. Henry St.
  Little Lord's—410 N. 2nd St.
  Adam St.—523 N. Adams St.

ROANOKE
HOTELS
  Dumas—Henry St. N. W.
TOURIST HOMES
  Y. M. C. A.—23 Wells Ave. N. W.
  Y. W. C. A.—208 2nd St. N. W.
TAVERNS
  Tom's Place
  F & G—114 N. Henry St.
GARAGES
  Maple Leaf—High St. at Henry

SOUTH HILL
HOTELS
  Brown's—Melvin Brown, Prop.
  Groom's—John Groom, Prop.

STAUNTON
TOURIST HOMES
  Pannell's Inn—613 N. Augusta St.
  F. T. Jones—515 Baptist St.
RESTAURANTS
  Johnson's—301 N. Central Ave.

TAPPAHANNOCK
HOTELS
  McGuire's Inn—Marsh St.
TOURIST HOMES
  Way Side Inn—Main St.

WARRENTON
RESTAURANTS
  Bill's—5th Street
  Phil's—5th Street
TOURIST HOMES
  Lawson—227 Alexanderia Pike
BARBER SHOPS
  Walker's—5th Street
BEAUTY PARLORS
  Fowlers—123 N. 3rd St.
TAXICABS
  Joyner's—Phone 292
  Bland—Phone 430
  Parker's—Phone 491

IN PATRONIZING THESE PLACES

WINCHESTER
HOTELS
  Evans—224 Sharp St.
TOURIST HOMES
  Mrs. Joe Willis—N. Main St.
  Dunbar Tea Room—21 W. Hart St.
RESTAURANTS
  Ruth's—128 E. Cecil Street

WASHINGTON

EVERETT
TOURIST HOMES
  J. Samuels—2214 Wedmore Ave.
  Mrs. J. T. Payne—2912 Pacific
  Mrs. G. Samuels—3620 Hoyt Ave.

SEATTLE
HOTELS
  Atlas—420 Maynard St.
  Y. W. C. A.—102-21 North St.
  Green—711 Lane St.
  Idaho—505 Jackson St.
  Olympus—413 Maynard St.
  Dunbar—328 N. W. 5th St.
  Eagle—408½ Main St.
RESTAURANTS
  Evelyn Inn—2229 E. Madison Ave.
  Palm Garden—1040 Jackson St.
  Pacific—417 Maynard St.
  Paramount—518 Jackson St.
  Egyptian—2040 E. Madison St.
  Elite—428 - 21st Street
  Shanty Inn—110 12th Ave.
  Sid's—2330 E. Madison Ave.
  Cozy Inn—66 N. E. Broadway
  Victory—652 Jackson St.
ROAD HOUSE
  Rendezvous—Empire Highway 2½ Mile S.
BEAUTY PARLORS
  Pauline's—2221 E. Madison
  Modernistic—674 Jackson St.
  Streamline—1212 Jackson St.
  LaMode—2036 E. Madison St.
  Bert's—2301 E. Denny Way
  Ruth Whiteside—614 Jackson
BARBER SHOPS
  Hayes—2227 E. Madison St.
  Stockards—2032 E. Madison St.
NIGHT CLUBS
  Pltyhouse—1238 Main St.
LIQUOR STORES
  Jackson's—707 Jackson Street
TAVERNS
  Stoemer—2047 E. Madison St.
  Hill Top—1200 Jackson St.
  Sea Gull—673 Jackson St.
  Pacific Cafe—417 Maynard St.
  Lucky Hour—1315 Yesler Way

SERVICE STATIONS
  Richfield—707 Jackson
  Bob's—19th & E. Madison St.
  Burnham's—2211 E. Madison St.
  Moszee—19 E. Madison St.
DRUG STORES
  Bon-Rot—14th & Yesler St.
  Bishop's—507 Jackson St.
  Chikata—114 12th Ave.
  Madison—22nd & Madison
TAILORS
  Gilt Edge—611 Jackson St.

TACOMA
TOURIST HOMES
  Mrs. A Robinson—1906 S. "I" St.
  J. H. Carter—1017 S. Trafton St.
BEAUTY PARLORS
  Catherine's—1408 South "K" St.

YAKIMA
TOURIST HOMES
  H. C. Deering—508 S. Third St.
  Mrs. W. H. Jones—310 Third Ave.

WEST VIRGINIA

BECKLEY
HOTELS
  New Pioneer—340 S. Fayette St.
TOURIST HOMES
  Mrs. E. Morton—430 S. Fayette St.
RESTAURANTS
  Home Service—338½ S. Fayette St.
BEAUTY PARLORS
  Katie's Vanity—S. Fayette St.
  Fuqua's—Fuqua Bldg. S. Fayette
BARBER SHOPS
  Paynes—338 S. Fayette St.
  Simpson's—New Pioneer Hotel
NIGHT CLUBS
  Beckino Club—S. Fayette St.
  Chesterfield Club—New Pioneer Hotel
SERVICE STATIONS
  Moss—501 South Fayette Street
DRUG STORES
  Morton Drug—S. Fayette St.
TAXICABS
  Robertson's—Dial 6542
  Nuway—Dial 3301

BLUEFIELD
TOURIST HOMES
  Traveler's Inn—602 Raleigh St.

CHARLESTON
HOTELS
  Ferguson
TAVERNS
  White Front—1007 Washington St.
  Palace Cafe—910 Washington St.

PLEASE MENTION "THE GREEN BOOK"

HUNTINGTON

HOTELS
 The Ross House—911-8th Ave.
 Southern—921 8th Ave.
 Massey's—837 7th Ave.

TOURIST HOMES
 Mrs. R. J. Lewis—1412 10th Ave.
 Mrs. C. J. Barnett—810 7th Ave.

RESTAURANTS
 J. Gross—839 7th Ave.

BEAUTY PARLORS
 Louise's—821 19th St.

TAVERNS
 Monroe's—1616 8th Ave.
 The Alpha—1624 8th Ave.

SERVICE STATIONS
 Sterling—Cor. 12th St. & 3rd Ave.

GARAGE
 South Side—716 8th Ave.

PARKERSBURG

NIGHT CLUBS
 American Legion—812 Avery St.

WELCH

HOTELS
 Capehart—14 Virginia Ave.

WHEELING

TOURIST HOMES
 Mrs. W. Turner—114 12th St.
 Mrs. C. Early—132 12th St.
 R. Williams—1007 Chapline St.

RESTAURANTS
 Singelery—1043 Chapline St.

BEAUTY PARLORS
 Miss Hall—Chapline St.
 Miss Taylor—Chapline St.

NIGHT CLUBS
 American Legion—1516 Main St.
 Elks Club—1010 Chapline St.

WHITE SULPHUR SPRINGS

TOURIST HOMES
 Brook's—138 Church Street
 Haywood Place—Church St.

WISCONSIN

FOND DU LAC

TOURIST HOMES
 Mrs. E. Pirtle—45 E. 11th St.
 V. Williams—97 S. Seymour St.

OSHKOSH

TOURIST HOMES
 L. Shadd—37 King St.
 F. Pemberton—239 Liberty St.

WYOMING

CASPER

TOURIST HOMES
 Mrs. J. E. Edwards—347 N. Grant
 H. Keeling—331 N. Grant
 G. Anderson—320 N. Lincoln St.

CHEYENNE

HOTELS
 Barbeque Inn—622 W. 20th St.

TOURIST HOMES
 Mrs. L. Randall—612 W. 18th St.

RAWLING

YELLOW FRONT

111 EAST FRONT ST.

See The Golden West

Barbeque Served Every Day

Phone: 1195W

Robert Westbrook, Mgr.

ROCK SPRINGS

TOURIST HOMES
 Mrs. R. Collins—915 7th St.

THIS GUIDE

is Consulted Throughout

the Year

by Thousands of Travelers

—♦—

Are You

Represented?

ADVERTISING SOLICITORS

We have a few territories open for representatives. The opportunity is open to a fine energetic and ambitious man or woman.

There may be an opening in your territory sometime. Liberal Commissions. Write for particulars, state your qualifications.

VICTOR H. GREEN & CO.
200 West 135th Street
Room 215-A
New York 30, N. Y.

The Negro Travelers' Green Book

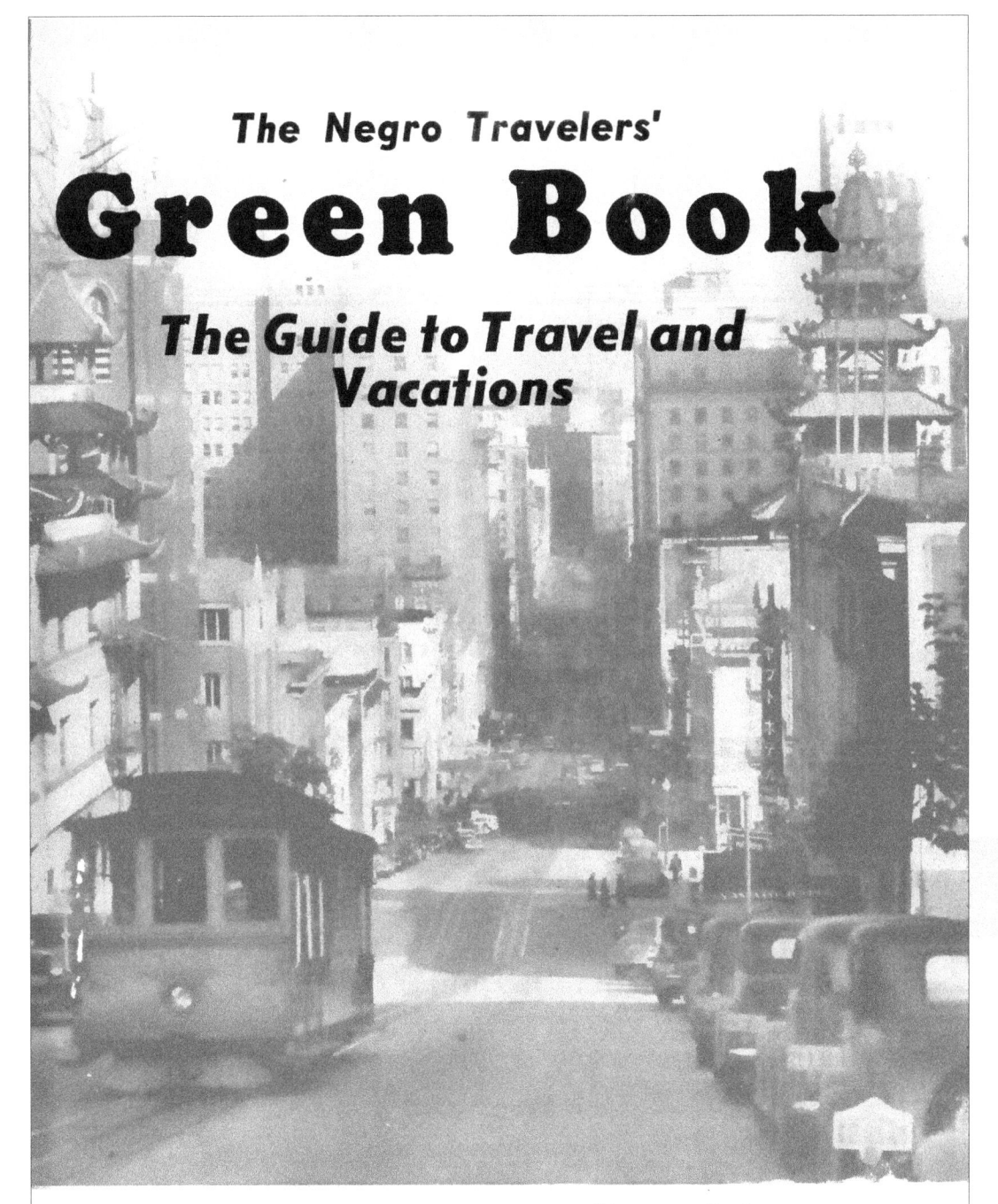

The Guide to Travel and Vacations

Travel-Wise People Travel by THE GREEN BOOK

For 16 years the guide used by experienced travelers.

Carry your GREEN Book with you — you may need it.

EASY MONEY FOR YOU!

You'll earn money—Yes, even if you've never tried before. Because people want to buy our guides. Never has there been a greater demand than now. — People don't know where to purchase them — We make it possible for you to make the sale. Join our agents staff now. Write for information on how to get started, so that you can make some easy money with little or no effort.

VICTOR H. GREEN & Co.
Publisher
200 West 135th St.
New York 30, N. Y.

A Chat With The Editor

TRAVELING is one of the large industries of this era. Millions of people hit the road as soon as the warm weather sets in. They want to get away from their old surroundings: to see—to learn how people live —to meet old and new friends.

In this era of the automobile, trains, buses, boats and fast flying air liners, we have an assortment of transportation which will take one to any place that they might wish to go. With all of these transportation facilities at hand, modern travel has brought thousands of people out of their homes to view the wonders of the world.

Thousands and thousands of dollars are spent each year in the various modes of transportation. Money spent like this brings added revenue to trades people throughout the country.

The white traveler for years has had no difficulty in getting accomodations, but with the Negro it has been different. He before the advent of Negro Travel Guides has had to depend on word of mouth and then sometimes accommodations weren't available. But now a days things are different—he has his own travel guide, that he can depend on for all the information that he wants and with a selection. Hence these guides have made traveling more popular and without running into embarrassing situations.

Since 1936, THE GREEN BOOK has been published yearly. A few years after its publication, THE GREEN BOOK was recognized as the official Negro Travel Guide by the United States Travel Bureau, a part of the Department of Commerce, which bureau has been closed, due to the lack of funds. By being such an important piece of literature, white business has also recognized its value and it is now in use by the Esso Standard Oil Co., The American Automobile Assn. and its affiliate automobile clubs throughout the country, other automobile clubs, air lines, travel bureaus, travelers aid, libraries and thousands of subscribers.

Hence we have filled one of our life's ambitions, to give the Negro a travel guide that will be of service to him, by this method we have established ourselves in the minds of the traveling public. THE GREEN BOOK is known from coast to coast as the source of information for travel and vacations.

VICTOR H. GREEN,
Editor & Publisher

THE NEGRO TRAVELERS' GREEN BOOK

The Guide to Travel and Vacations

VICTOR H. GREEN, Editor & Publisher

IN THIS ISSUE

Motel Section	5	Travel Section	8
San Francisco, Calif.	11	Sightseeing in New York	47
Reservation Bureau	36	Travel Bureau	50

Vacation Section, 77

INDEX

Alabama	8	New York	44
Arkansas	8	New Hampshire	51
Arizona	8	New Mexico	51
California	10	Nevada	51
Colorado	20	North Carolina	52
Connecticut	21	Ohio	54
Delaware	21	Oklahoma	57
Washington, D.C.	22	Oregon	58
Florida	22	Pennsylvania	58
Georgia	24	Rhode Island	60
Illinois	25	South Carolina	60
Idaho	26	South Dakota	62
Indiana	26	Tennessee	62
Iowa	27	Texas	63
Kansas	28	Utah	66
Kentucky	29	Vermont	66
Louisiana	30	Virginia	66
Maine	31	Washington (State)	68
Maryland	32	West Virginia	69
Massachusetts	32	Wisconsin	70
Michigan	34	Wyoming	72
Minnesota	35	Alaska	72
Mississippi	35	Canada	75
Missouri	37	Bermuda	75
Nebraska	39	Mexico	75
New Jersey	39	Caribbean	75

THE NEGRO TRAVELERS' GREEN BOOK, published yearly by Victor H. Green & Co., 200 West 135th St., New York 30, N. Y. ADVERTISING RATES, write to the publishers, last forms close Dec. 1. We reserve the right to reject any advertising which does not conform to our standards. SUBSCRIPTIONS: Prices in the United States, $1.25 post paid; Foreign (Outside the U. S.) $1.50 in advance. RUSH ORDERS: send 9c, first class; air mail, 18c; Special delivery, 29c. Copyrighted 1953 by Victor H. Green.

Dreams or Problems Worry You? Send in Your Dream or Problem Today!

Prof. Diamond's DREAM Formula

Opportunity . . .

At Last It's Here!

A Sure Way!

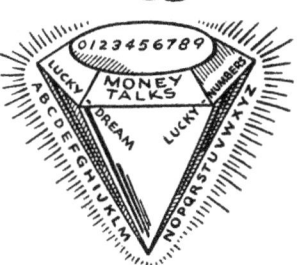

Respect Your Dreams. They May Mean Wealth Success Happiness

INTRODUCTION

For many years men have traveled all over the world trying to find an accurate method of analyzing life's DREAMS and PROBLEMS. Unfortunately, few have succeeded in discovering the secrets of DREAMS and the PROBLEMS of life.

Not only do I analyze your DREAM, which guides your every move in life, but I also solve your PROBLEMS by use of the AMAZING DREAM FORMULA. We have helped thousands with their DREAMS and PROBLEMS.

Mail in your DREAM or PROBLEM together with $1.00 to Prof. DIAMOND P. O. Box 172, G. P. O. New York 1, N. Y. When you mail in your DREAM or PROBLEM, you automatically become a member of the DIAMOND DREAM CLUB, which entitles you to many FREE benefits. The DREAM FORMULA will not fail you.

Send in for information regarding Prof. DIAMOND'S DREAM CHART, which reveals the secret numbers you live under, as compounded by the DIAMOND DREAM FORMULA.

Distributed and Copyrighted 1949 by Prof. Diamond, P.O. Box 172, G.P.O., N.Y.C.

PHOTO CREDITS: First & fourth covers, also pages 12, 13, 15, 16, 17 by courtesy of The Californians, Inc., San Francisco, California.

U. S. BOND'S MOTEL, MADISON, ARKANSAS

On Highway 70, 40 miles west of Memphis, Tennessee, 100 miles East of Little Rock, Ark, ½ mile west of Madison, Arkansas. Strictly Modern baths, Beauty Rest mattresses, built-in wall furnaces air-conditioned and ventilated fans. Room service. Meals served in rooms. Phone No. 1334J1

The South's finest and one of America's best Motels for Colored. Garages in rear.

The Green Book Motel Guide

We herewith supply you with these listings of Colored and White Motel owners throughout the United States. They are all first class motels and desire your patronage. Each place has been contacted. If in applying for accommodations you are refused, kindly notify us about same, giving us the reasons, we shall contact this particular place and remove their listing. DON'T BE DISAPPOINTED—make advance reservations. State date of arrival, number of persons in your party—adults or children and number of single or double beds required. After confirmation of reservation, send one nights lodging to be certain reservations will be held.

ARKANSAS

HOT SPRINGS
McKenzie Unique, 301 Henry St.

MADISON
Bond's, Rt. 70 1/" Mile West of Madison (see ad. opposite page)

ARIZONA

KINGMAN
White Rock, Rt. 66, East end of Town

CALIFORNIA

LOS ANGELES
Roberson's, 2111 E. Imperial Blvd
Johnson's, 1186 So. Wilmington Western, Cor. W. 37th St. & Western Ave.
Thomas, 2050 W. Jefferson Blvd.
Haye's, 960 E. Jefferson Blvd.

NEEDLES
El Adobe, Rt. 66

COLORADO

MONTROSE
Davis Auto Court

CONNECTICUT

POMFRET
The Willow Inn, Rt. 44, ½ Mile West of Conn. Rt. 101 & U. S. 44

DELAWARE

REBOBOTH BEACH
Mallory Cabins, Phone 8991
Rehoboth Ave. Ext.

FLORIDA

FERNANDINA
American Beach

JACKSONVILLE
A. L. Lewis, P. O. Box 660

OCALA
Carmen Manor Hotel
1044 W. Broadway St.

EBONY MOTEL
Kings Road at Cleveland St.
New, Modern - Air Conditioned
Steam Heat - Private Bath
Located near Railway and Bus Stations, Amusements, Business
On Highway No. 1
REASONABLE RATES
JACKSONVILLE, FLA.

IOWA

CEDAR RAPIDS

MOTEL SEPIA
CECIL & EVELYN REED, Props.
Clean, Modern, Air Conditioned
On Coast to Coast Highways 30 & 150
3 Miles East of Cedar Rapids
CEDAR RAPIDS, IOWA
Phone: 9736 or 3-8881

Please Mention the "Green Book"

ILLINOIS
FULTON
Twin Oaks, Rt. 30, 4 Miles east of Fulton

INDIANA
FURNESSVILLE
Roby's Country Club, Rt. 20
GARY
Roby's Country Club
20 miles N. E. of Gary

NEVADA
ELKO
Louis Motel
2 Miles West of Elko

OKLAHOMA
TULSA
Avalon Motel
2411-13 E. Aapache St.
Phone: 6-2572

PENNSYLVANIA
WASHINGTON
Motel Todd,
12½ Linn Avenue
Phone 4972
POTTSTOWN
Cedar Haven, Pa. Rt. 422, bet. Reading & Pottstown

TEXAS

RITZ MOTEL

The South's Finest

Coffee Shop

REFRIGERATED AIR CONDITIONING

Vented Heat - Telephone & Television
Innerspring Mattresses
Modern Furniture

All Tile Shower with Glass Door

Phone Circle 4-6607
2958 EAST COMMERCE ST.
SAN ANTONIO, TEXAS

MARSHALL
La Casa Motel, Route 5, Box 32
La Casa, Rt. 80, 2 Miles West
TEXARKANA
Sunset, 1508 North St.
SAN ANTONIO
Ritz Motel & Coffee Shop
2958 E. Commerce
Phone: Circle 4-6607

KANSAS
BOGUE
Tourist Court, Junction Rt. U. S. 24
STOCKTON
L. D. Fuller

MAINE
ROBBINSTON
Brook's Bluff Cottage, Rt. 1, 12 Miles E. of Calais
DIXFIELD
Marigold Cabins, Rt. 2 10 Miles East of Rumford

MASSACHUSETTS
TRAILER PARK
Mrs. Mary B. Pina, 26 Heed St.
WAREHAM
Mrs. L. Anderson, 294 Elm St.

MICHIGAN
VANDALIA
Copper, Rt. M 60, bet. Chicago & Detroit

NEW JERSEY
SOUTH PLEASANTVILLE
Fuller's, Rt. 9, Rt. 4
ASBURY PARK
Waverley, 138 DeWitt Ave.

NEW YORK STATE
ALBANY
White Birch Motel. Rt. 9, 15 Miles N. of Albany

NEW HAMPSHIRE
RUMNEY DEPOT
Whispering Pines, Rt. 25, 8 Miles North of Plymouth

NEW MEXICO
VADO
Fuller's, 3 N 1, Highway 80
LORDSBURG

HIGHTOWER'S MOTEL
Modern with Private Bath
Lunch Room
Located 1 mile east of Lordsburg,
Routes 70 & 80
Direct Route to and from the West Coast
Phone: 243-R-3   Rochester & Leona
LORDSBURG, N. M.

in Patronizing These Places

NORTH CAROLINA
HAMLET
C. B. Covington, North Yard

SOUTH CAROLINA
MYRTLE BEACH
MOTOR COURT
Fitzgerald's, Carver St.
Charles' Place
DARLINGTON
Mable's Motel

SOUTH DAKOTA
CUSTER
Rocket Court, 211 Custer Ave. on U. S. Rt. 16 & 85
WATERTOWN
5th Ave. & 212 Motel, U. S. Rt. 212

VIRGINIA
PETERSBURG
Lord Nelson, Rts. 1 & 301, bet. Petersburg & Richmond
ROANOKE
Pine Oak Inn, Rt. 460
Bet. Salem & Roanoke

WEST VIRGINIA
CHARLESTON
Hall's Park, U. S. Rt. 60
West of Charleston

EXPLANATION

No travel Guide is perfect! The changing conditions as all know, contribute to this condition, particularly in the United States.

The listings in this Guide are carefully checked and, despite this, past experiences have shown that our minute inspection had failed to notice errors which would be an inconvenience to the traveler. Therefore, at this point may we emphasize that these listings are printed just as they are presented to us and we would like your cooperation and understanding, that the publishers are not responsible for miscalculations or errors after this check has been made.

We appreciate letters from you, our patrons, donating advice and addresses of places not listed herein, that would be in accord with our level. We also welcome adverse criticism, in that, it might improve our standards, and, in the end, afford more comfortable conditions for you and others.

This Guide Book is not sold on newsstands but in bookstores. They make appreciative gifts to friends and neighbors. Inasmuch as the sale of these Guide Books depend mostly upon the friend-to-friend oral advertising system, it would be particularly interesting if more of our patrons would pass the word along concerning our "Green Book."

For further information concerning this matter you may contact our agents or the publishers: Victor H. Green & Co., 200 West 135th St., Room 215A, New York 30, N. Y.

Please Mention the "Green Book"

ALABAMA
BIRMINGHAM
HOTELS
Dunbar, 323 N. 17th St.
Fraternal, 1614 4th Ave. N.
Palm Leaf, 328½ N. 18th St.
New Home, 1718½ 4th Ave.

GADSDEN
TOURISTS HOMES
Mrs. A. Sheperd, 1324 4th Ave.
Mrs. J. Simons, 233 N. 6th St.

MOBILE
HOTELS
Blue Heaven, 361 Morton St.
TOURISTS HOMES
Midway Traders, 107 N. Dearborn
E. Reed, 950 Lyons St.
E. Jordan, 256 N. Dearborn St.
F. Wildins 254 N. Dearborn St.

MONTGOMERY
HOTELS
Hotel Ben Moore
Cor. High & Jackson Sts.
Ben Moore, Cor. High & Jackson
Douglass, 121 Monroe Ave.
TAVERNS
Douglas, 121 Monroe Ave.

SHEFFIELD
HOTELS
McClain, 19th St.
TOURISTS HOMES
Mrs. Mattie Herron, 1003 E. 19th St.

TUSCALOOSA
TOURISTS HOMES
Mrs. Clopton, 1516 25th Ave.

ARIZONA
DOUGLAS
TOURIST HOMES
Faustina Wilson, 1002 16th St.

NOGALES
RESTAURANTS
Bell's Cafe, 325 Morley Ave.

PHOENIX
HOTELS
Paducah Hotel
14 No. 6th Street
Winston Inn
1342 E. Jefferson St.
TOURIST HOMES
Swindall's Tourist Home
1021 E. Washington St.
Louis Jordan, 2118 Violet Dr. E.
Mrs. L. Stewart, 1134 E. Jefferson
Gardener's, 1229 E. Washington St.
Mrs. Bea. Jackson, 811 E. Monroe
RESTAURANTS
Alhambia, 1246-48 E. Wash. St.
Jefferson, 1303 E. Jefferson St.
Tapp's, 209 W. Hadley St.
Rose, 947 W. Watkins Rd.
BEAUTY PARLORS
Thelma's, 33 So. 1st Ave.
C. Jackson, 1238 E. Madison St.
BARBER SHOPS
Hagler's, 345 E. Jefferson
Bryant's, 620 S. 7th Ave.
TAVERNS
Vaughn's, 1248 E. Washington Ave.
SERVICE STATIONS
Super, 1245 Washington St.
GARAGES
DRUG STORES
Johnson's, 1140 E. Washington St.
LIQUOR STORES
Broadway, 1606 East Broadway

TUCSON
TOURIST HOMES
Mrs. Louise Pitts, 722 N. Perry St.

YUMA
HOTELS
Brown's, 196 N. Main St.
TOURIST HOMES
Mrs. John A. Gordon, 192 N. 5th

ARKANSAS
ARKADELPHIA
HOTELS
Hill's, 1601 W. Pine St.
TOURISTS HOMES
Mrs. B. Dedman, W. Caddo St.
Mrs. L. Cooper, W. Pine St.
RESTAURANTS
Hill's, River St.
BARBER SHOPS
Scott's, 6th & Clay St.
Richie's Upright, 16th St.

BRINKLEY
TOURISTS HOMES
Davis, 709 S. Main St.

CAMDEN
HOTELS
Summer Hotel
754½ Adams St. S.W.
TOURIST HOMES
Mrs. Benj. Williams, N. Main St.
Mrs. Hugh Hill, S. Main St.
RESTAURANTS
Jim Summers, 719 S. Main St.
TAVERNS
Daniel's, North Adams St.
Jones, 309 Monroe St.
TAXI CABS
Bradford, Phone 6-9396
LIQUOR STORES
Summers, 715½ S. Main St.

8

in Patronizing These Places

SOUTH CAMDEN
ROAD HOUSES
Henry Hanson, 415 Progress S. E.

EL DORADO
HOTELS
Green's, 303 Hill St.
TOURISTS HOMES
C. W. Moore, 5th & Lincoln Ave.
Dr. Dunning, 7th & Columbia Ave.
SERVICE STATIONS
Davidson's

FAYETTEVILLE
TOURIST HOMES
Mrs. S. Manuel, 313 Olive St.
N. Smith, 259 E. Center St.

FORT SMITH
HOTELS
Ullery Inn, 719 N. 9th St.
TOURISTS HOMES
Mrs. Clara E. Oliver
906 North 9th St.
Mrs. Clara E. Oliver, 906 N. 9th St.

HOPE
HOTELS
Lewis-Wilson, 217 E. 3rd St.
RESTAURANTS
Green Leaf, Old 67 Hiway
BEAUTY PARLORS
Unique, 501 S. Hazel St.
BARBER SHOPS
Yeager's, 401 S. Hazel St.
SERVICE STATIONS
Tarfly's Esso, 104 E. 3rd St.
GARAGES
Nun-McDowell, 3rd and Walnut St.
ROAD HOUSES
Fred's, 4th and Hazel Sts.

HOT SPRINGS
HOTELS
Crittenden, 314 Cottage St.
TOURISTS HOMES
New Edmondson, 243 Ash St.
Barabin Villa, 717 Pleasant St.
J. W. Rife, 347½ Malvern Ave.
Mrs. N. Fletcher, 416 Pleasant Ave.
Mrs. C. C. Wilson, 232 Garden St.
BEAUTY SCHOOLS
Hollywood, 310 Church St.
SANITARIUMS
Pythian Baths, 415½ Malvern Ave.

LITTLE ROCK
HOTELS
The Marquette, 522 W. 9th St.
Graysonia, 809 Gaines St.
New Vincent, 522½ West 9th St.
Tucker's, 701½ W. 9th St.
Honeycut, 816 West 9th St.
Charmaine, 820 W. 14th St.

TOURIST HOMES
Mrs. T. Thomas, 1901 High St.
RESTAURANTS
Lafayette, 904 State St.
College, 16th & Bishop
Johnson's, 610 W. 9th St.
DeLuxe, 724 W. 9th St.
Tucker's, 919 Victory St.
C & C, 522½ W. 9th St.
Rainbow, 620 W. 9th St.
Ed's, 1015 Gaines St.
BEAUTY PARLORS
Velvatex, 1004 State St.
Velvia, 814 Chester Ave.
Woods, 1523 High St.
Woods, 16th & High St.
Sue's, 919 W. 9th St.
Fontaine's, 714 West 9th St.
NIGHT CLUBS
Lafayette, 9th & State St.
BARBER SHOPS
Century, 608 W. 9th St.
Elite, 622 W. 9th St.
Fontaine's, 710 West 9th St.
Century, 610 West 9th St.
Woods, 1523 High St.
Friendly, 911 Victory St.
TAVERNS
Majestic, 708 W. 9th St.
LIQUOR STORES
Ritz, 1511 Wright Ave.
Jones, 528 W. 9th St.
Victory, 528 West 9th St.
GARAGES
Lee's, 1401 High St.
TAILORS
Metropolitan, 618 West 9th St.
Crenshaw, 709 W. 9th St.
Ideal, 1005 Apperson St.
SERVICE STATIONS
Lee's, 1401 High St.
Anderson, 8th & State St.
Wrecker, 9th & Gaines St.
GARAGES
Fosters, 1400 W. 10th St.
DRUG STORES
Floyd, 602 W. 9th St.
Children's, 700 W. 9th St.

NORTH LITTLE ROCK
HOTELS
Oasis, 1311 E. 3rd St.
TOURIST HOMES
De Lux Court, 2720 E. Broadway
RESTAURANTS
Jim's, 908 Cedar St. N. L. R.
Nov-Vena, 1101 E. 6th St.
ROAD HOUSES
Oasis, 1311 East 3rd St.

PINE BLUFF
HOTELS
Pee Kay, 300 E. 3rd St.
TOURIST HOMES
M. J. Hollis, 1108 W. 2nd Ave.

Please Mention the "Green Book"

RESTAURANTS
Shelton's, 200 E. 3rd St.
Duck Inn, 405 N. Cedar St.
BARBER SHOPS
Nappy Chin, 217 State St.
BEAUTY PARLORS
Pruitt's, 1317 W. Baraque St.
BEAUTY SCHOOLS
DeLuxe, 221 E. 3rd St.
Jefferson, 1818 W. 6th Ave.
GARAGES
Alley's, 1101 N. Cedar St.

FORDYSE
RESTAURANTS
Harlem, 211 1st St.

HELENA
SERVICE STATIONS
Stark's, Rightor & Walnut Sts.

RUSSELLVILLE
TOURIST HOMES
E. Latimore, 318 S. Huston Ave.

TEXARKANA
HOTELS
Brown's, 312 W. Elm St.
TOURIST HOMES
G. C. Mackey, 102 E. 9th St.
RESTAURANTS
Grant's Cafe, 830 Laurel St.
BEAUTY PARLORS
M. B. Randell, 1105 Laurel St.

CALIFORNIA

BERKLEY
BEAUTY PARLORS
Little Gem, 1511 Russell St.
BARBER SHOPS
Success, 2946 Sacramento St.

EL CENTRO
RESTAURANTS
Pearl McKinnel Lunch, Box 1049
HOTELS
Roland, 201 E. Main St.

FRESNO
TOURIST HOMES
La Silve, 841 F St.
RESTAURANTS
DeLux, 2193 Ivy St.
New Jerico, 101 Church St.
BEAUTY PARLORS
Rosebud's, 835 G St.
Ruth's, 1816 F St.
Golden West, 1032 F St.
BARBER SHOPS
Golden West, 1032 'F' St.
Magnolia, 602 F St.
Sportsman's, 855 G St.

TAVERNS
20th Century, 1401 F St.
GARAGES
Buddy Lang's, 1658 F St.
Frank's 1326 Fresno St.

HOLLYWOOD
TAILORS
Billy Berg's, 707 N. Ridgewood

IMPERIAL
TOURIST HOMES
Mrs. Albert Bastion, Cor. 7th & M Sts.

LOS ANGELES
HOTELS
Clark Hotel & Annexes
Cor. Washington Blvd. &
   Central Ave.
Phone: Prospect 5357
Clark, 1816 So. Central Ave.
La Dale, 802 E. Jefferson Blvd.
Watkins, 2022 N. Adams Blvd. (23)
Lincoln, 549 Ceres Ave.
Norbo, 529 E. 6th St.
Mack's Manor Hotel
1085 W. Jefferson Blvd.
McAlpin, 648 Stanford Ave.
Elite, 1217 Central Ave.
Olympic, 843 S. Central Ave.
Regal, 815 E. 6th St.
Kentucky, 1123 Central Ave.
Dunbar, 4225 S. Central Ave.
TOURIST HOMES
Cashbah Apartments
1189 W. 36th Place
Phone Republic 8290
Vallee Vista, 2408 Cimarron St.
RESTAURANTS
Ivie's, 1105½ E. Vernon Ave.
Henry Bros., 10359 Wilmington
Eddie's, 4201 S. Central Ave.
Zombie, 4216 S. Central Blvd.
Waffle Shop, 1063 E. 43 St.
Clifton's, 618 S. Olive St.
BEAUTY PARLORS
Sherwoods, 5113 S. Central Ave.
Studio, 2515 S. Central
Continental, 5203 Hopper Ave.
Triangle, 43 San Pedro & Walls Sts
Colonial, 1813½ S. Central Ave.
Dunbar, 4225 S. Central Ave.
Beauty Salon, 1195 East 35th St.
BARBER SHOPS
Bertha's, 1434 W. Jefferson Blvd.
Personality, 4222 S. Central Ave.
Echo, 43rd & Central Ave.

(Los Angeles, continued on 19)

10

The Golden Gate
San Francisco, Calif.

SAN FRANCISCO, the fabulous city by the Golden Gate, offers a mixture of adventure to the tourist.

This great metropolis of the West is said to have become a city overnight. In 1841, just thirty families comprised the entire village now known as San Francisco and in 1850 this same place recorded a population of 25,000 persons of every race, creed and color. Every able-bodied man on receiving news of the precious discovery made by one James W. Marshall on the South Fork of the American River in January of 1848, hurried towards the Golden Gate in pursuit of wealth. Many huge fortunes were amassed during this period. Since that time, San Francisco has never had a dull decade. Its life span has been more exciting than that of many Eastern cities, three times as old. The tourist will observe how the warm shadows of great events and vivid people linger on in this city, keeping it gay and carefree, wise and tolerant. San Franciscans share a common love of and desire to preserve their city's friendly, cosmopolitan way of life.

The strategic location of the city, its magnificent harbor and extensive shipping make it a major port. It possesses one of the finest land-locked harbors in the world. The crescent-shaped street known as the EMBARCADERO, is lined with piers and wharves, which parellels the bay shore for three and one half miles. Here, amid the seething activity of international trade, the newcomer may stop and pay tribute to the incredible beauty of this harbor whose scenic splendors, it is claimed, rivals Rio de Janiero. Shipping from every quarter of the globe testifies of this city's industrial importance to its country and the world. In the recent Pacific conflict this great port proved its value in another way, by serving as the principal embarkation point for servicemen on their way to uphold the American tradition of honor.

Geography is the element blamed the most, for San Francisco's peculiar weather. The fog and cool summer climate is caused when the heat of the interior valleys sucks the fog and cool air through the Golden Gate. There is no great range of temperature so San Francisco might best be described as enjoying a kind of perpetual autumn. Rain falls mostly in the winter half of the year dividing the seasons into what would normally be winter and summer. September usually heralds San Francisco's bright, sparkling weather which usually lasts until Christmas. However, it is suggested and very strongly too, that a topcoat accompany the newcomer any time of the year because the mornings are cold and the evenings are laughingly described as cool. Despite this strange weather San

GREAT BRIDGE SPANS GOLDEN GATE AT SAN FRANCISCO, CALIFORNIA

At this storied entrance to the continent, where the Pacific Ocean meets San Francisco Bay, stands this monumental red-orange bridge, its towers rising above the strait to the height of a 65-story building ... the highest, longest-spanned bridge in the world. Its towers are 746 feet high, its center span is 4200 feet long. It has six automobile traffic lanes and two sidewalks.

The Negro Traveler's Green Book

Francisco is wrapped in atmosphere of enchantment.

San Francisco was once a barren stretch of sand dunes and rocky hills, scattered with swamps and lagoons. In order to provide for its increasing populations its valleys, tidal marshes and lagoons have been filled in and its smaller hills leveled. Today, San Francisco is a city that is largely man-made. The city's famed bridges have united San Francisco with its neighboring municipalities, blending them into one metropolitan area. These bridges consist of two suspensions and one cantilever which when combined, covers over eight miles in length and adds up to the largest bridge structure yet built. The Golden Gate Bridge regarded as the most beautiful bridge structure is also the longest single suspension span in the world. By walking out on it for the price of one dime the tourist can behold this bridge in all its majesty. The San Francisco-Oakland Bay Bridge cannot be seen in this manner though none of its splendor is lost in viewing it from the harbor on a Southern Pacific ferryboat.

Though, the bridges have contributed to their economic and social growth the neighboring communities resent becoming known as San Francisco's bedrooms. Oakland which is California's third largest city is in the same unfavorable position as New York City's, Brooklyn. Industries and assembly plants have turned Oakland into a Western Detroit. Its outstanding symbol of activity is the Latham Square Building, headquarters for Henry Kaiser's vast industrial empire. This city has the largest Negro population on the Pacific Coast.

The University of California is located in Berkeley, the town adjoining Oakland. With more than forty thousand students attending classes on the eight, scattered campuses of the University, Berkeley still manages to be tidy, serene and cordial. It comes closest to achieving the cosmopolitan ease desired by other communities because of its casual acceptance of people regardless of their race, creed or color.

San Francisco however, is fast becoming the focal point of the Negroes' future. Before World War II this city had fewer than 5,000 Negroes. High war wages attracted these people from all over the country to this boom town. More than 45,000 Negroes are squeezed into two areas of San Francisco today, with an estimated thirty-five per cent unemployed. Though, comfortable housing facilities and business opportunities are limited to Negroes at this time, tribute should be paid to the encouraging attitude held by San Franciscans toward the improvement and eventual erasure of these existing conditions. They pride themselves on living in the most cultured, cosmopolitan and liberal com-

SAN FRANCISCO'S CHINATOWN

13

The Negro Traveler's Green Book

munity in the entire west and as a result are truly, exerting a sincere effort to maintain this position. Many Negroes are of course, proving their value to this community daily and justifying the opportunities presented to them.

In order to pursue their earnest interest in the cultural side of life, San Franciscans dig deep into their private and public funds. Their city is one of the very few where the symphony and opera groups are maintained by the support of every taxpayer. Its symphonic orchestra is one of the foremost in the country while its operatic group is fast gaining recognition. It should be mentioned that art of every kind is appreciated year-round and include fine art shows, lectures, concerts and theatres, for the tourist and art lovers' benefit. San Francisco owns its Opera House which is magnificent and famed as the place where the United Nations' charter was framed. It seems appropriate to San Franciscans that their city, with its people from many lands, was the birthplace of an organization designed to bring world peace.

The Cable Cars, which are a source of amazement and amusement to the newcomer, are a San Francisco institution. The city's hills account for their continued use. In their early days of existence they enabled the town to expand up these steep hills. A beautiful marine view is enjoyed by tens of thousands of San Franciscans from their living room windows atop these hills today, as a result of these comic yet picturesque vehicles. When a more modern method of transportation was proposed by the Transportation Committee, it was overwhelmingly voted against by a group, who represented those San Franciscans who, dismiss any inconveniences suffered enroute from their homes on high to their downtown office and who, rather enjoy the thrill of being crushed inside or hanging helter-skelter from any side of these quaint cars.

San Francisco's downtown area is compact and accesible as clusters of skyscrapers house banks, public buildings and business houses. The shopping district centers on Union Square where department stores, smart women's shops, furriers, fine book stores, hotels, theaters and specialty shops can all be located. It is an area of bustling activity and hurrying throngs, punctuated on every other street corner by the inevitable sidewalk flower stand which offers a colorful assortment of flowers to the busy yet appreciative passer-by. This downtown area is not only the center of San Francisco's economic life but also a point from which every fascinating district in the city can be found.

Like every famous city, San Francisco has its cherished land marks. The Presidio, which was formerly a garrison for Spanish soldiers is steeped in California's early history and heads the list of interesting sights in this city, as does Portsmouth Square, known as San Francisco's birthplace; the Mission District, the very oldest and most densely populated area; the San Francisco Terminal Building and the Donahue Monument. Of course Lotta's Fountain is a MUST on every visitor's list. It was formerly a watering trough for horses presented by the greatest Western belle of them all, Miss Lotta Crabtree, to the city of gold, during the exciting days of old. This gift has been transformed into a drinking fountain for humans and is the pride of every San Franciscan's heart. Yacht Harbor, Seal Rocks and the Fleishhacker Pool

14

THE SAN FRANCISCO-OAKLAND BAY BRIDGE, SAN FRANCISCO, CALIFORNIA

This bridge is the largest in the world. 8¼ miles long; 4½ miles over navigable water. The view is toward San Francisco from Yerba Buena Island in mid-bay, through which rocky island of 140 acres the bridge passes by a tunnel and then goes on by leaps of mighty spans to Oakland. The west half of the bridge, seen in the picture, consists of two suspension bridges anchored in the center to a concrete pier. The bridge is double-decked, with six lanes for automobiles on its upper deck, and three lanes for trucks and buses and two tracks for electric trains on its lower deck.

OCEAN BEACH AT SAN FRANCISCO, CALIFORNIA

San Francisco meets the Pacific Ocean on a long white beach, which extends some three and a half miles between the Cliff House and Fleishhacker Zoo. It is skirted by the Esplanade and the Great Highway; flanked by Playland-at-the-Beach and Golden Gate Park. Here people wade into waves from China; cast in the surf for striped bass and other fish; bask around picnic fires on the sand; point their cars west and watch the sea and ships or a sunset; enjoy entertainment at the playland. Golden Gate Park extends from here four miles to the center of the city.

16

The Negro Traveler's Green Book

Fishermen's Wharf is one of the sights of San Francisco. Located some three miles within the Golden Gate, it is like a bit of the Bay of Naples set down on the shore of San Francisco Bay. From the piers of the lagoons where some 350 fishing vessels berth, one has an excellent view of the Golden Gate Bridge and of the hills of the north shore piling up to the 2600 feet height of lordly Mount Tamalpais. Behind the wharf is Telegraph Hill with high Coit Tower on top. It is the visual center of the Latin Quarter in the North Beach section of San Francisco.

provide varied interests in water sports, while Golden Gate offers an atmosphere of great natural beauty with its 1,013 acres of flowers, shrubs, trees and lawns along with its recreational activities, refreshment enclosures and educational facilities.

Fisherman's Wharf is located at the end of the Embarcadero and is one of the most picturesque areas in San Francisco. Crews, of the gaily painted fishing fleet, tend their business, completely oblivious of the tourists' interest. A spirit of good fellowship prevails among these men as they share their boats, their gear and their profits. Their naturalness is an education and delight to the stranger. Along the street are stands displaying shellfish and at the curb, big, iron cauldrons boil large freshly caught crabs for the purchaser's immediate or delayed consumption. Neighboring restaurants have captured this Old World atmosphere and presents it, and recently caught dinners in a more fashionable manner to their patrons.

The Latin Quarter is one of the biggest tourist attractions in this city because it is a section of many nationalities. French, Negro, Spanish, Portugese and Italians are all found here. These people are devoted to the entertainment requirements of its many visitors. Everyone turns to its interesting district for a variety of foods and cabarets. From bawdy examples of San Francisco's hospitality, one may turn to more elegance and sophistication within a few short steps in this fascinating part of the city.

San Francisco's Chinatown is the largest Chinese settlement outside the Orient. It is an orderly section today. The old Chinatown of brothels, gambling houses, opium dens and slums was destroyed in the great fire

17

in Patronizing These Places

of 1906. Today exotic, pagoda roof tops and iron grilled balconies appear side by side with American tin roofs and straight fronts while men and women of Old China, mingle harmoniously with those who have adopted the latest occidental fashions. In exploring this part of San Francisco, the visitor's interest is captivated by the Chinese Telephone Exchange. This is a triple-pagoda building of traditional Chinese architecture completed with red and gold trimmed, lacquer dragons. Here, attractive Chinese girls operate the switchboards and are acquainted with every subscriber's street and telephone number. Naturally these girls have created a precedent in telephone operating efficiency. Chinatown on the whole is a section which offers fine silks, carved ivory, lacquer-ware and trinkets of every kind to the newcomer along with famous eating places and night clubs. The Chinese New Year celebration brings forth, with increased vigor, this section's best qualities. The streets are gaily lined with flower stands and every shrine in every shop is lavishly decorated while a spirit of genuine good will and revelry prevails.

The tourist will find San Francisco adaptable, elastic and truly cosmopolitan through the blending of the talents provided by its people. The Italians' love of operatic music, the Mexicans' joy of festivals, the French flair for style and the Spaniards' interest in romance are tempered by the wisdom of the Chinese, the vigor of Midwestern and Eastern settlers and most recently, the beloved humor and wit of the Negro. They have all contributed to San Francisco's mixed flavor and provide it with a viewpoint unlimited by horizons. Your trip to this Western city will be a thrilling experience indeed.

(First cover photo)

CABLE CARS CLIMB STEEP HILLS IN SAN FRANCISCO, CALIFORNIA

Cable cars were invented in San Francisco, in 1873, to climb that city's hills. People find them charming and festive there today in their roller-coaster, bell-Street cable line climbs from Market Street to the top of Nob Hill, passing ringing journeys. Here the California through the financial district and Chinatown on the way. On the height, where once stood the palaces of railroad and bonanza millionaires, are hotels and apartment houses. From the Top of the Mark there one enjoys superlative views of the city, bay and surrounding hills.

(Fourth cover photo)

MISSION SAN FRANCISCO DE ASIS, SAN FRANCISCO, CALIFORNIA

With the founding of Mission San Francisco de Asis, on June 29, 1776, San Francisco was begun—five days before the Liberty Bell in Philadelphia rang forth its historic tidings Situated near the center of the city, it is popularly known as Mission Dolores. Within its adobe walls, which are four feet thick, one sees ancient altars from Mexico and original decorative work of Indian neophytes on ceiling and walls. The "new church" next the old mission, is an example of Spanish architecture. On the other side of the mission is its ancient cemetery, with its "Grotto of Lourdes" and headstones recalling many notables and others of San Francisco's early days.

Please Mention the "Green Book"

(Los Angeles, cont. from p. 10)
TAVERNS
Margot, 5259 S. Central Ave.
Golden Gate, 1719 E. 103rd St.
Paradise, 5505 S. Central Ave.
Samba, 5th & Towns Ave.
Tip Top Cafe, 4631 S. Central Ave.
Johnson's, 4201 S. Main St.
Elks Lounge, 10123 Beach
NIGHT CLUBS
Basket Room, 3219 S. Central Ave.
Harlem, 11812 Parmalee
Wakeki, 3741 So. Western Ave.
Last Word, 4206 So. Central Ave.
LIQUOR STORES
Dunbar, 4223 S. Central Ave.
Jackson's, 5501 S. Central Ave.
Esquire, Vernon & Central Ave.
W. M. Davis. 4321 Long Beach Ave.
Fred Little John, 3503 Avalon Blvd.
SERVICE STATIONS
Valentine's Service, 2657 S. Western Ave.
Carner's, 4500 S. Avalon Ave.
Simpkins & Cower, 2227 S. Central Ave.
Tom's, 1424 W. Jefferson Blvd.
Hughes, 2901 W. Jefferson Blvd.
Brock, 1246 W. Jefferson Blvd.
Garcia, 52nd Pl. & Central
Wilkens, 4924 S. Central Ave.
Gracis, 5201 S. Central Ave.
Watson Bros., 4000 So. Pedro St.
GARAGES
Parkers, 10229 Alameda
Alexander's, Jefferson & Griffith
DRUG STORES
Allums, 4375 S. Central Ave.
Doctor's, 4012 S. Central Ave.
Medical, 3112 S. Western Ave.
TAILORS
Bader's, 1840 E. 103rd St.
Delta, 8512 Compton Ave.
Benjamin, 5016 So. Central Ave.
REAL ESTATE
Herndon, 3419 So. Central Ave.

LAKE ELSIMORE
HOTELS
Geo. Moore, 407 Scrivener St.
Lake Elsimore, 416 N. Kelogg St.

OAKLAND
HOTELS
Paradise, 1793 7th St.
Ebony Plaza, 3908 San Pablo Ave.
Carver, 1412 Market St.
Warren, 1252 7th St.
TOURIST HOMES
Mrs. A. C. Clark, 805 Linden St.
Mrs. H. Williams, 3521 Grove St.
RESTAURANTS
The Villa, 3016 Adeline St.

TAVERNS
Overland Cafe, 1719 7th St.
SERVICE STATIONS
McCabe, 5901 Adeline St.
Signal, 800 Center St.
GARAGES
Bufford's, 5901 Aldine St.

PERRIS
TOURIST HOMES
Muse-A-While

PASADENA
SERVICE STATIONS
Penn Mobile, 1096 Lincoln Ave.

SACRAMENTO
HOTELS
Center Hotel, 420½ Capitol Ave.
TOURIST HOMES
Mrs. R. C. Peyton 2202½ 4th St.
RESTAURANTS
Dunlap's, 4372 4th Ave.
BARBER SHOPS
Mrs. Mikes, 1350 56th St.
BEAUTY PARLORS
Twigg's, 421 Capitol Ave.
Leftridge, 3102 Sacramento Blvd.
Nannette's, 1214 5th St.
Larocco's, 1630 7th St.
NIGHT CLUBS
Mo-Mo, 600 Capitol Ave.
DRUG STORES
Taylors, 1230 6th St.

SAN DIEGO
HOTELS
Douglas, 206 Market St.
Simmons, 542 6th Ave.
Y.W.C.A., 1029 C St.
RESTAURANTS
Sun, 421 Market St.
Brown Hostess, 2816 Imperial Ave.
SERVICE STATIONS
Webber's, 1655 1st Ave.
Woodson's, 3126 Franklin Ave.
LIQUOR STORES
Robinson's, 2876 Imperial Ave.
TAILORS
Clever, 2606 Imperial Ave.
Imperial, 2751 Imperial Ave.
Ramona, 2244 Logan Ave.
Maryann, 1317 Market St.

SAN FRANCISCO
HOTELS
The Scaggs, 1715 Webster St.
New Pullman, 232 Townsend St.
Edison, 1540 Ellis St.
Texas, 1840 Filmore St.
Buford, 1969 Sutter St.
TOURIST HOMES
Mrs. F. Johnson, 1788 Sutter St.
Thadd's DeLux, 2040 Sutter St.

Please Mention the "Green Book"

RESTAURANTS
Hi-Lo, 1686 O'Farrell St.
BARBER SHOPS
Hillside, 5267 3rd St.
TAVERNS
Jack's, 1931 Sutter St.
NIGHT CLUBS
Town Club, 1963 Sutter St.
The Plantation, 1628 Post St.
Flamingo, 1836 Filmore St.
DRUG STORES
Riggan's, 2600 Sutter St.
Olympic, Cor. Jones & Post
Jim's, 1698 Sutter St.
LIQUOR STORES
Sullivan, 1623 Post St.
Coast, 1567 Tillmore St.

TULARE
TOURIST HOMES
South "K" St., 330 South "K" St.
TAVERNS
King's, 322-24 South K St.

VALLEJO
TAVERNS
Cotton Club, Virginia & Branciforte

VICTORVILLE
TOURIST HOMES
Murray's Dude Ranch
Raglan Guest Ranch, Box 437

COLORADO

BOULDER
RESTAURANTS
Ray's Inn, 2038 Goss St.

COLORADO SPRINGS
TOURIST HOMES
G. Roberts, 418 E. Cucharras St.

DENVER
HOTELS
Bean Hotel, 2152 Arapahoe St.
TOURIST HOMES
Mrs. G. Anderson, 2119 Marion St.
Mrs. George L. Anderson
2119 Marion St.
Mrs. Ila G. Burton, 3430 Race St.
Mrs. Harney E. Blair,
2936 Gaylord St.
Mrs. Hattie Graves, 3052 Humboldt St.
RESTAURANTS
Green Lantern, 2859 Fremont
Da-Nite, 1430 22nd Ave.
Atlas, 611 27th St.
B & E, 2847 Gilpin St.
BEAUTY PARLORS
Landers, 2460 Marion St.
Ford, 2527 Humboldt St.

BARBER SHOPS
Roxy, 2559 Welton St.
20th Century, 2727 Welton St.
TAVERNS
Rossonian Lounge, 2650 Welton St.
Arcade, 739 E. 26th Ave.
Archie's, 2449 Larimer St.
LIQUOR STORES
Lincoln, 2636 Welton St.
Aristocrat, 3101 William St.
18th Ave., 1314 E. 17th Ave.
SERVICE STATIONS
Da-Nite, 729 E. 26th Ave.
White, 2655 Downing St.
Plazer, E. 22nd & Humboldt Sts.
TAXI CABS
Ritz, 2721 Welton St.
DRUG STORES
T. K., 27th & Larimer Sts.
Ideal, 28th & Downing
V. H. Meyers, 22nd & Downing Sts.
Radio, Welton at 26th St.
TAILORS
Arcade 739 E. 26th St.
White House, 2863 Welton St.
Ace, 2200 Downing St.

DUMONT
LODGES
Mountain Studio

GREELEY
TOURIST HOMES
Mrs. E. Alexander, 106 E. 12th St.

LA JUNTA
TOURIST HOMES
Mrs. Moore, 301 Lewis Ave.

LA MAR
HOTELS
Alamo
RESTAURANTS
Joe's

MONTROSE
HOTELS
Adams
RESTAURANTS
Chipeta Cafe
BEAUTY SHOPS
Ace
SERVICE STATIONS
Sorenson Sinclair Station
GARAGES
Gilbert Motor Co.

PUEBLO
TOURIST HOMES
Mrs. T. Protho, 918 E. Evans Ave.
TAVERNS
Blue Bird, 705 N. Main St.
Mecca Grill, 719 N. Main St.
Grand, 114 W. 4th St.

20

in Patronizing These Places

CONNECTICUT

BRIDGEPORT
HOTELS
Y.W.C.A., Golden Hill St.
TOURIST HOMES
Mrs. M. Barrett, 83 Summer St.

HARTFORD
TOURIST HOMES
Mrs. Johnson, 2016 Main St.
BEAUTY SHOPS
Quality, 1762 Main St.
BARBER SHOPS
Williams, 1978 Main St.
DRUG STORES
Bellevue, 256 Bellevue St.
LIQUOR STORES
Harry's, 2574 Main St.
Canton, 1736 Main St.
Ben's, 1988 Main St.
The Paramount, 107 Canton St.
Bacon, 81 Homestead Ave.
TAVERNS
Bancroft's, Main & Elmer Sts.
Club Sundown, 360 Windsor St.
Franks Tavern, 257 Windsor St.
SERVICE STATIONS
Ware's, 34 Spring St.
Cauls, 2750 Main St.

NEW HAVEN
HOTELS
Portsmouth, 91 Webster St.
TOURIST HOMES
Dr. M. F. Allen, 65 Dixwell Ave.
RESTAURANTS
Monterey, 267 Dixwell Ave.
Belmonts, 156 Dixwell Ave.
BEAUTY PARLORS
Mme. Ruby, 175 Goffe St.
Glaly's, 624 Orchard St.
Ethel's, 152 Dixwell Ave.
Harris, 734 Orchard St.
SCHOOL OF BEAUTY CULTURE
Modern, 170 Goffe St.
NIGHT CLUBS
Elk's, 204 Goffe St.
Lillian's Paradise, 137 Wallace St.
LIQUOR STORES
Shiffrins, 221 Dixwell Ave.
DRUG STORES
Proctor's, 180 Dixwell Ave.

NEW LONDON
TOURIST HOMES
Mrs. E. Whittle, 785 Bank St.

SOUTH NORWALK
HOTELS
Palm Gardens, Post Rd.

STAMFORD
HOTELS
GLADSTONE, Gay St.
TOURIST HOMES
Robert Graham, 37 Hanrahan Ave.
NIGHT CLUBS
Sizone, 136 W. Main St.

WATERBURY
HOTELS
Elton
TOURIST HOMES
Community House, 34 Hopkins St.
DRUG STORES
Rhineharts, 471 N. Main St.
McCarthy, Main, Bishop & Grove Sts.
TAILOR SHOPS
Sam's, 149 South Main St.

WEST HAVEN
HOTELS
Dadds, 359 Beach St.
Seaview, 392 Beach St.
TAVERNS
Hoot Owl, 374 Beach St.

DELAWARE

DOVER
HOTELS
Cannon's, Kirkwood St.
Dean's, Forrest St.
Mosely's, Division St.

LAUREL
RESTAURANTS
Joe Randolph's, W. 6th St.
BARBER SHOPS
Joe Randolph's, W. 6th St.
BEAUTY PARLORS
Orchid, W. 6th St.

TOWNSEND
HOTELS
Rodney, Dupont Highway-Rt. 13
GARAGES
Hood's, Dupont Hiway

WILMINGTON
HOTELS
Royal, 703 French St.
Lawson, 208 Poplar St.
Y.M.C.A., 10th & Walnut Sts.
Y.W.C.A., 10th & Walnut Sts.
TOURIST HOMES
Miss W. A. Brown, 1306 Tatnall St.
Mrs. E. Till, 1008 French St.
RESTAURANTS
Christian Assn. Bldg., 10th & Walnut Sts.

21

Please Mention the "Green Book"

BEAUTY SHOPS
Mrs. M. Anderson, 916 French St.
Dora's, 314 East 10th St.

NIGHT CLUBS
Spot, 7th & 8th on French St.

SERVICE STATIONS
Esso, 8th & 9th on King

DISTRICT OF COLUMBIA

WASHINGTON, D. C.

HOTELS
Johnson's Hotel, 1505 13th St. N. W.
Whitelaw, 13th & "T" Sts. N. W.
Johnson, Jr., 1509 Vermont Ave., N. W.
Dunbar, U St. & 15th St., N. W.
Y.M.C.A., 1816 12th St., N. W.
Y.W.C.A., 901 Rhode Is. Ave., N. W.
Logan, 13th & Logan Circle N. W.
Clore, 614 'S' St. N. W.
Cadillac, 1500 Vermont St. N. W.
Ken Rod, 621 Rhode Island Ave., N. W.
Charles, 1334 'R' St. N. W.

TOURIST HOMES
Jannie's, 939 Rhode Is. Ave. N. W.
Buddie's, 1320 5th St. N. W.
Towles, 1321 13th St. N. W.
Towles, 1342 Vermont Ave., N. W.
Modern, 3006 13th St., N. W.
Rivers, 1021 Monroe St., N. W.
Patsy's, 2026 13th St., N. W.
Cottage Grove, 1531 Vermont Ave., N. W.
Terry's, 939 Rhode Is. Ave., N. W.
Boyd's, 1744 Swann St., N. W.
Edward's, 1837 16th St., N. W.

TAVERNS
Grand Casa Blanca, 3413 Georgia Ave. N. W.
New Hollywood, 1940 9th St. N. W.
Holleywood, 1940 9th St., N. W.
Harrison's Cafe, 455 Florida Ave., N. W.
Off Beat, 1849 7th St., N. W.
Kenyon, Ga. Ave. & Kenyon St., N. W.
Herbert's Stage Door, 618 "T" St., N. W.

RESTAURANTS
Republic Gardens, 1355 'U' St. N. W.
Alfreds, 1610 'U' St. N. W.
Keys, 7th & "T" St., N. W.
Chicken Paradise, 1210 U. St., N. W.
Earl's, 1218 U. St., N. W.

Sugar Bowl, 2830 Georgia Ave., N. W.
Shrimp Hut, 807 Florida Ave., N. W.
Uptown, 807 Florida, N. W.
Johnson's, 1909 14th St., N. W.
The Hour, 1937 11th St., N. W.
Cozy, 708 Florida Ave., N. W.
Kenyon Grill, 3119 Georgia Ave., N. W.
The Hour, 1837 11th St., N. W.

LIQUOR STORES
Peoples, 719 11th St., N. W.
S & W, 1428 9th St., N. W.
Shuster's, 101 H St., N. W.
Ney's, 1013 Penna. Ave., N. W.
Carter's, 1927 14th St., N. W.

BARBER SHOPS
Florida, 1803 Florida Ave., N. W.
Blue Bird, 3219 Georgia Ave. N. W.
Harpers, 703 Park Rd.
York, 3634 Georgia Ave. N. W.

BEAUTY PARLORS
Modes, 3100 Georgia Ave. N. W.
Al, Lenes 3551 Georgia Ave. N. W.
Henretta's, 3616 Georgia Ave. N. W.
Apex, 1417 'U' St., N. W.
The Royal, 1800 'T' St., N. W.
Elite, 1806 Florida Ave., N. W.
Lil's, 1416 9th St., N. W.
Green's, 1825 18th St., N. W.
Bandbox, 2036 18th St., N. W.
La Salle, 541 Florida Ave., N. W.

NIGHT CLUBS
Republic Gardens, 1355 U St., N. W.
Club Bali, 1901 14th St., N. W.
Club Caverns, 11th & U St., N. W.
Ebony, Cor. 7th & 'S' Sts. N. W.

SERVICE STATIONS
Brown's, 3128 Ga. Ave., N. W.
Engelberts, 1783 Florida Ave., N. W.

TAILORS
W. R. Reynolds, 1808 Florida Ave., N. W.

FLORIDA

DAYTONA BEACH

LIQUOR STORES
Hank's, 531 S. Campbell St.

DELRAY BEACH

TAVERNS
Manfield, N. W. 1st St.

FORT LAUDERDALE

HOTELS
Hill, 430 N. W. 7th Ave.

22

in Patronizing These Places

JACKSONVILLE

HOTELS
Richmond, 422 Broad St.
Blue Chip, 514 Broad St.
TOURIST HOMES
Craddock, 45th & Moncrief
E. H. Flipper, 739 W. Church St.
L. D. Jefferson, 1838 Moncrief Rd.
B. Robinson, 128 Orange St.
C. H. Simmons, 434 W. Ashley St.
NIGHT CLUBS
Two Spots, 45th & Moncrief Rd.
Manuel's, 624-629 W. Ashley St.
BARBER SHOPS
Blue Chip, 516 Broad St.
RESTAURANTS
Sunrise, 829 Pearl St.
Blu-Goose, 1303 Davis St.
DRUG STORES
Imperial, Broad & Ashley Sts.
Smith's, 613 Ashley St.

LAKE CITY

TOURIST HOMES
Mrs. M. McCoy, 730 E. Leon St.
Rivers, 931 Taylor St.
Mrs. B. J. Jones, 720 E. Leon St.
RESTAURANTS
Bill Rivers, 931 Taylor St.
BARBER SHOPS
George's, 302 E. Railroad St.
SERVICE STATIONS
Farmenis, 300 E. Washington St.
GARAGES
Chicken's, E. Railroad St.

LAKELAND

TOURIST HOMES
Mrs. J. Davis, 842½ N. Fla. Ave.
Mrs. A. Davis, 518 W.. 1st St.

LAKE WALES

RESTAURANTS
Hills Dew Drop Inn
47 "B" St.

MIAMI

HOTELS
Mary Elizabeth, 642 N. W. 2nd Ave.
Dorsey, 941 N. W. 2nd Ave.
Lord Calvert, 216 N. W. 6th St.
BEAUTY PARLORS
..lizabeth, 175 N. W. 11th Terrace
BEAUTY SCHOOLS
Sunlight, 1011 N. W. 2nd Ave.
TAVERNS
Star, 3rd Ave. & 15th St., N. W.

LIQUOR STORES
Cuban, 1701 N. W. 4th Ave.
Ideal, 175 N. W. 11th St.
Henry's, 379 N. W. 14th St.
TAILORS
Valet, 506 N. W. 14th St.

ORLANDO

HOTELS
Wells Bilt, 509 W. South St.

PENSACOLA

HOTELS
Grand, 2618 N. Guillemarde St.
RESTAURANTS
Rhumboogie, 509 E. Salamanca St.
TAILORS
Reese, 307 E. Wright St.
New-Way, 1021 N. 9th Ave.
DRUG STORES
Hannah, 198 N. Palafax
LIQUOR STORES
Two Spot, 316 N. Devillier St.
RESTAURANTS
Brown's, 406 Lemon St.

SOUTH JACKSONVILLE

RESTAURANTS
Cool Spot, 2619 Kings Ave.

ST. PETERSBURG

Mrs. M. C. Henderson, 2580 9th St.

ST. AUGUSTINE

TOURIST HOMES
F. H. Kelly, 83 Bridge St.

TAMPA

HOTELS
Afro, 722 La Salle St.
Rogers, 1025 Central Ave.
Pyramid, 1028 Central Ave.
Dallas, 829 Zack St.
TAVERNS
Little Savoy, Central & Scott
Peach, 1002 6th Ave.
Manuel's Place, 1608 N. Blvd.
Brittwood, 1320 Main St.
Paradise, 201 Robert St.
Atomic, 3813 29th St.
TAILORS
Elizabeth, 175 N. W. 11th Terrace
Alvarez, 931 E. Broadway
DRUG STORES
Wells, "K" & Nebraska Ave.
LIQUOR STORES
Reo-Franklin, Cor. Lafayette
Tampa St. Liquor Store
GARAGES
Calvins, 1408 Orange St.

Please Mention the "Green Book"

GEORGIA

ADRIAN
TOURIST HOME
Wayside, U. S. Rt. 80

ALBANY
TOURIST HOMES
Mrs. A. J. Ross, 514 Mercer St.
Mrs. L. Davis, 313 South St.
Mrs. C. Washington, 228 S. Jackson St.

ATLANTA
HOTELS
Hotel Royal, 214 Auburn Ave., N. E.
Mack, 548 Bedford Place, N. E.
Shaw, 245 Auburn Ave., N. E.
Y.M.C.A., 22 Butler St.
Waluhaje, 239 W. Lake Ave., N. W.
Savoy, 239 Auburne Ave., N. E.
TOURIST HOME
Connally, 125 Walnut St., S. W.
RESTAURANTS
Suttons, 312 Auburn Ave., N. E.
Joe's Coffee Bar, 200 Auburn Ave.
Paschal Bros., 837 Hunter St. N. W.
TAVERNS
The Blackaret, 848 Mayson Turner Ave.
Yeah Man, 256 Auburn Ave., N. E.
Sportmans Smoke Shop, 242 Auburn Ave., N. E.
Butler's, 1868 Simpson Rd.
BEAUTY PARLORS
Poro, 250½ Auburn Ave.
Camolene, 859½ Hunter St.
BARBER SHOPS
R. W. Woodard, 160 Elm St., S. W.
Artistic, 55 Decatur
Gate City, 240 Auburn Ave., N. W.
Silver Moon, 202 Auburn Ave.
NIGHT CLUBS
Posnciana, 143 Auburn Ave.
SERVICE STATIONS
Hall's, 215 Auburn Ave., N. E.
GARAGES
South Side, 539 Fraser St., N. E.
TAILORS
Spic & Span, 907 Hunter St., N. W.

AUGUSTA
HOTELS
Crimm's, 725 9th St.
LQIUOR STORES
Bollinger's, 1114 Gwennett St.

BRUNSWICK
TOURIST HOMES
The Palms, 1309 Glouster St.
Melody Tourist Inn, 1505 G. St.
RESTAURANTS
Green Lantern, 1615 Albany St.
BARBER SHOPS
Battle's, 1304 Gloucester St.
BEAUTY PARLORS
Ethel's, 1501 London St.
GARAGE
Gould's, 1608 New Castle St.
TAXI CABS
Murphy's, 201 "F" St.
TAVERNS
Duncan, 1100 Gloucester St.

COLUMBUS
HOTELS
Lowe's, 724 5th Ave.
Y.M.C.A., 521 9th Ave.
RESTAURANTS
BEAUTY PARLORS
BARBER SHOPS
Sherrell's, 1st Ave.
NIGHT CLUBS
Golden Rest, 1026 7th Ave.
GARAGES
Seventh Avenue, 816 7th Ave.

DOUGLAS
HOTELS
Economy, Cherry St.
TOURIST HOMES
Lawson's, Pearl St.
RESTAURANTS
Thomas', Pearl St.
BARBER SHOPS
Tucker & Mathis, Cherry St.
BEAUTY PARLORS
Rosella's, Gaskin St.
SERVICE STATIONS
Lonnie A. Pope, Peterson St.
TAVERNS
Sport Harold's, Coffee St.
ROAD HOUSES
Violet Tyson, Cherry St.

DUBLIN
TOURIST HOMES
Mrs. R. Hunter, 504 S. Jefferson

EASTMAN
TOURIST HOMES
J. P. Cooper, 211 College St.

MACON
HOTELS
Richmond, 335 Broadway
RESTAURANTS
Jean's, 545 Cotton Ave.
BEAUTY PARLORS
Lula Life, 283 2nd St.
TAILORS
Herschel, 284 Broadway
SERVICE STATIONS
Anderson's, Pursley at Pond St.

SAVANNAH
TOURIST HOMES
Elizabethian, 512 W. Park Ave.
BEAUTY PARLORS
Rose, 348 Price St.

24

in Patronizing These Places

SERVICE STATIONS
Gibson's, 442 West Broad St.
DRUG STORES
Moore's, 37th & Florence

STATESBORO

TOURIST HOMES
Debbie's, 210 Roundtree Ext.

THOMASVILLE

HOTELS
Imperial, Tallahassee Highway

WAY CROSS

HOTELS
TOURIST HOMES
Mrs. K. G. Scarlett, 843 Reynolds
RESTAURANTS
Paradise, Oak St.
BARBER SHOPS
Johnson's, Oak St.
SERVICE STATIONS
Union Cab, State St.

ILLINOIS

CHICAGO

HOTELS
Manor House, 4635 So. Parkway
Ritz Hotel, 409 East Oakwood Blvd.
Hotel Como, 5204-6 South Parkway
Du Sable, 764 Oakwood Blvd.
Evans Hotel, 733 East 61st St.
Pershing Hotel, 6400 Cottage Grove Ave.
Southway Hotel, 6014 S. Parkway
Spencer Hotel, 300 E. Garfield Blvd.
Grand Hotel, 5044 South Parkway
Y.M.C.A., 3763 South Parkway
S & S, 4142 South Parkway
Y.W.C.A., 4559 South Parkway
Monarch Hotel, 4530 Prairie Ave.
Albion Hotel, 4009 Lake Park Ave.
Prairie Hotel, 2836 Prairie Ave.
Eberhart Hotel, 6050 Eberhart Ave.
The Don Hotel, 3337 Michigan Ave.
Harlem Hotel, 5020 S. Michigan Ave.
South Central, 520 E. 47th St.
Loretta, 6201 Vernon Ave.
Garfield, 231 E. Garfield Blvd.
Vienna, 3921 Indiana Ave.
Wedgewood Towers, 64th & Woodlawn
Sutherland, 47th & Drexel Blvd.
Strand, Cottage Grove & 63 St.
TOURIST HOMES
Day's, 3616 South Parkway
Poro College, 4415 S. Parkway

RESTAURANTS
Morris' 410 E. 47th St.
Wrights, 3753 S .Wabash Ave.
A. & J. 105 E. 51st St.
Pitts, 812 E. 39th St.
Pioneer, 533 E. 43rd St.
Parkway, 429 East 45th St.
BEAUTY PARLORS
Matties', 4212 Cottage Grove Ave.
BARBER SHOPS
Bank's, 209 E. 39th St.
TAVERNS
The Palm, 466 E. 47th St.
El Casino, 823 E. 39th St.
Key Hole, 3965 S. Parkway
NIGHT CLUBS
Show Boat, 6109 Parkway
820 Club, 820 E. 39th St.
Delux, 6323 So. Parkway
SERVICE STATIONS
Parkway, 340 W. Grand Ave.
Standard, Garfield & S. Parkway
GARAGES
Zephyr, 4535 S. Cottage Grove Ave.
AUTOMOTIVE
Charles Baron, 3840 Michigan Ave.
DRUG STORES
Thompson, 545 E. 47th St.
TAILORS
Perkin, 4109 So. State St.
LIQUOR STORES
Sam's, 2255 W. Madison St.

DANVILLE

HOTELS
Stewarts, East North St.
Just A Mere Hotel, 218 E. North St.
TOURIST HOMES
Mrs. Lillian Wheeler, 109 Hayes St.

CENTRALIA

TOURIST HOMES
Mrs. Claybourne, 303 N. Pine St.
BEAUTY SHOPS
M. Coleman, 503 N. Poplar St.
BARBER SHOPS
P. Coleman, 503 N. Poplar St.
SERVICE STATIONS
Langenfield, 120 N. Poplar St.

EAST ST. LOUIS

TOURIST HOMES
P. B. Reeves, 1803 Bond Ave.
W. E. Officer, 2114 Missouri Ave.

PEORIA

TOURIST HOMES
Clara Gibons, 923 Monson St.
BARBER SHOPS
Stone's, 323 N. Adams St.
NIGHT CLUBS
Bris Collins, 405 N. Washington St.

SPARTA

HOTELS
Midtown Hotel & Country Club

Please Mention the "Green Book"

SPRINGFIELD
TOURIST HOMES
Dudley Tourist Rest
130 So. 11th St.
Madell Dudley, 1211 E. Adams
Mrs. L. Jones, 1230 E. Jefferson
Mrs. M. Rollins, 844 S. College St.
Mrs. B. Mosby, 1614 E. Jackson St.
Mrs. G. Bell, 625 N. 2nd St.
Mrs. E. Brooks, 705 N. 2nd St.
Dr. Ware, 1520 E. Washington St.
Mrs. Lula Stuart, 1615 E. Jefferson St.
Mrs. Bernie Eskridge, 1501 E. Jackson St.
BEAUTY PARLORS
Mrs. Mildred Ousley, 1228 So. 14th St.
Cozy Corner, 1229 E. Adams St.
BARBER SHOPS
Streamline, 835 E. Washington St.
Clem & Sikes, 120 So. 11th St.
TAVEVRNS
Cansler, 807 E. Washington St.
George White, 817 E. Washington St.
Panama, 120 So. 11th St.
Rose Lee, 1015 So. 17th St.
SERVICE STATIONS
Leon Stewart, 1400 E. Jefferson St.
DRUG STORES
Ideal Drug Store, 801 E. Washington St.

ROCKFORD
HOTELS
Briggs, 429 S. Court St.
TOURIST HOMES
Mrs. C. Gorum, 301 Steward Ave.
S. Westbrook, 630 Lexington Ave.
Mrs. Brown, 927 S. Winnebago St.

IDAHO
BOISE
TOURIST HOMES
Mrs. S. Love, 1164 River St.
Open Door Mission, 1159 River St.
RESTAURANTS
Union Pacific Greyhound Depot, 9th & Bannock St.

POCATELLO
TOURIST HOMES
A.M.E. Parsnge, 625 E. Fremont
Tourist Park, E. Fremont St.

INDIANA
ELKHART
TOURIST HOMES
Miss E. Botts, 336 St. Joe St.

EVANSVILLE
TOURIST HOMES
Mrs. Lauderdale, 608 Cherry St.
Miss F. Snow, 719 Oak St.
Community Ass'n, 620 Cherry St.

FORT WAYNE
HOTELS
Hotel Howell
1803 S. Hanna St.
Phone: H 5304
TOURIST HOMES
Mrs. B. Talbot, 456 E. Douglas
RESTAURANTS
Leo Manuals', 1329 Lafayette St.
Stewart's, 621 E. Brackenridge St.
Martin & Rankin, 1329 S. Lafayette St.
BEAUTY PARLORS
Service, 840 Lewis St.

GARY
HOTELS
Hotel Toledo
22nd Ave. & Adams St.
Phone: 5-2242
States', 1700 Washington St.
Hayes, 2167 Broadway
DRUG STORES
Haley's, 1600 Broadway
DRY CLEANING
Bufkin, 2472 Broadway

INDIANAPOLIS
HOTELS
Ferguson, 1102 N. Capitol Ave.
Y.M.C.A., 450 N. Senate Ave.
Y.W.C.A., 653 N. West St.
Hawaii, 406 Indians Ave.
Harbour, 617-19 N. Ill. St.
Marquis, 406 Indiana Ave.
Severin, 201 So. Illinois Ave.
TOURIST HOMES
Estelle, 455 W. 10th St.
RESTAURANTS
Lasley's, 510 Indiana Ave.
Parkview, 321 N. California Ave.
Log Cabin, 524 Indiana Ave.
Taylor's, 427 W. Mich. St.
Westmorland, 1309 E. 15th St.
Blue Eagle, 648 Indiana Ave.
Courtesy, 1217 Senate St.
Perkins, 793 Indiana Ave.
BEAUTY PARLORS
Burgess, 909 W. 29th St.
Beauty Box, 2704 Clifton St.
Dancy's, 436 N. California Ave.
Mignor's, 2457 Northwestern Sun
Home Beauty Parlor, 2704 Clifton St.
Majorette, 1509 E. 25th St.
Fannie Bowles, 418 W. 28th St.
Campbell, 2439 N. Western Ave.
Noonie's, 547 N. Senate Ave.

26

in Patronizing These Places

Crawford's, 450 Blake St.
Home Beauty Shop, 2704 Clifton St.
Terry's, 233 Indiana Ave.
Mary Childs, 721 Indiana Ave.
TAVERNS
Downbeat, 977 Indiana Ave.
Mayes Cafe, 503 Indiana
Ritz, Sinate & Indiana
Sunset, 875 Indiana
M. C., 544 W. Maryland St.
Panama, 306 Indiana
Downbeat, 1005 Indiana Ave.
Andrew Perkins, 793 Indiana Ave
Glenn's Place, 1771 Boulevard Pl.
Sunset, 875 Indiana Ave.
Cassa De Amor, 924 N. W. St.
CAFES
Sugar Boul, 952 N. West St.
SERVICE STATIONS
Al's Auto Laundry, Mich. & Blake Sts.
GARAGES
25th St. Garage, 560 W. 25th St.
DRUG STORES
Ethical, 628 Indiana Ave.
TAILORS
Lee's, 401 W. 29th St.
Meyer O. Jacobs, 212-214 E. 16th St.
Leon, 235 Mass. Ave.
LIQUOR STORES
Anna Bell's, 956 N. W. St.
Park Package, 1320 E. 25th St.
799 Liq. Store, 799 Indiana Ave.
Little Chum, 1422 N. Capitol Ave.
Avenue Liquor, 402 Indiana Ave.
Jimmy's, Cor. Blackford & New York St.
Steve's, 747 W. New York St.
Carl's, 2817 Clifton
NIGHT CLUBS
Savoy, 25th & Martendale
Blue Bird Inn, 502 Agnes St.
Blue Eagle Inn, 648 Indiana Ave.

JEFFERSONVILLE
TOURIST HOMES
Charles Thomas, 607 Missouri Ave.

MARION
TOURIST HOMES
Mrs. Violet Rhinehardt, 425 W. 10th
Mrs. Albert Ward, 324 W. 14th St.
RESTAURANT
Custer's Last Stand
State Rts. 15 & 37
Marshal's, 414-418 E. 4th St.
SERVICE STATION
Dave's, 2nd & By Pass

KOKOMO
TOURIST HOMES
Mrs. C. W. Winburn, 1015 Kennedy St.
Mrs. Charles Hardinson, 812 Kennedy St.
Mrs. S. D. Hughes, 1045 N. Kennedy St.

MICHIGAN CITY
TOURIST HOMES
Allen's, 210 E. 2nd St.

MUNICE
HOTELS
Y.M.C.A., 9065 Madison

SOUTH BEND
RESTAURANTS
Smokes, 432 S. Chapin St.

TERRE HAUTE
HOTELS
Booker, 33½ No. 3rd St.
Booker, 306 Cherry St.

WEST BADEN SPRINGS
HOTELS
Waddy

IOWA

CEDAR RAPIDS
TOURIST HOMES
Brown's, 818 9th Ave. S. E.

DES MOINES
HOTELS
Y.W.C.A., 512 9th St.
La Marguerita, 1425 Center St.
RESTAURANTS
Sampson, 1246 E. 17th St.
Cunningham's, 1602 E. University
Ida Bell's, 783 11th St.
Gertrudes, 1308 Keo Way
Peck's, 1180 13th St.
Community, 1202 Center St.
Ida Bell's, 783 Eleventh
Buzz Inn, 1000 Center St.
Erma & Carrie's, 1008 Center St.
William's, 1200 East 16th St.
BEAUTY PARLORS
Miniature, 1145 Enos
Vo-Pon, 1656 Walker St.
Berlin, 1022 13th St.
Polly's, 1544 Walker St.
Evalon, 1206 Center St.
Bernice's, 911 W. 16th St.
Miniature, 1145 Enis St.
Ruth's, 905 Laurel St.
TAVERNS
Herb's, 1002 Center St.
SERVICE STATIONS
Eagle, 2246 Hubble Blvd.
Mumford's, 4th & Euclid Ave.

The Negro Travelers' Green Book 1954

Please Mention the "Green Book"

GARAGES
4th St. 417 4th St.
TAILORS
National, 808 12th St.
Clean Craft, 1300 6th Ave.
DRUG STORES
Adams, E. 5th & Locust St.

DUBUQUE
TOURIST HOMES
Mrs. P. Martin, 712 University Ave.
Mrs. Edwin Weaver, 795 Roberts Ave.

KEOKUK
CAFES
Bradley's Blessed Mart in Cafe 1103 Main St.

OTTUMWA
TOURIST HOMES
William Bailey, 526 Center Ave.
Harry Owens, 814 W. Pershing

SIOUX CITY
RESTAURANTS
Prince Henry, 704 W. 7th St.
BEAUTY PARLORS
Fannie Mae's, 611 Cook St.

WATERLOO
TOURIST HOMES
Mrs. B. F. Tredwell, 928 Beach St.
Mrs. Spencer, 220 Summer St.
Mrs. E. Lee, 745 Vinton St.

KANSAS

ATCHISON
TOURIST HOMES
Mrs. M. McDonald, 1001 So. 7th St.
Mrs. Geneva Miles, 924 N. 9th St.

BETHEL
COUNTRY CLUB
Penrod, R. F. D. 1

COFFEYVILLE
TOURIST HOMES
Roberts Rooms, 8 E. 5th St.

CONCORDIA
TOURIST HOMES
Mrs. B. Johnson, 102 E. 2nd St.
Mrs. Glen McVey, 328 East St.

EMPORIA
TOURIST HOMES
Elliott's, 816 Congress St.

EDWARSVILLE
TOURIST HOMES
Road House, Anderson's Highway 32 & Bitts Creek

FORT SCOTT
HOTELS
Hall's, 223½ E. Wall St.

HIAWATHA
TOURIST HOMES
Mrs. Mary Sanders, 1014 Shawnee

HUTCHINSON
TOURIST HOMES
Mrs. C. Lewis, 400 W. Sherman

JUNCTION CITY
HOTELS
Bridgeforth, 311 E. 11th St.
TOURIST HOMES
Mrs. B. Jones, 229 E. 14th St.

LARNED
TOURIST HOMES
Mrs. C. M. Madison, 828 W. 12th St.
Mrs. Mose Madison, 815 W. 10th St.
Mrs. John Caro, 218 E. 4th St.
RESTAURANTS
Carrie's Bar-B-Q, 218 E. 4th St.

LAURENCE
HOTELS
Snowden's, 1933 Tennessee St.

LEAVENWORTH
TOURIST HOMES
Mrs. W. Shelton, 216 Poplar St.

KANSAS CITY
RESTAURANT
Keystone Club, 4th & Freemen
BARBER SHOPS
Dabb's, 10th & Oakland
BEAUTY PARLORS
Sander's, 1813 N. 5th St.
ROAD HOUSES
De Moss, 44th & Sorta Rd., Rt. 3
GARAGES
Economy, 1935 N. 5th St.
Arthur's, 2414 N. 5th St.
DRUG STORES
Whitney's, 5th & Virginia
Cundiff, 5th & Quindarf

MANHATTAN
MOTEL
George's, 826 Tuma St.
TOUSIST HOMES
Mrs. E. Dawson, 1010 Yuma St.

OTTAWA
TOURIST HOMES
Mrs. H. W. White, 821 Cypress

28

PAGE 152

in Patronizing These Places

TOPEKA

HOTELS
Dunbar, 400 Qunicy St.
Palma House, 313 Quincy St.
TOURIST HOMES
Mrs. E. Slaughter, 1407 Monroe
RESTAURANTS
Jenkins, 112 East 4th St.
Blue Heaven, 301 E. 1st St.
Joe Andy's, 1000 Washington St.
BARBER SHOPS
Lytle's, 107 E. 4th St.
Power's, 402 Quincy St.
BEAUTY PARLORS
Newton's, 1316 Van Buren St.
Avalia's, 1800 Van Buren St.
TAVERNS
Macks', 400 Quincy St.
SERVICE STATIONS
Powers, 401 Quincy St.

WICHITA

TOURIST HOMES
Mrs. E. Reed, 517½ N. Main St.
BEAUTY PARLORS
Veluntex, 532 Wabash Ave.
RESTAURANTS
Oklahoma Cafe, 517 N. Main St.
DRUG STORES
Jackson's, 1411 N. Hydraulic

KENTUCKY
BOWLING GREEN

NANCY'S TEA ROOM
Good Food Served Right

Dinners - Short Orders - Sandwiches
½ Block off 31W - Open 6 A.M.
NANCY BROWN, *Proprietor*
415 THIRD STREET
Bowling Green, Ky.   Tel. 5233

ELIZABETHTOWN

TOURIST HOMES
A. Johnson, Valley Creek Rd.
Mrs. B. Tyler, Mile St.

HAZARD

TOURIST HOMES
Mrs. J. Razor, 436 E. Main St.

HOPKINSVILLE

TOURIST HOMES
Mrs. E. Davis, 901 E. Hayes St.
L. McNary, 113 Liberty St.
J. C. Hopkins, 128 Liberty St.

LANCASTER

TOURIST HOMES
Burn's, Buford St.
Hord's, Buford St.

RESTAURANTS
Plum's, Buford St.
BEAUTY PARLORS
Hilltop, Buford St.
GARAGES
Warren & Francis, N. Campbell St.

LINCOLN RIDGE

TOURIST HOMES
Lincoln Institute

LOUISVILLE

HOTELS
Brown's Guest House
1121 W. Chestnut St.
Allen, 2516 W. Madison St.
Y.W.C.A., 528 S. 6th St.
Y.M.C.A., 920 W. Chestnut St.
TOURIST HOMES
Brown's, 1121 W. Chestnut St.
RESTAURANTS
Jones Chicken Shack
525 South 13th St.
Jones, 525 So. 13th St.
Brown Derby, 563 So. 10th St.
Betty's Grill, 547 So. 9th St.
Sara's, 1617 W. Jefferson St.
Miller's, 630 W. Walnut St.
Sally's, 1104 W. Walnut St.
Paddock, 617 So. 24th St.
Eatmore, 964 S. 12th St.
Harry's, 28th & Chestnut Sts.
Pedra's, 619 Walnut St.
Kelman's, 1832 Magazine St.
DRIVE IN
Jones Bar-B-Q, 771 S. Clay St.
BEAUTY PARLORS
Elizabeth's, 1200 W. Kentucky
Scotty's, 442 So. 21st St.
Bellonia, 1625 Callagher St.
Jones, 409 S. 18th St.
Va's, 221 S. 28th St.
Beauty Box, 922 W. Walnut St.
Rose's, 1813 W. Walnut St.
Willie's, 1815 W. Madison St.
Lov-Lee, Ladies, 529 S. 12th St.
Va's, 221 So. 28th St.
BARBER SHOPS
Hunter's, 1502 W. Chestnut St.
Miller's, 818 W. Walnut St.
TAVERNS
Herman, 1601 W. Walnut St.
Dave's, 13th & Magazine
Shiek's, 12th & Zane St.
NIGHT CLUBS
Top-Hat, 1210 W. Walnut St.
ROAD HOUSES
LIQUOR STORES
Palace, 12th & Walnut St.
Lyons, 16th & Walnut St.
GARAGES
Eade's, 3509 Dumesril
Lone Wolf, 1500 Garland Ave.

Please Mention the "Green Book"

SERVICE STATIONS
F. & M. 8th and Walnut St.
DRUG STORES
Camers, 18th & Broadway
TAXI CABS
Lincoln, 705 W. Walnut
Dependable, 1835 W. Walnut St.

PARIS
RESTAURANTS
Webster's, 112 W. 8th St.
BARBER SHOPS
Webster, 110 W. 8th St.
BEAUTY PARLORS
Robinson, Lilleston St.

PADUCAH
HOTELS
Metropolitan House
724 Jackson St.
Jefferson, 514 So. 8th St.
Metropolitan, 724 Jackson St.

LEXINGTON
TOURIST HOMES
Mrs. K. Wallace, 600 W. Maxwell

LOUISIANA

BATON ROUGE
HOTELS
Ever-Ready, 1325 Government St.
TOURIST HOMES
T. Harrison, 1236 Louisiana Ave.
RESTAURANTS
Ideal Cafeteria, 1501 E. Blvd.
TAVERNS
Waldo's, 712 Peach St.
BEAUTY PARLORS
Carrie's, 561 S. 13th St.
SERVICE STATIONS
Horatio's Esso, No. 1. 1150 South St.
Horatio's Esso, No. 3, 1607 Govt. St.
ROAD HOUSE
Apex, 978 Louise St.

BOGALUSA
TOURIST HOMES

LAFAYETTE
TOURIST HOMES
Bourges, 416 Washington St.

LAKE CHARLES
HOTELS
Lewis, 515 Boulevard
TOURIST HOME
Combre's Place, 601 Boulevard

LAKE PROVIDENCE
SERVICE STATIONS
Armstrong's, 817 Sparrow St.

MANSFIELD
TOURIST HOMES
W. Simpkins, Jenkins St.

MONROE
HOTELS
Turner, 1015 Desiard St.
Dudley's Hotel, 1015 Desiard St.
RESTAURANTS
Red Union, 705½ Desiard

MORGAN CITY
TOURIST HOMES
Mrs. L. Williams, 719 Federal Ave.
Mrs. V. Williams, 208 Union St.

MARREO
BEAUTY PARLORS
Shirley, 101 Robertson Ave.

NEW ORLEANS
HOTELS
Creole Ritz, 1314 Varondelet St.
Hotel Foster, 2926 LaSalle St.
Patterson's, 802½ S. Rampart St.
Vogue, 2231 Thalia St.
North Side, 1518 La Harpe St.
Gladstone, 3435 Dryades St.
Astoria, 235 S. Rampart St.
Paige, 1038 Dryades Ave.
Riley, 759 S. Rampart St.
New Roxy, 759 S. Rampart St.
Golden Leaf, 1209 Saratoga St.
Caldonia Inn, St. Claude & St. Phillip
TOURIST HOMES
Mrs. J. Montgomery, 2134 Harmony St.
Mrs. F. Livaudais, 1954 Jackson
N. J. Bailey, 2426 Jackson Ave.
Mrs. King, 2826 Louisiana Ave.
Mrs. Edgar Major, 2739 Jackson Ave.
RESTAURANTS
Honey Dew Inn, 115 Front St.
Place-of-Joy, 2700 Melpomene St.
Dooky, Cor. Orleans & Miro
Foster's Chicken Den, Cor. LaSalle & 7th St.
Hayes Chicken Shack, La. & Saratoga St.
Portia's, 2426 Louisiana Ave.
Gumbo House, 1936 La, Ave.
BARBER SHOPS
Lopez's, 447 S. Rampart St.
BEAUTY PARLORS
Bessie's, 1841 St. Ann St.
Ola's, 1320 St. Bernard Ave.
BEAUTY CULTURE SCHOOLS
Poro, 2217 Dryades St.
TAVERNS
Di Leo, 3911 Fairmont
Wonder Bar, 2304 London Ave.
Astoria, 235 S. Rampart St.
Club Crystal, 1601 Dumaine

30

in Patronizing These Places

Le Rendez-vous, 7 Mile Post Gentitly Highway
Horseshoe, Thalia & S. Rampart St.
Robin Hood, 2069 Jackson Ave.
Caldonia Inn, St. Phillips & Claude Ave.
Martin's, 1341 St. Anthony St.
Robin Hood, 2140 Loyla St.

NIGHT CLUBS
Dew Drop Inn, 2836 La Salle St.
Shadowland, 1921 Washington Ave.
Hi-Hat, N. Villere at St. Ann
Deside, 2604 Desire St.
Dileo, 3911 Fairmont Dr.
Caldonia Inn, St. Claude & St. Phillip Sts.
Bradshaw Wonder Bar, 2440 London Ave.

SERVICE STATIONS
Bill Board, 2900 Claiborne Ave.
Ross, 1330 S. Broad St.

TAXI CABS
Ed's, 315 S. Rampart St.
V-8 Cab Line, Felicity & Howard Sts.
Logan, 2730 Felicity St.

NEW IBERIA
TOURIST HOMES
M. Robertson, 116 Hopkins St.
N. E. Cooper, 913 Providence St.

OPELCUSAS
TOURIST HOMES
B. Giron, S. Lombard St.

SCOTLANDVILLE
SERVICE STATIONS
Horatio's Esso No. 2, Hiway 61

SHREVEPORT
TOURIST HOMES
Mrs. Ed. Turner, 309 Douglas St.
Mrs. J. Jones, 1950 Hotchkiss
Mrs. W. Elder, 1920 Hotchkiss

RESTAURANTS
Wilson's, 840 Williamson St.
Grand Terrace, Pierre & Looney St.

TAVERNS
Grand Terrace, Pierre Ave. at Looney
New Tuxedo, 611 East 70th St.

SERVICE STATIONS
Pat's, Milam at Lawrence St.
Ross', 901 Pierre St.
William's-Milan & Ross-Milan Ave.

BARBER SHOPS
Clay's, 1017 Texas Ave.

TAILORS
3 Way, 2415 Milam St.
Sprague St., 1459 Murphy St.

DRUG STORES
Peoples, 912 Pierre St.
New Avenue, 1062 Texas Ave.

LIQUOR STORES
Dandy, 918 Harwell St.

WASHINGTON
SERVICE STATIONS
Stephen's, Main St.

MAINE

GARDNIER
TOURIST HOMES
Pond View, Pleasant Pond Rd.

OLD ORCHARD
TOURIST HOMES
Mrs. R. Cumming's, 110 Portland Ave.

AUGUSTA
TOURIST HOMES
Mrs. Joseph McLean, 16 Drew St.

PORTLAND
TOURIST HOMES
Thomas House, 28 'A' St.

White Rice Inn

Chinese and American Restaurant

1306 PENNSYLVANIA AVE.   Phone LAfayette 3-7614
BALTIMORE, MARYLAND

For the Best in Chinese and American Dishes visit us. It will be our pleasure to welcome you on all your visits and endeavor to make you comfortable.

Now Open at 4 p.m. to 4 a.m. Daily

Real Cantonese Family Dinners

Robert Lew, *Proprietor*

31

Please Mention the "Green Book"

MARYLAND

ANNAPOLIS
RESTAURANTS
Alsop's, Northwest & Calvert Sts.

BALTIMORE
BARBER SHOPS
Scotty's, 1501 Penna. Ave.
Goldsborough, 524 Bloom St.
HOTELS
York, 1200 Madison Ave.
Smith's, Druid Hill Ave. & Paca St.
Majestic, 1602 McCulloh St.
Y.W.C.A., 1916 Madison Ave.
Honor Reed, 667 N. Franklin
Y.M.C.A., 1617 Druid Hill Ave.
TOURIST HOMES
Mrs. E. Watsons, 340 Blura St.
RESTAURANTS
Sphinx, 2107 Pennsylvania Ave.
Upton, Cor. Monroe & Edmondson
Sess, 1639 Division St.
G. & L., Fayette & Gilmore Sts.
Spot Bar-B-Q, 1530 Penna. Ave.
Club Barbeque, 1519 Penna. Ave.
BEAUTY PARLORS
M. King, 1510 Penna. Ave.
Scott's, 1526 Penna. Ave.
Young's, 613 W. Lafayette Ave.
La Blanche, 1531 Penna. Ave.
TAVERNS
Sugar Hill, 2361 Druid Hill Ave.
Velma, Cor. Penn & Baker St.
The Alhambra, 1520 Penna. Ave.
Gamby's, 1504 Penna. Ave.
Mayflower, 905 Madison Ave.
Dixie, 558 Baker St.
Frolic, 1401 Fenna. Ave.
NIGHT CLUBS
Little Comedy, 1414 Penn Ave.
Ubangi, 2213 Penna. Ave.
Wonderland, 2043 Penna.
Gambie's, 1502 Penna. Ave.
Casino, 1517 Penna. Ave.
ROAD HOUSES
Bertie's, 2432 Annapolis Ave.
LIQUOR STORES
D & D, 890, Linden Ave.
Fine's, 1817 Penna. Ave.
Hackerman's, 1733 Penna.
SERVICE STATIONS
Esso-Presstman & Fremont
GARAGES
Service, 1415 Etting St.

BOWIE
HOTELS
Stephens Bowie, Bowie-Laurel Rd.

CUMBERLAND
TOURIST HOMES
Glennwood Manor, 927 Glenwood St.

GLENBURNE
DRIVE INN
Brook's, 113 Crainway N. E., Rt. 301

FREDERICK
TOURIST HOMES
Mrs. J. Makel, 119 E. 5th St.
Mrs. W. W. Roberts, 316 W. South
RESTAURANTS
Crescent, 16 W. All Saint St.

HAGERSTOWN
TOURIST HOMES
Harmon, 226 N. Jonathan St.
RESTAURANTS
Ship Tea Room, 329 N. Jonathan St.

HAVRE DE GRACE
HOTELS
Johnson's, 415 S. Stokes St.

PRINCESS ANNE
RESTAURANTS
Victory, 137 Broad St.

TURNERS STATION
NIGHT CLUBS
Adam's
DRUG STORES
Balnew's, 101 Sollers Pt. Rd.

UPPER MARLBORO
HOTELS
Midway

WALDORF
RESTAURANTS
Blue Bird Inn

MASSACHUSETTS

ATTLEBORO
TOURIST HOMES
J. R. Brooks, Jr., 54 James St.

BOSTON
HOTELS
Mothers Lunch, 510 Columbia Ave.
Lucille, 52 Rutland Sq.
Harrett Tubman, 25 Holyoke St.
Columbus Arms, 455 Columbus Ave.
TOURIST HOMES
Julia Walters, 912 Fremont
Holeman, 212 W. Springfield St.
M. Johnson, 616 Columbus Ave.
Mrs. E. A. Taylor, 192 W. Springfield St.
Guest House, 191 Humbolt St.
Randolph House, 153 Worcester St.
Mrs. P. J. Reynolds, 613 Columbus Ave.
Smith's, 14 Yarmouth St.
RESTAURANTS
Edyth's, 170 W. Springfield St.
Slades, 958 Tremont St.
Charlie's, 429 Columbus Ave.
Sunnyside, 411 Columbus Ave.
Western, 415 Mass. Ave.
Estelles, 888 Tremont St.

32

in Patronizing These Places

BEAUTY PARLORS
Mme. F. S. Blake, 363 Mass. Ave.
E. L. Crosby, 11 Greenwich Park
Mme. Enslow's, 977 Tremont St.
W. Williams, 62 Hammond St.
E. West, 609 Columbus Ave.
House of Charms, 169-A W. Springfield
Josephine Bolt, 374 Columbus Ave.
Ruth Evans, 563 Columbus Ave.
Rubinetta, 961 Tremont St.
Lucile's, 226 W. Springfield St.
Constance, 414 Mass. Ave.
Easter's, 168A Springfield St.
Arizona, 563 Columbus Ave.
Betty's, 609 Columbus Ave.
Clark-Merrill, 507 Shawmut Ave.
Amy's, 782 Tremont St.
Doris, 767 Tremont St.
La Newton, 462 Mass. Ave.
Belleza De La Casa, 360 Mass. Ave.

BARBER SHOPS
Amity, 1028 Tremont St.
Abbott's, 974 Tremont St.

NIGHT CLUBS
Savoy, 410 Mass. Ave.

TAVERNS
4-H Lounge, 411 Columbus Ave.

TAILORS
Baltimore, 1013 Tremont St.
Chester's, 189 W. Newton St.

CAMBRIDGE
TOURIST HOMES
Mrs. S. P. Bennett, 26 Mead St.

EVERETT
BEAUTY PARLORS
Ruth's, 20 Woodward St.

GREAT BARRINGTON
TOURIST HOMES
Mrs. I. Anderson, 28 Rossiter St.
Mrs. J. Hamilton, 118 Main St.
Crawford's Inn, 14 Elm Court

HYAMIS
TOURIST HOMES
Zilphas Cottages, 134 Oakneck Rd.

NORTH ADAMS
TOURIST HOMES
F. Adams, 32 Washington Ave.

NORTH CAMBRIDGE
TOURIST HOMES
Mrs. L. G. Hill, 39 Hubbard Ave.

NEEDHAM
TOURIST HOMES
B. Chapman, 799 Central Ave.

PITTSFIELD
TOURIST HOMES
M. E. Grant, 53 King St.
Mrs. T. Dillard, 109 Linden St.
J. Marshall, 124 Danforth Ave.

RANDOLPH
RESTAURANTS
Mary Lee Chicken Shack, 482 Main St.

ROXBURY
BEAUTY PARLORS
Ruth E. Colery's, 132 Warren St.
Janett's, 132 Humboldt Ave.
Charm Grove, 90 Humboldt St.
Mme. Lovett, 68 Humboldt St.
Belinda's, 429 Shawmut Ave.
Cherrie Charm Cove, 90 Humboldt Ave.
Mae's, 140 Lenox St.
Lovett's, 69 Humboldt Ave.
Ruth's, 185 Warren St.

BARBER SHOPS
Wright's, 51A Humboldt St.
Metropolitan, Ruggles & Ashburn Sts.

SERVICE STATIONS
Thompson's, 1105 Tremont St.
Atlanta, 1105 Tremont St.

TAILORS
Morgan's, 355 Warren St.

DRUG STORES
Douglas Square, 1002 Tremont St.
Jaspan's, 134 Harold St.
Kornfield's, 2121 Washington St.

SOUTH HANSON
TOURIST HOMES
Modern, 26 Reed St.

SPRINGFIELD
HOTELS
Springfield

BARBER SHOPS
Joiner's, 97 Hancock St.

BEAUTY PARLORS
Mrs. Law's, 18 Hawley St.

TAILORS
American Cleaners, 433 Eastern Ave.

SWAMPSCOTT
TOURIST HOMES
Mrs. M. Home, 3 Boynton St.

WOBURN
TOURIST HOMES
Mrs. A. E. Roberts, 128 Dragon Ct.

WORCESTER
HOTELS
Worcester, Washington Square

SERVICE STATIONS
Kozarian's, 53 Summer St.

GARAGES
Bancroft, 24 Portland St.

DRUG STORES
Bergwall, 238 Main St.

The Negro Travelers' Green Book 1954

Please Mention the "Green Book"

MICHIGAN

ANN ARBOR
HOTELS
American, 123 Washington St.
Allenel, 126 El Huron St.

BATTLE CREEK
TOURIST HOMES
Mrs. F. Brown, 76 Walters Ave.

BALDWIN
LODGES
Teresa's, Rt. 1
TOURIST HOMES
Whip-or-Will Cottage, Rt. No. 1, Box 178B
NIGHT CLUBS
El Morocco

BENTON HARBOR
NIGHT CLUBS
Research Pleasure Club, 362 8th St.

BITELY
HOTELS
Royal Breeze, Woodland Park

KELSONIA INN
Enjoy the Country, Air, Swimming & Boating - Cottages by the Week or Month - Rooms, Modern Conveniences
Get Good Food - How You Want It
For Res., phone Baldwin 37F21
Woodland Pk. Resort   Biteley, Mich.
ROSCOE C. TERRY, *Proprietor*

NEW BUFFALO
RESTAURANTS
Fire Side, U. S. Rt. 12

COVERT
HOTELS
Star

DETROIT
HOTELS
Capitol, 114 East Palmer
McGraw, 5605 Junction St.
Gotham, 111 Orchestra Place
Mark Twain, E. Garfield & Woodward
Biltmore, 1926 St. Antoine St.
Elizabeth, 413 E. Elizabeth St.
Fox, 715 Madison St.
Norwood, 550 E. Adams St.
Russell, 615 E. Adams St.
Touraine, 4614 John R. St.
Terraine, John R. & Garfield
Northcross, 2205 St. Antoine
Dewey, 505 E. Adams St.
Davidson, 556 E. Forest Ave.
Edenburgh, 758 Westchester Ave.
Old Rivers, 2036 Hastings
Sportman's, 3767 W. Warren Ave.
Carlton Plaza, John R at Edmund
Paradise, 710 Madison St.
Ebony, 110 Chandler St.
Summers, 412 Frederick St.
Australian, 5464 Rivard
TOURIST HOMES
Labland, 39 Orchestra Place
RESTAURANTS
Pelican, 4613 John R. St.
BEAUTY SCHOOLS
Bee-Dew, 703 E. Forest Ave.
Hair Health, 1332 Gratiot Ave.
BARBER SHOPS
Swanson's, 3415 Hastings St.
Arcade, Hastings & Napoleon
Universal, 3129 Hastings St.
TAVERNS
Champion, Oakland & Holbrook
Horseshoe, 606 Club
Broad's, 8825 Oakland
Herman's, 3458 Buchanan
Flame, 4264 John R. St.
Bizerte, 9006 Oakland
Frolic, 4450 John R. St.
Royal Blue, 8401 Russell
NIGHT CLUBS
Congo, 2337 Gratiot St.
Uncle Tom's, 8206 W. 8 Mile Rd.
SERVICE STATIONS
Johnson's, McGraw & 25th St.
Cobb's, Maple & Chene Sts.
Homer's, 589 Madison Ave.
AUTOMOBILES
Davis Motor Co., 421 E. Vernon Highway
TAILORS
Kenilworth, 131 Kenilworth
Blair, 277 Gratiot St.
DHUG STORES
Clay, Clay & Cameron Ave.
Kay, 4766 McGraw Ave.

FLINT
TOURIST HOMES
T. L. Wheeler, 1512 Liberty St.
Mrs. F. Taylor, 1615 Clifford St.

GRAND JUNCTION
TOURIST HOMES
Hamilton Farms, RFD No. 1

IDLEWILD
HOTELS
Lydia Inn, Box 81
Casa Blanca
Oakmere
Paradise Gardens
McKnight's
Phil Giles
Club El Morocco, Rt. No. 1, Box
TOURIST HOMES
Edinburgh Cottage, Miss Herrone
B. Riddles
Rainbow Manor
Douglas Manor
Bash Inn, B'way at Hemlock
Spizerinktom
Rest Haven

34

in Patronizing These Places

RESTAURANTS
 Rosanna's
 Whiteway Inn
 Navajo
TAVERNS
 Rosana
 Purple Palace
 Paradise Gardens

JACKSON
TOURIST HOMES
 Mrs. W. Harrison, 1215 Greenwood Ave.

LANSING
TOURIST HOMES
 Mrs. M. Gray, 1216 St. Joseph St.
 Mrs Lewis, 816 S. Butler St.
 Mrs. Gaines, 1406 Albert St.

LAWRENCE
TOURIST HOMES
 Flora Giles Farm

MUSKEGON
TOURIST HOMES
 R. C. Merrick, 65 E. Muskegon Ave.

OSCODA
TOURIST HOMES
 Jesse Colbath, Van Eten Lake

SAGINAW
TOURIST HOMES
 Mrs. J. Curtley, 439 N. Third St

SOUTH HAVEN
TOURIST HOMES
 Mrs. M. Johnson, Shady Nook Farm

VANDALIA
HOTELS
 Hill's Hotel, Rt. No. 1
TOURIST HOMES
 Mrs. Mayme Cooper, P. O. Box 96

THREE RIVERS
TOURIST HOMES
 Jordan's, Route No. 2

NILES
TOURIST HOMES
 Jones Place, Rt. No. 2, Box 227

MINNESOTA

MINNEAPOLIS
HOTELS
 Serville, 246½ 4th Ave.
 Golden West, 307 Wash. Ave. S.
TOURIST HOMES
 Phyllis Wheatley House, 809 N. Aldrich Ave.
RESTAURANTS
 Bells Cafe, 207 South 3rd St.
TAVERNS
 North Side, 1011 Olson H'way
LIQUOR STORES
 Walston's, 28 South 6th St.
 Harold's, 619 Marq Ave.
 Safro, 236 3rd Ave. So.
 Mac's, 119 Washington Ave. So.
 Labrie's, 324 Plymouth Ave. So.
 Cook's, 239 Cedar Ave.
SERVICE STATIONS
 Dirk's, 2921 5th Ave. S.
TAILORS
 Ann's, 919 7th St. No.
 Franklin, 3510 Cedar Ave.

MOTLEY
TOURIST HOMES
 Motley's Camp
RESTAURANTS
 Herman Stelcks
SERVICE STATIONS
 Geo. Thorn

ROCHESTER
HOTELS
 Avalon, 303 North Broadway

ST. CLOUD
HOTELS
 Grand Central, 5th & St. Germaine
RESTAURANTS
 Spaniol, 13 61h Ave. N.

ST. PAUL
TOURIST HOMES
 Villa Wilson, 697 St. Anthony Ave.
RESTAURANTS
 G. & G. Bar-B-Q, 291 No. St. Albans
 Jim's, St. Anthony and Kent
SERVICE STATIONS
 Gardner's, Western and Central
GARAGES
 Milligan's, 1008 Rondo Ave.
TAILORS
 Drew, 1597 University Ave.
LIQUOR STORES
 Bond, 471 Wabasha
 First, Robert at Fifth
 Commerce, 2163 Ford Parkway
 Seven Corners, 158 West 7th St.
 St. Paul's, 200 East 7th St.
 Rite, 442 Wabasha
 Jack's, 517 Wabasha

MISSISSIPPI

BILOXI
TOURIST HOMES
 Mrs. G. Bess, 630 Main St.
 Mrs. A. J. Alcina, 443 Washington

D'LO
SERVICE STATIONS
 Dades, Hi'Way 49 So.

CANTON
RESTAURANTS
 Tolliver's, 115 N. Hickory
NIGHT CLUBS
 Blue Garden, 5 Liberty St.

CLEVELAND
SERVICE STATIONS
 7-11, Highway 61 at 8

Please Mention the "Green Book"

COLUMBUS
HOTELS
Queen City, 15th St. & 7th Ave.
TOURIST HOMES
M. J. Harrison, 915 N. 14th St.
H. Sommerville, 906 N. 14th St.
Mrs. I. Roberts, 12th & 5th Ave. N.
Mrs. Chevis, 1425 11th Ave. N.

GREENVILLE
SERVICE STATIONS
Peoples, Nelson & Eddie St.

GRENADA
TOURIST HOMES
Mrs. K. D. Fisher, 72 Adams St.
F. Williams, H'way 51 & Fairground Rd.
Mrs. Leola C. Fisher, 700 Govan St.

HATTIESBURG
TOURIST HOMES
W. A. Godbolt, 409 E. 7th St.
Mrs. A. Crosby, 413 E. 6th St.
Mrs. S. Vann, 636 Mobile St.

JACKSON
HOTELS
Summers Hotel, 619 W. Pearl St.
Edward Lee, 144 W. Church St.
RESTAURANTS
Shepherds Kitchenette, 604 N. Farish
TOURIST HOMES
Wilson House, 154 W. Oakley St.
BEAUTY PARLORS
Davis Salon, 703 N. Farish St.
BARBER SHOPS
City, 127 N. Farish St.
TAILORS
Paris, 800 N. Parish St.
DRUG STORES
Palace, 504 N. Farish St.
SERVICE STATIONS
Johnson's, 536 N. Farish
GARAGES
Farish St., 752 N. Farish
TAXI CABS
Veterans, 116 W. Amite St.

LAUREL
HOTELS
Bass, S. Pine St.
TOURIST HOMES
Mrs. E. L. Brown, 522 E. Kingston
Mrs. S. G. Wilson, 802 S. 7th

MACOMB
TOURIST HOMES
D. Mason, 218 Denwidde St.

MENDENHALL
SERVICE STATIONS
Bob's, H'way 49
Smith's, Hi'way 49 No.

MERIDIAN
HOTELS
E. F. Young, 500 25th St.
Beales, 2411 Fifth St.
TOURIST HOMES
C. W. Williams, 1208 31st St.
Mrs. M. Simmons, 5th St. betw. 16 & 17 Ave.
Charley Leigh, 5th St. & 16th Ave.

MOUND BAYOU
TOURIST HOMES
Mrs. Sallie Price
Mrs. Charlotte Strong
GARAGES
Liddle's

RESERVATION BUREAU

Going to take a trip, attend some convention—make sure of your accommodations before you leave.

Housing Conditions Make This Necessary

Reservations for all Hotels, Tourist Homes and Vacation Resorts throughout the United States, Alaska, Mexico and Bermuda can be made for you through our Reservation Bureau.

We have contacts with all Hotels, Tourist Homes and Vacation Resorts. Send us a list of the cities that you expect to pass through, the dates wanted, how many in your party and have us make your reservations. Fees are moderate.

Saves You Time and Money — Write Reservation Bureau

VICTOR H. GREEN & CO.

200 West 135th Street   Room 215A   New York 30, N. Y.

in Patronizing These Places

NEW ALBANY
HOTELS
Foot's, Railroad Ave.
TOURIST HOMES
S. Drewery, Church St.

PASSAGOULA
TOURIST HOMES
Mrs. Minnie B. Wilson, 1001 Kenneth Ave.

YAZOO CITY
HOTELS
Caldwell, Water & Broadway Sts.
TOURIST HOMES
Mrs. A. J. Walker, 321 S. Monroe

MISSOURI

CAPE GIRADEAU
TOURIST HOMES
W. Martin, 38 N. Hanover St.
J. Randol, 422 North St.

COLUMBIA
HOTELS
Austin House, 108 E. Walnut St.
TOURIST HOMES
Mrs. W. Harvey, 417 N. 3rd St.
E. Williams, 314 McBain St.
Williams' Home, 223 Lynn St.
BEAUTY PARLOR
Buckner's Beauty Shop, 502 N. 3rd St.

CHARLESTON
TAVERNS
Creole Cafe, 311 Elm St.

EXCELSIOR SPRINGS
HOTELS
The Albany, 408 South St.
Moore's, 302 Maine St.
Excelsior Springs Hotel, 302 Main St.

HANNIBAL
TOURIST HOMES
Mrs. E. Julius, 1218 Gerard St.

JEFFERSON CITY
HOTELS
Lincoln, 600 Lafayette St.
Booker T.
TOURIST HOMES
Miss C. Woodridge, 418 Adams St.
R. Graves, 314 E. Dunklin St.
RESTAURANTS
De Luxe, 601 Lafayette St.
Blue Tiger, Chestnut & E Atchenson St.
College, 905 E. Atchenson St.
BARBER SHOPS
Tayes, Elm & Lafayette Sts.
BEAUTY PARLORS
Poro, 818 Lafayette St.

TAVERNS
Tops, 626 Lafayette St.
NIGHT CLUBS
Subway, 600 Lafayette St.
Lone Star, 930 E. Miller St.
TAXI CABS
Veteran, 515 Lafayette St.
TAILORS
Rightway, 903 E. Atchenson St.

JOPLIN
TOURIST HOMES
Williams, 308 Penna. St.
J. Lindsay, 1702 Penna. St.
Mrs. F. Echols, 901 Missouri Ave.

KANSAS CITY
HOTELS
Cadillac, 1429 Forest
Booker T. Hotel, 1823 Vine St.
921 Hotel, 921 East 17th St.
Parkview, 10th & Paseo
Street's, 1510 E. 18th St.
Lincoln Hotel, 13th & Woodland Sts.
Square Deal, 1305 E. 18th St.
TOURIST HOMES
Thos. Wilson, 2600 Euclid
Y.W.C.A., 1908, The Paseo
Mrs. Vallie Lamb, 1914 E. 24th St.
RESTAURANTS
Old Kentucky's, 2401 Brooklyn
Oven, 17th & Vine St.
Elmora's Cafe, 1518 E. 18th St.
Famous, 12th & Forest
M. & T., 2013 E. 12th St.
Mim's Cafe, 1603 East 12th St.
TAVERNS
Forest Bar, 1200 E. 18th St.
Vine St., 1519 E. 12th St.
Blackhawk, 1410 E. 14th St.
Green Duck, 2548 Prospect
NIGHT CLUBS
El Capitan, 1610 E. 18th St.
BEAUTY PARLORS
Queen Ann, 1504 E. 11th St.
Hazel Graham, 1836 Vine St.
Arlene, 2409 Vine St.
Katherine's, 1024 East 19th St.
Haley's, 1521 E. 18th St.
Labell, 2614 Tracy
Queen Ann, 1504 East 11th St.
BARBER SHOPS
Ever-Ready, 1810A Vine St.
Barber Shop, 2603½ Prospect Ave.
LIQUOR STORES
Cardinal, 1515 E. 18th St.
Monarch, 2300 Prospect Ave.
Dundee, 1701 Troost
Virginia, 1601 Virginia
Golden Crown, 2218 Vine
Ace, 2404 Vine
Tracy's, 2001 Olive
Donnell, 18th & Troost Sts.
Rubin's, 19th & Vine
Donnich, 18th & Troost

Please Mention the "Green Book"

SERVICE STATIONS
Mobile Station, 1502 E. 19th St.
GARAGES
DRUG STORES
Community, 2432 Vine St.
Johnson's, 2300 Vine St.
Regal's, 2462 Brooklyn Ave.
Prospect, 18th & Prospect
Truman Rd., 2133 Truman Rd.
TAILORS
Spotless, 2303 Prospect Ave.
Courtney, 1715 Brooklyn Ave..

KIMLOCK
BEAUTY PARLORS
Hall's, 659 Carson Rd.
DRUG STORES
Kimlock, Lix & Carson Rd.

MOBERLY
TOURIST HOMES
Ralph Bass, 517 Winchester St.

SEDALIA
TOURIST HOMES
Mrs. T. L. Moore, 505 W. Cooper
Mrs. C. Walker, 217 E. Morgan
W. Williams, 317 E. Johnson

ST. LOUIS
HOTELS

Once Our Guest - Always Our Guest"
BOOKER WASHINGTON
Hotel & Courts
Private Baths - Air Conditioned
Connected Garage - Radios &
Telephones in Every Room
209 N. JEFFERSON AVE.
St. Louis 3, Mo. Tel.: JEfferson 0774

Antler, 3502, Franklin Ave.
Alcorn, 4165 Washington Ave.
Poro Hotel
4300 St. Ferdinand Ave.
West End, 3900 W. Beele St.
Grand Central, Jefferson & Pine
Calumet, 611 N. Jefferson Ave.
Midtown Hotel
2935 Lawton Ave.
Harlem, 3438 Franklin
Atlas, 4267 Delmar
Adam's, 4295 Olive St.
TOURIST HOMES
Y.W.C.A., 2709 Locust St.
RESTAURANTS
Bell's, 3867 Delmar Blvd.
DeLuxe, 10 N. Jefferson Ave.
Northside, 2422 N. Pendleton Ave.
Snack Shop, 1105 N. Taylor
Harlem Grill, 3438 Franklin
Nick's Snack House, 1109 Sarah
Wike's, 1804 N. Taylor Ave.

Ding-Ling End, 7915 Shaftsbury Ave.
Roma, 3839 Finney Ave.
Hunter's, 2610 Delmar Blvd.
Bells, 3867 Delmar Blvd.
Harlem, 3438 Franklin
BEAUTY PARLORS
Parkway, 4218 E. Moffit St.
Allen's, 2343 Market St.
Shaw's, 4356 Easton 13
Juvill, 4141 Easton 13
Young's, 2005 Pine St.
Azalie, 4716A Ashland
Amanda's, 1021 N. Cardinal Ave. 6
Boulevard, 4554 Newberry Ter.
Parkway, 4284 W. St. & Ferdinand
Montgomery, 1033 N. Compton Ave.
Harris, 919 Ohio Ave.
Marcella's, 2306 Cole St.
Tillie's, 2600 Cole St.
Long's, 3134 Bell
De Luxe, 727 Walton Ave.
M. & M., 3975 Delmar Blvd.
Argus, 1008 N. Sarah St.
Casalonia, 4067 A Easton At Sarah
Majestic, 3894 Enright Ave.
A. V's, 919 A Compton
Gloria's, 3151 Sheridan
BARBER SHOPS
Bullock's, 3320 Franklin Ave.
TAVERNS
Calumet, 759 Shaftsbury Ave.
Glass Bar, 2933 Lawson St.
Carioca, 1112½ N. Sarah St.
20th Century, 718 N. Vanderventer
West End, 939 N. Vanderventer Ave.
Hawaiian, 3839 Finney Ave.
Play House, 4071 Page Blvd.
Pullman Club, 2033 Market St.
Roma, 3839 Finney Ave.
Casbah, 2605 Cass Ave.
Duck's, 4384 St. Louis Ave.
Atlas, 4267 Delmar
Bob's, 3855 Pafe Blvd.
NIGHT CLUBS
West End, 911 N. Vanderventer
Riviera, 4460 Delmar Blvd.
20th Century, 718 N. Vanderventer St.
Carioca, 112½ N. Sarah
SERVICE STATIONS
Mack's, 4067 Delmar
Midville, 1913 Pendleton Ave.
Anderson's, 930 N. Compton
Brame's, 4324A Evans
GARAGES
Garfield, 4247 Garfield
TAILORS
Jackson's, 4501 W. Easton Ave.
Orchard, 4480 Easton Ave.
LIQUOR STORES
Siegals, 3015 Locust St.
Harlem, 4161 Easton Ave.
K. & F., 215 N. Jefferson Ave.
Sid's, 1223 N. 13th St.

38

in Patronizing These Places

TAXI CABS
Blue Jay, 2811 Easton Ave.
DeLuxe, 16 N. Jefferson Ave.
DRUG STORES
Taylor Page, 4503 Easton Ave.
Williams, 2801 Cole St.
Douglas, 3339 Laclede
Harper's, 3145 Franklin
Ream's, 1319 N. Grand

RICHMOND
TOURIST HOMES
Harrison, 130 So. Hill St.

SPRINGFIELD
HOTELS

When in Springfield Stop at
**ALBERTA'S HOTEL &
SNACK BAR**
617 NORTH BENTON
3 blocks north of City - Route 66
ALBERTA NORTHCUTT, *Proprietor*

NEBRASKA

AINSWORTH
HOTELS
Midwest
TOURIST HOMES
Skinner's Cabins
RESTAURANTS
Top Notch
SERVICE STATIONS
Weston
Skinner's
Phillips 66
Conoco
GARAGES
House of Chevrolet
Clark's Service
Gil's Body Shop

FREMONT
Gus Henderson, 1725 N. Irving St.

LINCOLN
TOURIST HOMES
Mrs. R. E. Edwards, 2420 'P' St.
DRUG STORES
Smith's, 2146 Vine St.
TAILORS
Zimmerman, 2355 O St.

OMAHA
HOTELS
Broadview, 2060 N. 19th St.
Patton, 1014-18 S. 11th St.
Willis, 22nd & Willis
TOURIST HOMES
L. Strawther, 2220 Willis Ave.
G. H. Ashby,, 2228 Willis Ave.

TAVERNS
Myrtis, 2229 Lake St.
Len's, 25th & Q St.
Apex, 1818 N. 24th St.
LIQUOR STORES
Thrifty, 24th & Lake St.
SERVICE STATIONS
Gabby's, 24th & Ohio
Kaplan, 24th & Grant
TAILORS
Tip Top, 1804 N. 24th St.
DRUG STORES
Hermansky's, 2725 Q St.
Duffy, 24th & Lake St.
Johnson, 2306 N. 24th St.
Reid's, 24th & Seward Sts.

SCOTTSBLUFF
HOTELS
Welsh Rooms, 10th St. & 10th Ave.
TOURIST HOMES
Pickett's, Cabins, East Overland
RESTAURANTS
Eagle,'s, 1603 Broadway

NEW JERSEY

ASBURY PARK
HOTELS
Royal, 216 3rd St.
Reevy's, 135 DeWitt Ave.
Whitehad, 25 Atkins Ave.
TOURIST HOMES
Mrs. W. Greenlow, 1315 Summerfield Ave.
Mrs. C. Jones, 141 Sylvan Ave.
Mrs. V. Maupin, 25 Atkins Ave.
E. C. Yeager, 1406 Mattison Ave.
Anna Eaton, 23 Atkins Ave.
Mrs. Margaret Wright, 153 Sylvan Ave.
RESTAURANTS
Black Diamond, 106 Sylvan Ave.
West Side, 1136 Springwood Ave.
Nellie Tutt's, 1207 Springwood Ave.
BEAUTY PARLORS
Imperial, 1107 Springwood Ave.
Opal, 1146 Springwood Ave.
Marions, 1119 Springwood Ave.
BARBER SHOPS
Consolidated, 1216 Springwood
John Milby, 1216 Springwood Ave.
TAVERNS
**Capitol Tavern,
1212 Springwood Ave.**
Aztex Room, 1147 Springwood Ave.
Hollywood, 1318 Springwood Ave.
2-Door, 1512 Springwood Ave.
Palm Garden, Springwood & Myrtle Aves.

Please Mention the "Green Book"

NIGHT CLUBS
Cuba's, 1147 Springwood Ave.
SERVICE STATIONS
Johnson, Springwood & DeWitt Pl.
Bomar's, Springwood & Ridge
GARAGES
West Side, 1010 Asbury Ave.

ATLANTIC CITY

HOTELS
Bay State, N. Tenn. Ave.
Randell, 1601 Arctic Ave.
Ridley, 1806 Arctic Ave.
Wright, 1702 Arctic Ave.
Lincoln, 911 N. Indiana Ave.
Attucks, 1120 Drexel Ave.
Villanova, 1124 Drexel Ave.
Burton's, 10 No. Delaware Ave.
Johnson's, 11 N. Kentucky Ave.
Albright, 228 N. Virginia Ave.
Liberty, 1519 Baltic Ave.
TOURIST HOMES
Murphy's, 234 Virginia Ave.
Washington, 1109 Arctic Ave.
Shore, 800 Arctic Ave.
Newsome's, 225 N. Indiana Ave.
A. R. S. Goss, 324 N. Indiana Ave.
E. Satchell, 27 N. Michigan Ave.
Bailey's Cottage, 1812 Arctic Ave.
D. Austin, 813 Battic Ave.
R. Brown, 113 N. Penn. Ave.
M. Conte, 128 N. Indiana Ave.
Burton's, 10-12 N. Delaware Ave.
Mrs. V. Jones, 1720 Arctic Ave.
Robert's, 303 No. Indiana Ave.
RESTAURANTS
J & J, 1700 Arctic Ave.
Golden's, 41 N. Kentucky Ave.
Kelly's, 1311 Arctic Ave.
BEAUTY PARLORS
C. E. Newsome, 225 N. Indiana Ave.
Grace's, 43 N. Kentucky Ave.
BARBER SHOPS
42 N. Illinois Ave.
Hollywood, 811 Arctic Ave.
Hunter's, 1816½ Arctic Ave.
TAVERNS
Mack's, 132 N. New York Ave.
Tom Buck's, 1608 Arctic Ave. ..
Lighthouse, 1605 Arctic Ave.
Wonder Bar, 1601 Arctic Ave.
Little Belmont, 37 N. Kentucky Ave.
Hattie's, 1913 Arctic Ave.
Daddy Lew's, Bay & Baltic Ave.
Popular, 1923 Arctic Ave.
Elite, Baltic & Chalfonte Ave.
Herman's, Maryland & Arctic
Prince's, 37 N. Michigan Ave.
Austin's, Maryland & Baltic
Elks Bar & Grill, 1613 Arctic
New Jersey, N. J. & Mediterranean
Circus, 37 N. Michigan Ave.
Tom Buck's, 1608 Arctic Ave.
My Own, 701 Baltic Ave.

Bill Marks, 1923 Arctic
Fannie's, 2001 Arctic Ave.
Shangri-La, Kentucky & Arctic Av.
Perry's, 1228 Arctic Ave.
Johnson's, 10 No. Kentucky Ave.
Hi-Hat, 1317 Arctic Ave.
NIGHT CLUBS
Harlem, 32 N. Kentucky Ave.
Paradise, 220 N. Illinois Ave.
LIQUOR STORES
Tumble Inn, Delaware & Baltic
SERVICE STATIONS
Mundy's, 1818 Arctic St.
DRUG STORES
London's, Cor. Ky. & Arctic Ave.

BARRINGTON
SERVICE STATIONS
Atlantic

BAYONNE
TAVERNS
John's, 463 Ave 'C'
TAILORS

BELMAR
HOTELS
Riverview, 710 8th Ave.
TOURIST HOME
Sadie's Guest House, 1304 "E" St.

BELL MEADE
HOTELS
Bell Meade, Rt. 31

BERLIN
TAVERNS
Tipping Inn, Or Rt. S41

BLOOMFIELD
RESTAURANTS
Lucy's, 376 Broughton Ave.

BRIDGETOWN
TAVERNS
The Ram's Inn, Bridgeston & Millville Pike

CAMDEN
CHINESE RESTAURANTS
Lon's, 806 Kaign Ave.
TAVERNS
Nick's, 7th & Central Ave.
TAILORS
Merchant, 743 Kaighor Ave.

CAPE MAY
HOTELS
New Cape May, Broad & Jackson Sts.
De Griff, 83 Corgie St.
TOURIST HOMES
Mrs. B. Hillman, Johnstown Lane
Stiles, 821 Corgie St.
RESTAURANTS
Billy Boy and Lees, 220 Jackson St.

40

in Patronizing These Places

EAST ORANGE
BEAUTY PARLORS
Ritz, 214 Main St.
Milan's, 232 Halstead St.
TAILORS
Vernon's, 182 Amherst St.
Charles, 49 N. Park St.
TAXI CABS
Whitehurst, Cor. Central & Halstead St.

EATONTOWN
NIGHT CLUBS
The Greenbriar, Pine Bush

EGG HARBOR
HOTELS
Allen House, 625 Cincinnati Ave.
TAVERNS
Red, White & Blue Inn, 701 Phila. Ave.

ELIZABETH
TOURIST HOMES
Mrs. T. T. Davis, 27 Dayton
TAVERNS
One & Only, 1112 Dickerson St.
Hunter's, 1197 E. Broad St.

ENGLEWOOD
TAVERNS
The Lincoln, 1-3 Englewood Ave.
LIQUOR STORES
W. E. Beverage Co., 107 William St.
Giles, 107 William St.

HACKENSACK
BEAUTY PARLORS
Mary, 206 Central Ave.
BARBER STORES
Tip Top, 174 Central Ave.
Crosson, Railroad Place
TAVERNS
Rideout's, 204 Central Ave.
NIGHT CLUBS
Majestic Lodge, 351 1st St.
SERVICE STATIONS
Five Point, 1st & Susquehanna St.

HASKELL
RECREATION PARKS
Thomas Lake

HIGHTSTOWN
TAVERNS
Paul's Inn, Rt. 33 E. Windsor TWP
Old Barn, 104 Daws St.

JERSEY CITY
BEAUTY PARLORS
Beauty, 74A Atlantic Ave.
TAILORS
Bell's, 630 Cummunipaw Ave.
BEAUTY PARLORS
N. J. Academy, 374 Forest St.

KINGSTON
ROAD HOUSES
Merrill's

KEYPORT
TAVERNS
Green Grove Inn, Atlantic & Halsey Sts.
Major's, 215 Atlantic Ave.

KENNELWORTH
TAVERNS
Driver's, 17th & Monroe Ave.

LAWNSIDE
HOTELS
Inman, White Horse Pike
TOURIST HOMES
Hi-Hat, White Horse Pike
TAVERNS
Acorn Inn, White Horse Pike
Dreamland, Evesham Ave.
La Belle Inn, Gloucester Ave.
Wilcox, Evesham Ave.
BEAUTY PARLORS
Thelma Thomas, Warwick Blvd.
BARBER SHOPS
Henry Smith, Mouldy Rd.
RECREATION PARK
Lawnside Park
SERVICE STATIONS
Newton's, White Horse Pike

LINDEN
TAVERNS
Victory, 1305 Baltimore Ave.

LONG BRANCH
TAVERNS
Club '45', Liberty St.
Sam Hall, 180 Belmont St.
Tally-Ho, 44 Liberty St.

MADISON
TAXI CABS

MAGNOLIA
TAVERNS
Sunshine, 540 White Horse Pike

MAHWAH
TAVERNS
Paul's Lunch, Brook St.

MONMOUTH JUNCTION
TOURIST HOMES
Macon's Inn, H'way Rt. No. 1-26

MONTCLAIR
TOURIST HOMES
Y.M.C.A., 39 Washington St.
Y.W.C.A., 159 Glenridge Ave.
RESTAURANTS
Tabard's, 144 Bloomfield Ave.
Blue Front, 154 Bloomfield Ave.

41

The Negro Travelers' Green Book 1954

in Patronizing These Places

BEAUTY SHOPS
Lula's, 270 Bloomfield Ave.
McGhee, 307 Orange Rd.
Gamble's, 146 Bloomfield Ave.

BARBER SHOPS
Stewart Bros., 139 Bloomfield Ave.
Walkers, 180 Bloomfield Ave.
Paramount, 215 Bloomfield Ave.

TAVERNS
Elm's, 231 Bloomfield Ave.

TAILORS
Cut Rate, 274 Bloomfield Ave.
Raveneau, 224 Bloomfield Ave.
Eay-Ayer's, 190 Bloomfield Ave.

SERVICE STATIONS
Whitefields, 175 Bloomfield Ave.
Montclairs, 170 Bioomfield Ave.

GARAGES
Cardell's, 323 Orange Rd.
Maple Ave., 91 Maple Ave.

TAXI CABS
Edmonds, 173 Bloomfield Ave.
Davenport, 152 Lincoln St.

DRUG STORES
Elm Pharmacy, 220 Bloomfield Ave.

NEPTUNE

RESTAURANTS
Hampton Inn, 1718 Springwood Ave
Samuel's, 351 Fisher Ave.
Gottlings, 118 Bradley Ave.

BEAUTY PARLORS
Priscilla's, 261 Myrtle Ave.

NEWARK

HOTELS
Rio Plaza Hotel, 92 S. 13th St.
Coleman, 59 Court St.
Grand, 78 W. Market St.
Y.M.C.A., 153 Court St.
Y.W.C.A., 20 Jones St.
Harwin Terrace, 27 Sterling St.

TOURIST HOMES
RESTAURANTS
Bar-B-Q, 9 Monmouth St.

BEAUTY PARLORS
Mae's, 161 W. Kinney St.
Wilson, 118 Springfield Ave.
La Vogue, 227 W. Kinney St.
Farrar, 35 Prince St.
Billy's, 206 Belmont Ave.
Algene's, 120 Spruce St.
Queen, 155 Barclay St.
Five-Star, 185 Kinney St.

BARBER SHOPS
El Idellio, 30 Wright St.

TAVERNS
Little Charles, 581 Central Ave.
Harlem, 109 Belmont Ave.
Howard, Springfield Ave. & Howard St.
Bert's, 211 Renner Ave.
Dan's, 245 Academy St.
Little Johnny's, 47 Montgomery

Kesselman's, 13th & Rutgers St.
Alcazar, 72 Waverly Place
Rosen's, 164 Spruce St.
Dave's, 202 Court St.
Kleinbergs, 88 Waverly St.
Afro, 19 Quitman St.
Welcome Inn, 87 West St.
'570', 570 Market St.
Corprew's, 297 Springfield Ave.
Dug-Out, 188 Belmont Ave.
Harry's, 60 Waverly Ave.
Ernie's, 104 Wallace St.
Trippe's, 121 Halstead St.
Mulberry, 302 Mulberry St.
Frederick, 2 Boston St.
Hi Spot, 166 W. Kinney St.
Harold, 71 Bloomfield
Wood's, 258 Prince St.

NIGHT CLUBS
Piccadilly, 1 Peshine Ave.
Club Caravan, 8 Bedford St.
Hi Spot, 166 W. Kinney St.
New Kinney Club, 36 Arlington St.
Boston Plaza, 4 Boston St.
Golden Inn, 192 S. Pruce St.
Nest Club, Warren & Norfolk St.
Alcazar, 72 Waverly Ave.
Night Cap, 1079 Broad St.

CHINESE RESTAURANTS
Chinese-American, 603 W. Market

SERVICE STATIONS
Estes, 77 Tillinghast St.

GARAGES
Branch, 45 Rankin St.

OCEAN CITY

HOTELS
Comfort, 201 Bay Ave.
Washington, 6th & Simpson St.
Brydson's, 2878 6th & Simpson Ave.

TOURIST HOMES
Edna Mae's, 921 West Ave.

ORANGE

HOTELS
Y.M.C.A., 84 Oakwood Ave.
Y.W.C.A., 66 Oakwood Ave.

RESTAURANTS
Triangle, 152 Barrow St.
Joe's, 120 Barrow St.

CHINESE RESTAURANTS
Orange Gardens, 132 Parrow St.

DRUG STORES
Central, Parrow & Hickory Sts.

TAILORS
Fitchitt, 99 Oakwood Ave.
Triangle, 101 Hickory St.

PAULSBORO

RESTAURANTS
Elsie's, 246 W. Adams St.

42

in Patronizing These Places

PATERSON
TAVERNS
Idle Hour Bar, 53 Bridge St.
Joymakers, 38 Bridge St.
GARAGES
Brown's, 57 Godwin St.

PERTH AMBOY
HOTELS
Lenora, 550 Hartford St.

POINT PLEASANT
TAVERNS
Joe's, 337 Railroad Ave.

PINE BROOK
TOURIST HOMES
RESTAURANTS

PLAINFIELD
TOURIST HOMES
Miss Daisy Robinson, 658 Essex St.
TAVERNS
Liberty, 4th St.

PLEASANTVILLE
TOURIST HOMES
Marionette Cot., 604 Portland Ave.
Virginia Inn, 1505 S. New Rd.
Garden Spot, 300 Doughty Rd.
TAVERNS
Harlem Inn, 1117 Washington Ave.
ROAD HOUSES
Martin's, 304 W. Wright St.

RED BANK
HOTELS
Robins Nest, 615 River Rd.
RESTAURANTS
Vincents, 263 Shrewsbury Ave.
TAVERNS
West Bergen, 103 W. Bergen Place
BARBER SHOPS
A. Dillard, 250 Shrewsbury Ave.
BEAUTY PARLORS
R. Alleyne, 124 W. Bergen Place
Suries, 261 Shrewsbury Ave.
SERVICE STATIONS
Galatres, Shrewsbury & Catherine
TAILORS
Dudley's, 79 Sunset Ave.

ROSELLE
TAVERNS
Omega, 302 E. 9th St.
St. George, 1139 St. George Ave.
RESTAURANTS
Hill Top, 60 Jerusalem Rd.
ROAD HOUSES
Villa Casanova, Jerusalem Rd.
COUNTRY CLUBS
Shady Rest, Jerusalem Rd.

SALEM
TAVERNS
Stith's, 111 Market St.

SEA BRIGHT
RESTAURANTS
Castle Inn, 11 New St.

SEWAREN
TAILORS
Quality, 13 Pleasant Ave.

SHREWSBURY
SERVICE STATIONS
Rodney's, Shrewsbury Ave.

SUMMIT
HOTELS
Y.M.C.A., 393 Broad St.

TOMS RIVER
TAVERNS
Casaloma, Manitan Park

TRENTON
HOTELS
Y.M.C.A., 40 Fowler St.
RESTAURANTS
Spot Sandwich, 121 Spring St.
BEAUTY PARLORS
Bea's, 114 Spring St.
Geraldine's, 17 Trent St.
BARBER SHOPS
Sanitary, 199 N. Willow St.
Bill's, 105 Spring St.
NIGHT CLUBS
Famous, 228 N. Willow St.
ROAD HOUSES
Crossing Inn, Eggertt's Crossing

VAUX HALL
TAVERNS
Carnegie, 380 Carnegie Place

WILDWOOD
HOTELS
Pondexter Apts., 106 E. Schellinger Ave.
Glen Oak, 100 E. Lincoln St.
The Marion, Artic & Spicer Ave.
Artic Ave., 3600 Artic Ave.
V'esta, 4118 Park Blvd.
TOURIST HOMES
Dean's, 166 W. Young Ave.
Lilian's, 134 W. Baker Ave.
Mrs. E. Crawley, 3816 Artic
BEAUTY PARLORS
B. Johnson's, 407 Garfield Ave.
BARBEH SHOPS
R. Morton, 4010 New Jersey Ave.
NIGHT CLUBS
High Steppers, 437 Lincoln Ave.

WOODBURY
RESTAURANTS
Robinson's, 225 Park Ave.

WEST PLEASANTVILLE
COUNTRY CLUB
Pine Acres Country Club

43

Please Mention the "Green Book"

NEW YORK STATE

ALBANY

HOTELS
Hotel Broadway,
603 Broadway
Kenmore, 76 Columbia Ave.

TOURIST HOMES
Mrs. Aaron J. Oliver
42 Spring St.

RESTAURANTS
Dorsey's, Cor. Van Trumpet & B'way

BEAUTY PARLORS
Buelah Foods, 96 2nd St.
Westner, 643 Broadway

BARBER SHOPS
Martin's, 4 Vantromp St.
Westner, 643 Broadway

NIGHT CLUBS
Rythm Club, Madison Ave.

TAVERNS
King's, Cor. Green & Madison Sts.

ANGOLA

ROAD HOUSES
Leroy's Hacienda
Rt. No. 5, 20 miles west of Buffalo

BATH

TOURIST HOMES
Tuskegee, 364 West Morris St.

BUFFALO

HOTELS
Little Harlem, 494 Michigan Ave.
Y.M.C.A., 585 Michigan Ave.
Montgomery, 486 Michigan Ave.
Vendome, 177 Clinton St.
Claridge, 38 Broadway

TOURIST HOMES
Miss R. Scott, 244 N. Division St.
Mrs. F. Washington, 172 Clinton St.
Mrs. G. Chase, 194 Clinton St.
William Campbell, 342 Adam St.

RESTAURANTS
Horseshoe, 212 William St.
Crystal, 534 Broadway
Bar-B-Q, 413 Michigan Ave.
Empire, 454 Michigan Ave.
Elite, 280 Broadway
Apex, 311 William St.
Alfreda's, 192 Broadway
Peter Dubil, 535 Broadway
New China's, 172 Genesse St.
Panama, 378 Jefferson St.

CHINESE RESTAURANTS
Kam Wing Loo, 433 Michigan Ave.

BEAUTY PARLORS
Middleton, 229 Bond St.
Lady Esther's, 94 Florida St.
Orchid, 419 Pratt St.
Melisey's, 196 Hickory St.
La Ritz, 348 Jefferson Ave.
Matchless, 169 William St.
Edwards, 530 William St.
Jean's, 142 Adams St.
Laura's, 643 Broadway
La Mae, 437 Jefferson Ave.
Jessie's, 560 Spring St.
Fuqua's, 587 Clinton St.
Middleton, 384 Clinton St.
Bonita's, 254 William St.

BARBER SHOP
People's, 433 Williams St.

TAVERNS
Jay G. Stamper, Prop., 192 B'way
Pearls, 474 Michigan Ave.
Clover Leaf, 443 Michigan Ave.

TAVERNS
Apex, 311 Williams St.
Balser, 416 William St.
Kern's, 382 William St.
Hickory, Hickory & Williams
Horse Shoe, Williams & Pine
Toussaint, 292 Williams St.
Joe's, 416 William St.
Glass Horseshoe, 214 Williams St.
Jamboree, 339 Williams St.
Mandy's, 278 Williams St.
Polly's, 483 Jefferson St.
Dubil's, 535 Broadway
Zarin, 557 Clinton St.
Parkside, 452 William St.

NIGHT CLUBS
Moonglow, Michigan & Williams
Horseshoe, William & Pine Sts.

LIQUOR STORES
Swan, Swan & Hickory St.
Aqui-Line, 141 Broadway
Ferry, 192 E. Ferry St.
Stenson's, 133 William St.

SERVICE STATIONS
Fraas, Clinton & Jefferson
Your Tire, 250 Broadway

TAILORS
Eagle, 414 Eagle St.
Reeve's, 119 Clinton St.
Mickey's, 544 Williams St.
Sam's, 270 William St.
Byrd's, 473 Broadway
Bell, 197 William St.
Sam's, 270 William St.
Empire's Star, 234 Broadway

TAXI CABS
Veterans, 120 William St.

DRUG STORES
Wilmar's, 432 William St.
Roebrts, 467 William St.

ELMIRA

TOURIST HOMES
Green Pastures, 670 Dickinson St.

ITHACA

NIGHT CLUBS
Elk's, 119 So. Tioga St.
Forest City, 119 So. Tioga St.

44

in Patronizing These Places

GLENN FALLS
TOURIST HOMES
Hayes Cottage, 99 Sanford St.
Mrs. M. Mayberry, 16 Ferry St.

HUGUENOT
TOURIST HOMES
Janeal Lodge, P. O. Box 23

JAMESTOWN
TOURIST HOMES
Mrs. I. W. Herald, 51 W. 10th St.
Mrs. J. M. Brown, 108 W. 11th St

KINGSTON
HOTELS
Gordon, 3 Canal St.

MECHANICVILLE
TOURIST HOMES
Green's, R.F.D. No. 1

NIAGARA FALLS
TOURIST HOMES
The Hutchinson's
1050 Center Ave.
TOURIST PLACEMENT for GROUPS
W. L. Parker, 627 Erie Ave.
Mack Hayes House, 437 1 St.
Mrs. Ralph W. Reynolds
419 1st St.
Mrs. Alice Ford, 413 First St.
Mrs. Brown, 1202 Haeberie Ave.
Mr. & Mrs. T. R. Davis
319 12th St.
A. E. Gabriel, 635 Erie Ave.
Mrs. M. Francis, 219 10th St.
Mrs. F. T. Young, 421 1st St.
TAVERNS
Cephas, 621 Erie Ave.

NYACK
NIGHT CLUBS
Paradise, Cedar Hill Ave.

PORT JERVIS
TOURIST HOMES
R. Pendelton, 26 Bruce St.

POUGHKEEPSIE
TOURIST HOMES
Mrs. S. Osterholt, 16 Crannell St.

ROCHESTER
HOTELS
Gibson, 461 Clariss St.
TOURIST HOMES
Mrs. Allie O. King, 456 Clarissa St.
Mrs. Latimer, 176 Clarissa St.
RESTAURANTS
La Rue, 491 Clarissa St.
Chicken Shack, 371 Clarissa St.
BEAUTY PARLORS
Beauty Salon, 481 Clarissa St.
Hawkins, 36 Favor St.

BARBER SHOPS
Blackstone's, 399 Clarissa St.
Hawkins, 36 Favor St.
TAILORS
Bright Star, 367 Clarissa St.
Walker's, 149 Adams St.
TAVERNS
Dawn, 314 Clarissa St.
Vallot's, 439 Clarissa St.
Rollin's, 118 Joseph Ave.
Cotton Club, 222 Joseph Ave.
Dan's, 293 Clarissa St.
LIQUOR STORES
Kaplan's, 346 Clarissa St.
GARAGES
Clarissa St., Cor. Spring & Clarissa Sts.
Derham's, 40 Cypress St.
SERVICE STATIONS
A & A, Cor. Beaver & Clarissa

SCHENECTADY
TOURIST HOME
Mrs. Grant Thomas, 1024 Albany
HOTELS
Foster House, 310 Dakota St.
BEAUTY PARLORS
Nixons, 558 Broadway
La Belle Femme, 806 Hamilton St.
Elizabeths, 545 Liberty St.
BARBER SHOPS
Russell's, 351 Broadway
Lee Washington, 530 Liberty St.
TAVERNS
Eljor, 348 Broadway
TAXI CABS
Billy, 348 Broadway

SARATOGA SPRINGS
RESTAURANTS
Spuyten Duyvil, 157 George St.
TOURIST HOMES
LaFleur, 21 Cowan St.
James, 17 Park St.
Mrs. John Parker, 18 Cherry St.

SYRACUSE
BEAUTY PARLORS
Tifferroa's, 422 Harrison St.
BARBER SHOPS
New York, 612 So. Townsend St.
HOTELS
The Savoy, 518 E. Washington St.
TOURIST HOMES
The Sylvan, 815 E. Fayette St.
Y.M.C.A., 340 Montgomery St.
W. R. Farrish, 809 E. Fayette St.
RESTAURANTS
Aunt Edith's, 601½ Harrison St.
TAVERNS
Coles, 825 Townsend St.
Penguin, 822 S. State St.
Copacabana, 725 S. Townsend St.
BEAUTY PARLORS
Tifferroa's, 313 S. McBride St.
Webb's, 512 Almond St.

Please Mention the "Green Book"

BARBER SHOPS
Smith's, 600½ E. Washington St.
New York, 62 So. Townsend St.
John Dove's, 529 Harrison St.
Smith's, 600½ E. Washington St.
NIGHT CLUBS
Goldie's, 423 Harrison St.
LIQUOR STORES
MulRoy's, 301 E. Genessee St.
Ben's, 601 Harrison St.
La Rock's, 442 E. Jefferson St.
DRUG STORES
A & B, 724 S. McBride St.
Singer's, 833 E. Genessee St.
Thornton's, 900 E. Fayette St.
Horton's, 615 Almond St.
TAILORS
Jackson's, 904 E. Fayette St.
Bennie's, 512 Harrison St.

UTICA
TOURIST HOMES
Broad St. Inn, 415 Broad St.
Howard Home, 413 Broad St.

WATERTOWN
HOTELS
Woodruff, Public Square
TOURIST HOMES
E. F. Thomas, 123 Union St.
V. H. Brown, 502 Binase St.
G .E. Deputy, 711 Morrison St.
Mrs. Ruth Thomas, 556 Morrison St.
RESTAURANTS
Capitol, Court Square
BARBER SHOPS
Chicago, Court St.
BEAUTY PARLORS
Mrs. Nancy Williams, 496 Edmonds
SERVICE STATIONS
Reilly Esso Station, 496 Edmonds
GARAGES
Guilfoyle, Stone St.

WESTBROOKVILLE
TOURIST HOME
White Horse Lodge

NEW YORK, N.Y.
(HARLEM)
HOTELS
Braddock, 126th & 8th Ave.
El Melrah, 19 W. 135th St.
Woodside, 2424 7th Ave.
Grampion, 152 St. Nicholas Ave.
Y.M.C.A., 180 W. 135th St.
Y.W.C.A., 175 W. 137th St.

HOTEL FANE
FRANK G. LIGHTNER, Manager
Formerly Hotel Dumas
In the Heart of Harlem
Rooms with Private Bath, Hot-Co
Water, Radio in Rooms
Phone Reservations
205 WEST 135th STREET
Tel.: AUdubon 6-7188

Hotel Revella
307 West 116th St.
Phone: UNiversity 4-9825
Elton, 227 W. 135th St.
Cadillac, 235 W. 135th St.
Rich's Plaza, 35 Bradhurst Ave.
Mel's Plaza, 151 W. 118th St.
America, 145 West 47th St.
Garret Hotel, 314 W. 127th St.
Crosstown, 515 W. 145th St.

Richard Hotel,
6 Bradhurst Ave.
Harriet Hotels, 313 W. 127th St.
Cambridge, 141 W. 110th St.
Martha, 6 W. 135th St.
Welthon, 2057 7th Ave.
Dewey Square, 201-203 W. 117th St.
The Tenrub, 328 St. Nicholas
Beakford, 300 W. 116th St.

Hotel Theresa,
2090 7th Ave.
Mariette, 170 W. 121st St.
Currie, 101 W. 145th St.
Cecil, 208 W. 118th St.
Revella, 307 W. 116th St.
Hudson, 1649 Amsterdam Ave.
Barbera, 501 W. 142nd St.

Crosstown Hotel
515 West 145th St.
Hotel Elmeneh, 845 St. Nicholas
Douglas, 809 St. Nicholas Ave.
Manhattan, 504 Manhattan Ave.
Delta, 409 W. 145th St.
Edgecombe, 345 Edgecombe
Crosstown, 515 W. 145th St.
Parkview, 55 W. 110th St.
RESTAURANTS
Pete's, 2534 7th Ave.
Surprise, 2319 7th Ave.
Lulu Belle's, 317 W. 126th St.
Four Star, 2433 7th Ave.

46

Please Mention the "Green Book"

for...
for Sightseeing
in New York

By Bus   By Boat

Special Rates for Groups of 25 or More

No Service Charge

Write or Contact

VICTOR H. GREEN & COMPANY
200 West 135th Street   Room 215A   New York 30, N. Y.

Esquire Lunchonette, 2201 7th Ave.
Brown's, 210 W. 135th St.
E & M, 2016 7th Ave.
Em & Bee, 458 Lenox Ave.
Davis', 2066 7th Ave.
Pals Inn, 307 W. 125th St.
Little Shack, 2267 7th Ave.
Jimmy's, 763 St. Nicholas Ave.
Rose Meta, 9 W. 125th St.
The Lotus, 454 Lenox Ave.
Jennie Lou's, 2297 7th Ave.
Hamburg Paradise, 377 W. 125th St.
Jimmie's, 307 W. 125th St.
Beverly Hills, 303 W. 145th St.
Frazier's, 2067 7th Ave.
Shalimar, 2065 7th Ave.

TOURIST HOMES
Mrs. Agnes Babb, 68 E. 127th St.

CHINESE RESTAURANTS
Mayling, 1723 Amsterdam Ave.

BEAUTY PARLORS
Frankie's, 2380 7th Ave.
Elite, 2544 7th Ave.
Myers & Griffin, 65 W. 134th St.
National, 301 W. 144th St.
Neuway, 143 W. 116th St.
Beard's, 322 St. Nicholas Ave.
Bonnie's, 165 W. 127th St.
Mme. Ruth's, 259 W. 116th St.

BARBER SHOPS
Sportsman, 268½ W. 135th St.
Davis, 69 W. 138th St.
Renaissance, 2349 7th Ave.
Delux, 92 St. Nicholas Pl.
World, 2621 8th Ave.

Dunbar, 2808 8th Ave.
Hi-Hat, 2276 7th Ave.
Ideal, 716 St. Nicholas Ave.
Modernistic, 2132 7th Ave.
Service, 2296 7th Ave.
Blue Castle, 1861 Amsterdam Ave.
Early Dawn, 2570 7th Ave.
The Esquire, 2265 7th Ave.
Tuxedo, 1925 Amsterdam Ave.

TAVERNS
El Favorito Bar, 2055 8th Ave.
International, 2150 5th Ave.
Arhtur's, 2481 8th Ave.
Red Tip, 2470 7th Ave.
John Allen's, 207 W. 116th St.
Brittwood, 594 Lenox Ave.
Frankie's Cafe, 2328 7th Ave.
Bank's, 2338 8th Ave.
Brownie's, 2571 7th Ave.
Bogan's, 2154 8th Ave.
Frank Lezama, 3578 Broadway
Palm, 209 W. 125th St.
Frank's, 313 W. 125th St.
William's, 2011 7th Ave.
Harris' Corner, 132nd St. & 7th Ace.
Dawn, 1931 Amsterdam Ave.
Pasadena, 2350 8th Ave.
Jack Carters, 1890 7th Ave.
Poor John's, 2268 8th Ave.
Farrell's, 2175 7th Ave.
Chico's, 2014 Fifth Ave.
Braddock, Cor. 126th St. & 8th Ave.
Jock's, 2350 7th Ave.
Tom Farrell's, 128th St. & Convent Ave.

47

Please Mention the "Green Book"

George's, 630 Lenox Ave.
Sugar Ray's, 2074 7th Ave.
Hawkin's, 308 W. 125th St.
Apollo, 303 W. 125th St.
Baby Grand, 319 W. 125th St.
Al's, 415 W. 125th St.
Horseshoe, 2474 7th Ave.
Lou's, 1985 Amsterdam Ave.
Welcome Inn, 2895 8th Ave.
Tom Delaney, 7th Ave. & 137th St.
Blue Heaven, 378 Lenox Ave.
Colonial, 116 Bradhurst Ave.
Eddie's, 714 St. Nicholas Ave.
Hot-Cha, 2280 7th Ave.
La Mar Cheri, 739 St. Nicholas Ave.
Logas, 2496 7th Ave.
Monte Carlo, 2247 7th Ave.
Murrain, 635 Lenox Ave.
Victoria, 2418 7th Ave.
Fat Man, St. Nicholas Ave. & 155th
Jimmie Daniels, 114 W. 116th St.
Moon Glow, 2461 7th Ave.
George Farrell's, 2711 8th Ave.
Novelty Bar & Grill, 1965 Amsterdam Ave.
L-Bar, 3601 Broadway
Chick's Bar & Grill, 2501 7th Ave.
Sport's Inn, 2308 8th Ave.
Clover Bar & Grill, 1735 Amsterdam Ave.
Daniel's, 2461 7th Ave.
Coran's, 2359 7th Ave.
Pelican, 45 Lenox Ave.
Mandalay, 2201 7th Ave.
Dawn Cafe, 1931 Amsterdam Ave.
Chateau Lounge, 379 W. 125th St.
Well's, Musical Bar, 2249 7th Ave.
Firpo's, 503 Lenox Ave.
Zambezi, 2267 7th Ave.
Mardi Gras, 1951 Amsterdam Ave.
Casbah, 163rd St. & St. Nicholas
Bowman's, 92 St. Nicholas Pl.
Renny, 2359 7th Ave.
Elk Scene, 439 Lenox Ave.
Magnet, 570 Lenox Ave.
Fez, 1958 7th Ave.
Frankie's, 2328 7th Ave.
Bird Cage, 2308 7th Ave.
Bali, 2096 Amsterdam Ave.

NIGHT CLUBS
Savannah Club, "66" 68 W. 3rd St.
Reno, 549 W. 145th St.
Elk's Rendezvous, 133rd & Lenox
Celebrity Club, 35 E. 125th St.
Murrain's, 132nd & 7 Ave.
Hollywood Club, 116th & Lenox
Lenox Rendezvous, 75 Lenox Ave.
Harlem, 266 W. 145th St.
Lido, 35 W. 125th St.
Club Harlem, 266 W. 145th St.
Gold Coast Lounge, 2017 5th Ave.
Well's Musical Bar, 2249 7th Ave.
Bowman's, 92 St. Nicholas Pl.
Paradise, 8th Ave. at 110th St.

LIQUOR STORES
Convent, 42 Convent Ave.
Charity, 483 W. 150 St.
Daniel Burrows, 760 St. Nicholas
Eulace Peacock, 200 W. 140th St.
Ferguson, 271 W. 126th St.
Fitton & Telesford, 300½ W. 116th
Green's, 161 W. 120th St.
H. & S., 5 W. 131st St.
Harlem, 85 W. 128th St.
Inez Gumbs, 347 W. 120th St.
C. D. Kings, 2087 Madison Ave.
Padam's, 1963 Amsterdam Ave.
Chas. Arshen, 2501 8th Ave.
Forbes, 272 W. 154th St.
Hamilton Place, 150 Hamilton Pl.
H & R, 273 W. 121st St.
Roy Campanella, 7th Ave. & 134 St.
Goldman's, 483 W. 155th St.

DRUG STORES
M. Boutte, 1028 St. Nicholas Ave.

GARAGES
Colonial Park, 310 W. 144th St.
Polo Grounds, 155th St. & St. Nicholas Ave.
Dumas, 226 W. 135th St.
Park Lane, 1890 Park Ave.

TAILORS
Robert Lewis, 1980 7th Ave.
Globe, 2894 8th Ave.
7th Ave., 2051 7th Ave.
Little Alpha, 200 W. 136th St.
Dig-By, 300 W. 111th St.
La Fontaine, 470 Convent Ave.
Hill Side, 513 W. 145th St.
Dillette's, 101 ..dgecombe Ave.

SERVICE STATIONS
Park Lane, 1890 Park Ave.

DANCE HALLS
Savoy, Lenox Ave. & 140th St.
Golden Gate, Lenox Ave. & 142th

BROOKLYN
HOTELS

GARFIELD HOTEL
Newly Furnished and Decorated
160 REID AVE., BROOKLYN, N. Y.
Bet. Gates Ave. & Monroe St.
Tel.: GLenmore 5-1094

Pleasant Manor, 218 Gates Ave.
Garfield, 160 Reid Ave.
Lincoln Terrace, 1483 Pacific St.
Y.M.C.A., 405 Carlton Ave.
Burma, 145 Gates Ave.
Lefferts, 127 Lefferts Place
Garfield, 160 Reid Ave.

RESTAURANTS
Commodore, 486 Thompkins Ave.
Continental, 706 Nostrand Ave.
Jackson's, 1558 Fulton St.

48

in Patronizing These Places

Dew Drop, 363 Halsey St.
Little Roxy, 490A Summer Ave.
Bernice's Cafeteria, 105 Kingston Ave.
Spick & Span, 70 Kingston Ave.
G & H, 382 Summers Ave.
Caravan, 377 Hancock St.

CHINESE RESTAURANTS
Chung King, 1139 Fulton St.
New Shanghai, 361 Nostrand Ave.
Fulton Palace, 1139 Fulton St.

BEAUTY PARLORS
Berlena's, 186 Jefferson
Bartley's, 1125 Fulton St.
Katherine's, 345 Sumner Ave.
Ideal, 285A Sumner Ave.
Mariett's, 451 Nostrand Ave.
Edith's, 389 Tompkins Ave.
LaRoberts, 322 Macon St.

BEAUTY CULTURE SCHOOLS
Theresa, 304 Livonia Ave.

TAVERNS
Riviera, Bedford & Brevoort Pl.
Brownie's, 714 St. Marks Pl.
Flamingo, 259 A Kingston Ave.
Topside, 537 Marcy Ave.
Palm Gardens, 491 Summer Ave.
Royal, 1073 Fulton St.
Parkside, 759 Gates Ave.
Decatur Bar & Grill,, 301 Reid Ave.
Kingston Tavern, 1496 Fulton St.
Arlington Inn, 1253 Fulton St.
Disler's, 759 Gates Ave.
Veorna Leafe, 1330 Fulton St.
K & C Tavern, 588 Gates Ave.
Smitty's, 286 Patchen Ave.
Casablanca, 300 Reid Ave.
Country Cottage, 375 Franklin Ave.
Bombay, 377 Christopher St.
Capitol, 1550 Fulton St.
Traveler's, Inn, 5A Hull St.
Marion's, 125 Marion St.
Ward's, 480 Halsey St.
Tip Top, 1750 Fulton St.
Topside, 537 Marcy Ave.
Berry Bros., 1714 Fulton St.
Logan's, 1165 Bradford Ave.
Bar 688, 688 Halsey St.
Brooklyn Fraternal, 1068 Fulton St.
Jefferson, 397 Tompkins Ave.
Bushwick, 375 Bushwick Ave.
Lorene's, 373 Nostrand Ave.
Turbo Village, 249 Reid Ave.
Elmo, 243 Reid Ave.
Summer, 693 Gates Ave.
New Durkin, 1285 Fulton St.
Esquire, Atlantic & Kingston Aves.
Frank's Caravan, 377 Hancock St.
Hollywood, Cor. Gates & Nostrand Aves.
Cross Roads, Cor. Bedford & Fulton Sts.
Laredo Bar, 1624 Fulton St.

NIGHT CLUBS
Ebony, 1330 Fulton St.
Baby Grand, 1274 Fulton St.

DRUG STORES
Provident, 1265 Bedford Ave.
Bancroft, Franklin & Bergen St.

WINE & LIQUOR STORES
Yak, 1361 Fulton St.
Lincoln, 401 Tompkins Ave.
York, 1361 Fulton St.
Stuyvesant, 1551 Fulton St.
Allen Rose, 106 Kingston Ave.
Turner's, 249 Sumner St.
Gottesman's, 41 Albany Ave.
Sexton's, 616 Halsey St.

TAILORS
Bea Jay, 1722 Fulton St.

BRONX

HOTELS
Guest House, 744 Kelly St.
Carver, 980 Prospect Ave.
Crotona, 695 E. 170th St.

RESTAURANTS
Daniel's, 1107 Prospect Ave.

BEAUTY PARLORS
Grayson, 874 Prospect Ave.
Glennada, 875 Longwood Ave.

BARBER SHOPS
Modern, 1174 Boston Rd.

TAVERNS
Freddie's Bar, 1204 Boston Rd.
Harty's Mid-Way, 458 E. 165th St.
Neighborhood, 3344 Third Ave.
Louis' Tavern, 3510 Third Ave.
Kennie's, 853 Freeman St.
Lucille's, 3800 Third Ave.
Jimmy's, 267 E. 161st St.
Zombie Bar, 1745 Boston Rd.
Rainbow Gardens, 977 Prospect Ave.
B & P, 823 E. 169th St.
Trinity, 163rd & Trinity Ave.
Ralph Rida's, 1155 Tinton Ave.
Crystal Lounge, 1035 Prospect Ave.
Five Corners, 169th St. & Boston Rd
Sporting Life, 950 Prospect Ave.
Central, 267 E. 161st St.
DeLuxe, 270 E. 161st St.
Alamo, 1056 Boston Rd.

WINE AND LIQUOR STORES
Franklin Ave., 1214 Franklin Ave.
Prospect, 889 Prospect Ave.
West Farms, 2026 Boston Rd.
O'Connell's, 1311 Boston Rd.

NIGHT CLUBS
845-845 Prospect Ave.

BALLROOM
McKinley, 1258 Boston Rd.

SERVICE STATIONS
Al & Jim's, Boston Rd. & 170th St.

49

Please Mention the "Green Book"

LONG ISLAND

AMITYVILLE
RESTAURANTS
Watervliet, 158 Dixon Ave.
ROAD HOUSES
Freddy's, Albany & Banbury Court
BARBER SHOPS
Jimmy's, Albany & Brewster
BEAUTY PARLORS
Boyd's, 21 Banbury Court

CORONA
TAVERNS
Big George, 106 Northern Blvd.
Prosperity, 32-19 103rd St.
NIGHT CLUBS
New Cameo, 108 Northern Blvd.
BEAUTY PARLORS
Myrt's, 105-09 Northern Blvd.
RESTAURANTS
Encore, 105-13 Northern Blvd.

FREEPORT
NIGHT CLUBS
Celebrity, 77 E. Sunrise H'way

HEMPSTEAD
TAVERNS
BARBER SHOPS
Modernistic, 96 So. Franklin St.
BEAUTY PARLORS
Sykes, 98 So. Franklin St.

INWOOD
NIGHT CLUBS
Club Carib, 333 Bayview Ave.

JAMAICA
TAVERNS
Palm Gardens, 107-02 Merrick
Tolliver's, 112-27 New York Blvd.
Mandalay, 114-16 Merrick Rd.
Hank's, 108-04 New York Blvd.
Old Sweet, 158-11 South Rd.
TAILORS
Klugh's, 107-21 171st St.
BEAUTY PARLORS
Roslyn, 106-53 New York Blvd.

LINDENHURST
NIGHT CLUBS
Club Ebony, Sunrise H'way 40th St.

SPRINGFIELD
BEAUTY PARLORS
Gorja, 126-17 Merrick Blvd.

ST. ALBANS
LIQUOR STORE
Frank Maybrs, 119-06 Merrick Blvd
NIGHT CLUBS
Ruby, 175-02 Baisley Blvd.

STATEN ISLAND

WEST BRIGHTON
BEAUTY PARLORS
Etta's, 1652 Richmond Terr.
BARBER SHOPS
Dozier, 192 Broadway
NIGHT CLUBS
Williams, 208 Broadway
TAILORS
A. Higgs, 721 Henderson
Tucker, 260 Broadway
SERVICE STATIONS
Rispoli, 46 Barker St.

Yes! We Can Arrange Your Vacation . . . Everyhere in the United States

CRUISES   TOURS   TICKETS

**WEST INDIES   CALIFORNIA   MEXICO
BERMUDA   EUROPE   CANADA
AFRICA   SOUTH AMERICA**

No Service Charge

VICTOR H. GREEN & CO.
200 West 135th Street   Room 215A
New York 30, N. Y.

50

in Patronizing These Places

WESTCHESTER

ELMSFORD
TAVERNS
Clarke, 91 Saw Mill River Rd.

MT. VERNON
TOURIST HOME
Mrs. Lloyd King, 343 So. 10th Ave.
RESTAURANTS
Hamburger, 15 W. 3 St.
Friendship, 50 W. 3rd St.
TAVERNS
Mohawk Inn, 142 S. 7th Ave.
Friendship Center, 50 W. 3rd St.

NEW ROCHELLE
HOTELS
Huguenot, 242 Huguenot St.
RESTAURANTS
Harris, 29 Morris St.
Week's, 68 Winyah Ave.
BEAUTY PARLORS
A. Berry, 50 DeWitts Pl.
B. Miller, 54 DeWitts Pl.
Ocie, 41 Rochelle Pl.
BARBER SHOPS
Field's, 66 Winyah Ave.
Bal-Mo-Ral, 56 Brook St.
LIQUOR STORES
A. Edwards, 112 Union Ave.
DRUG STORES
Daniel's, 57 Linclon Ave.

NORTH TARRYTOWN
BARBER SHOPS
Lemon's, Valley St.

TUCKAHOE
RESTAURANTS
Butterfly Inn, 47 Washington St.
BEAUTY PARLORS
Shanhana, 144 Main St.
BARBER SHOPS
Al's, 144 Main St.

YONKERS
RESTAURANTS
The Brown Derby, 125 Nepperham Ave.

WHITE PLAINS
HOTELS
Rel Rio, 122 Lafayette Ave.
RESTAURANTS
Walnard's, 79 Martine Ave.
Waldorf, 102 Grove St.
Tarks, 372 Central Ave.
Field's, 338 Tarrytown Rd.
BEAUTY PARLORS
Reynold's, 144 Main St.
Maudie's, 122 Martine Ave.
BARBER SHOPS
Mitchell's, 100 Grove St.
NIGHT CLUBS
Shelton's, 53 Grove St.

LIQUOR STORES
Martine, 120 Martine Ave.
TAVERNS
Field's, 538 Tarrytown Rd.
Sonny's, 397 Tarrytown Rd.
TAXI CABS
Martine, 85 Martine Ave.
Bower, 106 Grove St.
TAILORS
Johnson's, 121 Martine Ave.

NEVADA
RENO
TOURIST HOMES

HAWTHORNE GUEST
Catering to Tourists - Phone 3-7386
OPEN YEAR ROUND
Rec. by Chamber of Commerce,
also A.A.A.
J. R. HAMLET, Prop.
542 Valley Road   Reno, Nevada

Floyd Garner, 857 E. 2nd St.

LAS VEGAS
TOURIST HOMES
Harrison's Guest House
1001 North 8 'F' St.
Shaw Apts., 619 Van Buren St.

NEW HAMPSHIRE
WHITEFIELD
TOURIST HOMES
Mrs. Homer Mason, Greenwood St.

NEW MEXICO
ALBUQUERQUE
TOURIST HOMES
Mrs. Kate Duncan, 423 N. Arno St.
Mrs. W. Bailey, 1127 N. 2nd St.
RESTAURANTS
Aunt Brenda's, 406 North Arno St.

CARLSBAD
TOURIST HOMES
Mrs. A. Sherrell, 502 S. Haloquens
BARBER SHOPS
Garland Johnson, West Bronson St.

GALLUP
TOURIST HOMES
Mrs. Sonnie Lewis, 109 Wilson St.

ROSWELL
TOURIST HOMES
Mrs. Mary Collins
121 East 10th St.
R. Brown, 313 W. Math
RESTAURANTS
Sun Set Cafe, 115 E. Walnut St

51

Please Mention the "Green Book"

TUCUMCARI
TOURIST HOMES
Rockett Inn
524 W. Campbell St.
Jone's Rooms, Box 1002
J. E. Mitchell, 406 N. 3rd S.
Mitchell's Rooms
406 North 3rd St.
GARAGES
Swift's, Hi'way 66

NORTH CAROLINA

ASHEVILLE
HOTELS
James Keys, 409 Southside Ave.
Y.W.C.A., 360 College St.
Booker T. Washington, 409 Southside
TOURIST HOMES
Savoy, Eagle & Market Sts.
RESTAURANTS
Palace Grille, 19 Eagle St.
BARBER SHOPS
Wilson's, 13 Eagle St.
Jamison, 211 Ashland Ave.

BLADENBORO
BEAUTY PARLORS
Lacy's Beauty Shop

CHARLOTTE
HOTELS
Alexander, 523 N. McDowell St.
RESTAURANTS
Ingram's, 304 So. McDowell St.
BEAUTY PARLORS
Martha's, 509 E. 2nd St.
BARBER SHOPS
2nd St., 500 E. 2nd St.
Martha's, 508 E. 2nd St.
DRUG STORES
Charlotte, 200 E. Trade St.
Carolina, 401 E. Trade St.
TAILORS
New Way, 935 E. 9th St.
SERVICE STATIONS
Bishop Dale, 1st & Brevard Sts.
Bob Roberson's, 701 Trade St.

DURHAM
HOTELS
Biltmore, 332½ E. Pettigrew St.
Jones, 502 Ramsey St.
RESTAURANTS
Elivira's, 801 Fayetteville St.
Bull City, 412 Pettigrew
Cu-Cu, 916 Pickets
College Inn, 1306 Fayetteville

BEAUTY PARLORS
De Shazors, 809 Fayetteville St.
D'Orsay, 120 S. Mangum St.
Friendly City, 711 Fayetteville St.
Burma's, 536 E. Pettigrew St.
Vanity Fair, 1508 Fayetteville St.
BARBER SHOPS
Friendly, 711 Fayetteville St.
TAVERNS
Hollywood, 118 S. Mangum St.
College Inn, 1306 Fayetteville St.
Jack's Grill, 706 Fayettev ille St.
SERVICE STATIONS
Granite, Main & 9th St.
Pine Ctreet, 1102 Pine St.
Williams, Cor. Pettigrew & Pine Sts.
Biltmore, 402 E. Pettigrew St.
Clay's, 406 1-2 Pettigrew St.
Speight's, Fayetteville & Pettigrew
Sulton's Esso, 400 Pine St.
DRUG STORES
Garrett's Biltmore, E. Pettigrew St.
Bull City, 610 Fayetteville St.
TAILORS
Royal Cleaners
538 E. Pettigrew St.
Boykin, 715 Fayetteville St.
Service, 612 Fayetteville St.
Union, 418 Dowd St.
Scott & Roberts, 702 Fayetteville

ELIZABETH CITY
TAVERNS
Blue Duck Inn, 404½ Ehringhaus
SERVICE STATIONS
Small's, Cor. S. Rd. & Roanoke Ave.

ELIZABETHTOWN
BEAUTY PARLORS
Liola's Beauty Salon
TAVERNS
Gill's Grill
Royal Cafe
DRUG STORES
McKay & Neal

ENFIELD
RESTAURANTS
Royal, 301 Highway St.

FAYETTEVILLE
HOTELS
Restful Inn, 418 Gillespie St.
TOURIST HOMES
Jones' Tourist Home
311 Moore St.
Mrs. L. C. McNeil, 418 Gillespie St.
RESTAURANTS
Mayflower Grill, N. Hillsboro St.
Silver Grill, 115 Gillespie St.
Arthur's Seafood rGill, 637 Person
"Vpoint", Murchison Rd.
Silver Girll, 115 Gillespie St.

52

in Patronizing These Places

BEAUTY PARLORS
Brown's, 133 Person St.
Royal Beauty Parlor, 127½ Person
Modiste, 130½ Person St.
Ethel's, Gillespie St.

BARBER SHOPS
DeLux, Pesno St.
Mack's, 117 Gillespie St.

TAVERNS
Jack's, 213 Hillsboro St.

SERVICE STATIONS
Moore's, 613 Ramsey St.

GARAGES
Jeffrie's, Blount St.

TAILORS
Gregory's, 1219 Ft. Bragg Rd.

GOLDSBORO
DRUG STORES
Jackson's, So. James St.

TAILORS
Garris, 208 N. Center St.

RESTAURANTS
Scott's, 404 Gully St.

SHAVING PARLORS
Thornton's, Teenage, 507 Alvin St.

BEAUTY PARLORS
Raynard's, 619 Devereaux St.

GREENSBORO
HOTELS
Plaza Manor, 511 Martin St.
Legion Club, 829 E. Market St.

TOURIST HOMES
T. Daniels, 912 E. Market St.
Mrs. Lewis, 829 E. Market St.
I. W. Wooten, 41 Lindsay St.

TAVERNS
Paramount, 907 E. Market St.

TAILORS
Shoffners, 922 E. Market St.

TAXI CABS
MacRae, 106 S. Macon St.

GREENVILLE
RESTAURANTS
Paradise, 314 Albermale Ave.
Bell's, 310 Albermarle Ave.

BEAUTY SHOPS
Spain, 614 Atlantic Ave.

DRUG STORES
Harrison's, 908 Dickerson St.

HALLSBORO
BEAUTY PARLORS
Leigh's, Route No. 1

HAMLET
CABINS
C. B. Covington, North Yard

HENDERSON
TOURIST HOMES
Adams Tourist Home
526 Chestnut St.

TAXI CABS
Green & Chavis, 720 Eaton St.

HIGH POINT
HOTELS
Kilby's, 627½ E. Washington St.

KINGS MOUNTAIN
TOURIST HOMES
Mrs. L. E. Ricks

KINGSTON
SERVICE STATIONS
Daves, 205 E. South St.

LITTLETON
HOTELS
Young's Hotel

LUMBERTON
HOTEL
Spring's Inn, 103 Chestnut St.

LEXINGTON
SERVICE STATIONS
D. T. Taylor, Esso Service

MT. OLIVE
RESTAURANTS
Black Beauty Tea Room

NEW BERN
HOTELS
Rhone, 42 Queen St.

TOURIST HOMES
H. C. Sparrow, 06 West St.

RALEIGH
DRIVE IN RESTAURANTS
Nile-Congo, Rt. 70 & Garner Rd.
2½ Miles East

HOTELS
De Luxe Hotel
220 E. Cabarrus St.
Arcade, 122 E. Hargett St.
Y.M.C.A., 600 So. Bloodworth St.
Lewis Hotel, 200 Cabarrus St.

TOURIST HOMES
Starksville Guest House
809 E. Bragg St.
Mrs. Charles Higgs, 219 E. Lenoir
Mrs. Pattie Higgs, 313 N. Tarboro

RESTAURANTS
Owens, 125 E. Hargett St.
New York, 108 E. Hargett St.
Stanton's, Cafe, 319 South East St.

TAVERNS
Tip Toe Inn, Cor. Davis & Bloodworth Sts.

BEAUTY PARLORS
Hall's, 322 N. Tarboro St.
Sales, 222 S. Tarboro St.

TAILORS
G. & M., 106 Hargett St.
Lewis, 220 E. Cabarrus St.
Arcade, 122 E. Hargett St.
Peerless, 516 Fayetteville St.
Snakenburg, 123 So. Salisbury St.

53

The Negro Travelers' Green Book 1954

Please Mention the "Green Book"

GARAGES
Richradson & Smith, 108 E. Lenoir St.
TAXI CABS
East End, Dial 2-2086

PINEHURST
TOURIST HOMES
Foster's
SERVICE STATIONS
Foster's

ROCKY MOUNT
RESTAURANTS
Dixie, 106 E. Thomas
SERVICE STATIONS
Atlantic, 216 E. Thomas St.
Shaws, 440 Raleigh Rd.

SALISBURY
TAXI CABS
Safety, 122 N. Lee St.

SANFORD
DRUG STORES
Bland's, 300 S. Steele St.

SUMTER
TAVERNS
Silver Moon, 20 W. Liberty St.

WELDON
HOTELS
Pope
Terminal Inn, Washington Ave.

WHITEVILLE
TOURIST HOMES
Mrs. Fannie Jeffers, Mill St.

WILSON
HOTELS
The Wilson Biltmore, 539 E. Nash
TAXI CABS
M. Jones, 1209 E. Queen St.

WINSTON SALEM
HOTELS
Belmont, 601½ No. Patterson St.
Lincoln, 9 E. 3rd St.
Y.M.C.A., 410 N. Church St.
TOURIST HOMES
Charles H. Jones, 1611 E. 14th St.
Mrs. H. L. Christian, 302 E. 9th St.

WILMINGTON
HOTELS
Murphy, 813 Castle St.
TOURIST HOMES
Charles F. Payne
417 North 6th St.
RESTAURANTS
Johnson's, 1007 Chestnut St.
Ollie's, 415½ S. 7th St.
Blue Bird, 618 Castle St.
BEAUTY PARLORS
Beth's, 416 Anderson St.
Lezora, 609 Red Cross St.
Germany's, 715 Red Cross St.
Lou's, 820 Red Cross St.
Newkirk's, 1217 Castle St.

Pierce's, 615 Kedder St.
Apex, 613 Red Cross St.
Dickson, 1101 S. 7th St.
Gertrude, 415 S. 7th St.
Howard's, 121 S. 13th St.
Vanity Box, 115 S. 13th St.
La May, 703 S. 15th St.
Thelma's, 207 S. 12th St.
Zan-Zibar, 403 Nixon St.
McCleese, 9th & Red Cross Sts.
BARBER SHOPS
Johnson's, 6 Market St.
Brown's, 607 S. 7th St.
NIGHT CLUBS
TAVERNS
William's, 8th & Dawson Sts.
SERVICE STATIONS
Brooklyn, 4th & Taylor Sts.
GARAGES
Fennell's, 124 So. 13th St.
DRUG STORES
Lane's, 4th & Bladen Sts.
TAXI CABS
Star, Dial 9259
Mack's, Dial 7645
Dixie, 516 S. 7 St.
Tom's, 418 McRae St.
Crosby's, Dial 9246
Greyhound, Dial 2-1342
TAILORS
New Progressive, 525 Red Cross St.

OHIO

AKRON
HOTELS
Green Turtle, Federal & Howard
Garden City, Howard & Furnace
Matthews, 77 N. Howard St.
TOURIST HOMES
R. Wilson, 370 Robert St.
BARBER SHOPS
Goodwill's, 422 Robert St.
Matthew's, 77 N. Howard St.
Allen's, 43 N. Howard St.
TAVERNS
Garden City, 124 N. Howard St.
SERVICE STATIONS
Dunagan, 834 Rhoades Ave.

ALLIANCE
TOURIST HOMES
Mrs. W. Jackson, 774 N. Webb Ave.

CADIZ
TOURIST HOMES
Mrs. James Pettress, RFD 2

CANTON
HOTELS
Phillis Wheatly Asso., 612 Market Ave. So.
DRUG STORES
Southside, 503 Cherry Ave., S. E.

54

PAGE 178

in Patronizing These Places

CINCINNATI

HOTELS
Y.W.C.A., 702 W. 8th St.
Manse, 1004 Chapel St.

TOURIST HOMES
O. Steele, 3065 Kerper St.
Ethel Buckner, 505 W. 8th St.

RESTAURANTS
Miniature Grill, 1132 Chapel St.
Mom's, 6th & John Sts.
Perkins, 430 W. 5th St.
Loc-Fre, 1634 Freeman St.
Williams, 1053 Freeman St.
Hide Away, 524 W. 5th St.
Hill's, 645 Richmond St.
Naomi's, 667 Linn St.
Harry Bruce, 404 W. 5th St.
Helen Johnson, 622 Mound St.
Ida Miller, 611 W. 6th St.
Felix Savage, George & John St.
Wm. Taylor's, 400 W. Court St.

CHINESE RESTAURANTS
Tim Pang, 514 W. 6th St.

BEAUTY PARLORS
Neighborhood, 927 Linn St.
Efficiency, 878 Beecher St.
Mill's, 2639 Park Ave.
E. N. Anderson, 1533 Blair Ave.
E. Anderson, 701 Cutter St.
Carrie Brown, 749 W. Court St.
Breck's, 1569½ Central Ave.
Margaret Brown, 924 Linn St.
Cleaver Mae's, 1018 John St.
Rosebud, 719 W. Court St.
Ludie's, 444 Chestnut St.
Pattie Lounds, 927 Linn St.
Mrs. Mahan, 551 W. Liberty St.
Margaret Peak, 2614 Park Ave.
Callie P. Smith, 709 Mound St.
Martha Williams, 506 W. 5th St.
B. Wilkins, 639 Richmond St.

BARBER SHOPS
5th Ave., 528 W. 5th Ave.
Clifford Brown, 1213 Linn St.
R. E. Crump, 500 W. 6th St.
George Cannon, 434 W. 5th St.
C. Lewis Handy, 810 John St.
Rev. Wm. Halbert, 703 Kenyon Ave.
Charles Humphrey, 528 W. 5th St.
Flowers Slaughter, 435 W. 5th St.

TAVERNS
Travelers Inn, 1115 Hopkins St.
Log Cabin, 608 John St.
Kitty Kat, 417 W. 5th St.
Barr & Linn, 760 Barr St.
Shuffle Inn, 638 Baymiller St.
Wright's, 776 W. 5th St.
Ben, 723 W. 5th St.
Silver Fleet, 810 W. 8th St.
Felder's, 810 W. 8th St.
Hotel, 542 W. 7th St.

DRUG STORES
Sky Pharmacy, 5th & John Sts.
Hoard's, 937 Central Ave.

Fallon's, 6th & Mound Sts.
West End, 709 W. Court St.
Mangrum, Chapel & Park Ave.
Dr. Russel, 612 W. 9th St.

NIGHT CLUBS
Cotton Club, 6th & Mound St.
Downbeat, Beecher & Gilbert Sts.

ROAD HOUSES
Shuffle Inn, 7th & Carr Sts.

TAILORS
De Luxe, 1217 Linn St.
Charles Bell, 603 W. 6th St.
Walthal, 732 W. 5th St.

SERVICE STATIONS
S. & W., 9th & Mound Sts.
Coursey, 2985 Gilbert Ave.
9th St., 9th & Mound St.

TAXI CABS
Calvin, 9th & Mound Sts.

CLEVELAND

HOTELS
Ward's Apartment Hotel
4113 Cedar Ave.
Ward, 4113 Cedar Ave.
Phyllis Wheatly, 4300 Cedar Ave.
Carnegie, 6803 Carnegie Ave.
Geraldine, 2212 E. 40th St.
Y.M.C.A., E. 76th & Cedar
Majestic, 2291 E. 55th St.

TOURIST HOMES
Mrs. Fannie Gilmer, 10519 Kimberley Ave.
Mrs. Edith Wilkins, 2121 E. 46th

RESTAURANTS
Williams, Central & E. 49th St.
Cassie's, 2284 E. 55th St.
Manhattan, 9903 Cedar Ave.
State, 7817 Cedar

BEAUTY PARLORS
Alberta's, 8203 Cedar Ave.
Wilkin's, 12813 Kinsman Rd.

BARBER SHOPS
Bryant's, 9808 Cedar Ave.
Driskill, 1243 E. 105th St.

TAVERNS
Brown Derby, 40th & Woodland Ave
Cedar Gardens, 9706 Cedar Ave.
Cafe Society, 966 E. 105th St.
Gold Bar, 105th St. & Massic Ave.

NIGHT CLUBS
Douglas, 7917 Cedar Ave.

BEAUTY CULTURE SCHOOLS
Wilkins, 2112 E. 46th St.

SERVICE STATIONS
Kyer's, Cedar & 79th St.
Amoco, 1416 E. 105th St.

DRUG STORES
Benjamin's, E. 55th St. & Central

TAILORS
Grant's, 9502 Cedar Ave.

55

Please Mention the "Green Book"

COLUMBUS

HOTELS

HOTEL ST. CLAIR
Service and Comfort Is Our Motto
Completely Air Conditioned
Dining Room Service - Elevator, Valet
Laundry - Telegraph
A. J. McKibbon, *Manager*
338-46 ST. CLAIR AVE.
Tel.: Fairfax 1181-2-3

Hotel St. Clair
338 St. Clair Ave.
Phone: Fairfax 1181-82-83
Ford, 179 N. 6th St.
Lexington, 180 Lexington Ave.
Macon Hotel, 366 N. 20th St.
Charlton, 439 Hamilton Ave.
Hawkins, 65 N. Monroe Ave.
Litchferd, N. 4th St.
Newford, 452½ E. Long St.
Deshler-Wallick, Board & High Sts.
Fort Hayes, 31 W. Spring St.
Garden Manor, 91 Miami Ave.
Neil House, 415 High St.
St. Clair, 338 St. Clair Ave.

TOURIST HOMES
Hawkins, 70 N. Monroe Ave.
Cooper, 259 N. 17th St.

RESTAURANTS
Cottage Restaurant & Sandwich Shop, 540 N. 20th St.
B. & B., 318 Barthman Ave.
Southern Tea Room, 618 Long St.
Bruce Latham, 317 Hosacks St.
Belmont, 689 E. Long St.
Turner's, 452½ E. Long
Edward's, 318 Barthman Ave.
Atcheson, 1288 Atcheson St.
Duck Inn, 382 E. 5th St.
Bessie's, 423 W. Goodale St.

TAVERNS
Mickey's, 425 Goodale St.
Lincoln, 389 W. Goodale St.
Royal, 752 E. Long St.
Paradise, 878 Mt. Vernon Ave.
Duck Inn, 382 E. 5th Ave.
Novelty, 741 E. Long St.
Poinciana, 758 E. Long St.
Village, 1219 Mt. Vernon Ave.

NIGHT CLUBS
Club Rogue, 772½ E. Long St.
Belmont, 689 Long St.
Skurdy's, 1074 Mt. Vernon Ave.
Club 169, Cleveland Ave.
Club Regal, 772 E. Long St.
Yatch, Cor. 20th & Mt. Vernon
McCown's, St. Clair & Mt. Vernon

BEAUTY PARLORS
Evelyn's, 947 Mt. Vernon Ave.
Long's, Charlie Mae's, 925 Mt. Vernon Ave.

Helena's, 336 Carsons Ave.
Vi's, 281 N. 18th St.
The Ave. Beauty Shop, 881 Mt. Vernon
Shingle House, 1409 Granville St.
Our Beauty Shop, 1163 Atcheson
The Classics, 925 Mt. Vernon Ave.
Justa Mere Beauty Shop, 345 N. 20th.
Ola's, 434 N. Monroe Ave.
Elaum's, 172 Lexington Ave.
Mond's Classic, 920 E. Long St.

BARBER SHOPS
Sugg & Bennie, 621 Long St.
Whaley's, 614 E. Long St.
Pierce's, 483 E. Long St.

GARAGES
Smith's, 492 Charles St.

AUTOMOTIVE
Brooks, 466 S. Washington St.

SERVICE STATIONS
King's, E. Long & Monroe
Peyton Sohio's, E. Long & Monroe
Brook's, 466 S. Washington Ave.

DAYTON

HOTELS
Y.M.C.A., 907 W. 5th St.

TOURIST HOMES
B. Lawrence, 206 Norwood St.

RESTAURANTS

TAVERNS
Palmer House, 1107 Germantown

SERVICE STATIONS
Poorer's, Shio, 1200 W. 5th St.

LIMA

TOURIST HOMES
Sol Downton, 1124 W. Spring St.
Edward Holt, 406 E. High St.
Mrs. A. Turner, 1215 W. Spring St.
George Cook, 230 S. Union St.

BEAUTY PARLORS
Nancy's, 1431 Norval Ave.

LORAIN

TOURIST HOMES
Mrs. Alex Cooley, 114 W. 26th St.
Mrs. W. H. Hedmond, 201 E. 22nd
Worthington, 209 W. 16th St.
Porter Wood, 1759 Broadway
H. P. Jackson, 2383 Apple Ave.

INNS
Wood's Social Inn
Beer, Wine, Food & Liquor
1759 Broadway

MANSFIELD

HOTELS
Lincoln, 757 N. Bowman St.

DRUG STORES
Mayer, 243 N. Main St.

MARIETTA

TOURIST HOMES
Mrs. E. Jackson, 213 Church St.

56

in Patronizing These Places

MIDDLETOWN
RESTAURANTS
TAILORS
Tramell, 1308 Garfield

OBERLIN
HOTELS
Oberlin Inn, College & Main

SANDUSKY
HOTELS
Hunter, 407 W. Market St.
BARBER SHOPS
Peoples, 218 W. Water St.

SPRINGFIELD
HOTELS
Posey, 209 S. Fountain Ave.
Y.M.C.A., Center St.
Y.W.C.A., Clarke St.
TOURIST HOMES
Mrs. M. E. Wilborn, 220 Fair St.
RESTAURANTS
Posey, 211 S. Fountain Ave.
BEAUTY PARLORS
Powder Puff, 638 S. Wittenberg Ave.
BARBER SHOPS
Griffith & Martin, 127 S. Center St.
Harris, 39 W. Clark St.
TAVERNS
Posey's, 211 S. Fountain Ave.
NIGHT CLUBS
K. P. Imp. Club, S. Yellow Spring
SERVICE STATIONS
Underwood, 1303 S. Yellow Spring
GARAGES
Green's, 1371 W. Pleasant St.
Ben's, 935 Sherman Ave.

TOLEDO
HOTELS
Pleasant, 15 N. Erie Ave.
TOURIST HOMES
Cook's Tourist Home
1736-38 Washington St.
G. Davis, 532 Woodland Ave.
Mrs. J. Jennings, 729 Indiana Ave.
J. F. Watson, 399 Pinewood Ave.
P. Johnson, 1102 Collingwood Blvd.
Cook's, 1736 Washington St.

COOK'S TOURIST HOME
"Toledo's Finest"
Fans, Radios, Air Conditioners in Most Rooms
1736-38 WASHINGTON ST.
Tel.: Emerson 1640

BARBER SHOPS
Chiles, Indiana & Collingwood
TAVERNS
Indiana, 529 Indiana Ave.
Midway, 764 Tecumsik St.
SERVICE STATIONS
Darling's, 835 Pinewood Ave.
Hobb's, 714 Palmwood

YOUNGSTOWN
HOTELS
Hotel Allison
212 North West Ave.
Y.M.C.A., 962 W. Federal St.
Rideuot, 383 Lincoln Ave.
McDonald, 442 E. Federal
Royal Palms, 625 Hemrod
Gold Inn, 851 W. Federal
Mohoning, 3411 Nelson Ave.
TOURIST HOMES
Belmont, 327 Belmont Ave.
RESTAURANTS
"Y," 962 Federal St.
Central, 137 S. Center
Bagnet, 316 Covington
BARBER SHOPS
Harris, 701 W. Rayen Ave.
BEAUTY PARLORS
Renee's, 321 E. Federal St.
Francine, 427 W. Chicago Ave.
TAVERNS
Sponteno, 377 E. Federal
State, 130 E. Broadman
TAILORS
H. V. Walker, 371 E. Federal
GARAGES
Underwood, 543 5th Ave.
NIGHT CLUBS
40 Club, 399 E. Federal St.
40 Club, 369 E. Federal
West Side Social, 552 W. Federal
A. A. Social, 703 W. Rayen Ave.

ZANESVILLE
HOTELS
Park, 1561 W. Main St.
RESTAURANTS
Little Harlem, Lee St.
TOURIST HOMES
L. E. Costom, 1545 N. Main St.
BARBER SHOPS
Nap Love, Second St.

OKLAHOMA

BOLEY
HOTELS
Berry's, South Main St.

CHICKASHA
TOURIST HOMES
Boyd's, 1022 Shepard St.

ENID
TOURIST HOMES
Mrs. Eliza Baty, 520 E. State St.
Mrs. Johnson, 217 E. Market St.
Edward's, 222 E. Park St.

GUTHRIE
TOURIST HOMES
James, 1002 E. Springer Ave.
Mrs. M. A. Smith, 317 E. Second St.

57

Please Mention the "Green Book"

MUSKOGEE

HOTELS
People's, 316 N. 2nd St.
Elliots, 111½ So. 2nd St.
RESTAURANTS
People's, 316 N. 2nd St.
BARBER SHOPS
Central, 228 N. Second St.
Robbins, 114 Court St.
BEAUTY PARLORS
Lenora's, 228 N. 2nd St.
SERVICE STATIONS
Smith's, 228 N. 2nd St.
AUTOMOTIVE
Smith Tire Co., 2nd & Denison Sts.
GARAGES
Middleton's, 420 N. 2nd St.
Nelson's, 940 S. 20th St.
London's, 209 Denison
TAILORS
Williams, 321 N. 2nd St.
Ezell's, 208 S. 2nd St.

OKLAHOMA CITY

HOTELS
4th St. Branch Y.M.C.A.
614 N.E. 4th St.
Y.M.C.A., 614 N. E. 4th St.
Canton, 200 N. E. 2nd St.
Little Page, 219 N. Central
Littlepage Hotel
219 N. Central St.
Phone: Regent 9-8779
Hall, 308½ N. Central
TOURIST HOMES
Scrugg's, 420 N. Laird St.
Cortland Rms., 629 N. E. 4th St.
Tucker's, 315½ N. E. 2nd St.
Mrs. Lessie Bennett, 500 N. E. 4th
RESTAURANTS
Eastside Food Shop, 904 N. E. 2nd
BEAUTY PARLORS
W. B. Ellis, 505 N. E. 5th St.
Lyons, 316 North Central
BARBER SHOPS
Golden Oak, 300 Block N. E. 2nd
Clover Leaf, 300 Block N. E. 2nd
SERVICE STATIONS
Richardson's, 400 N. E. 2nd St.
Mathues, 1023 N. E. 4th St.
DRUG STORES
Randolph, 331 N. E. 2nd St.

OKMULGEE

RESTAURANTS
Simmons, 407 E. 5th St.
TAXI CABS
H. & H., 421 E. 5th St.

SHAWNEE

HOTELS
Olison, 501 S. Bell St.
Slugg's, 410 So. Bell St.
TOURIST HOMES
M. Gross, 602 S. Bell St.

TULSA

HOTELS
Avalon, 2411 Apache St.
Y.W.C.A., 1120 East Pine
Lafayette, 604 E. Archer St.
McHunt, 1121 N. Greenwood Ave.
Small, 615 E. Archer
Del Rio, 607½ N. Greenwood
Miller, 124 N. Hartford St.
TOURIST HOMES
W. H. Smith, 124½ N. Greenwood
C. U. Netherland, 542 N. Elgin St.
RESTAURANTS
Chicken Shack, 316 N. Elgin
Art's Chili Parlor, 110 N. Greenwood
The Upstairs Dining Rm. 119½ N. Greenwood
BEAUTY PARLORS
Eula's, 205 N. Greenwood
BARBER SHOPS
Swindall's, 203 N. Greenwood
TAILORS
Lawson, 1120 Greenwood Ave.
Carver's, 125 N. Greenwood Ave.
SERVICE STATIONS
Mince, 2nd & Elgin Sts.
DRUGS
Meharry Drugs, 101 Greenwood St.

OREGON

PORTLAND

HOTELS
Medley, 2272 N. Interstate Ave.
Y.W.C.A., N. E. Williams Ave. & Till.
RESTAURANTS
Barno's, 84 N. E. Broadway
BEAUTY PARLORS
Bakers, 6535 N. E. Grand Ave.
Redmond, 2862 S. E. Ankeny
Mott Sisters, 2107 Vancouver Ave.
BARBER SHOPS
Holliday's, 511 N. W. 6th Ave.
NIGHT CLUBS
Oregon Fat., 1412 N. Wms.
ROAD HOUSES
Spicers, 1734 N. William Ave.
TAXI CABS
Broadway DeLuxe Cab, Br. 1-2-3-4

PENNSYLVANIA

ALLENTOWN

RESTAURANTS
Southern, 372 Union St.

ALTOONA

TOURIST HOMES
C. Bell, 1420 Wash. Ave.
Mrs. E. Jackson, 2138 18th St.
Mrs. H. Shorter, 2620 8th St.

in Patronizing These Places

BEDFORD SPRINGS
HOTELS
Harris Hotel, Penn. & West Sts.

CHAMBERSBURG
TOURIST HOME
Pinn's, 68 W. Liberty St.

COATESVILLE
HOTELS
Subway

CHESTER
HOTELS
Harlem, 1909 W. 3rd St.
Moonglow, 225 Market St.
BEAUTY PARLORS
Rosella, 413 Concord Ave.
Alex. Davis, 123 Reaney St.
BARBER SHOPS
Bouldin, 1710 W. 3rd St.
TAVERNS
Wright's, 3rd St. & Central Ave.

CRESCO
TOURIST HOMES
Mrs. Daniel L. Taylor

DARBY
TAVERNS
Golden Star, 10th & Forrester

ERIE
HOTELS
Pope, 1318 French St.

GETTYSBURG
TOURIST HOMES

GERMANTOWN
HOTELS
Y.M.C.A., 132 W. Rittenhouse
TAVERNS
Terrace Grill, 75 E. Sharpnack St.

HARRISBURG
HOTELS
Jackson, 1004 N. 6th St.
Jack's, 1208 N. 6th St.
TOURIST HOMES
Mrs. W. D. Jones, 1531 No. 6th St.
Mrs. H. Carter, 606 Foster St.
BARBER SHOPS
Jack's, 1002 N. 6th St.

LANCASTER
BEAUTY PARLORS
E. Clark, 505 S. Duke St.
J. Carter, 143 S. Duke St.
A. L. Polite, 540 North St.

NEW CASTLE
HOTELS
Y.W.C.A., 140 Elm St.

OIL CITY
TOURIST HOMES
Mrs. Jackson, 258 Bissel Ave.

PHILADELPHIA
HOTELS
Southwest Y.W.C.A., Res. 756 S. 16th St.
Paradise, 1527 Fitzwater St.
Bellevue-Stratford, Broad & Walnut
Benjamin Franklin, 9th & Chestnut Sts.
Essex House, 13th & Fillbert Sts.
Chesterfield, Broad & Oxford Sts.
Baltimore, 1438 Lombard St.
Attucks, 801 S. 15th St.
Elizabeth, 756 S. 15th St.
Woodson, 1414 Lombard
The Grand, 420 So. 15th St.
Douglas, Broad & Lombard Sts.
Elrae, 805 N. 13th St.
LaSalle, 2026 Ridge Ave.
New Roadside, 514 S. 15th St.
Paradise, 1627 Fitzwater St.
Y.M.C.A., 1724 Christian St.
Y.W.C.A., 1605 Catherine St.
Y.W.C.A., 6128 Germantown Ave.
Horseshoe, 12th & Lombard
New Phain, 2059 Fitzwater
La Reve, Cor. 9th & Columbia Ave.
Ridge, 1610 Ridge Ave.
Pitts, 1301 Poplar St.
Carlyle, 1425 W. Poplar St.
Doris, 2219 N. 13th St.
RESTAURANTS
Marion's, 20th & Bainbridge Sts.
Trott Inn, 5030 Haverford Ave.
Mattie's, 4225 Pennsgrove St.
Ruth's, 1818 N. 17th St.
BEAUTY PARLORS
A. Henson, 1318 Fairmont Ave.
LaSalle, 2036 Ridge St.
Lady Ross, 718 S. 15th St.
Rose's, 16th & South St.
F. Franklin, 2115 W. York St.
Motom's, 816 So. 15th St.
Redmond's, 4823 Fairmont Ave.
A. B. Tooks, 1702 Diamond St.
SCHOOL OF BEAUTY CULTURE
Carter's School, 1811 W. Columbia
BARBER SHOPS
S. Jones, 1423 Ridge Ave.
TAVERNS
Irene's, 2345 London Ave.
Trott Inn, 5030 Haverford Ave.
Wander Inn, 18th & Federal St.
Butler's Tavern, 17th & Carpenter
Campbell's, 18th & South St.
Loyal, 16th & South Sts.
Irene's, 2329 Ridge Ave.
Lyons, 12th & South St.
Blue Moon, 1702 Federal St.
Butler's, 2066 Ridge Ave.
Cotton Grove, 1329 South St.
Wayside Inn, 13th & Oxford St.
Preston's, 4043 Market St.
Casbah, 39th & Fairmont St.
Last Word, Haveriford & 51st St.
Cathrine's, 1350 South St.
Postal Card, 1504 South St.
Emerson's, 15th & Bainbridge St.
Brass Rail, 2302 W. Columbia Ave.
Club 421, 5601 Wyalusing Ave.

Please Mention the "Green Book"

NIGHT CLUBS
  Cotton Club, 2106 Ridge Ave.
  Cafe Society, 1306 W. Columbia Ave.
  Paradise, Ridge & Jefferson
  Progressive, 1415 S. 20th St.
  Cotton Bowl, Master St. & 13th St.
GARAGES
  Bond Motor Service, 6726 N. 8th St.
  Booker Bros., 1245 So. 21st St.
SERVICE STATIONS
  Witcher, 1856 No. Judson St.
DRUG STORES
  Bound's, 59th & Race St.

PITTSBURGH
HOTELS
  Flamingo, 2407 Wylie Ave.
  Ave., 1538 Wylie Ave.
  Bailey's, 1533 Center Ave.
  Colonial, Wylie & Fulton Sts.
  Palace, 1545 Wylie Ave.
  Ellis, 5 Reed St.
TOURIST HOMES
  Agnes Taylor, 2612 Center St.
  Birdie's Guest House, 1522 Center Ave.
  B. Williams, 1537 Howard St.
  Mrs. Williams, 5518 Claybourne St.
RESTAURANTS
  Dearling's, 492 Culver St.
  Vee's Dining Room, 2403 Centre Ave.

READING
TOURIST HOMES
  C. Dawson, 441 Buttonwood St.

SCRANTON
TOURIST HOMES
  Mrs. Elvira R. King, 1312 Linden St.
  Mrs. J. Taylor, 1415 Penn. Ave.

SELLERSVILLE
TOURIST HOMES
  Mrs. Dorothy Scholls, Forest Rd.

SHARON HILL
TAVERNS
  Dixie Cafe, Hook Rd., Howard St.

WASHINGTON
TOURIST HOMES
  Richardson, 140 E. Chestnut St.
RESTAURANTS
  W. Allen, N. Lincoln St.
  M. Thomas, N. Lincoln St.
BARBER SHOPS
  Yancey's, E. Spruce St.
NIGHT CLUBS
  Thomas Grill, N. Lincoln St.

WAYNE
NIGHT CLUBS
  Plantation, Gulf Rd. & Henry Ave.

WESTCHESTER
  Magnolia, 300 E. Miner St.

WILLIAMSPORT
TOURIST HOMES
  Mrs. Edward Randall, 719 Matle St.

WILKES BARRE
HOTELS
  Shaw, 15 So. State St.

YORK
TOURIST HOMES
  Mrs. I. Grayson, 32 W. Princess St

RHODE ISLAND
NEWPORT
TOURIST HOMES
  Ma Gruber, 82 William St.
  Mrs. F. Jackson, 28 Hall Ave.
  Mrs. L. Jackson, 35 Bath Rd.

PROVIDENCE
HOTELS
  Biltmore
TOURIST HOMES
  Hines, 462 North Main St.
  Retlaw House, 24 Camp St.
TAVERNS
  Dixieland, 1049 Westminster St
BEAUTY PARLORS
  B. Boyd's, 43 Camp St.
  Geraldine's, 205 Thurbus Ave.

SOUTH CAROLINA
ANDERSON
RESTAURANTS
  Ess-Tee, 112 E. Church St.
TOURIST HOMES
  Mrs. Sallie Galloway, 420 Butler St.

AIKEN
TOURIST HOMES
  C. F. Holland, 1118 Richland Ave.

ATLANTIC BEACH
HOTELS
  Theretha

BEAUFORD
SERVICE STATIONS
  Peoples, D. Brofn, Prop.

CHARLESTON
TOURIST HOMES
  Mrs. Gladsen, 15 Nassau St.
  Mrs. Mayes, 82½ Spring St.

CHERAW
TOURIST HOMES
  Mrs. M. B. Robinson, 211 Church
  Mrs. Maggie Green, Church St.
  Liveoak, 328 2nd St.
RESTAURANTS
  College Inn, 324 2nd St.
  Gate Grill, 2nd St.
  Watson, 2nd St.
TAVERNS
  College Inn, 2nd St.

60

in Patronizing These Places

ROAD HOUSES
Hill Top, Society Hill Rd.
BARBER SHOPS
Imperial, 276 2nd St.
BEAUTY PARLORS
Bell's, Huger St.
SERVICE STATIONS
Motor Inn, 2nd St.

COLA
BEAUTY PARLORS
Workman's, 1825 Taylor St.

COLUMBIA
HOTELS
Y.W.C.A., 1429 Park St.
Nylon, 918 Senate St.
TOURIST HOMES
Mrs. Irene B. Evans, 1106 Pine St.
College Inn, 1609 Harden St.
Mrs. S. H. Smith, 929 Pine St.
Mrs. H. Cornwell, 1713 Wayne
Mrs. W. D. Chappelle, 1301 Pine St.
Beachum, 2212 Gervais St.
Mrs. J. P. Wakefield 816 Oak St.
RESTAURANTS
Green Leaf, 1117 Wash. St.
Savoy, Old Winnsboro St.
Cozy Inn, 1509 Harden St.
Mom's, 1005 Washington St.
Brown's, 1014 Lady St.
Blue Palace, 1001 Washington St.
Waverly, 2515 Gervais St.
BEAUTY PARLORS
Amy's, 1125½ Washington St.
Obbie's, 119½ Washington St.
BARBER SHOPS
Holman's, 2138 Gervais St.
BEAUTY SCHOOLS
Poro, 2481 Millwood Ave.
Madare Bradley, 2228 Hampton St.
TAVERNS
Moon Glow, 1005 Washington St.
SERVICE STATIONS
A. W. Simkins, 1331 Park St.
Caldwell's, Oak & Taylor Sts.
Waverly, 2202 Taylor St.
Leevy's, 1831 Taylor St.
DRUG STORES
Count's, 1105 Washington St.
TAXI CABS
Blue Ribbon, 1024 Washington St.

CROSS HILL
RESTAURANTS
Willie Miller

FLORENCE
TOURIST HOMES

You're Always Welcome at
EBONY GUEST HOUSE
FLORENCE'S FAMOUS GUEST HOUSE
Your Home—Away from Home
712 NO. WILSON ST.
Florence, S. C.

Richmond, 108 S. Griffin St.
John McDonald, 501 So. Irby St.
Mrs. B. Wright, 1004 E. Cheeve St.
RESTAURANTS
Ace's Grill, 114 E. Cheeve St.
Wright's, 110 S. Griffin St.

GEORGETOWN
TOURIST HOMES
Mrs. R. Anderson, 424 Broad
Mrs. D. Atkinson, 811 Duke
Jas. Becote, 118 Orange
T. W. Brown, Merriman & Emanuel
Mrs. A. A. Smith, 317 Emanuel

GREENVILLE
TOURIST HOMES
Dr. Gibbs, 914 Anderson Rd.
Miss M. J. Grimes, 210 Mean St.
Mrs. W. H. Smith, 212 John St.
RESTAURANTS
Fowlers, 16 Spring St.
BEAUTY PARLORS
Broadway, 11 Spring St.
BARBER SHOPS
Broadway, 8 Spring St.
GARAGES
Whittenburg, 600 Anderson St.
PHARMACY
Gibbs, 101 E. Broad St.

MULLINS
TOURIST HOMES
E. Calhoun's, 535 N. Smith St.
BARBER SHOPS
Noham Ham, Front St.
NIGHT CLUBS
Calhoun Nite Club, 535 Smith St.
ROAD HOUSES
Kate Odom, 76 H'way
SERVICE STATIONS
Ed. Owins', Front St.

ORANGEBURG
DRUG STORES
Danzier, 121 W. Russell St.

SPARTANBURG
TOURIST HOMES
Mrs. O. Jones, 255 N. Dean St.
Mrs. L. Johnson, 307 N. Dean
RESTAURANTS
Mrs. M. Davis, S. Wofford
BEAUTY PARLORS
Clowney's, 445 S. Liberty St.
BARBER SHOPS
R. Browning, 122 Short Wofford
TAVERNS
Victory, Union Highway
SERVICE STATIONS
Collins, 398 S. Liberty St.
South Side, S. Liberty St.
TAXI CABS
Collin's, 389 S. Liberty St.

Please Mention the "Green Book"

ROCK HILL
BEAUTY SCHOOLS
Jefferson's, 168 W. Black St.

SUMTER
TOURIST HOMES
Edmonia Shaw, 206 Manning Ave.
Mrs. Julia E. Byrd, 504 N. Main
C. H. Bracey, 210 W. Oakland
Johnnie Williams, Hi'way 15A
TAVERNS
Steve Bradford, N. Main St.
SERVICE STATIONS
Esso Gas Station
Mutual, 208 Bartlee St.
DRUG STORES
People, 5 W. Liberty St.

WALTERBORO
TOURIST HOMES
Mrs. Rebecca Maree, 14 Savage St.
RESTAURANTS
Keynote, Gruber St.

SOUTH DAKOTA
ABERDEEN
HOTELS
Alonzo Ward, S. Main St.
RESTAURANTS
Virginia, 303 S. Main St.
BEAUTY PARLORS
Marland, 321 S. Main St.
BARBER SHOPS
Olson, 103½ S. Main St.
SERVICE STATIONS
Swanson, H'way 12 & Main Sts.
GARAGES
Spaulding, S. Lincoln St.
Wallace, S. Lincoln St.

SIOUX FALLS
TOURIST HOMES
Mrs. J. Moxley, 915 N. Main
Chamber of Commerce, 131 S. Phillips Ave.

TENNESSEE
BRISTOL
TOURIST HOMES
Mrs. M. C. Brown, 225 McDowell
Mrs. A. D. Henderson, 301 McDowell St.
TAVERNS
The Morocco, 800 Spencer St.

CHATTANOOGA
HOTELS
Y.M.C.A., 793 E. 9th St.
Dallas, 230½ E. 9th St.
Lincoln, 1101 Carter St.
Martin, 204 E. 9th St.
Peoples, 1104 Carter St.
Dallas, 230½ E. 9th St.
Harris, 110½ Carter St.
TOURIST HOMES
Mrs. Etta Brown, 1129 E. 8th St.
Mrs. J. Baker, 843 E. 8th St.
Y.W.C.A., 839 E. 8th St.
J. Carter, 1022 E. 8th St.
RESTAURANTS
Thomas Chicken Shack, 235 E. 9th St.
La Grand, 205 E. 9th St.
Manhattan, 324 E. 9th St.
Brown Derby, 331 E. 9th St.
TAVERNS
Gamble's, 108 W. Main St.
Brown Derby, 331 E. 9th St.
Dandy's, 1101 W. 12th St.
Mrs. Annie Ruth Conley, 205 E. 9th St.
LIQUOR STORES
Pat's, 727 James Blgd.
Walter Johnson, 213 E. 8th St.
Cap's, 422 E. 9th St.
Watt's, 320 E. 9th St.
DRUG STORES
Rowland's, 326 E. 9th St.
Moore & King, 836 Market St.
GARAGES
Volunteer, E. 9th St. & Lindsay
TAXI CABS
Simms, 915 University Ave.

CLARKSVILLE
TOURIST HOMES
Mrs. H. Northington, 717 Main St.
Mrs. Kate Stewart, 500 Poston St.
RESTAURANTS
Foston's Grill, 853 College St.
Foston's, 853 College St.
BEAUTY PARLORS
Johnson's, 10th St.

KNOXVILLE
Y.W.C.A., 329 Temperance St.
Hartford, 219 ... Vine St.
TOURIST HOMES
Rollins, 302 E. Vine St.
Anderson's, 501 E. Church St.
RESTAURANTS

Visit the
RON-DOO-VOO TEA ROOM
Dining Room Service
A-Rating
Breakfast - Lunch - Dinner
Home Made Cakes and Pies
a Good - Steaks - Chicken in Baske
Sleeping Accommodations
Mrs. Wm. Weatherby, Prop.
1206 E. MAIN AVE.

62

in Patronizing These Places

LEXINGTON
TOURIST HOMES
C. Timberlake, Holly St.

MEMPHIS
HOTELS
Marguette Hotel, 500 Linden St.
Travelers, 347 Vance
Mitchells, 160 Hernando St.
Larraine, Mulberry At Huling
Eosary, 181 Beale Ave.
TOURIST HOMES
Mrs. E. M. Wright, 896 Polk Ave.
RESTAURANTS
Scott's, 368 Vance Ave.
Davidson's, 345 S. 4th St.
Bessie's, 338 Vance Ave.
NIGHT CLUBS
Tony's Place, 1404 Lyceum Rd.
BEAUTY SCHOOLS
Burchitta, 201 Hernando St.
Superior, 1550 Florida Ave.
Johnson, 316 S. 4th St.
DRUG STORES
So. Memphis, 907 Florida Ave.
Pantaza, Main & Beale

MURFREESBORO
TOURIST HOMES
Mrs. M. E. Howland, 439 E. State

NASHVILLE
HOTELS
Y.M.C.A., 4th & Charlotte Aves.
Grace, 1122 Cedar St.
Carver Courts, White's, Creek Pike
Y.W.C.A., 436 5th Ave. N.
Brown's, 1610 Jefferson St., North
Bryant House, 500 8th Ave. So.
BEAUTY PARLORS
Queen of Sheba, 1503 15th Ave., N.
Myrtles, 2423 Eden St.
BEAUTY SCHOOLS
Bowman's, 409 4th Ave., N.
RESTAURANTS
Martha's, 309 Cedar St.
Peacock Inn. Jefferson & 18th Ave.
BARBER SHOPS
'Y', 34 4th Ave. N.

TEXAS

ABILENE
TAVERNS
Hammond Cafe, 620 Plum St.

AMARILLO
HOTELS
Watley, 112 Van Buren St.
Tennessee, 206 Van Buren St.
RESTAURANTS
Tom's Place, 322 W. Third St.
New Harlem, 114 Harrison St.
BARBER SHOPS
Foster's, 204 Harrison St.

BEAUTY PARLORS
Unique, 312 W. Third St.
ROAD HOUSES
Working Man's Club, 202 Harrison
TAVERNS
Carter Bros., 323 W. Third St.
TAILORS
Mitchell's, 314 W. Second St.
RECREATION CLUBS
Blue Moon, 107 Harrison St.
Watley, 202 Harrison St.
DRUG STORES
G. & M. 204A Harrison St.
Knighton, 422 W. Third St.
Corner, 118 Harrison St.

ATLANTA
TOURIST HOMES
Mrs. Lizzie Simon, 308 N. Howe St.

AUSTIN
TOURIST HOMES
Mrs. J. W. Frazier, 810 E. 13th St.
Mrs. J. W. Duncan, 1214 E. 7th St.
Mrs. W. M. Tears, 1203 E. 12th St.
Porter's, 1315 E. 12th St.

BEAUMONT
HOTELS
Whitney, 2997 Pine St.
Hotel Theresa, 875 Neches St.
TOURIST HOMES
Mrs. Pearl Freeman, 730 Forsythe
Mrs. B. Rivers, 730 Forsythe St.
RESTAURANTS
Long Bar-B-Q, 539 Forsythe St.

CORPUS CHRISTIE
TOURIST HOMES
Horace Crecy's, 1710 Lexington Ave.
RESTAURANTS
Avalon, 1510 Ramirez
Skylark, 1216 N. Staples
Blue Willow, 806 Winnebago
Square Deal, 810 Winnebago
Royal, 1222 N. Staples St.
Fortuna, 1307 N. Staples St.
BEAUTY PARLORS
Mitchell's, 1519 Ramirez St.
Bessie's, 1526½ Sam Rankin
BARBER SHOPS
Steen's, 1303 N. Alameda St.
NIGHT CLUBS
Alabam, 1503 Ramirez
Elite, 1216 N. Staples St.
LIQUOR STORES
Savoy, 1220 N. Staples St.
GARAGES
Crecy's, 1502 Ramirez

CORSICANA
TOURIST HOMES
Mrs. R. Lee, 712 E. 4th St.
BARBER SHOPS
Mrs. Dellum, 117 E. 5th Ave.

Please Mention the "Green Book"

DALLAS
HOTELS
Howard Hotel
3118 San Jacinto St.
Phone: Ta 5970
  Lewis, 302½ N. Central St.
  Powell, 3115 State St.
  Y.M.C.A., 2700 Flora St.
  Y.W.C.A., 3525 State St.
  Hall's, 1825½ Hall St.
RESTAURANTS
Shalimar Grill,
2219 Hall St.
  Beaumont Barbeque, 1815 N. Field
  Davis, 6806 Lemmon Ave.
  Palm Cafe, 2213 Hall St.
BEAUTY PARLORS
  S. Brown's, 1721 Hall St.
BARBER SHOPS
  Washington's, 3203 Thomas Ave.
DRUG STORES
  Smith's, 2221 Hall St.

EL PASO
HOTELS
  Phillips Manor, 218 So. Mesa
  Murray Theater, 218 S. Mesa Ave.
  Daniel Hotel, 413 S. Oregon St.
TOURIST HOMES
  A. Winston, 3205 Almeda St.
  Mrs. S. W. Stull, 511 Tornillo
  C. Williams, 1507 Wyoming St.
  E. Phillips, 704 S. St. Vrain St.
DRUG STORES
  Donnel, 3201 Nanzana St.

FORT WORTH
HOTELS
  Del Ray, 901 Jones St.
  Jim, 413-15 E. Fifth St.
TOURIST HOMES
  Evan's, 1213 E. Terrell St.
RESTAURANTS
  Y.M.C.A., 1604 Jones St.
  Green Leaf, 315 E. 9th St.
BEAUTY PARLORS
  Dickerson's, 1015 E. Rosedale
SERVICE STATIONS
  South Side, 1151 New York St.

GALVESTON
HOTELS
  Oleander, 421½ 25th St.
  Gus Allen, 2710 Ave. F.
TOURIST HOMES
  Mrs. J. Pope, 2824 Ave. M.
TAVERNS
  Gulf View, 28th & Blvd. Houston
NIGHT CLUBS
  Manhattan, 2802 Ave. R½
BARBER SHOPS
  Imperial, 1814-O½
GARAGES
  Sunset, 3928 Ave. H.

HENDERSON
RESTAURANTS
  Chat & Chew, 615 N. Mill St.
BARBER SHOPS
  Mucklerogs, 617 N. Mill St.
SERVICE STATIONS
  Johnson's, Kilgore & Tyler Hi'way
GARAGES
  Holman's, Kilgore & Tyler Hi'way

HITCHCOCK
RESTAURANTS
  Rose Bud, Hi'way 6
BARBER SHOPS
  Fairwood, Hi'way 6
BEAUTY PARLORS
  Mae's, Hi'way 6
SERVICE STATIONS
  Brown's, Hi'way 6

HOUSTON
HOTELS
  Crystal, 3308 Lyons Ave.
  Y.M.C.A., 1217 Bagby St.
  Cooper's, 1011 Dart St.
  Ajapa, 2412 Dowling St.
  New Day, 1912 Dowling St.
RESTAURANTS
  Lincoln, Conti & Jenson
  Lincoln, 2502 E. Alabama
  Eva's, 1617 Dowling St.
CHINESE RESTAURANTS
  Oriental, 2751 Lyons Ave.
TAVERNS
  Black, 1808 Dowling St.
  Welcome Cafe, 2409 Pease Ave.
  Savoy Inn, 3321 Winbern
  Potomic, 2721 Holman St.
BARBER SHOPS
  Harris, 508 Louisiana St.
  Grovey's, 2303 Dowling St.
  Beau Brummel, 1512 Benson
BEAUTY PARLORS
  School & Parlor, 222 W. Dallas
  Lou Lillie's, 2108½ Jenson Dr.
  Franklin, 2014 Dowling St.
NIGHT CLUBS
  Club Matinee, 3224 Lyons Ave.
  Bronze Peacock, 4104 Lyons
  El Dorado, 2310 Elgin St.
  Casino Club, 2004 Jensen Dr.
SERVICE STATIONS
  Crystal White, 3222 Lyons Ave.
  Lan's, 4312 Lyons Ave.
GARAGES
  Jessie Jones, 1906 Dowling St.
  Whiteside, 117 W. Dallas
TAXI CABS
  Crystal, 3222 Lyons Ave.
DRUG STORES
  Rolston, 3318 Lyons Ave.
  Langford's, 3026 Pierce St.
  Lion's, 618 Prarie & Louisiana
  Eureka, 2322 Dowling St.
  Forest Homes, 3033 Holman St.

64

in Patronizing These Places

MARSHALL
TOURIST HOME
Rev. Bailey, 1103 W. Grand Ave.
TAVERNS
Singleton, W. Grand Ave.
BARBER SHOPS
Craver's, So. Carter St.

MEXIA
HOTELS
Carleton, 1 W. Commerce St.
RESTAURANTS
Mrs. M. Carroll, 109 N. Belknap St.
BEAUTY PARLORS
Mrs. B. Smith, N. Denton
BARBER SHOPS
Mr. C. Carter, N. Belknap
TAVERNS
R. Houston, N. Belknap
NIGHT CLUBS
Payne's, West Side
ROAD HOUSES
Jim Ransom, N. Carthage
SERVICE STATIONS
Joe Brooks, 107 N. Belknap
GARAGES
Rev. T. Sparks, N. Belknap

MIDLAND
HOTELS
Watson's Hotel
RESTAURANTS
King Sandwich, 301 N. Lee
TAXI CABS
Johnnie's, 209 North Lee

PARIS
HOTELS
Brown Rigg, 322 N. E. 2nd St.
TOURIST HOMES
Mrs. I. Scott, 405 N. E. 2nd St.

PORT ARTHUR
RESTAURANTS
Shadowland, 632 W. 7th St.
Tick Tock, 536 W. 7th St.
BARBER SHOPS
Manhattan, 440 W. 7th St.
LIQUOR STORES
Messina's, 2147 Woodrow Dr.
Coleman's, 735 Texas Ave.

SAN ANTONIO
HOTELS
Manhattan, 735 E. Commerce
Nolan, 525 Nolan St.
Ross, 126 N. Mesquite St.
TOURIST HOMES
Mundy, 129 N. Mesquite St.
RESTAURANTS
Mamie's, 1833 E. Houston St.
Silver Slipper, 506 S. Gevers
BEAUTY SHOPS
Vessie's, 125 Canton St.
Jones, 209 N. Swiss St.
Optimistic, 105 Anderson St.
Band Box, 135 N. Mesquite St.
Mitts, 115 N. Swiss St.

Arritha's, 113 Alabama St.
R. & B., 126 N. Mesquite St.
Briscoe's, 518 S. Pine St.
Three Point, 716 Virginia Blvd.
Maggie Jones, 413 Center St.
NIGHT CLUBS
Wood Lake Country Club, New Sulphur Spring Rd.
Key Hole, 1619 West Poplar
DRY CLEANING
C. L. Baho, 1843 E. Commerce St.
Dependable, 205 Losoya
Esquire, 212 Broadway
SERVICE STATIONS
Eason's, 1605 E. Houston St.
GARAGES
Eason's, 1606 E. Houston St.
DRUG STORES
W. H. Leonard, 701 S. Pine St.

TYLER
TOURIST HOMES
Mrs. Thomas, 516 N. Border St.
W. Langston, 1010 N. Border St.

TEXARKANA
RESTAURANTS
Casino, 504 West 3rd St.
GARAGES
Carl Hill's, 936 W. 20th St.

WACO
HOTELS
College View, 1129 Elm Ave.
TOURIST HOMES
B. Ashford, 902 N. 8th St.
BEAUTY PARLORS
Cendivilla, 107½ N. Second St.
Cinderella, 1133 Earle St.
Ideal, 1029 Taylor St.
Earle St., 1113 Earle St.
Mayfair, 112 Bridge St.
Modern, 1406 Taylor St.
Hine's, 1125 Earle St.
Murphy's, 115 So. 2nd St.
Odessa's, 920 Dawson St.
RESTAURANTS
Harlem, 123 Bridge
Ideal, 902 No. 8th St.
NIGHT CLUBS
Waco Loughorn, 19th & LaSalle
ROAD HOUSES
Golden Lilly, 426 Clifton
TAVERNS
Green Tree, 1325 S. 4th St.

WAXAHACHIE
TOURIST HOMES
Mrs. A. Nunn, 413 E. Main St.
Mrs. M. Johnson, 427 E. Main St.
Mrs. N. Lowe, 418 E. Main St.
Mrs. N. Jones, 430 E. Main St.

WICHITA FALLS
HOTELS
Bridges, 404 Sullivan St.
TOURIST HOMES
E. B. Jeffrey, 509 Juarez St.

Please Mention the "Green Book"

UTAH
OGDEN
HOTELS
Royal, 2522 Wall Ave.

SALT LAKE CITY
HOTELS
Jenkin's Hotel
250 West South Temple
Sam Sneed, 250 W. South Temple
Y.W.C.A., 306 E. 3rd St.
St. Louis Hotel
242½ West South Temple
Phone: 5-0838

VERMONT
BURLINGTON
HOTELS
The Pates, 86-90 Archibald St.
TOURIST HOMES
Mrs. William Sharper, 242 North St.

MANCHESTER
HOTELS
Clyde Blackwells

NORTHFIELD
TOURIST HOMES
Cole's Tourist Home, 7 Sherman Ave.

RUTLAND
TOURIST HOMES
Mead Cottage, 24 High St.

VIRGINIA
ALEXANDRIA
TOURIST HOMES
J. T. Holmes, 803 Gibbon St.
J. A. Barrett, 724 Gibbon St.

BEDFORD
TOURIST HOMES
Marinda Jones, R. F. D. No. 1, Box 7A

BRISTOL
TAVERNS
Morocco, 800 Spencer St.

BUCKROE BEACH
HOTELS
Bay Shore
NIGHT CLUBS
Club 400

CARET
TAVERNS
Sessons Tavern

CHARLOTTESVILLE
HOTELS
Carver Inn, 701 Preston Ave.
Paramount, West Main St.
TOURIST HOMES
Chauffeur's Rest, 129 Preston Ave.
Alexander's, 413 Dyce St.
BARBER SHOPS
Jokers, North 4th St.

CHRISTIANBURG
HOTELS
Eureka

COVINGTON
TOURIST HOMES
Mrs. Loretta S. Watson, 219 Lexington St.
RESTAURANTS
Silver Star, 208 So. Maple Ave.

CULPEPER
TOURIST HOMES
Maple Rest,
1018 South Main St.
Mrs. Mary L. Taylor, 1018 S. Main

DANVILLE
TOURIST HOMES
Mrs. P. M. Logan, 328 No. Main St.
Yancey's, 320 Holbrook St.
Mrs. M. K. Page, 434 Holbrook St.
Mrs. S. A. Overby, Holbrook St.
Mrs. Mary L. Wilson, 401 Holbrook
RESTAURANTS
Blue Room, 358 Holbrook St.

FARMVILLE
TOURIST HOMES
Mrs. K. Wiley, 626 Main St.
RESTAURANTS
Reid's, 236 Main St.
TAVERNS
Reid's, 200 Block, Main St.
SERVICE STATIONS
Clark's, Main St.

FREDERICKSBURG
HOTELS
McGuire, 521 Princess Anne St.
Rappahannock, 520 Princess St.
RESTAURANTS
Taylor's, 505 Princess Anne St.

HAMPTON
HOTELS
Savoy, 140 W. Queen St.
RESTAURANTS
Abraham's, 39th St. & Hi'Way
BARBER SHOPS
Paul's, 154 Queen St.
BEAUTY PARLORS
Tillie's, 215 N. King St.
SERVICE STATIONS
Lyle's, 40 Armitsead Ave.
GARAGES
Walton's, W. Mallory Ave.
TAXI CAB
Abraham's Taxi Service

66

in Patronizing These Places

HARRISONBURG
TOURIST HOME
Mrs. Ida M. Francis, 252 N. Main

HEWLETT
TAVERNS
Beverly Bros., R. F. D. No. 1

LEXINGTON
TOURIST HOMES
The Franklin, 9 Tucker St.
RESTAURANTS
Washington, 16 N. Main St.
TAVERNS
Rose Inn, 331 N. Main St.

LURAY
TOURIST HOMES
Camp Lewis Mountain, Skyline Dr.

LYNCHBURG
HOTELS
Hotel Douglas,
Route 29, North & South
Phone: 28841
Douglas, Rt. 29
Phyllis Wheatley Y.W.C.A., 613 Monroe St.
TOURIST HOMES
Mrs. C. Harper, 1109 8th St.
Mrs. N. P. Washington, 611 Polk
Mrs. Smith, 504 Jackson
Happyland Lake, 812 5th Ave.
BEAUTY PARLORS
Selma's, 1002 5th St.

NEWPORT NEWS
HOTELS
Cosmos Inn,
620 25th St.
TOURIST HOMES
Ritz, 636 25th St.
Mrs. W. E. Barron, 2123 Jefferson
Thomas E. Reese, 636 25th St.
Mrs. C. Stephens, 1909 Marshall
RESTAURANTS
Stop Light, 601 25th St.
Webb, 619 25th St.
BEAUTY PARLORS
Alice, 628 25th St.
SERVICE STATIONS
Ridley's, Orcutt Ave. & 30th St.
BARBER SHOPS
V. & R., 636 25th St.
TAILORS
Faulk, 638 25th St.
DRUG STORES
Woodard's, 25th St. & Madison

NORFOLK
HOTELS
Wheaton, 633 E. Bramleton Ave.
Tatum Inn, 453 Brewer St.
Plaza, 1757 Church St.
Y.M.C.A., 729 Washington Ave.
RESTAURANTS
Russell's, Grill. 816 Church St.
BEAUTY PARLORS
Jordan's, 526 Brambleton Ave.
Yeargen's, 1685 Church St.
Betty's, 641 E. Brambleton Ave.
Hazel, 363 E. Brambleton Ave.
DRUG STORES
Arthur's, 744 Church St.
Woods, 1000 Church St.
TAVERNS
Russell's, 835 Church St.
SERVICE STATIONS
Alston's, Cor. 20th & Church St.

PETERSBURG
HOTELS
The Walker House, 116 South
NIGHT CLUBS
Chatter Boy, 143 Harrison St.

PHOEBUS
HOTELS
Horton's, County & Mellon Sts.
RESTAURANTS
Horton's, County & Mellon Sts.
DRUG STORES
Langley, County & Mellon Sts.
TAILORS
Perry, Mellon St.
SERVICE STATIONS
Ward's, County Nr. Fulton St.

RICHMOND
HOTELS
Slaughters, 529 N. 2nd St.
Harris, 200 E. Clay St.
Eggleston Miller's, 2nd & Leigh
TOURIST HOMES
Mrs. E. Brice, 14 W. Clay St.
Y.W.C.A., 515 N. 7th St.
BEAUTY PARLORS
Rest-a-Bit, 619 N. 3rd St.
BARBER SHOPS
Scotty's, 505 N. 2nd St.
TAVERNS
Market Inn, Washington Park
SERVICE STATIONS
Harris, 2205 Rockwood Ave.
Vaughn, 1701 Chamberlayne Ave.
Cameron's, Brook Ave. & W. Clay
Adam St., 523 N. Adam St.

67

Please Mention the "Green Book"

ROANOKE

HOTELS
Dumas, Henry St. N. W.
TOURIST HOMES
Y.W.C.A., 208 2nd St. N. W.
DRUG STORES
Brook's, 221 N. Henry St.

COLVIN'S TOURIST HOME
All Modern Conveniences
Write or Phone for Reservations
Rate $3.00 and up
MRS. MARY B. COLVIN, Prop.
16 Gilmer Ave., N.W., Roanoke 17, Va.
Tel.: 2-3813

SOUTH HILL
HOTELS
Brown's, Melvin Brown, Prop.

STAUNTON
TOURIST HOMES
Pannell's Inn, 613 N. Apgusta St.
RESTAURANTS
Johnson's, 301 N. Central Ave.

SUFFOLK
BEAUTY PARLORS
Lonely Hour Inn, Rt. 460

TAPPAHANNOCK
HOTELS
McGuire's Inn, Marsh St.
Mark, Haven Beach

WARRENTON
TOURIST HOMES
Lawson, 227 Alexander Pike
BARBER SHOPS
Walker's, 5th St.
BEAUTY PARLORS
Fowlers, 123 N. 3rd St.
Pinn, 121 5th St.
TAXI CABS
Joyner's, Phone: 292
Bland, Phone: 430
Parker's, Phone: 491
TAILORS
McLain, 205 Culpepper St.

WILLIAMSBURG
HOTELS
Baker House, 419 Nicholson St.

WINCHESTER
HOTELS
Evans, 224 Sharp St.
RESTAURANTS
Ruth's, 128 E. Cecil St.
Dunbar Tea Room, 21 W. Hart St.

WASHINGTON

EVERETT
TOURIST HOMES
Mrs. J. T. Payne, 1632 Rainier St.

SEATTLE
HOTELS
Y.W.C.A., 709 29th Ave.
Atlas, 420 Maynard St.
Y.W.C.A., 709 29th Ave.
Green, 711 Lane St.
Idaho, 505 Jackson St.
Olympus, 413 Maynard St.
Eagle, 408½ Main St.
Mar, 520 Maynard Ave.
Welcome Annex, 613½ Jackson St.
TOURIST HOMES
Zora Rooms, 1826 23rd Ave.
M. Mathis, 1826 23rd Ave.
RESTAURANTS
Shanty Inn, 110 12th Ave.
Victory, 652 Jackson St.
BARBER SHOPS
Hayes, 2600 E. Valley St.
Stockards, 2032 E. Madison St.
Atlas, 410 Maynard Ave.
BEAUTY PARLOS
Catherine's, 410 Main St.
Pauline's, 2221 E. Madison
LaMode, 2039 E. Madison St.
Bert's, 2301 E. Denny Way
Glenarvons, 657 Jackson St.
NIGHT CLUBS
Playhouse, 1238 Main St.
LIQUOR STORES
Jackson's, 707 Jackson St.
TAVERNS
Mardi Gras, 2047 E. Madison St.
Hill Top, 1200 Jackson St.
Sea Gull, 673 Jackson St.
Lucky Hour, 1315 Yesler Way
Banquet, 1237 Jackson St.
Victory, 652 Jackson St.
Banquet, 1237 Jackson St.
Dumas, 1040 Jackson St.
GARAGES
Commercial Auto, 9th & Denny
DRUG STORES
Bon-Rot, 14th & Yesler St.
Bishop's, 507 Jackson St.
Chikata, 114 12th Ave.
Madison, 2051 E. Madison
Gosho, 656 Jackson St.
Tokuda, 1724 Yesler Way
Jackson St., Jackson & Maynard
TAILORS
Gilt Edge, 611 Jackson St.

TACOMA
HOTELS
Monte Carlo, 1555 Tacoma Ave.
RESTAURANTS
Monte Carlo, 1555 Tacoma Ave.
Travelers, 1506½ Pacific Ave.

68

in Patronizing These Places

WEST VIRGINIA

BECKLEY
HOTELS
New Pioneer, 340 S. Fayette
BEAUTY PARLORS
Katie's Vanity, S. Fayette
Fuqua's, Fuqua Bldg., S. Fayette
BARBER SHOPS
Payne's, 338 S. Fayette
Simpson's, New Pioneer Hotel
GARAGES
Moss's, 501 S. Fayette
DRUG STORES
Morton's, S. Fayette
TAXI CABS
Nuway, Dial 3301

BLUEFIELD
HOTELS
Travelers' Inn, 602 Raleigh St.
Hotel Thelma, 1047 Wayne St.
DRUG STORES
Kingslow's, Bland St.

CHARLESTON
HOTELS
Brown's, Capitol & Donnelly Sts.
Ferguson's, Washington St.
Penn's, West Charleston
RESTAURANTS
The Hut, 1329 Washington St.

SERVICE STATIONS
Bridge's Esso, Wash. & Truslow
TAXI CABS
Red Star, Dial 39-331

CHESTER
BARBER SHOPS
Kenneth B. Johnson, 505 Carolina

CLARKSBURG
LODGINGS
Mrs. Ruby Thomas, 309 Water St.
NIGHT CLUBS
American Legion, Monticello St.
Pythian, 119 Harper St.
Elks, First St.
TAVERNS
Johnson's, Monticello St.

FAIRMONT
HOTELS
Monongahela, Madison St.
RESTAURANTS
Whittaker's Grill, Pennsylvania
BEAUTY SCHOOLS
Parker's, Pennslyvania Ave.

GRAFTON
LODGINGS
Mrs. Geo. Jones, Front St.
RESTAURANTS
Jones', Latrobe St.
TAVERNS
Boston's, 36 Latrobe St.

HINTON
HOTELS
The Price House,
109 9th Ave.
GUEST HOUSE
Maya's, State St.
DRY CLEANING
Emile's Cleaning & Pressing

HUNTINGTON
HOTELS
The Ross House, 911 8th Ave.
LODGINGS
Mrs. C. J. Barnett, 810 7th Ave.
RESTAURANTS
The Spot, 1614 8th Ave.
BEAUTY PARLORS
Louise's, Artisan Ave.
TAVERNS
Monroe's, 1616 8th Ave.
Finley's 8th & 16th
TAXI CABS
Party Taxi, Tel. 28385
SERVICE STATIONS
Sterling, Cor. 12th & 3rd

INSTITUTE
SERVICE STATIONS
White's Superette, Hi'Way 25
Pack's Esso

THE HUT
Charleston's Finest

We Always Serve You With
a Smile - Snappy Service

Sizzling Steaks, Chops, Sea Food
Bar-B-Q Fried Chicken Our Specialty

Breakfast - Lunch - Dinner

PHONE: 29-584

1329 E. Washington Street
Charleston, W. Va.

69

Please Mention the "Green Book"

KEYSTONE
HOTELS
Franklin
DRUG STORES
Howard's Pharmacy
RESTAURANTS
Sam Wade's Cafe

KIMBALL
HOTELS
City Hotel
BEAUTY SHOPS
Smith's
RESTAURANTS
Palace

MONTGOMERY
HOTELS
New Royal, 223 Gaines St.
BEAUTY PARLORS
Snyder's, Fayette Pike
TAVERNS
The Green Front, 188½ 3rd Ave.
TAXI CABS
Gray's, 212 Gaines St.

MORGANTOWN
LODGINGS
Mrs. Linnie Mae Slaughter, 3 Cayton
Mrs. Jeannette O. Parker, 2 Cayton
NIGHT CLUBS
American Legion, University Pl.

MOUNDSVILLE
LODGINGS
Mrs. Blance Campbell, 1206 4th St.

NORTHFORK
HOTELS
Houchins Hotel & Cafe
BARBER SHOPS
Hough's

PARKERSBURG
NIGHT CLUBS
American Legion, 812 Avery St.

PRINCETON
TAVERNS
Twilight Inn, High St.
Spotlight Grill, Beckley Rd.

WEIRTON
LODGINGS
Mrs. Robert Wililams, Kessel St.

WELCH
HOTELS
Capehart, 14 Virginia Ave.

WHEELING
HOTELS
Blue Triangle, Y.W.C.A.
108 12th St.
Verse, 1042 Market St.
LODGINGS
Mrs. W. C. Turner, 114 12th St.

RESTAURANTS
Blue Goose, 1035 Chapline St.
BEAUTY PARLORS
Mode-Craft, 1028½ Chapline St.
NIGHT CLUBS
American Legion, 1045 Chapline
Elk's Club, 1005½ Chapline St.
DRUG STORES
North Side Pharmacy, Chapline St.

WHITE SULPHUR SPRINGS
LODGINGS
Brooks, 138 Church St.
Haywood Place, Church St.
Slaughter's, Tel. 9280

WILLIAMSON
LODGINGS
Mrs. A. Wright, 605 Logan St.
DRUG STORES
Whittico's
NIGHT CLUBS
Elk's Club, Vinson St.
TAILOR SHOPS
Garner's, Logan St.

WISCONSIN

FOND DU LAC
TOURIST HOMES
Mrs. E. Pirtle, 45 E. 11th St.
V. Williams, 97 S. Seymour St.

MILWAUKEE
HOTELS
Hillcrest Hotel
504 W. Galena St.
ROOMING HOUSES
Mrs. Nettie M. Brown
920 W. Wright St.
Phone: Franklin 4-1965
Pastell Lampkins, 2427 N. 14th St.
Mrs. Margaret Burns
1241 North 6th St.
Johnson's Rooms
1033 W. Somers St.
Mrs. Sally King
2328 West 12th St.
RESTAURANTS
North Side, 2141 N. 10th St.
Black King, 1342 N. 5th St.
Larry's, 619 W. Walnut St.
Carl's Ideal Eat Shoppe
628 W. Juneau Ave.
Christine's, 614 W. Juneau
Hargroves, 1443 N. 3rd St.
Barnes, 409 W. Brown St.
Hickory, 1243 W. McKinley St.
Kiner, 1457 N. 7th St.
Sun Flower, 500 W. Vine St.
Boatner's, 709 W. Walnut St.

in Patronizing These Places

Knights Restaurant
1501 North 7th St.
  Moseby's, 1602 N. 7th St.
Our Chicken Shack
537 W. Walnut St.
  Huff 7 Puff, 1504 W. Juneau
  Gay Paree, Cor. 7th & Galena Sts.
Eddie's Restaurant
504 W. Galena St.
BARBER SHOPS
  Hollywood, 2676 N. 5th St.
  Handsome, 828 W. Walnut St.
  Veterans, 1017 W. Walnut St.
  Matthew's, 800 W. Lloyd St.
  Peoples, 504 W. Juneau Ave.
  Colonial, 610 W. Walnut St.
  Corley's, 903 W. Walnut St.
  De Luxe, 939 W. Walnut St.
  Rainbow, 1646 N. 6th St.
  Sterling, 837 W. Walnut St.
  William's, 831 W. Walnut St.
BEAUTY PARLORS
  Poro, 1820 N. 7th St.
  House of Beauty, 822 W. N. Ave.
  Rosa Lee, 2245 North 6th St.
  Victory, 1426 West N. Ave.
  Blanche's, 726 West Walnut St.
  Enchanted, 815 W. North Ave.
  Apex, 2101 North 7th St.
  Augusta's, 1649 North 10th St.
  Freddie's, 1820 North 6th St.
  Little's, 635 West Walnut St.
  Moderne, 1909 N. 12th St.
  Novelty, 905 W. Walnut St.
  Sally's, 1116 W. Walnut St.
  Vogue, 923 W. Walnut St.
  Unique, 717 W. Somers St.
TAVERNS
Midway Inn,
1000 W. Galena St.
Vine Street Tavern
341 West Vine St.
  Lucille's, 2052 N. 7th St.
  Liberty, 1745 N. 3rd St.
  Tally-Ho, 600 W. Lloyd St.
  Fat's, 1810 N. 3rd St.
  Bronze Bar, 1239 N. 6th St.
  Jon & Lou's, 823 W. Walnut St.
  High Step, 908 W. Galena
  Star, 2479 N. 8th St.
  Thelma's, 701 W. Juneau Ave.

TIP TOP TAVERN

WE HAVE ALL POPULAR BRANDS
Meals & Sandwiches Served

1800 N. 10th St., Milwaukee 5, Wisc.
Tel.: Concord 9819

  Curley's, 1744 N. 3rd St.
  Butch's, 1008 W. Somers St.
  Andy's, 1748 N. 7th St.
  Floyd's, 1222 N. 7th St.
  Cork & Bottle, 1601 N. 12th St.
  Nino's, 1111 W. Vliet St.
  Gold Coast, 638 W. Walnut St.
  Knox's, 608 W. Walnut St.
  Milt's, 1039 W. Walnut St.
NIGHT CLUBS
  Flame, 1315 N. 9th St.
CHINESE RESTAURANTS
  Loy's, 705 W. Juneau Ave.
LIQUOR STORES
  Wisconsin House, 336 W. Walnut
DRUG STORES
Dr. Edgar Thomas
440 W. Galena St.
  Community, 440 W. Galena St.
  Neighborhood, 1802 N. 7th St.
  Lloyd's, 725 W. Walnut St.
  Shaw's, 1701 W. State St.
  Schroeder, 1951 N. 3rd St.
TAILORS
Helens, 1249 N. 7th St.
  Hiawatha, 512 W. Center St.
Wilcher's Tailoring Shop
1830 North 12th St.
  Comet, 916 W. North Ave.
W. A. Mason,
732 W. Walnut St.
  General, 2018 N. 10th St.
  Ideal, 214 W. Wells St.
SERVICE STATIONS
Paul's, 200 No. 8th St.
  Paul Schraven, 12th & Garfield
  Abbott's, 1319 W. North Ave.
  Park's, 1616 N. 7th St.
  Gary's, No. 11th & W. Vliet Sts.
  Derby's, 603 W. Walnut St.
  Huff & Barker, 539 W. Cherry St.
  Tankar, 735 W. Walnut St.
GARAGES
  Adolph's, 1625 A North 9th St.
  A. & E., 750A W. Winnebago St.
  Community, 1920 N. 9th St.
  McGee's, 624 W. Juneau Ave.
  St. Paul, 1218 N. 7th St.
  Universal, 2244 N. 34th St.
  T. & H., 1218 N. 7th St.
GROCERY STORES
Patterson's Grocery
2109 North 6th St.
Triangle Market
1767 North 7th St.
Rhodes Grocery
901 W. Galena St.
Keene's Grocery
1953 North 8th St.

Please Mention the "Green Book"

TAXI CABS
Apex Amusement
819 W. Walnut St.
HABERDASHERY
Matherson Haberdashery
623 W. Walnut St.
PHOTOGRAPHER
Hillside Photographic Studio
1243 A North 7th St.
UNDERTAKER
Raynor & Reed, 1816 N. 7th St.

BELOIT
BARBER SHOPS
  Hobson's, 441 St. Paul
RESTAURANTS
  Hobson's, 102 Park Ave.
SERVICE STATIONS
  Collins, Colby St.
TAVERNS
  Clover Leaf, 103 Prospect

MADISON
RESTAURANTS
  Twilight, 838 W. Washington
BEAUTY PARLORS
  Emily's, 16 So. Murray
TAILORS
  Guy's, 316 E. Main St.

RACINE
RESTAURANTS
  Hadley's, 2121½ Meade St.

OSHKOSH
TOURIST HOMES
  F. Pemberton, 239 Liberty St.

WYOMING

CASPER
TOURIST HOMES
  Mrs. David J. Rudd, 646 E. "A" St.

RAWLINGS
RESTAURANTS
  Yellow Front, 11 E. Front St.
TOURIST HOMES
  Hobert Westbrook, 111 E. Front St.

ROCK SPRINGS
TOURIST HOMES
  Collins Tourist Home, 915 7th St.

ALASKA

FAIRBANKS
HOTELS
  Savoy

Please Mention the "Green Book"
in Patronizing These Places

PEMBROKE, BERMUDA
SWANSTON GUEST HOUSE
Newest Guest House in Bermuda
Large Airy Rooms - Luxuriously Fitted - Near the Capitol
HERE YOU WILL FIND CORDIALITY AND HOSPITALITY
RATES (All With Meals)
Double Room—Private Bath—$8.00 per Person, a Day
Double Room $7.50 — Single $7.00

Mrs. Florence Swan, Prop.   Berkeley Road
PEMBROKE, WEST

72

in Patronizing These Places

Bermuda

Out in the Mid-Atlantic, south east of the Virginia Capes, beyond the Gulf Stream's flying fish and phosphorous, lie the most famous coral islands in the World. It is the Bermudas . . . less than 20 square miles in size and so formed that in few spots it is possible to get more than a mile away from the sea. The north and south shores are utterly different and might belong to countries hundreds of leagues apart.

The Bermudas, with startling clarity of sunlight, their gentle tropical sea, their special flash of white washed roofs, pink-tinted walls and flaming poinciana trees, and their island nights glittering with more stars than any other sky in the Atlantic. They are collectively called "Bermuda." Here we find a place of coveted ease, unhurried charm and relaxed living.

Here it may mean building castles in the cleanest pink and white sand on earth, wandering over coral beaches into ocean that is the greenest green, the bluest blue. It may mean cycling along South Shore Road between tall hedges of Oleander, with youngster and picnic lunches safely tucked in a basket on handle bars.

Or it may be the velvety greens and fairways of one of Bermuda's many golf courses. Or where attractive shops show choicest merchandise of the British Empire.

There are many beautifully kept tennis courts, hidden picnic beaches, delightful roads and coral rocks from which a native fisherman's net may be cast, ensnaring everything including prancing, sea-horses and mermaids singing! For, like a jewel set in Mid-Atlantic, Bermuda is the wish at sunset and romance is starlight.

HOW DO I GET TO BERMUDA?

You go from one Parish to another by boat, by bicycle, by the small motor car. Everywhere the place is leisurely. The motor car convenient for visits from one end of the islands to the other, travels (by law) only a few miles faster than average horse and carriage.

You fly by the latest aircraft or

St. Peter's Church, St. Georges

Please Mention the "Green Book"

you go by luxury liner. The plane takes a few hours, boats from New York, 35 hours. Departures from Baltimore, Boston, Halifax, Montreal and England. When you make reservations inquire about special rates for children

CURRENCY

Although sterling is the legal tender in Bermuda, American and Canadian currencies are accepted everywhere. **United Kingdom Bank Notes are still not negotiable.**

FACTS ABOUT BERMUDA

Entry Requirements—No one requires passports or visas for visits to Bermuda, for periods of less than eight months. **United States** citizens require same form of identification and proof of citizenship when **returning** to the U. S. A.

THINGS TO SEE IN BERMUDA

Somerset Tour — One day, Ferry from Hamilton to Somerset Island, returning by taxi, carriage or bicycle. Several interesting places in Somerset for lunch. See unique Somerset Bridge, visit U. S. Naval Base, enjoy panorama of Bermuda from gallery of Gibbs Hill Lighthouse.

ST. GEORGES TOUR— ONE DAY

Because of long journey to the town of St. George, you will have more time to see if you go by taxi. Points of especial interest in St. George, St. Peter's Church, the old **United States House, St. George's Historical Museum, Gates Fort and David's Lighthouse.**

TEMPERATURE

Mild and Equable, never far off 70.7. No sudden changes occur. Rainfall brief and skies clear very quickly after a shower.

WHAT TO WEAR

During warmer months (mid-March to mid-November) cotton dresses and afternoon dress, a long one for evening, summer sportsclothes. For Men — Light weight suits, sport clothes, Bermuda shorts, white dinner jackets. During cooler months (mid-November to mid-March) light wool dresses, sweaters and skirts, warm suit, dinner dresses, top coat. For Men — tweed jacket, slacks, tweed or flannel suits, sportswear, afternoon clothes, sweaters, dinner jacket, top coat.

Queen Street, St. Georges, Bermuda

in Patronizing These Places

BERMUDA

ST. GEORGES
GUEST HOUSE
"Archlyn Villa," Wellington St.
LIQUOR STORE
Packwood's, Walter St.
BICYCLES
Dowling's Cycle Livery, York St.

PENBROKE
HOTELS
Richmond House, Richmond Rd.
GUEST HOUSE
Milestone, Coxs Hill

W. PEMBROKE
GUEST HOUSE
Sunset Lodge, P. O. Box 413

WARRICK
GUEST HOUSE
Mrs. Leon Eve, Snake Rd.
Homeleigh, Mrs. D. Eave, Prop.
Hilton Manor, Mrs. W. Tucker, Prop.

HAMILTON
HOTELS
Imperial, Church St.
GUEST HOUSES
Ripleigh, Mrs. Doris Pearman,
RESTAURANTS
Blue Jay, Church St.
The Spot, Burnaby St.

CANADA

COLLINGWOOD
TOURIST HOMES
Cedar Inn, P. O. Box 265

MONTREAL
TOURIST HOMES
Mrs. Cummings, 764 Atwater Ave.
Davis, 1324 Torrence St.
Mrs. N. P. Morse, 932 Calumet Pl.
Au Repos Rooms
1824 Dorchester St., West.
BEAUTY PARLORS
Mendes, 2036 St. Antoine St.

CARIBBEAN

BARBADOES, St. Michael
GUEST HOUSES
West Gate, West Gate, Landsend

ST. JOHN'S, ANTIGUA
American House, Redcliff St.

PORT-AU-PRINCE, HAITI
Beau Site, Frank Cardozo, rPop.

NASSAU, BAHAMAS
Shalimar, P. O. Box 606

MEXICO

ENSENADS
MOTELS
James Littlejohn, Highway 101

MONTERREY
HOTELS
Hotel Genova, Madero Blvd.
RESTAURANT
El Tapinumba

JACALA
TOURIST HOMES
Pemex

TAMAZUNCHALE
TOURIST HOMES
Pemex

IXQUIMILIPAN
TOURIST HOMES
Pemex

CUERNAVACA
TOURIST HOME
Butch's Manhattan, on the Hi'way

MEXICO CITY
HOTELS
Hotel Carlton, Ignacia Marisca
NIGHT CLUB
The Waikiki, Paseo de la Reforma

SAN JOSE, COSTA RICA, CENTRAL AMERICA

HOTELS
Castilla, Calle 6, Ave. 1/3
Continental, Calle 3, Ave. 3/5
Europa, Calle Av., Ave. 5
Latimo, Calle 6, Ave. 3
Pan American, CS. 3/5, Ave. F. G.
Rex, Calle 2, Ave. F.G./2
Anexo, CS. 7/9, Ave. F.G.
Central, Calle 6, Ave. 2
Costa Rica, Calle 3, Aves. F.G/2
Las Americas, Calle 8, Ave. 3/5
Metropoli, CS. 1/3, Ave. F.G.
Regina, Calle 5, Ave. 3
Ritz, Calle 11, Ave. 3
Trebol, CS. 8/9, Ave. 3
RESTAURANTS
El Torino, Calle 6, Ave. 5
La Eureka, CS. 4/6, A.F.G.
El Imperio, Calle 6/8, Ave. 3
El Nido, Calle 6, Ave. 1/3
Roma, Calle 3, Ave. 1
El Moderino, Calle 2, Ave. 6
La Esmeralda, C. Av., F.G./2
La nava, Calle 9, Avs. 12/14
Tavernsperial, Calle 6, Ave. 2

75

in Patronizing These Places

THE GREEN BOOK VACATION GUIDE

Introduction . . .

To assist you in planning your vacation, to help you make it a better and a more enjoyable holiday than it has ever been, this section is dedicated.

Choose the Vacation which most perfectly matches your mood and pocketbook. By listing the names and addresses of the various resorts, it is easy to write and secure your reservations. Where no address is supplied, write to the city mentioned during the summer months.

This year make it a grand and glorious vacation and use this booklet to help you to decide where you would like to go.

Our Vacation Reservation Service will be ready each year to make your reservation from the places advertised.

Our advertisers are ready and willing to give you the best there is, to make you comfortable — to see to it that you have an enjoyable time, so that you may return from your vacation feeling fit for your job.

To select the perfect place in which to spend your vacation, and to get the most out of your stay, it is suggested that you:

Select the state that you wish most to visit.

Make your reservations far enough in advance through VICTOR H. GREEN & Co. to be sure that you can be accommodated.

COLORADO
PINE CLIFF
  Wink's Panorama Lodge

CONNECTICUT
WEST HAVEN
  Dadd's Hotel, 359 Beach St.
  Sea View Hotel, 392 Beach St.
  Home of Hawkins, 372 Beach St.

DELAWARE
MILLSBORO
  Rosedale Beach
FRANKFORD
  Briarwood Farm
REHOBOTH BEACH
  Mallory Cabins, Mrs. Mary E. Mallory

FLORIDA
FERNANDINA
  Hotel American Beach, P. O. Box 195

MAINE
OGUNQUIT
  Viewland
  Mace Guest House, 20 Agamenticus
GARDNIER
  Pond View, R.F.D. 1*A
FAYETTE
  Pine Cone Lodge, P. O. Box 12
NORCROSS POND
  Lodge Norcross
WEST SCARBOROUGH
  Elcla Acres
  Spring Hill Farm, R. F. D. 1
SACO
  Coley Acres, Portland St.
WELLINGTON
  Picturesque Manor
  Mrs. E. E. Walker
  743 Chestnut St. Camden 3, N. J.

76

Please Mention the "Green Book"

MARYLAND

ANNAPOLIS
  Carr's Beach
  Sparrow's Point, P. O. Box 266
BENEDICT
  Violet Belles Hotel
COLTON
  Shirley K Hotel
WESTMINSTER
  Scarletts Country Club

INDIANA

ANGOLA
  Pryor's Country Place, R. R. No. 2

MASSACHUSETTS

FALMOUTH
  La Casa Linda, Indiana Ave.
FRANKLIN
  The Franklin House, 509 Maple St.
OSTERVILLE
  The Roost, P. O. Box 488
OAK BLUFFS
  Brownies Cottage, P. O. Box 788
  The Eastman's, P. O. Box 1221
HYANNISPORT
  Dr. M. C. Tohmpson, 181 Windsor
  Hilltop, P. O. Box 205
BILLERICA
  Galehurst, P. O. Box 583
CANTON
  Peter Pan House, 808 West St.
  Whispering Willow, 808 West St.
EAST BROOKFIELD
  Camp Atwater
KINGSTON
  Camp Twin Oaks
  Kingston Inn
MASHPEE
  Camp Maushop, P. O. Box 7
  The Guest House, P. O. Box 234
NORWELL
  Norwell Pines, P. O. Box 234
OAK BLUFFS
  The O'Brien House
  220-222 Circuit Ave.
  Shearer Cottage
  Scott's Cottage, P. O. Box 1131
  Maxwell Cottage, P. O. Box 1354
  Lill & Delta Cottage, School St.
VINEYARD HAVEN
  Araujo Rooms, P. O. Box 518
WAREHAM
  Clipper Cabins, 294 Elm St.
  Stockbridge, Mass.
  Parkview, Park St.
WEST HYANNIS
  West Hyannis Port, Craryville Rd.
WILLIAMSTOWN
  Hart's Camp

MINNESOTA

PINE RIVER
  Ware's Resort, 50 Lakes Rt.
BACKUS
  Pine Mt. Camp

NEW YORK STATE

ACCORD
  Rock Hill Farm Camp
ALLABEN
  Camp Bryton Rock
ATHENS
  Riverview, R. F. D. 1
BLOOMINGBURG
  Harper's Lodge
CATSKILL
  Camp Sky Mountain, R. F. D. 1.
  Box 195
  Johnson's Inn, Cauterskill Ave.
CHESTERTON
  Crystal Lake Lodge
CLINTON CORNERS
  The Patches, Jameson Hill Rd.
CUDDEBACKVILLE
  Paradise Farm
EDDIEVILLE
  Boston Terrace
  Arrow Lodge
GREENWOOD LAKE
  La Part Cabins in the Sky
  Just Haven
  Mrs. Louise Taylor, P. O. Box 314
  Farm Lake House
GLEN FALLS
  McFerson's Hotel, 52 Glen St.
GLENWILD
  Camp Napretep
HUNTER
  Notch Mountain House P. O.
  Box 5
HIGH FALLS
  Clove Valley Dude Ranch
HOLMES
  Lake Drew Lodge, 100 W. 138th St.
ROSENDALE
  Rosendale Gardens, P. O. Box 154
  Jumping Hooster Country Club
STUYVESANT
  Simmons Farm
NAPANOCH
  Shangri-La Country Club
KINGSTON
  Lang's Ranch, Route 4, Box 302
HIGH FALLS
  Wickie Wackie Club
STONE RIDGE
  Hy Charles Farm, Box 303
WEST BROOKVILLE
  Glen Terrace Hotel
WARWICK
  Appalachian Lodge, R. D. 1,
  Box 33
  Lakeland

77

Please Mention the "Green Book"

KERHONKSON
　Rainbow Acres
KINGSTON
　Moulton's Retreat, R. F. D. 4,
　　Box 251
LAKE GEORGE
　Woodbine Cottage, 75 Dieskau St.
LAKE PLACID
　Dreamland Cottage, 41 Mckinley St.
　Camp Parkside, Woodland Terrace
LIVINGSTON MANOR
　Hillside Camp
MECHANICVILLE
　Comfort Inn, R. F. D. 1
MONROE
　Lakeside Farm
　Mrs. Lottie Henderson, R. F. D. 1
　Randolph's Mt. Lake Lodge
　R. F. D. 1, Box 198
MONTGOMERY
　Sumphaven Lodge, R. F. D. New Rd
OTISVILLE
　King's Lodge
　Mountainside Farm, P. O. Box 207
NEW YORK CITY, N. Y.
　Brucewood, 321 W. 125th St.
PLEASANT VALLEY
　Brown Hill Farm, R. F. D. 1
RIFTON
　Maple Tree Inn, P. O. Box 116
ROXBURY
　New Mt. Viek House, P. O. Box 120
SARATOGA SPRINGS
　Nimmo Manor, 21 Federal St.
　Richards, 29 Ballston Ave.
　Jemmott's Inn, 22 Cowen St.
　Branchcomb Cottage, 18 Cherry St.
　James' Guest House, 17 Park St.
STAATSBURG
　White Wall Manor
STORMVILLE
　Mountain View Farm, R. F. D. 16
　The Cecil Lodge, R. F. D.
SPRING VALLEY
　White Birches, S. Pascack Rd.
WINGDALE
　Camp Unity
WHITE LAKE
　Fur Workers Resort
VERBANK
　Sunset Hill Farm
VALLEY COTTAGE
　Mtn. View Lodge, Mt. View Ave.

LONG ISLAND

AMITYVILLE
　Van Winn Villa, Albany Ave.
　　& Reed Rd.
DEER PARK
　Deer Haven, 1531 Deer Park Ave.
EAST MEREDITH
　Stone House, Mrs. C. B. Simkins,
GREENPORT
　Sea Breeze Cottage, 321 7th St.
　　R. F. D.
MEDFORD
　Gordon Hgts. Rest
　Flor's Cottage, P. O. Box 211
HAMMELS
　The Cherokee, 217 Beach 76th St.
JAMAICA
　Lillie's Cottage, 147-11 Ferndale
PATCHOGUE
　Martin Acres, Yaphank Rd.
QUOGUE
　Shinnecock Arms, Jessup Ave.
　Williams Cottage
　Arch Cottage, P. O. Box 761
ROCKAWAY BEACH
　Regina House, 223 Beach 77th St.
　Ocean View, 232 Beach 77th St.
　The Cherokee, 217 Beach 76th St.
SAG HARBOR
　Douglas Cottage
SOUTHOLD
　Cherry-Wells Brung., P. O. Box 571
SOUTHAMPTON
　Starlight Rest, 111 Pelletreau St.
　Kellis Rest, P. O. Box 112
　Ross Acres, Box 536

NEW JERSEY

ATLANTIC CITY
　Jones Cottage, 1720 Arctic Ave.
　Apex Rest, Indiana & Ontario Aves
　Wright's Hotel, 1702 Arctic Ave.
　Gregory Frances House, 232
　　N. Virginia Ave.
ASBURY PARK
　Wright's Cottage, 153 Sylan Ave.
　Ada's Cottage, 1404 Sumerfield
　Gladstone Cottage, 1701 Bangs Ave.
　Hotel Carver, 312 Myrtle Ave.
　Rhine Cliff Cottage, 138 Reage Ave.
BELMAR
　Pleasant View House, 504 11th Ave.
　LaPetite Cottage, 502 16th Ave.
　Baldwin Cottage, 610 11th Ave.
　Riverview Inn, 710 8th Ave.
　Sadie's Guest House, 1304 E. St.
CAPE MAY
　Stiles, 821 Corgie St.
CLIFFWOOD
　Forbes Beach, P. O. Box 231
FARMINGDALE
　Mrs. N. Perry, R. F. D. No. 1,
　　Box 400
　Blue Top Cottage, Shark River Rd.
LONG BRANCH
　Albreco Anchorage, 395 Atlantic
LONG BRANCH, West End
　Metropolitan Seashore Home,
　　8 Cottage Ave.
MAHWAH
　Josie Rue Acres, P. O. Box 184
OCEAN CITY
　Hotel Comfort, 201 Bay Ave.
　Bryson's, 6th & Simpson Ave.

78

in Patronizing These Places

NEPTUNE
  Busy Bee Cottage, 446 Fisher Ave.
  Shore Villa, 316 Myrtle Ave.
MILLINGTON
  Playland Farms
MIDVALE
  Camp Midval
NORTH LONG BRANCH
  Shady Nook Cot., 71 Atlantic Ave.
LAKEHURST
  Robertson's Farm
NEW GRENTA
  Oaklawn Country Club
PLEASANTVILLE
  Morris Beach, 401 Bayview Ave.
  Garden Spot, 300 Doughty Rd
  Marionette Cottage, 604 Portland
RICHLAND
  Red Oaks Rest
SKILLMAN
  Rainbow End
SPRINGLAKE BEACH
  Laster Cottage, 419 Morris Ave.
TOMS RIVER
  McDaniel Farm, 2 Rover Rd.
WILDWOOD
  Poindexter Cottage,
    106 E. Schellenger Ave.
  Mrs. J. B. Quarles, 100 Young Ave.

MICHIGAN

BALDWIN
  Whip-or-Will Cot. Rt. 1,
    Box 178B
  Three Sisters
CONSTANTINE
  Double J. Ranch, Jean S. Jones,
BAY SHORE
  Zac White Pines
BUCHANAN
  Waters Farm
BITLEY (Woodland Park Resort
  Old Dears Rest, Rt. 1
  Dagg's Cottage, Rt. 1
  Everett Rest Haven, Rt. 1
  Royal Breeez Hotel, Rt. 1
  Caslen's Blue Bell Garden, Rt. 1
COVERT
  Scott's, Country Villa, Rt. 1, Box 53
  Pitchford's, Big Tower Child.
    Camp. Tel. OA 4-4749
  Mable's Place
HART
  Bryson's, on the Hilltop
    202 N. State St.
HARTFORD
  Matthew Burgess' Place
IDLEWILD
  The Pomiserania Lodge
  Mildred Williams
    Club El Morocco, Rt. 1, Box 186A
    Bask-Inn, Broadway & Hemlock
    Douglas Manor, P. O. Box 794
    McKnight's Par. Pal., P. O. Box 75

White Way Inn, Broadway
Lydia Inn, P. O. Box 81
Rosana Tavern, Lake Drive
Nichol's Home, P. O. Box "B"
Morton's Motel, P. O. Box 116
LAWRENCE
  FloraGiles Farm, Rt. 1
PAW PAW
  Trails End Resort
  Pit's Resort, Rt. 1, Box 131
ROSE CENTER
  Medicine Acres, 8775 Water St.
SOUTH HAVEN
  Thornton's Resort, Rt. 3, Box 41
  Johnson's Shady Nook, Rt. 1,
    Box 102
  Twin Star Resort, Rt. 3, Box 245
  Clare Harris' Resort, Rt. 4, Box 38
  Evergreen Resort
THREE RIVERS
  Wilson's Farm, Rt. 2, Box 344
  Jordan's Home, Rt. 2, Box 546
VANDALIA (Paradise lk. Resort
  Three Sisters, Rt. 1

PENNSYLVANIA

STROUDSBURG
  Stroudsburg Mt. View House,
    14 No. 2nd St.
EAST STROUDSBURG
  Fern Board. House, 387 Lincoln
ESPY
  Sunrise, P. O. Box 65
MONROETON
  Dorsey Wood Park Farm,
    R. F. D. 1
MT. POCONO
  The Carter House, 15 Quay St.
SWIFTWATER
  Alenia's Inn, Box 236
WILLOW GROVE
  Laster Chateau, 428 S. Easton Rd.

GLOVER'S CHI-ACRES Trail's End Resort

You'll Be Delighted

WITH THE FRIENDLY HOSPITALITY, WELCOME ECONOMY AND COMFORTABLE ACCOMMODATIONS AT GLOVER'S CHI-ACRES ON BEAUTIFUL EAGLE LAKE

Write for a Brochure

Boating, Fishing, Swimming

ROUTE 1, PAW PAW, MICHIGAN

Please Mention the "Green Book"

RHODE ISLAND
WESTERLY
Orchard House

SOUTH CAROLINA
OCEAN DRIVE
Atlantic Beach
Hotel Gordon, Atlantic Beach

VERMONT
MANCHESTER
Limberlock
NORTHFIELD
Cole's Brown Bung. 7 Sherman Ave.

VIRGINIA
CROZET
Mtn. View Farm, R. F. D. 1, Box 52
ORANGE
Mrs. B. Wood, R. F. D. 2
BEDFORD
Mrs. M. Jones, R. F. D. 1, Box 7A
CATAWBA
Mrs. E. Sorano, R. F. D. 1, Box 32A
LYNNHAVEN
Ocean Breeze Beach
TAPPAHANNOCK
Mark-Haven Beach

WISCONSIN
FORT ATKINSON, WISCONSIN

BURNS' RESORT
House-Keeping Cabins
Good Fishing, Boats & Bait
For Reservations write:
Rt. 3, Box 266   Phone: 850-J-2

SPOONER
Lone Star Resort, Rt. 2
Channey's Resort, Rt. 2
TOMAHAWK
Somom Heights Resort

CANADA
COLLINGWOOD (ONTARIO)
Cedar Inn, P. O. Box 265
SHEFFIELD'S CEDAR INN
P. O. BOX 265
MUSKOKA
Black & Tan Resort
QUEBEC
Husband's Resort, 6 Calixa
MONTREAL
TOURIST HOMES
Mrs. N. P. Morse, 922 Calumet Pl.
Mrs. A. Cummings, 764 Atwater
Davis Home, 1324 Torrence St.
AuRepos Rooms, 1824 Dorchester
Grant House, 1432 St. Antoine St.

THIS GUIDE

is Consulted

Throughout

the Year

by

Thousands

of

Travelers

—

Are You

Represented?

FREE
to your friends...
a copy of The
GREEN BOOK

Want to show them what a valuable guide this is and why you order same?

You can send a FREE sample copy to as many friends as you like. Just give their names and addresses and we'll do the rest—at no cost to you or your friends. Of course, we will send it to them with your compliments and ours.

VICTOR H. GREEN & CO.
Publishers

200 West 135th Street
New York 30, N. Y.

YES, send a sample copy of *THE GREEN BOOK* to the folks listed below:

YOUR NAME ....

CITY AND STATE ....

SEND A SAMPLE COPY OF *THE GREEN BOOK* TO:

NAME ....
ADDRESS ....
CITY AND STATE .....

NAME ....
ADDRESS ....
CITY AND STATE .....

NAME ....
ADDRESS ....
CITY AND STATE .....

NAME ....
ADDRESS ....
CITY AND STATE .....

The Negro Travelers' Green Book 1954

TRAVELERS' Green Book

$1.95

INTERNATIONAL EDITION 1963-64

for vacation without aggravation

Plus BONUS BOOKLET

HOTELS · MOTELS · VACATION RESORTS
RESTAURANTS · TOURIST HOMES

green book's HISTORY-MAKERS

JIM BECKWOURTH
1798–1867

HUNTER AND TRAPPER, HE CAME FROM ST. LOUIS WHERE HE WAS A BLACKSMITH. A U.S. SCOUT, HE WON FAME AS A FIGHTER AND BECAME A CHIEF OF THE CROW INDIANS! HE WAS ONE OF THE FOUNDERS OF DENVER, COLORADO!

© HERITAGE FEATURES

© 1961 New York World's Fair 1964-1965 Corp.

The Unisphere, symbol of the 1964-1965 New York World's Fair, represents the basic theme of "Peace Through Understanding" and was given by the United States Steel Corporation.

Don't miss your special New York World's Fair 1964 edition of the Travelers' GREEN BOOK. Order your copy NOW!

All the excitement and glamour of this "Greatest Fair of Them All" in the greatest city, with the dramatic details in pictures and stories, will be in the 64-65 Travelers' GREEN BOOK ... plus many new features designed to help you "VACATION WITHOUT AGGRAVATION." Send check or money order (Special Advance Price $1.50) to Victor H. Green Co., 200 W. 135th St., N. Y.

L. Waller

27th Consecutive Issue

FOUNDED 1936
By Victor H. Green

Travelers' GREEN BOOK
"Assured Protection for the Negro Traveler"

1963-64 EDITION
Published by
VICTOR H. GREEN CO.

L. A. WALLER
MELVIN TAPLEY
Co-Publishers

This edition of Travelers' Green Book is dedicated to our many friends and advertisers whose cooperation and encouragement made it possible: Mrs. Alma Green, Reginald Pierrepointe, Carlton Bertrand, Atty. J. J. Fieulleteau, Atty. Hope Stevens, Constance Curtis, Al Lockhart, William Capitman, Hy Schneider, Wendell Colton, Peter Celliers, Ken Brown, Thomasina Norford, Dr. P. M. H. Savory, Ted Shearer, Vondel Nichols, Frank Palumbo, and YOU.

INSIDE
- THE 50 States 4-77
- Canada 79-80
- Caribbean 77, 81
- Latin America 80, 85
- Europe 86
- Africa 92

Features:
- Your Rights 23
- Guideposts 95
- Convention Calendar 78
- Gee Bee 97
- History-Makers 99
- Travel Trunklines 99
- Baseball Circuit 97

Copyright 1963 by Victor H. Green Co.
All Rights Reserved—Editorial & Advertising
Offices are located at 200 W. 135th St., New York 30, N. Y.

LOCKHART AGENCY

Cover by
WILLARD SMITH

Travelers' Green Book 1963–64

RIGHTS GUARDIANS—Congressmen William L. Dawson, Ill.; Augustus C. Hawkins, Calif.; Adam C. Powell, N. Y.; Robert N. C. Nix, Pa.; Charles C. Diggs, Mich., are five stalwarts
ROBT. COTTROL

YOUR RIGHTS, BRIEFLY SPEAKING!

Most people who 'go on holiday,' as they say in England, the Caribbean and other places where the accent is English, are seeking someplace that offers them rest, relaxation and a refuge from the cares and worries of the work-a-day world.

The Negro traveler, to whom the Travelers Green Book has dedicated its efforts since 1936, is no exception. He too, is looking for "Vacation Without Aggravation".

Of course, this is no surprise. The National Association for the Advancement of Colored People, the National Urban League, the Congress on Racial Equality, the Students Non-Violence Committee, the Southern Christian Leadership Association and other groups fighting for minority rights make it very clear that the Negro is only demanding what everyone else wants . . . what is guaranteed all citizens by the Constitution of the United States.

In fact, the militancy of these civil right groups exhibited in sit-ins, kneel-ins, freedom rides, other demonstration and court battles has widened the areas of public accommodations accessible to all.

Realizing that a family planning a vacation hopes for one that is free of tensions and problems, the Travelers Green Book includes the following brief summary of various state statutes on discrimination as they apply to public accommodations or recreation:

ALASKA	Law bans jimcro in recreational facilities. Violators are subject to criminal punishment (court proceedings).
CALIFORNIA	Anti-jimcro law in recreational facilities. Violators are subject to civil suits for damages plus $250.
COLORADO CONNECTICUT	Anti-jimcro law in recreational facilities, including discriminatory advertising. Administrative enforcement machinery. Alternatively, enforcement through court proceedings (criminal punishment).
DISTRICT OF COLUMBIA	Anti-jimcro law in recreational facilities. Violators subject to criminal punishment, forfeiture of licenses (court proceednigs).
IDAHO	Anti-jimcro in recreational facilities. Violators subject to criminal punishment (court proceedings).
ILLINOIS	Anti-jimcro law in recreational facilities, including discriminatory advertising. Violators subject to civil damages, criminal punishment and injunction (court proceedings).

INDIANA	Anti-jimcro law in recreational facilities. Violators are subject to civil damages and criminal punishment (court proceedings).
IOWA	... Violators subject to criminal punishment (court proceedings).
KANSAS	... Violators subject to fines (court proceedings).
MAINE	... including discriminatory advertising. Violators subject to criminal punishment (court proceedings).
MASSACHUSETTS	... including ... advertising. Administrative enforcement machinery. Alternatively, enforcement through court proceedings (civil damages, criminal punishment).
MICHIGAN	... including ... advertising. Violators are subject to civil suits for treble damages, criminal punishment, and revocation or suspension of license (court proceedings).
MINNESOTA	... Violators subject to civil damages and criminal punishment ...
MONTANA	... No specific sanctions.
NEBRASKA	... Violators subject to criminal punishment (court proceedings).
NEVADA	Law declares jimcro in recreational facilities to be against public policy. Administrative investigating machinery.
NEW HEMPSHIRE	... Violators subject to fines ...
NEW JERSEY	... including discriminatory advertising. Administrative enforcement machinery. Alternatively, enforcement through court proceedings (civil damages, criminal punishment).
NEW MEXICO	... No specific sanctions.
NEW YORK OREGON PENNSYLVANIA	... including discriminatory advertising. Administrative enforcement machinery. Alternatively, enforcement through court proceedings (civil damages, criminal punishment).
NORTH DAKOTA	... Violators subject to criminal punishment ...
OHIO	... Administrative enforcement machinery. Alternatively, enforcement through court proceedings (civil damages, criminal punishment).
RHODE ISLAND	... Administrative enforcement machinery.
VERMONT	... Violators subject to criminal punishment (court proceedings).
VIRGINIA	Prohibition of advertisements discriminating because of religion. Violators are liable to injunction suits (court proceedings).
VIRGIN ISLANDS	... Violators subject to civil damage (actual damages plus punitive damages up to $5000), criminal punishment and revocation or suspension of licenses (court proceedings).
WASHINGTON	... including discriminatory advertising. Administrative enforcement machinery. Alternatively, enforcement through court proceedings ...
WEST VIRGINIA	No law prohibiting discrimination in recreational facilities. Human Rights Commission authorized to investigate charges of discrimination.
WISCONSIN	... Violators subject to civil damages and criminal punishment ...
WYOMING	... Violators subject to criminal punishment ...

Travelers' Green Book 1963–64

This information was condensed from "Civil Rights and Minorities" by Paul Hartman, associate director of the law department of the Anti-Defamation League of B'nai B'rith. Other excellent reference material is the "Report On State Anti-Discrimination Agencies and the Laws They Administer" prepared by the Commission on Law and Social Action of the American Jewish Congress. Shad Polier is chairman of the Commission; Leo Pfeffer, director; and Joseph Robison, assistant director. Mr. Robison is author of these AJC reports.

By-the-way, if you encounter any problems in these states that have this legislation (incidentally, Massachusetts had a law banning discrimination in recreational facilities open to the general public as far back as 1865 . . . the first of its kind) you can take your complaint to:

Alaska — Dept. of Labor — Juneau, Alaska
California — Div. of Fair Employment Practices, Dept. of Industrial Relations — 455 Golden Gate Ave., San Francisco 1, Calif.
Colorado — Anti-Discrimination Commission — 1525 Sherman St., Denver
Connecticut — Commission on Civil Rights — State Office Bldg., Hartford 15
Illinois — Fair Employment Practices Commission — Chicago
Indiana — Civil Rights Commission — 1004 State Office Bld., Indianapolis 4, Ind.
Kansas — Commission on Civil Rights — State Office Bldg., Topeka, Kan.
Massachusetts — Commission Against Discrimination — 41 Tremont St., Boston, Mass.
Michigan — Fair Employment Practice Commission — 900 Cadillac Sq. Bldg., Detroit 26, Mich.
Minnesota — Minnesota Fair Employment Practices Commission — Rm. 12, State Office Bldg., St. Paul 1
Missouri — Commission on Human Rights — Rm 131B, State Capitol Bldg., Jefferson City, Mo.
New Jersey — Div. on Civil Rights, Dept. of Education — 1100 Raymond Blvd., Newark 5, N. J.
New Mexico — Fair Employment Practices Commission — Capitol Bldg., Santa Fe, New Mexico
New York — Commission on Human Rights — 270 Broadway, N. Y. 7
Ohio, Civil Rights Commission — 22 E. Gay St., Columbus 15
Oregon — Civil Rights Division, Bureau of Labor — 1216 S.W. Hall St., Portland 1
Pennsylvania — Human Relations Commission, Dept. of Labor and Industry — 1401 Labor & Industry Bldg., Harrisburg
Rhode Island — Commission Against Discrimination — State House, Providence 2
Washington — State Board Against Discrimination — 206 Capitol Park Bldfi., Olympia
Wisconsin — Fair Employment Practices Division — 634 2nd St., Milwaukee Industrial Commission

ALABAMA
Hotels — Motels — Tourist Homes — Restaurants

ATMORE

FREEMANVILLE SERVICE STATION & GARAGE
Complete Auto Service — Picnic Supplies

4 Mis. N. W. of Atmore
East of Jackspring Rd.
2 Mis. W. of Hwy 21

Rte. 3, Box 148
Atmore, Alabama

Paris Motel ....173 Ashley Street

★The SNACK BAR .... 70 Carver Avenue
Where They Have A Knack For Delicious Snacks

"The Best Place In Birmingham For Food & Rest"

FRATERNAL CAFE
Famous for Our Homecooked Food

Open:
6:30 A.M. to 8 P.M.

1624 Fourth Avenue
N. Birmingham, Ala.

★PALM LEAF HOTEL .... 328½ North 18th Street
Your Gracious Hostess . . . Mrs. Eva Lou Russell

Satisfaction Guaranteed

FOURTH AVENUE SERVICE STATION

B. F. Davis, Owner

1601 Fourth Avenue No.
AL 2-9177

★PARKVIEW CAFE & RAYMOND'S SNACK BAR .... 1701 Fifth No.

DOTHAN
William Washington Hotel .... 216 W. North Street

FLORENCE
Hawkin's Bar-B-Que .... 837 W. Mobile Avenue

GADSDEN
Mrs. A. J. Shepard Tourist Home .... 1324 4th Avenue
Barnes Motel .... 422 North 9th Street
James Service Station & Body Shop .... 213 N. 6th Street

---

LI 3-3911

JAMES SERVICE STATION

SUNDRY & SNACK BAR

Courtesy Service

213 N. 6th Street
Gadsden, Alabama

W. J. Wills
Manager

James Sundry & Snack Bar .... 554 Meighan Blvd.

Travelers' Green Book 1963–64

    Skyline Recreation Center .... 550-C Meighan Blvd.
    The Marisue Apartment & Motel .... 550-C Meighan Blvd.
HUNTSVILLE
    Glaly's Jane Motel .... 1302 Posey Avenue
    Mrs. India Herndon Tourist Home .... 515 Oak Street
    Mrs. Rose Allen Tourist Home .... 212 Lowe Street
    Patten Service Station .... 329 North Church Street
MOBILE
    E. Jordan Tourist Home .... 256 North Dearborn Street
    F. Wildins Tourist Home .... 254 North Dearborn Street
    Le Grand Hotel .... 1461 Davis Avenue

"The Ultimate In Southern Hospitality"
MIDWAY HOTEL ... Rest at Midway
5 Minute Walk to Churches of All Denominations, Western Union,
P. O., Railroads, Courthouse, Union Halls, and Places of Pleasure.
Mrs. Lovie Beck Johnson   107 N. Dearborn Street

MONTGOMERY
    Alexander's Blue & Gray Inn .... 1415 Wilcox
    Hotel Ben Moore .... 902 Highland Avenue
    Mrs. Dave Sims Tourist Home .... 900 Cleveland Avenue
    Mrs. Dave Sims Tourist Home .... 322 Cleveland Street
MOULTON
    Triangle Shopping Center .... Sommerville Avenue
PHENIX CITY
    Rayfus Parham Tire Shop & Service Station .... 1725 Seale Road
TUSCALOOSA
    G. W. Clopton Tourist Home .... 1516 25th Avenue
    Hotel Preston .... 101 University Avenue
TUSKEGEE
    Flossie's Fashion .... Carver Shopping Center, Southside & Jericho Streets
    Gunn's Grocery, Garage & Gas .... 2 Mi. East of Tuskegee
TUSKEGEE INSTITUTE
    Rogers Shoe Shop & Shoe Store, Inc. .... Phone 944
    Snowden's Garage & OK Rubber Welders .... Phone 582
    Typewriter Sales & Service Co. .... Chambliss Bldg.
    Wiley's Eat Shop .... Montgomery Hiway, U.S. 80 at Greenforks

ALASKA
Hotels — Motels — Tourist Homes — Restaurants
ANCHORAGE
    Parsons Hotel .... 300 M Street
    The Westward Hotel .... 3rd Ave. & F St.
    Traveler's Inn .... 720 Gambell Street
FAIRBANKS
    Fairbanks Hotel
    Savoy Hotel
    Traveler's Inn .... 813 Noble Street
JUNEAU
    Baranof Hotel .... 2nd & Franklin St.
KETCHIKAN
    The Ingersoll Hotel .... Front & Mission St.

ARIZONA
Hotels — Motels — Tourist Homes — Restaurants

BISBEE
   Hotel Copper Queen

DOUGLAS
   Faustina Wilson Tourist Home .... 1002 16th Street

FLAG STAFF
   El Rancho Flag Staff .... Box 1241
   Park Plaza Motel .... Rts. 66 & 89

GRAND CANYON
   Bright Angle
   El Toya Hotel

KINGMAN
   Mountain Villa Motel .... Hwy. 66, East
   ★White Rock Court .... 843 E. Andy Dr.

MESA
   Peter Pan Motel .... 620 Main St.

NOGALES
   Coronado .... 900 Grand Ave.
   El Porto Motel .... Tucon Road

PHOENIX
   Alhambia Restaurant .... 1246-48 East Washington St.
   Hotel Rice .... 535 East Jefferson Street
   Lucille's Motel .... 2021 E. Van Buren St.
   ★PADUCAH HOTEL AND APARTMENTS .... 14 North 6th Street
   254-0938 — Reasonable Rates — Write for Reservations
   Rose Restaurant .... 947 West Watkins Street
   ★SWINDALL'S TOURIST HOME .... 1021 East Washington St.

PRESCOTT
   Mission Lodge .... 1211 E. Gurley

TUCSON
   Mrs. Louise Pitts Tourist Home .... 722 North Perry Street
   Rio Motel .... 3031 So. 6th

YUMA
   Rev. James Coleman's Downtown Lodge
   113 S. Gila Street
   Yuma, Arizona

ARKANSAS
Hotels — Motels — Tourist Homes — Restaurants

ARKADELPHIA
   Hill's Hotel .... 1601 West Pine Street
BLYTHESVILLE
   St. Francis Sundry Store .... 1204 Heans Street
CAMDEN
   Burnell's Service Station .... 204 Grinstead S. E.
   Mrs. Benjamin Williams .... North Main Street
CONWAY
   Deluxe Diner .... 1151 Markham Street
ELDORADO
   C. W. Moore Tourist Home .... 618 Cordell
   Dr. Dunning Tourist Home .... 709 Columbia Avenue
   Green's Hotel .... 303 Hill Street
FAYETTEVILLE
   N. Smith Tourist Home .... 259 East Center Street
FORDYSE
   Harlem Restaurant .... 211 1st Street
FORT SMITH
   Mrs. Clara Oliver Tourist Home .... 718 North 9th Street
   Ullery Inn Hotel .... 719 North 9th Street
HELENA
   Barbour's Tourist Home .... 814 Richtor St.
HOPE
   Green Leaf Restaurant .... Highway 67
   Lewis-Wilson Hotel .... 217 East 3rd Street
HOT SPRINGS
   Arkansas Loan Company .... 428 Malvern Avenue
   Barabin Villa .... 717 Pleasant Street
   C. & D. Hotel .... 320 Church Street
   Crittenden Hotel .... 314 Cottage Street
   Gray's Hotel .... 436 Church Street
   Harris Hotel .... Church & Cottage Sts.
   Home Rooms for Rent .... $10.50—$6.50 week .... 120 Gaines Ave.
   J. W. Rife Tourist Home .... 347½ Malvern Avenue
   Jewell Apartments .... 711 Pleasant Street
   Little Palace Cafe .... 403½ Silver Street
   ★McKENZIE MOTEL .... 401 Henry St., 2 blocks off Hwy. 270 East
   South's Finest — Air Conditioned — Phone NA 3-7849
   National Baptist Sanitarium .... 501 Malvern Ave.
   New Edmondson Tourist Home .... 207 Ash Street
   Palm Lounge Restaurant .... 415 Malvern Ave.
   Pythian Baths .... 415½ Malvern St.
   Rest-A-While Tourist Home .... 121 Grove St.

Smith's Steak House	435 Malvern Avenue
The Harlem Chicken Shack	518 Malvern Avenue
The Royal Liquor Store	526 Malvern Avenue
The Texan Inn	605 Pleasant Street
Town Talk Barbeque	500 Pleasant St.
Wadkins Tourist Home	212 Garden St.

LITTLE ROCK

College Restaurant	16th and Bishop
Graysonia Hotel	809 Gaines Street
Honeycut Hotel	816 West 9th Street
Miller Hotel	812½ West 9th Street
Mrs. H. Gilmore Tourist Home	1324 West 19th St.
Tucker's Hotel	701½ West 9th Street

MADISON

U. S. Bond's Motel	U. S. Hway. 70, ½ mile w. of Madison

NORTH LITTLE ROCK

Cat's Motel & Cafe	Highway 67W
De Lux Court	2720 East Broadway
Ideal Beauty Shop	Rt. 5, Box 360
Jim's Restaurant	908 Cedar Street N.L.R.
Nov-Vena Restaurant	1101 East 6th Street
Waters Drive-In	Rt. 5, Box 360

PINE BLUFF

Duck Inn Restaurant	405 North Cedar Street
M. J. Hollis Tourist Home	1108 West 2nd Avenue
Pee Kay Hotel	300 East 3rd Street

RUSSELLVILLE

E. Latimore Tourist Home	318 South Huston Avenue

TEXARKANA

Brown's Hotel	312 West Elm Street
G. C. Mackey Tourist Home	102 East 9th Street
Grant's Cafe Restaurant	830 Laurel Street

TUCKERMAN

Freeman's Tourist Court	Hwy. 67

WEST MEMPHIS

RE 5-9177   Mr. & Mrs. James Williams, Props.   Open 24 Hours

WILLIAMS APARTMENT & BABY GRAND SANDWICH SHOP

Home Cooked Meals — Air Conditioned Rooms — Free Parking

314 S. 11th Street   West Memphis, Ark.

Travelers' Green Book 1963–64

CALIFORNIA
Hotels — Motels — Tourist Homes — Restaurants

ALTURAS
  Niles ....P. O. Box 891

ANAHEIM
  Disneyland ....1441 So. West Street

BERKELEY
  Berkeley Inn ....2501 Taste St.
  Berkeley Plaza ....1175 University Ave.
  Bonanza Motel ....1720 San Pablo Ave.
  Claremont Hotel ....Ashby and Claremont Ave.
  Durant Hotel ....2600 Durant Ave.

FRESNO
  De Lux Restaurant ....2193 Ivy Street
  Fresno Hacienda ....Hwy. 99 and Clinton
  Palm Motel ....Hwy. 99, North
  Poplar Grove Motel ....Hwy. 99

HOLLYWOOD
  Carlton Lodge ....2011 N. Highland Ave.
  Hollywood Plaza ....1637 N. Vine
  Hollywood Roosevelt ....7000 Hollywood Blvd.
  Hallmark House Motor Hotel ....7023 Sunset Blvd.
  Hollywood Thunderbird Inn ....8300 Sunset Blvd.
  Hollywood Wilcox Hotel ....6500 Selma Ave.
  Imperial "400" Motel ....6826 W. Sunset Blvd.
  Sands-Sunset Hotel ....8775 Sunset Blvd.

LOS ANGELES
  Alexandria ....210 W. 5th Street
  Ambassador ....3400 Wilshire Blvd.
  Astor Motel ....2901 S. Flower St.
  Bel Air Motel ....701 Stone Canyon Rd.
  Biltmore ....515 S. Olive Street
  Californian ....1907 W. 6th Street
  ★**CASBAH APARTMENTS AND ROOMS**................................**1189 W. 36th Place**
    Reasonable Rates — Comfort — Privacy — Good Accommodations
    For Information and Reservations Write or Tel.: 735-8290
  Clark ....425 S. Hill Street
  Cortez ....375 Columbia Ave.
  EC Eastsider ....2133 S. Central
  EC Motel ....3501 S. Wesetrn
  HAYES MOTEL ....**960 Jefferson Blvd.**
  HAYES WESTERN MOTEL ....**3700 S. Western Avenue**
  Harmon Motel ....700 W. Florence
  Manchester Motel ....800 E. Manchester
  Mayfair ....1256 W. 7th Street
  New Casa Motel ....7720 S. Main St.
  Notel Motel ....4766 S. Main St.
  PALM VUE ....**3922 South Western**
  Raywood Motel ....8200 S. Figueroa St.

10

Santa Barbara Motel	1758 W. Santa Barbara Ave.
Sky Terrace Motel	Normandie & Jefferson Blvd.
Statler-Hilton	930 Wilshire Blvd.

LAKE ELSIMORE
Lake Elsimore Hotel	416 North Kelogg Street

MADERA
Casa Grand Motel	Hwy. 99

NEEDLES
El Adobe Motel	U. S. Highway, 66

OAKLAND
California Hotel	3501 San Pablo Street
Carver Hotel	1412 Market Street
Fifty-Fifth Motel	2320 55th Ave.

PERRIS
Muse-A-While	Highway 395

SACRAMENTO
Dunlop's Restaurant	4322 4th Ave.

SAN DIEGO
Douglas Hotel	206 Market St.
Ebony Inn Motel	740 32nd St.
Manor Hotel	2223 El Cajon Blvd.
Motel Western Shores	6345 Pacific Hwy.
Simmons Hotel	542 6th Avenue
Y.W.C.A.	1012 C. Street

SAN FRANCISCO
Booker T. Washington Hotel	1540 Ellis St.
Bullford Hotel	843 Hayes Street
Edison Hotel	1540 Ellis Street
New Pullman Hotel	232 Townsend Street
Sir Francis Drake Hotel	450 Powell St.
Texas Hotel	1840 Filmore Street
The Scaggs Hotel	1715 Webster Street

SAN LUIS OBISPO
Ranchotel	1900 Montgomery St.

STOCKTON
El Camino Motel	1506 Mariposa
Sunset Motel	1305 So. Wilson Way

VALLEJO
Bell Motel	1308 Lincoln Hwy.
Charlotte Hotel	518 Sacramento St.

YOSEMITE NATIONAL PARK
- Camp Curry
- Glasier Point Hotel
- High Sierra Hotel
- Hotel Ahwanne
- Yosemite Lodge

COLORADO
Hotels — Motels — Tourist Homes — Restaurants

ADAMS CITY
Crestline Motor Hotel	7330 Hiway 85

COLORADO SPRINGS
    G. Roberts Tourist Home .... 418 East Cucharras Street
GREELEY
    Mrs. E. Alexander Tourist Home .... 106 East 12th St.
LA MAR
    Alamo Hotel .... La Mar, Colorado
MESA VERDE NATIONAL PARK
    Spruce Tree Lodge
MONTROSE
    Adams Hotel .... Montrose, Colorado
    Chipeta Cafe .... Montrose, Colorado
PUEBLO
    Coronado Lodge .... 2130 Lake

CONNECTICUT
Hotels — Motels — Tourist Homes — Restaurants

BRIDGEPORT
    Hotel Barnum .... 150 Fairfield
    Arcade Hotel .... 1001 Main Street
    Bridgeport Motor Inn .... 100 Kings Highway Cut-off
                                                                       Rte 1A, Exit 24, Conn Turnpike
    Stratfield Hotel .... 1241 Main Street
CLINTON
    Clinton Hotel .... 14 E. Main Street
    Coastway Motel .... U.S. Hwy No. 1
DANBURY
    New Englander Motor Hotel .... Main Street
DARIEN
    Howard Johnson's Motor Lodge .... Conn. Turnpike Exit 11
EAST HARTFORD
    Howard Johnson's Motor Lodge .... 490 Main Street
GREENWICH
    Indian Harbor Motel .... 34 E. Putnam Ave.
    New Englander Motor Hotel .... 1114 Post Rd. (U.S. 1)
HARTFORD
    Bond Hotel .... 338 Asylum St.
    Farmington Ave. Motor Lodge .... 226 Farmington Ave.
    Georgian Motor Hotel & Apts. .... 725 Asylum Ave.
    Hartford Hotel .... 240 Church St.
    Mrs. Johnson Tourist Home .... 2016 Main St.
    Statler Hilton .... Ford and Pearl Streets
MOODUS
    Banner Lodge .... Banner Rd.
    Dawn Lodge .... TRiangle 3-9015
    Moodie's Lodge .... TW 8-9573
    Ted Hilton's .... Rte 151
NEW HAVEN
    Duncan Hotel .... 1151 Chapel St.
    Hotel Garde .... 4 Columbus Ave.
    Howard Johnson's Motor Lodge .... 2260 Whitney Ave.
    Monterey Restaurant .... 267 Dixwell Avenue
    Nathan Hale Motor Inn .... 1605 Whalley Ave.

Rip Van Winkle Hotel ....1548 Whalley Ave.
Taft Hotel ....Chapel & College St.
Three Judges Motel ....1560 Whalley Ave.
NEW LONDON
Crocker House ....178 State St.
Lighthouse Inn ....Lower Blvd.
Mohican Hotel ....281 State St.
Mrs. E. Whittle Tourist Home ....46 Hempstead St.
POMFRET CENTER
Willow Inn ....Highway 44, 1/2 Mile W. of Conn. Rts 101 & 44
SHARON
Gordon's Tourist Home
SOUTH NORWALK
Palm Gardens Hotel ....Post Road
STAMFORD
Robert Graham Tourist Home ....37 Hanrahan Ave.
WATERBURY
Community House Tourist Home ....34 Hopkins St.
Elton Hotel ....Waterbury, Conn.
Putt Meadow Motel ....U. S. Hwy. 6-A
WEST HAVEN
Dadds Hotel ....359 Beach Street
Seaview Hotel ....392 Beach Street
Dixon's ....379 Beach Street
Home of Hawkins ....372 Beach Street

DELAWARE
Hotels — Motels — Tourist Homes — Restaurants

DOVER
Dean's Hotel ....Forrest Street
Mosely's Hotel ....Division Street

Free Radio   Central Heating   Private Bath

CORA ANN'S MOTEL

9 Miles South of Dover, Del. U. S. Rte. 13 — 2 Miles North of Felton, Del.

Ph. 284-4074   Wm. & Cora Gibbs, Props.

LAUREL
Joe Randolph's Restaurant ....West 6th Street
REBOBOTH BEACH
Mallory Cabins ....Reboboth Avenue Ext.
TOWNSEND
Rodney Hotel ....Dupont Highway—Rt. 13
WILMINGTON
Christian Assn. Bldg. Restaurant ....10th and Walnut St.
Miss W. A. Brown Tourist Home ....1306 Tatnall Street
Y.M.C.A. ....10th and Walnut Street

DISTRICT OF COLUMBIA
Hotels — Motels — Tourist Homes — Restaurants

WASHINGTON, D. C.

★ALFRED'S RESTAURANT ....1610 "U" Street, N.W.
Ambassador Hotel ....Fourteenth & K Street, N.W.
Bellevue Hotel ....15 E. St., N.W.
Buddie's Tourist Home ....1320 5th Street
Burlington Hotel ....1120 Vermont Ave., N.W.
Cadillac Hotel ....1500 Vermont Street, N.W.
Carlyle Hotel ....500 N. Capital Street
Commodore ....No. Capitol & F Street, N.W.
Charles Hotel ....1338 R Street, N.W.
Clore Hotel ....614 S Street, N.W.
Cozy Restaurant ....708 Florida Avenue, N.W.
Dupont Plaza ....1500 New Hampshire Avenue, N.W.
Earl's Restaurant ....1218 U Street, N.W.
Edward's Tourist Home ....1837 16th Street, N.W.
Executive House ....Scott Circle, N.W.
International Inn ....Thomas Circle, 14th & M Streets, N.W.
Johnson, Jr. Hotel ....1509 Vermont Avenue, N.W.
Ken Rod Hotel ....621 Rhode Island Ave., N.W.
Kenyon Grill Restaurant ....3119 Georgia Avenue, N.W.
Madison ....15th & M St., N.W.
Manger Annapolis Hotel ....1111 H Street, N.W.
Manger Hamilton Hotel ....14th & K St., N.W.
Manger Hay-Adams Hotel ....16th & H St., N.W.
Modern Tourist Home ....3006 13th St., N.W.
Patsy's Tourist Home ....2026 13th St., N.W.
Pitts' Tourist Home...1451 Belmont St., N.W.
Raleigh Hotel ....12th St. & Pennsylvania Ave.
Republic Gardens Restaurant ....1355 U St., N.W.
Rivers Tourist Home ....1021 Monroe St., N.W.

14

Roger Smith Hotel	Pennsylvania Ave. & 18th St., N.W.
Sheraton-Carlton Hotel	923 16th St., N.W.
Sheraton-Park Hotel	Conn. Ave. & Woodley Rd., N.W.
Statler Hilton	16th & K Sts., N.W.
Sugar Bowl Restaurant	2830 Georgia Ave., N.W.
The Hour Restaurant	1837 11th St., N.W.
Towles Tourist Home	1321 13th St., N.W.
Y.M.C.A.	1816 12th St., N.W.
Y.M.C.A.	901 Rhode Island Ave., N.W.

FLORIDA

Hotels — Motels — Tourist Homes — Restaurants

COCONUT GROVE
Brown's Grove 66 Station .... 3685 Grand Avenue

BOYNTON BEACH
Bahama Motel .... 114½ N.E. 10th Ave.

DAYTONA

CL 3-9271   CL 2-9514

CAMPBELL'S HOTEL & BAR
Nightly and Weekly Rates

537-541½ Second Avenue
Elijah Campbell, Prop.   Daytona Beach, Fla.

KAT TAVERN .... 325 Mississippi Street
Friendly Atmosphere .... Phone CL 2-9632

Phone 255-3917   Isaac L. Purcell, Mgr.

CLUB EIGHT - EIGHTY
Cocktail Lounge - Restaurant

Daytona's Leading Social Center
Cocktails served daily, 2 p.m. until 2a.m. in the Blue Room
Guest Stars Entertain in the Celebrity Room
Tuesday, Friday, Saturday and Sunday

Complete Banquet and Party Facilities Available

1408 Mason Avenue   Daytona Beach, Fla.

Phone CL 2-5410 Phone CL 2-7247

SHEPPARD'S RESTAURANT

Specializing in Fine Foods

Rooms

Day — Week — Month

706 Cypress Street Daytona Beach, Fla.

GRAY'S SERVICE STATION
Riley M. Gray, Prop.
693 Cypress St., Daytona Beach
Paradise Inn .... 328 Alabama Street
James Cooper, Mgr. .... Daytona Beach, Fla.

DELAND

Specializing In Brakes & Tuning RE 4-3263

WEST SIDE SERVICE STATION & CAB SERVICE

Your One-Step Auto Center

Bill Bruten, Mgr. & Owner 242 W. Voorhis

DELRAY BEACH
    Fifth Avenue Pharmacy .... 104 N. W. 5th Avenue
    Kemp's Paradise Restaurant .... 103 N. W. 5th Avenue
    La France Hotel .... 104 N. W. 5th Avenue

FERNANDINA BEACH
    American Beach Apts.

FT. LAUDERDALE
    Cooper's Sundries & Cafe .... 615 N. W. 6th Street
    Catherine's Better Food Cafe .... 515 N. W. 4th Street
    The Friendly Place to Find the Best Home Cooking
    Chester's Place .... 1312 N. W. 5th Street
    Osborn's Restaurant .... 1904 N. W. 6th Street
    Five Point Service Station .... 2590 N. W. 22nd Rd.
    Hankerson's Gulf Service Station .... 1201 N. W. 6th Street
    Hill Hotel .... 430 N. W. 7th Avenue
    Johnson's Service Station .... 1100 N. W. 6th Street
    O'Dell's Bar & Grill & Rooms .... 2930 N. W. 7th Street
    Tasty Luncheonette .... 315A N. W. 5th Avenue

HOLLYWOOD
  Dew Drop Inn ....2243 Simms Street
HOMESTEAD
  Ida's Cafe ....739 S. W. 8th Avenue
JACKSONVILLE
  ★ASTOR MOTEL..................................1111 Cleveland St., on U.S. #1 North
  Jaxonville's FINEST STOP TO MIAMI Rates $5 up
  Pvt. BATHS — AIR COND. — Leave U.S. 95 EXIT AT KINGS RD.

THE FIESTA MOTEL

One of the South's Finest In The Gateway City

Free TV • Private Bath with Shower in Every Room. Electrically Heated

1251 Kings Rd.   Jacksonville, Fla.

  B. Robinson Tourist Home ....128 Orange Street
  Blue Chip Hotel ....514 Broad Street
  C. H. Simmons Tourist Home ....434 W. Ashley Street
  Gwendolyn Hotel ....722 W. Monroe Street
KEY WEST
  Little Charles Hotel ....713 Whitmarsh Lane
LAKE CITY
  Bill Rivers Restaurant ....931 Taylor Street
  Mrs. B. J. Jones Tourist Home ....720 E. Leon Street
  Mrs. M. McCoy Tourist Home ....730 E Leon Street
  Rivers Tourist Home ....931 Taylor Street
LAKELAND
  Mrs. A. Davis Tourist Home ....518 West 1st Street
  Mrs. J. Davis Tourist Home ....842½ N. Fla. Avenue
  Rainey's Tourist Home..152 Lake Beulah Dr.
MIAMI
  Booker T. Motel ....4200 N.W. 27th Ave.
  Dorsey Hotel ....941 N.W. 2nd Ave.
  Hampton House ....4200 N.W. 27th Ave.
  Leonard's Bakery ....1655 N.W. 3rd Ave.
  Mary Elizabeth Hotel ....642 N.W. 2nd Ave.
  Miami-Carver Hotel ....899 N.W. 3rd Ave.
  Sir John Hotel ....276 N.W. 6th St.

SOUTH MIAMI
Alexander & Sons Grill .... 6454 S.W. 59th Place
OCALA
The Brown Derby .... 902 Lincoln St.
OPA LOCKA
Grant's Drive Inn .... 15055 N.W. 22nd Ave.
Bunche Park Service Station .... 15525 N.W. 22nd Ave.
Stewart's City Service Garage .... 14585 N.W. 22nd Ave.
ORLANDO
Brigg's Restaurant & Rooming House .... 619 & 619½ S. Parramore St.
Sun-Glo Motel .... 737 So. Orange Blossom Trail
Wells Bilt Hotel .... 509 W. South Street
Coleman's Cross Country Gas Station .... cor. Ivey Lane & Gore Ave.
PERRINE
J. J.'s Gulf Service .... 17690 Homestead Avenue
PLANT CITY
Chat & Chew .... 420 Laura Street

Phone: 752-1725

HARGRETT'S ORANGE GROVE
We Ship Everywhere
One half mile North of Highway #60 — 20 miles East of Tampa

Route 6, Box 209　　　　　　　　　　　　　　　　　　　Plant City, Fla.

POMPANO BEACH
Kidd's Place .... 745 Hammond Road
Ali's Hotel & Bar .... 312 N.W. 6th Avenue
Hotel Grisham .... 407 N.W. 4th Avenue
RICHMOND HEIGHTS
Mondell Gulf Service .... 14600 Lincoln Blvd.
RIVIERA BEACH
Davis Bros. Garage .... 819 Old Dixie Highway
Ebony Motel .... 1101 Old Dixie Highway
ST. AUGUSTINE
F. M. Kelly Tourist Home .... 83 Bridge Street
ST. PETERSBURG
Club Moton .... 642 22nd Street, South
Seymoure Service Station .... 1079 3rd Avenue, South
TALLAHASSEE
Abner—Virginia Motel .... Bragg Dr. at Railroad Avenue
TAMPA
Afro Hotel .... 722 La Salle Street
Anthony's Drive Inn .... 1501 Main Street
Anthony's Coffee Shop .... 720 La Salle Street
Pyramid Hotel .... 1028 Central Ave.
WEST PALM BEACH
West Virginia Hotel .... Cor. 3rd & Sapodilla Ave.
Palm Garden Drug Store .... 332 Rosemary Avenue

18

GEORGIA
Hotels — Motels — Tourist Homes — Restaurants

ADRIAN
    Wayside Tourist Home .... U. S. Route 80

ATLANTA
    Connally Tourist Home .... 125 Walnut Street, S.W.
    Forrest Arms Hotel .... 325 Butler Street, N.W.
    Henry's Grill & Lounge .... 180 Auburn Avenue
    Hotel Royal .... 214 Auburn Avenue, N.E.
    Joe's Coffee Bar .... 200 Auburn Avenue
    Mack Hotel .... 548 Bedford Place, N.E.
    Paramount Grille .... 688 East Avenue, N.E.
    Paschal Bros. Restaurant .... 837 Hunter Street, N.W.
    Savoy Hotel .... 239 Auburn Avenue, N.E.
    ★STRATTON'S TEA ROOM .... **2991 Peachtree Rd.**
    Waluhaje Hotel .... 239 W. Lake Avenue, N.W.
    Y.M.C.A. .... 22 Bulter Street
    Haugabrook's Funeral Home .... 364-66 Auburn Avenue, N.E.

AUGUSTA
    Crimm's Hotel .... 725 9th Street
    Foster Tourist Home .... 1110 12th Street
    Paramount Motel

BRUNSWICK
    Melody Tourist Inn .... 1403 G Street
    The Palms Tourist Home .... 1309 Glouster Street

CHICKAMAUGA, GA.
    C. D. Halerig & Sons .... R.F.D. 2

COLUMBUS
    Carver Heights Motel .... Rigon Road
    Lowe's Hotel .... 724 5th Avenue
    Miles Auto Wrecking .... 1807 Cussetta Road
    Y.M.C.A. .... 521 9th Avenue

DOUGLAS
    Economy Hotel .... Cherry Street
    Lawson's Tourist Home .... Pearl Street
    Thomas' Restaurant .... Pearl Street

DUBLIN
    Dudley's Motel & Cafe .... 505 E. Jackson (U.S. 80)
    Mrs. R. Hunter Tourist Home .... 504 S. Jefferson Street

EASTMAN
    J. P. Cooper Tourist Home .... 211 College Street

JEKYLL ISLAND
    DOLPHIN CLUB & MOTOR HOTEL .... Jekyll Island

JESUP
    Robinson Motel .... 391 No. 4th Street

MACON
    Douglas Hotel .... 373 Broadway
    Mabell's Place .... 247 5th Street

Travelers' Green Book 1963–64

Hotel Richmond .... 335 Broadway
Jean's Restaurant .... 545 Cotton Avenue
MARIETTA
East Side Cab Stand .... 399 N. Fairground Street
Hunter's Lunch & Lounge .... 501 Hunt Street
PERRY
Ebony Motor Court .... U. S. Hwy. 41 South
SAVANNAH
Blay Boy Motel .... 52nd St. Exit
Southside Motel .... Rt. 17 Ogeecheer, 1/2 Mile
STATESBORO
Gross Motel
THOMASVILLE
Imperial Hotel .... Tallahassee Highway
VALDOSTA
Mae's Tourist Home .... 414 North Street
WAY CROSS
Paradise Restaurant .... Oak Street

HAWAII
Hotels — Motels — Tourist Homes — Restaurants

HILO
Hilo Hotel .... 142 Kinoole St.
Lanai Motel .... 103 Banyan Dr.
Naniloa Hotel .... 495 Kilohana St.
HONOKAA
Honokaa Club Hotel .... P. O. Box 185
KAILUA-KONA
King Kamehameha Hotel
Kona Inn .... Kailua Bay

Island of Kauai
HANALEI
Hanalei Plantation
LIHUE
Coco Palms Resort Hotel
Kauai Inn

Island of Maui
HANA
Hana-Maui Resort Hotel
Sheraton-Maui Hotel

Island of Oahu
HONOLULU
Aina Luana Apartment Hotel .... 358 Royal Hawaiian Ave.
Ala Koa Apartment Hotel .... 2439 Koa Ave.
Ala Moana Ebbtide Hotel .... 1920 Ala Moana

20

Coconut Grove Hotel	205 Lowers Rd.
Coco Palms Apartment Hotel	2465 Koa Ave.
Coral Strand Hotel	2979 Kalakaua Ave.
Hawaiiana Hotel	260 Beach Walk
Hawaiian Village	2005 Kalia Rd.
Islander Hotel	400 Seaside Ave.
Moana Hotel	2365 Kalakaua Ave.
Princess Kaiulani Hotel	120 Kaiulani Ave.
Waikikian	1811 Ala Moana Blvd.
Waikiki Biltmore Hotel	2424 Kalakaua Ave.
Waikiki International Hotel	2310 Kuhio Hotel
Waikiki Surf Hotel	412 Lewers Rd.
Reef Hotel	2169 Kalia Rd.
Royal Hawaiian Hotel	2259 Kalakaua Ave.
Royal Tropicana Hotel	340 Royal Hawaiian Ave.
Surfrider Hotel	2365 Kalakaua Ave.
The Tradewinds	1720 Ala Moana

IDAHO
Hotels — Motels — Tourist Homes — Restaurants

ASHTON
  Lone Court .... 7th Ave. & Main St.

BLACKFOOT
  Colonial Motel .... 695 So. Broadway

CALDWELL
  Holiday .... 5th Ave. & Highways 20-26-30

COEUR D'ALENE
  Hart's Hotel .... 1830 No. 4th St.
  Pine Grove Motel .... Highway 10, West of Coeur D' Alene

IDAHO FALLS
  Campbell's Hotel Rogers .... 545 Shoupe Ave.
  Kruse Court Motel .... West Broadway
  Ray's Motel .... 248 No. See

LEWISTON
  Lewis Clark .... 2nd and Main

MONTPELIER
  Swiss Motel .... 125 South 5th Street

POCATELLO
  Banner Motel .... 1406 N. Main St., U. S. 30
  Bidwell's Motel .... 1304 So. 5th Avenue
  Fred's Motel .... 1333 No. Main Street

TWIN FALLS
  Covey's Motel .... 121 4th Ave., South
  Monterey Court Motel .... 433 West Addison

ILLINOIS
Hotels — Motels — Tourist Homes — Restaurants

CARTHAGE
  Hap's Hotel .... U. S. Hwy. 136

CENTRALIA
    Mrs. Claybourne .... 303 N. Pine Street

CHICAGO
    A & J Restaurant .... 105 East 51st Street
    Alamac Hotel .... 1934 W. Jackson Blvd.
    Ambassador East & West .... N. State Pkwy & Goethe
    Archway Supper Club .... 356 E. 61st Street
    Ascot House .... 11th St. & Michigan Ave.
    Belmont Hotel .... Sheridan Rd. at Belmont Ave.
    Bennie's Restaurant .... 6256 South Parkway
    Bismarck .... 171 W. Randolph St.
    Clark's Beauty Bazaar .... 810 E. 75th St.
    C & C Club & Lounge .... 6513 Cottage Grove
    Club Baby Doll .... 7309 Vincennes Ave.
    Conrad Hilton .... 7th & 8th St. & Michigan Blvd.
    Deluxe Beauty Shop .... 620½ East 79th Street
    Dixon's Beauty Shop .... 311 East 47th Street
    Drake .... Lake Shore Dr. & Upper Michigan Ave.
    Earl's 74th Street Lounge .... 7404½ Cottage Grove
    Eberhart Hotel .... 6050 Eberhart Avenue
    Edgewater Beach Hotel .... 5300 N. Sheridan Rd.
    Executive House .... 71 E. Wacker Dr.
    E's Lounge .... 456 East 43rd Street
    Evans Hotel .... 733 East 61st Street
    Friendship Beauty Shop .... 1356 East 61st Street
    Garfield Hotel .... 231 East Garfield Blvd.
    Gold Coast Lounge .... 5701 S. State Street
    Grand Hotel .... 5044 South Parkway
    Harlem Hotel .... 5020 So. Michigan Avenue
    Hayes Hotel .... 6345 So. University
    Hotel Alcazar .... 3000 W. Washington Blvd.
    Hotel Woodmere .... 4641 S. Woodlawn
    Impala Lounge .... 100 East 71st Street
    Kitty Kat Club .... 611 East 63rd Street
    Madeline's Beauty Salon .... 5107 S. Michigan Avenue
    Manfield Hotel .... 6434 Cottage Grove Ave.
    Manor House .... 4635 So. Parkway
    McGowan's Lounge .... 933 East 43rd Street
    McKie's Disc Jockey Show Lounge .... 6325 S. Cottage Grove
    Payton's New Brass Rail .... 329 East 47th Street
    Pershing Hotel .... 6400 S. Cottage Grove
    Playboy Club .... 232 E. Ohio Street
    Ritz Hotel .... 409 East Oakwood Blvd.
    Robert's Show Club .... 6622 South Park
    Roberts Motel .... 6625 S. Parkway
    Royal Canton Cafe .... 354 East 43rd Street
    Royalton Hotel .... 1810 W. Jackson Blvd.
    S & S Hotel .... 4142 South Parkway
    Southway Hotel .... 6018 S. P'way
    Spencer Hotel .... 300 E. Garfield Blvd.
    ★**STELZER'S RESTAURANT** .... **3455 So. Parkway**
    Strand Hotel .... Cottage Grove & 63rd Street

Sutherland Hotel	47th & Drexel Blvd.
The Corner	111th & Vincennes (Morgan Park)
The Place	619 East 63rd Street
Tippin-Inn Lounge	325 East 35th Street
Trocadero Lounge	4719 Indiana
Vel-Mar Hotel	2120 W. Washington St.
★WEDGEWOOD TOWERS HOTEL	6401 So. Woodlawn Ave.
Y.M.C.A.	500 S. Indiana Avenue

CARBONDALE
Plaza Court	600 E. Main Street

DANVILLE
Just—A—Mere Hotel	218 East North Street

EAST ST. LOUIS
38 CLUB	34th & St. Clair Sts.
Bond Food Shop	628 Bond Street
Bush's Rib Station	1836 Missouri Avenue
Hotel Harlem	1426 Broadway
Mid-Town Service Station	1501 Broadway
Murray's Standard Service	3765 Bond Avenue
Nichol's Drive Inn	900 Missouri Avenue
Rock Grill	1433 Brady

PEORIA
Wind's Motel	3527 W. Harmon Way
★MRS. CLARA EUBANK'S TOURIST HOME	741 N. Monson Street

ROCKFORD
Briggs Hotel	429 Court Street
Mrs. Brown Tourist Home	927 S. Winnebago Street
Mrs. C. Gorum Tourist Home	301 Steward Avenue
S. Westbrook Tourist Home	630 Lexington Avenue

SPRINGFIELD
Dr. Ware Tourist Home	1520 E. Washington Street
Mrs. B. Mosby Tourist Home	1614 E. Jackson Street
Mrs. Bernie Eskridge Tourist Home	1501 Jackson Street
Mrs. G. Bell Tourist Home	625 No. 2nd Street
Mrs. L. Jones Tourist Home	1230 East Jefferson Street

VIENNA
McCormick Motel	Highway 45 & 146, ½ Mile So. of Vienna

INDIANA
Hotels — Motels — Tourist Homes — Restaurants

ANGOLA
Pryor's Lodge	East Side Fox Lake Resort, RR 2
The Mar-Fran Motel	U. S. 20, 1 mi. West of Angola, then ½ mi. So.

ELKHART
Miss E. Botts Tourist Home	336 St. Joe Street

EVANSVILLE
Hotel Rena	661 Governor Street
Mrs. H. Best Tourist Home	658 Lincoln Avenue

Travelers' Green Book 1963-64

FRANKLIN
   Tanyika Inn ....751 W. King Street

FORT WAYNE
   Howell Hotel ....1803 S. Hanna Street
   Mrs. B. Talbot Tourist Home ....456 E. Douglas
   Stewart's Restaurant ....621 E. Brackenridge Street
   West Acres Motel ....1301 Goshen Avenue

GARY
   ★HOTEL TOLEDO ....**22nd Avenue & Adams Street**
   Hayes Hotel ....2167 Broadway

INDIANAPOLIS
   Blue Eagle Restaurant ....701 Indiana Avenue
   Foster Hotel ....2154 N. Illinois Street
   Guest House ....31 West 22nd Street
   Perkins Restaurant ....793 Indiana Avenue
   Severin Hotel ....201 So. Illinois Avenue
   Trade Winds Motel ....2922 Madison Avenue
   Y.M.C.A. ....Senate Avenue Branch
   Y.M.C.A. ....806 W. 10th Street
   Y.W.C.A. ....329 N. Penn Street

KOKOMO
   Mrs. C. W. Winburn Tourist Home ....1015 Kennedy Street
   Mrs. Charles Hardinson Tourist Home ....812 Kennedy Street
   Mrs. S. D. Hughes Tourist Home ....1045 N. Kennedy Street

LAFAYETTE
   Green Acres Motel ....Hwy. 52, North

MARION
   Marshal's Restaurant ....414-418 East 4th Street
   Mrs. Albert Ward Tourist Home ....324 West 14th Street

MICHIGAN CITY
   Allen's Tourist Home ....210 East 2nd Street

MUNCIE
   Gray's Motel ....3600 No. Broadway
   Y.M.C.A. ....9065 Madison Street

SOUTH BEND
   Alou Tourist Hotel ....2261 Dixie Way, North
   Smokes Restaurant ....432 So. Chapin Street

VINCENNES
   Grand Hotel ....P. O. Box 118

WEST BADEN SPRINGS
   Waddy Hotel

IOWA
Hotels — Motels — Tourist Homes — Restaurants

CEDAR RAPIDS
   Brown's Tourist Home ....818 9th Avenue, S.E.
   Sepia Motel ....Mt. Vernon Road, S.E.

CLINTON
   Mississippi View Motel ....2626 Harding

24

COUNCIL BLUFFS
   Grove Motel .... So. Omaha Bridge Rd.
   Woodland Echoes Village .... 429 N. 27th

DAVENPORT
   Davenport Hotel

DES MOINES
   Community Restaurant .... 1202 Center Street
   Erma & Carrie's Restaurant .... 1008 Center Street
   Maple Grove Motel .... 6500 Hickman Rd.
   Peck's Restaurant .... 1180 13th Street
   Y.W.C.A. .... 512 9th Street
   Sampson Restaurant .... 1246 East 17th Street

DUBUQUE
   Canfield Hotel

IOWA CITY
   Oak Grove Motel .... Hwy. 6
   Skyway Motel .... Hwy. 218, South

NEWTON
   Hillcrest Motel .... 3120 1st Ave., E., Hwy. 6

OTTUMWA
   Park Hotel .... Box 375
   William Bailey Tourist Home .... 526 Center Avenue

SIOUX CITY
   Floyd Park Motel .... 2236 Williams Avenue
   Prince Henry Restaurant .... 818 Hamilton Street
   West Hotel

WATERLOO
   Hotel Ellis
   Mrs. B. F. Tredwell Tourist Home .... 928 Beach Street
   Mrs. E. Lee Tourist Home .... 745 Vinton Street
   Mrs. Spencer Tourist Home .... 220 Summer Street
   Swing Inn Motel .... 821 Washington

KANSAS
Hotels — Motels — Tourist Homes — Restaurants

ABILENE
   Diamond Court Motel .... 1403 N.W. 3rd Street
   Sunflower Hotel .... Box 237

ATCHISON
   Mrs. M. McDonald Tourist Home .... 1001 South 7th Street

CONCORDIA
   Mrs. B. Johnson Tourist Home .... 102 East 2nd Street

DODGE CITY
   Shangri-La Motel

EMPORIA
   Elliott's Tourist Home .... 816 Congress Street

EDWARDSVILLE
   Road House Tourist Home .... Anderson's Hwy., 32 & Bitts Creek

FORT SCOTT
   Hall's Hotel .... 223½ East Wall Street
   Harrison's Court Motel .... 1916 E. Wall
   Todds Motel .... Rt. 69

GARDEN CITY
   Trail Inn Court Motel .... Hwy. 50

HIAWATHA
   Mrs. Mary Sanders Tourist Home .... 1014 Shawnee

HUTCHINSON
   Beauty Rest Motel .... 2927 East 4th Street
   Mrs. C. Lewis Tourist Home .... 400 West Sherman

JUNCTION CITY
   Bridgeforth Hotel .... 311 East 11th Street

KANSAS CITY
   Crown Court Motel .... 4120 State Street
   Hale's Court .... 4110 State Street
   Y.W.C.A. .... 644 Quindaro Blvd.

LARNED
   Carrie's Bar-B-Q Restaurant .... 218 East 4th Street
   Mrs. C. M. Madison Tourist Home .... 828 West 12th Street
   Mrs. John Caro Tourist Home .... 218 East 4th Street
   Mrs. Mose Madison Tourist Home .... 518 West 10th Street

LAWRENCE
   Snowden's Hotel .... 1933 Tennessee Street

LEAVENWORTH
   Leavenworth Motel .... 2100 So. 4th Street

MANHATTAN
   George's Motel .... 826 Yuma Street
   Mrs. E. Dawson Tourist Home .... 1010 Yuma Street

SALINA
   Canary Motor Court .... 510 No. Broadway

STOCKTON
   L. D. Fuller

TOPEKA
   Ace Motel .... Junction Hwys. 75-24-40
   Ace Motor Court .... 2117 Central
   Capitol Hotel .... 105 East 5th Street
   F. W. Woolworth Co. Cafeteria .... 627 Kansas Avenue
   Mrs. E. Slaughter Tourist Home .... 1407 Monroe
   Palma House Hotel .... 1811 W. 8th Street
   Pennant Cafeteria .... 915 Kansas Avenue
   Purple Cow Coffee Shop .... Box 118
   Senate Cafeteria .... 822 Kansas Avenue

WICHITA
   Allis Hotel .... Broadway & William Sts.
   Lassen Hotel .... E. 1st & Market Streets
   Osage Motel .... 3358 S. Broadway

KENTUCKY
Hotels — Motels — Tourist Homes — Restaurants

BOWLING GREEN
   Hotel Southern Queen .... State Street, Hwy. 31-w

ELIZABETHTOWN
   Mrs. B. Tyler Tourist Home .... 224 No. Niles Street
HOPKINSVILLE
   L. McNary's Tourist Home .... 113 Liberty Street
   Mrs. E. Davis Tourist Home .... 901 E. Hayes Street
LEXINGTON
   Greystone Motel .... Race Street
   Huggins Service Center .... 7th & Lime
   Mrs. K. Wallace Tourist Home .... 600 W. Maxwell
LOUISVILLE
   Brown Derby Lounge .... 563 S. 10th Street
   Elite Tavern & Grill .... 2801 W. Walnut
   Frank's Service Station .... 729 W. Walnut
   Hook's Hotel .... 8th & Chestnut Street
   Mickey's Bar & Grill .... 633 S. 10th Street
   The Allen Hotel .... 2516 W. Madison Street
   Turner's Drive In .... 3671 Newburg Road
   Y.M.C.A. .... 920 W. Chestnut Street
   Y.W.C.A. .... 206 W. Broadway
MAMMOTH CAVE NATIONAL PARK
   Mammoth Cave Hotel .... Open year round
PADUCAH
   Jefferson Hotel .... 514 South 8th Street

LOUISIANA
Hotels — Motels — Tourist Homes — Restaurants

ALEXANDRIA
   The Orient Hotel .... 725½ Lee Street
BASTROP
   Blue Front Cafe .... 423 W. Madison
BATON ROUGE
   Ever Ready Hotel .... 1325 Government Street
   Ideal Cafeteria .... 1501 E. Boulevard
   Lincoln Hotel .... 400 South 13th Street
   Pearson's Tourist Home .... 1515 Oleander Street
   T. Harrison Tourist Home .... 1236 Louisiana Avenue
KENNER
   Tanner's Motel .... Rte. 1, Box 1096
LAFAYETTE
   Bourges Tourist Home .... 416 Washington Street
LAKE CHARLES
   Combre's Place Tourist Home .... 601 Boulevard
   Grand Terrace Hotel .... 531 Boulevard
   Lewis Hotel .... 515 Boulevard
MONROE
   Blue Moon Restaurant .... 1811 Conover Street
   Crane's Hotel .... 503 Adams Street
   Dudley's Hotel .... Desiard Street
   Nelson's Motel
   Red Union Restaurant .... 705½ Desiard Street
MORGAN CITY
   Mrs. L. Williams .... 719 Federal Avenue
   Mrs. V. Williams .... 208 Union Street

Travelers' Green Book 1963–64

NEW ORLEANS
Astoria Hotel .... 235 So. Rampart Street
Caladonia Inn Hotel .... St. Claude & St. Phillip
Dooky Restaurant .... Cor. Orleans & Miro
Foster's Chicken Den Restaurant .... Cor. LaSalle & 7th Sts.
Gladstone Hotel .... 3435 Dryades Street
Golden Leaf Hotel .... 1209 Saratoga Street
Gumbo House Restaurant .... 1936 Louisiana Avenue
Harris House Hotel .... 1383 St. Bernard Avenue
Honey Dew Inn Restaurant .... 115 Front Street
Hotel Foster .... 2926 LaSalle Street
Marsalis Motel .... 110 Shrewsbury Road
★MASON'S MOTEL .... 3923 Melpomene Street
Mrs. J. Montgomery Tourist Home .... 2134 Harmony
Mrs. King Tourist Home .... 2826 Louisiana Avenue
Mrs. P. Robinson Tourist Home .... 9038 Olive Street
N. J. Bailey Tourist Home .... 2426 Jackson Avenue
North Side Hotel .... 1518 La Harpe Street
Place-Of-Joy Restaurant .... 2700 Melpomene Street
Portia's Restaurant .... 2426 Louisiana Avenue
Riley's Guest House .... 1983 N. Rocheblave Street
Robin Hood Hotel .... 2132 Simon Bolivar Street
Robinson's Tourist Home .... 3300 Hamilton Street
Shadowland Hotel .... 1921 Washington Avenue
Vogue Hotel .... 1116 N. Dorgenois Street
Roosevelt Haney .... 2112 Felicity Street

NEW IBERIA
M. Robertson Tourist Home .... 116 Hopkins Street
N. E. Cooper Tourist Home .... 913 Providence Street

OPELCUSAS
B. Giron Tourist Home .... 510 So. Lombard Street

SHREVEPORT
Castle Hotel .... 1000 Sprague Street
George Washington Carver Branch Y.M.C.A. .... 1051½ Texas Avenue
Hollywood Cities Service Station .... 3807 Hollywood
King's Circle Inn Bar-B-Que .... 4054 Miles
Lloyd's Hotel .... 1229 Milan Street
Mrs. A. Harris Tourist Home .... 2848 Milan Street
Mrs. Ed. Turner Tourist Home .... 309 Douglas Street
Sprague Hotel .... 1032 Sprague Street
The New Airport Motel .... 4416 Hollywood
Will Steward Hotel .... 1249 Oakland

Visit George Washington Carver Branch Y.M.C.A.
1051½ Texas Ave.   Phone 2-0391 — Shreveport, La.

WEST MONROE
Jackson's Motel .... 2004 Cypress Street
Myles' Auto Parts & Wrecking Co. .... 2122 Cypress Street

MAINE
Hotels — Motels — Tourist Homes — Restaurants
BANGOR
THE BANGOR HOUSE Motor Hotel .... Main at Union Streets

Downtown Bangor, Family Plan, TV, AAA, Duncan Hines, Dining Room,
Coffee Shop & Cocktail Lounge — Tel Ban 7321
DIXFIELD
Marigold Motel .... Hwy. 2, 10 Miles East of Rumford
OLD ORCHARD
Mrs. R. Cumming's Tourist Home .... 110 Portland Avenue
PORTLAND
Thomas House Tourist Home .... 28 "A" Street
Swampscotta Lodge .... Rt. 302, 9 miles from Portland
ROBBINSTON
Brook's Bluff Cottage .... Hwy. 1, 12 Miles East of Calais

MARYLAND
Hotels — Motels — Tourist Homes — Restaurants
ANNAPOLIS
Alsop's Restaurant .... Northwest & Calvert Sts.
Brown Hotel .... 50 Clay Street
BALTIMORE
Club Bargeque .... 1519 Penn. Avenue
Honor Reed Hotel .... 667 No. Franklin
Majestic Hotel .... 1602 McCulloh Street
Sphinx Restaurant .... 2107 Pennsylvania Avenue
Sess Restaurant .... 1639 Division Street
Spot Bar-B-Q Restaurant .... 1530 Penn. Avenue
White Rice Inn .... 1306 Penn. Avenue
Y.M.C.A. .... 1617 Druid Hill Avenue
Y.W.C.A. .... 1916 Madison Avenue
BOWIE
Stephen Bowie Hotel .... Bowie-Laurel Road
ELKRIDGE
Bass Motel .... U. S. Rt. No. 1
FAULKNER
Blue Star Motel .... Rt. 301, 6 miles N. of Potomac River Bridge
FREDERICK
Crescent Restaurant .... 16 W. All Saint Street
Mrs. J. Makel Tourist Home .... 119 East 5th Street
Mrs. W. W. Roberts Tourist Home .... 316 W. South Street
HAGERSTOWN
Harmon Tourist Homes .... 226 N Jonathan Street
Ship Tea Room .... 329 N. Jonathan Street
HAVRE DE GRACE
Johnson's Hotel .... 415 So. Stokes Street
SALISBURY
Franklin Hotel .... U. S. Hwy. 50, 6 blocks W. of Rt. 13
WALDORF
Blue Jay Motel .... U. S. 301

MASSACHUSETTS
Hotels — Motels — Tourist Homes — Restaurants
BOSTON
Bedford Motel .... Rt. 4, Exit #36, Off Rt. 128
Charlie's Restaurant .... 429 Columbus Avenue
Columbus Arms Hotel .... 455 Columbus Avenue

29

Travelers' Green Book 1963–64

Harriet Tubman Hotel .... 25 Holyoke Street
Holeman Tourist Home .... 212 W. Springfield Street
Julia Walters Tourist Home .... 912 Fremont
M. Johnson Tourist Home .... 616 Columbus Avenue
Mrs. E. A. Taylor Tourist Home .... 192 W. Springfield Street
Slades Restaurant .... 958 Tremont Street
Sunnyside Restaurant .... 411 Columbus Avenue
The Manger .... Causeway & Nashua Streets
Western Restaurant .... 415 Mass. Avenue

BUZZARDS BAY P.O.
Wagon Wheels .... Savary Avenue, R.F.D.

CAMBRIDGE
Mrs. S. P. Bennett Tourist Home .... 26 Mead Street

GREAT BARRINGTON
Mrs I. Anderson Tourist Home .... 28 Rossiter Street
Mrs. J. Hamilton Tourist Home .... 118 Main Street

HYANNIS
Cape Traveler Motel .... Rt. 28, 2 miles east of Hyannis
Zilphas Cottages Tourist Home .... 134 Oakneck Road
Hyannisport .... Hilltop, P. O. Box 205

KINGSTON
Kingston Inn .... Kingston, Mass.
Camp Twin Oaks .... Tel. Kingston 468

NANTUCKET ISLAND
The Skipper Restaurant

NORTH CAMBRIDGE
Mrs. L. G. Hill Tourist Home .... 39 Hubbard Avenue

OAK BLUFFS
Brownie's Cottage .... P. O. Box 788
Cinderella Cottage .... 36 Pequot Avenue
Dunmere-By-The-Sea .... 5 Penacock Avenue
Maxwell Cottage .... P. O. Box 1354
O'Brien House .... 220 Circuit Avenue
Oliver W. Moody .... Box 327
Scott's Cottage .... P. O. Box 1131
Shearer Cottage

PITTSFIELD
J. Marshall Tourist Home .... 124 Danforth Avenue
M. E. Grant Tourist Home .... 53 King Street
Mrs. T. Dillard Tourist Home .... 109 Linden Street

PROVINCETOWN
Kalmar Village .... Rt. 6

RANDOLPH
Chickenshack .... 428 Main Street

SPRINGFIELD
Hotel Springfield .... 1827 Main Street

MICHIGAN
Hotels — Motels — Tourist Homes — Restaurants

ANN ARBOR
Allenel Hotel .... 126 El Huron Street
American Hotel .... 123 Washington Street

30

BATTLE CREEK
 Mrs. F. Brown Tourist Home ....76 Walters Avenue
BALDWIN
 Whip-Or-Will Cottage ....Rt. No. 1 Box 153
BITLEY
 Kelsonia Inn ....Woodland Park
 Royal Breeze Hotel ....Woodland Park
CASSOPOLIS
 Idlehour Country Club ....Phone: State 2-2834
 Caslen's Blue Bell Garden..................Rt. 1
 Dagg's Cottage ....Rt. 1
 Everett Rest Haven..................Rt. 1
 Royal Breeze Hotel..................Rt. 1
DETROIT
 Capitol Hotel ....114 East Palmer
 Capri-Plaza Hotel ....7541 Linwood Street
 Ebony Hotel ....110 Chandler Street
 Gotham Hotel ....111 Orchestra Place
 Mark Twain Hotel ....52 E. Garfield
 McGraw Hotel ....5605 Junction Street
 Mt. Royal Hotel..................8841 Woodward Ave.
 Russell Hotel ....615 E. Adams Street
 Summers Hotel ....412 Frederick Street
 Summers Hotel ....2940 Harding Street
 Thomas Hotel ....244 E. Kirby Street
 Town Motel ....2127 W. Grand Blvd.
FLINT
 Elms Park Motel ....2801 So. Dort Hwy.
 Mrs. F. Taylor Tourist Home ....1615 Clifford Street
 T. L. Wheeler Tourist Home ....1512 Liberty Street
GRAND RAPIDS
 Villa Court Motel ....5451 So. Division
HART
 Bryson's Lake View ....202 N. State Street
IDLEWILD
 B. Riddles Tourist Home
 Bask Inn Tourist Home..................Broadway at Hemlock
 Casa Blanca Hotel
 Club El Morocco Hotel ....Rt. No. 1
 Douglas Manor Tourist Home
 Edinburgh Cottage, Miss Herrons Tourist Home
 McKnight's Hotel
 Navajo Restaurant
 Oakmere Hotel
 Paradise Gardens Hotel
 Phil Giles Hotel
 Rainbow Manor Tourist Home
 Rest Haven Tourist Home
 Rosanna's Restaurant
 Spizerinktom Tourist Home
 The Pomiserania Lodge ....Box 815
 Whiteway Inn Restaurant

31

Travelers' Green Book 1963-64

INKSTER
   Mona Lisa Motel ....28725 Michigan Ave.
JACKSON
   Mooreman Tourist Lodge ....1120 So. Milwaukee Street
   Mrs. W. Harrison Tourist Home ....126 Moore
LANSING
   Mrs. Gaines Tourist Home ....1406 Albert Street
   Mrs. James Lewis Tourist Home..816 S. Butler Street
   Sonny's Tropicana Lodge..Division & Williams Streets
MACKINAW CITY
   Parkview Cabins ....114 Depeyster Street
MUSKEGON
   R. C. Merrick Tourist Home ....65 E. Muskegon Avenue
NEW BUFFALO
   Fireside Restaurant ....U. S. Route 12
OSCODA
   Jesse Colbath Tourist Home ....Van Eten Lake
PONTIAC
   Motel Morocco ....597 Franklin Rd.
VANDALIA
   Copper Motel ....Hwy. M 60, Bet. Chicago & Detroit
   Mrs. Mayme Cooper Tourist Home ....P. O. Box 96
THREE RIVERS
   Jordan's Tourist Home ....Rt. 4, Box 289
   Wilson's Farm ....Rt. 3, Box 196

MINNESOTA
Hotels — Motels — Tourist Homes — Restaurants

AUSTIN
   Fox Hotel ....501 N. Main Street
BENSON
   Earl's Motel ....Hwy. 9
DULUTH
   London Road Court ....2521 London Rd.
GRAND RAPIDS
   Holiday Village Motel ....Junction U.S. 2 & 169-E
MINNEAPOLIS
   Parkway Motor Court ....4757 Hiawatha Avenue
MOTLEY
   Herman Steick's Restaurant
ROCHESTER
   Avalon Hotel ....303 North Broadway
   De Luxe Motor Court ....Hwys. 14 & 52
ST. CLOUD
   Grand Central Hotel ....5th & St. Germaine
   Kays Motel ....102 Lincoln Avenue
   Spaniol Restaurant ....13 6th Avenue No.
ST. PAUL
   Coleman's Restaurant ....2239 Ford Parkway
   Covered Wagon ....320 Wabasha
   Hotel Lowery ....339 Wabasha
   Hotel Ryan ....402 Robert
   Hotel St. Paul ....363 St. Peter

32

Jean's French Restaurant	748 Grand
Lee's Village Inn	800 Cleveland
Lexington Restaurant	1096 Grand
Lindy's Steak House	1581 University
Lowry	339 Wabasha
Port's Restaurant	1046 Grand
Radisson	
Ryan	6th and Robert Streets
Sarrack Motel	946 McKnight Rd.
Sugar's Restaurant	201 East 4th Street
Y.M.C.A.	123 West 5th Street

WINONA
Hotel Winona	
Red Top Motel	Hwy. 61, West
Winn Tee Pee—Cottage Motel	Hwys. 61-14-43, ½ Mile East

MISSISSIPPI
Hotels — Motels — Tourist Homes — Restaurants

BILOXI
Mrs. A. J. Alcina Tourist Home	443 Washington
Mrs. G. Bess Tourist Home	630 Main Street

CLARKSDALE
Riverside Hotel	615 S. Sunflower Avenue

COLUMBUS
Mrs. Chevis Tourist Home	1425 11th Avenue N.
M. J. Harrison Tourist Home	915 N. 14th Street
Queens City Hotel	15th Street & 7th Avenue

FOREST
The Sky Way Motel	Mrs. Guise, Prop., Box 53

GREENVILLE
El Moroco Hotel	1039 Nelson Street
Hotel Montrol	Nelson Street

HATTIESBURG
Crosby's Hotel	512 Mobile Street
Mrs. A. Crosby Tourist Home	413 E. 6th Street
Mrs. S. Vann Tourist Home	636 Mobile Street
W. A. Godbolt Tourist Home	409 E. 7th Street

HOLLY SPRINGS
Clark's Dairy Bar & Taxi Service	On Hiway 78N
College Court Motel	U. S. Hwys. 78 & Miss. 7

JACKSON
Edward Lee Hotel	144 W. Church Street
Summers Hotel	619 W. Pearl Street

LAUREL
Mrs. S. G. Wilson Tourist Home	806 So. 7th Street

McCOMB
De Soto Hotel	601 Summit Street
White Castle Hotel	Highway 51

MERIDIAN
Beales Hotel	2411 Fifth Street
Charley Leigh Tourist Home	1425 Fifth Street
Hotel E. F. Young, Jr.	500 25th Avenue
Hotel Henderson	2507 5th Street

Travelers' Green Book 1963-64

MOUND BAYOU
    Leggette's Fan-Cee Freeze ....On Highway 61
    Marzel Motel
    Mrs. Charlotte Strong Tourist Home
    Mrs. Sallie Price Tourist Home
NATCHEZ
    Mrs. S. Miller Tourist Home ....31 Bishop Street
    Riverside Restaurant ....200 S. Broadway
NEW ALBANY
    S. Drewery Tourist Home ....Church Street

HOWARD'S MOTEL & SNACK BAR —
540 Oak Street
New Albany, Miss.

Room Rate $1 - $7.50 per night
Night Phone: 634-5829
Day Phone: 534-5829

PASSAGOULA
    Mrs. Milline B. Wilson Tourist Home ....1001 Kenneth Avenue
    Jabo's Motel & Restaurant ....706 E. Live Oak Street
TOUGALOO
    Zebra Motel ....Hwy. 51, By Pass, 7 miles N. of Jackson
VICKSBURG
    Y.M.C.A. ....923 Walnut Street
YAZOO CITY
    Mrs. A. J. Walker Tourist Home ....321 S. Monroe

MISSOURI
Hotels — Motels — Tourist Homes — Restaurants

CAPE GIRARDEAU
    J. Randol Tourist Home ....422 North Street
    W. Martin Tourist Home ....38 N. Hanover Street
COLUMBIA
    Austin House Hotel ....1 West Ash Street
    Williams Tourist Home ....110 Lynn Street
EXCELSIOR SPRINGS
    Moore's Hotel ....Main Street
HANNIBAL
    Mrs. E. Julius Tourist Home ....1218 Gerard Street
JACKSON
    Eulinberg's Place ....U.S. Hiway 61, 14 Mi. of Jackson
JEFFERSON CITY
    Blue Tiger Restaurant ....Chestnut & E. Atcheson Street
    Booker T. Hotel
    Lincoln Hotel ....600 Lafayette Street
    Miss C. Woodridge Tourist Home ....418 Adams Street
KANSAS CITY
    Annabelle's Beauty Nook ....2306 E. 12 Street
    Broyles Brothers Auto Service ....3031 Prospect
    Drumm's Cleaners & Dyers ....Prospect at 35 St.
    Eddie's Hickory House..17th & Vine
    Gather Inn ....1734 E. 31 Street
    Gill-Hodges Pharmacy ....1512 N. 5th Street
    Gladyes Briscoe's Beauty Salon ....1800 N. 5th Street
    Ideal Barber Shop ....1308 N. 5th Street

Jacqulyn's Cleaners & Launderers	29th & Treost
Katz Drug Co.	
Last Round-Up	1611 E. 12 Street
Levell's Pharmacy	1101 Quindaro
Lincoln Hotel	13th & Woodland St.
Lock's Beauty Salon	3401 Prospect
Lou's Pharmacy	N.E. Cor. 31st & Brooklyn
M & T Restaurant	2013 E. 12th Street
Mardi Gras Night Club	19th & Vine
Marmadell's Beauty Salon	2118 E. 39th Street
Martha's Cafe	1406 N. 5th Street
Mattie's Dinette	1820 N. 7th
Melody Lanes Bowling Alley	41st & Indiana
Mim's Cafe	1603 E. 12th Street
Mr. Burger Drive-In	81230 Santa Fe
Mr. J's Beauty Salon	2108 E. 39th Street
Mrs. Vallie Lamb Tourist Home	1914 E. 24th Street
921 Hotel	921 E. 17th Street
Old Kentucky's Restaurant	1221 Brooklyn
Oven Restaurant	17th & Vine Streets
Parkview Hotel	10th & Paseo
Party House	510 E. 31st Street
Santa Fe Discount Drugs	2701 Prospect
Smith's Ultra Modern Drug Store	3839 Prospect
Square Deal Motel	1305 E. 18th Street
Street's Motel	1510 E. 18th Street
Y.W.C.A.	1908 the Paseo
Lincoln Hotel	13th & Woodland Sts.
M & T Restaurant	2013 E. 12th Street
Mim's Cafe	1603 East 12th Street
Mrs. Vallie Lamb Tourist Home	1914 E. 24th Street

MOBERLY
Ralph Bass Tourist Homes	517 Winchester Street

ST. CHARLES
Virginia's Bar-B-Q Stand	824 Clark Street (Rear)

ST. CLAIR
Mrs. L. Hilliard Motel	U. S. Hiway 66

ST. LOUIS
Abernathy's Adams Hotel	4295 Olive Street
Alcorn Hotel	4165 Washington Avenue
Anderson's Service Station	4950 Northland Pl.
Atlas Hotel	4267 Delmar
Booker T. Washington Hotel	3930 N. Kings Highway
Collin's Service Station	4190 Delmar
Gordon's Rib Station	4269 Delmar
Lucille's Food Shop	4401 Aldine Street
Northside Grill	347 Peardon Drive
Poro Hotel	4300 St. Ferdinand Avenue
Sara-Lou Cafe	4069 St. Louis Avenue
St. Louis Service Station	1906 Whittier Street
West End Hotel	3900 W. Beele Street
Wilke's Eat Shop	4664 Fairlin Avenue

Travelers' Green Book 1963-64

SPRINGFIELD
   Alberta's Hotel ....617 No. Benton

MONTANA
Hotels — Motels — Tourist Homes — Restaurants
BILLINGS
   General Custer Hotel
   Rimrock Lodge ....1200 No. 27th Street
BUTTE
   Ham's Court ....3702 Harrison Avenue
GREAT FALLS
   Motel Central ....715 Central Ave., West
GLACIER NATIONAL PARK
   All Hotels Open — June 15 to Sept. 15
   Glacier Park Hotel
   Porter's De Luxe Cabins ....Hwy. 2
HELENA
   Capitol Court ....1150 11th Avenue
   Placer Hotel ....Helena, Montana
LIVINGSTON
   Murry Hotel ....201 West Park
   Willow Park Cottages ....U. S. 89
   Yellowstone Motel ....So. Main Street
MISSOULA
   Hotel Florence

NEBRASKA
Hotels — Motels — Tourist Homes — Restaurants
AINSWORTH
   Midwest Hotel
   Skinner's Cabins
CHARDRON
   Oak's Court Motel ....West Hwy. 20
FREMONT
   Gus Henderson Tourist Home ....1725 N. Irving Street
   Shady Nook Cabins ....P. O. Box 45
LINCOLN
   Deluxe Court ....4433 No. 70th Street
   Lincoln Hotel ....9th & "P" Streets
OMAHA
   Broadview Hotel ....2060 N. 19th Street
   Patton's Hotel ....2425 Erskine Street
SCOTTSBLUFF
   Eagle's Restaurant ....1603 Broadway
   Welsh Roome Hotel ....1015 9th Avenue
SIDNEY
   Long Pine Court ....1701 Illinois
VALENTINE
   Hotel Marion

NEVADA
Hotels — Motels — Tourist Homes — Restaurants
BOULDER CITY
   Boulder Dam Hotel

Lake Meade Lodge
ELKO
  ★LOUIS MOTEL ....West Elko, Hwy. 40
  Phone RE 8-6188   —   Family Units   —   No Pets
LAS VEGAS
  Carver House ....Jackson and "D" Streets
  Hotel Jackson ....405 W. Jackson Street
  Shaw Apt. Tourist Home ....619 Van Buren Street
  West Motel ....950 Bonanza Road
RENO
  Hawthorne Tourist Home ....542 Valley Road
  New China Club ....260 Lake Street

NEW HAMPSHIRE
Hotels — Motels — Tourist Homes — Restaurants
LITTLETON
  White Wall Motel ....Rt. 302
MANCHESTER
  Floyd Hotel ....614 Elm Street
NEW LONDON
  Twin Lake Village
TWIN MOUNTAIN
  The Last Chance Motel ....U. S. Highway 3
WHITEFIELD
  Mrs. Homer Mason Tourist Home ....Greenwood Street
  Mrs. Wm. Nolan..Union Street

NEW JERSEY
Hotels — Motels — Tourist Homes — Restaurants
ASBURY PARK
  E. C. Yeager Tourist Home ....1406 Mattison Ave.
  Mrs. C. Jones Tourist Home ....141 Sylvan Ave.
  Mrs. V. Maupin Tourist Homes ....25 Atkins Ave.
  Mrs. W. Greenlow Tourist Home ....1315 Summerfield Ave.
  Nellie Tutt's Restaurant ....1207 Springwood Ave.
  Reevy's Hotel ....135 DeWitt Ave.
  Waverly Motel ....138 DeWitt Ave.
  West Side Restaurant ....1136 Springwood Ave.
  Whitehead Hotel ....25 Atkins Ave.
ATLANTIC CITY
  Attucks Hotel ....1120 Drexel Ave.
  Burton's Hotel ....10 North Delaware Ave.
  Carver Hall Hotel ....500 North Carolina Ave.
  Gambrill's ....501 N. Indiana Ave.
  Golden's Restaurant ....41 North Kentucky Ave.
  Hawkin's ....1114 Baltic Ave.
  Hotel McCracken ....1701 Arctic Ave.
  Jamaica Motel ....1140 Adriatic Avenue
  Johnson's Hotel ....11 North Kentucy Ave.
  Jones Cottage ....1720 Arctic Ave.
  Kathryn Guest House...1817 Arctic Ave.
  Liberty Hotel ....1579 Baltic Ave.
  Lincoln Hotel ....15 North Indiana Ave.

Travelers' Green Book 1963–64

    Livingston's Guest House .... 38 N. Rhode Island Ave.
    Murphy Tourist Home .... 234 Virginia Ave.
    Newsome's Cottage .... 126 N. Indiana Ave.
    PARK PLAZA MOTEL .... Illinois Ave. at Bachrach Blvd.
    Phone 348-9131 — 26 modern units — Air Conditioned
    Perry's Restaurant .... 1222 Arctic Ave.
    R. Brown Tourist Home .... 113 North Pennsylvania Ave.
    Randell Hotel .... 1601 Arctic Ave.
    Stigare Motel .... Absecon Blvd. & Drexel Ave.
    Village Inn .... 1806 Arctic Ave
    Villanova Hotel .... 1124 Drexel Ave.
    Wash's Sea Food Restaurant .... 710 N. Michigan Ave.
    Washington Tourist Home .... 1109 Arctic Ave.
    Wright Hotel .... 1702 Arctic Ave.

BELMAR
    Sadie's Guest House .... 1304 "E" Street

BELL MEADE
    Bell Meade Hotel .... U. S. Route 31

BURLEIGH
    Indian Trail Motel .... Indian Trail Road

CAPE MAY
    Admiral Arms .... 226 Jackson St.
    De Griff Hotel .... 83 Corgie Street
    Dot's Guest House .... 230 Jackson St.
    Indian Trail Motel .... Rt. No. 2
    Richardson's Hotel .... Broad & Jackson Streets
    Stiles Tourist Home .... 821 Corgie Street

EGG HARBOR
    Allen House Hotel .... 625 Cincinnati Avenue

ELIZABETH
    Mrs. T. T. Davis Tourist Home .... 27 Dayton

ESTELLE MANOR
    Lake La-Will Motel .... First Avenue

FAIR HAVEN
    Robin's Nest Hotel .... 83 Navesink Avenue

LAWNSIDE
    Hi-Hat Tourist Home .... White Horse Pike
    Inman Hotel .... White Horse Pike

MONMOUTH JUNCTION
    Macon's Inn Tourist Home .... Highway Rotue No. 1-26

MONTCLAIR
    Y.M.C.A. Tourist Home .... 39 Washington Street
    Y.W.C.A. Tourist Home .... 159 Glenridge Avenue

NEPTUNE
    Busy Bee Cottage .... 418 Fisher Avenue
    Gottling's Restaurant .... 118 Bradley Avenue
    Hampton Inn Restaurant .... 1718 Springwood Avenue
    Samuel's Restaurant .... 351 Fisher Avenue

NEWARK
- Alpine House ..... 345 Washington Street
- Coleman Hotel ..... 59 Court Street
- Grand Hotel ..... 78 W. Market Street
- Park Lane Hotel ..... 81 Lincoln Park
- Y.M.C.A. ..... 52 Jones Street
- Y.W.C.A. ..... 20 Jones Street

OCEAN CITY
- Benning Hotel ..... 6th St. & Simpson Ave.
- Comfort Hotel ..... 201 Bay Avenue
- Edna Mae's Tourist Home ..... 921 West Avenue

ORANGE
- Triangle Restaurant ..... 152 Barrow Street
- Y.M.C.A. ..... 84 Oakwood Avenue
- Y.W.C.A. ..... 66 Oakwood Avenue

PERTH AMBOY
- Lenora Hotel ..... 550 Hartford Street

PLEASANTVILLE
- Fuller's Motel ..... 1401 So. New Road
- Garden Spot Tourist Home ..... 300 Doughty Road
- Lin-Mar Hotel ..... 1420 So. New Road, Hwy. 9
- Marionette Cottage Tourist Home ..... 604 Portland Avenue
- Morris Beach ..... 401 Bayview Ave.
- Virginia Hotel ..... 1505 New Road
- Virginia Inn Tourist Home ..... 1505 S. New Road

RED BANK
- Vincents Restaurant ..... 263 Shewsbury Avenue

SEA BRIGHT
- Castle Inn Restaurant ..... 11 New Street

SPRING LAKE BEACH
- Laster Cottage ..... 419 Morris Ave.

TRENTON
- HOTEL DE LAINE — ½ Blk. from Bus Terminal ..... 152 Perry Street
  Clean Attractive Rooms & Baths
  Your Home Away from Home — Phone EX 2-9226
- Y.M.C.A. ..... 40 Fowler Street

WILDWOOD
- Arctic Ave. Hotel ..... 3600 Arctic Avenue
- Dean's Tourist Home ..... 166 W. Young Avenue
- Elfra Court Motel ..... 119 W. Robert Street
- Ivy Hotel ..... 436 W. Garfield Avenue
- Lilian's Tourist Home ..... 134 W. Baker Avenue
- Mrs. E. Crawley Tourist Home ..... 3816 Arctic Avenue
- Poindexter Apts. Hotel ..... 106 E. Schellinger Avenue
- The Harmon Motel ..... 4308 Hudson Avenue
- The Marion Hotel ..... Arctic & Spencer Avenue
- The Norris House ..... 107 W. Roberts Avenue

NEW MEXICO
Hotels — Motels — Tourist Homes — Restaurants

ALAMOGORDO
  Travelers Court Motel .... Hwys. 54 & 70

ALBUQUERQUE
  Aunt Brenda's Restaurant .... 331 53 St., N.W.
  Cactus Motel .... 5930 Central Ave., S.W.
  Mrs. Kate Duncan Tourist Home .... 331 53 St., N.W.
  Mrs. W. Bailey Tourist Home .... 1127 N. 2nd Street

CARLSBAD
  Black River Village

DEMING
  Darling Courts Motel .... West Hwys. 70 & 40
  La Mesa .... 822 W. Soruce Street

LORDSBURG, N. M.

Modern with Private Bath   Phone: 54 2-9002
HIGHTOWER MOTEL & CAFE
One Mile East of Lordsburg, N. M.
On Highways 70 & 80

Mr. and Mrs.   Box 291
Rochester Hightower   Lordsburg, N. M.

ROSWELL
  Apache Lodge .... 1401 So. Main Street
  B. Brown .... 313 W. Math.

SANTE FE
  El Ray Court .... 2500 Cerellios Road

SANTA ROSE
  Will Rogers Court .... Will Rogers Drive

TRUTH OR CONSEQUENCES
  Black Range Court .... 711 Date Street

TUCUMCARI
  Amigo Motel .... 1823 East Gaynell Avenue
  Jones' Rooms Tourist .... Box 1002
  Rockett Inn Tourist Home .... 524 W. Campbell Street

VADO
  Fullers Motel .... Highway 80

NEW YORK STATE
Hotels — Motels — Tourist Homes — Restaurants

ALBANY
Dorsey's Restaurant .... Cor. Van Trumpet & Broadway
Hotel Broadway .... 603 Broadway
Kenmore Hotel .... 76 Columbia Avenue

BUFFALO
Al Fras Service Station .... William & Michigan Sts.
Art's Lounge .... 1164 Jefferson Ave.
BOB & LOU'S TAVERN .... 925 Jefferson
The Friendly Tavern, Good Food, Pleasant Atmosphere
Bon Ton Oasis Cocktail Lounge .... William St.

TT 4-1000

CAMERON'S LIQUOR STORE
Fast Free Delivery — Free Parking

153 E. Utica Street   Buffalo, N. Y.

Costello Cafe & Hotel .... 605 Michigan Street
Claridge Hotel .... 38 Broadway
Crystal Restaurant .... 534 Broadway
DAIRY ISLE .... 263 Jefferson
The Best In Everything To Eat!
Dennis Snack Bar .... 208 William Street
DUBIEL'S LAS VEGAS RESTAURANT .... 535 Broadway
The Best of Food

Travelers' Green Book 1963–64

TL 6-4154   TL 4-9026
GERALD'S RESTAURANT
Delightful Dinners for Particular People — Open 24 hours

165 Broadway, near Michigan Ave.   Buffalo, N. Y.

Hickory Tavern	352 William
Horseshoe Restaurant	212 William Street
J. B.'s Gulf Service Station	#1 — 419 Broadway, #2 — 120 William
Montgomery Hotel	486 Michigan Avenue
MOTHER DEAR'S BAR-B-QUE	**582 William Street**
Perry's Snack Bar	360 William Street
Perry's Cleaners	368 William Street
Pixie's Bar	317 Glenwood Avenue
Pine Grill	Jefferson Avenue & E. Ferry
THE S & L GRILL	**264 E. Uticar Street**

Phone: TL 2-9827   Wholesome Environment

SAM'S RESTAURANT

Specializing in the Best of Barbecue

534 Broadway   Buffalo, N. Y.

When Passing Through Buffalo Be Our Guest . . .
THE WILLIAMS HOTEL
9 Sycamore Street   TL 2-9319   Buffalo, N. Y.
WILLIAMS LIQUOR STORE
206 Seneca Street   TL 3-7722   Buffalo, N. Y.

Sperry's Tan Tempo Lounge	757 Michigan Avenue
STINSON'S LIQUOR STORE	**134 William Street**
We Deliver — TL 3-9000 — William Stinson, Prop.	
William Campbell Tourist Home	210 Brunswick Street
Texas Red Hot Stand	1411 Jefferson Avenue

The New Skateland..Main & Riley Sts.
Y.M.C.A. ....585 Michigan Avenue

CASTLETON
　Mrs. A. Oliver Tourist Home ....Maple Hill

CENTER BRUNSWICK
　Twin Acres Motel ....Highway 7, 6 miles North of Troy

CROTON-ON-HUDSON
　Watergate Motel ....Albany Post Rd.

CUDDEBACKVILLE
　Paradise Farms
　Little Lake Lodge

EAST GREENBUSH
　Motel Blue Stone ....P.O. Box 417, 6 mi. East of Albany

ELMIRA
　Green Pastures Tourist Home ....670 Dickinson Street

GLEN FALLS
　★McFERSON'S HOTEL ....52 Glen Street
　Hayes Cottage Tourist Home ....99 Sanford Street

GODEFROY
　Resnick's Motel

GREENWOOD LAKE
　La Part Cabins
　Farm Lake House
　Jus Haven
　Mrs. Louise Taylor..P. O. Box 314

HIGH FALLS
　Glove Valley Dude Ranch
　Wickie Wackie Club

HYDE PARK
　Dutch Patroon Garden Hotel St..............................Rt. 9, 4 miles north Pokips

JAMESTOWN
　Mrs. I. W. Herald Tourist Home ....511 W. 10th Street

KERHONKSON
　Rainbow Acres
　Pegleg Bates

KINGSTON
　Gordon Hotel ....3 Canal Street
　Lang's Ranch..................................Rte. 4, Morgan Hill Lodge, Tel. Federal 8-9664

LACKAWANNA
　GREEN'S RESTAURANT ....25 Gates Ave.
　Old Fashioned Home Cooking & Barbecue

43

Travelers' Green Book 1963–64

LAKE GEORGE
Woodbine Cottage ....75 Deskau Street
Georgian Motel ....U. S. 9, in Lake George Village

LAKE HUNTINGTON
Sister Lillian Resort, Villa Theresa

LAKE PLACID
Dreamland Cottage...41 McKinley Street
Camp Parkside ....Woodland Terr.

LARCHMONT
Larchmont Motel ....50 Boston Rd.

MECHANICSVILLE
Green's Tourist Home ....R.F.D. No. 1
Comfort Inn

NAPANOCH
Pine Oak Guest House

NIAGARA FALLS
★MRS. ALICE FORD TOURIST HOME ....413 1st Street
3 Blocks from the Falls
Anchor Motel...N. Y. 384 & 265
High Light Barber Shop..513 Erie Avenue
Hotel Niagara
Hutchinson Tourist Home ....1050 Center Avenue
Mrs. Brown Tourist Home ....1202 Haeberie Avenue
Mrs. Eugene Ellis Tourist Home ....3501 Royal Avenue
Mrs. R. Reynolds Tourist Home.....................................419 1st Avenue
Seventos Creamy Day...3214 Cleveland Avenue
W. L. Parker Tourist Home ....627 Erie Avenue

BU 2-9370

CARVER'S LUNCHEONETTE
Best Food in Town

216 13th Street   ¼ Mile to the Falls

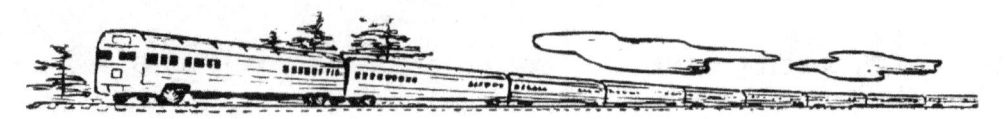

44

NEW YORK CITY

HOTEL	RATES SINGLE	DOUBLE
Abbey, 151 W. 51 St.	$ 8.50-10.50	$11.50-16.50
Algonquin, 59 W. 44 St.	10.00-13.00	13.00-17.00
Allerton House, 130 E. 57 St.	8.00-10.00	11.00-16.00
America, 145 W. 47 St.	5.00- 7.00	7.00-10.00
Americana, 52nd St. & 7th Ave.	12.00-28.00	16.00-32.00
Arlington, 18 W. 25 St.	5.00- 8.00	6.00-12.00
Astor, 44 St. & Broadway	9.00-18.00	14.00-24.00
Barbizon-Plaza, 106 Central Pk.	9.50-15.00	15.00-23.00
Belmont Plaza, 49 St. & Lexington Ave.	8.50-16.00	14.00-20.00
Biltmore, 43 St. & Madison Ave.	14.95-25.00	18.95-30.00
Buckingham, 101 W. 57 St.	10.50-14.50	12.50-17.50
Claridge, B'way & 44 St.	7.00-10.00	9.00-15.00
Commodore, 42 St. at Park & Lexington Aves.	11.00-19.00	16.00-24.00
Diplomat, 108 W. 43 St.	7.50- 9.00	9.50-12.00
Drive-In Hotel, 75 Macombs Place		
Edison, 228 W. 47 St.	8.50-12.00	13.50-18.50
Empire, 63rd St. & Broadway	7.00-10.00	10.00-16.00
Essex House, 160 Central Pk., So.	16.00-28.00	20.00-28.00
Executive, 37 St. & Madison	12.50-15.50	15.50-19.50
Fifth Avenue, 5th & 9th Sts.	10.00-14.00	15.00-19.00
George Washington, 23 St. & Lexington Ave.	7.00-10.00	11.50-16.00
Gladstone, 114 E. 52 St.	13.00-17.00	17.00-22.00
Governor Clinton, 371 7 Ave.	8.00-14.00	11.00-21.00
Great Northern, 118 W. 57 St.	7.50-11.00	10.50-14.00
Hadson, 1234 B'way	5.00- 8.00	7.00-12.00
Hamilton, 141 W. 73 St.	5.00- 7.00	7.00- 9.00
Henry Hudson, 353 W. 57 St.	7.25-12.00	11.00-18.50
Holiday Inn, 57 St. - 9th & 10th Aves.	13.00-14.00	17.00-18.00
Howard Johnson's Motor Lodge, 51 St. & 8 Ave.	12.00-20.00	14.00-22.00
Kimberly, 203 W. 74 St.	7.00- 9.00	10.00-14.00

45

Travelers' Green Book 1963–64

Save for your vacation — Save for travel
Carver Federal Savings & Loan Association
New York City   4% Dividends Paid Annually   Brooklyn
75 W. 125th Street   1273 Fulton Street
TRafalgar 6-4747   ULster 7-5515
"Where personal pride and community interests meet"

King Edward, 120 W. 44 St.	5.50- 8.00	8.00-12.00
Knickerbocker, 120 W. 45 St.	6.00-10.00	9.00-16.00
Lexington, Lexington & E. 48 St.	10.75-15.95	14.95-20.95
Lincoln Square Motor Inn, 155 W. 66 St.	14.00-18.00	14.00-18.00
Mayfair House, 610 Park Ave.	$18.00-20.00	$20.00-24.00
Mayflower Hotel, 15 Central Park W.	14.00-17.00	16.50-19.00
Meurice Hotel, 145 W. 58th St.	10.00-11.00	15.00-16.00
Murray Hill Hotel, 42 W. 35th St	7.00-10.00	10.00-13.00
Nassau Hotel, 56 E. 59th St.	3.00- 5.00	4.00- 6.00
National Hotel, 592 7th Ave.	6.00- 7.00	9.00-10.00
Navarro Hotel, 112 Central Park S.	16.50-22.00	19.50-26.00
New York Hilton, Ave. of the Americas & 53 & 54	14.00-22.00	18.00-29.00
New Yorker, 34th St. & 8th Ave.	9.00-15.00	13.00-21.00
One Fifth Avenue, 1 5th Ave.	13.00-17.00	16.00-20.00
Paramount Hotel, 235 W. 46th St.	7.50-10.50	10.50-15.00
Paris Hotel, 752 West End Ave.	5.00-8.75	7.50-13.50
Park Crescent Hotel, 150 Riverside Dr.	8.00-15.00	11.00-18.00
Park Lane Hotel, 299 Park Ave.	19.00-22.00	25.00-28.00
Park Plaza, 50 W. 77th St.	4.50- 6.00	7.00-10.00
Park Royal, 23 W. 73rd St.	8.00-12.00	10.00-18.00
Park Sheraton Hotel, 870 7th Ave.	8.50-15.50	13.90-19.50
Peter Cooper Hotel, 130 E. 39th St.	14.00-16.00	16.50-18.50
Piccadilly, 227 W. 45th St.	8.00-12.00	11.00-17.00
Pierre Hotel, 2 E. 61st St.	23.00-27.00	28.00-33.00
Plaza Hotel, 5th Ave. at 59th St.	15.00-29.00	20.00-34.00
Plymouth Hotel, 143 W. 49th St.	7.00-10.00	10.00-17.00
President Hotel, 234 W. 48th St.	7.00-10.00	11.00-15.00
Prince George Hotel, 14 E. 28th St.	11.00-13.00	12.00-17.00
Regency Hotel, Park Ave. at 61st St.	22.00-30.00	27.00-36.00
Riviera Congress Motor Inn, 550 10th Ave.	12.00-16.00	16.00-20.00
Roger Smith Hotel, 501 Lexington Ave.	9.00-14.50	13.00-18.50
St. Moritz, 50 Central Pk. S	11.00-18.00	15.00-21.00
Savoy-Hilton, 5th Ave. at 58th St.	13.00-35.00	18.00-35.00
Schuyler Hotel, 57 W. 45th St.	6.00- 9.00	8.00-11.00
Seventy Park Hotel, 70 Park Ave.	12.50-20.00	17.00-24.00
Shelburne Hotel, 303 Lexington Ave.	10.85-13.85	13.85-16.85
Shelton Towers Lexington Ave., 48-49th Sts.	8.85 11.85	17.85
Sheraton Atlantic, 34th St. & Bway	8.75-14.00	13.75-18.00
Sheraton-East, 341 Park Ave.	19.00-26.00	23.00-30.00
Sheraton Motor Inn, 42nd St. & 12th Ave.	11.50-17.00	17.75-21.00
Skyline Motor Inn, 725 10th Ave.	14.00-18.00	14.00-20.00
Stanhope Hotel, 995 5th Ave.	16.00-24.00	20.00-28.00
Statler-Hilton, 401 7th Ave.	11.00-19.00	14.50-25.00
Summit Hotel, E. 51st St. & Lexington Ave.	14.00-28.00	16.00-32.00
Taft Hotel, 7th Ave at 50th St.	8.50-13.75	11.50-19.75

46

Theresa Hotel, 7th Ave. at 125th St.	10.48-11.48	10.48-12.48
Times Square Motor Hotel, 255 W. 43rd St.	6.00- 8.00	9.00-12.00
Tudor Hotel, 304 E. 42nd St.	6.00-11.00	10.00-17.00
Tuscany Hotel, 39th St. E. of Park Ave.	18.80-24.80	24.80-30.80
Waldorf-Astoria, 301 Park Ave.	10.00-22.00	16.00-32.00
Warwick Hotel, 65 W. 54th St.	14.00-25.00	18.00-29.00
Wellington Hotel, 59th & 56th Sts. at 7th Ave.	7.75-14.75	11.50-19.50
Wentworth Hotel, 59 W. 46th St.	8.00-12.00	10.00-16.00
Westbury Hotel, Madison Ave. at 69th St.	14.00-20.00	18.00-25.00
Westover Hotel, 253 W. 72nd St.	8.00-10.00	10.00-12.00
Windermere Hotel, 666 West End Ave.	7.00-10.00	10.00-12.00
Winslow Hotel, 45 E. 55th St.	8.00-11.00	12.00-15.00
Wolcott Hotel, 4 W. 31st St.	7.00- 9.00	10.00-14.00
Woodstock Hotel, 127 W. 43rd St.	6.50- 9.00	10.00-14.00
Woodward Hotel, 210 W. 55th St (Broadway)	5.00-8.00	8.00-12.00
Wyndham Hotel, 42 W. 58th St.	11.00-13.00	12.00-14.00
Y.M.C.A. Wm. Sloane House, (Men Only) 356 W. 34th St.	7.50	

The Bronx

Bronx Park Motel, 2500 Crontona Ave.	12.00	14.00-16.00
Concourse Plaza Hotel, 900 Grand Concourse	7.50-10.00	13.00-19.00
Deegan Motel, 3600 Bailey Ave.	10.00-12.00	12.00-20.00
Riverdale Motor Inn, 6355 Broadway	12.00-14.00	14.00-16.00
Stadium Motor Lodge, W. 167th St.-Major Deegan Expwy.	10.00-12.00	14.00-16.00
Town & Country Motor Lodge, 2244 Tillotson Ave	11.00-13.00	13.00-17.00
Van Cortlandt Motel, 6393 Broadway	8.00-10.00	10.00-14.00

Brooklyn

Franklin Arms Hotel, 66 Orange St.	6.50- 7.00	8.50-10.00
Golden Gate Motor Inn, Belt Pkwy.-Knapp St.	11.00-13.00	15.00-19.00
Granada Hotel, Lafayette Ave. & Ashland Pl.	8.50-12.00	11.00-16.00
Gregory Hotel, 8315 4th Ave.	8.00	10.00-11.00
Manhattan Beach Hotel, 156 West End Ave.	7.50-16.50	10.00-22.00
St. George Hotel, 51 Clark St.	6.50-14.00	10.00-17.00
Sea Isle Motor Inn, 3900 Shore Pkwy. (Ex. 14 Belt Pkwy)	12.00-18.00	14.00-22.00
Towers Hotel, 25 Clark St.	7.00- 8.00	10.00-13.00

Queens

Beach Haven Hotel, 243 Beach 19th St., Far Rockaway 91, N. Y.	10.00	15.00-18.00
Crossway Airport Inn At La Guardia, 100-30 Ditmars Blvd., Flushing 69, N. Y.	14.00-18.00	18.00-24.00
Crossway Idlewild Inn, 152-25 138th Ave., Jamaica 34, N. Y.	14.00-15.00	18.00-19.00
Forest Hills Inn, 1 Station Square, Forest Hills 75, N. Y.	8.50-14.00	12.00-20.00
Franklin Hotel, 89-05 163rd St., Jamaica 32, N. Y.	6.00- 8.00	6.00- 9.00
Grand Central Motor Inn, 71-11 Astoria Blvd., Astoria 2, N. Y.	12.00-15.00	15.00-26.00
Homestead Hotel, 82-45 Grenfall St., Kew Gardens 15, N. Y.	9.00-12.00	12.00-15.00

47

Travelers' Green Book 1963-64

International Hotel, N. Y. Int. Airport,
   Jamaica 30, N. Y. 12.00-17.00   18.00-22.00
Kew Motor Inn, 80-05 Grand Central Pkwy.,
   Kew Gardens Hills 35, N. Y. 12.00-16.00   16.00-30.00
La Guardia Hotel, 99-11 Ditmars Blvd.,
   E. Elmhurst 69, N. Y. 13.00-17.00   17.00-22.00
Pan American Motor Inn, 79-10 Queens Blvd.,
   Elmhurst 73, N. Y. 15.00-22.00   18.00-28.00
Riviera Idlewild Hotel, N. Y Int. Airport (Belt Pkwy.)
   Jamaica 30, N. Y. 16.00-20.00   22.00-32.00
Sanford Hotel, 140-40 Sanford Ave.,
   Flushing 55, N Y. 9.00-10.00   13.00-14.00
Schine Inn at Forest Hills, 108-25 Horace Harding Expwy,
   Flushing 68, N. Y. 12.00-16.00   16.00-18.00
Seaway Idlewild Hotel, N. Y. Int. Airport (Belt Pkwy.)
   Jamaica 30, N. Y. 16.00-20.00   22.00-32.00
Sheraton-Tenney Inn At La Guardia, 90-10 Grand Central Pkwy.,
   E. Elmhurst 69, N. Y. 12.50-16.50   14.50-20.00
Skyway Hotel, 132-10 S. Conduit Ave.,
   Jamaica 30, N. Y. 13.00-15.00   17.00-22.00
Skyway Hotel La Guardia, 102-10 Ditmars Blvd.,
   Flushing 69, N. Y. 13.00-15.00   17.00-20.00
Sunchester Hotel, 37-52 80th St.,
   Jackson Hts. 72, N. Y. 12.00-14.00   12.00-14.000
Travelers Hotel-Motel, 9400 Ditmars Blvd.,
   (La Guardia Airport), E. Elmhurst 69, N. Y. 13.00   17.00-18.00
Treadway Inn, 114th St. & 37th Ave. (near the Fair)
   Flushing 52, N. Y. 15.00-17.00   19.00-24.00
Whitman Hotel, 160-11 89th Ave., Jamaica 2, N Y. ... 9.00-12.00   12.00-15.00

Richmond (Staten Island)
Richmond Hotel, 71 Central Ave., ... 8.40   10.50

Nassau
Bar Harbour Motel, 5050 Sunrise Hwy. (Rt. 27),
   Massapequa Park, N. Y. 10.00-11.00   12.00-15.00
Bayberry Great Neck Hotel, 75 N. Station Plaza,
   Great Neck, N. Y. 13.00   18.00
Bethpage Motel, Hempstead Tpke., Bethpage, N. Y. 10.00-12.00   12.00-20.00
Colony Arms Hotel, 190 Glen Cove Ave.,
   Glen Cove, N. Y. 8.00   11.00-13.00
Colony Hotel, 10 Bond St., Great Neck, N. Y. 9.50-12.00   14.00-18.00
Courtesy Inn Sea-Horse Marina, S. Main St.,
   Freeport, N. Y. 11.00-13.00   12.00-19.00
Farmingdale Motor Lodge, Rt. 110
   Broadhollow Rd.), Farmingdale, N. Y. 9.00   10.00-12.00
Garden City Hotel 7th St. & Park Ave.,
   Garden City, N. Y. 12.00-16.00   17.00-21.00
Gateway Motel, Sunrise Hwy., Merrick, N. Y. 12.00-16.00   14.00-18.00
Hempstead Motor Hotel, 130 Hempstead Ave.,
   West Hempstead, N. Y. 12.00-14.00   14.00-20.00
Heritage Quality Court Motor Inn, Jericho Tpke.
   (Rt. 25), Syosset, N. Y. 11.00-12.00   15.00-19.00
Island Inn, Old Country Rd., Westbury, N Y. 12.00-15.00   16.00-22.00

Island Lodge Motel, 274 Jericho Tpke., Syosset, N. Y.	11.00	16.00-18.00
Jericho Motel, Jericho Tpke., Jericho, N. Y.	9.00-11.00	12.00-20.00
Lynbrook Motor Hotel, 5 Freer St., Lynbrook, N. Y.	12.00-16.00	15.00-30.00
Mansion Hotel, 54 Lincoln Ave., Rockville Cent., N. Y.		
Meadowbrook Motor Lodge, 4400 Jericho Tpke., Jericho, N. Y.	11.00	16.00-18.00
Mineola Hotel, 193 2nd St., Mineola, N. Y.	6.50	8.50-10.00
Promenade Hotel on the beach, 102 W. Broadway, Long Beach, N. Y.	15.00-25.00	25.00-35.00
Raceway Inn Motel, Old Country Rd., at Post Ave., Westbury, N. Y.	12.00-14.00	14.00-18.00
Roosevelt Inn, 1650 Hempstead Tpke., East Meadow, N. Y.	11.00-13.00	14.00-20.00
Roslyn Harbor Hotel, 22 Bryant Ave., Roslyn, N. Y.		
Tivoli Motel, 3400 Brush Hollow Rd., Westbury, N. Y.	12.00	15.00-18.00
Towne & Country Motel, 49 Old Country Rd., Westbury, N. Y.	12.00	15.00-18.00
Turnpike Motel, 434 Hempstead Tpke., W. Hempstead, N. Y.	12.00 15.00	15.00-26.00
Westbury Motel, Jericho Tpke., Westbury, N. Y.	12.00-16.00	12.00-21.00

Orange
Thayer Hotel, West Point, N. Y.	7.00- 9.00	10.00-12.00

Rockland
Ashley Motor Court, U. S. Rt. 59, Nanuet, N. Y.		12.00-14.00
Courtesy Inn, N. Y. Thruwy. (Ex. 11), Nyack, N. Y.	11.00-13.00	15.00-19.00
Motel on the Mountain, N. Y. Thruwy (Ex. 15), Suffern, N. Y.	12.00-14.00	17.00-22.00
Pascack Motel, Rt. 59 (N. Y. Thruwy. Ex. 14), Spring Valley, N. Y.	8.00-10.00	10.00-14.00

Suffolk
Bayshore Inn, 400 Bayshore Rd., Bayshore, N. Y.	11.00-13.00	13.00-16.00
Beacon Motel, Smithtown Bypass & Jericho Tpke., Nesconset, N. Y.	8.00-10.00	12.00
Chevy Chase Motel, 436 Sunrise Hwy., Babylon, N. Y.		10.00-12.00
Eden Rock Motel, 3055 Veterans Memorial Hwy., Ronkonkoma, N. Y.	8.00-12.00	10.00-17.00
Fontenac Motor Lodge, Jericho Tpke.- Bridge Branch Rd., Smithtown, N. Y.	11.00-13.00	14.00-18.00
Huntington Motel, 331 W. Jericho Tpke. (Rt. 25), Huntington, N. Y.	8.00-10.00	10.00-12.00
Jerimac Motel, 2231 Jericho Tpke., Commack, N. Y.	8.00-10.00	10.00-12.00
Lindenhurst Motel, W. Montauk Hwy. & Chestnut St., Lindenhurst, N. Y.	8.00-10.00	10.00-12.00
The 112 Motel, Rt., 112, Medford, N. Y.	8.00-10.00	10.00-14.00
Patchogue Motel & Country Club, Sunrise Hwy. (Rt. 27), Patchogue, N. Y.	8.50	12.00-13.00
Pines Motor Lodge, Rt. 109 near Straight Path, North Lindenhurst, N. Y.	10.00-11.00	10.00-12.00

Travelers' Green Book 1963–64

St. Moritz Motel, Yacht Club Rd., Babylon, N. Y. 12.00-18.00   12.00-18.00
Sky Motel, 7th St. & 3rd Ave. (Rt. 109),
    N. Lindenhurst, N. Y. 8.00- 9.00   10.00-13.00
Starlite Motel, 760 Little E. Neck Rd. (Sunrise Hwy.),
    West Babylon, N. Y. 10.00-14.00   10.00-16.00
Three Village Inn. Dock Rd., Stony Brook, N. Y. 6.00   12.00
Walt Whitman Motel, 295 E. Jericho Tpke. (Rt. 25),
    Huntington St., N. Y. 8.00-10.00   10.00-16.00

Westchester

Ardsley Acres Hotel Court, 560 Saw Mill River Rd.
    (Rt. 9A), Ardsley, N. Y. 8.00   12.00-14.00
Central Motel Court, 441 Central Ave.,
    White Plains, N. Y. 9.00   10.00-12.00
Dunwoodle Motor Inn, 300 Yonkers Ave.,
    Yonkers, N. Y. 10.00-12.00   14.00-17.00
Gramatan Hotel, Pondfield Rd., Bronxville 8, N. Y.   8.00-12.00   14.00-18.00
Hawthorne Circle Motor Inn, 20 Saw Mill River Road,
    Hawthorne, N. Y. 9.00-12.00   11.00-16.00
Hilton Inn, 455 S. Broadway, Tarrytown, N. Y. 12.00-15.00   16.00-20.00
Holiday Inn of Yonkers, 125 Tuckahoe Rd.,
    Yonkers, N. Y. 10.00-14.00   12.00-18.00
Roger Smith Motor Hotel, 1 Chester Ave.,
    White Plains, N. Y. 8.00-13.00   11.50-17.00
Saw Mill River Motel, 25 Valley Rd.,
    Elmsford, N. Y. 10.00-12.00   13.00-17.00
Scarsdale Inn, School La. off Popham Rd.,
Scarsdale, N. Y. 10.00   15.00
Tarryrest Motel, 542 Tarrytown Rd.,
    White Plains, N. Y. 9.00   11.00-15.00
Trade Winds Motor Court, 1141 Yonkers Ave.,
    Yonkers 2, N. Y. 10.50-12.00   12.00-18.00
Tuckahoe Motel, 307 Tuckhoe Rd., Yonkers, N. Y. 11.00   14.00-15.00
Watergate Motor Hotel, Albany Post Rd. (Rt. 9),
    Croton-on Hudson, N. Y. 8.00   12.00-14.00
Westchester Town House Motor Inn, 165 Tuckahoe Rd.
    (N. Y. Thrwy Ex. 6), Yonkers, N. Y. 14.00-16.00   16.00-24.00
Yorktown Motor Lodge, U. S. Rt. 202-Taconic Pkwy.,
    Yorktown Hts., N. Y. 12.00-14.00   14.00-20.00

NEW JERSEY

Bergen

Courtesy Inn, Rt. 4, Fort Lee, N. J. 10.00   12.00-20.00
Horizon Motel, U. S. Rt. 46, S. Hackensack, N. J. 10.00-16.00   10.00-22.00
Howard Johnson's Motor Lodge, Rt. 17,
    Ramsey, N. J. 10.00-12.00   14.00-16.00
Marriott Motor Hotel at Geo Washington Bridge, Hudson
    Ter. & The Bridge Plaza, Fort Lee, N. J. 10.00-17.00   14.00-25.00
New Orleans Motel, Rt. 4, Fort Lee, N. J. 6.50-11.00   8.00-16.00
Oritani Motor Hotel, 414 Hackensack Ave. (Rt. 4),
    Hackensack, N. J. 8.00-10.00   10.00-16.00
Palisades Motor Lodge, Rt. 46, Fort Lee, N. J. 8.00   12.00-14.00
Peter Pan Motel, Rt. 3, E. Rutherford, N. J. 8.00-12.00   10.00-16.00
Skyview Motel, Rts. 1 & 9 & 46, Fort Lee, N. J. 9.00-12.00   11.00-13.00

Suburban Motor Hotel, Rt. 4 & Intersection 208,
   Fair Lawn, N. J. 10.00-12.00   14.00-16.00
Swiss Court Motel, N. J. Hwy. 17,
   Upper Saddle River, N. J. 7.00- 8.00   9.00-12.00

New York City

THEATRES
- Apollo ....W. 125th Street
- Astor ....Broadway at 45th Street
- Capitol ....1639 Broadway
- Carnegie Hall Cinema ....Seventh Ave. at 57th Street
- Criterion ....Broadway at 45th Street
- Embassw Newsreel...46th Street and Broadway
- Guild 50th ....32 W. 50th Street
- Little Carnegie ....146 W. 57th Street
- Palace ....Broadway and 47th Street
- Paramount ....Times Square
- Plaza ....58th Street E. of Madison Ave.
- Poet's ....39 W. 54th Street
- Radio City Music Hall ....1260 Sixth Ave.
- Rivoli ....1620 Broadway
- Sutton ....57th Street and 3rd Ave.
- Trans-Lux ....52nd Street on Lexington Ave.
- Victoria ....Broadway and 46th Street
- Warner ....Broadway and 47th Street

Brooklyn

- Al's Restaurant ....1550 Fulton Street
- Caravan Restaurant ....175 Willoughby Avenue
- Dew Drop Restaurant ....363 Halsey Street
- G. & H Restaurant ....382 Sumner Avenue
- Hotel St. George ....51 Clark Street
- La Marchal ....1200 President Street
- Lefferts Hotel ....127 Lefferts Place
- Lincoln Plaza Hotel ....153 Lincoln Place
- Lincoln Terrace Hotel ....1483 Pacific Street
- Little Roxy Restaurant ....490A Sumner Avenue
- Mohawk Hotel ....379 Washington Avenue
- Pleasant Manor Hotel ....218 Gates Avenue

BARS
- La Marchal Supper Club ....1873 Nostrand Ave., Near President Street

Bronx

- Blue Morocco ....1185 Boston Rd.
- Carver Hotel ....980 Prospect Avenue
- Crotona Hotel ....695 E. 170th Street
- Concourse Plaza ....Grand Concourse at E. 161st Street
- Fountainhead

NEW ROCHELLE
- Harris Restaurant ....29 Morris Street
- Huguenot Hotel ....242 Huguenot Street
- Three 4s ....444 North Avenue
- Week's Restaurant ....68 Winyah Avenue

New York City

SHOPS AND STORES
From 34 to 59th Street

Macy's	Herald Square
Gimbals	Broadway at 33rd Street
Saks 34th Street	34th Street at Broadway
Altman's	5th Avenue at 34th Street
Lord and Taylor	5th Avenue at 38th Street
Best's	5th Avenue & 51st Street
Bonwit Teller	721 Fifth Avenue
Saks Fifth Avenue	5th Avenue & 49th Street
Tailored Woman	742 Fifth Avenue
Bergdorf Goodman	5th Avenue & 58th Street

IMPORTANT MEN'S SHOP

Wallach's	5th Avenue & 46th Street
Roger's Peet	600 Fifth Avenue, at 48th St.
Weber and Heilbroner	5th Avenue & 47th Street
John David	Broadway & 32nd Street
Browning Fifth Avenue	
Tripler's	366 Madison Avenue
Brooks Bros.	346 Madison Avenue
Saks Fifth Avenue	5th Avenue & 49th Street
DePinna's	650 Fifth Avenue
Abercrombe & Fitch	Madison Avenue & 45th St.
Jarrell John Inc.	518 Fifth Avenue

IMPORTED OR SPECIAL MERCHANDISE

American House (Artistic American handicrafts)	32 E. 52nd Street
Bazaar Francais (Imported kitchen articles)	666 Sixth Ave.
Bonnier's (Scandinavian arts and crafts)	605 Madison Ave.
Delgado's (Latin-American jewelry, textiles)	31 W. 8th Street
Leighton's (Mexican handicraft)	15 E. 8th Street
Irish Industries (Latin and South American decorative objects)	876 Lexington Ave.
Scottish Products (Scotch delicacies, woolens)	24 E. 60th Street
Sweden House (Scandinavian vases, pottery)	12 W. 50th Street
United Nations Gift Shop (Articles from all over the world)	

PARKS, ZOOS, AQUARIUM and GARDENS

Battery Park	Lower Broadway at the Battery
Botanical Gardens	
Bryant Park	42nd St. at 6th Ave.
Central Park Zoo	59th Street to 110th Street
City Hall Park	Broadway and Park Row
Fort Tyron	Myrtle and Nagle Streets
Jacob Riis	Rockaway, Queens
Prospect	Flatbush Ave. and Empire Blvd.
Van Cortlandt	Broadway and 242nd Street
Washngton Square	5th Ave. and 4th Street

POINTS OF INTEREST
- Bowery
- Cathedral of St: John Divine
- Central Park and its Zoo
- Chinatown
- City Hall
- Columbia University
- Coney Island
- Empire State Building
- Freedomland
- Grand Central Terminal
- Grant's Tomb
- Greenwich Village
- Hayden Planetarium
- International Airport
- La Guardia Field Airport
- Lever Building
- Little Italy
- New York Harbor
- Penn Station
- Port Authority Bus Terminal
- Riverside Church
- Rockefeller Center
- Schomburg Collection, Countee Cullen Branch Library
- Statue of Liberty
- Stuyvesant Town
- United Nations
- Wall Street
- Washington Square

RESTAURANTS

Avenue	509 Fifth Ave.
Blue Bird Inn	121½ E. 17th Street
Bombay Indian	465 W. 125th Street
Brass Rails	100 Park Ave.
	521 Fifth Ave.
	745 Seventh Ave.
	500 Eighth Ave.
Bus Stop Restaurant	21 Macombs Place
Cattlemen's	48th St. & Lexington Ave.
China Bowl	152 W. 44th Street
Chinese Rathskeller	45 Mott Street
Danny's Corner	2154 Amsterlam Ave.
Davy Jones Sea Food House	103 W. 49th Street
Dawn Cafe	1702 Amsterdam Ave.
Eddie's Restaurant	714 St. Nicholas Ave.
El Charro	4 Charles Street
El Mundial	222 W. 116th Street
Frank's	315 W. 125th Street
Jack Dempsey's	1619 Broadway off 49th Street
King of the Sea	879 Third Ave.
Living Room	915 Second Ave.
Lobster Box	34 City Island Ave.
Lundy's	739 St. Nicholas Ave.
Mama Laura	230 E. 58th Street
McGinnis	Broadway at 48th Street
Palm Cafe	209 W. 125th Street
Patricia Murphy's Candlelight Rest.	33 E. 60th Street
Pete's	18 Irving Place
Phil's Rest.	187 Third Ave.
Prelude	3219 Broadway
Stella D'Oro	5806 Broadway
Wells Restaurant	2249 7th Ave.
Xochitl Mexican Restaurant	146 W. 46th Street

Seafood:

Fisherman's Net	495 Third Ave

53

Travelers' Green Book 1963-64

Grand Central Oyster House ....Grand Central Terminal
Harvey's Seafood House ....509 Third Ave.
King of the Sea ....879 Third Ave.
Sea Fare ....1033 First Ave. also 44 W. 8th Street

Steaks:
Barney's ....2125 Eighth Ave.
Harlem Embers ....W. 125th Street
Hickory House ....839 Second Ave.
Lloyd's ....W. 125th Street
Pen and Pencil ....205 E. 45th Street
Steak Joint ....58 Greenwich Ave.

American Specialties:
Hearthstone ....102 E. 22nd Street
Patricia Murphy ....33 E. 60th Street

Chinese:
House of Chan ....52nd Street and Seventh Ave.
Ruby Foos ....240 W. 52nd Street
Lum Fong ....150 W. 52nd Street

MUSEUMS
American Museum of Natural History ....79th St. and Central Park West
American Neumismatic Society ....Broadway and 155th Street
Brooklyn ....Washington Ave. and Eastern Parkway
Cloisters ....Fort Tryon Park
Frick Collection ....5th Ave. and 70th Street
Jewish ....5th Ave. and 92nd Street
Metropolitan ....5th and 82nd Street
American Indian ....Broadway at 155th Street
City of New York ....5th Ave. and 103rd Street
Modern Art ....11 West 53rd Street
New York Historical Society ....Central West and 77th Street
Solomon R. Gugginheim ....5th Ave. and 88th Street
Spanish ....Broadway and 155th Street
Whitney ....22 W. 54th Street

NIGHT CLUBS & BARS
African Room ....730 Third Ave.
Basin Street ....137 E. 48th Street
Bell, Cook & Candle....................................Amsterdam Ave. at 158th Street
Birdland ....1678 Broadway
Blue Angel ....152 E. 55th Street
Bon Soir ....40 W. 8th Street
Copacabana ....10 E. 60th Street
Count Basie's ....2245 Seventh Ave.
Danny's Hide-A-Way ....151 E. 45th Street
Dawn Cafe ....1702 Amsterdam Ave.
Dragon Inn ....140 W. 40th Street
El Morocco ....307 E. 54th Street
Fireside Inn ....411 W. 24th Street
Flash Inn ....107 McCombs Pl.
Gold Brick Inn...157th Street & Amsterdam Ave.
Hawaiian Room ....515 Lexington Ave.
Jimmy Ryan's ....53 W. 52nd Street
Jock's Place ....2350 Seventh Ave.

54

La Famille	2017 5th Ave.
Linnette's	714 St. Nicholas Ave.
Living Room	915 Second Ave.
Latin Quarter	200 W. 48th Street
Midway Lounge	415 W. 125th Street
Nicks'	10th Street and Seventh Ave.
Prelude	3219 Broadway
Red Rooster	2354 Seventh Ave.
Sapphire's	271 W. 47th Street
7 Ports	1604 Broadway
Smalls'	Seventh Ave. at 135th St.
Sugar Ray's	2074 7th Ave.
Sweet Chariot	225 W. 46th Street
The Round Table	151 E. 50th Street
Top Club	354 W. 125th Street
Upstairs at the Downstairs and Downstairs at the Upstairs	37 W. 56th Street

OSSINING

Depot Square Hotel	2 Water Street
Hotel Ossining	120 Main Street

PEEKSKILL

B & J Service Station	Corner Broad & Lincoln Terr.
Greene the Tailor	11 Nelson Ave.
Green's Lounge	Depew Street & Central Ave.
Granberry's	Park Street
Peekskill Motor Inn	Rte. 202 Cor. Rte. 9
Towne Lyne Motel	Rte. 202 Crompond Rd.

PORT JERVIS

R. Pendelton Tourist Home	26 Bruce Street

POUGHKEEPSIE

Poughkeepsie Motor Hotel	Rte. 9

RIVERHEAD

Peter's Motel	223 Flanders Road

ROCHESTER

A & A Garage	368 Clarissa St.
Arthur's Pharmacy	300 Joseph Ave.
Bowers Drug Store	553 Plymouth Ave., S.
Gibson Hotel	461 Clarissa St.
Headley Dry Cleaners	45 South Ave.
La Rue	491 Clarissa St.
Lawrence Soda Bar	581 S. Plymouth Ave.
Miller's Gulf Service	Troup and Clarissa
Shamrock Gas & Quaker State Proucts	494 South Ave.
Shepard's Barber Shop	508 Clinton St., N.
Sol Jeffries Service Station	121 Reynolds St.
Stanfield Hotel	34 Joseph Ave.

SCHENECTADY

Foster House Hotel	310 Dakota Street
Mrs. Grant Thomas Tourist Home	1024 Albany

Travelers' Green Book 1963-64

SARATOGA LAKE
White Sulphur Restaurant .... Rte. 9P

SARATOGA SPRINGS
G. & G. Restaurant .... 445 Broadway
Gideon Putnam
James Tourist Home .... 17 Park Street
Mrs. John Parker Tourist Home .... 18 Cherry Street
Playmore Motel .... S. Broadway, Rte. 9
Reds Seafood Restaurant .... Rte. 9

SYRACUSE
Aunt Edith's Restaurant .... 601½ Harrison Street
The Sylvan Tourist Home .... 815 E. Fayette Street
Y.M.C.A. .... 340 Montgomery Street

TARRYTOWN
Hilton Inn .... 455 S. Broadway

TICONDEROGA
Belfred Court .... Corner Montcalm Street & Wayne Avenue

VALATIE
Blue Spruce Motel .... Rt. 9, 16 mi. So. of Albany

WATERTOWN
G. E. Deputy Tourist Home .... 711 Morrison Street
V. H. Brown Tourist Home .... 502 Binase Street
Woodruff Hotel .... Public Square

WHITE PLAINS
Roger Smith Motor Hotel .... 123 E. Post Road
Del Rio Hotel .... 160 Lafayette Avenue
Tarks Restaurant .... 374 Central Avenue
4 Leaf Clover Restaurant .... 70 Dobbs Ferry Road
Waldorf Restaurant .... 102 Grove Street
Winbrook Restaurant .... 136 Brookfield Street
Fields Rotisserie & Motel .... 538 Tarrytown Road

YONKERS
Patricia Murphy's Candlelight Restaurant .... Central Ave.
Trade Winds Motor Ct. .... 1141 Yonkers Ave.

LONG ISLAND

JAMAICA
Boulevard Restaurant .... 110-33 Sutphin Blvd.

ST. ALBANS
Bonvivani Supper Club .... 114-16 Merrick Blvd.
Bowman's Show Place .... 111-59 Farmers Blvd.
Locust Restaurant .... 117-02 Merrick Blvd.
Staghead Club .... 189-29 Linden Blvd.

SPRINGFIELD GARDENS
Club Zanzibar .... 137-08 New York Blvd.

56

PAGE 264

NORTH CAROLINA
Hotels — Motels — Tourist Homes — Restaurants

ASHEVILLE
- Booker T. Washington Hotel .... 409 Southside Avenue
- James Keys Hotel .... 409 Southside Avenue
- Mrs. S. Foster Tourist Home .... 88 Clengman Avenue
- Savoy Tourist Homes .... Eagle & Market Sts.
- Y.W.C.A. .... 194 Ashland Avenue

CHARLOTTE
- Addie Motel .... 516 N. Meyers Street
- Alexander Hotel .... 523 N. McDowell Street
- Ingram's Restaurant .... 304 S. McDowell Street
- Alexander's Barber Shop .... 1310 S. Independence Blvd.
- Ballard's Barber Shop .... Five Points
- Biddleville Luncheonette .... 1116 Beatties Ford Rd.
- Chicken 'N' Ribs .... 1100 Beatties Ford Rd.
- Cleanway Cleaners .... University Park Shopping Center
- Davis Sandwich Shop .... 1108 Spring St.
- Ebony Cleaners .... 318 McDowell St. South
- Edith's Snack Bar .... 716 S. Caldwell St.
- Excelsior Club .... 921 Beatties Ford Rd.
- Fairview Barber Shop .... 1001 Oaklawn Ave.
- Ingram's Inn .... 419 S. Cedar St.
- J. C. Hart's Shoe Shop .... 329 S. McDowell
- J. C. Sandwich Shop .... 504 S. McDowell St.
- Joe's Auto Repair Service .... 2810 Statesville Ave.
- Johnson's Barber Shop .... 318 Cedar St. So.
- Mack's Paint & Body Shop .... 1422 Statesville Ave.
- Maxie's Coffee House .... 1425 Oaklawn Ave.
- McDowell's Barber Shop .... 502 McDowell St. So.
- McGowan's Boarding House .... 811 Oaklawn Ave.
- Oaklawn Tavern .... 1133 Oaklawn
- Orr's Washerette .... 1100 Seaboard St.
- Randolph's Grill .... 806 S. Mint St.
- Shu-Fixery .... 425 W. 11 St.
- The Griffith Street Luncheonette .... Griffith St.
- The Ideal Smoke Shop .... 1122 Beatties Ford Rd.
- The Igloo Dairy Bar .... 1500 Beatties Ford Rd.
- The Musical Grille .... 802 S. McDowell St.
- Third Ward Barber Shop .... West Hill & Poplar St.
- Welcome Grill .... 207 N. McDowell St.
- White Gable Cafe .... 233 Frazier Ave.
- White's Rendezvous .... 2435 Lucene Ave.

DURHAM
- Biltmore Hotel .... 323 E. Pelligrew Street
- Bull City Restaurant .... 412 Pettigrew Street
- College Inn Restaurant .... 1306 Fayetteville
- DeShazor's Hostelry .... 809 Fayetteville Street

FAYETTEVILLE
- Arthur's Sea Food Grill Restaurant .... 637 Person
- Coral Motor Court .... U. S. 301, 3 mi. South
- Jones Tourist Home .... 311 Moore Street

57

King Cole Motel ....2418 Murchison Rd.
Silver Grill Restaurant ....115 Gillespie Street

"Where the Guest is King"

KING COLE MOTEL

Individual Heat & Air Conditioned

2418 Murchison Road

Tel. 433-3775

On Highway #210 One Mile No. of Fayetteville, N. C.

GREENSBORO
Plaza Manor Hotel ....511 Martin Street
T. Daniels Tourist Home ....922 E. Market Street
GREENVILLE
Bell's Restaurant ....604 Albemarle Avenue
HENDERSON
Adams Tourist Home ....526 Chestnut Street
HIGH POINT
KILBY HOTEL ....**627 E. Washington Street**
Comfort, Convenience and Cleanliness
KINGS MOUNTAIN
Mrs. L. E. Ricks Tourist Home
KINSTON
Mark's Tourist Home & Cabins ....105 W. South St.
NEW BERN
H. C. Sparrow Tourist Home ....731 West St.
Rhone Hotel ....512 Queen St.
RALEIGH
Bloodsworth St. Tourist Home ....425 So. Bloodsworth St.
Deluxe Hotel ....220 E. Cabarrus St.
Home Eckers Hotel ....122 E. Hargett St.
Legion Home Restaurant ....416 E. Cabarrus St.
New York Restaurant ....108 E. Hargett St.
Stanton's Cafe-Restaurant ....319 South East St.
Starksville Guest House ....809 E. Bragg Street
Y.M.C.A. ....600 So. Bloodworth St.
ROCKY MOUNT
Wright's Motel ....P. O. Box 43
Lincoln Park Motel ....1000 Leggett Rd.
STATESVILLE
CARSON'S SERVICE STATION ....636 S. Center Street
Stop in for the best in general auto service.

58

Evening Breeze Motel .... On Hiway 70
FRANK'S GRILL .... 640 S. Center Street
Best of Foods — Phone 873-9250
STOKESDALE

Phone: Midway 3-3530   Open Year Round
JOHNSON'S SERVICE STATION & GROCERY
On Highway 158   Paul Johnson, Prop.
1½ Miles West of Stokesdale, N. C.
20 Miles East of Winston Salem, N. C.

WELDON
  Pope Hotel
  Terminal Inn Hotel .... Washington Avenue
WHITEVILLE
  Mrs. Fannie Jeffers Tourist Home .... Mill Street
WILMINGTON
  Johnson's Restaurant .... 1007 Chestnut Street
  Owens Club 900 Restaurant .... 900 No. 9th Street
  Paynes' Tourist Home .... 417 No. 6th Street
WINSTON SALEM
  Charles H. Jones Tourist Home .... 1611 E. 14th Street

NORTH DAKOTA
Hotels — Motels — Tourist Homes — Restaurants

BISMARK
  Grand Pacific Hotel
  Motel Court .... Box 724
FARGO
  Home Sweet Home Motel .... Hwys. 10 & 52
MINOT
  Le Grand-Parker Hotel
MEDORA
  Rough Riders Motel
WILLISTON
  Clack Court Motel .... 2nd St., West at 11th St.

OHIO
Hotels — Motels — Tourist Homes — Restaurants

AKRON
  Green Turtle Hotel .... Federal & Howard Street
  Matthews Hotel .... 77 N. Howard Street
CINCINNATI
  Club Tavern Hotel .... 2017 Seymour
  Jim Williams Sohio Service Station .... 552 W. 9th Street
  Lincoln Hotel .... 3166 Madison Road
  Manse Hotel .... 1004 Chapel Street
  O. Steele Tourist Home .... 3065 Kerper Street
  Sinton .... Walter Latscha, Mgr. 4th & Vine
  Y.W.C.A. .... 821 Lincoln Park Drive
CLEVELAND
  Carnegie Hotel .... 6803 Carnegie Avenue
  Majestic Hotel .... 2291 E. 55th Street

Travelers' Green Book 1963–64

Manhattan Restaurant	9903 Cedar Avenue
Mrs. Edith Wilkins Tourist Home	2121 E. 46th Street
Mrs. Fannie Gilmer Tourist Home	12421 Benham Street

HOUSING FOR WOMEN & GIRLS
125 Rooms — 10 Minutes from downtown Cleveland

THE PHILLIS WHEATLEY ASSOCIATION
4450 Cedar Avenue — Cleveland 3, Ohio
EXpress 1-4443

Nominal Rates for
Temporary Guests — Permanent Gueets
Food Service In Building

State Restaurant	7817 Cedar Avenue
Ward Hotel	4113 Cedar Avenue
Y.M.C.A.	E. 76th & Cedar

COLUMBUS

Atcheson Restaurant	1288 Atcheson Street
B. & B. Restaurant	2015 Persons Avenue
Belmont Restaurant	1105 Oak Street
Bruce Latham Restaurant	317 Hosacks Street
Cooper Tourist Home	259 N. 17th Street
Deshler-Wallick Hotel	Board & High Sts.
Duck Inn Restaurant	883 No. 4th Street
Hawkins Hotel	65 N. Monroe Avenue
Litchford Hotel	North 4th Street
Macon Hotel	366 N. 20th Street
Neil House Hotel	35 South High Street
Newford Hotel	452½ E. Long Street
St. Clair Hotel	338 Ct. Clair Avenue
Turner's Restaurant	452½ E. Long Street

DAYTON

Cox's Cut Rate Drugs & Gifts	842 W. 5th Streeet
Vina's Luncheonette & Delicatessen	837 W. 5th Street
Whitey's Garage	512 S. Broadway
Y.M.C.A.	907 W. 5th Street

LIMA

George Cook Tourist Home	230 S. Union Street
Mrs. A. Turner Tourist Home	1215 W. Spring Street
Turner Hotel	1215 West Spring Street

LONDON

Mrs. James Pettress Tourist Home	26 E. Lincoln Avenue

LORAIN

H. P. Jackson Tourist Home	2383 Apple Avenue
Mrs. Alex Cooley Tourist Homes	114 W. 26th Street
Porter Wood Tourist Home	1759 Broadway
Worthington Tourist Home	209 W. 16th Street

60

Travelers' Green Book 1963–64

PLAIN CITY
   Madry's Travel Inn .... U. S. Hwy. 33, 20 mi. N.W., Columbus
PORT CLINTON
   Woodlawn Cabins .... Rts. 2 & 163, ½ mile E. of Port Clinton
SANDUSKY
   Hunter Hotel .... 407 W. Market Street
SPRINGFIELD
   Mrs. M. E. Wilborn Tourist Home .... 220 Fair Street
   Posey Hotel .... 209 S. Fountain Avenue
   Posey Restaurant .... 211 S. Fountain Avenue
   Y.M.C.A. .... Center Street
TOLEDO
   COOK'S TOURIST HOME .... 1736-38 Washington Street
   Collingwood Motel .... Collingwood & Indiana Avenue
   J. F. Watson Tourist Home .... 399 Pinewood Avenue
   Mrs. J. Jennings Tourist Home .... 729 Indiana Avenue
YOUNGSTOWN
   ★HOTEL ALLISON .... 212 North West Avenue
  Fine Foods - Room Service - Free Parking — Tel. RI 6-9057
   Belmont Tourist Home .... 327 Belmont Avenue
   Central Restaurant .... 137 S. Center Street
   Gold Inn Hotel .... 851 W. Federal Street
   McDonald Hotel .... 442 E. Federal Street
   Red Lion Motel .... 2019 Hubbard-Coitsville Rd.
   Royal Palms Hotel .... 625 Hemrod Street
   Y.M.C.A. .... 962 W. Federal Street
   "Y" Restaurant .... 962 Federal Street
   Blue Haven Cafe .... 371 E. Federal
   Wee Motel .... 2705 McGuffey Rd.
ZANESVILLE
   L. E. Costom Tourist Home .... 1545 W. Main Street
   Little Harlem Restaurant .... Lee Street

OKLAHOMA
Hotels — Motels — Tourist Homes — Restaurants
ENID
   Mrs. Johnson Tourist Home .... 217 E. Market Street
MUSKOGEE
   Elliots Hotel .... 111½ So. 2nd Street
   People's Hotel .... 316 N. 2nd Street
OKLAHOMA CITY
   Canton Hotel .... 200 N.E. 2nd Street
   Hall Hotel .... 308½ N. Central
   Hotel Youngblood .... 4th & Stiles Sts.
   Mrs. Lessie Bennett Tourist Home .... 500 N.E. 4th Street
   Tucker's Tourist Home .... 315½ N.E. 2nd Street
   Wayside Motel .... 2028 N. Bryan Street
   Y.M.C.A. .... 614 N.E. 4th Street
SHAWNEE
   Olison Hotel .... 702 S. Bell
   Slugg's Hotel .... 118 East Bently

SAPULA
   Brooklyn Hotel .... 511 E. Hobson Street
SEMINOLE
   Due Drop Inn .... 110 W. Wewaha Street
TULSA
   Avalon Motel .... 2411 East Apache Street
   C. U. Netherland Tourist Home .... 542 N. Elgin Street
   Del Rio Hotel .... 607½ N. Greenwood
   McHunt Hotel .... 1121 N. Greenwood Street
   Miller Hotel .... 124 N. Hartford Street
   Small Hotel .... 615 E. Archer
   W. H. Smith Tourist Home .... 124½ N. Greenwood
   Y.W.C.A. .... 1120 East Pine

OREGON
Hotels — Motels — Tourist Homes — Restaurants

ASTORIA
   Astoria Court Motel .... 55 Olney Avenue
BEND
   Cascade Court .... 846 South 3rd Street
CRATER LAKE
   Crater Lake Lodge
EUGENE
   City Center Lodge .... 476 E. Broadway
KLAMATH FALLS
   Crater Cottages .... 2045 Oregon Avenue
PENDLETON
   Pendleton Hotel
PORTLAND
   Capitol Hill Motel .... 9110 S.W. Barbur Blvd.
   Hotel Multnomah .... 319 S. W. Pine
SALEM
   Salem Hotel .... Box 230
WALDPORT
   Sea Stones Cottage .... 5 miles South on Hiway 101

PENNSYLVANIA
Hotels — Motels — Tourist Homes — Restaurants

ALLENTOWN
   Southern Restaurant .... 372 Union Street
BEDFORD SPRINGS
   Harris Hotel .... Penn. & West Sts.
CARLISLE
   Lincoln Motel .... Box 114
CHESTER
   Harlem Hotel .... 1909 W. 3rd Street
   Vesta Vesta .... 311 Farnall Street
COATESVILLE
   DeLoach Motor Lounge .... 420 Harry Rd.
   Hotel Subway .... Coatesville
CRESCO
   Mrs. Daniel L. Taylor Tourist Home

EAST STROUDSBURG
- Fern Boarding House ..... 387 Lincoln
- Hillside Inn ..... R.F.D. No. - (Hwy. 209)

ERIE
- **KINTUCKY BAR-B-QUE** ..... 1438 Parade Street
  Visit us for the best ribs in town!
- Pope Hotel ..... 1318 French Street
- **WILSON'S SINCLAIR SERVICE STATION** ..... 17th & French Streets
  General Repairs and Tune-ups — Service calls
- Stake's House & Bar ..... 1435 Parade Street

GERMANTOWN
- Y.M.C.A. ..... 132 W. Rittenhouse

HARRISBURG
- Jack's Hotel ..... 1002 North 6th Street
- Mrs. W. D. Jones Tourist Home ..... 1531 North 6th Street
- Palace Hotel ..... 1602 North 7th Street
- Wishing Well Motel ..... Hwy. 22, E. of Harrisburg

NEW CASTLE
- Y.W.C.A. ..... 312 N. Jefferson

OIL CITY
- Mrs. Jackson Tourist Home ..... 258 Bissel Avenue

HENRYVILLE
- Lang's Orchard Cottage

MT. POCONO
- Alenia's Inn — Anchor Inn

PHILADELPHIA
- Bea's Hotel & Dining Room ..... 1857 N. 17th Street
- Bellevue-Stratford Hotel ..... Broad & Walnut Sts.
- Benjamin Franklin Hotel ..... 9th & Chestnut Sts.
- Brown's Restaurant ..... N.E. Cor. 17th & Columbia Ave.
- Burrell's Tourist Houses ..... 306 N. 40th Street
- Butler's Tavern ..... S.W. Cor. 17th & Carpenter
- Camp Mohawk ..... 27 Upsal St.
- Chesterfield Hotel ..... Broad & Oxford Sts.
- Essex House Hotel ..... 13th & Filbert Sts.
- Hoard's Southern Style Bar-B-Que ..... 1841 Ridge Avenue
- Hotel Linconia ..... 1907 Fairmount Avenue
- Horseshoe Hotel ..... 12th & Lombard Sts.
- Marriott Motor Hotel ..... City Line & Monument Avenue
- Tally's Paradise Hotel ..... 1527 Fitzwater Street
- Travelers Hotel ..... 316 So. Broad Street
- West End Hotel ..... 420 N. 40th Street
- Woodson Hotel ..... 1330 Catherine Street

PITTSBURGH
- B. Williams Tourist Home ..... 1537 Howard Street
- Birdie's Guest House ..... 1522 Center Avenue
- Elmore Hotel ..... 2153 Webster Avenue
- Flamingo Hotel ..... 2407 Wylie Avenue
- Hotel Webster Hall ..... 4415—5th Avenue
- Palace Hotel ..... 1545 Wylie Avenue
- Sherwyn Hotel
- **THE ELLIS HOTEL** ..... 2044 Center Avenue
  Cocktail Bar & Lounge — Phone: 281-3269

POWELL
    Winter's Farm
READING
    Hotel Abraham Lincoln .... 100 North 5th Street
    Mrs. C. Dawson .... 441 Buttonwood Avenue
SCRANTON
    Hotel Scranton .... Vine & Wyoming
SELLERSVILLE
    Mrs. Dorothy Scholls Tourist Home .... Forest Road
SWIFTWATER
    Rose Tree Inn
WASHINGTON
    Harley's Mapleview Motel .... U. S. Hwy. 19
WILKES BARRE
YORK
    Mrs. I. Grayson Tourist Home .... 276 S. Belvidere Avenue
    Yorktowne Hotel .... Market & Duke Sts.

RHODE ISLAND
Hotels — Motels — Tourist Homes — Restaurants

NEWPORT
    Mrs. F. Jackson Tourist Home .... 28 Hall Avenue
PROVIDENCE
    Hines Tourist Home .... 462 North Main Street

Why not a JOURNAL of your club's affair? Picnics, Dances, Conventions . . . No event too small or large! We will compile these important, historic moments in photos and story . . . A journal that will capture today's excitement for tomorrow. Details FREE! Box 172, Manhattanville Station, N. Y. 27, N. Y

SPEAKERS NEEDED?

For prominent speakers on any subject for YOUR affair CONTACT our SPEAKERS BUREAU, Box 172, Manhattanville Station, N. Y. 27, N. Y.

FOR INEXPENSIVE LUXURY VACATIONS

If you have a boat, home, cabin, vacation spot, etc. and are interested in "Exchange Vacations", write us about a listing in our "EXCHANGE VACATIONS JOURNAL". Spend a wonderful, trouble-free, money-saving vacation ANYWHERE. Box 172, Manhattanville Station, N. Y. 27, N. Y.

CELEBRITY ESCORT SERVICE

Our armed escorts can meet your plane, train, ship, etc. and you can have a care-free visit to the Big City, celebrity-style. For details: Box 172, Manhattanville Station, N. Y. 27, N. Y.

SOUTH CAROLINA
Hotels — Motels — Tourist Homes — Restaurants

AIKEN
   C. F. Holland Tourist Home .... 602 Richland Avenue East

ANDERSON
   Ess-Tee Restaurant .... 112 E. Church Street
   Mrs. Sallie Galloway Tourist Home .... 420 Butler Street

BEAUFORT
   DONALDSON'S FISHING .... Broad River
   Camp & Lodge .... School Rd.

CHARLESTON
   James Hotel .... 238 Spring Street
   Mrs. Gladsen Tourist Home .... 15 Nassau Street
   Mrs. Mayes Tourist Home .... 82½ Spring Street

CHERAW
   College Inn Restaurant .... 324 2nd Street
   Gate Grill .... Second Street
   Mrs. Maggie Green .... 209 Church Street
   Valerie Motor Inn .... 7 miles, south of Cheraw, S. C. on U. S. # 1
   Live Oak Tourist .... 328 Second Street

Electric Heat
Air Conditioned
Complete Private Bath

NEW ULTRA-MODERN

VALERIE MOTOR INN

7 miles south of Cheraw, S. C. on U. S. No. 1

| Family Rooms | Office & Eating |
| TV | Accommodations Adjoining |

COLUMBIA
   Beachum Tourist Home .... 212 Gervais Street
   College Inn Tourist Home .... 1609 Harden Street
   Cozy Inn Restaurant .... 1509 Harden Street
   Green Leaf Restaurant .... 1117 Wash. Street
   Mom's Restaurant .... 1005 Washington Street
   Mrs. H. Cornwell Tourist Home .... 1713 Wayne
   Mrs. Irene B. Evans Tourist Home .... 1106 Pine Street
   Mrs. J. P. Wakefield Tourist Home .... 816 Oak Street
   Mrs. S. H. Smith Tourist Home .... 929 Pine Street
   Mrs. W. D. Chappelle Tourist Home .... 1301 Pine Street
   Nylon Hotel .... 918 Senate Street
   Savoy Restaurant .... Old Winnsboro Street
   Waverly Restaurant .... 2515 Gervais Street
   Y.W.C.A. .... 230 Taylor Street

DARLINGTON
   Mable's Motel .... Box 309

FLORENCE
   Spring Valley Restaurant .... H'wa, 301

Travelers' Green Book 1963-64

SOUTH DAKOTA
Hotels — Motels — Tourist Homes — Restaurants

ABERDEEN
Alonzo Ward Hotel .... S. Main Street
Virginia Restaurant .... 303 S. Main Street

BROOKINGS
Modern Wayside Motel .... 1430 6th Street

CUSTER
Rocket Court .... 211 Custer Ave. (U. S. 16 & 85)

PHILLIP
A. B. C. Motel .... U. S. 212

SIOUX FALLS
Mrs. J. Moxley Tourist Home .... 915 N. Main

WATERTOWN
5th Ave. & 212 Motel .... U. S. 212

TENNESSEE
Hotels — Motels — Tourist Homes — Restaurants

BRISTOL
MOROCCO MOTEL & GRILL .... 1200 Moore Street
Clean, Comfortable, Courteous Service.
Welcome to travelers.
Mrs. M. C. Brown Tourist Home .... 225 McDowell
Mrs. A. D. Henderson Tourist Home .... 320 Nelson St.

CHATTANOOGA
Dallas Hotel .... 230½ E. 9th Street
Kat's Korner Restaurant .... 601 Lincoln
La Grand Eat Shop .... 206 East 9th Street
M-Y-B Package Store .... 320 East 9th Street
Martin's Esso Center .... 3701 Alton Park Blvd.
Millender's Pharmacy .... 1800 East 3rd Street
Peoples Hotel .... 1104 Carter Street
Reuben's Place .... 411 East 9th Street

---

48 Rooms   AM 6-9979

QUINN'S HOTEL
The most fabulous Hotel for colored.

227 West Main at Cowart St.,
Chattanooga, Tenn.

4 Blocks from Downtown
on Highway 58, 11, 64, South

Mrs. Ressie Harris, Owner

66

"JUST A STONE'S THROW FROM ROCK CITY AND LOOKOUT MOUNTAIN"

THE ROSETTA MOTELS, Inc.

"CHATTANOOGA'S AND THE SOUTH'S NEWEST AND FINEST"

AIR CONDITIONED • FREE TELEVISION

PRIVATE BATH   AMPLE PARKING

COFFEE SHOP

37th & WILLIAM STREETS
CHATTANOOGA, TENN.   AMherst 7-2068

JAMES B. McCLELLAN, JR., Mgr.

EARL "SQUARE" WASHINGTON, President

JAMES "FATS" McCLELLAND, Vice President

LA GRAND EAT SHOP

"Food Like Mother Used to Cook"

Annie R. Conley

206 E. 9th Street, Chattanooga, Tenn.

M. Y. B. PACKAGE STORE

320 East 9th Street   Chattanooga, Tenn.

Ruby's Drive-In	101 E. 46th Street
Y.M.C.A.	915 Park Street
Y.W.C.A.	924 E. 8th Street

CLARKSVILLE

Northington Tourist Home	717 Main Street
Virginia's Cafe	908 E. College Street

CLEVELAND

Kline Rest Home	680 E. Inman Street, East
Quality Cafe	795 Inman Street

COLUMBIA

Stop & Rest Motel & Restaurant	4 mi. South on Hiway 31

HUMBOLDT

Booker T. Motel	U. S. 79 & 70A

Phone 9-3-5449   Mr. & Mrs. Arthur D. Miller, Props.

MILLER'S MODERN MOTEL & RESORT
Comfort, Convenience and Courtesy
On the Highway U. S. 11-W — 7 Miles East of Knoxville

Route 5, Box 485   Knoxville, Tenn.

KNOXVILLE

Anderson's Tourist Home	501 E. Church Street
College Cafe	1518 University Ave., N.W.
Graves Drug Store	1901 Texas Avenue
Miller's Modern Motel & Resort	On Hiway 11-W, 7 mi. East of Knoxville
Rosebud Tavern & Restaurant	120 E. Vine Avenue
Streamline Snack Bar	125 E. Vine Street
The Pink House	1514 University Ave., N.W.
Tommy's Service Station	1304 Vine Ave., S.E.

68

Toussaint L'Ouverture Post No. 80, American Legion .... 112 Main Ave., S.E.
Y.M.C.A. Cansler Branch...716 E. Church Avenue
Y.W.C.A. ....2026 McCalla Avenue

MEMPHIS
Annie's Cafe ....155 Beale Street
Cain Bros. Gulf Service & Garage ....1252 Breedlove Street
Carnes Ave. Gulf Service Station & Garage........................2585 Carnes Avenue
Eosary Hotel ....181 Beale Avenue
Four Way Grill ....998 Mississippi Blvd.
Georgia's Cafe ....671 Mississippi Avenue
Handy House ....995½ Mississippi Blvd.
Hotel Queen Ann ....228 Vance Avenue
J. A. Ewing Service Station ....Mississippi & Alston Avenues
Jiffy Sundry ....2509 Park Ave.
Lorraine Motel & Hotel ....406 Mulberry Street
Marquette Hotel ....507 Linden Street
Mitchells Hotel ....160 Hernando Street
Mrs. Young's Tourist Home ....1191 Smith Street
Nu-Way Service Station & Garage ....855 Porter Street
Presley Gulf Station ....181 W. Brooks Road
Ragland's Mobilgas Service Station..282 Beale Street
Sue's Bakery & Snack Bar...2902 Bradley Street
The Ann's Grill ....186 E. Calhoun
The Cosmos Cafe ....3514 Boxtown Road
The Friendly Three Cafe ....416 Peoples Road
Travelers Hotel ....347 Vance Avenue
United Taxi ....240 Linden Avenue
Walker's Shell Service Station & Garage ....Bellevue at Vollintine
Ware's Super Market ....226 W. Brooks Road
Ware's Texaco Station ....337 W. Mitchell Road
Washburn's Mobilgas Service Station ....941 Mississippi Avenue
Wells Sundry & Cafe ....516 N. 3rd Street
White Star Cleaners ....225 S. 4th Street

MURFREESBORO
Benford's Amoco Service Station ....429 Maney Avenue
Moore's Tourist Home ....State & University Streets

NASHVILLE
Cozy Corner Restaurant & Tavern ....1137 Jefferson Street
Eldorado Mofel ....2806 Buchanan Street
Family Service Grocery ....1601 Jefferson
Jet Restaurant ....1815 Jefferson — 1510 Charlotte Ave.
Price's Dinner Club & Tavern ....3020 Centennial Blvd.
R & R Liquor Store ....1043 Jefferson
White's Lunch Room ....2116 Meharry Blvd.
Y.M.C.A. ....4th & Charlotte Avenues   Y.W.C.A. ....1708 Pearl Street
Driver's Shell Station..AL 5-9370

Phone: 242-9589   Spruell Driver, Prop.

DRIVER'S MOTEL
"Newest In Motel Designing"

3 Blocks W. of A. & I. State U. ....3910 Centennial Blvd.
1 Mile W. of Fisk U.   Nashville, Tenn.

TEXAS
Hotels — Motels — Tourist Homes — Restaurants

ABILENE
Mrs. Guy E. Rogers Tourist Home .... 550 No. 8th Street

AMARILLO
Tennessee Hotel .... 206 Van Buren Street
Tom's Place Restaurant .... 322 W. Third Street
Watley Hotel .... 112 Van Buren Street

ATLANTA
Mrs. Lizzie Simon Tourist Home .... 308 N. Howe Street

AUSTIN
Mrs. J. W. Duncan Tourist Home .... 1214 E. 7th Street
Porter's Tourist Home .... 1315 E. 12th Street
Southern Restaurant .... 1010 East 11th Street

BEAUMONT
Hotel Theresa .... 875 Neches Street
Long's Bar-B-Q .... 539 Forsythe Street
Mrs. B. Rivers Tourist Home .... 730 Forsythe Street

CORPUS CHRISTIE
Horace Crecy's Tourist Home .... 1710 Lexington Avenue
Avalon Restaurant .... 1510 Ramirez

DALLAS
Beaumont Barbeque Restaurant .... 1815 N. Field
Bogel Hotel .... 821 Bogel Street
Green Acres Motel .... 1711 McCoy Street
Howard Hotel .... 3118 San Jacinto Street
Powell Hotel .... 3115 State Street
Shalimar Restaurant .... 2219 Hall Street
Y.M.C.A. .... 2700 Flora Street
Y.W.C.A. .... 3525 State Street

DEL VALLE
Mayco Motel .... F. M. Rd. 973, Hwy. 71

EL PASO
C. Williams Tourist Home .... 1505 Wyoming Street
Daniel Hotel .... 413 S. Oregon Street
La Luz Motel .... 8064 Alameda (U. S. 80, East)
Mrs. S. W. Stull Tourist House .... 511 Tornillo

FORT WORTH
Clover Hotel .... 1901 East 4th Street
Evan's Tourist Home .... 1213 E. Terrell Street
Green Leaf Restaurant .... 315 E. 9th Street
Hotel Jim .... 413-15 E. Fifth Street
Monterey Hotel .... 1055 Evans Avenue
Y.M.C.A. .... 1604 Jones Street

GALVESTON
Gus Allen Hotel .... 2710 Ave. F
Little Shamrock Motel .... 1207 31st Street
Mrs. J. Pope Tourist Home .... 2824 M 1/2 Ave.
Oleander Hotel .... 421 1/2 25th Street

HENDERSON
Chat & Chew Restaurant .... 615 N. Mill Street

HOUSTON
- Ajapa Hotel .... 2412 Dowling Street
- Crystal Hotel .... 3308 Lyons Avenue
- Kirk Courts .... 2121 Kirk Street
- La Jayo Hotel .... 4024 Lyons Avenue
- Lincoln Restaurant .... Conti & Jenson
- Mingo Motel .... 4749 Reed Road
- New Day Hotel .... 1912 Dowling Street
- Oriental Restaurant .... 2751 Lyons Avenue
- Robinson's Manor .... 3211 Jackson Street
- Sid's Ranch .... 8051 W. Montgomery

LONGVIEW
- Eastman Road Motel .... Route 1, on Eastman Road

MARSHALL
- Adkins West End Texaco Service Station .... 310 N. Bishop
- Bailey Tourist Home .... 1103 W. Grand Avenue
- La Casa Motel .... U. S. 80, 2 miles from Marshall
- New Deal Ser. Station .... 618 S. Carter
- Tucker's Gulf Service Station .... 900 Wiley

MEXIA
- Mrs. M. Carroll Restaurant .... 109 N. Belknap Street

PORT ARTHUR
- Ritz Hotel .... 708 Texas Avenue
- Shadowland Restaurant .... 632 W. 7th Street
- Tick Tock Restaurant .... 536 W. 7th Street

SAN ANTONIO
- Mamie's Restaurant .... 1833 E. Houston Street
- Manhattan Hotel .... 735 E. Commerce
- Nolan Hotel .... 525 Nolan Street
- Ritz Motel .... 2958 Commerce Street
- Ross Hotel .... 126 N. Mesquite Street
- Silver Slipper Restaurant .... 506 S. Gevers

TEXARKANA
- Casino Restaurant .... 504 W. 3rd St.
- The Wheel Motel .... 2207 W. 18th St.
- Moore's Hotel .... 807 W. 4th St.

TYLER
- Franklin Service Station .... Palace at Morris
- Hotel Alfreda .... 1009 W. Morris Street
- Mrs. Thomas Tourist Home .... 516 N. Border Street
- North Palace Gulf Service Station .... 903 W. Lincoln
- The Downbeat Cafe .... 906 Barret
- W. Langston Tourist Home .... 1010 N. Border Street
- White Sandwich Shop .... 420 N. Border Street
- Wickware's Cities Service Station .... 628 N. Bois DArc

VAN HORN
- McVay Courts .... Hwys. 80 - 90 & 54, 120 mi E. of El Paso

VICTORIA
- Hotel Hayes .... 707 E. Stayton

WACO
- B. Ashford Tourist Home .... 902 N. 8th Street
- College View Motel .... East Elm Street

Ebony Motel ..... 4723 Sanger
Ideal Restaurant ..... 902 N. 8th Street
WAXAHACHIE
   Mrs. M. Johnson Tourist Home ..... 427 E. Main Street
   Mrs. N. Lowe Tourist Home ..... 418 E. Main Street
WICHITA FALLS
   Bridges Hotel ..... 404 Sullivan Street
   E. B. Jeffrey Tourist Home ..... 509 Juarez Street
   Johnson's Restaurant ..... 803 Harding Street
   Mrs. L. Winson Tourist Home ..... 607 Juarez Street
   Plaza Hotel ..... 423 Flood Street

UTAH
Hotels — Motels — Tourist Homes — Restaurants

BRYCE CANYON NATIONAL PARK
   Bryce Canyon Inn ..... Opens May 15th to Oct. 15th
   Bryce Canyon Lodge ..... Opens June 15th to Sept. 15th
CEDAR CITY
   Cedar Crest Lodge Motel ..... 555 So. Main Street
OGDEN
   Royal Hotel ..... 2522 Wall Avenue
PROVO
   El Rancho Provo ..... 1015 So. State
SALT LAKE CITY
   Harlem Hotel ..... 528½ West 2nd Street
   Jenkins Hotel ..... 250 W. South Temple
   Sam Sneed Hotel ..... 250 W. South Temple
   St. Louis Hotel ..... 242½ West South Temple
   Y.W.C.A. ..... 306 E. 3rd Street
ZION NATIONAL PARK
   Zion Lodge ..... Opens June 15th to Sept 15th
   Zion Inn ..... Opens May 15th to Oct. 15

VERMONT
Hotels — Motels — Tourist Homes — Restaurants

BURLINGTON
   The Pates Hotel ..... 86-90 Archiband Street
NORTHFIELD
   Cole's Tourist Home ..... 7 Sherman Avenue
RUTLAND
   Meade Cottage Tourist Home ..... 24 High Street

VIRGINIA
Hotels — Motels — Tourist Homes — Restaurants

AMHERST
   Sam & Sarah Hudson Tourist Home ..... Rte. 2, Box 256
   Southern Style Bar-B-Que ..... Norfolk Ave.
   For Reservation Call 946-8721
BUCKROE BEACH
   Bay Shore Hotel ..... Buckroe Beach
CHARLOTTESVILLE
   Carver Inn Hotel ..... 701 Preston Avenue
   Chauffeur's Rest Tourist Home ..... 129 Preston Avenue
   Alexander's Tourist Home ..... 413 Dyce Street

CHASE CITY
RED DOOR RESTAURANT ....8 East 5 Street
For the best flavor fo good food, give us a visit
THE GREEN DOOR RESTAURANT ....12 West 5th Street
Unsurpassed for quality food and courteous service!
CHESTER
Colbrook Inn ....Rt. 3, Box 207
CHRISTIANBURG
Eureka Hotel
COVINGTON
Mrs. Loretta S. Watson Tourist Home ....219 Lexington Street
DANVILLE
Mrs. M. K. Page Tourist Home ....434 Holbrook Street
Mrs. Mary L. Wilson Tourist Home ....401 Holbrook
Mrs. S. A. Overby Tourist Home ....Holbrok Street
Yancey's Tourist Home ....320 Holbrook Street
DISPUTANTA
Forest View Motel ....460 Norfolk Hwy.
DOSWELL
Hill Top Restaurant & Cabins ....Highway #1
EMPORIA
ATLANTIC ESSO STATION ....107 E. Atlantic Street
C. A. Harris, Prop. — Phone: ME 4-2077

Phone: ME 4-2594   Reasonable Rates

M. L. WEAVER
Tourist Home

Rest. Accommondations All Hours

115 Main Street   Emporia, Virginia

GLOUCESTER
Watkins Motel ....Gloucester
HAMPTON
Harriet's Drive-In ....130 W. Pembroke Ave.
Kellam's Motel ....185 Atlantic Ave.
JAMAICA
Oliver's Motel ....Highway 17 at Center Cross, Va.
LANEXA
R. & D. Motel ....Rte. 60
PHOEBUS-HAMPTON
The Rendezvous Cafe ....58 Fulton St.
LAWRENCEVILLE
CORNER INN ....409 N. Main Street
Beverly Taylor, Mgr.
LEXINGTON
Rose Inn ....331 No. Main Street
The Franklin Tourist Home ....9 Tucker Street
LURAY
Camp Lewis Mountain Tourist Home ....Skyline Drive
HOLLOWAY INN ....RFD 2
Special Attention to Families, Travelers, Hunters

Travelers' Green Book 1963–64

LYNCHBURG
- Happyland Lake Tourist Home .... 812 5th Avenue
- Mrs. C. Harper Tourist Home .... 1109 8th Avenue
- Mrs. N. P. Washington Tourist Home .... 611 Polk
- Phyllis Wheatley Y.W.C.A. .... 613 Monroe St.

NEW KENT
- Road Side Inn .... New Kent, Va.

NEWPORT NEWS
- Al Smith's Service Station .... 2701 Marshall Ave.
- Bob & Sam's Drive Inn .... 2811 Jefferson Ave.
- Cosmos Hotel .... 620 25th St.
- Grant's Restaurant .... 2108 Jefferson Ave.
- Huggins Bar-B-Que .... 631 25th St.
- Johnson's Room & Board .... 553 23rd St.
  Clean, Comfortable Rooms — Phone' CH 7-5656
- New York Barber Shop .... 2002 Jefferson Ave.
- Norman's Service Station .... Hampton — Jefferson Ave.
- Palm Tea Room .... 2146 Jefferson Ave.
- Plaza Drive Inn .... 13537 Warwick Boulevard

NORFOLK
- Foodarama .... 577 Church St.
- ★**PLAZA HOTEL** .... **1757 Church St.**
- Morning Glory Funeral Home .... 600 Chapel St.
- Russell's Restaurant & Grill .... 816 Church St.
- Regent Drive-In .... Shell Rd. & Delaware Ave.

PETERSBURG
- Atlantic Cafe .... 103 Halifax St.
- Colbrook Motel .... U. S. Rte. 1 & 301

PHOEBUS
- Horton's Hotel .... County & Mellon Streets
- Horton's Restaurant .... County & Mellon Streets

PORTSMOUTH
- Benjamin's Confectionery & Dining Room .... 223 S. Green St.
- Beuie's Esso Service Station .... 1701 Effingham St.
- Blue Haven Hotel .... 401 S. Green St.
- Combo Terrace .... On Hiway #13 and 460
- Sportsman's Restaurant & Motel .... On Rte. 2 nr. Portsmouth
- Fagan's Seaford Restaurant .... Cor. Gosport Rd. & Pine St.
- Holmes Bros. Sinclair Service Station .... 3415 Gosport Rd.
- Jimmie's Flying A Service Station .... 1201 Langley Blvd.
- Kelly's Restaurant & Motel .... 801 County St.
- Marshall's Cities Service Station .... 1808 Gosport Rd.
- Ransdell's Motel .... 630 London St.

RICHMOND
- Eggleston Hotel .... 2nd & Leigh
- Harris Hotel .... 200 E. Clay Street
- Slaughter Hotel .... 529 N. 2nd Street
- Y.WC.A. .... Orange Avenue
- Perry's Restaurant .... 519 N. 2nd St.
- Skinney's Bar-B-Que .... Fairmount Ave. at 25th St.
- Otto's Inn .... 314 No. 2nd St.

ROANOKE
- Colvin's Tourist Home .... 16 Kilmer Avenue, N. W.

74

PAGE 282

Dumas Hotel	Henry Street, N. W.
Y.W.C.	416 Gainbore Rd., N. W.
Colvin's Tourist Home	16 Gilmer Avenue, N. W.
Brooks Pharmacy	221 N. Henry Street

SOUTH HILL
Brown's New Cafe	105 E. Virginia St.

STAUNTON
Pannell's In, Tourist Home	613 N. Augusta Street

STORMONT
Midway Auto Repair	Urbanna Road
G. L. Davis Service Station	Cook's Corner

SUFFOLK
E & L Lassiter Pur Oil Station	802 E. Washington St.
Nansemond Co-Op Servicenter	133 Tyne sStreet
Suffolk Professional Pharmacy, Inc.	362 E. Washington St.

TAPPAHANNOCK
Mark Haven Beach Hotel	Tel.: Hillcrest 3-3871
McGuire's Inn Hotel	Marsh Street

WEST POINT
Jordan's Enterprises	14th & Kirby Streets
Morton's Restaurant	221 15th Street

WILLIAMSBURG
Grove's Esso Service Center	Route 2 - Box 228

WINCHESTER
Ruth's Restaurant	128 E. Cecil Street

WASHINGTON
Hotels — Motels — Tourist Homes — Restaurants

BELLINGHAM
Bell's Auto Court	208 Samish Highway
Leopold Hotel	1224 Cornwall Ave.

BREMERTON
Enetai Hotel	318 Washington Ave.

GRAND COULEE
Continental Hotel

OLYMPIA
Hotel Olympian

RANIER NATIONAL PARK
Paradise Inn
Paradise Lodge

SEATTLE
Atlas Hotel	420 Maynard Street
Eagle Hotel	408½ Main Street
Benjamin Franklin	5th Ave. & Virginia
Commodore Hotel	2013 2nd Ave.
Doric Mayflower	4th & Olive Way
Doric New Washington	2nd & Stewart St.
Edmond Meany Tourist Home	45th & Brooklyn East
Green Hotel	711 Lane Street
Mar Hotel	511 Maynard Avenue
New Richmond Hotel	308 4th Avenue
Olympus Hotel	413 Maynard Street
Welcome Annex Hotel	613½ Jackson Avenue

TACOMA
   Dittemore's Court .... 12701 Pacific Highway
   Monte Carlo Hotel .... 1555 Tacoma Avenue
   Travelers Restaurant .... 1506½ Pacific Avenue
   Winthrop Western Hotel .... 9th and Broadway

VANCOUVER
   Ricketon's New Motel .... 4010 Main Street

YAKIMA
   Senator Hotel

WEST VIRGINIA
Hotels — Motels — Tourist Homes — Restaurants

BECKLEY
   New Pioneer Hotel .... 340 S. Fayette Street

BLUEFIELD
   Travelers' Inn Hotel .... 1039 Wayne Street

CHARLESTON
   Ferguson's Hotel .... Washington Street
   Penn's Hotel .... West Charleston

CLARKESBURG
   Mrs. Ruby Thomas Lodgings .... 126 Maud St.

FRANKLIN
   Hotel Franklin .... 129½ Main Street

GRAFTON
   Jones' Restaurant .... Latrobe Street

HINTON
   Maya's Guest House .... State Street
   The Price House Hotel .... 109 2nd Avenue

HUNTINGTON
   Mrs. C. J. Barnett Lodgings .... 810 7th Avenue
   Spot Restaurant .... 1614 8th Avenue
   The Ross House Hotel .... 911 8th Avenue

MONTGOMERY
   New Royal Hotel .... 223 Gaines Street

MORGANTOWN
   Mrs. Jeannette O. Parker Lodgings .... 2 Cayton
   Mrs. Linnie Mae Slaughter Lodgings .... 3 Cayton

MOUNDSXILLE
   Mrs. Blanche Campbell Lodgings .... 1206 4th Street

NORTHFORK
   Houchins Hotel & Cafe

WELCH
   Capehart Hotel .... 14 Virginia Avenue

WHITE SULPHUR SPRINGS
   Slaughter's Tourist Home

WISCONSIN
Hotels — Motels — Tourist Homes — Restaurants

ASHLAND
   Stone's Motel .... RFD #3

BELOIT
   Beloit Hotel
   Hobson Motel .... 102-110 Park Avenue

76

ELM GROVE
  Sleepy Hollow Motel ....12600 W. Blue Mound Rd.
GREEN BAY
  Beaumont Hotel ....Box 643
LA CROSSE
  Linker Hotel
  Nuttleman's Lodge Motel ....Hwy. 16
MILWAUKEE
  Ambassador Motel Hotel ....2308 W. Wisconsin Ave.
  Astor ....924 E. Juneau Ave.
  Milwaukee Inn ....E. State St. & Lake
  Schroeder ....509 W. Wisconsin Ave.
  Shorecrest ....1962 N. Prospect Ave.
  Carl's Restaurant ....628 W. Juneau Avenue
  Chicken Shack Restaurant ....537 W. Walnut Street
  Hillcrest Hotel ....504 W. Galena Street
  Mrs. M. Burns, Rooming House ....1241 N. 6th Street
  Pastell Lampkins Roming House ....2427 N. 14th Street
  Y.W.C.A. ....915 W. Wisconsin Avenue
OSHKOSH
  Hotel Raulf ....530 N. Main St.
RACINE
  Hotel Racine ....535 Main St.
SUPERIOR
  Hotel Saratoga
WISCONSIN DELLS
  Lazy "M" Dude Ranch ....Route 2, River Road

WYOMING
Hotels — Motels — Tourist Homes — Restaurants
CASPER
  Blue Spruce Motel ....1914 Yellowstone, East
CHEYENNE
  ★MINNEHAHA MOTEL ....1905 E. Lincolnway
ROCK SPRINGS
  Collins Tourist Home ....915 7th Avenue
  Liberty Motel ....U. S. 30
YELLOWSTONE NATIONAL PARK
  Grand Canyon
  Mammoth Hot Springs Hotel
  Old Faithful Inn

BERMUDA
HAMILTON
  Blue Jay Restaurant ....Church Street
  Imperial Hotel ....Church Street
  Ripleigh Guest House ....Mrs. Doris Pearman
  The Spot Restaurant ....Burnaby Street
PEMBROKE
  Milestone Guest House ....Coxs Hill
  Richmond House Hotel ....Richmond Road

ST. GEORGE'S
"Archlyn Villa," Guest House..Wellington Street
St. George's Hotel
TUCKER'S TOWN
Castle Harbor Hotel
WARRICK
Hilton Manor Guest House..Mrs. W. Tucker, Prop.
Homeleigh Guest House..Mrs. D. Eave, Prop.
Mrs. Leon Eve Guest House..Snake Road
W. PEMBROKE
Sunset Lodge Guest House..P. O. Box 413

CONVENTION AND CONFERENCE CALENDAR

May   3- 5 National Epicureans, Inc., Washington, D. C. (Presidential Arms)
May 17-19 The Moles, Inc., Washington, D. C.
May 24-25 Girl Friends, Inc., Chicago, Ill.
May 29-31 National Alliance of Postal Employees, Miami, Fla. (Hampton House)
May 18   National Council of Negro Women, Inc., Washington, D. C. (Commem-
           ration meeting)
June 7- 9 Chi Delta Mu Fraternity, Washington, D. C. (Statler-Hilton)
June 25-28 National Association of Ministers' Wives, Atlanta, Ga.
           oration Meeting
June 25-30 Chi Eta Phi Sorority, Inc., Durham, N. C.
July 1- 7 National Association For the Advancement of Colored People, Chicago,
           Ill. (Morrison Hotel)
July 15-21 Bible Way Church of Our Lord Jesus Christ World Wide, Inc., Washing-
           ton, D. C.
July 16-20 Zeta Phi Beta Sorority, Inc., Miami, Fla. (Miami Municipal Auditorium)
July 16-21 National Assn. of Fashion And Accessory Designers, Inc. Chicago, Ill.
           (Sheraton)
July 22-26 National United Church Ushers Assn. of America, Inc. Baltimore, Md.
July 25-27 Lambda Kappa Mu Sorority, Inc., Syracuse, N. Y.
July 28-Aug. 1 National Urban League, Los Angeles, Calif. (Statler-Hilton)
July 31-Aug 3 American Teachers Assn., Dallas, Tex.
Aug. 3- 9 Woman's Home & Foreign Missionary Society, AME Zion Church, St.
           Louis Mo. (Washington Metropolitan AMEZ Ch.)
Aug. 4- 8 National Beauty Culturists League, Inc., Chicago, Ill.
Aug. 4- 9 National Dental Assn., Inc., Philadelphia, Pa. (Sheraton)
Aug. 5- 9 National Convention of Gospel Choirs & Chouses, Inc. Pittsburgh, Pa.
Aug. 6-11 National Sorority of Phi Delta Kappa, Los Angeles, Calif.
Aug. 10-16 Iota Phi Lambda Sorority, Inc., Youngstown, Ohio
Aug. 11-15 National Funeral Directors & Morticians Assn., Columbus, O.
           (Deshler-Hilton)
Aug. 13-18 Tau Gamma Delta Sorority, New York, N. Y. (Waldorf Astoria)
Aug. 12-15 National Medical Assn., Los Angeles, Calif. (Statler Hilton)
Aug. 12-15 Women's Auxiliary to the National Medical Assn., Los Angeles, Calif.
Aug. 12-17 Sigma Gamma Rho Sorority, Inc., Denver, Colo. (Brown Palace)
Aug. 14-18 National Assn. of College Women, Chicago, Ill. (Morrison)
Aug. 16-22 Alpha Phi Alpha Fraternity, Inc., Boston, Mass. (Statler Hilton)
Aug. 17-24 National Supreme Council Ancient & Accepted Scottish Rite Masons,
           Miami, Fla. (Hampton House)
Aug. 17-24 National Grand Chapter Order of Eastern Star, Miami, Fla.

Aug. 18-21 Supreme Lodge Knights of Pythias, Hot Springs, Ark. (Pythian Hotel)
Aug. 18-23 Ancient Egyptian Arabic Order Nobles of the Mystic Shrine, Pittsburgh, Pa. (Penn-Sheraton)
Aug. 18-23 Imperial Court-Daughters of Isis, Pittsburgh, Pa. (Penn-Sheraton)
Aug. 18-23 National Assn. of Negro Musicians, Columbus, Ohio
Aug. 19-23 National Insurance Assn., Chicago, Ill. (Sheraton-Chicago)
Aug. 20-23 Frontiers International, Inc., Chicago, Ill. (Sheraton)
Aug. 25-29 National Assn. of Real Estate Brokers, Inc., Chicago, Ill. (Sherman House)
Aug. 26-30 Improved Benevolent Protective Order of Elks of the World, Boston, Mass.
Aug. 26-30 Grand Temple Daughters of I.B.P.O.E. of W. Boston, Mass
Aug. 28-Sept. 2 National Technical Assn., Chicago, Ill.
Sept. 3- 8 National Baptist Convention, U.S.A., Inc., Cleveland, Ohio
Oct. 13-16 National Hotel Assn., Inc., New Orleans, La. (Mason's Motel)
Dec. 26-30 Phi Beta Sigma Fraternity, Inc., Nashville, Tenn. (Tenn. A & I State U.)
Excerpts from "When They Meet" compiled by Joseph V. Baker Associates, Inc. for Hamliton Watch Company.

CANADA
Hotels — Motels — Tourist Homes — Restaurants
ONTARIO

BRANTFORD
 Graham Bell Hotel...48 Dalhousie St.
CORNWALL
 Lloyd George Hotel ....15 Pitt St.
FT. WILLIAM
 Adanae Hotel ....227 Simpson St.
HAMILTON
 Crestwood Hotel
  4 miles east on #2 Hwy.
 Fischer Hotel ....51 York St.
 Sheraton-Connaught Hotel
  & Motor Inn............112 King St., E.
 Wentworth Arms Motor Hotel
  Main & Hughson St.
LONDON
 London Hotel
  Dundas & Wellington St.
NIAGARA FALLS
 Foxhead Motor Inn
  Falls Ave. & Clifton Hill
 Park Hotel ....Clifton Hill
 Sheraton-Breck Hotel
  1685 Falls Ave.
OTTAWA
 Bytown Inn ....73 O'Connor St.
 Chateau Laurier
  Rideau St. (Hwy 17)
 Lord Elgin ....Elgin & Laurier Ave.
 Rock Haven Motel
  597 Montreal Rd.

PORT ARTHUR
 Port Arthur Motor Hotel
  N. Cumberland St.
SAULT STE. MARIE
 Sault Windsor Hotel
  617 Queen St., E.
TORONTO
 Anndore Hotel ......15 Charles St., .E
 Constellation Hotel
  Dixon Rd. & Renforth Dr.
 Four Seasons Motor Hotel
  Jarvis & Carlton St.
 Frontenac Arms ....306 Jarvis St.
 Glenview Terraces Hotel
  2904 Yonge St.
 King Edward Sheraton
  37 King St., E.
 Lido Motel..........West Hill P. O.
 Lord Simcoe
  University Ave. & King St.
 Park Plaza ......Bloor St. & Avenue Rd.
 Regency Towers ....89 Avenue Rd.
 Royal York ....Front St.
 Skyline Hotel ....655 Dixon Rd.
WINDSOR
 Bali-Hi Motor Hotel
  1280 Ouellette Ave.
 Norton Palmer ....130 Park St., W.

Travelers' Green Book 1963-64

MONTREAL
Berkeley Hotel
　　　　1188 Sherbrooke St., W.
Capri ....6445 Decarie Blvd.
Cartier Motel
　　　　14070 Sherbrooke St., E.
De La Salle ....1240 Drummond St.
Laurentien Hotel ...1130 Windsor St.
New Carlton ....915 Windsor St.
Queen Elizabeth
　　　　900 Dorchester St., W.
Queen's Hotel ....700 Windsor St.
Ritz Carlton ....Sherbrooke St., W.
Sheraton-Mt. Royal........1455 Peel St.
Skyline Hotel
　　　　6050 Cote de Liesse Rd.

QUEBEC
Chateau Frontenac ......Place d'Armes
Chateau Laurier .....695 Grand Allee
Manoir St. Castin
　　　　P. O. Lae Beauport, Que.

MOOSE JAW
Harwood Hotel .....30 Fairford St., E.

REGINA
King's Hotel ....1746 Searth St.
Saskatchewan Hotel
　　　　Victoria Ave. (Hwy 1)

SASKATEEN
Albany Hotel ....20th St. & Ave. B
Bessborough
　　　　Spadina Crescent & 21st
King George ......157 Second Ave., N.
Senator ....243 - 21st St., E.

MEXICO

ACAPULCO
Acapulco Hilton
　　　　Avenida Miguel Aleman
Boca Chica ....Playa Caletilla
Caleta ......P.O. Box 76, Caleta Beach
Club De Pesea
　　　　Costera Miguel Aleman 60
Del Monte
　　Cerro de la Pinzina (P.O. Box 55)
El Morador ....La Quebrada
El Presidente
　　　　Avenida Miguel Aleman
Las Brisas Hilton ....Escenica Hwy.

CUERNAVACA
Motor Hotel Mandel
　　　　Blvd. & Zapata 801 (Hwy 95)

GUADALAJARA
California Courts ...Av. Vallarta 2525
Camino Real
　　　　Calz. del Nino & Vallarta
Turiservicios, S. A..........Vallarta 2785

GUAYMAS
Playa de Cortes ....Bahia de
　　　　Bacochibampo (P.O. Box 66)

JUAREZ
Hotel Continental.................Lerdo 178
Hotel San Antonio
　　　　Av. 16 de Septiembre 634
Hotel Sylvias
　　　　Av. 16 de Septiembre 1587
Tourist Camp—Jardin Fronterizo
　　　　American H'way #7
Hotel Moran.............Av. Juarez 238

MEXICAN GOVT. TOURIST BD.

80

MAZATLAN
    Playa Mazatlan ....P. O. Box 207
MERIDA
    Panamericana ....59th St., No. 455
MEXICO CITY
    Alameda ....Ave. Juarez 50
    Ambassador ....Humboldt No. 38
    Continental Hilton
            Paseo de la Reforma 166
    Cortes ....Ave. Hidalgo 85
    Del Prado Hotel ....Av. Juarez 70
    El Presidente ....Hamburgo 135
    Francis
            Paseo de la Reforma & Morelos
    Geneve ....130 Londres St.
    Guardiola ....Madero 5
    Luma ....Orizaba 16
    Majestic ....Madero No. 73
    Meurice ....Calle Marsella 28
    Monte Cassino ....Genova 56

Prado-Aiffer ....Revillagijedo 18
Ritz ....Madero 30
MONTERREY
    Ambassador
            Hidalgo & Galeana St.
    Anfa Super Motel
            Hwy 85 N., Kilometer 995
    Gran Hotel Aneira ......Plaza Hidalgo
MORELIA
    Virrey de Mendoza
            Portal Matameros 16
PATZCUARE
    Posada De Don Vasco
            Av. Americas Unidas
TAXCO
    Loma Linda Motel
            Hwy 95 at Kilometer 161
    Posada De La Mision
            Calle de la Mision 32

THE CARIBBEAN
Hotels — Motels — Tourist Homes — Restaurants

BARBADOS TOURIST BD.

ANTIGUA
    Admirals Inn ....English Harbour
    Anchorage ....Dickenson Bay
    Antigua Beach ....Hodges Bay
    Antigua Horizons ....Long Bay
    Balgowne Guest House ......St. John's
    Barrymore ....Fort Rd.
    Beachcomber ....Coolidge
    Blue Waters ....Soldier Bay
    Caribbean Beach Club
            Dickejsen Bay
    Curtain Bluff ....Old Road
    Galley Bay Surf Club ......Galley Bay
    Half Moon Bay ....Half Moon Bay
    Hawksbill ....Five Islands

Jolly Beach ....Jolly Hill Bay
Kensington House ....St. John's
Long Bay ....Long Bay
Lord Nelson Club ....Coolidge
Stephendale ....St. John's
Sugar Mill ....Coolidge
The Inn ....English Harbour
Trade Winds ....Dickenson Bay
White Sands ....Hodges Bay
ARUBA
    Aruba Caribbean Hotel ....Casino
BARBADOS
    Abbeville ....Christ Church
    Accra Beach ....Christ Church

81

Travelers' Green Book 1963–64

BARBADOS TOURIST BD.

Aquatic Club	St. Michael
Bagshot House	Christ Church
Blue Water	Christ Church
Bonnie Dundee	Christ Church
Bowden	Christ Church
Cacrabank	Christ Church
Caribbee	Christ Church
Colony Club	St. James
Coral Reef	St. James
Crane	St. Philip
Eastry House	St. Peter
Edgewater	St. Joseph
Island Inn	St. Michael
Marine	Christ Church
Miramar	St. James
Ocean View	Christ Church
Paradise Beach Club	St. Michael
Powell Spring	St. Joseph
Rockley Beach	Christ Church
Royal Caribbean	Christ Church
Royal-On-Sea	Christ Church
St. Lawrence	Christ Church
Sam Lord's	St. Philip
Sandy Beach	Christ Church
Sandy Lane	St. James
San Remo	Christ Church
Sea View	Christ Church
Shoe String	Christ Church
Stonehaven Inn	St. Philip
South Winds	Christ Church
Sunset Lodge	St. Peter
Swiss Chalet	St. James
White Sands	Christ Church

BRITISH GUIANA

Park	Georgetown
Tower	Georgetown
Woodbine	Georgetown

BRITISH HONDURAS

Bellevue	Belize
Fort George	Belize

DOMINICA

Cherry Lodge	Roseau
Clarke Hall	Layou
South Chiltern	St. Paul
Springfield	Imperial Rd.
Sutton	Roseau

GRAND CAYMAN

Bay View	Georgetown
Beach Club Colony	West Bay Beach
Buccaneer's Inn	Cayman Brac
Coral Caymanian	Georgetown
Emerald Beach Apts.	South Sound
Galleon Beach	Georgetown
Pageant Beach	Georgetown
Rum Point	Rum Point
Sea View	Georgetown
Sunset House	Georgetown

GRENADA

Antilles	St. George's
Crescent Inn	Belmont-Grand Anse
Elite Guest House	St. George'
Green Gables	St. George'
Grenada Beach	Grand Anse
St. James	St. George'
Silver Sands	Grand Anse
Spice Island	Grand Anse
The Islander	St. George'

GUADELOUPE

Au Grand Corsaire	Gosie

82

Dole-Les-Bains ....Gourbeyre
Grand ....Pointe-A-Pitre
Normandie ....Pointe-A-Pitre
Royal ....Basse-Terre
Vielle Tour ....Gosier

JAMAICA (Kingston Area)
Abahati ....Kingston
Abbey Court ....Kingston
Blue Mt. Inn ....Gordon Town
Courtleigh Manor ....Kingston
Flamingo ....Kingston
Green Gables ....Kingston
Kingsley ....Kingston
Liguanea Terrace ....Kingston
Manor House ....Kingston
Melrose ....Kingston
Mimosa ....Kingston
Mona ....Kingston
Morgan's Harbour ....Pt. Royal
Myrtle Bank ....Kingston
Sheraton Kingston ....Kingston
South Camp ....Kingston
Stony Hill ....Kingston
Strawberry Hill ....Irish Town
Terra Nova ....Kingston

(Mandeville Area)
Mandeville ....Mandeville
Mayflower ....Mandeville

(Montego Area)
Bay Roc ....Montego Bay
Beach View ....Montego Bay
Black Swan ....Montego Bay
Blairgowrie ....Montego Bay
Casa Blanca ....Montego Bay
Casa Montego ....Montego Bay
Chatham ....Montego Bay
Colony ....Montego Bay
Coral Cliff ....Montego Bay
Corniche Studio Apts. Montego Bay
Gloucester House ....Montego Bay
Good Hope Plantation ......Falmouth
Hacton House ....Montego Bay
Half Moon ....Montego Bay
Harmony House ....Montego Bay
Miranda Lodge ....Montego Bay
Montego Beach ....Montego Bay

Montego Inn ....Montego Bay
Montego Bay Racket Club
....Montego Bay
Richmond Hill ....Montego Bay
Round Hill ....Montego Bay
Royal Caribbean ....Montego Bay
Silver Sands ....Duncans
Sunset Lodge ....Montego Bay
Tropical Terrace..................Montego Bay
Tryall ....Sandy Bay

(Ocho Rios & North Shore)
Arawak ....Ocho Rios
Carib-Ocho ....Ocho Rios
Casa Maria ....Port Maria
Eaton Hill ....Runaway Bay
Falcondip ....Ocho Rios
Golden Head Beach ......Oracabessa
Hibiscus Lodge ....Ocho Rios
Jamaica Inn ....Ocho Rios
Marrakesh Beach ....Ocho Rios
Plantation Inn ....Ocho Rios
Runaway Bay Hotel ......Runaway Bay
Sans Souci ....Ocho Rios
Shaw Park Beach Club ......Ocho Rios
Silver Seas ....Ocho Rios
Tower Isle ....Ocho Rios
Windsor ....St. Ann's Bay

(Port Antonio)
Domontevin Lodge ....Port Antonio

MARTINIQUE
Atlantique ....Lorrain
Auberge de L'Anse Mitan
....Treis-liest
Auberge du Manoir
....Route de Moutte
Auberge du Vieux Chalet
....Morne-Rouge
Berkeley ....Fort-de-France
Bristol ....Fort-de-France
Gallia
Hotel Central et Europe
Hotel de France ....Mormo-Rouge
Imperatrice ....Fort-de-France
La Dunette ....Sainte-Anne
Les Pitons ....Balata
Lido ....Fort-de-France

PUERTO RICO

AGUADILLA
   Montemar Hotel
ARECIBO
   Mir Hotel

BARRANQUITAS
   El Barranquitas Hotel
DORADO
   Dorado Beach Hotel

Travelers' Green Book 1963–64

PONCE
  El Ponce Intercontinental
SAN JUAN
  Americana of San Juan
            P. O. Box 5628, Isla Verde
  Atlantic Beach
            Vendig St. (Santurce)
  Bird El Hato Rey
            452 Ponce de Leon Ave.
  Caribe Hilton
  Condado Beach .... Box 3552
  Condado Lagoon
            Jeffre & Clemenceau St.
  El Miramar Charterhouse
            Av. Olimpio 60
  El San Juan .... P. O. Box 389
  Escambron
  International Airport
            Airport Terminal Bldg.
  Sheraton-San Juan
  Normandie
  Pierre

ST. KITTS
  Blakeney .... Bassəterro
  Palms .... Bassəterro
  Royal
  Seaside
  The Cockleshells .... Salt Pond
ST. LUCIA
  Blue Waters Beach .... Castries
  James
  St. Antoine
  St. Lucia Beach .... Gres Islet
  Villa .... Castries
ST. VINCENT
  Blue Caribbean .... Kingstown
  Blue Lagoon .... Rathe Mill
  Hadden .... Kingstown
  Heron
  Olive's
  Sugar Mill Inn .... Rathe Mill
  Sunny Caribbee .... Bequia
  Villa Lodge .... Villa

VIRGIN ISLANDS

ST. CROIX
  Buccaneer Hotel
  Club Comanche
  Cottages By the Sea
  The Cruzana
  Estate Belvedere
  Estate Good Hope
  Grapetree Bay Hotel
  Hotel-On The Cay
  King Christian Hotel
  Mahogany Inn
  Pink Fancy Apts.
  Sprat Hall
  St. Croix Beach Hotel
  Sunset Cottages
  Turquoise Bay Cottages
  Village At Cane Bay
  The Waves
ST. JOHN
  Caneel Bay Plantation
  Gallows Point
ST. THOMAS
  Adams Guest House
  Bluebeard's Castle
  Bluebeard's Beach Club
  Caribbean Beach Hotel
  Cromwell House
  Domini Hus
  Dorothea Beach Club
  Enchanted Hill Guest House

  Estate Contant
  Flamboyant Hotel
  Gramboko Inn
  Harbor View
  Holiday House
  Holland House
  Island Beachcomber
  Kriss Guest House
  La Borde's Guest House
  Mafloie Apartment Hotel
  Midtown Guest House
  Miller Manor
  Morning Star Beach Resort
  Mountain Top
  Nibbs-Ville
  Sapphire Bay Beach Club
  Sea Horse Inn
  Smith's Fancy
  Surfside
  The Gate
  Trade Winds Hotel
  Tropic Isle Hotel
  Vialet's Villa Guest House
  Villa Santana
  Virgin Island Hilton
  Water Isle Hotel & Beach Club
  Yacht Haven Cottage Resort
TOBAGO
  Arnes Vale .... Plymouth
  Bacolet .... Scarborough

84

Bird of Paradise	Speyside
Bluehaven	Scarborough
Castle Cove	Scarborough
Crown Point	Crown Point
Della Mira	Scarborough
Robinson Crusoe	Scarborough

TRINIDAD

Bel Air	Piarco
Bergerac	Port of Spain
Bretton Hall	
Normandie	
Pelican Inn	
Piarco Guest House	Piarco
Queen's Park	Port of Spain
Simpson's Shoreland	Point Cumana
Trinidad Hilton	Port of Spain
Tropical	Maraval

COSTA RICA
SAN JOSE
Europa Hotel
    Central St. at 5th Ave.

SAN SALVADOR
El Salvador Intercontinental

GUATAMALA
GUATAMALA CITY
Guatamala-Biltmore
    La Reforma y 15 Calle
Maya Excelsior ......7a Ave. No. 12-46

HONDURAS
TEGUEIGALPA, D. C.
Gran Hotel Lincoln

NICARAGUA
MANAGUA
Gran Hotel ....Av. Central N. 41

PANAMA
PANAMA CITY
Siesta Hotel ....nr. Locumen Airport
Panama Hilton ....via Estana
Hotel Continental ....via Estana
Hotel Internacional,
    Plaza Cinco de Mayo

SOUTH AMERICA
ARGENTINA
BUENOS AIRES
City Hotel ....Bolivar 160
Claridge ....Tucuman 535
Continental
    Av. Reque Saenz Pena 725
Plaza Hotel ....Florida y Charcas

BRAZIL
BRASILIA
Nacional-Brasilia ......Seter Hoteleiro
CAMPINAS
Terminus
    Avenida Francisco Glicerio 1075
RECIFE
Grande
    Avenida Martins de Barros, 593
Guararapes ....Rua da Palma s/n
RIO DE JANEIRO
Excelsior Copacabana
    Avenida Atlantica 1800
Ouro Verde
    Avenida Atlantica, 1456 Copabana

BARBADOS TOURIST BD.

PANAMA TOURIST BD.

Travelers' Green Book 1963–64

SALVADOR
  Plaza de Salvador
    Avenida Sete de Setembro, 212
SAO PAULO
  Excelsior Hotel ....Ov. Ipiranga 770
  Iaragua ....Rua Major Quedinho 40

CHILE
SANTIAGO
  Carrera Hilton Hotel
    Teatinos No. 180

COLOMBIA
BARRANQUILLA
  Central Hotel ......Calle 38 #41-122
BOGOTA
  Tequendama Hotel
    Carrera 10, #26-21

PERU
LIMA
  Gran Hotel Bolivar
    Plaza San Martin
  Savoy ....Caylloma 224

URUGUAY
MONTEVIDEO
  Victoria Plaza
    Plaza de la Independencia 759

VENEZUELA
CARACAS
  Avila
  El Conde
  Macuto-Sheraton

EUROPE

AUSTRIA
  Altausee ....House Eibl
  Badgastein ....Mozart
  Graz ....Hotel Daniel
  Heiligenblut ....Alpenhotel Kaiser
  Innsbruck ....Hotel Tyrol, Hotel Kreid
  Obergurgl ....Hotel Haus Burger
  Portschach ....Hotel Minerva
  Salzburg ....Pension Eibl
  Seeboden am Millstattersee ....Royal Hotel Seehof
  Vienna ....Hotel Bristol, Hotel de France

BELGIUM
  Antwerp ....Grand Hotel Londres, Queen's Hotel, Metropole Hotel
  Bastogne ....Hotel Lebrun
  Blankenberge ....Hotel Petit Rouge, Hotel Ideal
  Bouillon ....Hotel De La Post, Hotel Du Panorama
  Bruges ....Hotel Memlinc
  Brussels ....Hotel Mayfair, Hotel Plaza, Hotel des Colonies
  Charleroi ....Grand Hotel Siebertz
  De Haan (Le Coq) ....Hotel Astoria
  Ghent ....Hotel Cour St-Georges
  Rochefort ....Grand Hotel du Centre
  Spa ....Grand Hotel Britannique

DENMARK
  Aalborg ....Hotel Phoenix
  Copenhagen ....Hotel d'Angleterre, Grand Hotel, Hotel Excelsior
  Fredensborg ....Hotel Frederik IV
  Fredrikshavn ....Hoffmanns Hotel
  Helsingor ....Hotel Marienlyst
  Snekkersten ....Hotel Kystens Perle
  Mon ....Hotel Store Klint

EIRE
  Bantry ....Ballylickey House

86

Bray	Glencormac House
Carrick-On-Shannon	Bush
Dublin	Gresham Hotel, Jury's, Moira
Galway	Warwick
Lisdoonvarna	Imperial, Hydro
Oughterard	Corrib Hotel
Salthill	Golf Links Hotel
Sutton	Marine Hotel

FRANCE

Aix-Les-Bains	Hotel Splendide-Royal and Excelsior, Hotel Astoria
Andorre La Vieille	Hotel Meritxell
Annecy	Imperial Palace, Hotel Beau-Rivage
Antibes	Grand Hotel Du Cap d'Antibes
Avignon	Hotel D'Europe
Bagnoles-de-L'Orne	Lutetia-Reine Astrid
Barbotan	Grand Hotel des Thermes
Biarritz	Hotel Miramar, Hotel Regina Et Du Golf
Bordeaux	Splendid-Hotel
Boulogne	Hotel Marmin
Cannes	Hotel Carlton, Hotel Gray d'Albion, Hotel Splendid
Chamonix	Savoy Hotel
Deauville	Royal, Normandy
Dijon	De la Cloche
Fontainebleau	Aigle Noir
Juan-Les-Pins	Hotel Provencal
Lourdes	Grand Hotel De La Grotte
Lyon	Carlton Hotel
Marseille	Hotel Beauvau, Select Hotel
Monte Carlo	Hotel de Paris, New Beach Hotel
Nancy	Grand Hotel
Nantes	Duchesse Anne
Nice	Hotel Negresco, Hotel Royal, Hotel Westminster
Paris	Hotel Continental, Hotel George-V, Hotel Meurice, Hotel California, Hotel Elysee-Park, Hotel Vendome
Reims	Lion D'or
St. Jean Cap Ferrat	Grand Hotel Du Cap Ferrat
St. Raphael	Hotel Continental
Soissons	Hotel Du Lion Rouge
Strasbourg	Hotel Terminus Gruber
Touquet	Westminster Hotel
Versailles	Hotel Trianon-Palace
Vichy	Thermal Palace, Elysee Palace Hotel

GERMANY

Aachen	Kurhotel Quellenhof
Augsburg	Parkhotel Wiesses Lamm
Baden-Baden	Hotel Bellevue
Bad Durkheim	Kurparkhotel
Bad Harzburg	Bodes Hotel, Harzburger Hof
Badenweiler	Hotel Roseneck-Kurhotel Saupe
Berlin	Hilton, Hotel Kempinski, Hotel Fruling am Zoo, Hotel Savigny
Bonn	Sternhotel
Bremen	Park Hotel

Dusseldorf	Hotel Eden
Elten-Gelderland	Kurhotel
Frankfurt	Hotel Frankfurter Hof, Hotel Momopol-Metropole
Garmisch	Hotel Garmischer Hof
Hamburg	Hotel Berlin, Hotel Continental
Heidelberg	Schloss-Hotel
Koblenz	Rheinhotel Koblenzerhof
Mainz/Rhein	Hotel Mainzer Hof, Europahotel
Munich	Bayerischer Hof, Hotel Schottenhamel
Oberammergau	Hotel Alois Lang
Reclinghausen	Europahotel
Tubingen	Touring-Motel

ENGLAND
GREAT BRITAIN

Arundel	Norfolk Arms Hotel
Ascot	Berystede Hotel
Bath	Pratt's Hotel
Birmingham	Grand
Blackpool	Imperial Hotel
Bournemouth	Carlton, Highcliff Hotel
Brighton	Bedford Hotel, Royal Albion
Bristol	Grand Hotel
Burford	The Lamb Inn
Cambridge	Blue Boar
Canterbury	Abbots Barton Hotel
Chester	The Blossoms Hotel
Chipping Campden	Noel Arms Hotel
Cirencester	King's Head Hotel
Coventry	The Hall Hotel
Deal	Queen's Hotel
Doncaster	Punch's Hotel
Dover	White Cliffs
Droitwich Spa	Worcestershire Hotel
East Grinstead	Ye Olde Felbridge Hotel
Evesham	Crown Hotel
Exeter	Gipsy Hill Hotel
Hampton Court	Mitre
Haslemere	Georgian
Haytor	Moorland Hotel
Leamington Spa	Regent Hotel
Liverpool	Lord Nelson
London Airport	Skyway
London	The Carlton Tower, Dorchester Hotel, Ritz Hotel, Savoy, Westbury, Hyde Park, Londoner, Piccadilly, Washington, Rembrandt, Rubens, St. Ermins, Green Park, Mostyn
Maidenhead	Skindles Hotel
Manchester	Queen's Hotel
Newcastle Upon Tyne	Royal Turk's Head
Newmarket	Bedford Lodge Hotel
Newquay	Headland
Nottingham	County Hotel
Oxford	Mitre Hotel

88

Plymouth	Grand Hotel
Salisbury	White Hart Hotel
Scarborough	Royal Hotel
Sheffield	Grand
Southampton	Dolphin
Stratford-Upon-Avon	Shakespeare
Torquay	Imperial, Torbay, Rosetor Hotel
Weymouth	Gloucester Hotel
Windermer	Old England Hotel
York	Abbey Park Hotel

SCOTLAND

Aberdeen	Caledonian Hotel
Aviemore	Lynwilg Hotel
Ayr	Hotel Dalblair
Banff	Fife Arms Hotel
Edinburgh	Carlton, Grosvenor Hotel
Glasgow	More's Hotel, Ivanhoe
Killin	Killin
Pitlochry	Fishers Hotel
St. Andrew's	Rusack's Hotel

GREECE

Athens	Hotel St. George, New Angleterre, Cosmopolite, Palladion
Chalkis	Lucy Hotel
Kifissia	Hotel Cecil, Theoxenia
Rhodes	Hotel Des Roses
Thessaloniki	Mediterranean Hotel

HOLLAND

Amsterdam	Amstel Hotel, Grand Hotel Krasnapolsky
Arnheim	Hotel Haarhuis
Delft	Hotel Wilhelmina
Groningen	Hotel De Doelen
Haarlem	Hotel Lion d'Or
The Hague	Hotel Des Indes, De Hertenkamp, Du Passage
Rotterdam	Hotel Atlanta, Parkhotel
Utrecht	Hotel Terminus
Zandvoort	Hotel Bouwes

ITALY

Abano Terme	Grand Hotel Trieste
Alassio	Mediterranee
Cortina D'Ampezzo	Cristallo Palace
Cremona	Hotel Impero
Florence	Hotel Excelsior Italie, Savoy, Grand Hotel
Gardone Riviera	Savoy Palace
Genoa	Colombia Excelsior Hotel
Loreto	Grand Hotel Marchigiano
Mantova	Jolly Hotel
Milan	Cavalieri Hotel, Grand Hotel Continental, Garden Hotel, Diana Majestic, Palace Hotel, Principe and Savoia
Montecatini Terme	Grand Hotel Croce di Malta
Naples	Hotel Excelsior
Pisa	Hotel Dei Cavalieri
Portofino	Hotel Splendido

Rimini	Grand Hotel
Rome	Hotel Excelsior, Le Grand Hotel, Hassler-Villa Medici, Commodore, Bricktop's
San Remo	Grand Hotel and Des Anglais
Sestriere	Principi Di Piemente Hotel
Stresa	Grand Hotel et des Iles Borromees, Regina Palace
Taormina	S. Domenico and Grand Hotel
Torino	Turin Palace
Venice	Danieli Royal Excelsior, Grand Hotel Europa and Britannia, Hotel Regina and Di Roma, Excelsior Palace, Grand Hotel Des Bains and Palazzo Al Mare, Grand Hotel Lido

NORWAY

Bergen	Orion Hotel
Fevik	Strand Hotel
Kristiansand	Ernst Hotel
Oslo	Grand Hotel, Hotel Bristol
Solfonn	Solfonn
Voss	Fleischers Hotel

PORTUGAL

Bucaco	Palace Hotel
Lisbon	Ritz Hotel, Hotel Condestavel, Avenida Palace Hotel
Nazare	Pensao Central
Porto	Hotel Infante De Sagres, Grande Hotel Do Porto, Batalha

MEXICAN GOVT. TOURIST BD.

SPAIN

Alicante	Hotel Carlton
Andorre La Vielle	Hotel Meritxell
Barcelona	Hotel Avenida Palace, Gran Hotel Cristina
Bilbao	Hotel Carlton
Cadaques	Rocamar Hotel
Cordoba	Cordoba Palace
Granada	Nevada Palace Hotel, Hotel Alhambra Palace
Lloret de Mar	Gran Hotel Monterrey
Madrid	Castellana Hilton, Hotel Fenix, Hotel Menfis
Playa De Aro	Park Hotel San Jorge
Puerto De La Cruz	Europahotel "Oro Negro"
S'Agaro	Hostel De La Gavina

San Sebastian ....Londres E. Inglaterra
Sevilla ....Hotel Cristina, Alfonso XIII
SWEDEN
Goteborg ....Park Avenue Hotel
Granna ....Hotel Gyllene Uttern
Jonkoping ....Stora Hotellet
Malmo ....Savoy Hotel
Stockholm ....Carlton Hotel, Hotel Malmen
Tallberg ....Greens Hotell
SWITZERLAND
Aarau ....Hotel Aarauerhof
Adelboden ....Nevada Palace

UNITED NATIONS

Arosa	Hotel Arosa-Kulm
Basel	Hotel Trois Rois au Rhin, Hotel Greub
Gstaad	Royal Winter and Gstaad Palace
Interlaken	Grand Hotel Victoria-Jungfrau, Hotel Du Nord
Lausanne	Lausanne Palace, Central Bellevue
Lucerne	Hotel Astoria
Lugano	Hotel Splendide-Royal, Hotel Bellevue Au Lac
Montreux	Montreuv-Palace Hotel, Continental
St. Moritz	Hotel Carlton, Albana
Vevey-La Tour De Peilz	Hotel Rive-Reine
Wengen	Palace
Zurich	Hotel Baur Au Lac, Hotel Carlton Elite
Chateau D'Oex	Grand Hotel du Parc
Geneva	Hotel Beau-Rivage, de la Paix
Grindelwald	Belvedere

AFRICA

ALGERIA

ALGIERS
- Aletti .... $7 up
- Albert .... $6 up
- Oasis .... $5 up
- Suisse .... $6 up
- St. George .... $7 up

BONE
- Hotel Orient .... $6 up

CONSTANTINE
- Transatlantique .... $6 up

ORAN
- Grand Hotel .... $7 up
- Martinez .... $7 up

BURUNDI

USUMBURA
- Urundi Palace
- Paguidas
- LeGrillon

CAMEROUN

DOUALA
- Akwa Palace .... $6 up
- Des Cocotiers .... $8 up

N'GAOUNDERE
- Hauts Plateaux $3.50

GAROUA
- Relais Aeriens $3.25
- Relais St. Hubert $4

YAOUNDE
- Relais Aeriens $7
- Bellevue $5
- Terminus $6

CENTRAL AFRICAN REPUBLIC

BANGUI
- Rock Hotel .... $11 to $13

CHAD

ABECE
    MOREAU
        FT. LAMY
- Air Hotel .... $9 up
- du Chari .... $12 up

FT. ARCHAMBAULT
- L'Escale .... $4.50 up
- des Chasses .... $4.00 up
- Grand Hotel .... $10 up
- du Parc .... $10 up

92

CONGO REPUBLIC
BRAZZAVILLE
   Congo Ocean ....$4 up   Grand ....$5 up
   de Maya Maya ....$8 up   Relais Aeriens ....$8 up
POINTE NOIRE
   Victory Palace ....$6   du Mayombe ....$5 up

CONGO
LEOPOLDVILLE
   Astoria ....$4.50 up   Palace ....$7 up
           Regina $8
BUKAVU
   Riviera ....$7   Royal Residence ....$5 up

DAHOMEY
COTONOU
   Babo ....$3 up   de la Plage ....$8 up

ETHIOPIA
ADDIS ABABA
   D'Itegue ....$5 up   Guenet ....$4 up
   Ghion ....$8 up   Ras ....$6 up
ASMARA
   Alb. Mamasien ....$2.50 up   C.I.A.A.O. ....$6 up

GABON
LIBREVILLE
   de La Residence ....$5.50 up   de l'Estuaire ....$4 up
           du Roi Denis ....$8 up
LAMBARENE   **PT. GENTIL**
   de L'Ogooue ....$6 up   du Grand Tarpon $8

GHANA
ACCRA
   Ambassador ....$12 up   Avenida ....$10 up
   Lisbon ....$ 6 up   Ringway ....$ 8 up
TAKORADI
   Hillcrest ....$6 up   Windsor ....$6 up

GUINEA
CONAKRY
   Camayenne Plage ....de France, de La Gare, du Niger

IVORY COAST
ABIDJAN
   de La Vigie ....$3.50   International ....$4 up
   du Parc ....$8 up   Le Grand ....$7 up
           Relais de Cocody ....$10 up

LIBERIA
MONROVIA
   Ducor Palace ....$11 up   Pan Am Hotel ....$6 to $10
   Johnson's ....$ 8   Paramount ....$ 8

LIBYA
BENGHAZI
   Berenice ....$7   Grand ....$3 up
TRIPOLI
   Casino Uaddan ....$6   Del Mehari ....$3 up
           Grand ....$3 up

MALAGASY
TANANARIVE
- Fumaroli, Terminus ....$2 up
- Lido ....$2.75 up
- Colbert $2.50
- de Franco $3.25

MALI
BAMAKO
- de La Gare ....$ 5
- Grand ....$10 up
- Le Lido ....$ 7 up
- Majestic ....$ 7 up

MAURITANIA
NOUAKCHOTT
- Oasis ....$3 up

PT. ETIENNE
- de l'Etoile ....$5 up

MOROCCO
CASABLANCA
- El Mansour ....$7 up
- Anfa ....$4 up

RABAT
- Balima ....$6 up
- Rex ....$5 up
- Tour Hassan $4

NIGER
NIAMEY
- Grand ....$8 up
- Relais Aeriens ....$5 up
- Rivoli
- Terminus ....$3 up

NIGERIA
LAGOS
- Ambassador ....$6 up
- Federal Palace ....$17 up

KANO
- Central ....$12 up

RWANDA
KISENYI
- Beau Sejour ....$5 up
- Bugoyi Guest House ....$8 up
- Palm Beach ....$6 up

SENEGAL
DAKAR
- Grand de N'Gor ....$8 up
- Clarice ....$5 up
- De la Croix du Sud ....$8 up
- Vichy ....$5 up
- Majestic ....$ 6

SIERRA LEONE
FREETOWN
- City Hotel ....$6 up
- Government Rest House ....$7 up
- Paramount ....$9 up
- Riviera ....$7 up

BO
- Demby ....$5 up

MAGBURAKA
- Adams ....$5 up

SOMALIA
MOGADISCIO
- Croce del Sud ....$3 up
- Giuba ....$3.50 up
- Savoia ....$2.50 up
- Scepelle ....$4 up

SUDAN
KHARTOUM
- Acropole ....$9 up
- Grand ....$7 up

TANGANYIKA

ARUSHA
New Arusha ....$6 up
Safari House ....$5.50 up

DAR ES-SALAAM
New Africa ....$6 up
Etiennes ....$4 up
Rex ....$5.50 up
Seaview ....$6 up

TANGA
Park ....$5.50 up

TOGO

LOME
Benin ....$10 up   du Golfe ....$4 up

TUNISIA

TUNIS
Majestic ....$6 up   Palace ....$7 up

UGANDA

ENTEBBE
Victoria ....$7 up

KAMPALA
Kampala Imperial ....$9 up
Speke ....$6 up

JINJA
Ripon Falls $5

MBALE
Mt. Elgon ....$7 up

UNITED ARAB REPUBLIC

CAIRO
Nile-Hilton ....$16.80 up   Continental Savoy ......$4.50 up
Longchamps ....$ 4.50 up   Semaris ....$6 up

UPPER VOLTA

OUAGADOUGOU
Central ....$8 up   de La Gare ....$4 up
            Chez Fanny ....$2.50 up

BOBO-DIOULASSO
Potiniere ....$4 up   Provencal ....$3 up
            Royan ....$8 up

VISA INFORMATION

Usually the traveler must have innoculation certificates for Small Pox.. Visa requirements of U. S. citizens is usually that they have a valid United States Passport and Inoculation certificates attesting to their vaccinations for Small Pox and Yellow Fever. The number of copies of the applications and photos for the applications as well as the amount of the visa fees depends on the individual countries.

GUIDE POSTS FOR A PLEASANT TRIP
By Thomasina Norford

So you're off on that "dream trip"? How can you make it really a dream trip? Or will it be a nightmare?

In travelling, like most other situations — a lot will depend on you. Knowing what to do and how to do it the easy way can mean the difference between coming home with the memories of a lifetime or saying, "Gee, I'm glad to be home".

So you have packed light and are off by car, boat, train or plane — now what?

Knowing where to stop and what is expect is provided in The Travelers Green

Book. You already know whether the place you're going to stop at, in what town, has a swimming pool or not and what other facilities are available. You have already checked on the price scale. Your reservations have been accepted and you arrive.

The first person to greet you will be the taxi driver, if you don't drive. Before you get in the taxi tell him where you are going and ask him approximately how much it will cost to get there. If the price seems exorbitant — talk to the sky cap or red cap or an official.

The next persons you meet will be the doorman and bell boy who will take your luggage into the lobby and after room assignment is made will take your luggage to the room.

Rooms vary in price. The higher up the room the more expensive, usually, and rooms "with a view" are more than inside or court rooms. Many hotels have public places such as ballrooms, rooms normally used by salesmen and party rooms. Getting on the same floor with them can be annoying. However, if you are the gregarious type — "if you can't lick 'em jine 'em."

Meals can be a joy, if you know what to order! Usually every hotel or restaurant has a house specialty. Try it. Maybe you won't like Creole Gumbo in Louisiana, but maybe you will. After all aren't you out for adventure? Then have it! If you don't like Gumbo (or any other food you've ordered) — don't blame the cook — blame only your own provincial taste and go down the street and order some ham and eggs.

So you want to "see the town"? Good! Some home work before going can be very helpful as a starter. Read some travel book, road maps and talk to some folks who have lived there. Then supplement this by a chat with some of the folks you meet in the town, such as service folk. Take a look at the picture postcards in the five and ten and take off.

If you are motoring get a road map. If you are using a sightseeing service you will know what you will see and the cost. If you are using a taxi or a private conveyance, by all means get his price and what it will cost before you engage him. It's better to hire them by the hour in most towns.

Plan your sightseeing while the townspeople are at work so as not to get involved in a traffic jam. Yes, every town has its traffic problem, or "rush hour".

So you brought the children? How nice! Well, I am sure you have prepared well for them in terms of games they can play while traveling; dressed them in comfortable clothes and told them all about the trip beforehand.

And surely you want them to have a good time, but please don't allow them to spoil other persons trips! Their "manners will be magic". Of course Papa orders all foods in the dining room. Children should come in and sit down and "act like little ladies and gentlemen" like you have trained them. This goes for public conveyances, too. And please, no running up and down the corridors and lobbies of the hotel you are in!

If you are going to visit relatives or friends in a town with the hotel as a "base of operation" call them first and find out when you will see them and for what type of activity so you will know how to dress. Then plan your other activities after that schedule is set.

So you're now ready to move to the next town or home but you must get some "gifts for the folks back home." What will it be?" Two rules are pretty simple to start with. 1. What would the recipient like? 2. What is typical of the place you've visited that fits what the person would like.

Some of the unusual things are cook books of favorite recipes of the town; charms of the most famous place or historical place; maps of the place on a hanky, scarf or towel; a travel book about the place or something that is made in the town.

Be pleasant, ask questions, don't complain (just don't go THERE again is the way to handle that!) because what you complain about will not be rectified while you are there anyway in most instances; be adventuresome; and most of all don't expect any place to be "like home". After all, that's why you took the trip in the first place, wasn't it?

THE BASEBALL CIRCUIT

AMERICAN LEAGUE

BALTIMORE ORIOLES
Memorial Stadium:
Seating capacity—49,373
33rd Street, Ellerslie Avenue,
36th Street and Ednor Rd.

CHICAGO WHITE SOX
Comiskey Park:
Seating capacity—46,550
35th Street and Shields Avenue,
Chicago 16, Ill.

CLEVELAND INDIANS
Municipal Stadium:
Seating capacity—73,811
Foot of West Third Street,
Cleveland 14, Ohio

BOSTON RED SOX
Fenway Park:
Seating capacity—33,357
Jersey Street, Landsdowne Street
and Ipswich Streets

DETROIT TIGERS
Tiger Stadium:
Seating capacity—52,850
Michigan Avenue, National Avenue,
Cherry Street and Trumbull Avenue

KANSAS CITY ATHLETICS
Municipal Stadium:
Seating capacity—32,561
Twenty-second Street and
Brooklyn Avenue

LOS ANGELES ANGELS
Chavez Stadium (Dodger Stadium):
Seating Capacity—56,000
1000 Elysian Park Avenue,
Los Angeles, Calif.

MINNESOTA TWINS
Metrpolitan Stadium:
Seating capacity—39,525
8001 Cedar Avenue,
Bloomington 20, Minn.

NEW YORK YANKEES
Yankee Stadium:
Seating capacity—70,000
East 161st Street and River Avenue,
Bronx, N. Y.

WASHINGTON SENATORS
District of Cloumbia Stadium:
Seating capacity—42,000
Twenty-second and East Capitol St.
Washington 3, D. C.

NATIONAL LEAGUE

CHICAGO CUBS
Wrigley Field
Seating capacity—36,755
Addison Street, Clark Street,
Waveland and Sheffield Avenues

GEE BEE SAYS: IF YOU PLAN YOUR TRIP, YOU'LL KNOW WHERE YOU'VE BEEN BEFORE YOU GET THERE!

© HERITAGE FEATURES

97

Travelers' Green Book 1963–64

HOUSTON COLT .45s
Colt Stadium:
Seating capacity—32,000
Old Spanish Trail and Main Street,
Houston, Texas

LOS ANGELES DODGERS
Dodger Stadium:
Seating capacity—56,000
1000 Elysian Park Avenue,
Los Angeles, Calif.

MILWAUKEE BRAVES
Milwaukee County Stadium:
Seating capacity—43,826
South 44th Street off Bluemound Rd.
Milwaukee 46, Wis.

NEW YORK METS
Polo Grounds:
Seating capacity—55,000
155th Street and 8th Avenue,
New York 39, N. Y.
(Shea Stadium, 126th Street and
Roosevelt Avenue, Flushing 68, N. Y.

PHILADELPHIA PHILLIES
Connie Mack Stadium:
Seating capacity—33,608
Lehigh Avenue, Somerset Street,
North 20th and North 21st Sts.
Philadelphia 32, Pa.

PITTSBURGH PIRATES
Forbes Field.
Seating capacity—35,000
Cor. of Bouquet and Sennott Streets
Pittsburgh, Pa.

ST. LOUIS CARDINALS
Busch Stadium:
Seating capacity—30,500
Grand Boulevard, Dodier Street,
Sullivan Avenue and Spring Avenues
St. Louis 7, Mo.

SAN FRANCISCO GIANTS
Candlestick Park:
Seating capacity—42,500
Bayshore Blvd., San Francisco, Caif.

CURRENCY EXCHANGE

The following list gives the approximate rates of exchange, quoted on the U.S.A. dollar, as we went to press. Since exchange rates vary from day to day, to be accurate it is advisable that you check with your bank or travel agent.

CURRENCY EXCHANGE		per U.S.$
AUSTRIA	Shilling (Groschen)	26
BELGIUM	Franc (Centimes)	50
DENMARK	Kroner	6.90
FRANCE	Nouveau Franc	4.90
GERMANY	Deutschmark (pfennig)	4.001
GREAT BRITAIN	Pounds (Shillings and Pennies)	7/-
GREECE	Drachma	30
HOLLAND	Gulder (Cent)	3.60
ITALY	Lire	620
NORWAY	Kroner (Ore)	7.1
PORTUGAL	Escudo (Centavo)	28.50
SPAIN	Peseta (Centimo)	59
SWEDEN	Kroner (Ore)	5.17
SWITZERLAND	Franc (Centimes)	4.31
YUGOSLAVIA	Dinar	700
CANADA		1.08
BRAZIL		Free Fluctuating
COLOMBIA		Free Fluctuating
EGYPT	(Pound-100 piastres)	.434
MEXICO	Peso	.08

green book's HISTORY-MAKERS

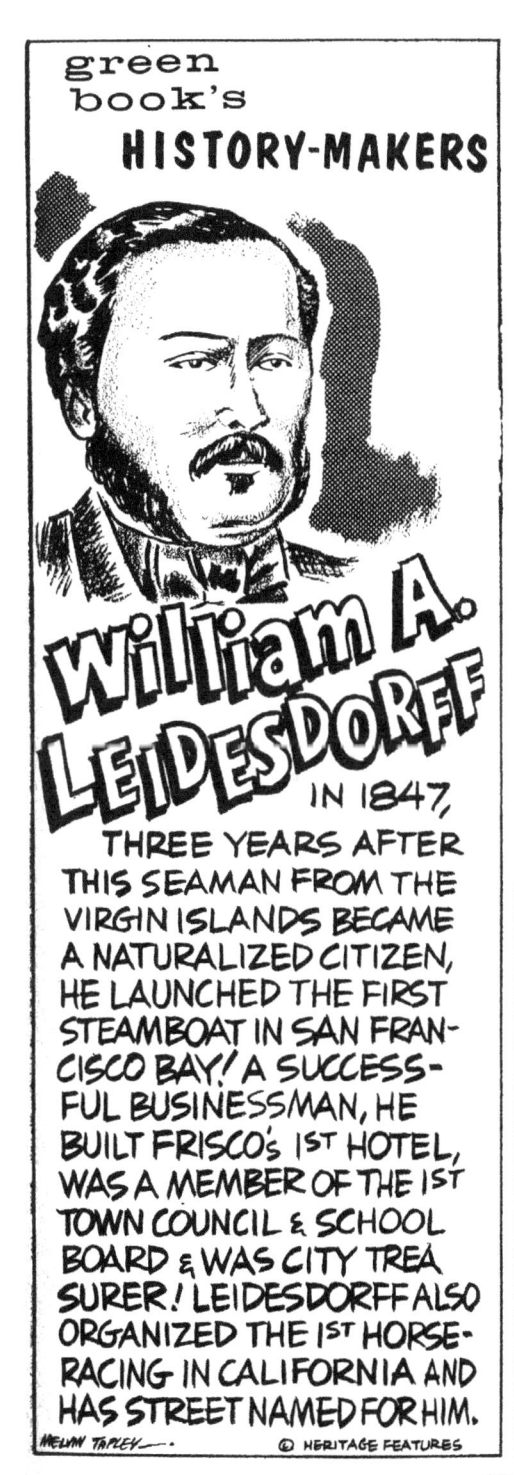

William A. Leidesdorff

IN 1847, THREE YEARS AFTER THIS SEAMAN FROM THE VIRGIN ISLANDS BECAME A NATURALIZED CITIZEN, HE LAUNCHED THE FIRST STEAMBOAT IN SAN FRANCISCO BAY! A SUCCESSFUL BUSINESSMAN, HE BUILT FRISCO'S 1ST HOTEL, WAS A MEMBER OF THE 1ST TOWN COUNCIL & SCHOOL BOARD & WAS CITY TREASURER! LEIDESDORFF ALSO ORGANIZED THE 1ST HORSE-RACING IN CALIFORNIA AND HAS STREET NAMED FOR HIM.

MELVIN TAPLEY — © HERITAGE FEATURES

TRAVELING TRUNKLINES

Have most of your travel wardrobe wash 'n' wear. A dip, splash and drip keeps your things fresh as a daisy.

Simple, basic travel togs save space. As usual, hubby won't need much... slacks, several jackets, etc. will keep him neat. You can give the impression of a large wardrobe with an interesting variety of accessories without excess luggage.

Pack heavier articles together at the bottom of the suitcase and the larger garments, carefully and smoothly folded, over them. Keep plastic bags that those new shirts came in for shoes. Put toiletries in leakproof containers. This will save your things from damage. By-the-way, the things you use first or most often put them on top.

Be protected. Go to the bank and get travelers' checks. These are replaceable and always negotiable.

Don't forget the weather, girls! Unless you're going au naturel, have enough 'hair aids' to keep you confident in humid or dry conditions.

DEAR READERS:

During 27 dedicated years of publishing your Travelers' GREEN BOOK we have constantly sought to improve our service to you. We want you to enjoy yourself. In fact, we are in business to help you "VACATION WITHOUT AGGRAVATION."

If you will drop us a line and tell us how you enjoyed your travel accommodations, we certainly would appreciate it. If you have any suggestions how we can be of more help, let us know... it will help us to maintain our high standards and keep Travelers' GREEN BOOK your favorite travel guide.

Sincerely,
Victor H. Green Co.

Don't

Pack

Without

LANGSTON HUGHES'

"FIGHT FOR FREEDOM"

The Story Of The NAACP

A moving drama of the 54-year struggle of a dedicated group of men and women.

Here in 205 fascinating and easy-to-read pages is the chronicle of the hard-fought battle, its triumphs and its setbacks, and the people who gave their time, their energies and sometimes their lives in the fight for equal rights.

This exciting document of living history is yours for only 50¢ for the paperback, $4.50 for the hard cover. Available at any local branch or the NAACP national office, 20 West 40th Street, New York 18, N. Y.

STETSON BELMONT
STYLE 1006
$29.99

STETSON
SHOES FOR MEN
1885

STETSON
GENUINE ALLIGATOR
STYLE 1290 ... $69.99

STETSON
SARATOGA
STYLE 1288
$28.99

ORDER BY MAIL...
Just send $2 Deposit with each order.

VISIT OUR STORE WHENEVER YOU ARE IN NEW YORK CITY

FREE CATALOG!
WRITE FOR YOUR COPY OF DAVINS BIG, NEW, STYLE CATALOG WITH MORE SHOES, HATS, AND CLOTHING.

STETSON
ITALIANO
STYLE 1010
$29.99

DAVINS
Stetson
Shoes for Men

155 W. 125 ST.   N.Y.C. 27

RATE CARD

SPECIAL – TO ADVERTISERS – FREE

We are assembling our material for the next edition of our guide and, as a progressive business person, you want to reach as many people as you can at a small cost.

You will want to include your business along with the hundreds of others who advertise successfully.

An advertisement is primarily an introduction. It makes new friends and holds the old ones. It makes people know you and regard you in a friendly light.

The following number of guides are given **FREE** with your contract.

1 Page – 6"	–	$225.00	– 25 Copies Free
2/3 Page – 4"	–	$175.00	– 25 Copies Free
1/2 Page – 3"	–	$150.00	– 25 Copies Free
1/3 Page – 2"	–	$ 80.00	– 15 Copies Free
1/4 Page – 1½"	–	$ 65.00	– 10 Copies Free
1/8 Page – 3/4"	–	$ 40.00	– 5 Copies Free
3 Lines.......		$ 25.00	– 1 Copy Free
2 Lines.......		$ 20.00	– 1 Copy Free

Space left blank on cover for your name and address; you can use a rubber stamp or write in.

FREE COPIES are not to be sold. They are for **FREE** distribution to your guests and clients.

CUTS will be made **FREE** when photos are supplied for the 1/3 page and larger spaces.

VICTOR H. GREEN & CO., Publishers
200 WEST 135th STREET   NEW YORK 30, N. Y.

Green Book rate card circa 1963

Also available:

California Negro Directory 1942–43

What the *Negro Motorist Green Book* was for the traveler, the *California Negro Directory* was for those staying close to home. Covering cities not just in California but along the whole US west coast, this World War II-era guide includes listings and photo-filled ads for Black-owned and Black-friendly businesses; a white pages-style directory of local African Americans; a Who's Who of the African-American community; introductory comments by the Governor of California and by the mayor of Los Angeles; and more.

Ask for it where you got this book!

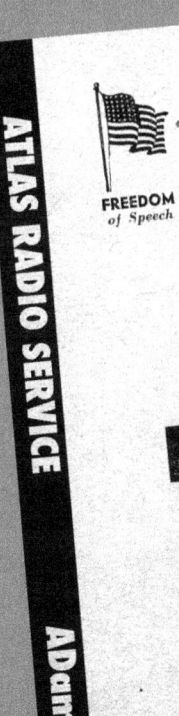

Green Book Facsimile Editions

About Comics publishes facsimile editions of individual Green Book editions. These acclaimed reprints have been discussed by The Guardian, Newsweek, and BBC News, are carried by the gift shops of major museums, and were used in promoting a certain major motion picutre.

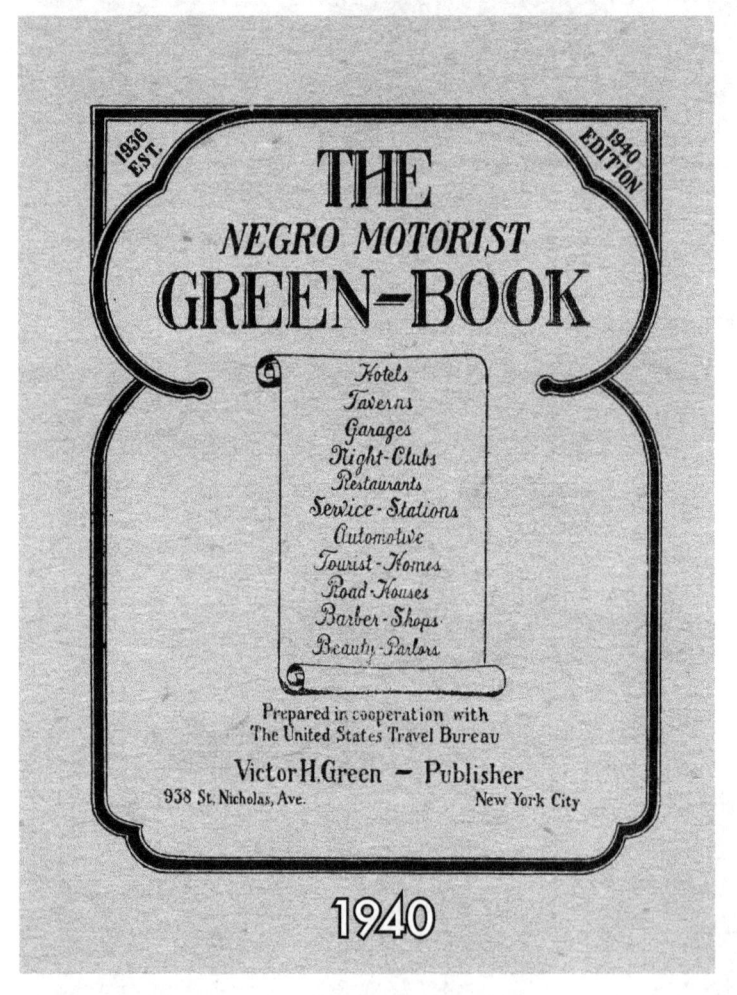

1940

1947

1949

1954

1959

1962

1963

More information available at www.AboutComics.com

CPSIA information can be obtained
at www.ICGtesting.com
Printed in the USA
BVHW010919021020
590167BV00013B/100

9 781949 996104

The Chateau of Prince Polignac

Anthony Trollope

Table of Contents

The Chateau of Prince Polignac..1
    Anthony Trollope..1

The Chateau of Prince Polignac

Anthony Trollope

Kessinger Publishing reprints thousands of hard−to−find books!

Visit us at http://www.kessinger.net

The Chateau of Prince Polignac

Few Englishmen or Englishwomen are intimately acquainted with the little town of Le Puy. It is the capital of the old province of Le Velay, which also is now but little known, even to French ears, for it is in these days called by the imperial name of the Department of the Haute Loire. It is to the south-east of Auvergne, and is nearly in the centre of the southern half of France.

But few towns, merely as towns, can be better worth visiting. In the first place, the volcanic formation of the ground on which it stands is not only singular in the extreme, so as to be interesting to the geologist, but it is so picturesque as to be equally gratifying to the general tourist. Within a narrow valley there stand several rocks, rising up from the ground with absolute abruptness. Round two of these the town clusters, and a third stands but a mile distant, forming the centre of a faubourg, or suburb. These rocks appear to be, and I believe are, the harder particles of volcanic matter, which have not been carried away through successive ages by the joint agency of water and air.

When the tide of lava ran down between the hills the surface left was no doubt on a level with the heads of these rocks; but here and there the deposit became harder than elsewhere, and these harder points have remained, lifting up their steep heads in a line through the valley.

The highest of these is called the Rocher de Corneille. Round this and up its steep sides the town stands. On its highest summit there was an old castle; and there now is, or will be before these pages are printed, a colossal figure in bronze of the Virgin Mary, made from the cannon taken at Sebastopol. Half-way down the hill the cathedral is built, a singularly gloomy edifice,—Romanesque, as it is called, in its style, but extremely similar in its mode of architecture to what we know of Byzantine structures. But there has been no surface on the rock side large enough to form a resting- place for the church, which has therefore been built out on huge supporting piles, which form a porch below the west front; so that the approach is by numerous steps laid along the side of the wall below the church, forming a wondrous flight of stairs. Let all men who may find themselves stopping at Le Puy visit the top of these stairs at the time of the setting sun, and look down from thence through the framework of the porch on the town beneath, and at the hill-side beyond.

Behind the church is the seminary of the priests, with its beautiful walks stretching round the Rocher de Corneille, and overlooking the town and valley below.

The Chateau of Prince Polignac

Next to this rock, and within a quarter of a mile of it, is the second peak, called the Rock of the Needle. It rises narrow, sharp, and abrupt from the valley, allowing of no buildings on its sides. But on its very point has been erected a church sacred to St. Michael, that lover of rock summits, accessible by stairs cut from the stone. This, perhaps—this rock, I mean—is the most wonderful of the wonders which Nature has formed at La Puy.

Above this, at a mile's distance, is the rock of Espailly, formed in the same way, and almost equally precipitous. On its summit is a castle, having its own legend, and professing to have been the residence of Charles VII., when little of France belonged to its kings but the provinces of Berry, Auvergne, and Le Velay. Some three miles farther up there is another volcanic rock, larger, indeed, but equally sudden in its spring,—equally remarkable as rising abruptly from the valley,—on which stands the castle and old family residence of the house of Polignac. It was lost by them at the Revolution, but was repurchased by the minister of Charles X., and is still the property of the head of the race.

Le Puy itself is a small, moderate, pleasant French town, in which the language of the people has not the pure Parisian aroma, nor is the glory of the boulevards of the capital emulated in its streets. These are crooked, narrow, steep, and intricate, forming here and there excellent sketches for a lover of street picturesque beauty; but hurtful to the feet with their small, round-topped paving stones, and not always as clean as pedestrian ladies might desire.

And now I would ask my readers to join me at the morning table d'hote at the Hotel des Ambassadeurs. It will of course be understood that this does not mean a breakfast in the ordinary fashion of England, consisting of tea or coffee, bread and butter, and perhaps a boiled egg. It comprises all the requisites for a composite dinner, excepting soup; and as one gets farther south in France, this meal is called dinner. It is, however, eaten without any prejudice to another similar and somewhat longer meal at six or seven o'clock, which, when the above name is taken up by the earlier enterprise, is styled supper.

The dejeuner, or dinner, at the Hotel des Ambassadeurs, on the morning in question, though very elaborate, was not a very gay affair. There were some fourteen persons present, of whom half were residents in the town, men employed in some official capacity, who found this to be the cheapest, the most luxurious, and to them the most comfortable mode of living. They clustered together at the head of the table, and as they

The Chateau of Prince Polignac

were customary guests at the house, they talked their little talk together—it was very little—and made the most of the good things before them. Then there were two or three commis-voyageurs, a chance traveller or two, and an English lady with a young daughter. The English lady sat next to one of the accustomed guests; but he, unlike the others, held converse with her rather than with them. Our story at present has reference only to that lady and to that gentleman.

Place aux dames. We will speak first of the lady, whose name was Mrs. Thompson. She was, shall I say, a young woman of about thirty- six. In so saying, I am perhaps creating a prejudice against her in the minds of some readers, as they will, not unnaturally, suppose her, after such an announcement, to be in truth over forty. Any such prejudice will be unjust. I would have it believed that thirty-six was the outside, not the inside of her age. She was good-looking, lady-like, and considering that she was an Englishwoman, fairly well dressed. She was inclined to be rather full in her person, but perhaps not more so than is becoming to ladies at her time of life. She had rings on her fingers and a brooch on her bosom which were of some value, and on the back of her head she wore a jaunty small lace cap, which seemed to tell, in conjunction with her other appointments, that her circumstances were comfortable.

The little girl who sat next to her was the youngest of her two daughters, and might be about thirteen years of age. Her name was Matilda, but infantine circumstances had invested her with the nickname of Mimmy, by which her mother always called her. A nice, pretty, playful little girl was Mimmy Thompson, wearing two long tails of plaited hair hanging, behind her head, and inclined occasionally to be rather loud in her sport.

Mrs. Thompson had another and an elder daughter, now some fifteen years old, who was at school in Le Puy; and it was with reference to her tuition that Mrs. Thompson had taken up a temporary residence at the Hotel des Ambassadeurs in that town. Lilian Thompson was occasionally invited down to dine or breakfast at the inn, and was visited daily at her school by her mother.

"When I'm sure that she'll do, I shall leave her there, and go back to England," Mrs. Thompson had said, not in the purest French, to the neighbour who always sat next to her at the table d'hote, the gentleman, namely, to whom we have above alluded. But still she had remained at Le Puy a month, and did not go; a circumstance which was considered singular, but by no means unpleasant, both by the innkeeper and by the gentleman in

The Chateau of Prince Polignac

question.

The facts, as regarded Mrs. Thompson, were as follows:– She was the widow of a gentleman who had served for many years in the civil service of the East Indies, and who, on dying, had left her a comfortable income of—it matters not how many pounds, but constituting quite a sufficiency to enable her to live at her ease and educate her daughters.

Her children had been sent home to England before her husband's death, and after that event she had followed them; but there, though she was possessed of moderate wealth, she had no friends and few acquaintances, and after a little while she had found life to be rather dull. Her customs were not those of England, nor were her propensities English; therefore she had gone abroad, and having received some recommendation of this school at Le Puy, had made her way thither. As it appeared to her that she really enjoyed more consideration at Le Puy than had been accorded to her either at Torquay or Leamington, there she remained from day to day. The total payment required at the Hotel des Ambassadeurs was but six francs daily for herself and three and a half for her little girl; and where else could she live with a better junction of economy and comfort? And then the gentleman who always sat next to her was so exceedingly civil!

The gentleman's name was M. Lacordaire. So much she knew, and had learned to call him by his name very frequently. Mimmy, too, was quite intimate with M. Lacordaire; but nothing more than his name was known of him. But M. Lacordaire carried a general letter of recommendation in his face, manner, gait, dress, and tone of voice. In all these respects there was nothing left to be desired; and, in addition to this, he was decorated, and wore the little red ribbon of the Legion of Honour, ingeniously twisted into the shape of a small flower.

M. Lacordaire might be senior in age to Mrs. Thompson by about ten years, nor had he about him any of the airs or graces of a would-be young man. His hair, which he wore very short, was grizzled, as was also the small pretence of a whisker which came down about as far as the middle of his ear; but the tuft on his chin was still brown, without a gray hair. His eyes were bright and tender, his voice was low and soft, his hands were very white, his clothes were always new and well fitting, and a better-brushed hat could not be seen out of Paris, nor perhaps in it.

The Chateau of Prince Polignac

Now, during the weeks which Mrs. Thompson had passed at La Puy, the acquaintance which she had formed with M. Lacordaire had progressed beyond the prolonged meals in the salle a manger. He had occasionally sat beside her evening table as she took her English cup of tea in her own room, her bed being duly screened off in its distant niche by becoming curtains; and then he had occasionally walked beside her, as he civilly escorted her to the lions of the place; and he had once accompanied her, sitting on the back seat of a French voiture, when she had gone forth to see something of the surrounding country.

On all such occasions she had been accompanied by one of her daughters, and the world of Le Puy had had nothing material to say against her. But still the world of Le Puy had whispered a little, suggesting that M. Lacordaire knew very well what he was about. But might not Mrs. Thompson also know as well what she was about? At any rate, everything had gone on very pleasantly since the acquaintance had been made. And now, so much having been explained, we will go back to the elaborate breakfast at the Hotel des Ambassadeurs.

Mrs. Thompson, holding Mimmy by the hand, walked into the room some few minutes after the last bell had been rung, and took the place which was now hers by custom. The gentlemen who constantly frequented the house all bowed to her, but M. Lacordaire rose from his seat and offered her his hand.

"And how is Mees Meemy this morning?" said he; for 'twas thus he always pronounced her name.

Miss Mimmy, answering for herself, declared that she was very well, and suggested that M. Lacordaire should give her a fig from off a dish that was placed immediately before him on the table. This M. Lacordaire did, presenting it very elegantly between his two fingers, and making a little bow to the little lady as he did so.

"Fie, Mimmy!" said her mother; "why do you ask for the things before the waiter brings them round?"

"But, mamma," said Mimmy, speaking English, "M. Lacordaire always gives me a fig every morning."

The Chateau of Prince Polignac

"M. Lacordaire always spoils you, I think," answered Mrs. Thompson, in French. And then they went thoroughly to work at their breakfast. During the whole meal M. Lacordaire attended assiduously to his neighbour; and did so without any evil result, except that one Frenchman with a black moustache, at the head of the table, trod on the toe of another Frenchman with another black moustache— winking as he made the sign—just as M. Lacordaire, having selected a bunch of grapes, put it on Mrs. Thompson's plate with infinite grace. But who among us all is free from such impertinences as these?

"But madame really must see the chateau of Prince Polignac before she leaves Le Puy," said M. Lacordaire.

"The chateau of who?" asked Mimmy, to whose young ears the French words were already becoming familiar.

"Prince Polignac, my dear. Well, I really don't know, M. Lacordaire;—I have seen a great deal of the place already, and I shall be going now very soon; probably in a day or two," said Mrs. Thompson.

"But madame must positively see the chateau," said M. Lacordaire, very impressively; and then after a pause he added, "If madame will have the complaisance to commission me to procure a carriage for this afternoon, and will allow me the honour to be her guide, I shall consider myself one of the most fortunate of men."

"Oh, yes, mamma, do go," said Mimmy, clapping her hands. "And it is Thursday, and Lilian can go with us."

"Be quiet, Mimmy, do. Thank you, no, M. Lacordaire. I could not go to-day; but I am extremely obliged by your politeness."

M. Lacordaire still pressed the matter, and Mrs. Thompson still declined till it was time to rise from the table. She then declared that she did not think it possible that she should visit the chateau before she left Le Puy; but that she would give him an answer at dinner.

The most tedious time in the day to Mrs. Thompson were the two hours after breakfast. At one o'clock she daily went to the school, taking Mimmy, who for an hour or two

The Chateau of Prince Polignac

shared her sister's lessons. This and her little excursions about the place, and her shopping, managed to make away with her afternoon. Then in the evening, she generally saw something of M. Lacordaire. But those two hours after breakfast were hard of killing.

On this occasion, when she gained her own room, she as usual placed Mimmy on the sofa with a needle. Her custom then was to take up a novel; but on this morning she sat herself down in her arm-chair, and resting her head upon her hand and elbow, began to turn over certain circumstances in her mind.

"Mamma," said Mimmy, "why won't you go with M. Lacordaire to that place belonging to the prince? Prince—Polly something, wasn't it?"

"Mind your work, my dear," said Mrs. Thompson.

"But I do so wish you'd go, mamma. What was the prince's name?"

"Polignac."

"Mamma, ain't princes very great people?"

"Yes, my dear; sometimes."

"Is Prince Polly-nac like our Prince Alfred?"

"No, my dear; not at all. At least, I suppose not."

"Is his mother a queen?"

"No, my dear."

"Then his father must be a king?"

"No, my dear. It is quite a different thing here. Here in France they have a great many princes."

The Chateau of Prince Polignac

"Well, at any rate I should like to see a prince's chateau; so I do hope you'll go." And then there was a pause. "Mamma, could it come to pass, here in France, that M. Lacordaire should ever be a prince?"

"M. Lacordaire a prince! No; don't talk such nonsense, but mind your work."

"Isn't M. Lacordaire a very nice man? Ain't you very fond of him?"

To this question Mrs. Thompson made no answer.

"Mamma," continued Mimmy, after a moment's pause, "won't you tell me whether you are fond of M. Lacordaire? I'm quite sure of this,— that he's very fond of you."

"What makes you think that?" asked Mrs. Thompson, who could not bring herself to refrain from the question.

"Because he looks at you in that way, mamma, and squeezes your hand."

"Nonsense, child," said Mrs. Thompson; "hold your tongue. I don't know what can have put such stuff into your head."

"But he does, mamma," said Mimmy, who rarely allowed her mother to put her down.

Mrs. Thompson made no further answer, but again sat with her head resting on her hand. She also, if the truth must be told, was thinking of M. Lacordaire and his fondness for herself. He had squeezed her hand and he had looked into her face. However much it may have been nonsense on Mimmy's part to talk of such things, they had not the less absolutely occurred. Was it really the fact that M. Lacordaire was in love with her?

And if so, what return should she, or could she make to such a passion? He had looked at her yesterday, and squeezed her hand to- day. Might it not be probable that he would advance a step further to-morrow? If so, what answer would she be prepared to make to him?

She did not think—so she said to herself—that she had any particular objection to marrying again. Thompson had been dead now for four years, and neither his friends, nor

The Chateau of Prince Polignac

her friends, nor the world could say she was wrong on that score. And as to marrying a Frenchman, she could not say she felt within herself any absolute repugnance to doing that. Of her own country, speaking of England as such, she, in truth, knew but little—and perhaps cared less. She had gone to India almost as a child, and England had not been specially kind to her on her return. She had found it dull and cold, stiff, and almost ill-natured. People there had not smiled on her and been civil as M. Lacordaire had done. As far as England and Englishmen were considered she saw no reason why she should not marry M. Lacordaire.

And then, as regarded the man; could she in her heart say that she was prepared to love, honour, and obey M. Lacordaire? She certainly knew no reason why she should not do so. She did not know much of him, she said to herself at first; but she knew as much, she said afterwards, as she had known personally of Mr. Thompson before their marriage. She had known, to be sure, what was Mr. Thompson's profession and what his income; or, if not, some one else had known for her. As to both these points she was quite in the dark as regarded M. Lacordaire.

Personally, she certainly did like him, as she said to herself more than once. There was a courtesy and softness about him which were very gratifying to her; and then, his appearance was so much in his favour. He was not very young, she acknowledged; but neither was she young herself. It was quite evident that he was fond of her children, and that he would be a kind and affectionate father to them. Indeed, there was kindness in all that he did.

Should she marry again,—and she put it to herself quite hypothetically,—she would look for no romance in such a second marriage. She would be content to sit down in a quiet home, to the tame dull realities of life, satisfied with the companionship of a man who would be kind and gentle to her, and whom she could respect and esteem. Where could she find a companion with whom this could be more safely anticipated than with M. Lacordaire?

And so she argued the question within her own breast in a manner not unfriendly to that gentleman. That there was as yet one great hindrance she at once saw; but then that might be remedied by a word. She did not know what was his income or his profession. The chambermaid, whom she had interrogated, had told her that he was a "marchand." To merchants, generally, she felt that she had no objection. The Barings and the Rothschilds were merchants, as was also that wonderful man at Bombay, Sir Hommajee Bommajee, who was worth she did no know how many thousand lacs of rupees.

That it would behove her, on her own account and that of her daughters, to take care of her own little fortune in contracting any such connection, that she felt strongly. She would never so commit herself as to put security in that respect out of her power. But then she did not think that M. Lacordaire would ever ask her to do so; at any rate, she was determined on this, that there should never be any doubt on that matter; and as she firmly resolved on this, she again took up her book, and for a minute or two made an attempt to read.

"Mamma," said Mummy, "will M. Lacordaire go up to the school to see Lilian when you go away from this?"

"Indeed, I cannot say, my dear. If Lilian is a good girl, perhaps he may do so now and then."

"And will he write to you and tell you how she is?"

"Lilian can write for herself; can she not?"

"Oh yes; I suppose she can; but I hope M. Lacordaire will write too. We shall come back here some day; shan't we, mamma?"

"I cannot say, my dear."

"I do so hope we shall see M. Lacordaire again. Do you know what I was thinking, mamma?"

"Little girls like you ought not to think," said Mrs. Thompson, walking slowly out of the room to the top of the stairs and back again; for she had felt the necessity of preventing Mimmy from disclosing any more of her thoughts. "And now, my dear, get yourself ready, and we will go up to the school."

Mrs. Thompson always dressed herself with care, though not in especially fine clothes, before she went down to dinner at the table d'hote; but on this occasion she was more

The Chateau of Prince Polignac

than usually particular. She hardly explained to herself why she did this; but, nevertheless, as she stood before the glass, she did in a certain manner feel that the circumstances of her future life might perhaps depend on what might be said and done that evening. She had not absolutely decided whether or no she would go to the Prince's chateau; but if she did go –. Well, if she did; what then? She had sense enough, as she assured herself more than once, to regulate her own conduct with propriety in any such emergency.

During the dinner, M. Lacordaire conversed in his usual manner, but said nothing whatever about the visit to Polignac. He was very kind to Mimmy, and very courteous to her mother, but did not appear to be at all more particular than usual. Indeed, it might be a question whether he was not less so. As she had entered the room Mrs. Thompson had said to herself that, perhaps, after all, it would be better that there should be nothing more thought about it; but before the four of five courses were over, she was beginning to feel a little disappointed.

And now the fruit was on the table, after the consumption of which it was her practice to retire. It was certainly open to her to ask M. Lacordaire to take tea with her that evening, as she had done on former occasions; but she felt that she must not do this now, considering the immediate circumstances of the case. If any further steps were to be taken, they must be taken by him, and not by her;— or else by Mimmy, who, just as her mother was slowly consuming her last grapes, ran round to the back of M. Lacordaire's chair, and whispered something into his ear. It may be presumed that Mrs. Thompson did not see the intention of the movement in time to arrest it, for she did nothing till the whispering had been whispered; and then she rebuked the child, bade her not to be troublesome, and with more than usual austerity in her voice, desired her to get herself ready to go up stairs to their chamber.

As she spoke she herself rose from her chair, and made her final little bow to the table, and her other final little bow and smile to M. Lacordaire; but this was certain to all who saw it, that the smile was not as gracious as usual.

As she walked forth, M. Lacordaire rose from his chair—such being his constant practice when she left the table; but on this occasion he accompanied her to the door.

The Chateau of Prince Polignac

"And has madame decided," he asked, "whether she will permit me to accompany her to the chateau?"

"Well, I really don't know," said Mrs. Thompson.

"Mees Meemy," continued M. Lacordaire, "is very anxious to see the rock, and I may perhaps hope that Mees Lilian would be pleased with such a little excursion. As for myself—" and then M. Lacordaire put his hand upon his heart in a manner that seemed to speak more plainly than he had ever spoken.

"Well, if the children would really like it, and—as you are so very kind," said Mrs. Thompson; and so the matter was conceded.

"To-morrow afternoon?" suggested M. Lacordaire. But Mrs. Thompson fixed on Saturday, thereby showing that she herself was in no hurry for the expedition.

"Oh, I am so glad!" said Mimmy, when they had re-entered their own room. "Mamma, do let me tell Lilian myself when I go up to the school to-morrow!"

But mamma was in no humour to say much to her child on this subject at the present moment. She threw herself back on her sofa in perfect silence, and began to reflect whether she would like to sign her name in future as Fanny Lacordaire, instead of Fanny Thompson. It certainly seemed as though things were verging towards such a necessity. A marchand! But a marchand of what? She had an instinctive feeling that the people in the hotel were talking about her and M. Lacordaire, and was therefore more than ever averse to asking any one a question.

As she went up to the school the next afternoon, she walked through more of the streets of Le Puy than was necessary, and in every street she looked at the names which she saw over the doors of the more respectable houses of business. But she looked in vain. It might be that M. Lacordaire was a marchand of so specially high a quality as to be under no necessity to put up his name at all. Sir Hommajee Bommajee's name did not appear over any door in Bombay;—at least, she thought not.

And then came the Saturday morning. "We shall be ready at two," she said, as she left the breakfast-table; "and perhaps you would not mind calling for Lilian on the way."

The Chateau of Prince Polignac

M. Lacordaire would be delighted to call anywhere for anybody on behalf of Mrs. Thompson; and then, as he got to the door of the salon, he offered her his hand. He did so with so much French courtesy that she could not refuse it, and then she felt that his purpose was more tender than ever it had been. And why not, if this was the destiny which Fate had prepared for her?

Mrs. Thompson would rather have got into the carriage at any other spot in Le Puy than at that at which she was forced to do so—the chief entrance, namely, of the Hotel des Ambassadeurs. And what made it worse was this, that an appearance of a special fate was given to the occasion. M. Lacordaire was dressed in more than his Sunday best. He had on new yellow kid gloves. His coat, if not new, was newer than any Mrs. Thompson had yet observed, and was lined with silk up to the very collar. He had on patent leather boots, which glittered, as Mrs. Thompson thought, much too conspicuously. And as for his hat, it was quite evident that it was fresh that morning from the maker's block.

In this costume, with his hat in his hand, he stood under the great gateway of the hotel, ready to hand Mrs. Thompson into the carriage. This would have been nothing if the landlord and landlady had not been there also, as well as the man-cook, and the four waiters, and the fille de chambre. Two or three other pair of eyes Mrs. Thompson also saw, as she glanced round, and then Mimmy walked across the yard in her best clothes with a fete-day air about her for which her mother would have liked to have whipped her.

But what did it matter? If it was written in the book that she should become Madame Lacordaire, of course the world would know that there must have been some preparatory love-making. Let them have their laugh; a good husband would not be dearly purchased at so trifling an expense. And so they sallied forth with already half the ceremony of a wedding.

Mimmy seated herself opposite to her mother, and M. Lacordaire also sat with his back to the horses, leaving the second place of honour for Lilian. "Pray make yourself comfortable, M. Lacordaire, and don't mind her," said Mrs. Thompson. But he was firm in his purpose of civility, perhaps making up his mind that when he should in truth stand in the place of papa to the young lady, then would be his time for having the back seat in the carnage.

The Chateau of Prince Polignac

Lilian, also in her best frock, came down the school-steps, and three of the school teachers came with her. It would have added to Mrs. Thompson's happiness at that moment if M. Lacordaire would have kept his polished boots out of sight, and put his yellow gloves into his pocket.

And then they started. The road from Le Puy to Polignac is nearly all up hill; and a very steep hill it is, so that there was plenty of time for conversation. But the girls had it nearly all to themselves. Mimmy thought that she had never found M. Lacordaire so stupid; and Lilian told her sister on the first safe opportunity that occurred, that it seemed very much as though they were all going to church.

"And do any of the Polignac people ever live at this place?" asked Mrs. Thompson, by way of making conversation; in answer to which M. Lacordaire informed madame that the place was at present only a ruin; and then there was again silence till they found themselves under the rock, and were informed by the driver that the rest of the ascent must be made on foot.

The rock now stood abrupt and precipitous above their heads. It was larger in its circumference and with much larger space on its summit than those other volcanic rocks in and close to the town; but then at the same time it was higher from the ground, and quite as inaccessible, except by the single path which led up to the chateau.

M. Lacordaire, with conspicuous gallantry, first assisted Mrs. Thompson from the carriage, and then handed down the two young ladies. No lady could have been so difficult to please as to complain of him, and yet Mrs. Thompson thought that he was not as agreeable as usual. Those horrid boots and those horrid gloves gave him such an air of holiday finery that neither could he be at his ease wearing them, nor could she, in seeing them worn.

They were soon taken in hand by the poor woman whose privilege it was to show the ruins. For a little distance they walked up the path in single file; not that it was too narrow to accommodate two, but M. Lacordaire's courage had not yet been screwed to a point which admitted of his offering his arm to the widow. For in France, it must be remembered, that this means more than it does in some other countries.

The Chateau of Prince Polignac

Mrs. Thompson felt that all this was silly and useless. If they were not to be dear friends this coming out feting together, those boots and gloves and new hat were all very foolish; and if they were, the sooner they understood each other the better. So Mrs. Thompson, finding that the path was steep and the weather warm, stood still for a while leaning against the wall, with a look of considerable fatigue in her face.

"Will madame permit me the honour of offering her my arm?" said M. Lacordaire. "The road is so extraordinarily steep for madame to climb."

Mrs. Thompson did permit him the honour, and so they went on till they reached the top.

The view from the summit was both extensive and grand, but neither Lilian nor Mimmy were much pleased with the place. The elder sister, who had talked over the matter with her school companions, expected a fine castle with turrets, battlements, and romance; and the other expected a pretty smiling house, such as princes, in her mind, ought to inhabit.

Instead of this they found an old turret, with steps so broken that M. Lacordaire did not care to ascend them, and the ruined walls of a mansion, in which nothing was to be seen but the remains of an enormous kitchen chimney.

"It was the kitchen of the family," said the guide.

"Oh," said Mrs. Thompson.

"And this," said the woman, taking them into the next ruined compartment, "was the kitchen of monsieur et madame."

"What! two kitchens?" exclaimed Lilian, upon which M. Lacordaire explained that the ancestors of the Prince de Polignac had been very great people, and had therefore required culinary performances on a great scale.

And then the woman began to chatter something about an oracle of Apollo. There was, she said, a hole in the rock, from which in past times, perhaps more than a hundred years ago, the oracle used to speak forth mysterious words.

The Chateau of Prince Polignac

"There," she said, pointing to a part of the rock at some distance, "was the hole. And if the ladies would follow her to a little outhouse which was just beyond, she would show them the huge stone mouth out of which the oracle used to speak."

Lilian and Mimmy both declared at once for seeing the oracle, but Mrs. Thompson expressed her determination to remain sitting where she was upon the turf. So the guide started off with the young ladies; and will it be thought surprising that M. Lacordaire should have remained alone by the side of Mrs. Thompson?

It must be now or never, Mrs. Thompson felt; and as regarded M. Lacordaire, he probably entertained some idea of the same kind. Mrs. Thompson's inclinations, though they had never been very strong in the matter, were certainly in favour of the "now." M. Lacordaire's inclinations were stronger. He had fully and firmly made up his mind in favour of matrimony; but then he was not so absolutely in favour of the "now." Mrs. Thompson's mind, if one could have read it, would have shown a great objection to shilly– shallying, as she was accustomed to call it. But M. Lacordaire, were it not for the danger which might thence arise, would have seen no objection to some slight further procrastination. His courage was beginning, perhaps, to ooze out from his fingers' ends.

"I declare that those girls have scampered away ever so far," said Mrs. Thompson.

"Would madame wish that I should call them back?" said M. Lacordaire, innocently.

"Oh, no, dear children! let them enjoy themselves; it will be a pleasure to them to run about the rock, and I suppose they will be safe with that woman?"

"Oh, yes, quite safe," said M. Lacordaire; and then there was another little pause.

Mrs. Thompson was sitting on a broken fragment of a stone just outside the entrance to the old family kitchen, and M. Lacordaire was standing immediately before her. He had in his hand a little cane with which he sometimes slapped his boots and sometimes poked about among the rubbish. His hat was not quite straight on his head, having a little jaunty twist to one side, with reference to which, by–the–bye, Mrs. Thompson then resolved that she would make a change, should ever the gentleman become her own property. He still wore his gloves, and was very smart; but it was clear to see that he was not at his ease.

The Chateau of Prince Polignac

"I hope the heat does not incommode you," he said after a few moments' silence. Mrs. Thompson declared that it did not, that she liked a good deal of heat, and that, on the whole, she was very well where she was. She was afraid, however, that she was detaining M. Lacordaire, who might probably wish to be moving about upon the rock. In answer to which M. Lacordaire declared that he never could be so happy anywhere as in her close vicinity.

"You are too good to me," said Mrs. Thompson, almost sighing. "I don't know what my stay here would have been without your great kindness."

"It is madame that has been kind to me," said M. Lacordaire, pressing the handle of his cane against his heart.

There was then another pause, after which Mrs. Thompson said that that was all his French politeness; that she knew that she had been very troublesome to him, but that she would now soon be gone; and that then, in her own country, she would never forget his great goodness.

"Ah, madame!" said M. Lacordaire; and, as he said it, much more was expressed in his face than in his words. But, then, you can neither accept nor reject a gentleman by what he says in his face. He blushed, too, up to his grizzled hair, and, turning round, walked a step or two away from the widow's seat, and back again.

Mrs. Thompson the while sat quite still. The displaced fragment, lying, as it did, near a corner of the building, made not an uncomfortable chair. She had only to be careful that she did not injure her hat or crush her clothes, and throw in a word here and there to assist the gentleman, should occasion permit it.

"Madame!" said M. Lacordaire, on his return from a second little walk.

"Monsieur!" replied Mrs. Thompson, perceiving that M. Lacordaire paused in his speech.

"Madame," he began again, and then, as he again paused, Mrs. Thompson looked up to him very sweetly; "madame, what I am going to say will, I am afraid, seem to evince by far too great audacity on my part."

The Chateau of Prince Polignac

Mrs. Thompson may, perhaps, have thought that, at the present moment, audacity was not his fault. She replied, however, that she was quite sure that monsieur would say nothing that was in any way unbecoming either for him to speak or for her to hear.

"Madame, may I have ground to hope that such may be your sentiments after I have spoken! Madame"—and now he went down, absolutely on his knees, on the hard stones; and Mrs. Thompson, looking about into the distance, almost thought that she saw the top of the guide's cap—"Madame, I have looked forward to this opportunity as one in which I may declare for you the greatest passion that I have ever yet felt. Madame, with all my heart and soul I love you. Madame, I offer to you the homage of my heart, my hand, the happiness of my life, and all that I possess in this world;" and then, taking her hand gracefully between his gloves, he pressed his lips against the tips of her fingers.

If the thing was to be done, this way of doing it was, perhaps, as good as any other. It was one, at any rate, which left no doubt whatever as to the gentleman's intentions. Mrs. Thompson, could she have had her own way, would not have allowed her lover of fifty to go down upon his knees, and would have spared him much of the romance of his declaration. So also would she have spared him his yellow gloves and his polished boots. But these were a part of the necessity of the situation, and therefore she wisely took them as matters to be passed over with indifference. Seeing, however, that M. Lacordaire still remained on his knees, it was necessary that she should take some step toward raising him, especially as her two children and the guide would infallibly be upon them before long.

"M. Lacordaire," she said, "you surprise me greatly; but pray get up."

"But will madame vouchsafe to give me some small ground for hope?"

"The girls will be here directly, M. Lacordaire; pray get up. I can talk to you much better if you will stand up, or sit down on one of these stones."

M. Lacordaire did as he was bid; he got up, wiped the knees of his pantaloons with his handkerchief, sat down beside her, and then pressed the handle of his cane to his heart.

"You really have so surprised me that I hardly know how to answer you," said Mrs. Thompson. "Indeed, I cannot bring myself to imagine that you are in earnest."

The Chateau of Prince Polignac

"Ah, madame, do not be so cruel! How can I have lived with you so long, sat beside you for so many days, without having received your image into my heart? I am in earnest! Alas! I fear too much in earnest!" And then he looked at her with all his eyes, and sighed with all his strength.

Mrs. Thompson's prudence told her that it would be well to settle the matter, in one way or the other, as soon as possible. Long periods of love-making were fit for younger people than herself and her future possible husband. Her object would be to make him comfortable if she could, and that he should do the same for her, if that also were possible. As for lookings and sighings and pressings of the hand, she had gone through all that some twenty years since in India, when Thompson had been young, and she was still in her teens.

"But, M. Lacordaire, there are so many things to be considered. There! I hear the children coming! Let us walk this way for a minute." And they turned behind a wall which placed them out of sight, and walked on a few paces till they reached a parapet, which stood on the uttermost edge of the high rock. Leaning upon this they continued their conversation.

"There are so many things to be considered," said Mrs. Thompson again.

"Yes, of course," said M. Lacordaire. "But my one great consideration is this;—that I love madame to distraction."

"I am very much flattered; of course, any lady would so feel. But, M. Lacordaire—"

"Madame, I am all attention. But, if you would deign to make me happy, say that one word, 'I love you!'" M. Lacordaire, as he uttered these words, did not look, as the saying is, at his best. But Mrs. Thompson forgave him. She knew that elderly gentlemen under such circumstances do not look at their best.

"But if I consented to—to—to such an arrangement, I could only do so on seeing that it would be beneficial—or, at any rate, not injurious—to my children; and that it would offer to ourselves a fair promise of future happiness."

"Ah, madame; it would be the dearest wish of my heart to be a second father to those two young ladies; except, indeed—" and then M. Lacordaire stopped the flow of his speech.

The Chateau of Prince Polignac

"In such matters it is so much the best to be explicit at once," said Mrs. Thompson.

"Oh, yes; certainly! Nothing can be more wise than madame."

"And the happiness of a household depends so much on money."

"Madame!"

"Let me say a word or two, Monsieur Lacordaire. I have enough for myself and my children; and, should I every marry again, I should not, I hope, be felt as a burden by my husband; but it would, of course, be my duty to know what were his circumstances before I accepted him. Of yourself, personally, I have seen nothing that I do not like."

"Oh, madame!"

"But as yet I know nothing of your circumstances."

M. Lacordaire, perhaps, did feel that Mrs. Thompson's prudence was of a strong, masculine description; but he hardly liked her the less on this account. To give him his due he was not desirous of marrying her solely for her money's sake. He also wished for a comfortable home, and proposed to give as much as he got; only he had been anxious to wrap up the solid cake of this business in a casing of sugar of romance. Mrs. Thompson would not have the sugar but the cake might not be the worse on that account.

"No, madame, not as yet; but they shall all be made open and at your disposal," said M. Lacordaire; and Mrs. Thompson bowed approvingly.

"I am in business," continued M. Lacordaire; "and my business gives me eight thousand francs a year."

"Four times eight are thirty–two," said Mrs. Thompson to herself; putting the francs into pounds sterling, in the manner that she had always found to be the readiest. Well, so far the statement was satisfactory. An income of three hundred and twenty pounds a year from business, joined to her own, might do very well. She did not in the least suspect M. Lacordaire of being false, and so far the matter sounded well.

The Chateau of Prince Polignac

"And what is the business?" she asked, in a tone of voice intended to be indifferent, but which nevertheless showed that she listened anxiously for an answer to her question.

They were both standing with their arms upon the wall, looking down upon the town of Le Puy; but they had so stood that each could see the other's countenance as they talked. Mrs. Thompson could now perceive that M. Lacordaire became red in the face, as he paused before answering her. She was near to him, and seeing his emotion gently touched his arm with her hand. This she did to reassure him, for she saw that he was ashamed of having to declare that he was a tradesman. As for herself, she had made up her mind to bear with this, if she found, as she felt sure she would find, that the trade was one which would not degrade either him or her. Hitherto, indeed,—in her early days,—she had looked down on trade; but of what benefit had her grand ideas been to her when she had returned to England? She had tried her hand at English genteel society, and no one had seemed to care for her. Therefore, she touched his arm lightly with her fingers that she might encourage him.

He paused for a moment, as I have said, and became red; and then feeling that he had shown some symptoms of shame—and feeling also, probably, that it was unmanly in him to do so, he shook himself slightly, raised his head up somewhat more proudly than was his wont, looked her full in the face with more strength of character than she had yet seen him assume; and then, declared his business.

"Madame," he said, in a very audible, but not in a loud voice, "madame—je suis tailleur." And having so spoken, he turned slightly from her and looked down over the valley towards Le Puy.

There was nothing more said upon the subject as they drove down from the rock of Polignac back to the town. Immediately on receiving the announcement, Mrs. Thompson found that she had no answer to make. She withdrew her hand—and felt at once that she had received a blow. It was not that she was angry with M. Lacordaire for being a tailor; nor was she angry with him in that, being a tailor, he had so addressed her. But she was surprised, disappointed, and altogether put beyond her ease. She had, at any rate, not expected this. She had dreamed of his being a banker; thought that, perhaps, he might have been a wine merchant; but her idea had never gone below a jeweller or watchmaker. When those words broke upon her ear, "Madame, je suis tailleur," she had felt herself to be speechless.

The Chateau of Prince Polignac

But the words had not been a minute spoken when Lilian and Mimmy ran up to their mother. "Oh, mamma," said Lilian, "we thought you were lost; we have searched for you all over the chateau."

"We have been sitting very quietly here, my dear, looking at the view," said Mrs. Thompson.

"But, mamma, I do wish you'd see the mouth of the oracle. It is so large, and so round, and so ugly. I put my arm into it all the way," said Mimmy.

But at the present moment her mamma felt no interest in the mouth of the oracle; and so they all walked down together to the carriage. And, though the way was steep, Mrs. Thompson managed to pick her steps without the assistance of an arm; nor did M. Lacordaire presume to offer it.

The drive back to town was very silent. Mrs. Thompson did make one or two attempts at conversation, but they were not effectual. M. Lacordaire could not speak at his ease till this matter was settled, and he already had begun to perceive that his business was against him. Why is it that the trade of a tailor should be less honourable than that of a haberdasher, or even a grocer?

They sat next each other at dinner, as usual; and here, as all eyes were upon them, they both made a great struggle to behave in their accustomed way. But even in this they failed. All the world of the Hotel des Ambassadeurs knew that M. Lacordaire had gone forth to make an offer to Mrs. Thompson, and all that world, therefore, was full of speculation. But all the world could make nothing of it. M. Lacordaire did look like a rejected man, but Mrs. Thompson did not look like the woman who had rejected him. That the offer had been made—in that everybody agreed, from the senior habitue of the house who always sat at the head of the table, down to the junior assistant garcon. But as to reading the riddle, there was no accord among them.

When the dessert was done, Mrs. Thompson, as usual, withdrew, and M. Lacordaire, as usual, bowed as he stood behind his own chair. He did not, however, attempt to follow her.

The Chateau of Prince Polignac

But when she reached the door she called him. He was at her side in a moment, and then she whispered in his ear –

"And I, also—I will be of the same business."

When M. Lacordaire regained the table the senior habitue, the junior garcon, and all the intermediate ranks of men at the Hotel des Ambassadeurs knew that they might congratulate him.

Mrs. Thompson had made a great struggle; but, speaking for myself, I am inclined to think that she arrived at last at a wise decision.